Amazir

Amazir

by
Tom Gamble

Beautiful
Books

First published 2010

Beautiful Books Limited
36-38 Glasshouse Street
London W1B 5DL

www.beautiful-books.co.uk

ISBN 9781905636976

9 8 7 6 5 4 3 2

A catalogue reference for this book is available
from the British Library.

Cover design by Ian Pickard.
Typesetting by Misa Watanabe.
Printed in and bound in the UK by CPI Mackays, Chatham ME5 8TD.

To the children of the Atlas
Si riches avec si peu

1

Looking back, 1938 was a year which should almost not have existed. It was like the empty, half-way moment in a gathering of people, the hollow time before it kicked back into life. The world was a wait.

It was the year Wilding's job took him outside the States, a brief stop over in Europe before setting to work exploring for oil in French and Spanish Mauritania. It was also the year he first met Harry Summerfield, in a bar in Gibraltar, in May.

As an American, Wilding viewed the whole European scene as practically theatrical. To a large extent, he was shrewd enough to understand that his ideas were shaped by a mix of cultural preconceptions, the satirical cartoons in the US press and Chaplin's grotesque spoof, the *Great Dictator*. The film, which he had seen several times back in the States, was more powerful for him than any Hemingway prose or any serious columnist he could have read. The threat of war seemed like an impossible, far off bad joke and in some ways Wilding guessed he was like the vast majority of people: there were just other more important things to be getting on with.

On the voyage down to Gibraltar from Southampton, Wilding read a whole packet of newspapers and reviews. These he passed on to a British family occupying the adjacent cabin and was very amused to catch the young son and daughter cutting out the various photos. They pasted them into a scrapbook, making a home-made comic strip by pencilling in speech balloons from the politicians' mouths and, in some cases, with fiendish, uncontrollable giggles, their noses and backsides. The children honoured Wilding with their artwork and duly reading it he noticed they had filled the balloons with mostly infantile remarks but sometimes, in that curious way kids have of hitting the nail on the head, electrifyingly pertinent comment.

Wilding chuckled—it really did seem as if it were all some big stage act—here the clowns in their outrageously decorated uniforms, elsewhere those in top hat and tails; others dressed in workers' fatigues, English royalty wearing lopsided sailor caps and Mediterranean leaders with tassels like Broadway curtain cords dangling from their regalia. And the more Wilding looked at these pictures, the more the thought came, until he actually laughed out loud, that it was all down to a pantomime war of outrageous ideological costumes. *Who would win the battle?* he joked with the family.

The cargo stopped over in Gibraltar, to Wilding a pokey, bustling little place dominated by a rocky outcrop and British shore batteries. From the beginning of his journey from New York, he'd spent the better part of two weeks cooped up in a ship's cabin and ached to put foot on dry land once again. The first thing he did was to stroll along the docksides and into town intent upon buying a beer.

A first bar looked too noisy, too full of ships' crewmen. A second bar, not so farther along the main street, looked quieter and more genuine. Wilding stepped into the cool interior, momentarily losing his bearings in the dimness, sat down at the first table and ordered.

As his sight grew accustomed, Wilding saw that the walls and ceiling were a sickly, tannin shade of brown—years of accumulated smoke and nicotine. It was practically empty and Wilding's eyes took in the silent clientele—a British sailor asleep at the nearest table, head in his hands and a copy of *Movie Times* covering his cap; a couple of bleary-eyed old locals dressed in cheap cotton suits and finally a fourth man, in his late twenties, probably English, judging from his clothes, and approximately his age—twenty-nine—guessed Wilding.

He was sitting some ten or so yards away, sweating, waiting. Judging from the expression on his face, it seemed as if his whole life had been just one long wait. Wilding watched him pick up his glass, notice it was nearly empty and measure the amount he drank so that one last mouthful remained. It was then that the

Englishman glanced up, his eyes a clear, sharp blue and almost fierce. With an obvious movement of irritation, he returned to the newspaper spread before him. Long seconds passed. He didn't seem to be reading, but thinking. Wilding decided to go over.

'James—*Jim*—Wilding,' said the American, offering his hand.

The Englishman looked up.

'You're a *Yank*.'

An English voice, dry and matter-of-fact. The man glanced at Wilding's outstretched hand, frowned and with a reluctant slowness shook it. Perhaps, thought Wilding, it wasn't a British thing to do.

'Harry Summerfield.'

The Englishman glanced at the door, then at Wilding who, expecting to be asked to take a seat, stood waiting before the table for the invitation which failed to come. Finally, scraping back a chair, he just sat down.

'Damn hot,' said Wilding, and made a gesture that suggested the heat was uncomfortable, though to tell the truth, he'd experienced temperatures in his job in the southern states that were on a par, if not higher. Summerfield grinned sheepishly, returned to gazing at the door, glanced once again at his wristwatch and finally exhaled in what Wilding took as a final decision to finish his glass and leave. Instinctively—he didn't know why—Wilding turned towards the bar and called for another beer. 'Have one on me,' he said, raising his glass to the strange Englishman. Summerfield seemed surprised, then embarrassed, worried and finally after one last look in the direction of the entrance, one last swallow of his remaining beer, nodded.

'*Thanks*, Yank.'

The most striking feature about Summerfield, noticed Wilding, was his eyebrows—or lack of them. Instead, the arcades of his eyes were marked by a prominent brow and this effect deflected attention to his eyes which were blue, fierce, lighter than Wilding's and somewhat bloodshot. This Wilding took for a sign of prolonged and uncomfortable travel. He started.

'So what are you up to in Gibraltar?' Summerfield had said, unexpectedly.

'I've just arrived from Southampton—a cargo ship called the Wader,' he answered.

'*Good name,*' interrupted Summerfield, ironically.

Wilding pursed his lips then relaxed. 'I'm catching a ferry across the Straight to Morocco and there on south to Mauritania.'

'So you're not going onto Spain?' The Englishman looked mildly surprised. 'I thought perhaps…'

'I'm not a writer or a journalist,' said Wilding, grinning. 'Not like all the other Americans around here seem to be. My company, Southern Star Petroleum, thinks there's oil down there.'

'Where there's money…' murmured Summerfield, returning to the ironical.

'There's *life,*' continued Wilding, deciding to play his game. 'Sometimes business can bring people together.'

'And sometimes tear them apart,' added the Englishman.

While Summerfield pretended to return to his newspaper, Wilding was beginning to regret having offered the sour Limey a beer. He could at least make the effort to communicate correctly, he heard himself thinking. *Asshole*—you're wasting my time. Suddenly Wilding found himself wanting to bring the meeting to an end.

'Well, tell me what you're up to Harry, and then I'll leave you in peace,' he said, bluntly.

'Waiting,' said Summerfield, glancing curiously at him.

'Is that right?' answered Wilding with a smile.

'For a contact,' added Summerfield, aware of the American's sudden aggressiveness and attempting at last to make amends. 'To go over there,' he added, nodding in the direction of the Spanish border. 'Bloody Spanish—so undependable. You'd think they didn't care.'

Wilding showed surprise. 'So *you're* a journalist?'

'God, no,' said Summerfield, 'Though I suppose you could say I write. I used to be a copywriter for ads—a word alchemist, lies to sell dreams. Soap, tins of corned beef, cigarettes, loo paper—you name it, I wrote it. No,' he continued, returning to Wilding's question. 'I was hoping to join in the mess across the frontier. I've been waiting in this hole for three days for the contact to show up.'

'You mean you want to fight?' asked Wilding, instantly feeling somewhat stupid and consequently lowering his voice. 'You're waiting to go to the front? You know it's a lost war.'

'I don't see what else I'd be doing in this place,' replied Summerfield, seeming not to notice Wilding's remark. 'All in all, I've been on the continent a month. I tried getting into Spain from the north, but the frontier is shut tight on either side— stopping people getting out. Someone gave me a name and said I could get a boat that'd drop me off up the coast.'

'There must be a thousand ways,' added Wilding. 'What about via Portugal? They *can't* control the entire border—not everywhere. It's too long.'

Summerfield suddenly grew cold again. 'Are you questioning my conviction, Wilding?'

Wilding stared at him, perplexed by the Englishman's sensitivity. 'Hell, no—I was just trying to offer an alternative idea,' he defended. The Englishman seemed to think about it and Wilding saw the tenseness go out of his body. The poor guy looked exhausted. 'I imagine you're quite tired,' he offered.

'It's the climate,' returned Summerfield, apologetically. 'I can stand the travel and the discomfort—I'm used to that—just that I hadn't quite expected this *bloody heat*. I'm afraid I haven't what they call the *gumption* that certain people have.'

'Come again?'

'I didn't go to the right school,' added Summerfield, sourly— '*I'm not of proper ilk.*' Seeing Wilding's continuing incomprehension, he added: 'I wasn't brought up to cope with what is expected of a *real gentleman.*'

Wilding guffawed. '*Oh, come on, Harry*! That stuff is so old-fashioned!'

'Not where I come from,' said Summerfield, reddening slightly as though he realised he might have sounded strange.

'Who cares?' shrugged Wilding. 'This isn't England—even if the Union Jack is flying from the top of the rock, it isn't. Drink your beer Harry. I need to walk and by the sound of you, you need a change of atmosphere.'

Over the next two days, Wilding and Summerfield explored most
of the colony, stopping frequently in various bars to quench their
thirst and watch, amused, the odd little piece of Britain passing by.
Wilding learnt how Summerfield came to believe in the necessity
of taking part in the civil war in Spain. He said he'd listened to
Orwell give a speech in London the year before and that the
writer had managed to spark off what he'd always felt but had
been unable to express: the need to take part in a *just* cause.

Strangely, Summerfield gave Wilding the impression of
someone who hadn't yet managed to find the adult in himself.
It was as though the Englishman believed in fairy tales, the fight
between good and evil, the prince coming to save the damsel
that was democracy. On several occasions Wilding very nearly
told him he thought it was a crusade of self-discovery more than
anything else; that there were other ways in which to find oneself
rather than shooting at people with different views. But then
again, the little remaining idealistic side to Wilding—or maybe
even creative side, for several family generations of scientists and
five years of geology studies at Princeton had all but erased any
artist in him—told him that both great and mad-hat achievements
were often born of the child in us rather than the adult. That naïve
belief that things could change through dreams and heroism—
that childish disrespect for reason—seemed to be characteristic of
Harry Summerfield.

There was also the writer in Summerfield that seemed to lead
him on: the writer and the rebel. For Wilding noted that the
Englishman often referred to himself as *one who hadn't followed the
usual path*. Most of the time, Wilding understood it was a cynical
reflection on the British class system, and Summerfield's particular
trouble in fitting in. Other times he was sure that Summerfield
had a damned big inferiority complex: Summerfield, the boy from
a modest background who'd gone through the grammar school
system, meeting with the invisible barriers at a later stage during
university—language studies apparently. Although he didn't
say it, Wilding guessed that Summerfield had flunked, hadn't
continued. In fact, he understood the Englishman was largely
self-taught. He certainly knew a lot—maybe more than his peers

who'd followed through and gained degrees. But there lacked the veneer. There lacked the accent. There lacked the annoyingly smug self-confidence that exuded from that type of Englishman who naturally and unquestionably *was* the best in this world *and* any other.

It was probably because of this last point that Wilding got to liking him. Summerfield was an Englishman apart, a doubter and a rebel, more Yankee than Brit. Strolling in the narrow streets of the colony, often half-drunk from the heat and beer, Summerfield played games, cockily saluting military officers whenever they crossed them, mimicking their peculiarly nonchalant and sloppy style. The goal of his game—that made Wilding almost cringe with embarrassment—was to receive the most salutes in return. It was like a kind of test to see if they could see through him. Sometimes, judging his victim as a particularly acute case of thoroughbred officer stock, Summerfield would let fly such an outlandish salute that it was difficult for anyone to decide if it was a blatant insult. The looks on the faces of his poor victims ranged from shock, distaste and scorn to—funniest of all for Wilding— sheer snobbish refusal to acknowledge his existence.

On the evening of his second night in Gibraltar and due to leave the following morning, Wilding took Summerfield to get drunk in the waterfront pubs. At 2 a.m., mulling over a double whisky in *The HMS Vengeance*, they found themselves pondering over the destiny of the world when Wilding blurted out an invitation for Summerfield to accompany him to Africa. Wilding told him the war could wait and that his artistic flair would be far better nourished by the cultures of this unknown continent than Spain. Summerfield replied, after some trouble in raising himself from his chair, glass in hand, that there would be other, bigger wars to fight in any case. How right Summerfield was to be.

The next morning saw Wilding and Summerfield on the ferry, chugging across the Straight to Tangiers. On the subsequent journey through the Spanish enclave on the northern coast to Casablanca—a gruelling train ride of forty-two stops, a public whipping and numerous hold ups due to herds of goats invading the tracks—Summerfield showed Wilding some of his journals in which he wrote and sketched. Wilding whistled through his clenched teeth. Summerfield's command of style was impressive— at least, impressive for him, a scientist by nature. He was able to write the driest of descriptive prose and the most soaring of verse; the funniest and most caustic of satire and the flattest, most cynical parody to beauty. The content, however, was less impressive, though Wilding didn't tell him. 'The idea will come,' said Wilding instead, 'most maybe on this journey.'

They stopped off at the Southern Star Petroleum offices in Casablanca; a bustling, buzzing, almost European city crammed with military presence, and then caught a train southbound the next day.

It was in Marrakesh that they parted, Summerfield saying that the name of the place seemed interesting. They sat in the lobby of Wilding's hotel and drank tea. A large, whirring ventilator sent a blessing of cool air upon them and then, with an obtrusive click, broke down.

'I'll be back in six months,' Wilding told him. 'Ten days' leave and then another stint, back to geological surveys and prospecting.' He mopped his forehead. 'If we strike oil, I suppose it would only be natural for me to move base permanently south. What about you, Harry?'

In a mirror gesture, Summerfield too wiped his forehead then blew air into his face. 'I think I'll stay on in Marrakesh, Jim—even if it *is* damn hotter than Gibraltar. I suppose it's a question of time—getting used to it, that's all,' he added. 'I've got some savings. And when I run out of money, I'm counting on my French and Spanish to land me a job.'

'How about a job at Southern Star?' suggested Wilding, raising a speculative eyebrow.

Summerfield shook his head, looking adamant. 'No thanks.' He hesitated, pondered for an instant and on an afterthought, changed his mind: 'But who knows, Jim. Perhaps I'll come back to that in the future. Thanks for the offer.'

Wilding scribbled down an address and handed it across,

though Summerfield was unable to give him one in return.

'I'll wire you with news once I've found a place to stay.'

At seven-forty—the train an hour late—they shook hands on the station platform. Wilding hoisted himself up into his compartment as the locomotive tugged and whistled away.

'Hey, Harry!' Wilding shouted from his window. 'Hope you don't regret me asking you here.'

'You may have saved my life, Jim,' Summerfield called back. 'You certainly saved me from waiting.'

'By the way, Harry—were you *really* going to go ahead with it? Somehow I don't see you as a slave to *any* cause,' Wilding yelled back.

The Englishman grinned, seemed to hesitate between keeping it secret and telling. He gave a shrug. 'Got to find *something* to believe in, Jim—*what else can we do?*'

It was the last Wilding saw of Summerfield for the next eight months.

2

Summerfield stood on the platform of the station and watched the train pull out of sight. The air was still cool, the sky a striking blue. Summerfield recognised it as the colour certain locals used, not only for their clothes but also in the decorative work of objects and buildings. The blue seized one's vision in an otherwise dominantly pink city—from the earth of the date groves beyond the city gates that sheltered the caravans from the south, to the great pale-pink ramparts surrounding the city and the colour of the palaces and the sprawling, rickety hovels of the medina within. There were pinks, reds, rusts, browns, the black shapes that were covered women and finally that almost phosphorescent blue. It was a festival, a magic that enchanted Summerfield's English eyes.

Realising he was not alone, realising that perhaps others were observing him watching the sky, feeling himself smiling from an inner joy—suddenly, after the tedious past weeks, how alive he felt—he turned, his hands in the pockets of his khaki slacks, and sauntered back to the hotel.

In the hotel lobby he signed in for another two days, the necessary time it would take to find lodgings, he thought. Leaving his two suitcases, he stepped out into the sun intent upon exploring the old town. The heat instantly pounced on him, a physical presence, a palpable weight. He searched in his knapsack for the hat he'd purchased at the Army & Navy stores in Oxford Street barely three weeks before. It was a bush model made of pale green cotton with a wide, floppy brim destined for the hotter Dominions. He felt conspicuously English—and rather embarrassed by the fact. Glancing at his reflection in the hotel doors, he looked like some Rhodes-type figure.

He set out across the wide, burning stretch of the *Djemaa El*

Fna square, deserted but for the detritus of the night before and a few fruit sellers sheltered under the canvas sheets of their makeshift stalls. He strode past a blind man dressed in a ragged *jellaba* who muttered something in Arabic to him. Too hot, already sweating, Summerfield then hopped into the shade afforded by a cluster of date trees and magnolias that were shelter to thirty or so people. It was like slipping into a cool bathing pool. Only a hundred yards and his clothes were sticking and patched with sweat. He sat down on a bench and was immediately approached by a young boy selling tea. Summerfield refused. The boy, shaven-headed and annoyingly insistent, thrust a terracotta bowl into Summerfield's hands, sealing his fate. He paid and the boy disappeared as quickly as he had appeared and without giving any change. He shook his head, took a cigarette from his case, lit up and exhaled.

To his left was the tall, imposing minaret of the *Koutubia*—the central mosque—with its chequered tiling. It brought back to him the five o' clock wail of Morning Prayer that had woken him and Wilding in their sleep. His first reaction had been to swear, but as the long, nasal verses had echoed in the chilly dawn air, endlessly repeating the same hypnotic chant, it became soothing, haunting. Even the notes, so twisted and painful—*like some cat mewling midnight serenades*, he had commented to Wilding—had become distinctively musical by the time he slipped back into sleep. He remembered that he hadn't thought he'd learn to accept so quickly. He pulled on his cigarette, took a sip of the burning tea—spearmint—and felt better.

Suddenly, feeling a presence, Summerfield glanced to his side and started. There were two gruesomely imploring faces staring at him. They laughed. Summerfield had never seen such large yellow teeth—it gave them a very dromedary air.

'*Piss off*,' muttered Summerfield, feeling uncomfortable, but they drew closer, nodding in the direction of his cigarette. '*Go away*,' he added, catching their smell in his nostrils, a mixture of sweat and hay. He repeated himself first in French, then in Spanish but to no avail. Perhaps they were deaf, thought Summerfield and, much in the way the British Naval officers had snubbed him in Gibraltar, he continued smoking and sipping

his tea as though they didn't exist. But they persisted, two pairs
of hands outstretched in a gesture of supplication. Summerfield
sighed irritably, opened his cigarette case and handed two ready-
rolled cigarettes across. Of all the cheek, they then gestured for a
light. '*Now* piss off!' hissed Summerfield, striking a match. They
grinned, rose and walked calmly away puffing nonchalantly on
their newly acquired treasure.

'You should have continued to ignore them,' suddenly came a
voice in French. 'They would have left you alone. It is just a matter
of time.' Summerfield turned to see a tall, heavily-built Moroccan
dressed in well-cut, royal blue native attire. A small, rather houndish
moustache—much in Clark Gable style—decorated his upper
lip and his large, smooth hands clasped a folded umbrella. He
smiled. What did they *mean* by that smile, thought Summerfield.
'That, or stare straight at them immediately with iron in your
eyes,' continued the man. 'Like this—' The Arab's face changed so
radically into an expression of ferociousness that it sent a shiver
through Summerfield. 'Just a tip,' continued the man, returning to
his disarming smile. 'Try it next time.'

Summerfield nodded, distrustful. He felt suddenly alone and
quite vulnerable.

'*Merci.*'

'With God's grace,' replied the man, leaning forwards in a
slight bow.

Bewildered, not knowing what to do, Summerfield pursed
his lips, hesitated, then with a slight cough decided to continue
walking. He rose, feeling the man's eyes on him like the damned
sun. For a second, it seemed as if he couldn't move—stuck fast on
the burning ground. Finally, with a noticeable lurch, Summerfield
started in the direction of a narrow street in the farthest corner
of the square.

'Your *tea*,' came the voice behind him, but Summerfield was
already away.

It was like stepping back into the Middle Ages. He would never
have seen this in Spain, the thought came to him. Silently, he
thanked Wilding for having helped steer him away from what

would surely have been the misery of the Spanish front.

Reaching the other side of the vast square, a myriad of streets and alleyways quickly swallowed him up. The streets were so narrow in places that the carts and other paraphernalia of transportation had to be lifted sideways so that one wheel clattered in the stinking gutter running through the middle of the passageway, while the other, elevated wheel ran along the wall. Summerfield noticed that in these narrow bottlenecks grooves had been worn over time in the stone at shoulder height.

There was noise everywhere, bedlam compared to the emptiness of the square barely two hundred yards away—a cacophony of laughter, sewing machines, lathes, clattering carts, dringing bicycles ridden without heed for life or limb, animals, music and the shrill warbling of women from behind the intricate wooden partitions that blocked out the windows. And then the two speeds, the mass of people. There were those who were static, in pairs or in threes or those, the vast majority, who walked at great haste, deftly slipping past the others, dodging the bicycles, rubbish and faeces collecting in the narrow streets. Summerfield the odd one out—neither static nor fast-moving. It was almost this, his gait, more than his attire that made him so obtrusive. Eyes followed him. The children, more daring, turned their heads or else tagged him for a while, imitating his walk and chattering with laughter. Once or twice, sombre-faced men spat at his feet—whether it was a challenge or not he couldn't know.

At first, nervous and unsure, Summerfield began to adapt, adopting the behaviour of someone who didn't care, someone who felt quite natural in these alien surroundings. It was almost like turning it all about-face: it was the *local* environment that was different, not he. Perhaps it was the advice of the large Moroccan man under the magnolias, perhaps (and he smiled at himself for this), his Britishness. He felt his eyes fill with hardness and he remembered a saying he'd once read in a book of Persian poems: *it is the look in a man's eye that determines what he has in his soul.* He met both the imploring and the aggressive with iron and calmness and they seemed to leave him alone.

After a while, he came to a halt, thirsty. He looked around

him, spotted a face which he thought he could trust and asked in French, then in Spanish, where he could rest and drink. The young man smiled and beckoned. Summerfield, calculating the risk, followed him through a network of passageways suddenly and quite deafeningly quiet, surprisingly clean and odourless. They came to a small, iron-embossed door. The young man stopped, nodded, smiled once more and opened it. Warily, Summerfield peered in, withdrew his head and smiled back.

'Here,' he said, dipping into his pocket. '*Merci*—thanks,' and placed a coin in the young man's palm.

A dim, arched entrance opened out into the most heavenly, most spectacular and most beautiful house he had ever seen. It was the first time he had ever seen a *riad* and Summerfield stood there, overwhelmed. Around the whitewashed sides of the structure he counted twelve open rooms, each decorated in coloured tapestries and tiles, rugs and intricately sculpted wood, each a separate colour: pale green, blue, white, orange, deep red, pastel yellow, pink; each containing a cluster of low tables surrounded by large, inviting cushions. There were no chairs. In the centre, under an open sky, was a pond, a date tree, lilies and magnolias, the lemon scent of which gave the air an ethereal, heavenly feel. In the middle of the pond, accessible by a small wooden bridge, was a glass kiosk with its private table and a set of luxuriant cushions of golden silk. Water flowed, birds cheeped and warbled, the sound of their beating wings the only interruption in the silence. *I have found paradise*, said Summerfield silently and closed his eyes.

Presently a young man appeared dressed in a white gown and made the customary greeting—the right hand to the heart followed by a swishing, open gesture. No words were exchanged and Summerfield let himself be ushered to a room—pale yellow—and a table. Tea in a huge brass urn was brought to him together with a tray filled with cakes dripping in sugar and honey. The young waiter filled a glass flute with mint tea. As he finished, the creak of the entrance door echoed in the courtyard. Only Summerfield turned his head. Into the *riad* stepped the man who had insisted on advising him in the square. Noticing Summerfield, the large Moroccan sent him that same, exaggerated smile and walked over.

'So you are here—certainly fate has decided that we meet this day.' A gesture of welcome, hand to heart.

'Perhaps,' answered Summerfield, warily. He rose and, for some reason, offered his hand in much the same way as the American, Jim Wilding, would have done.

'I am obliged to offer you this tea,' said the man, nodding at the great urn, 'In return for the tea you lost through no small fault of mine. I'm afraid I took you by surprise. Forgive me.'

'That's twice,' replied Summerfield, curtly. Then, more relaxed, he added. 'Please sit down—I accept your offer. And perhaps you can help me with more advice,' he added ruefully.

The man raised an eyebrow. 'Ah?'

'Yes,' said Summerfield. 'But first—'

'First let us introduce ourselves,' interrupted the Moroccan. 'I am Abrach.'

'Harry Summerfield. But I didn't quite catch your last name.'

'My first name, *Abrach*—that is sufficient,' grinned the man. 'My family name is long and rather complicated for your tongue, I imagine.' Summerfield hesitated, wondering whether to insist, but the Moroccan continued. 'I am a merchant. *Un commerçant* as we say in French. But not one shop—*several*.'

'And I'm not French, I'm afraid.'

'Indeed. I take your accent for English, maybe American,' replied Abrach, his voice remaining calm and too polite. 'But I should think you are English—you do not look like an American. And you do not behave like one, either for I have met several on my travels.'

'Your judgement is correct, Abrach,' said Summerfield, copying the over-polite tones. He sipped on his tea, feeling the bubbling of mischief inside him. 'I noticed you were someone of importance back there in the square. Your clothes,' added Summerfield, courteously. Abrach nodded and smiled, accepting the compliment. 'Tell me,' inquired Summerfield, suddenly remembering. 'Where does this incredible blue come from?'

'Ah, yes,' said Abrach. 'The blue that is so particular to this region.' He made a sign to the young waiter to serve him more tea. 'Believe it or not, a Frenchman invented it. *Majorelle* is his name, a painter. The city is his home and he paints many pictures in the Atlas Mountains to the east. The blue is worn by the Berber tribes and Majorelle mixed in other pigments to produce this unique colour. It is, by the way, called *bleu Majorelle*.'

'I should like to buy a headscarf of such colour if I decide to go up into the mountains,' commented Summerfield.

'A *cheiche* we call it,' said Abrach, in a voice that sounded like an invitation. And then, a smooth transition: 'And may I ask what brought you to Marrakesh?'

Summerfield laughed. 'An American!' For the first time, Abrach's expression of careful pleasantness changed to a frown. Summerfield explained. 'I was about to cross the Spanish frontier to take part in the war. He convinced me not to.'

'A wise man,' said Abrach, 'perhaps even a Godsend. I saw death when the Spanish and French hunted down the dissidents some years ago. A ghastly, ugly sight.'

They were silent for a few seconds and Summerfield's attention returned to the *riad* and he felt the greatest of calm enter him. The colours, the sound of trickling water and birdsong, the sweet nip of spearmint tea in his mouth made it all so complete, all so satisfying.

When he turned back, he saw that Abrach was observing him. But the merchant didn't seem to mind. Instead, he smiled and Summerfield thought he saw a note of sadness in the man's face.

'You mentioned that I could perhaps help you, Mr Summerfield,' said Abrach, his expression returning suddenly to the genial. 'And how?'

'You have a good memory,' nodded Summerfield. 'In fact, I thought you might provide me with an address. You see, I want somewhere to stay.'

'You surely have a hotel?'

'I would like somewhere where I can live among the people— the *real* people.'

'Indeed,' said Abrach, raising an eyebrow.

'It's a question of means,' added Summerfield, holding his gaze. 'When I first arrived in North Africa, I had a notion that one week would be sufficient. Now…' he paused, summing up the surroundings with an appreciative nod of his head, 'now I think I'd like to stay a while longer.'

'A wise man plans with both head and heart,' offered Abrach. 'You are right to be concerned.' Another silence before the merchant spoke again, delicately picking out his words. 'So then…you are not a *rich* man, Mr Summerfield?'

Summerfield grunted. 'No. And I'm not for the instant interested in being one.' Summerfield smiled ironically. 'You think I'm a fool, Abrach.'

'I think you are strange, complex.'

'The world is changing. Many people are beginning to believe in the good of all and not just the few.'

Abrach pondered this and released a sigh. 'I suppose it is how your world works, *Sidi* Summerfield. Here it is different—the people who wish to become wealthy try to become wealthy because it is their personal destiny and, I'm sure, they have good reason to.'

'Not so different,' said Summerfield, with a shake of his head.

'Let us not spoil our splendid surroundings with ideology and politics,' said Abrach. 'We will undoubtedly have another opportunity to discuss these things. You see, I am an educated man. I studied medicine for a while with our European rulers, and what with my Arabic instruction, I enjoy such intellectual sparring.' The merchant's smile remained unbroken for several seconds and it sent a distant flicker of alarm through Summerfield. 'But now,' continued Abrach, finally releasing his smile, 'Let me say that in answer to your question I can propose three ways: you may leave your hotel and be a welcome guest in one of my homes—I have several rooms which are empty and in need of presence. Secondly, I have a good friend who owns one of the better hotels in the city. He owes me a debt and will surely offer you rooms at a very generous fee. And finally, I can find you accommodation in the popular district of the old town, not far from here—another acquaintance, absent for some time, may I add. There you will see poverty, Mr Summerfield. You will see how most of the city dwellers live and there may be times when you will have to take guard over your belongings and your safety. A European in such places is practically unknown. It could be seen as an intrusion. These are my three proposals to help you.'

Summerfield looked keenly at the merchant. 'Your generosity is…'

'Worthy of a good Moroccan,' said Abrach. 'But I must also add that I perhaps have a job for you which will enable you to stay longer than you had expected. That is—*if you wish*.' Again, Summerfield shook his head. 'This is not work as you may think.' Summerfield glanced up and made a gesture for the merchant to continue. 'You see, I need *your* assistance, too. And above all, Harry Summerfield, *discretion*.'

'I don't see how…'

'Mr Summerfield—in the square I heard you speak three languages.'

'English, Spanish and French,' acknowledged Summerfield, looking away. 'I studied at university in England—it seems like a lifetime ago.'

'You can speak them—but can you also *write* them?'

The question took Summerfield by surprise. 'Yes, I can. In fact, I used to write for a living. Why?'

'Have you ever been in love, Mr Summerfield?'

'Who hasn't?'

'But so much in love with a particular woman that you feel as though your only reason to live is to live for her?'

'That's a little dramatic, Abrach.'

'But you said you were a writer.'

'An *unknown* writer—a copywriter for meaningless products and lies.'

'A writer is a writer under God, regardless of whether he is known to others or not. Don't you agree? Do you not *feel* as though you are a writer?'

'You make it sound as though I've failed the second part of a test,' commented Summerfield, growing irritable.

'I am simply stating my belief in your capacities, Harry. I also believe in signs. It was you who came to me on the bench in the square—a man who can assist me, if he so wishes.'

'And was it *me* who came to you *here*?' said Summerfield.

Abrach laughed. 'Sometimes a man must give that initial sign a further push in order to help things along.'

'So you followed me.'

'I simply asked the man who showed you the way. You see, the idea came to me the moment you stepped away. We must pursue our ideas in life.'

'I didn't go to Spain to fight.'

'But you did decide to stay longer in Marrakesh. Sometimes it is a question of choosing the *right idea*.' Summerfield pursed his lips. He detested being pressed into a situation. As if sensing Summerfield's resistance, Abrach added: 'I'm afraid I may appear too aggressive. Forgive me—my trade has much influenced my ways. I wish not to force you, *Sidi* Summerfield. I would like us to find an arrangement that suits us both.'

Again Summerfield remained silent. A finch flew overhead, barely a foot from their heads and rested on a branch. It was so close Summerfield could see the beat of its heart. He sighed. The offer was interesting, bizarre, but not without complications. His idea had been to be responsible only to himself. And then he thought that too many times in the past he had missed out on opportunities—and why? Because of his fear, he told himself. Fear of the unknown, fear of his capacities.

'Abrach—you want me to write love letters, is that it? Trick her? Isn't it a little Romanesque—'

'Just one letter—a *real* test. And then…'

'Can I ask why *you* do not write to her?'

'Because, my dear friend, I cannot write French as I speak it. It is one of the reasons I could not continue studying with the Europeans. And, to say the least, I am no poet. I was born to grow rich through selling.'

'Then why don't you simply tell her?'

A strange, sharp look momentarily came into Abrach's eyes and he laughed to himself. 'Because the woman in question is a *European*.'

'I *see*.'

'Do you, Mr Summerfield?'

'I suppose you mean that blood is not to be mixed?' Abrach nodded. 'In some of our British dominions, the same law applies,' added Summerfield. 'And I suppose you understand that I would be breaking one my people's codes of conduct.'

'Do you really consider yourself one of *them*, Harry? They are French, they are Spanish. You are British. And I believe that the British hold certain opinions about their *frères ennemis* across the English Channel? Am I wrong? I believe you are a person who values equality, *Sidi* Harry. And I also believe that you consider yourself more like us, the Moroccans, than either the French or Spanish and despite the colour of our skin. All foreigners empathise—and that is the great irony of it all. For us Moroccans, we are foreigners in our own land.'

They sat for several minutes in silence. Another two customers entered, greeted them and chose a room on the opposite side of the lily pond. Although speaking softly, their words came to Summerfield, as mysterious and as enchanting as the early morning prayer. He suddenly felt tired, his mind muddled by the heat, this man, their haggling conversation. He had no notion of time and could not bring himself to glance at his watch. It didn't matter.

'Abrach,' he said, tentatively—'do you believe in destiny?'

The merchant laughed softly. 'All men ask themselves this question. I think you know my answer. Though sometimes it is hidden—murky and dangerous. And other times it is as clear as the water in a mountain spring.'

'Ten months ago I listened to a great man, one of the greatest writers of our times and he gave me the strength to finally follow what I'd always wanted to do and be. Then I came up against setbacks in Spain and I didn't follow it through.'

'Some say a setback is a way of testing our will to achieve what we want. If you changed path, then it is a sign that you did not really mean to follow that path to Spain.'

'I am glad I am here,' said Summerfield, almost to himself. 'I hadn't expected to—to feel so close to what I really want. I had so many false ideas.'

'Which may indeed be put to the test,' said Abrach. 'And they may be proven right. It is for you to see.'

'It isn't easy. The American I met in Gibraltar, Jim Wilding, would have known,' said Summerfield, thinking aloud.

'Whatever way you choose, Harry Summerfield, remember that it is the good way. Otherwise, your life will be full of regret and of sorrow.'

'So?' said Summerfield.

'So you know the way,' replied Abrach, looking smug.

Summerfield looked steadily at the merchant for a few seconds and then drew breath. 'I agree to that third proposal of yours.'

'And the transaction, *Sidi* Summerfield?'

'And I agree to the transaction,' acquiesced Summerfield. 'My pen will write beauty like no other before it.'

'*Maktub*,' said Abrach—*It is written*—and shook Summerfield's hand.

3

Two days later, one of Abrach's employees, a small, tacit man in his mid-forties, arrived at the hotel with a calash drawn by a sorrowful looking donkey. Abrach was not to be seen and when Summerfield asked the employee, the latter stood mute and uncomprehending. Summerfield wondered if the merchant had decided not to come through snobbery and felt disappointed. He'd hoped Abrach had understood his argument, his beliefs. Apparently not. His trunk and suitcase were loaded onto the calash and he stepped up behind the employee who gave the donkey's hind quarters a sharp thwack with a cane. The beast pulled subserviently away, but not without a backwards and rather disdainful glance at the driver. Perhaps revenge in another life, thought Summerfield as they trotted along the track which ran parallel to the city walls.

They passed across the Djemaa El Fna, littered with the debris of the market, Summerfield recognising the spot where he'd first met Abrach. He thought he recognised the boy who had sold him tea, now leaning against the bench and without his cups and urn and waved, but the boy, although waving back, obviously didn't remember him. He recognised, too, in the far right-hand corner of the square, the street that had lead him to the *riad* and hoped (the comfort of the known, he thought afterwards) the calash would take him in that direction. But it didn't. Instead, the driver yanked the rein to the left and the donkey grudgingly changed direction, heading for a part of the city Summerfield hadn't yet explored.

They entered the extreme western tip of the medina for fifty or so yards, a narrow, cobblestone way of one-storey huts, the sun shut out by a makeshift roof made of whatever materials had been found—wooden slats, branches and leaves from the date trees, chicken wire, glass, canvas and cardboard. At certain points, the shanty roof had disappeared and here, great funnels of light beamed down highlighting the millions of particles of dust filling the air and the crazy swirl of flies. A mass of sellers with their goods spilling onto the cobblestones operated from the small shop fronts. The sheer variety of goods and colour and smells made Summerfield's head swirl but before he could focus on assembling the jigsaw into a clear picture, they were suddenly out into the blaring sunlight and a district which seemed entirely dedicated to bicycle repair work.

The smell of machine oil, rubber and the nauseating nip of aging metal filled his nostrils. It was like an open-air grave. Piles of parts, the skeletal remains of frames and twisted wheels, cogs in heaps of hundreds and the tragic, imploring clawing of mounds of handlebars and distorted spokes lay strewn either side of the street. Sometimes the piles lay slap bang in the middle of the way, so that Abrach's employee had to manoeuvre his way delicately round or else, on one occasion where the wheel got stuck, harangue a group of idlers into shifting the pile.

A feeling took hold of Summerfield that he recognised as excitement. Excitement mixed with a little fear. A sudden thought entered him that it was here that he was going to live—at least for a while. A completely foreign place, more than a thousand miles from home and a world away from his culture. Part of him wanted to resist. Part of him told him it was a filthy and lazy world. A world that, because it was different, was ultimately wrong. *It is not civilised*, said a voice in his head. *It is dangerous*, said another. But above these inner demons, another voice said, *I would simply like to see and live it and understand*.

Strangely, it was as though his instinct knew something, something that inextricably linked him to his future. It was the same feeling he'd felt last year, when in the crowd that spilled into the reading rooms of that London library, he'd listened to Orwell's description of the struggle in Spain. A sort of kindling flame in his stomach and in his heart. A flame that had sparked a rush of blood to his head. Everything, in that precise moment, had seemed to come together. It was the same now, he realised, the same sense that *this was what it meant*. Only now it was almost stronger, and at least more palpable, because he was here and receiving sparks constantly from everything around him. It was first hand, in vicarious rhythm with his environment, a companion.

The scores of little workshops with their piles of dissected bicycles were left behind as sharply as he had entered them and another district opened itself up. On the right, the rear walls of the medina with its shanty roofing. On the left, homes which were, to Summerfield's eyes, just the same type of huts but this time piled irregularly on top of each other to form constructions of three to four storeys high. Some had glass in their windows, others wooden blinds or rusting iron bars and others nothing at all. Here and there, quaint little shop fronts with their strange, Arabic writing above the door and, in smaller letters, French, announcing the nature of their trade: *Pharmacie, Dentiste, Epicerie, Coiffeur…* It was into these, at first a wide turning which quickly narrowed into a grid of tracks—themselves promising a future as an extension to the old medina—that the calash turned and came to a halt.

Summerfield made to get down, but the employee—who now introduced himself as Nassir—shook his head and motioned a gesture which suggested he should stay in the calash. Summerfield obeyed. The little man descended and shifted through the crowd, now and then rising on tiptoe, obviously looking for someone.

While Nassir searched, a small group of boys appeared, barefoot, grimy and dressed in an odd assortment of stained clothes, hand-me-downs from older brothers or cousins. Some of them, dirty-cheeked, beamed him smiles. Others just stared at him. Summerfield saw beyond what could have been mistaken for hostility to a deep wariness, a mix of concentrated distrust and fear and, above all, pure curiosity. They continued for some moments to stare at each other and then, feeling mischievous, Summerfield sharply raised his arm whereupon several of the boys flinched—one actually turning heel and beginning to run—and then brought it to a rest at his nape where he calmly began to scratch an imaginary itch. He did it again and the effect was less dramatic. This time he grinned and the boys chattered with laughter. One of them held out his hand for money, then another and another followed. Summerfield shrugged his shoulders but the boys pressed forward, pushing noisily against the phlegmatic donkey. Luckily, Nassir appeared and, brandishing his cane, scolded them in Arabic. The boys turned heels and ran, if only for a few yards or so. Summerfield had the distinct feeling that some of Nassir's words had also been directed at him and felt vaguely stupid. He was right, thought Summerfield. He was no longer a tourist, but one of them and had to respect the rules of his new home.

At last, Nassir beckoned him to get down from the calash. At ground level, things felt a little different and Summerfield was overcome by a brief sensation of being lost. There seemed to be people everywhere and they all seemed to look the same. The driver pulled on his arm and Summerfield followed, his rucksack in hand, along the street. There was a foul-smelling tree, the base of which had been liberally doused in urine, and it was here that Nassir turned left along a shaded pathway, roughly five yards wide, to a door. Summerfield raised his eyebrows inquisitively and the unsmiling Nassir looked upwards. Summerfield nodded back. At least, he thought thankfully, he wouldn't be at ground level.

When the driver had gone—hovering around for a tip that Summerfield begrudgingly handed over, he found himself alone behind a closed door of peeling green paint. The lack of noise was striking. It was part of the jigsaw that made up the city's puzzle—the ability to descend from the loudest din to a profound silence in all of a few yards. Turning, Summerfield set eyes on his new home.

In one corner, through the dimness, there was a rough oven made of bricks and clay and covered in a metal grid. A conduit ran vertically from the back of it and disappeared through the roof where a large patch of black stained the ceiling. Two threadbare carpets—almost impossible to discern the original colour—covered the middle of the room. There was a wooden bed, a chest of drawers and a low table with two cushions. An open doorway led to another room and Summerfield, unconsciously checking the door was rightly closed, went through to explore.

The second room was half-lit by sunlight from the street. It was empty but for a bucket, a small desk and, thank God, a chair which looked as though it had had a former life in one of the city's Franco-Spanish administrative offices. The window, or more specifically, the large gaping space in the wall, much to the delight of the flies which buzzed energetically in and out, was without glass. The walls were of pink plaster, rough and undulating, the smell non-descript if not slightly mossy.

But it was something else that caught Summerfield's attention more than anything else—a narrow set of steps that lead upwards to a wooden trap in the ceiling. He climbed up, pushed and received a shower of dust and grit. He pushed again, harder, and this time the trap flapped back with a loud bang. Summerfield squeezed carefully through and found himself on the roof. He remained squatting for a few seconds, determining the limits of this platform, slowly getting his eyes accustomed to the painful light. He immediately felt the sun on his skin, pressing down onto his face, neck, forearms and hands, gaining pressure, gaining heat. After some moments, he stood up, not a natural lover of heights, and almost shuffled the few steps across the baked surface to lean forwards and peer over. To his surprise, only six or seven feet below was another roof—or terrace as he now recognised—and below that another. The first-floor terrace was half-covered in a tarpaulin giving shade, the second in a large tent much like those Summerfield had seen in desert paintings of the Bedouins. There were also plants and spindly trees in pots and a large cistern for catching rain water (*if it ever rained*, he thought). He stood back, erect now and more assured and surveyed the clutter of roofs across the immediate horizon. The noise of the streets rose up to him, the smells of the city changing in the light breeze. In the not-too-far distance, the high minaret of the *Koutubia* and others, mostly angular, poking up from the sprawl of the medina. He glanced at his forearm, noticed it had turned quite a vivid pink, and decided to return to his rooms.

On the small desk before the large window was a letter. Abrach's employee must have left it there. Summerfield sat on the chair, lit up a cigarette and opened it.

'*Greetings indeed once more, Sidi Summerfield,*' it began and Summerfield couldn't help snorting a laugh at the quaint protocol. And then he remembered that Abrach disliked writing—he'd probably had it transcribed orally. He read on. '*I took care to ensure that the accommodation is furnished. You may add to those furnishings as seen necessary. A man of mine, Badr, will come once weekly to ensure that all is fine. He will also perform three duties I have entrusted him: he will collect the money owing for the accommodation, he will also hand you a sealed letter with payment for the letter you will write. And lastly, he will, if our business agreement may continue, hand you instructions as to any further correspondence to undertake and collect any previously written correspondence written* (a mistake, noticed Summerfield). *I would also wish to see you once weekly to discuss our business. I finish by reminding you of the conditions of our agreement, notably the faith I place in your discretion and your abilities in your craft. I also add that I am able to terminate the agreement when deemed fit. Naturally, any papers relating to the drafting and writing of our correspondence are to be destroyed. Badr is to witness this in your presence.*

Yours faithfully and soon…'

There was no signature. Summerfield sat back and stubbed out his cigarette in the bucket, immediately realising that it was perhaps there for other purposes. He thought about Abrach's words. All the secrecy. Perhaps it meant the possibility of danger, he wondered. Still, it was an agreement and Summerfield felt bound to the merchant if not for the fact that he appreciated him. And then, like an apple falling on his head, the realisation suddenly came to him that he hadn't discussed the price. *What a crafty*—began Summerfield and smiled. *Inchalla*, he said softly, turning to the window: *let it be God's will.*

Two days later, Summerfield journeyed out to the main post office to wire Jim Wilding his new address. When he returned there was a tall, sinewy young Moroccan waiting for him in the narrow street in front of his rooms.

'Badr,' said the adolescent, scratching his chin and Summerfield noticed the striking blue of his eyes—Berber blood. '*J'ai une lettre pour vous.*'

'Come in,' said Summerfield, and walked ahead, up the stairs to the third floor, Badr following. Despite being two steps behind, the young man's head was at the same level as Summerfield's. Once inside and the door closed, Summerfield turned to the messenger and made the customary gesture of welcome. 'So Abrach has sent you,' he said in French. 'May I have the letter?' He noticed for the first time the young man's vain attempt at growing a beard. It explained the tic of repeatedly and rather ferociously raising his hand to scratch his chin. The young man hesitated, taking his time to understand and then slid a hand inside his shirt to bring out the letter. He nodded and handed it across. It was damp from the boy's sweat. 'Does Abrach expect payment for my rooms?'

The messenger shook his head. 'After the work. Abrach will join you. You will talk and see.'

'Thank you, Badr.'

Alone once more, Summerfield peered out of the window and watched the tall young man enter the street and disappear round the corner by the tree which he had come to understand as the area's habitual place for relieving oneself. It was a wonder the tree was still standing.

He put some water on the boil, placed the letter on the desk and sharpened a couple of pencils while waiting for the tea to brew. He sought paper, placed three sheets on the writing desk and weighted them down with his watch, noting the shocking white band of untanned skin around his wrist, a legacy of England. He waited, teasing himself, putting the moment off, playing with his inspiration. He waited until the tea became cool enough to sip. Then he opened the letter. Again the bizarre, heavy-handed opening formula:

'Greetings indeed once more, Harry Summerfield,

I trust you are well. The time has come to write, Sidi Summerfield. You must be delicate and at the same time persuasive. The lady, I fear, is timid and will not appreciate an open declaration. I wish to begin formalities by stating my admiration, that I have already observed her and appreciate her beauty and softness becoming of a woman. I wish to inform her, in a diplomatic and most gentlemanly way, that she entered my heart the first time I saw her. For your information she is dark-haired,

neither tall nor small, has brown eyes and a most feminine silhouette.
She is also quite young, twenty to be exact, and intelligent. She also has
grace, like a gazelle.

Good luck, Sidi Summerfield.'

Summerfield shook his head. Why the merchant Abrach
couldn't simply send the very same words to the woman in
question was beyond him. Still, there was money involved and
Summerfield imagined that Abrach wished for something special,
something more poetic. A pity there wasn't anything to go on—
the description of the young woman could probably fit twenty
thousand others in Marrakesh.

He re-read the letter, picked up a pencil, waited some more.
Nothing came. Instead a small squiggle, a little like a coiled snake,
began to fill the sheet of paper under his distracted fingers. He
exhaled noisily and drank his tea. Eventually, after remaining in
his chair for what seemed an hour or so, he got up, impatient, and
strode once around the room. 'Nope, nope, *nope*! Won't do—*can't
do.*' He sat down again, then stood up and once more, his eyes
caught the trap door in the ceiling.

The sun was sinking westwards, early evening. The pink city had
turned red and the faint sound of the square and its preparations
for the nocturnal bustle of the salt and sugar sellers reached him.
He had come to understand this time of the day. The city would
soon enter a little death, just under an hour between the end of
the preparations for the night and the swaying mass of people
that would fill the huge square. Summerfield closed his eyes, felt
the cool, warm breeze lap against his skin and sucked in the smell
of smoke and of spices. '*Come on*, come to me,' he whispered. He
focused his mind and imagined her and began slowly to write.

4

S he had just passed through the entrance gates of the *Académie des Jeunes Demoiselles de Sainte Suzanne de Marrakesh*. It was five o'clock and the end of classes for the day. The rather ornate gates, a reduced model of those she had seen in books about the Palace of Versailles, had warped under the heat of ten Moroccan summers and now never drew completely shut. For want of a better solution, a rope knot was used to keep them from swinging open, held in place by a local man who had entrepreneured, several years ago, to loosen and tighten it as visitors passed in and out of the premises. The man was very old and very wrinkled and wore a hood and cape against the sun. His hands, knurled and arthritic, resembled the very knots he loosened and tied a hundred times a day. None of the young ladies attending the institute knew his name, but they all called him *Monsieur Quasimodo* and made up for their wickedness by offering him food and coins.

In front of the French academy was a square, the meeting point for three roads and a gravel track that led into the date and orange groves. There was a fountain that functioned only in the winter months, a lawn of thick rough grass and a dozen or so orange trees. A gaggle of pony traps and several cars, sent by the parents of the richer students, waited around the perimeter of the *place* for the young ladies to appear.

Jeanne parted with her friends, giving each three a *bise* and a wave as they walked off under the protection of their straw hats and parasols to their respective transportation. Soumia, Jeanne's chaperone and the family help for nearly fifteen years appeared, dressed in her pale blue working dress, and went through the ritual of fussing her to drink.

'But I've already had a glass of water, Soumia,' Jeanne protested, as she always did, and then finished by accepting, as was also custom.

Soumia was known to be a stubborn woman whose opinion regarding certain things was only to be considered as the absolute truth: things that neither her mother nor even her father would contest, like the amount of salt to put into the courgettes, the exact time of the day to brew tea, where to place jasmine in the house to ward away unpleasant smells and evil spirits and of course how many glasses of water to drink per day. Once, several years ago, her mother had dared to do differently and old Soumia (not so old, in fact—rather her mother's age—forty-five) had sulked for a full month before accepting an apology and returning full-hearted to her duties.

They walked together towards the awaiting trap, and Soumia halted. Before the Nanny opened her mouth, Jeanne knew what was coming next.

'Yes, Nanny Soumia,' she said, rolling down the sleeves of her blouse. 'But all my friends wear short sleeves. I feel so old-fashioned!'

'Do you want to be burnt, Jeanne?' said Soumia, adding a cluck, like an aspired *h*—her way of reproach. 'Do you want your skin to be brown and shrivelled like mine, like an old prune?'

'You have beautiful skin,' replied Jeanne. 'In fact—'

'No *in facts*, *'moiselle*,' said Soumia. 'You must keep your paleness. That's what makes a European lady so different, so precious.'

'All this fuss about skin,' said Jeanne, grumpily. 'And in any case, don't think I haven't noticed that even if the others do bare their arms, they are still whiter than me.'

'Stop it, Jeanne, or I shall tell your parents of your behaviour. You sound as if you are ashamed of them.'

'On the contrary, Soumia—but I just wish they'd speak to me.'

'Speak to you? What do you think they do every day?' But Soumia didn't finish. Instead, as they approached the trap, she stared at something across the square. Three ragged children from the medina had appeared, shouting noisily. 'Hmm—up to no good,' muttered Soumia. 'Come, Jeanne. Do not tarry. Into your seat and Mohammed will drive us home.' But the three children seemed to head straight towards them. '*Beggars!*' said Soumia. 'They should not be allowed to such an area.' The driver,

Mohammed, offered his hand for Jeanne to step in just as the children arrived. Mohammed turned to them, his voice low in a failed attempt to scare them off.

'We owe you nothing, little pests—go away!'

'God will be merciful to you! The Evil eye shall not shine— give us something, Oh Mistress. A little coin!'

Soumia, with a sigh of exasperation, born more of embarrassment than anger, stepped out again. 'You've mistaken us for someone else,' she said loudly in French and added a scolding in Arabic.

From her seat, Jeanne noticed one of the children was missing an arm, the stump of which showed smooth and round when he gesticulated. She shook her head. Why Mohammed couldn't just give them a coin or two, she thought. Just then, a shape—*a man*— brushed past the trap on the other side and released something white into the trap that span then fluttered crazily. Jeanne instinctively drew back and let out a gasp. In one second, the man was gone. The white object, lying at her feet, she recognised as a letter. She picked it up, glanced back to search for the man and then heard Soumia's voice turning to her.

'What is it? What's wrong?'

Why she made that decision she would never know. Instantly, Jeanne Lefèvre stuffed the letter into her satchel and frowned. 'I thought I'd forgotten something, Nanny Soumia—and for goodness sake, give the children a coin to shut them up. Can't you see the poor child is an invalid?'

Soumia rolled her eyes heavenwards and gabbled something to the driver. 'If we gave charity for every missing limb in this city, we'd be penniless within the week. Oh, go on! Give them some *sous*!'

She could have shown Soumia the letter. She could have opened it in front of her. She could even have given it, unread, to her father. Instead, she kept it, in her satchel, on her knees and clutched like a treasure. On the journey back, Soumia remarked that she seemed a little tense. Jeanne replied that the day had been rather tiring—tectonic plate theory—to which Soumia let out a gloomy sigh: '*Another new disease!*'

Both her father and mother were absent when she arrived home. Apparently, they had been invited to a *soirée* given by the Bridge Club and would be back late. Leaving Soumia to prepare tea, Jeanne climbed the stairs to her bedroom.

It was a medium-sized house, one built especially for civil servants coming from the French *Métropole,* and located in an avenue with twenty others built in exactly the same, whitewashed colonial style. There were four bedrooms upstairs and two in the outhouse where Soumia and Mohammed respectively slept. Downstairs there was a large, tiled kitchen, a double living room, a dining room and father's study. The garden was long and semi-wild, a continual struggle for Mohammed, whose hopeless monthly battle consisted in keeping the sand from invading the lawn. Thankfully, the architects had thought of a veranda and the planners had planted trees along the avenue and in the gardens to create blessed shade. It was here, too, that wild thyme and savory, seeds blown in on the winds from the Atlas, had taken root and grew in abundance. Their fragrance was such that Jeanne could sense the approach to her house even with her eyes closed. Once she had tested her theory—and it was true. Her street smelled of pepper and lemon.

Closing the door to her bedroom, Jeanne opened her satchel, rummaged through the books and papers and, when still unable to find the letter which had taken on the excitement of gold, emptied the contents onto her bed. There it was. Turning her back to the door, listening one last time for any footsteps, she first brought the letter to her face and smelt it—*fleur d'oranger*. It was a fragrance she had smelt a thousand times in the city. The women used it in their cooking, the men used it as eau de cologne to hide the smell of perspiration, the *riads* and restaurants offered it to wash one's hands with before and after a meal. Breathing in one last time, infinitely curious, smiling to herself with excitement, she carefully prised open the seal. But could it be a mistake? On an afterthought, she checked the front of the envelope—no signature, no address, not even her name. So the man *had* made a mistake. It *had* been an accident. She turned her attention back to the letter, teased it out, unfolded it and read.

The leaving of the day comes tender to my eyes, the grace of the setting shadow casting minutes' full and pleasant sigh; for another moment will come to wake, where you shall rise and once more be my day.

Rising by setting sun, such beauty as is yours can do no other than warm the admiration of Man; and, no doubt, sweet young woman, I am but one whose words you capture in your time.

Jeanne reddened, quite lost and decidedly bothered. Upon reading the last word, her eyes had seemed to revolve inwards and gaze longingly down into the deepness of her body. She looked around the room, as if scrabbling for help, then reached across and dipped her fingers into the water basin on her night table. She dabbed her neck and forehead, the cool drops seeming to evaporate as quickly as they had touched her skin. Her next feeling could almost be measured as anger. It was grossly perverse—how *dare he (it had to be a He, didn't it?)* write such things—and to *her*. But then curious again. The returning of her eyes to the text and, despite the indignation, the faint resistance, the second reading. And it was quite good, in fact, she concluded. Actually, when she became objective about it all, it was quite very beautiful. A third time. But the third reading was interrupted by Soumia's call for tea. Jeanne rose, quickly slid the letter beneath her pillow, then on second thoughts, under her mattress, and stepped out onto the landing.

'*Still* not changed!' cried Soumia, as if the world had come to an end. 'You've certainly had a day, young lady!'

'I certainly have, Soumia,' replied Jeanne, sheepishly.

It was one of those occasions when, despite how much effort Jeanne made to break free, she was disposed to sit with Soumia and listen. The more the seconds passed, the more she squirmed in her seat. The worst was when Soumia began to embark on a recapitulation of the day. Under normal circumstances, Jeanne would bear the monologue out, making noises and offering the odd comment until Soumia had finished. This time, she was frustratingly aware of Soumia's penchant for listing the most minute of futile detail—from the aspect of the water from the tap at six in the morning, to the insect Mohammed had found lodged in the spout of the watering can and the state of the gutters in the roads during the journey to fetch her at the *Académie*. Jeanne mentioned she had homework to complete to which Soumia replied that she had time, seeing as her parents were absent. But it was when Soumia doted on the appearance of the child beggars before the *Académie*, that Jeanne's impatience and frustration reached bubbling point. No matter how hard she tried to point Soumia in the direction of the mystery man, without of course directly mentioning him, Nanny Soumia branched off at tangents on a series of tirades against the police authorities, the city beggars, local taxes, the danger of being robbed and finally Mohammed's character, which she found too soft and tolerant to be of any use as a help to the family. In the end, Jeanne closed her ears and let herself be sucked in towards the subject that had really stolen her mind for the past hour-and-a-half.

In her shut-out world, the words of the letter came back to her, the smell of orange essence, snippets of memory that seemed to refuse to be put into any logical order. Had she seen the man's face? She tried hard to recollect and found herself forcing an image into her head. No, no—*try*, she said to herself.

'What did you say?' came Soumia's voice, suddenly causing Jeanne to jump in her seat.

'What?'

'Do you not agree, *Mademoiselle*?'

'I was just wondering if it was a trick,' floundered Jeanne.

'A trick you say? *The governor*?' Soumia frowned.

'The boys in front of the *Académie*. They might have been creating a diversion. Perhaps their father was at that very moment robbing those whose attention was taken—'

'Gracious God,' gasped Soumia, cupping her face in her hands in a gesture that Jeanne thought rather too theatrical. '*I'd never have thought*! We must check our belongings!'

'Did you see anyone?' pressed Jeanne, 'A man perhaps?' Soumia stopped and looked away, narrowing her eyes in the effort to remember. 'Think, Nanny Soumia.'

Soumia thought, long and intensely. 'Nope.'

'*Are you sure?*'

'I was giving the beggars a ticking off,' replied Soumia,

disappointed. 'I should have paid more attention!'

'I'm not saying there *was* a man,' said Jeanne, quickly, realising the danger that Soumia would now concentrate her energies on recounting the whole scene yet again. Soumia hummed and remained silent. Jeanne finished the last morsel of cake on her plate and placed her cup back in the saucer.

'Are you feeling under the weather, *Mademoiselle*?' ventured Soumia, distrustfully. Jeanne smiled and shook her head. 'You're not—'

'*I beg your pardon, Soumia?*' cut short Jeanne, all too aware of where Soumia was aiming for.

'Feeling *poorly* or anything,' said Soumia, rectifying her words from the warning Jeanne's voice had carried. 'No?'

'No, Soumia,' finished Jeanne. 'Certainly not *poorly* in the way *you* suggest. Just a little tired. I do enjoy our conversations, Nanny Soumia, but I do have work to finish for the *Académie*.'

'It's not that *tictonic plague* is it?' probed Soumia, one last time, getting it wrong. 'It is quite surprising how those samples you girls study don't escape from the classroom. Just think—the whole city infested with disease!'

'Well, they *do* sometimes try to jump out of the spawning jars, but the *Professeur* obliges us to keep lids on them,' replied Jeanne, ruefully.

'I should hope so,' answered Soumia, a little disappointed to hear otherwise. 'Right—perhaps I should let you get on with your work, Jeanne. But don't work too hard. And I'll just check my bag, just to make sure. And don't go sitting outside in the heat!' she added, regaining her share of authority.

'I won't,' smiled Jeanne, reassuringly. 'However, I will go to bed early this evening, I think. Could you bring me something to eat? I'll leave the tray on the landing.' And with that, controlling the urge to sigh out loud in relief, Jeanne rose and climbed the stairs to her bedroom.

Evening came. Resisting the urge to re-read the letter, concentrating on her homework and aware of the intense delight of putting off the excitement until later, Jeanne sat at her desk and wrote her geography essay. She giggled to herself whenever the words *tectonic plates* appeared and she found it almost irresistible not to replace it with Nanny Soumia's *tictonic plague*. She must remember to tell her friends! Indeed—should she tell them about the *letter* as well? It would certainly raise her esteem in the other girls' eyes—they would think her worldly, a woman. Though, on the other hand, it could cause quite a few jealous tongues to wag. And they may ridicule her. She would decide upon reading the letter again, she concluded and went back to finishing her essay.

Dusk fell and the night drew closer. Soumia had brought her a light dinner and a jug of fresh water which she then placed, as planned, back outside her door near the stairs. She called out— *bonne nuit*—and Soumia's voice faintly called back, wishing her a peaceful sleep.

Softly locking her door and moving across her room to the bed, Jeanne noticed that she still hadn't changed out of her school clothes. *Later*, she thought and slid her hand under the mattress to recover the envelope. Withdrawing the letter, the thought struck her that her hands were now touched with the scent and the perspiration of the man who had written it. At first alarmed, she crossed the room to wash her fingers, then stopped herself. It was silly. She wasn't going to read the letter wearing gloves! And, as she sat back down by the bedside lamp, the idea that she was in contact with part of the person who had written it sent a strange shiver through her—something indiscernible, hardly a pleasure as a feeling of fear and something deeper, out of reach.

She read the letter again, twice, the first time quickly, the second time taking care over each word. She thought she could hear the man's voice in her head and, strangely enough, it brought back the image of the young actor she had seen some several months before, interpreting Molière's *Le Bourgeois Gentilhomme*. He had had the finest of faces, rather bird-like and inquisitive and extremely expressive clear brown eyes. Several of her friends had written to him and two of them, including Cécile, her best friend, much to the dismay of all the others, had received warm replies.

Jeanne pondered over the words of the little text, searching the meaning, searching too for *hidden meanings*. Of course, the overall picture was one of admiration. Admiration of her beauty. *Beauty!* She giggled. The word had never occurred to her before! At least, not concerning herself. Her body was something that was just there—an unfelt presence for most of the time, a part of the whole that was ruled by the head. She did masturbate, of course, like her friends—though this had been deemed an unladylike occupation since early adolescence by her peers, notably the sisters at the *Académie*. What did *they* do? she suddenly wondered, and promptly readjusted her thoughts for fear of losing the effect of the letter. And she—Jeanne—had also kissed. Several times. Mostly sweet, endearing pecks from Edouard, one of father's colleague's sons. He seemed to like her. Perhaps, the letter was from him. No, it was too adult. Edouard was only nineteen and sadly rather lacking in literary skills, thought Jeanne. He was destined to be a chartered accountant.

The letter. The words. No one had ever written to her like that. If indeed it were not all some silly mistake. She paused, suddenly aware of something inside her, something churning. She drew in air through her lips. It was the sound of her heart. She listened and it grew faster, deeper, almost as if it wanted to race ahead of her thoughts. And then she felt the tingling, down there, in the intimate, unmentionable part of her womanhood. Again she breathed in, thinking of anything but the letter, bridling her beating heart and bringing it to a slow trot.

After that, her first reflex was to stand up, close the shutters and draw the curtains as if shutting out the world. The word *beauty* came back to her, a word invoking that same mild surprise and a distant feeling of guilt and embarrassment. She suddenly felt terribly alone and vulnerable. She switched on her bedside lamp and a soft warm halo spread instantly across her bed. It cast a warm glow over *Baudelaire*, her battered and faithful old teddy. She picked him up, brought him to her cheek, the faint sugary, sour odour of the fleece filling her with a sense of presence, of safety. Everything was all right.

She began to change into her nightclothes. It was just before ten and the cool air came through the shutters. Standing before the mirror, she took off her dress and blouse, folding them neatly and placing them on her dressing table. Then she slipped out of her underclothes, reached for her nightdress and hesitated. Her eyes turned to the mirror and caught her looking sideways at herself, at first embarrassed, then curious. But this time the reflection was somehow different. It was as though she had managed to step out from herself and was looking at the image of a person looking at another in the mirror. It was so curious. She stood up.

The image she saw was both familiar and unknown, the image of what she suddenly realised was a woman. This woman quite tall, slender in her age, her hair black in the light of night and wavy, falling to rest on her collar bone. Her eyes dark eyes, dark hazel. Two distinct black crescent moons that were the eyebrows; a thin mantle above the bridge of her nose, quite prominent, that cast a tiny shadow on her skin. Thin shoulders, childlike perhaps and fragile. The gentle slope of her breasts, falling firmly then tapering to a point, turned slightly outwards to the nipples, hard and dark like tenacious little rose buds. Her arms neither fat nor thin. Stomach and waist, venturing into womanhood, rising here, there flat like the water on a ripple-less lake. Her thighs both round and angular all at once, encompassing the nut of her sex, a delta of jet black. Then a glance sideways at a most precocious, impertinent pair of buttocks that almost seemed to defy gravity. It was indeed a woman she saw in the reflection, perhaps even a woman who could fit the words of the letter.

Stepping back even more, unfocusing, Jeanne saw the shape and colour as a whole, saw that the figure before her was not exactly European, the skin although clear beholding a quality that was richer, deeper and possessing a sort of pastel quality like the skin of a young green olive. *Very* curious, she thought. Who *is* this woman belonging to no definable point of the compass? Who could belong to no distinct definition? Finally, both tired and perplexed, Jeanne slipped on her nightdress and climbed into bed. She went to sleep that night with the letter under her pillow, conscious of her body against the sheets, a stranger that was her.

5

Abrach was in fine spirits. Sitting in the *Café Kasbah* by the crumbling royal palace, he ordered Summerfield a *caoua*—a coffee. The merchant wore that same habitual smile, but this time Summerfield noticed a perceptible deepening in it, a stamp of sincerity.

'I am very content with the results of your work, Harry Summerfield,' grinned Abrach. And then, as an aside: 'And forgive me for not coming to see you in your home. I try to remain discreet.'

'I imagine you would be greatly solicited,' offered Summerfield, accepting the coffee with a nod of his head.

'I help those who helped me—I always do,' continued Abrach. 'Though some try to make you believe they helped when in fact they did the exact opposite. It is often these people who ask the most!'

'How odd,' smiled Summerfield. He was beginning to feel a genuine liking for Abrach and his simple anecdotes.

The merchant made a sign for the waiter to refill their cups then turned back to Summerfield. 'So tell me—how are you, Harry? Are you still decided on staying that little while longer?'

'Every day is a discovery,' answered Summerfield. 'I'll stay until the novelty runs out rather than the money.'

'Good.' Abrach grinned. 'And it may take some time. Because, as you may understand, I wish to continue with your services.'

'In all honesty, I thought it would be the last I'd see of you, Abrach. So I passed the test, did I?'

'You succeeded well—and I thank you.'

'I was a little concerned,' began Summerfield. 'One tries to imagine how one's reader will interpret.'

'Which is a good sign, Harry. A sign that you are professional in your approach to your craft.'

Summerfield leant forwards. 'You see, the most difficult was trying to find the inspiration. I just couldn't fathom out how to tackle it.'

Abrach's mouth sagged. 'You make the most beautiful creature on Earth seem like an English rugby match! I must protest!'

Summerfield laughed. 'I wrote to the city of Marrakesh.' Abrach looked at him and frowned. 'Yes,' continued Summerfield, lighting up a cigarette, enjoying the conversation. 'The inspiration wouldn't come, so I climbed on the roof and when I saw the city and its lights and the sunset, I knew I had the subject matter!'

'I *see*,' answered the merchant, suddenly looking saddened. 'So if I had simply looked out from my terrace at the setting of day, I could have written the thing myself—and saved my money!'

Again they laughed. 'You could try,' said Summerfield and Abrach pondered for a second, then shook his head.

'A wise man leaves a craftsman to his craft. I would not entrust you with my shops. I would not entrust myself with poetry.'

They remained sitting at the table in the café, observing the flurry of people coming and going in the narrow street. Leaning his large frame forwards, Abrach pointed out the colour of the sky, an opaque creamy blue and informed Summerfield that this meant imminent rain. Surely enough the wind began to kick up, blowing with it particles of dust and sand that darted around the city walls, filtered through the streets, skittered the alleyways and came to rest on the tables of the café they were sitting in. Summerfield touched the dust with the tip of a finger and studied it.

'It comes from the desert,' mentioned Abrach, raising his eyebrows. 'All the way from Ouarzazate and beyond.' There was distance in his voice, as though it was the expanse of the desert itself speaking. Summerfield gave a nod of understanding.

'One day I will go there.'

The rain thickened. Summerfield tried to find a comparison to English rain—something approaching an August storm. But it wasn't quite that. Here the rain fell in visible, pear-shaped drops like the milky semi-precious stones the local artisans used for making pendants. Great pink and dusty explosions as they hit the ground. The people in the street did not run for shelter. Instead, there seemed to be even more of them, quickening their pace and pushing as they threaded their way over the cobblestones. On one side of the street, to the left and barely ten yards away was a hole—work being carried out on the sewers—and next to it a mound of excavated earth. Under the force of the rain, it soon began to subside. One passer-by lost his footing on it, slipped and fell over. Another passer-by quickly picked him up and moved on, the former shouting thanks and continuing his journey, his *jellaba* smeared with deep red mud. Summerfield looked at his companion and laughed—not through malice, but a sense of surprise and enchantment at the acceptance of it all. Falling over a pile of dirt that had been lazily heaped in the middle of a street seemed just as normal to the people as the rising of the sun.

After ten or so minutes, the downpour suddenly stopped, the cool air instantly saturated by the heat, giving rise to a heavy odour which Summerfield judged as something between a mixture of sweat, excrement and leather. He wrinkled his nose and tried not to appear disturbed by it. Abrach must have noticed however, for he called out into the street. Presently, an old man appeared with a basket under his arm. Abrach gave a small coin and delved into the basket, bringing out two sprigs of fresh mint.

'*Choukran,*' he said to the peddler and then, turning to Summerfield. 'Here—you take them. I am used to such things.' Summerfield took the mint, wondering whether to pick the leaves and chew them. 'Like this,' said Abrach, momentarily taking back the sprigs and holding them to his nose. 'It kills the bad odours. I see you haven't been to the tanners' district,' added Abrach, handing them back. Summerfield shook his head and Abrach beamed. 'My friend, you have many things to discover yet—but remember the mint. You will learn of its importance.'

After their coffee, Abrach invited Summerfield for a stroll in the King's gardens beyond the city gates. They hailed a calash and were soon trotting along to their destination. Summerfield tried to engage conversation during the trip, but the merchant remained silent, no doubt, thought Summerfield, in case the driver should overhear.

Blue sky appeared just as they stepped down from the calash and entered the ornate gardens. They began to stroll, Abrach ushering Summerfield on towards an ornamental lake. At last, sensing the moment was right, Summerfield posed the question he had been waiting impatiently to ask.

'You say the results of the letter were positive,' he began. 'So I take it she replied?'

His companion took off his hat and wiped his brow with his hand, which he then wiped on a handkerchief. He gave a little snort. 'Heavens no. If it could be so quick, so simple, my friend. It will take time. It is rare that one's quest for treasure ends in victory after the first strike of the spade.'

Summerfield hummed agreement. 'But then, what was the positive outcome you were so content with?'

'You are very direct, Harry. Indeed, there are two positive outcomes, barely visible but nonetheless victories in their own right.'

'Go on,' encouraged Summerfield, concentrating, for his mind had already begun to focus on the next letter he was to write.

'The first is that the young beauty in question did not reject the letter. She could have thrown the envelope into the gutter but she did not. The second is that she *read* the letter.'

'How do you know that?' asked Summerfield.

'Because on the following day, she appeared and searched the faces around her. She was obviously intrigued, did not seem bothered or angry. Indeed, according to my man she appeared rather curious and willing to make further contact.'

Summerfield chuckled. 'I can imagine her face when she read—'

'I do not wish you to laugh,' interrupted Abrach, stonily. Summerfield fell silent, taken aback by the merchant's sudden swing of mood. 'Your writing must continue to express respect, Harry. It will be helped by the fact that you respect her person. You see,' continued Abrach, his voice now mellowing, 'she is a beauty, a unique being for me and closer to my heart than you will ever imagine. Oh, if Allah wills—I tell you, Harry, I would donate my life and my wealth to the good and needy if I could have her in my presence.'

6

Nothing happened. Not on the second day, nor the third. Every day Jeanne left the *Académie* and stood by the gates until Soumia came to accompany her home. She must have looked at the faces a thousand times until they were all recognisable to her at a glance. And still she observed, wondering which one of those waiting would make the uncommon gesture, who would start walking towards her. But no one did. She lingered longer than usual by the calash until she felt Soumia begin to become suspicious and then, with a terse, *oui, Soumia*, she would climb in, frustrated and disappointed.

On the fourth day, it occurred to Jeanne that she had been concentrating on one specific thing—and it was perhaps this that had made her miss the man in white. It was the simple fact that she had been expecting the messenger to arrive in the evening, after classes. The morning she rushed, typically inattentive to detail, concentrating on being behind her desk when the bell rang for lessons. Why hadn't she doubted that he could be there at any time of the day? She felt stupid and also, as she left the house that morning with Mohammed, rather excited.

She was alert when the trap came to a halt and Mohammed opened the door for her to climb down. It was as if she sensed something would happen. This time, this morning, she waited until Mohammed had driven off to continue on towards the gates and the old knot tier. She looked around her, trying not to be too conspicuous, answered a couple of hellos from some other girls, but did not see the man or anything resembling a letter in anyone's hand. She looked down, beginning to question her supposition, ready to face the fact that she was wrong, when it happened. It was all very quick. Suddenly, there in front of her, was a man—a young Arab. She looked up, surprised and her face broke into a look of enquiry. *Is it you? Are you the writer of messages?* she wanted to say, but no words came. Instead, sensing the question, the young man shook his head. He was tall, thin, barely older than herself, clean-shaven and dressed in western clothes, rather too clean and smart. He looked a little uncomfortable in them.

'*Un deuxième message*,' he said, softly in French. 'I will be waiting if you wish to reply.' He brought out his hand, as if to shake hers, but it contained a small white envelope which he quickly slid into her palm.

Jeanne stood still, conscious of time slipping past and the sense of urgency less someone should notice them. 'Where?' she blurted out. 'When?'

'Do like this,' he replied quickly, making a fanning gesture with his hand. 'I will be waiting, do not worry.' And he smiled. '*Au revoir*.'

'Your name?' said Jeanne in a whisper, but the young Arab shook his head.

'Not me.'

The following hours were agonising. Once Jeanne had stepped inside the gates of the *Académie*, fate threw a thousand different obstacles in her way. For some reason, this particular day, everybody wanted to talk to her, everybody wanted to ask her assistance and everybody wanted to bother her. Cécile, her best friend, clung onto her as she entered the buildings, asking for this paper and that for the English test. Sarah Bassouin, the pretty Jewish girl who was already engaged to marry later that year—one of the Embassy staff, a young tax officer, had connections with her family—accosted her with an invitation to a party just as Jeanne was about to enter the ladies' room.

'Thanks, awfully,' returned Jeanne, 'we'll talk about it at break.' But Sarah Bassouin, much to Jeanne's horror, followed her into the toilets and continued chattering away as she reached for the handle. 'Look, Sarah, I'm sorry—' said Jeanne, finally, 'But—' The bell rang.

'No time!' squealed Sarah, gleefully. 'Come on—you know

what old Marthe will say if we're late!'

'But the loo!' replied Jeanne.

'Should've gone before. *Pisseuse!*'

'Sarah!' gasped Jeanne. 'Your *language!*'

And so classes commenced. *Sœur* Marthe, age unknown and unfathomable, already puffing from the heat at this time of the day, seemed to single her out. Jeanne couldn't keep her eyes from glancing down at her satchel and the hidden letter. Sister Marthe, her own eyes very much alert despite her Calvary—she was quite red in the face now and had brought out her habitual perfume flacon, an ornate bulb-like article filled with water and with a rubber pump attached to it that, when pressed, wheezed a spray of water onto her face—spotted her.

'*Mademoiselle Lefèvre,*' came Sister Marthe's voice. 'Am I right to conclude that you keep looking at your neighbour's work?'

Jeanne froze. 'No, Sister.'

'Then what are you up to, *Mademoiselle?*'

'Up to no good,' came a comment from somewhere at the back and a collective, but restrained giggle spread through the class, brought to an abrupt end by the gargoyle-like grimace suddenly appearing on Sister Marthe's face.

'Well?'

'Sorry, Sister Marthe,' returned Jeanne, blushing furiously and diverting all her energy to sitting up straight and attentive.

'You look a little flustered,' continued the teacher.

'She's in love!' came a whisper and this time, laughter and whoops, impervious to Sister Marthe's glowering, rose up from the students.

'That's not true!' returned Jeanne, immediately realising her mistake. For now, no one would ever believe her. The other students whooped loudly again.

'*Be quiet!*' shouted Sister Marthe, puffing from the effort. The class fell silent. Sister Marthe's perfume pump wheezed flatulently. 'Continue with the next paragraph, Lefèvre. Read.' And so began Jeanne's blurted, stumbling reading of Shakespeare's *The Tempest* until Sister Marthe, herself seemingly under torture, almost pleaded her to stop. 'Whatever is the matter, *Mademoiselle?*

Are you ill?'

Jeanne flushed a deep crimson, hesitated, then said: 'I would like to go to the ladies' room, please.'

'That's right, Sister,' came Sarah's voice. 'She wanted to go at the beginning of lessons. Her bladder must be bursting!' Again, the laughter.

'Sarah Bassouin!' shrieked Sister Marthe. 'Just because you are leaving us for marriage, doesn't mean you are exempt from civility! Now,' continued the old teacher, mopping her brow, 'why didn't you simply put your hand up, my girl?'

'I thought it was—'

'What?'

'I thought it was just…but it isn't.'

'*Lord*,' sighed Sister Marthe, phlegmatic. 'You're a little bit early this month—off you go. Quick!'

Jeanne stood up, clutching her bag and made her way out of the classroom as discreetly as possible, unfortunately knocking over the parasol stand in the effort. A loud clatter rang through the classroom, again followed by giggles. She stooped down, helped by Cécile who had left her seat, and then disappeared behind the door, closing it with the vision of Sister Marthe's eyes rolling heavenwards in despair.

Once in the toilets, Jeanne locked herself in a latrine and sat down. She was breathless. The excitement was unbearable, almost like fear. Her hands trembling, she reached down and brought her satchel to her knees. The letter seemed so precious, so delicate. Again the faint smell of *fleur d'oranger*, faint though strong enough to overcome the odour of bleach in the small cubicle. She was afraid she might tear it in two and again she leant back and caught her breath. Sister Marthe would be wondering. And the others. Mustn't be too long, the thought raced through her mind. Putting all her strength of concentration into the folded paper, she slowly peeled away the seal, whimpered when she made a slight tear, regained control of her fingers and continued until the seal was completely broken. The letter slipped out of the envelope and fluttered from her fingers to the floor. She picked it up, unfolded it and gasped—it was a poem!

With past-midnight eyes
the old, everlasting stars do shine
as they do over endless hearts
and endless words.
Countless they are
Both those silvery
points in night's pincushion
and metaphors for eyes,
heartbeats, fate and foolery:
for there are some ageless stories
that are born to live
and live they do—like stars.

Jeanne felt her body slide from under her. She opened her eyes.
Somehow, she had ended up on the floor, slumped in a crouching
position in the confines of the cubicle. She was unable to gauge
how much time had passed, but it felt like the years in the
poem—endless. She had fainted. Good God, she had *fainted*, she
said to herself, as though asking for confirmation. She tried to get
up, slipped back down and drew a deep breath, this time heaving
herself up to a sitting position. Quickly, she folded away the letter,
her fear now that of losing it. She chose not to put it back into
her satchel, instinctively tucking it under the waistband of her
skirt to the elastic of her drawers, against her skin, and covered it
up with the folds in her blouse.

When she opened the door to the classroom, she was met
with silence. The girls were sitting a test and Sister Marthe, for an
instant eyeing Jeanne with suspicion, then with concern, nodded
to her to sit down. Poor Jeanne. She could not, for one second,
concentrate. The text appeared aggressive, the letters blurred.
Again she felt herself reddening. She must have been staring at
the test paper, for a hand suddenly appeared on her desk top.
It was Sister Marthe's, with wrinkles, liver spots and all. Jeanne
closed her eyes, fearing the worst—fearing that she would ask
her to stand up. She saw it all: the letter would slip out and fall
to the floor; Sister Marthe would ask her to read it in front of
the whole class. The *shame*, she said inwardly. Instead, the hand

rose to rest, surprisingly lightly, on her shoulder. She looked up. Sister Marthe's face was different. There was a softness in it. The old teacher raised her eyebrows, a sign for Jeanne to rise. Silently, without fuss, she followed Sister Marthe out into the corridor.

'You are in trouble, Jeanne.' The Sister's voice was gentle.

Jeanne shook her head. 'No, Sister. I'm very tired, that's all. A little fatigue.'

This time Sister Marthe shook her head. 'You obviously have something worrying you, Jeanne. It would be wise to talk.'

Jeanne hesitated and a little whimper escaped her lips. 'I'm sorry, Sister Marthe—I can't. I'm sorry.'

The old lady pursed her lips and the gargoyle came fleetingly back to her expression, then disappeared. 'In that case, I prescribe a day or two of rest over the weekend. No going out, especially with Sarah Bassouin and those parties of hers. I shall write a note to your parents. Off you go. *Home*—Friday is finished for you.'

Jeanne could not have hoped for a more awful turning of events. Before she knew it, Sister Marthe had accompanied her to the infirmary and attended time enough for the nurse, a small, wiry woman called Mme. Hubert, to administer Jeanne two doses of quinine. The ghastly liquid was so bitter it brought tears to her eyes. She sat there, on the side of one of the two beds in the drab little room, painted pea-green, while Nurse Hubert went on to take her blood pressure.

Her heart was beating fast—not so much from the fact that she could feel the letter against the skin of her hips, but rather through the fear that nurse Hubert would ask her to undress for further examination and discover it. The envelope had become limp with her perspiration, a clinging presence against her hip, a source of growing irritation that turned into an annoying itch. She fought to stay still.

Twenty minutes later, Nanny Soumia appeared at the door. 'I knew something was wrong!' she fretted, giving the nurse an all-knowing scowl.

'Nothing so serious,' replied Nurse Hubert, 'Most likely just a case of stomach cramps. Make sure she drinks a lot.'

'I knew it!' shrieked Soumia—nurse had touched her on a

nerve-end. Jeanne winced with embarrassment.

'If it continues after this evening, call the doctor—just to make sure,' added nurse Hubert, frowning. She reached into a tray and pulled out a form. 'Now,' she said, turning to both Jeanne and Soumia. 'I need your signatures—*or your mark*—just here, at the bottom.'

Nanny Soumia took the pen. 'I can write,' she said, almost in defiance and signed, her tongue protruding from between her teeth, taking the utmost care with her loops, before passing the pen on to Jeanne.

Once home, Jeanne had hoped she could slip up to her bedroom and hide the letter. Her mother had decided otherwise. Instead, Soumia led the young woman to the veranda and seated her in the wicker armchair usually reserved for her father. Presently, her mother arrived, with Soumia reappearing at her sides carrying the tea tray.

Jeanne's mother was tall, pale and doted with a sort of serenity that spoke of manners and good company and a certain belief in boundaries that were not to be overstepped. Her eyes were steady and grey, her lips rather thin and delicate—lips that Jeanne knew both capable of uttering the softest compliment and the bitterest reproach. She had never quite managed to obtain her mother's attention in its entirety. Over all the years, their time together invariably left Jeanne with a sense that something was missing.

Jeanne's mother, dressed in one of her lemon-yellow dresses (she had several in her wardrobe), sat down next to her and took her hand.

'Sister Marthe phoned through before you left. How are you, my dear?'

'She said she would write a note,' replied Jeanne, a frown creasing her forehead. It seemed almost like treason. 'She didn't have to phone. There's really no need to worry, mother. Just a little tired lately.'

Her mother made a nodding motion with her head. Was that a smile Jeanne could detect? 'It seems to be a long-lasting tiredness,' said Mme Lefèvre, sending a glance to Soumia, a sign for her to leave. 'Nanny informed me of the same occurrence—almost a week ago. Tell me,' she continued, her voice calm. She poured tea and offered a cup across. 'What sort of tiredness is it? Perhaps an *Edouard* tiredness?'—the words emphasised, as though held aloft in a pair of tweezers.

'*Mother!*'

'Silly it may sound,' returned her mother, her lips showing a fleeting trace of amusement. 'But really—your father and I have noticed that he seems to *loiter* every time we meet.'

'He's a little serious,' replied Jeanne, suddenly quite interested in the conversation.

Her mother raised an eyebrow. 'I believe he collects insects.'

'*Stamps*, mother.'

'Much the same thing,' continued her mother. 'A nice boy. His father is one of Papa's friends—a good position, too.'

'Is that a criterion for matchmaking, *maman*? I thought that disappeared with the turning of the century.'

'Don't be so impertinent, dear Jeanne. I was just mentioning that it would be preferable to get to know a young man whose parents are—are one of our *own kind*, that's all.' She looked up, saw the shock on her daughter's face and smiled again. 'Edouard is indeed a *nice* boy.'

'And he indeed seems to like me,' said Jeanne, exploring.

'*Indeed*,' replied her mother, sipping her tea. 'Nice and… *dreadfully boring*. In fact, quite like his father—but for heaven's sake don't tell. Could you imagine, Jeanne, being made to accompany him to the *souk* every week to choose his specimens—beetles, cockroaches, spiders—*oh!*'

'I said he collected *stamps*, mother!' said Jeanne, joining in with her mother's laughter.

'You did, my dear, you did.' A silence, while they both gathered themselves. Her mother sipped again and placed the dainty tea cup back down on the tray. She looked across. 'Jeanne, I do wish you to fall in love, of course. It would make a relationship more special. More…*lasting*, perhaps.'

'You do?'

'Yes. But not now—and *not* with anybody.'

'You mean, court each other like you and papa did?'

Her mother's lips seemed to grow thinner, almost disappear. 'Yes, dear—like I and your father. Now,' she added, drawing breath. 'You seem better, already. I imagined a little chat would do some good. But you still haven't mentioned what it is that's causing your state. If it isn't Edouard...'

'The exams,' offered Jeanne, knowing full well that her mother was aware they were some months off. 'The weather—' Her mother cleared her throat, ever so softly, obviously a sign. Jeanne sighed. She thought of the letter. What would her mother's reaction be? What would her father say—he'd probably have guards placed around her night and day. She sighed again. 'It's me,' she said, finally, catching her mother unprepared.

'You?'

'I—I'm beginning to feel...that I'm different, mother.'

'*Different*?' Again the word held in her mother's tweezers. 'Of course you're different—we all are.'

'Mother, when I look at myself in the mirror, I see a woman who is neither like you nor papa.'

Her mother gave a little snort. 'Firstly, *woman*—perhaps the word is a little too precocious, Jeanne.'

'I'm twenty, mother—nearly twenty-one.'

'And I find it particularly insulting to hear you speak of *difference*,' continued her mother. 'Whatever's *different* about you, my girl?'

'The colour of my skin,' said Jeanne, perhaps too quickly. 'My features,' she added, only causing further damage.

'This is ridiculous!' cried her mother, making Soumia suddenly appear on the veranda. 'Go away,' ordered her mother in the same breath. 'Ridiculous and insulting. A little girl's fantasy—the poor little orphan syndrome. Jeanne—I could expect this from a girl of six and not—as you pretend to be—a woman of twenty.'

'Mother,' said Jeanne, wanting to justify herself, but her mother made a waving motion with her hand.

'Go up to your room and take a cold bath, girl. It will calm your wild mind. I don't know what it is that is causing this behaviour, but it must disappear in time for dinner. Do you understand. I want no further discussion on the matter.'

Jeanne hesitated then, seeing there was no use in continuing, rose and walked away. Dinner with her father, would surely see her crucified—forbidden to go out for the next month. God, how she felt miserable.

Jeanne finally found herself in her bedroom. She locked the door. Falling onto her bed, exhausted, she gazed at the ceiling for a long time, concentrating on the rise and fall of her chest, the heaviness disappearing from her limbs that became light, almost floating. After some time, she moved her hand to her hip pulling away the folds of her blouse tucked into her skirt. Her fingertips touched the letter, hot and damp and gently pulled. It would not come loose. It was stuck to her. She unclasped the waistband of her skirt, prised it apart and pulled down one side of her knickers. On her side now, propped up by her pillows, her free hand gently peeled away the envelope. There was ink on her skin—her dull skin—and the scent of orange essence. Again, she felt light, slightly dizzy. She lay on her back, the envelope between her hands. The seal came away in tendrils of glue. The letter, unfolded, smelled heavy, overpowering. She read and time passed, unimportant, unnoticed.

The last trial in her day, dinner, was a most bizarre occasion. Jeanne had descended at eight sharp, freshly washed and clothed in her pyjamas, determined to keep her composure. Her father, still in his working suit of white linen, back hunched and balding, the epitome of the government civil servant, accepted her kiss without moving from his seat at the table. Mother sat to his left, reading through the newspaper he had brought her back from the office. From time to time, she made a comment and engaged in a brief exchange with her. When Soumia served dinner, the conversation turned to her father's day at work, the situation in France and in Europe, the Hindenburg disaster that, although some months old, had etched in their memories forever with the newsreel they'd watched at the *Pathé* picture house. Jeanne's father, rinsing his mouth with local table wine, enquired how she was. Glancing across at her mother, Jeanne replied that she had been a little tired, but was now feeling better. Her mother said nothing, kept a mysterious silence and let herself drift along with the turn of conversation.

Jeanne returned to her room at nine, relieved and filled with mild surprise. Had mother been showing a sign of feminine solidarity? Perhaps, thought Jeanne, they were at last to be real friends, real equals.

Switching on her bedside lamp, again she read the poem. And once more, time passed, irrelevant. She had never been impulsive, never been in love. But she wanted to. She wanted to feel that great and noble feeling that some of her friends had experienced, had talked about. They had said it was like flying higher than any bird, on a current that just kept lifting you upwards, towards the sun and heaven. At other moments, they said it sent you plummeting desperately, uncontrollably downwards until it seemed you would die. And at the last instant, when all seemed lost, it would shoot you upwards again to soar high and free. They said it did strange things to your heart and sent the most exquisite shivers through the whole of your body. There were things, too, that they did not speak about, but which Jeanne, together with the other avid listeners, could imagine—dark things, forbidden things, things that went beyond upbringing and frontiers and colour and race. It was as if everything that stood for order was shattered. A soft and violent anarchy. Jeanne wanted to feel that. It seemed, at that precise moment, that her entire life had been devoted to leading her to this point in time.

She picked up her favourite pen and withdrew a piece of paper from a drawer, conscious that something grand and beyond her mortal control was about to take place. She was about to live, about to taste the world and all its glory. She began to write her reply.

7

The letter lay unfolded on his desk, backside up. Summerfield leant back, wiped the sweat from his hands and brow and tried to discern the faint scent that rose from the paper. Something like lemon and pepper, he thought. Thyme, perhaps? Citronella? Perhaps it was Abrach's smell—but wasn't his *orange*? Summerfield looked up.

Out in the small dead-end below his window, a dispute was going on—or at least it sounded like it. Summerfield got up and peered out of the open window. Two women—perhaps mother and daughter—were energetically haranguing a man who sat resignedly on a handcart. At one point, the man looked up and caught Summerfield's eye. Summerfield shrugged and the man shrugged back. *Women!* he seemed to say. Some language was universal.

Returning to his desk, Summerfield lit a cigarette, again wiped the sweat from his skin in what had become a mechanical gesture, and gently turned over the letter. It was a short text—one line, written with great care, in deep blue ink. The regularity and width of the ink told him that the pen was of good quality. Another tic—he put his spectacles on, despite the clear light and glancing at himself in the mirror—he thought he had a faint Orwellian air about him—he read:

A wish to write you those words you cannot tell me; soft, gentle words that only I could inspire in you…

Summerfield felt his chest wince. So simple, so clear, he thought, and so honest. He felt perplexed. His immediate reaction was to draw a comparison with his own words which now seemed so heavy and clumsy. What the young woman had succeeded in doing was, on a stylistic basis, so stripped of artifice that it stood out, loud and true. The thought that his own words had served as a trap, and that the trap had worked, made him feel suddenly cheap. He sat back in his chair and took a drag on his cigarette. It occurred to him that he had discovered a value, something he hadn't hit upon before and it surprised him: it was manipulation, or rather the negation of manipulation, of an innocent heart.

Rising, he went to the window again. The argument had stopped and the two women had disappeared. Only the man still sat there, leaning forwards on his handcart and staring into space. Summerfield studied the man's shaven head, the glow from the light that, at this angle, caught the silver stubble on his face. Seconds passed and Summerfield thought of nothing, his mind empty. He peered along the alleyway and into the main street. People passed by, neither speaking nor turning their heads, hurrying to some unknown destination. A little boy with his mother stopped to pee up the tree. And life went on, the rush, the incessant ebb and flow.

After some moments, Summerfield again returned to his desk. Another cigarette—harsh, brown local tobacco—which sent him into a momentary fit of coughing. He read the words again. He felt something. Something indiscernible and hidden deep inside. Perhaps it was the recognition that he had succeeded his initial task. But perhaps, it slowly dawned on him, it was the fact that his own words had been read, recognised and acknowledged in such a sweet way. The young woman had expressed sentiment. And she'd given her feelings with much courage to an unknown writer, an unknown man—Abrach, of course, being the proprietor but in reality himself, Harry Summerfield. Good God, was she to fall in love with him? The thought made him sadly ironical. And then, faintly, it rose up, glimmered a little in his mind and he felt strangely fulfilled.

8

The city was in effervescence. Everyday was a market day, but this particular day a caravan had entered the city to sell its wares in the red city, some two hundred merchants, having travelled up from French West Africa through Mauritania. *Djemaa El Fna* square was packed with a mass of people, whole families out to buy spices and materials, the shop owners of Marrakesh out to purchase new stock.

Summerfield found himself caught up in the great crowd. As far as he could see, he was the only European among ten or so thousand people. It was an odd sensation and his mind, in a playful frame, turned the situation around—what if he were the only Arab among ten thousand Europeans? What would he feel then?

He had no idea of a destination. He let the crowd, a great winding serpent with a will of its own, push him onwards through the hundreds of makeshift stands. The noise was tremendous—he had never experienced such collective abandon of constraint. Everybody seemed to be shouting and shoving—high-pitched women's voices, dirty-faced children who ducked and weaved and shrieked, men who haggled with such guttural vehemence that it seemed negotiation would come to blows. But among this explosion of noise, the play-fight, the chaos, great smiles appeared on the faces. Close to one such scene, a man had reached shouting level and, in a mock gesture of anger, drew back pushing into Summerfield. Summerfield's immediate reaction was to resist and when the man turned, Summerfield was astonished to see a broad grin on his face. He smiled back. The man, obviously unperturbed by the question of place and status, clapped him on the shoulder and gesticulated at the merchant. Summerfield let out a sound—a sort of gargle—which everyone seemed to understand. There was a great roar of laughter and the merchant, shrugging his shoulders, finally gave way and reached across to offer his hand to the buyer. They shook, grimy bank notes were exchanged in a flash and the man who had crashed into Summerfield disappeared, holding aloft his purchase—a saucepan. Summerfield shook his head and again caught another smile from a face in the crowd. A sweet tingle of happiness filled him. He felt—and this was the strange part—*one of them.*

After ten or so minutes of pushing, he found himself before a stall selling headwear. Next to the stall, a group of Berber musicians dressed in the most outrageous hats Summerfield had ever seen—like giant, conical sombreros from which hung strips of red and black cloth—were playing music. Approaching the stall to get a closer look at the goods, someone suddenly grabbed hold of him and pulled him aside. It was a small, bearded man who spoke excitedly. Summerfield frowned, immediately on his guard. The man pointed to the ground, to a large basket. Peering inside, Summerfield saw that it contained two, maybe three coiled cobras. '*Choukran,*' nodded Summerfield—'I nearly put my foot in it, didn't I?'

The hats did not interest him. Remembering the conversation with Abrach and the mysterious reference to the desert, Summerfield wanted a headscarf—a *cheiche*—like the desert people wore. And, thinking further, he wanted something that would blend him in more with the local people—some trousers and a linen top. The negotiation took ten minutes, followed the same pattern as the client he had seen at the other stand—though this time inverted: it was the seller who went into a frenzy—further complicated by the impossibility to understand each other's words. A crowd had gathered round the scene, entertained by this European and his bizarre wish to buy their clothing, entertained by the mix of French, Arabic, Spanish and that strange, singing, echoing-sounding language that was English; entertained, perhaps the most, by the importance that Summerfield's gestures took on. In the end, the deal concluded, the small crowd applauded. Coyly, Summerfield took his newly acquired clothes and rejoined the serpent flow.

He slept in the afternoon. Before closing his eyes, it occurred to him that he was increasingly taking on the habits of his surroundings. He would like to try some *khat,* he remembered saying to himself—not a thing of these parts, but occasionally those from further east, labourers mostly, could be seen chewing the sleep-inducing herbs in the afternoon.

He must have slept for two hours. He couldn't be bothered to look at his watch. The first thing he did was to wash down—even asleep and motionless, he had sweated. He then tried the clothes he had bought in the market. A white linen shirt, a little like a smock, black cotton trousers which hung loosely, letting in the air. And lastly a black *cheiche.* He looked at himself in the small mirror he used for shaving and tried to knot it into headwear. The men from the caravan wrapped their entire heads in such garments until only their eyes could be seen. It was not so easy a task. No matter how he twisted and turned the material, it wouldn't stay in place. In the end, losing his temper, he flung it in a corner. The heat, what with his effort, had become almost unbearable. He drank in a series of gulps. And then he remembered the man he had seen that morning, the ground floor neighbour.

Their door was open. He hesitated, searching, of all things, for a door bell. Perhaps nobody was in, he thought, hoping distantly that it would mean a return to his own rooms. But no—the sound of voices reached him. He called out. The voices stopped. He called again.

The man appeared, looking nervous, and then recognised Summerfield. *Bonjour,* he stammered and Summerfield asked him in French if he could show him how to use the scarf. The man stared blankly at him and scratched first the stubble on his cheek, then his shaven head. It had obviously been the only word of French he knew. Summerfield pointed to the head scarf in his hands. The man shook his head and then disappeared inside the doorway. Summerfield hesitated, wondering whether to leave. On the point of turning to go, the man reappeared with a young girl, one of his daughters. She was dressed in a long, dark blue gown and only her face was open to view. Summerfield repeated his request slowly and the little girl gabbled, in what seemed a hundred words too many, to her father. The man looked curiously at Summerfield, shrugged in much the same way as he had done that very morning, and beckoned for him to come in.

Summerfield stepped into the dark living space and stopped in his tracks. In front of him, the whole family had lined up—the man, what Summerfield now recognised as his two wives, two other daughters and two boys in their early teens. As Summerfield's eyes became accustomed to the dimness, he noticed they were staring at his feet. He had his boots on. Perhaps he should take them off, he thought and nodded downwards, whereupon the man—the husband—waggled a finger. *No need*, said the little girl in French and her mother sent her a sharp glance. Instinctively, Summerfield searched for a gesture of gratitude. Fumbling in his pockets, all he could find were his cigarettes and a couple of boiled sweets. He offered the packet across to the husband who nodded and took one and then rather clumsily passed the two sweets to the little girl who promptly popped both into her mouth regardless of her brothers and sisters.

'I live above—on the top. I'd like you to teach me how to put this on,' said Summerfield in slow French, holding out the *cheiche*. The girl translated uncertainly. Summerfield was aware of mixed feelings among his listeners. The boys laughed, the second girl giggled, as did one of the wives. The other, older wife frowned. The husband was devoid of expression, no doubt not wishing to repeat that morning's scene. To all appearances, it seemed as though he was leaving the decision to his unsmiling first wife.

'I would be greatly honoured,' said Summerfield, gallantly, looking directly at the first wife, who instantly dropped her gaze. 'Sorry,' said Summerfield, turning to the husband and repeating himself. The man looked sideways across, seemed to sum up the weight of the request and then said:

'*Atay*—tea.'

The girl sat at his side while preparations were made for refreshment. At least he had an ally—thanks to the sweets. He smiled at her. '*Comment dit-on je m'appelle Harry Summerfield. Quel est votre nom?*' He winked and she whispered Arabic into his ear. '*Ana Summerfield. Chnou smitek?*' he repeated. The husband clapped his chest.

'*Abdlakabir.*'

'*Ab...bl*—no sorry, it's too difficult,' said Summerfield and everyone laughed.

'Ab-lak-a-bir.'

'*Ablakakababir.*'

'Non! AB-LAK,' continued the husband, very slowly and very loudly. He did this three times before Summerfield got it right, with the result that everyone clapped, except the family chief— Abdlakabir's first wife—who continued, despite the warming welcome and despite the afternoon heat, with an expression that Summerfield likened to a November morning on Dover pier.

There seemed no hurry. The water for the tea boiled slowly on a slow fire. The afternoon flies buzzed slowly about the room. Summerfield took advantage to observe the space that constituted the kitchen and dining room. It had been painted many years ago, perhaps when the man and his first wife had first moved in, a thick coat of now discoloured white lime that in some places had flaked away leaving open wounds of powdery plaster. There were several wall carpets and Summerfield wondered if they hid more holes. Along one wall, on a score of nails, hung cooking pots and crockery. Opposite the stove and a chimney was a lonely piece of furniture made of reddish, dark wood, the doors of which had been carved into intricate interwoven stars picked out in mother-of-pearl. Summerfield caught the two women watching him studying the patterns and he made a complimentary nod in return. The first wife rose promptly and disappeared to return with the tea. Abdlakabir poured with great pomp and from great height, only missing, observed Summerfield, the cup once—that of his first wife. They drank. Summerfield made an appreciative sound and Abdlakabir, the husband, echoed him.

When he had finished, he reached across and took Summerfield's headscarf. The children crowded round, were pushed back. The elder son was made to remove his finger from his nose after a prolonged and fruitless probing.

Abdlakabir was a master. First he tied a simple slack knot, then slung the scarf over his head and in three seconds had wound the material into headwear that resembled the men of the caravan. Too fast for Summerfield. Again, this time slower, Abdlakabir went through the motions and then handed it back for Summerfield to try. Summerfield's first attempt was a disaster—he ended up with something approaching a conical turban on his head—which greatly amused the onlookers. Blushing, but aware that even the first wife had succeeded in smiling, he mimed frustration. Then a second attempt, this time the knot slipping loose and the whole thing falling into his lap. Again the squeals and shouts. Abdlakabir, wagging his head and clucking *la, la, la*—which the little girl thoughtfully translated as *non, non, non*—snatched it back and showed him an ultimate time. Summerfield concentrated hard, took back the *cheiche* and, after a hesitant start, finished up with something resembling success whereupon the whole family applauded. Abdlakabir spoke above the noise and, after some moments, the girl turned to Summerfield and explained.

'There are two ways to wear the *cheiche*—the desert way and the mountain way. Now father show you the mountain way?'

Summerfield smiled and said: '*La, la*—No, no—one is complicated enough! Another time—with many thanks.'

More tea was poured while Summerfield went through a second successful attempt of winding the headscarf. Then the first wife said something and to Summerfield's surprise everyone got up in a hurry. Instantly, mats were produced. He called across to the little girl.

'What's happening?'

'Afternoon prayer!' said the little girl and added, quite determinedly: 'You must take off your shoes!'

'Oh dear, I'd forgotten,' said Summerfield. Then: 'But I'm *C of E*! We don't do that sort of thing.' No sooner had he said it when an echoing wail, carried through the narrow streets via a megaphone in the local mosque, filled the air. The family immediately took up prayer position, leaving Summerfield sitting obtrusively with his cup in his hand.

He suddenly felt his presence rather disrespectful. Here he was, with his boots on, in the midst of a family who had welcomed him and taught him. He frowned, then put aside his tea and began to unlace his boots. The prayer chant continued. At first he stood, much as in a church, with his head bowed and his hands clasped—something he hadn't done since grammar school assembly in his teens. And Socialists certainly don't do that sort of thing—at least Socialists who went to fight in Spain, he heard his mind contest. But then he hadn't gone to Spain for the cause. He'd come to Morocco—for himself and, he was slowly beginning to realise, increasingly for the place and its people. Perhaps he should kneel—he didn't know if such a thing was permitted, but couldn't interrupt to ask. At last, summoning his humility, he unclasped his hands, dropped to his knees beside the girl who sent him an impertinent little grin, and closed his eyes. What would Orwell have thought of this? he wondered. What would Jim Wilding think? The chant, with its painfully laborious lament, became hypnotising, haunting. He drifted. And Orwell? And Wilding? Didn't matter. They would never know.

When evening came, he once more took the cramped stairs to the roof and sat there with a cushion, breathing in the cool air and watching the sunset over the pink city. He had his notebook with him, had already drafted the beginning of a reply to the letter, but felt dissatisfied. It wasn't the words he had written—they were, on an artistic level, quite good, he thought. It was rather the message itself, the reason for writing.

He hadn't seen Abrach for several days. The merchant was away on business of some sort and Summerfield had received the letter via his messenger, Badr. After some reflection, Summerfield realised that Abrach was a motivating factor for his writing. Quite apart from the fee he received, it was the contact with the man and his personality which gave Summerfield his belief in his work. Abrach needed him and thanks to him, Summerfield had received recognition. But now, since that first, simple reply, Summerfield felt uncomfortable. On the one hand, there was his patron with whom he had fostered a friendly and working relationship. On the other, a woman he hadn't even seen but whose words had given him a glimpse of her heart, of her character. She had become real. Those twenty or so words had told him something much more. Beyond them, inside them, there was courage and a hoping heart. There was vulnerability. She had placed herself at the mercy of her correspondent, *of him*. And the options now lying open to him required reflection, for the reply had made Summerfield hesitate. *Was it his own fear? What would happen to her? And Abrach—what would there be in all this for him?* He looked out over the roof tops to the distant outline of the Atlas Mountains, a deep purple against the deep blue of the sky. He was in a position of power. The *worm*—a horrible word, but it was the first to come to his mind—had already wriggled into her heart and mind and any path forward would lead to upheaval of some sort. Should he opt for the lesser pain and terminate his contract with Abrach now? Should he go on with it?

He glanced down at the three lines in his notebook. Three lines that had taken two hours to ease onto the paper. They were what Abrach would have written, if he could. Summerfield hesitated, his lips pursed. And then, on a second's impulse, he scribbled over them blackening them out completely. In five minutes, as if mirroring his anger, the sky over the city turned metal blue, then black. The rich quarters to the south and west were lit by the glow of lamps, the poorer districts to the north and east by firelight.

And then the idea came to him. Unformed, distant, but still solid, like a nut growing in size. He got up, disappeared into his rooms and resurfaced again holding an oil lamp. He placed it down by his notebook, excited now and remembering exactly what he had erased some ten minutes before. He picked up his pencil, rolled it between thumb and forefinger, tapped out a rhythm on his knee. Slowly, very slowly, he began to write.

I had not hoped for such a sweet and gentle reply. The simple truth of your words made me conscious of my clumsiness. I am a rock whereas you are water, clear and flowing. Already I am changing shape, smoothing my hardness, polishing the roughness of my stone. Like you, sweet lady, may my words trickle softly in reply while running deep and true. May I be at once both polished stone and rushing water.

Summerfield did not stop there. He stayed, lingering on the

roof until the air from the mountains reached him, cold and clear. He began to write freely and for himself—something he would have written for her, personally. It was when the Morning Prayer sounded across the city from the minaret, just before dawn, that he finally closed his book and descended from the roof to his bed.

9

The next day, he took the message to the district where Badr, the young go-between lived. Abrach had given express orders that it should be Badr who came to his rooms, but Summerfield, after initial formalities were dropped, had already accompanied the young messenger on a visit of his home patch in return for a meagre payment.

It had been a new discovery for Summerfield, for Badr lived in a district even poorer than his. It was there, among the disorderly sprawl of huts and tents made from corrugated metal, crudely shaped bricks, wood and canvas, that Summerfield had handed over the second message almost a week and a half before. Here, the faces were lined and hard and wore expressions of either distrust or outright displeasure at his presence, even with Badr at his side. After barely thirty minutes in the place, it was Summerfield who had decided to leave, filled with his first real presentiment that he was in danger. Badr, who had also become aware of the uneasy atmosphere, had seen him off with an apologetic shrug and the words (not without a hint of pride, Summerfield had noted) '*this is where the outcasts come, for there is no other place*'. It had intrigued him. The total lack of welcome, the unspoken language that told him he was a foreigner and therefore an enemy. And he knew he would return.

This time, Summerfield was intent upon getting closer to Badr's people. He dressed in his loose-fitting cotton trousers and shirt that he had bought in the market place, donned his open-toed sandals he usually kept for wearing in his rooms and lastly, still with effort, wound the black headscarf around his head, across the lower part of his face, and tucked the remaining material into the nape. Already tanned, only his blue-grey eyes seemed foreign. But then again, remembering that the Berber tribes from the mountains counted clear-eyed men and women among them, he wondered if it would pass off. He carefully slid the latest letter into a pocket and set out to find a calash.

At first sight, the driver refused to take him—a good sign. Coming closer to speak, Summerfield noticed a look of surprise on the driver's face followed by a frown which to all appearances seemed to suggest madness. This made Summerfield laugh and he climbed aboard, filled with a sense of mischief he hadn't felt since strolling Gibraltar streets with the American, Jim Wilding.

Purposefully, Summerfield left the calash some distance from the shanty district and went the rest of the way on foot. His first steps made him feel conscious of his gait—even that was different, European. Continuing, he tried to observe without drawing undue attention and finally chose a model—a man of roughly his height and build who seemed to walk slightly on his toes, giving him an unsteady, shambling air. Summerfield, his mind wholly into the game, adopted the gait as well as he could and walked on. He received no particular stares, no particular looks. He seemed to have succeeded.

The red, brick and plaster inhabitations resembling that of his own became steadily less frequent, replaced by the shanty housing he remembered from his first visit. It was as if a frontier had been crossed. The indications of poverty suddenly appeared. Groups of idle men sat on corners, the streets became increasingly unclean and rutted and filled with cast away rubbish and drying faeces. Old women huddled against their makeshift homes, children streaked with dirt and in rags, played or squabbled. There was the odd cart here and there, but mostly things were carried and mostly by women, some bent double with their loads. The same stares, in spite of his clothes.

Summerfield realised that it didn't matter who he was or even, to a lesser extent, how he dressed. He was a foreigner, one who did not belong to the usual, the known. This time, from behind his covered face, he stared back. And he noticed that those who stared at him finished by averting their eyes. He was beginning to think he really did pass as a Berber, when Badr bumped into him.

'*Monsieur Summerfield?*' said the young man, incredulous.

'*Harry*,' said Summerfield, caught between irritation and embarrassment. 'I've come with a letter.'

'The patron would not think well of it,' said Badr, drawing him aside.

'I had to get it to you quickly,' said Summerfield by way of justification. 'It's an important letter this time.'

'I see,' said Badr, scratching the soft, patchy stubble of his ever-nascent beard. He reminded Summerfield increasingly of a much clawed at teddy bear. 'Then let me invite you. Come.'

Summerfield followed slightly behind and Badr, occasionally glancing back, talked. 'You look very like us, *Monsieur*.'

'*Harry*,' replied Summerfield.

'But there are some things that told me clearly that you were not.'

'Oh?' said Summerfield, again feeling irritated. 'What?'

Badr stopped and turned to face him. 'First your clothes are too new. Look at those around you—their clothes are clothes of brothers and cousins, of fathers and even grandfathers—and maybe even of those they have killed.'

'Good God.' Badr laughed and Summerfield frowned. Perhaps the young man was trying to impress him with stories.

'And then,' continued Badr, once more scratching fiercely, 'your smell.'

'My smell.'

'When I walked into you, I smelt soap—European soap. We use—or try to use,' he corrected, 'liquid soap made from olives. Or orange essence.'

'Thanks for the tip,' said Summerfield and they continued walking. 'I'll remember it.'

'Lastly,' added Badr, grinning cockily, 'the watch you are wearing is a *very* expensive watch and one which we would never have the chance to wear.'

Summerfield glanced down then looked up in surprise. 'I'm not wearing a watch, Badr.'

'Correct,' replied the young man. 'It's in my pocket. I took it from you when we walked into each other. Here—'

Summerfield shook his head, defeated, and took it from the young man's hand. 'Thank you, Badr. You know—you could have kept it and I wouldn't have realised until later.'

Badr smiled and then his face darkened. 'In this part of the city most people never know if there will be a *later*—it is why I gave it back.'

Summerfield grunted. 'It's because you like me.'

The young man echoed him. 'It's perhaps because I like you, Harry. But do not mock me—my father died last year, one of my brothers the year before that. They did not see a *later*. And they were quite naturally robbed before I arrived to collect their bodies. It is a law here.'

'Against the rules of Islam,' mentioned Summerfield. 'What do the religious leaders say?'

'They risk their lives everyday. Things are changing, Harry,' said Badr. Summerfield looked sharply at him. He himself had said something of the same sort to Abrach only two weeks before.

'You mean the old rules are being forgotten?'

This time it was Badr who looked keenly at him. A thin smile appeared on his lips and his voice dropped in tone and volume. 'I think you, of all people, know what I mean. Is not Socialism a world religion, Harry?' Summerfield remained silent. 'Come—let us talk in a safer place.'

They entered a shack with a large overhang made of tarpaulin that gave protection from the fierce sun. From Badr's invitation, Summerfield had imagined something more intimate. Instead, the shack was crammed with men drinking and smoking black tobacco. The smell was overpowering and Summerfield breathed in short, sharp doses, the time it took for him to become accustomed.

'A drink of orange?' suggested Badr. 'It is the cheapest of drinks and the best. Allah made the fruit grow in abundance around here, even in the poorest districts.'

The juice was sweet, silky and surprisingly cool. It seemed out of place with their shabby surroundings. After a while, Summerfield turned to Badr, picking up on the previous conversation.

'And who do you believe, Badr? Allah or Marx? You don't

seem to mind mentioning both in the same breath.'

Badr leant forwards, suddenly earnest. 'Unlike some, I am beginning to believe that they are not incompatible.'

Summerfield cocked his head. 'A powerful combination. Does Abrach know of this?'

'My relationship with the *patron* is one of work and respect. I would not dare to trouble him with my views. He works hard and has many worries to solve concerning daily business.'

Summerfield nodded. 'I'm not surprised by what you say, Badr—it's rather you yourself who's surprising. I would—'

'*Never have thought a person of my status could be so aware?*' finished Badr.

'I suppose—perhaps said less bluntly,' continued Summerfield. 'And why did you speak to me about this?'

'I understand why you wish to dress like my people. And because you are of a similar belief.'

'I don't believe in God,' returned Summerfield.

'Then you will do before your life comes to an end,' replied Badr. 'Forgive my frankness—but here, in this land, you will finish by finding Him.'

'And what makes you so certain?'

'Easy,' grinned Badr, returning to his former self. 'Because this country is so beautiful.'

'And so is my own country.'

Badr pondered momentarily. 'I do not know England. But is He not present there, too? I believe you even have a song—*in England's pleasant pastures seen*,' he said, with a pronunciation that made Summerfield wince.

'Badr—you surprise me at each turn. Though you really do need some English lessons, if I may be so direct.'

'And you must learn our language—the real language of this country.'

'You're right,' nodded Summerfield and added, somewhat mysteriously, 'and perhaps I will.'

They talked on, the conversation leading to Abrach on whom Badr skilfully avoided any comment and then turning to the letter. Summerfield reached inside his pocket and handed it across.

'What does she look like?' said Summerfield, innocently.

'I did not know it was addressed to a woman,' replied Badr, evasively. 'My patron wishes to keep his life his own.'

'So you don't actually deliver the letter?' continued Summerfield.

Badr shook his head. 'Abrach is a clever man—and very prudent. I have a special place I must leave it and I never see who takes it.'

'But you could.'

'I wish to live,' replied Badr, curtly. 'I have…a lot of things to do in this life.' Summerfield grunted and looked down into his glass. 'And now,' added the young man, 'If you will excuse me, I must go immediately and put the letter in its place. And please do not try to follow me,' added Badr. 'I say this to ensure that we both will have a *later*.'

'Understood,' said Summerfield, realising it was useless to pursue the issue. 'I'll stay a little longer and have a walk. I'll be all right, won't I?' he added, as Badr rose.

'You'll be all right,' smiled Badr. 'You are *almost* one of us!'

Remaining in the makeshift café, Summerfield immediately regretted Badr's departure. Was it a case of creeping paranoia he was feeling, or were there indeed several pairs of eyes fixed on his back? Angry with himself, he ordered another drink, although part of him began to advise him urgently to leave. And then it happened, not from inside as he had expected. But from outside.

There was a sudden squeal of brakes and the sound of skidding. Even before the vehicle stopped, the shack became mayhem. Chairs and tables were upturned in a cloud of dust and before Summerfield knew it, everybody was pushing and clawing to get out. Bewildered, Summerfield half rose and looked around him. The rear exit was a mass of bodies. He even saw two men leap out of the side window, the capes of their *gandoras* flapping madly as they disappeared at a run. And then he felt someone tug violently on his arms. He resisted, pulled away and was tugged back. He span round with a shout of anger and stopped, his mouth agape.

A French *gendarme* stood before him, one hand clutching his arm, the other raised above his head and holding a cane. Summerfield frowned, perplexed. A long second passed. And then the cane came down with an agonising thwack across his shoulder. '*I'm British!*' he heard himself wail, before collapsing to the ground.

Unable to raise his head for fear of being beaten yet again, Summerfield let himself be pushed outside to join a group of men waiting by the tailgate of a lorry. He was bleeding and his shirt was ripped where the cane had repeatedly struck him. With a series of sharp orders and a few prods with their canes, the para-military *gendarmes*—a squad of them—managed to assemble the men in two rough lines. There were at least twenty and Summerfield, now risking a glance, noticed two of them as those who had glared so fiercely at him in the café. *Papiers!* The *gendarmes* strode along the line, addressing them one-by-one. Those who had papers presented them for inspection, those who didn't were pulled out of the line and made to climb aboard the lorry.

'*Toi! Papiers—yallah!*'

Summerfield looked up. A tall, red-haired *gendarme*, his upper lip sweating profusely, was staring at him. A strong mixture of sweat and eau de cologne wafted from his khaki uniform and filled Summerfield's nostrils. From the accent, Summerfield thought he might be from the north—not that far from Calais, almost England. It was ludicrous.

'First of all, I'm British,' said Summerfield. 'Secondly, don't *tutoye* me and thirdly—I want an apology.'

'What the hell—?' said the *gendarme*, wide-eyed. He turned. 'Sergeant Gautier!'

A sergeant appeared with a waxed moustache so intricately arranged it would, in normal circumstances, have made Summerfield laugh aloud. The man had a look in his eye that made Summerfield feel horribly ill at ease—the sort of look that indicated the sergeant was capable of anything.

'What's this bloody darkie want? He's bleeding like a pig.'

'I'm a British citizen,' said Summerfield, wincing.

The two policemen looked at each other. 'What the hell are you dressed in that clown outfit for, then? Where are your papers?'

'I don't have them on me.'

'Get into the lorry—immediately!'

'I'm British,' repeated Summerfield, almost with desperation in his voice. 'I just happened to be in the café—I'm visiting. *Please*.'

The gendarmes seemed suddenly unsure of what action to take and again, Summerfield felt that danger—he was clearly facing two individuals whose thought pattern was distinctively binary. Any abrupt action, words or movement and he was sure they'd be capable of shooting him on the spot. Slowly and painfully, Summerfield lifted his right arm and unwound the *cheiche* on his head, hoping his clear brown hair would serve as indisputable evidence to his nationality.

'We should really inform the lieutenant,' said the younger gendarme.

The sergeant shook his head and spoke quickly. 'No—it'd only land us in trouble. Think of all the shit paperwork. You,' he added, turning back to Summerfield. 'You *idiot*. Go away—*now*. And you didn't see any of this, understand?' His hand tightened its grip on the cane and Summerfield nodded timidly. The sergeant flicked his head. 'Fuck off now—*dégage!*' Summerfield stepped out of the line and walked away, conscious of the hostile stares of the other unfortunate men.

A day passed and the pain worsened. Upon arriving back in his rooms from the poor district—he couldn't remember the journey back—he had fallen into a deep sleep. It was the pain that awoke him in the night. Unable to move his left arm without a searing blade shooting through the whole side of his torso, he gingerly undressed. It took him almost twenty minutes and when, finally, he managed to uncover his shoulder, he almost fainted. There were two, distinct purple weals where the cane had struck him, surrounded by a dark red crust where the blood had seeped out and congealed. His whole shoulder had swollen into a blotchy red and blue and a truly gigantic, egg-shaped protrusion had appeared where one of the marks ran over his collarbone. The skin had split and wept a yellowish fluid. He hoped he hadn't fractured it and thanked God the cane hadn't hit his face—what a dreadful mess that would have made. He bathed the wounds with boiled water and covered himself up, wondering how he was going to find a doctor.

10

The following morning, Abrach knocked on his door carrying a satchel full of herbs and local medicines. He looked genuinely concerned.

'Can I offer you some tea?' was Summerfield's first remark after getting over his initial surprise.

'Very *British* of you, Harry,' said Abrach, shaking his head. 'Sit down and let me have a look at your wounds.' Summerfield hesitated then sat down by his writing desk. He drew away as the merchant uncovered his shoulder. 'Sorry,' said Abrach, this time grinning and then pulled a face. 'Rather unpleasant,' he commented, 'And rather unfortunate. So you had an accident falling out of a calash?' he offered, innocently.

Summerfield grunted. 'Badr told you, I suppose.'

'He was worried. I believe he witnessed the scene. And you were lucky.'

'It was a truly French way of welcoming me to Morocco.'

'Playing disguises landed you in trouble, Mr Summerfield,' replied Abrach, reproachfully. 'It happened to be the gendarmes who injured you—but it could have, given the place you were in, been the local people. So stupid.' He shook his head. 'I trust you will not go back.'

'It makes me even more determined to,' returned Summerfield, wincing as Abrach applied a dark, brownish-green liquid to his wound, 'Though more the wiser.' He noticed a fleeting frown appear on the merchant's face and added: 'I did not wish to cause you any trouble, Abrach. And I take full responsibility.'

'Badr tells me you are greatly interested in our culture,' replied Abrach. 'That is a good thing—but done properly.'

'I'm sorry,' repeated Summerfield and for a few moments was lost in reflection. 'I was shocked by it all. Why did they do that—and why so much anger and violence?'

'They were probably scared,' said Abrach. 'Fear turns easily to hatred. It is an excuse, a way to overcome it. The district has a reputation. They could not have done that at night—they would not dare.'

'So they were looking for criminals?'

'Perhaps. But criminals in their minds also include those whose thoughts do not exactly fit with their own.'

Summerfield raised an eyebrow. 'Go on.'

'You see, Harry,' said Abrach, finishing off by delicately posing a compress over Summerfield's collarbone. 'I know how to take care of wounds well. I didn't learn this from my studies but from a tribal doctor during the revolts.'

'When was that? I didn't know there'd been rebellion.'

'A long time ago, though in fact not quite so long,' added Abrach, almost as an afterthought. '1925. Only thirteen years ago, the Berber tribes of the northern Rif under Abd El-Krim declared independence from the French authorities. To the south, in the Atlas, Moha Ou Hammou Zayani, the great mountain warrior, took up the struggle. It was the first time, for many of us, that we became aware we had a proper identity. We even had a political party, the *Istiqlal*, who claimed a constitutional government and legal autonomy.'

'You say *we*, Abrach.'

'I was younger and more impetuous,' added Abrach, glancing up from Summerfield's shoulder. That disarming smile appeared on his face. 'I'm not sure I would carry the same convictions now.'

'And what happened?'

Abrach remained silent for a few seconds, the time it took to tie a sling for Summerfield's arm. 'The war lasted a year, but the struggle has been going on for twenty or more. Like the British with their own conquests, the French authorities did not want to lose their possession. There was a bloody repression— much fighting in the eastern regions. The French and Spanish used mustard gas which they dropped from planes. In the end— unconditional surrender.'

'And Krim and Zayani?'

'El-Krim,' rectified Abrach. 'He was exiled to Madagascar.

Moha Ou Hammou Zayani died in battle. And those who sympathised—I think you can imagine.'

'And *you?*'

Abrach snorted a laugh. 'Me? Oh, I was just an amateur doctor, administering aid whenever I could. I even helped the French, Harry. That is the work of a doctor. And perhaps,' he added, introspectively, 'I knew that such a role would give me a certain protection from either side. One has to survive.'

'You did what was necessary,' said Summerfield, feeling a certain sadness enter him. As Abrach stood back to view his work, Summerfield gingerly slid into his shirt. 'And thanks.'

Abrach stayed another hour. They drank tea and business was discussed. Summerfield took two envelopes the merchant offered him, one containing his payment and the other, the young woman's reply—the two symbolically separate, as if Abrach had taken pains not to tarnish one with the other. Abrach was pleased with the results and thanked Summerfield, suggesting a longer wait for the reply.

'It has come to a point in time where a little distance is necessary. Love needs space to breathe—like a tree, it needs to push downwards as well as grow upwards.'

Summerfield shook his head and smiled. 'I still can't understand why you don't write to her yourself. You have a good way of talking about such things.' Abrach did not reply. Instead he questioned Summerfield on his feelings about the progression of events.

'I feel the young woman in question is much attached to this exchange,' answered Summerfield. 'Week by week her replies are truer and clearer. I think there is solid sentiment in her words.'

'Would you say *love*, Harry?'

Summerfield thought for a moment, thought of her and Abrach and also of himself. He suddenly felt an urge to explain to Abrach the strange feeling he had experienced upon reading her last message. But he didn't. Later, he would analyse this as almost a reaction of possession—as though the young woman's sentiments were his and not his patron's.

'Not yet,' he said. 'But there is certainly a deepening of feeling.'

Abrach looked at him and Summerfield felt perplexed. What

was there in the merchant's eyes that spoke almost of certainty? A small, almost imperceptible smile of irony came to Abrach's lips and he spoke softly. 'I will not judge.'

Summerfield opened his mouth—what did he mean?—but Abrach raised a hand.

'*Inchalla*. And now,' he added, rising. 'I have business to do. Take care, Harry. I will leave you the medicines and if you need assistance, the family below will help. I have arranged it with them.'

After Abrach had left—from his rooms he heard the patron's voice, rather low and oddly harsh (he hadn't heard him speaking Arabic before) conversing briefly with Abdlakabir below— Summerfield leant over and slid the letter close to him. Clumsily, for his left arm was strapped to his chest, he managed to open it.

The young woman's message was longer this time, a letter. Abrach had blacked out parts of the text, a measure of discretion.

I thank you for your gentle message. You compare yourself to a rough and unyielding stone though I would say, through your words, one that is precious, one that shines. Your words are a comfort and I look forward to reading every one. I do not know who you are or even what you look like, but through your messages I have formed a picture. It is both a physical picture made up of many different people I have known or met (please forgive me, please do not mock me) and probably a hundred miles from reality, but also a picture made up of feelings which seems to me truthful.

Sometimes I am filled with astonishment at the thought that you happened to choose me and not any of the other young ladies at the Académie, for you must surely have observed us.

Every morning and every evening I search the faces of the people waiting, looking for a face that fits the picture I have made myself. But you do not come. Instead, your messenger will appear, as if by magic (and such a kind young man, he is) and despite my questioning does not reply to my curiosity. My reason tells me you are someone in my entourage, though however much I reflect the more unsure I am that you could be one of my father's environment. Indeed, I know of nobody who could write so beautifully. Therefore, you remain a mystery. And this further incites my curiosity.

I would like to see you, unless secrecy is due and in that case, I would request a photograph or a least a description, it being hardly fair for yourself to observe without being yourself observed.

I wonder how much you know of me? Of course, my studies at —— —— —— —— —— ——: my favourite subjects are Geography and English and I hope to pursue these at university next year, which would most probably mean returning to France...

Summerfield placed the letter down and sat back. So she would be leaving Morocco. It was in the natural flow of events, but the words still managed to sting him a little. He shook his head, feeling suddenly ridiculous. His job was just to write and his mind was wandering. *An idiot you are*, he said aloud, letting the words sink in.

After a while, his head cleared and he went back to the letter. This time his mind was clinical, professional and he read as though reading with a scalpel. And then he drew back. It had suddenly occurred to him that her letter, despite Abrach's crossing out, was sending him clues as to where and who she was. *Idiot*, he uttered again and this time for a different reason.

It was all so clear. All this while he had been in the possession of all the information he required, regardless of her name. He knew her age and her nationality. He knew her milieu. He also had, thanks to Abrach, a rough physical description of her. He knew she studied—there couldn't be that many schools in Marrakesh and the number dwindled when he put her age and background into context. He was also getting to know her likes and her personality. Much as she herself had concluded in her letter, he too could almost put a face to her words. Suddenly, the wild thought came to him that he could find her.

The afternoon drew on. Instead of sleeping, he was filled with restlessness and pottered aimlessly about his rooms, putting off the decision. Finally, realising that he was simply playing for time, he read her letter once more, this time with more distance, weighed up the idea of finding her. True, Abrach had said a little breathing space was necessary in order for her feelings to gestate and grow. He could use that time—a week, ten days, a fortnight?—to carry out his own investigation. He just wanted to see her. And maybe, he added, his resistance rapidly caving in, talk to her. Just a few words. He imagined the scenario—he, recognising her instantly, the way it happened in the films, walking up to her. And she too, filled with some sixth sense, or perhaps one of destiny. As in all great love stories their eyes would meet. He would open his mouth, but there would be no need for words. Instead, they would come closer until their lips touched. And then… And then? The last question, born of Summerfield's logic, stopped him dead. It was as if a bubble had popped and splattered his face.

It was preposterous. He reminded himself of his age. He reminded himself of his background. He also, swearing to himself, reminded himself of Abrach. It made him sober. The drunkenness of joy slowly dissipated and he sat down on the side of his bed. He sighed. *Abrach.* Suddenly tired, he gently lay down. His shoulder throbbed painfully—and that was another thing he had overlooked. Would she be impressed by a badly shaven, battered Englishman without a suit? Without money? Sunburnt pink and probably malodorous, too?

Perhaps it was his burst pride, perhaps the hard analytical side to his writer's personality, that made him focus, with clinical clarity, on his patron. A number of questions promptly presented themselves: questions he had smothered, unasked until this precise moment. He had always taken Abrach for granted—or at least their relationship: he had been hired by a rich Arab merchant to write love letters. That was all. His sole term of contract had been to imagine and to exercise loyalty and discretion. *But what about Abrach?* Summerfield stared up at the ceiling, studied a fly for a few, aimless moments and then pictured the merchant: late-forties, rather tall and thick-set, cumbersome almost. Clean. Good clothes. His skin quite clear compared to most of his compatriots. The neat little moustache, Clark Gable style. A large, strong nose which spoke of a solid character. Thick sharp eyebrows like two, curving blades beneath a protuberant brow, Turkish blood perhaps. He had intellect and wit. A changed man, thought Summerfield, judging from what Abrach had said about his youthful convictions and his now mellowed beliefs. The pull of comfort too strong for his convictions. Perhaps, rather a softer version than the truth, wondered Summerfield. And what about Abrach and the young woman? How had he first known of her? Why such an obsession with her and not a woman of his own people? Perhaps, the thought came to him, he already had a wife—or maybe several—Summerfield was ignorant of that aspect of custom. And what if Abrach were just realising a whim? A whim of a man who had succeeded, who was rich and needed the challenge of something he couldn't obtain from his own culture? So many questions and no clear answers. It irritated him.

Summerfield's mind turned to the outcome of it all. Until then, he had simply focused on the immediate goal—to trick the young lady to fall in love with Abrach. And now, he wondered just what Abrach's chances of success were. For it was one thing to make someone fall in love with an image, with a dream—but what about *after*? It was a sharp and brutal truth that entered Summerfield's mind at that instant: *Abrach could not win*. Everything was against him—his age, race, profession, language, perhaps even physique. In all appearances, Abrach hadn't lent any thought to that aspect, for the merchant seemed certain of what steps to take and when. But then again, countered Summerfield himself, when a man loves, he is impervious to logic, the only thing of any matter being the quest to triumph and conquer. Love could be one of the bloodiest of battles.

His thoughts meandered, back to the fly on the ceiling which seemed to have established permanent accommodation in a slight hollow in the plaster, and then to his own past. He had experienced that search himself, several years ago.

Her name had been Elisabeth Thornton. And he had lost. Strangely, some aspects of the sordid affair echoed in the present situation: different backgrounds, different values—Elisabeth the sister of a fellow teacher. Both women were from a society family. The hopelessness of yearning for a woman he would never get. Perhaps, thought Summerfield, it had also been a major factor— quite apart from witnessing Orwell's call for international commitment—that had led him to leave England for the civil war: just another way of burying failure and bereavement. He laughed out loud, ironic. It suddenly occurred to him that what made men pursue almost impossible challenges was in most cases just a simple obsession with proving themselves to someone else. Was he *still* trying to prove himself to Elisabeth Thornton and her family? Was his unconscious hatching plans to one day return and conquer? Summerfield again snorted aloud and almost as suddenly, a voice called up from below. It was the neighbour.

'Monsieur Summerfield. *Monsieur—un télégramme!*'

'I can't get up!' said Summerfield, irritably and winced. 'Read it aloud, please.' Silence. Summerfield immediately regretted his sharpness—he had forgotten that Abdlakabir probably couldn't read. He sat up. '*Listen—er sorry*. Abdlakabir, I'm—'

And then the girl's voice—Abdlakabir's daughter—rose up, sweet, slow and uncertain.

'*Dear Harry. Will arrive Marrakesh two-five-thh at 2pm. See you soon. Jim—*' she pronounced the American's name—'*Will-ding.*'

Summerfield let out a painful whoop. '*Choukran*, my little princess. *Thank you!*'

11

A change had taken place and Jeanne, in one of those rare moments in life, was able to notice the change as it happened. The birds still sang in the orange groves. Mohammed, like King Canute, still persisted every day in his hopeless battle to turn back the sands from the garden flowerbeds. The piquant fragrance of thyme and savory still told her that here was her home and Soumia, dear never-changing Soumia, still bothered her with water and trivia and generally treated her in much the same way as she had treated her when she was a child. Nothing had changed here. It was Jeanne.

She held a golden egg, wrapped in the secrecy of her mind, heart and soul, and shared it with no one. It made her walk in a perceptively different way—more upright, more assured. It made her look up from her school books and think about the unspoken—that studies were not, in fact, the most important thing in life and a way in which to meet all the influential young suitors. And, above all, it made her feel curiously *super-alive*. Aware of all things, living and innate, and aware of the life that each thing held inside it. Even trees, stones and sand had something to say to her— not a language studded with verbs and adjectives, but a language of truth, of noises and of feelings, perhaps even clearer than the spoken word. It was as though she had found a purpose. The word *destiny* often came to her, and although she couldn't discern what exactly her destiny was, where she was going or even whom she would meet, it certainly *felt* as though she were living out the omnipotent word. At night she read the messages, especially the poems. Her dreams had turned from vast and restless to warm and known, as if her heart had accepted. And she waited.

Half-term came. Descending the stairs for breakfast one morning, her mother gave her a probing glance. Jeanne did not look at her as she sat down and waited for Soumia to serve. But she could actually feel her mother's lips pursing with the effort she was making holding in her words until Soumia had left.

'Good morning, *'moiselle*,' said Soumia, arriving with the breakfast tray. 'Would you like a pancake—Mohammed's brother offered us some honey.' Jeanne nodded and smiled. 'The hive,' continued Soumia, a sign for Jeanne's mother to let out a sigh—they knew what was coming next—'was discovered by Abdul, who is, by the way, thinking of joining the Colonial Light Cavalry, the *Méhari*, that is, because he believes that his parents will sooner or later propose a whole series of not-so-well-natured, shall we say, young virgin brides which of course he doesn't—'

'*Delicious!*' interjected Jeanne. 'Mother—have you tried Mohammed's brother Abdul's honey?'

'Indeed I have, my dear,' replied her mother, dryly, glancing up from her month-old copy of *La Métropole*.

Soumia beamed a smile of gratitude that almost as quickly disappeared, to be replaced by a frown. 'Young Jeanne,' she said, in a low, worried voice—'Is there any more news on that *tictonic plague* epidemic you mentioned? I've been speaking to Fatima and she thinks she read somewhere that the Germans invented it for their war plans.'

Jeanne's cheeks bulged with the effort to keep herself from laughing and consequently the pancake from being ejected from her mouth. She looked at her mother with tears in her eyes. Her mother scowled and closed her magazine.

'Thank you, Soumia. I believe there is the salon to be dusted before father's guests arrive.'

'But that's this evening,' began Soumia and then, her mouth falling open, understood. '*Oui, Madame.*'

Jeanne's mother watched Soumia leave and turning to Jeanne shook her head. 'Whatever have you been filling her mind with, Jeanne? You know how susceptible she is to worries. We have enough with talk of war let alone plagues. And *tictonic*—where did you get that from?'

'In fact,' answered Jeanne, 'the real word's *tectonic*. It's a new geological theory that forwards the idea of the earth being formed of plates which, when in movement, collide to form the planet's relief—notably our mountain chains.'

Her mother gave her a disapproving glance. 'And I didn't, in fact, wish you to reply to that question. Especially so petulantly.'

'Sorry, mother,' said Jeanne, looking down at her pancake and grinning.

Silence. Jeanne sipped tea. Her mother re-opened her magazine, studied it and tutted. 'And what a silly idea,' she remarked, looking up with her sharp, grey eyes. 'If these so-called plates did move, then we'd feel it. Your silly theory surely pretends that we are, in fact, floating on a series of bits of land.'

'*Exactly*,' said Jeanne, nodding encouragement.

'Nonsense,' replied her mother. 'The inner earth is rock and fire, not water. Therefore we cannot float.'

'*Professeur* Duchene would call that *a limiting belief*,' explained Jeanne, unaware of the impact of her words. Her mother's lips all but disappeared from her face, becoming extremely thin and drawn, rather like a morsel of wire.

'I greatly resent that a minor civil servant should insinuate my beliefs are limited! It seems that what your *Professeur* Duchene is really doing is encouraging you to question both the truth and authority. I shall inform the bishop—who is, as you well know, Jeanne—the principal benefactor of the *Académie*.'

'Yes, mother,' said Jeanne, once again lowering her eyes, but this time through habit, that childhood fear. 'Sorry.'

'And for goodness sake, *no more impertinence!*'

There was another long, uncomfortable silence, Jeanne becoming increasingly conscious of the sound her jaws made as she chewed Soumia's pancake. She tried chewing more slowly and, after a while, experimenting with a sideways movement. Her jaw clicked dully. She looked up to find her mother staring at her.

Again a sigh. 'Jeanne.'

'Yes, mother.'

'The party. I'm not—something's happened—you've…you're different. You *will* tell me, won't you?'

Jeanne frowned. 'Sarah Bassouin's party? *Political* party?'

'*You're doing it again*!' said her mother, her voice rising in tone enough to make Soumia scurry back out onto the veranda. '*No,*' said her mother, curtly waving the nanny to go back inside. 'I meant,' she continued, piercing Jeanne with that gaze, 'If you are in trouble, I insist that you inform me before it gets to your father. You may not realise, but I have protected you on many occasions, young lady.'

Jeanne's expression was one of regret. Again she apologised and this time her mother accepted it for real. 'Mother—I would *dearly* love to be able to attend Sarah's party. It's probably one of the last times I'll see her. After the marriage they plan to leave for Europe. So, may I go—*please*? With your blessing?'

Her mother looked away and seemed to weigh up the request. She nodded and Jeanne expressed her thanks. 'That conversation, some time ago now—strange and unfounded as it was,' continued her mother, looking back—'you seemed to question your roots, Jeanne.'

Jeanne looked mildly surprised. 'I had forgotten, mother. Honestly.'

Her mother seemed to relax slightly. 'We all ask ourselves these questions at some time, my dear. I suppose what we're really doing is searching for our identity. Our real self.'

Jeanne stopped eating and looked at her mother, suddenly overcome by a feeling of complicity. It must have showed, for a slight and whimsical smile crossed her mother's lips.

'And this I understand. It's part of becoming an adult,' said her mother. 'Do you understand?' Jeanne nodded. 'But it doesn't mean you have to deny what identity you have created—or that we, your parents, have created for you, including your environment—up until this point. It will remain and your new identity will be formed from it and keep the stronger elements of the former. Believe me, daughter,' said her mother, so earnestly it almost frightened Jeanne, '*I* have done my best to ensure that the foundations of your future life are good, sound and solid.' Jeanne flinched with emotion, though a voice inside her, curious, raised the point that her mother had not included her father in this. Was it simply a question of egoism or a certain bitterness on her mother's part regarding her father's effort in bringing her up? Jeanne started. Suddenly, her mother sat back and laughed, something approaching relief. 'What I suppose I'm really asking is that you think about what is *right and wrong*. And if *Edouard*, our bug-or-stamp-collecting young friend, begins to court you, *please* tell me before anything silly happens.'

That evening, her father had arranged for a small group of friends to dine with them. Jeanne found it hard to believe her father had friends. In fact, they were more work colleagues and other men of decisional importance in the ruling French community.

Soumia, with the help of her sister's daughter, Faïza, served a *blanquette de veau*, oddly and undeniably tinted with a little local flavouring—cinnamon. But nobody said anything. The wine was complimented, as though it were a person, another guest. Berber goat's cheese replaced Camembert and dessert was simple, local and delicious—roundels of orange powdered with, again, cinnamon and presented with a sprig of fresh mint. The *Poste et Télégraphe* director, an over-jovial, grey haired bachelor named Fresquin, praised Soumia's work and she blushed a fierce purple before scuttling off in her pointed *babouches*. The wives present discussed recipes and fashions, the men discussed new advances in technology and sporting events. Jeanne, as daughter of the hosts, was obliged to stay and eat—and be silent. Apart from an opening sortie into how her studies were progressing, she was quickly forgotten. A sign that she hadn't yet been accepted as an adult.

She didn't mind. Instead, she seized upon the opportunity to study the guests. Indeed, now every time she met new people she keenly, though surreptitiously, observed them for any clues. For, filled with excitement at the very thought, it might very well be possible that her secret writer of words and rhyme was present. After all, how could an admirer admire her if he didn't know her? It was a simple deduction, but nonetheless, one that seemed most plausible.

She was alert, too, for any signs from the gathered men. Was there anything hidden behind that look? Why did Colonel Le Guédec, chief of the regional *gendarmerie*, look away so abruptly when she caught his gaze? What was the *real* meaning of the compliment that the director of the national bank made?

But this evening, the search seemed quite fruitless. They were all so serious and all so old—and that particular thought repulsed her somewhat—that not only could she not detect any clues, she didn't wish to either. It was her mother who, catching one of the wives looking at her daughter looking intently at the wife's husband, very diplomatically suggested that youth had other things to be getting on with than listening to grown-up chit-chat. Jeanne smiled gratefully and rose. As she left the room, cigars and cigarettes were lit and she lingered a little at the bottom of the stairs to hear the conversation turn earnestly towards the subject of war. At other dinners, the war in question had been the civil war in Spain. Now it had been forgotten for a new and different event. Apparently, her father had received a message from Paris. Hitler, that distant and funny-looking German with the little moustache and scary eyes, had ordered his troops into the Czechoslovakian border area that very day.

12

The preparations for Sarah Bassouin's party were long, good-natured and rather complex. Sarah, quite apart from being recognised as the prettiest girl in the whole *Académie*, was also known as a natural-born changer of minds. It was a miracle indeed that she had clearly chosen to accept her future husband's hand in marriage. Every one of Jeanne's friends thought the young tax officer at the embassy, *Chéri Henri* as Sarah called him, must be a very strong young man indeed to want to harness Sarah's ebullient character.

In the week leading up to the party, Sarah changed her mind three times on the theme. The first idea was a fancy dress idea, that of knights and damsels. This was much appreciated by the young ladies until one of the male guests raised the point that the chances of finding a full suit of armour in Marrakesh were rather slim. Edouard, also present during the planning phase, earnestly added that the armour would pose two major problems: first, the discomfort of wearing a steel suit in the oncoming summer temperature—now often rising to 40 degrees or so—and secondly the difficulty in undertaking any attempt at dancing. The knights and damsels idea, after Sarah had joked that it wouldn't make any difference since Henri always stepped on her toes in the best of circumstances, was thus dropped.

The second theme chosen—a decision that lasted two whole days, was to dress up in roaring twenties style. It was Jeanne, seconded by Cécile, objecting to the fact that they didn't want to look like their parents, who lead to the idea being discarded. *Boring*, the others agreed.

Finally, it was Robert de Montpommier, the bank director's second son, who hit upon the idea of dressing up in local native attire—*Simple and awfully fun*. And practical, too, Edouard had added—they could always borrow rags from their servants. And so the final theme was chosen. But there also remained the other and not altogether uncomplicated questions of food, musical accompaniment, last-minute requests for invitation from third-parties, transportation and presents. In true tradition, Sarah never managed to settle these questions before it was too late. But in fact, it didn't that much matter.

Sarah Bassouin's house, as opposed to the vast majority of other expatriate families, was located away from the European district and close to the centre of Marrakesh. It had been Sarah's father's idea—himself of *pied noir* stock and having been born and brought up mostly in French Algeria—that they should live the atmosphere of their environment. This would, under any other circumstances, have been considered highly distasteful. But Sarah's father was President of the Chambers of Commerce for the whole southern sector of Morocco, a much-valued advisor at the embassy and most importantly president of the Marrakesh Bridge Club. Nobody, not even those on a professional par, would dare to criticise his choice of habitat on that account.

From the outside, the house looked bleak and daunting. A sheer, dark pink, almost purple-washed wall with several small, barred windows greeted the visitor. The entrance was a small, thick door, slightly lopsided through age and embossed with iron. It was here that Jeanne stood, in her freshly ironed, white cotton summer dress and holding a bag in her hand. Mohammed and Soumia waited in the calash, checking that she was safely inside before setting off.

'I do hope Sarah's new maid will like the clothes,' Soumia had fretted, during the trip to the city centre. 'The last time I put them on was almost twenty years ago. But you *did say* she was young.'

'I'm sure she'll love them,' Jeanne reassured her, patting the bag stuffed full of clothes. 'And if she doesn't, you can always blame me for having chosen,' she added.

The door opened. It was Sarah's father, Jean Bassouin—another one of his odd habits.

'Oh,' said Jeanne, taken aback. 'I was expecting…'

'I always welcome my own guests,' beamed Sarah's father. 'Do come in—Jeanne Lefèvre, I presume? Yes—I know your father well. Good with the cards—very regular.' Jeanne entered and immediately heard the sound of voices from above, Sarah's characteristically the loudest among them. She followed Sarah's father through a cool, flagstone corridor and up a narrow flight of stairs. 'Your first time *chez nous*, I believe,' offered Bassouin, playing host. 'My daughter tells me you're a good friend of Cécile's.' He turned his head and Jeanne nodded. He stopped, looking mildly surprised: 'Aren't you supposed to be dressed up, though? I must say—the others do look a treat.'

Jeanne hung her head. 'I'm afraid my parents would have raised a fuss,' she said, apologetically.

'Oh, dear,' murmured Monsieur Bassouin, suddenly looking quite regretful, though not, as Jeanne thought, for any inconvenience her parents might have incurred. 'I imagine you must have quite a few difficult moments at times, young lady.'

Jeanne returned his complicit smile. 'But I did manage to sneak out some clothes in my bag,' she said.

'Well, that's good, then.'

'But please don't tell—I said they were for your maid.'

Jean Bassouin pondered for some moments then gave her a wink.

'I wish—' said Jeanne, before she could stop herself, but Sarah's father interrupted.

'They're probably trying to do their best, don't you think. You're a very pretty young woman. Parents are sometimes a little odd. In fact, I'm quite sure Sarah would even say that of me. Come.'

They continued upwards on the rough and winding stairs. The sound of voices became louder and suddenly they emerged from the gloom of the stairwell into a spacious and beautiful room, lit by the reds, greens, yellows and blues of a dozen or so Arabic lozenge lamps.

'I'll show you where you can change,' said Sarah's father, raising his voice, but it was too late. With a shriek, Sarah hurried over and grabbed her arm, apparently Jeanne's lack of disguise going unnoticed. 'Oh, well,' said Monsieur Bassouin sheepishly and glanced at his wife for help. 'Later, then.'

Jeanne had never been kissed on the cheek by so many people in such a small amount of time. Some people she knew, others she instantly forgot their names as she was introduced. Not only Sarah, but her other friends too seemed in a state which Jeanne could only describe as euphoria.

'Are you drunk?' hissed Jeanne, secretively.

'Of course not,' giggled Cécile. 'But don't worry—I've filched a few drops of papa's punch for later.'

Jeanne was about to enquire further about the high spirits when she suddenly saw the real reason why. She could almost feel her jaw drop. It was Sarah's fiancé, Henri, or more to the point, *the friend* he was leading towards her through the party goers.

'*Yes!*' wheezed Sarah, tugging on her arm. 'If I'd have only known Henri had a friend like that!'

'Sarah!' gasped Jeanne, shocked by her friend's brash hint at infidelity. But only a sort of cooing sound escaped Sarah's lips.

'His name's Ludovic,' said Sarah, as the two young men approached.

'*Ludo*,' corrected the young man in question.

'Isn't that a game?' said Jeanne, suddenly feeling quite foolish for having said it.

Ludovic cleared his throat, grinned and offered his hand. 'How do you do? Forgive me for not offering a *bise*,' he said, and Jeanne was struck by the sound of his voice, rich, mid-tone and polished. 'I would only blush at such prettiness.'

'You dog, Ludo,' said Henri, moving close to Sarah and touching her arm. 'But I do believe it's our poor Jeanne who's blushing!' They laughed. Jeanne turned from pink to red to purple and looked away in panic. Oh God, she heard herself saying, and it might even be *him*. She forced herself to turn back and smiled apologetically.

'I must say your costumes look—'

'That's it!' said Sarah. 'I *knew* something was wrong. Why aren't you dressed for the party?' Jeanne's face filled with a hard look and Sarah immediately understood. 'Hmm, Mater and Pater, *n'est-ce pas*. No need to worry. You'll change later. Come—let's talk to Cécile. She's with your Edouard.'

'Not *my* Edouard!' said Jeanne, and again shot a glance that mixed both panic and apology.

Ludo nodded at her as Sarah pulled her away. 'Perhaps later we'll dance?' he said as a baritone parting shot.

'Yes,' said Jeanne, craning her neck and then he was gone. 'Who is he?' she asked Sarah, once they were clear.

'Ludo is Henri's best friend.'

'I know that.'

'I see. Well, Ludo is fresh out from the *Ponts et Chaussées*,' continued Sarah, her voice deepening with respect upon uttering the name of the élite *grande école*. 'He's working as an engineer for the railways.'

'Here in Marrakesh?' frowned Jeanne.

'Unfortunately not, I believe. I think he spends his time between Rabat and Casablanca.'

'It can't be him,' murmured Jeanne.

'Beg your pudding?' said Sarah.

'What? Oh, nothing.'

Edouard and Cécile were engaged in earnest conversation. Edouard was dressed in a striped pair of Zouave trousers, a waistcoat and a tall, tasselled fez. On his feet were an awesome pair of yellow leather slippers that curved dangerously upwards to brass-tipped points.

'You look a bit Turkish to me,' said Jeanne, critically.

Edouard smiled nonchalantly. 'Much the same, in any case. And what about you, Jeanne? Too afraid to dress up?'

Jeanne let out a moan. 'No—my parents again. But I've a bag somewhere with my disguise. Every time I want to put it on, Sarah tugs me away.'

'She's drunk,' said Cécile, giggling.

'That's what *I* said.'

'Drunk with *love*,' winked Cécile, crooning the last word so that it came out as *lerrrrve*. Sarah let out a shriek which made Edouard cringe. 'Lucky you!' added Cécile.

'Yes,' said Sarah, suddenly sober, 'Lucky me.' A look rather like that of a lost child came across her face. 'Oh God…' she said, distantly. 'I think I need to get drunk. Come on, I'll show you where papa's punch is.'

Cécile moved off with her, but Jeanne stayed. 'I'll get changed first.' She turned back to Edouard and smiled and was about to go in search of her bag when Edouard put his hand on her elbow, gently pulling her back.

'Yes?' she said, sure that the young man had a question. Instead, Edouard stood riveted and quite ill-at-ease, staring at his coiled slippers. '*Yes, Edouard?*' inquired Jeanne again and frowned. 'You're not going to be sick or anything?'

It seemed to wake him up. 'Lord no!' he blurted. Another uneasy silence.

'Well?' insisted Jeanne. 'What is it, then?'

'What's happened, Jeanne?' Jeanne frowned in incomprehension and Edouard took another breath. 'You—seem—*different*.'

'Different? Why does everybody keep saying I'm *different*?'

'I—I don't mean *different* as in—as in *strange*,' said Edouard, moving closer. Unfortunately, the rashly curving points of his slippers immediately stabbed into Jeanne's shins.

'*Ow!!*' she cried, hopping back and rubbing her skin.

'Oh, God—did I hurt you?' said Edouard. '*Bloody slippers!* Oh God, I'm sorry Jeanne.'

'I'm fine,' said Jeanne, wincing. 'Well?'

'Well,' continued Edouard with great effort. 'I meant different as in—*pretty*.'

'Oh, dear.'

'Yes, you're—it's hard to put a finger on it,' battled Edouard.

'Edouard, I'm not a stamp,' said Jeanne.

'Quite. You see, it's—you're—it's almost as if you've become a *woman*.'

Jeanne frowned. 'A woman? But I've *always* been a woman.'

'No, silly. Woman as in grown-up—sort of a *real* woman.'

Jeanne remained silent. She looked at Edouard looking at her. And Edouard's look was suddenly and unashamedly roving, almost—to put it in his own terms—*male*. A strange sense of dawning came over her, a remote, questioning curiosity.

'Edouard?'

'Yes.' Edouard's voice had croaked to a whisper. 'Yes,' he added, more forcefully.

'We did…' she lowered her voice. 'We did kiss, didn't we.'

Edouard nodded. 'My first on any woman's lips.'

'Apart from your mother's,' added Jeanne.

'Not even,' replied Edouard.

'No—me neither,' said Jeanne, mechanically. 'But we kissed— on two occasions.'

'Not a real kiss, though. Not—*you know*.'

Jeanne felt her skin glow beneath her clothes. What an obscene, divine thought—kissing with tongues. 'I was curious,' she said, for no conscious reason. 'That's why I wanted to kiss you.'

'Hmm,' hummed Edouard, analysing the issue. 'Me too, I suppose.'

'Do you write poetry, Edouard?'

Edouard looked surprised. 'No—why d'you say that?' He shrugged his shoulders. 'I suppose I could do if I had to, though. Rhymes—it's all down to rhymes. That's what good poetry's all about.'

Jeanne laughed. 'Edouard—you sound like my father!'

'Well, it was him who told me,' defended Edouard. The look on Edouard's face was one of shock. And then she knew. It was like two threads coming together.

'You mean you've been talking to father about poetry? About—*about me*?'

'Jeanne,' he said, 'I'd like to show you—' But Edouard did not finish.

'Show me your *bug* collection, no doubt!' interrupted Jeanne, scathingly. '*Bugs!*' she hissed again, and walked away.

'Jeanne, I don't collect *bugs*,' Edouard called sulkily after her. 'I collect…*stamps*.'

Jeanne found them from the muted giggles coming from behind the door. She knocked. Silence. She knocked again, more softly.

'It's me—Jeanne.'

'*Come in*!' came a collective hiss, followed, instants later by the sound of a key turning.

Jeanne pushed open the door, which was then quickly shut again and locked. The room was gloomy, the window open though failing to dissipate the smell of cigarettes and the sickly-sweet cocktail of rum and orange juice. A glass was thrust in her hand. She sipped and pulled a face.

'Still haven't changed into your costume?' said Cécile.

'You look different,' added Sarah, unknowingly.

'Oh, *God*!' pleaded Jeanne. 'Not you, too!'

'What have I said?' shrieked Sarah only to be hushed by Cécile. 'Sorry—must be the booze. I need to piss.'

'Sarah—your *language*!'

Cécile burst into a fit of giggling, bringing Sarah with her. 'What's the matter, anyway? You look in a terribly dark mood.'

Jeanne sat down on the side of Sarah's bed, next to her two friends. Cécile's veil had fallen away and her mascara had run. '*Edouard*—that's the matter. The fool has been speaking to my father—*plotting*!' In a gesture of extreme interest, both Sarah and Cécile suddenly drew themselves closer. 'Plotting about my future.'

'You mean he wants to marry you?' gaped Cécile. '*Another one*! And what about me!?'

'We should never have kissed,' said Jeanne, and realised, too late, that she had let her secret escape.

'You *kissed*—with Edouard *the philatelist*, the future *chartered accountant*!?'

'But not with—*you know*.'

'*Tongues*,' said Sarah, with a worldly tone to her voice. 'Oh, poor girl. So you don't yet know…'

'What's it like?' said Jeanne, desperately looking to steer the conversation away from Edouard and herself.

'Must be sticky,' commented Cécile, taking a gulp from her glass.

'It's warm and moist and lovely and—and very tickly,' explained Sarah, inspired. Jeanne and Cécile giggled. Sarah continued. 'Henri is a sublime kisser. So *érotique*.' This time, Jeanne could hardly contain her imagination from moaning aloud. 'When he kisses me,' added Sarah, her voice becoming soft and husky, 'I feel like fainting with pleasure.'

'Go on, *go on*,' encouraged Cécile.

'At first he kisses me softly on the lips and then—not always, for I tease a little and remain in that position—'

'Closed lips,' informed Jeanne.

'Apparently it's the thing to do.'

'Why?' inquired Cécile, frowning.

'Well it's supposed to make men more appreciative of a woman, I think.'

'I should think it makes them rather annoyed,' commented Jeanne.

'That's the whole point,' said Sarah, shaking her head. 'Don't you see—it makes them more—*more brutal.*'

'Strange,' mumbled Cécile. 'Why would you want them to be brutal?'

'Not at all. Mother said it was like the relationship between a lion and a gazelle.'

'You spoke to your *mother* about sex??' gasped Jeanne. It was unthinkable.

'Of course—when I announced my feelings for Henri, it was the first thing we talked about. She took me aside when papa was at work and we had a marvellous chat.'

'God, you're lucky,' said Jeanne. 'I think my mother believes *sex* is just another word for *gender.*'

'Well—what else did Mater say?' asked Cécile, curling up and unconsciously baring her knees.

Sarah drank from her glass and held it out for Cécile to re-fill. 'Well—she spoke of the clitoris.'

'What's that?'

'The *clitoris*…' Sarah hesitated, letting the word linger and settle in, much as her mother had done during their talk. 'The *clitoris* is a jewel, a hidden and sacred treasure on a woman's body.' Silence. Somewhat baffled, Jeanne and Cécile exchanged glances. 'It's a metaphor,' explained Sarah, secretly hoping they'd understand, for it was, beyond all doubt, even for her, quite a delicate subject to explain.

'In fact I remember,' said Cécile, with effort, 'overhearing the word and asking mummy. I must have been fourteen, I think.'

'And what did she say, then?' asked Sarah, hoping a revelation would come to Cécile.

'I said *mother—what does it mean?* and mummy said *oh, something scientific—*'

Silence.

'Is *that* all?'

'Well—yes. I didn't dare ask more.'

'A *clitoris*,' said Sarah, once again taking up the forbidden subject, and this time with great wisdom and certitude filling her voice, 'is a small nodule of skin and muscle situated in a woman's sexual regions which becomes hard during loving encounter and which leads to the female reaching—reaching—'

'*Go on!*'

'*Reaching orgasm.*'

Jeanne gasped. Cécile said: '*What's that?*'

'Oh, *shut up!*' scolded Sarah. 'Use a *dictionary*, for heaven's sake!'

'Whatever it is, it sounds useful,' said Cécile.

'When you find it, you'll know it,' said Sarah, wistfully.

'I'll second that,' lied Jeanne, feeling herself blushing and fearing another question from Cécile. She took another sip— and a second—from her glass of punch. Cécile stared at them, miserably.

'Oh for heaven's sake!' blurted Sarah, irritably. 'Stop pulling that cow face. Here!' And suddenly, Sarah's hand darted up Cécile's dress and probed. Cécile looked at her, rigid and quite still and said nothing. A frown appeared on Sarah's face.

'You look as though you're rummaging for biscuits at the back of the cupboard,' whispered Jeanne, totally mesmerised, totally confused.

'It's a bit like that,' murmured Sarah. '*Hold still*! Maybe not every woman has one? Mother didn't mention that. *There*—that's it! It must be!'

'Oh, *God*!' Cécile looked as though she'd been electrocuted. She let out a squeal: 'Yes—that must be it!' Sarah withdrew her hand and Cécile fell back, relapsing into a fit of giggles. 'My God!

Thanks *awfully!*'

Sarah tipped her head, a heroine's recognition, a woman, took a puff of her cigarette and drank.

The sound of voices suddenly came from behind the door. Men's voices. The three friends froze then, not without a certain amount of clattering, quickly hid away the incriminating glasses.

'Are you in there?' It was Henri's voice. 'Sarah—come out. We're putting some music on the grammy. Time to dance.'

Arriving back in the reception room, a popular waltz was playing on the gramophone. Jeanne was surprised however to see that no one was dancing. And then Monsieur Bassouin, rather gallantly bowing to his wife, took the floor. Henri, dressed in his flowing desert robes, guided Sarah forwards. Ludo glanced across at Jeanne, Jeanne nodded and then Edouard stepped up, minus his fez, and took her by the elbow before Ludo could come to her.

They danced almost at arm's length, both through their lingering uneasiness and the fact that Edouard's ornate slippers forbade any closeness.

'You haven't changed,' commented Edouard, at last, glancing at her clothes.

'You said I *had*,' returned Jeanne, dryly.

'Not that—' Edouard began to explain and then pulled a face. 'Look, Jeanne—I do apologise. And—why did you say I collected *bugs* for heaven's sake?' He shook his head.

Jeanne pursed her lips. 'Oh, something my mother said,' returned Jeanne. And then, after a moment, 'look—I *do* think I like you. I just don't want anyone to suddenly surprise me by saying that I *had* to be friends with so-and-so. Do you understand?'

Edouard frowned.

'But isn't that how it works?'

'Maybe here—yes, but—'

Edouard shrugged his shoulders. 'So why should it bother you?'

'*Edouard!*' Jeanne looked shocked. '*Romance*—haven't you heard?'

'Oh, that,' said Edouard. 'We *kissed* didn't we?'

'But that was just curiosity.'

'Several times.'

'And poetry and messages and letters and mystery?'

Edouard sniggered and then grew serious. 'You know, Jeanne—I *am* capable of that. Every man, once he falls for a girl, is. Just look at the couples we know—just look at our parents! Some men are the oddest of sorts. But I'm sure even the ugliest, most idiotic of them managed to woo their wives with verse.'

'So you're not in love,' said Jeanne, the thought coming to her slowly, like gears setting into motion.

'Why, no,' said Edouard, momentarily letting his hold go. He frowned.

'Well, neither am I—at least…' said Jeanne, then thought it wiser to stop there. They danced in silence for a full verse.

'I like you, too,' said Edouard at last, as though he had analysed the situation thoroughly and was ready to pronounce his findings. Jeanne hummed and glanced away. Cécile's face, beaming with a grin, waltzed past—she was with Ludo, Henri's most handsome friend. Then she saw Monsieur Bassouin, who smiled at her and she forced herself to smile back.

'Well, I can't envisage any relationship without love coming into it,' she said, thinking aloud.

'Well,' said Edouard, his voice lowered. 'Neither can I.'

'So please don't plot with father.'

'Well, I was thinking,' Edouard offered, 'That perhaps it might happen—quite soon.'

'What?' Jeanne straightened. 'You mean…?' Edouard's face remained uncommitted, but she was sure she had understood. 'You mean like switching on an electric lamp?'

'No one knows how it happens,' said Edouard. 'Electric lamp—*not bad*.' Again Jeanne looked away, lost. Suddenly, his words seemed quite grown up, quite irrefutable. She knew he was expecting a reply, but what could she say? It was *almost* as if Edouard were proposing. The music stopped. Edouard pulled away and gave a slight bow. 'And I didn't step on your toes once,' he added, suddenly seeming quite full of himself. It was an Edouard she hadn't noticed before. Sure, confident and armed with a rueful smile. And then she saw a look of concern then alarm come over his face and before she could turn round to see what it was that had caused it, she felt herself be drawn into a pair of arms—Ludo's arms.

'Thanks awfully,' said Ludo, nodding brusquely at Edouard.

'A pleasure,' replied Edouard and then staggered back as Cécile collided with him.

'Let's dance, Edouard,' chirped Cécile. 'But *please*, take those bloody horns off your feet!'

The music began again. Jazz. Jeanne couldn't move. She looked sheepishly at Ludo, a whole head and a half above her. He smiled in return.

'Don't worry. Just follow me,' he said. 'It's an integral part of final year's study. Paris would not exist without jazz.'

Despite the advice, Jeanne at first tried to move to the rhythm, only to be gently but firmly guided otherwise. It was a far different cry from anything else she'd ever experienced. She felt like a rag doll and remembered *Baudelaire*, her teddy, and how she used to make him dance when she was a child. She wasn't really sure she liked it. It was violent—almost a struggle. Several times she felt Ludo's grasp tighten, his muscles flex. Like a lion and a gazelle, she thought, Sarah's words echoing in her head. She pushed back, glancing up and Ludo smiled strangely before he countered with his own push—one, two and the third time, she felt herself spinning round, his hands clasping hers, her back suddenly projected into his stomach. She felt the warmth of his body and—good God—he had actually *touched* her. Her immediate reaction was to push him away, but in that position her body only managed a rippling motion. He was on her back like the lion and she was indeed as helpless as his gazelle. She felt her body become limp, submissive. And his grip loosened too. He turned her, gently this time, so that they came back facing each other. The music seemed to slow, and it did—to a sort of march.

'You see,' said Ludo. 'You can do it. Well done.'

Jeanne looked troubled, glanced away and then looked back. 'Thank you.' Ludo said nothing, but she felt his hand squeeze her arm, ever so slightly. Could this be...*how it happens*? she said to herself, remembering her conversation with Edouard. Like a mortal struggle and then—and then metaphorical death, the strange serenity of it all, the acceptance?

'How old are you?' she said, involuntarily.

Ludo distanced himself to look at her, grinned, then drew close once more. 'Twenty-six. And I imagine you're twenty-five.'

Jeanne giggled. 'Not quite. Are you—are you what they call a seducer?'

This time Ludo let out a laugh. 'Ha! You're such a different kind of girl. What do *you* think?' Jeanne thought that Ludo must be the umpteenth person to have said she was different that week, but she didn't say this. Instead, she frowned. 'Please don't ponder too much,' said Ludo. 'You're much better when you don't. And I say that as a compliment.'

'I think you're very handsome, a little scary. Maybe it's because you're tall. Maybe it's your background.'

'My background?' smiled Ludo. 'Why, we're probably of the same. My father works for the *République*. He organises rail logistics for the army. Listen—'

'I'm listening.'

'I'm a little tired—I journeyed all day to be here. May we sit somewhere calm and chat? I'd like that.'

Jeanne looked into his eyes, felt reassured and nodded. 'That would be nice.'

13

The evening was turning to night and the air was cool and sharp. Summerfield sat on the uneven roof of his meagre rooms and contemplated the sky with his headscarf on, a cigarette and a thimble of whisky. It was his weekly treat, a ration he savoured from the bottle he'd bought in Gibraltar. Almost another life, he said to himself. *It was* another life, his thoughts confirmed.

The city murmured. The crowd still thronged in the Djemaa El Fna square to the east. It would only dissipate later upon midnight prayer, the main reason why he'd decided to come up and sit. Its long, quavering chant would send a shiver of excitement and curiosity through him and put him to bed to spice his sleep.

He studied the stars—Venus, the North Star, the constellation of the Plough, Cassiopeia. The moon was a crescent—the pupil in a cat's eye. It gave the sky its femininity.

He looked west and sipped. The city lay in darkness but for one or two scattered lights and one particular edifice, a house perhaps—but a big one. He had noticed it before on several occasions, all alit, an exception. He tried to focus his eyes, played with the thought that a telescope would make a good purchase. In the daylight he had seen the house was topped by a luxuriant garden. It was the house of a rich man. Perhaps it was Abrach's house, he wondered and the thought made him laugh.

It set his mind to imagining the young woman. She's out there somewhere, he said softly. Will I ever meet her? Oh, how I've trapped you—and forgive me. I teased you like a fish, tying an exotic fly to my hook. I dangled poetry before your heart and snagged your feelings. And still I play, letting off slack at present and soon to reel in. I was a hunter, using cunning and trickery. *Was*, his mind had said. Strange. Yes, *was*. For the hunter is himself now hooked—on the barbs of you. I do not know you—and yet I know you are truthful and real. You are a girl, but also a woman. Your beauty is most probable—I have been told of it—but you are truthfully beautiful through your innocence and your trust. And—perhaps it's the tot of whisky speaking—I would dearly love to kiss you, just once, and say: 'twas I who writ these rhyming words upon a hook and bit the catch of love myself.

14

She didn't know how they ended up on the roof-top veranda, but it enchanted her. It was as though they were figures in a film: now they were here and then they were there, a different scene, a different setting.

She could almost see herself, walking slowly beside Ludo, his tallness, his presence. They had chatted about his time in Paris and what it was like to study at such a prestigious school as *Ponts et Chaussées*. But also, she had noticed, he had enquired about her own life in French Morocco. It seemed rather boring in comparison, though Ludo—his family name was *Dekerque*, a northern name and indeed his family home was in Lille—seemed to find it full of interesting information.

They stepped out onto the veranda and the coolness of the night air made them fall suddenly silent. A Marrakeshi habitat, the veranda was in fact the roof of the floor below arranged in terrace style. It was large, landscaped with many potted plants and trees and even had a little shaded pond in which goldfish swam.

'Sarah's father certainly has a taste for originality,' commented Ludo and seemed to weigh up an inner question. 'I rather *like* it.'

'Me too,' said Jeanne. 'I only wish I'd had time to change. I look a little foolish being the odd one out. If I were dressed, then we'd look—' she didn't finish. Ludo raised an eyebrow. 'The same,' said Jeanne, flatly.

'Hmm.' Ludo looked amused.

'Look,' said Jeanne, trying to make amends. She walked over to the edge of the veranda and leant upon the balustrade. 'Isn't it wonderful?'

'It's not Paris,' said Ludo, joining her and added, 'but it's charming. I suppose the exoticism is having an effect on me. It reminds me of *a Thousand and One Nights*.'

'That's Turkey,' said Jeanne.

'I'm afraid we didn't learn that in higher studies,' replied Ludo, his rich, mellow voice filled with irony.

Jeanne exhaled, feeling foolish. 'Sorry. I don't suppose you appreciate learning trivia—especially from me. I haven't even sat my final exams yet.'

'Beauty has no exams to speak of as far as I know,' said Ludo, and glanced at her.

'Oh, no—' Jeanne shook her head—'I'm not the beautiful one!'

'Have you ever been in love?' Ludo leant forward, seeming to surprise himself with his question. 'Well?'

'I don't know,' said Jeanne, somewhat mysteriously.

'Oh, come on! That's an odd reply. An explanation, please.'

Jeanne looked out over the city, the glow of torches rising from the great square barely half a mile away, sunk out of sight in the clutter of rooftops and tinting the sky orange. To the east, the metal blue of the plain and the black horizon, the mountains. Here the sky was alive with stars. She thought of the poem, recited every word in her head. Suddenly, she was conscious of time and of her silence.

'I was being truthful,' she said, matter-of-factly. 'There is…'

'A young man—that *Edouard*, perhaps. Pity about the yellow slippers.'

'No.' Jeanne remained silent, then inhaled. 'I wish I could tell.'

'It must be something serious,' said Ludo, lightly.

'And you?' asked Jeanne, changing subject.

'I—' began Ludo, drawing closer, lowering his voice, 'I have loved, yes.'

'Which means…' worked Jeanne's mind, mechanically.

'Which doesn't necessarily mean I have been in love,' said Ludo.

'And…' said Jeanne, not fully understanding what he meant, 'I suppose you have kissed—*properly*.'

Ludo suddenly laughed. 'If that's what you want to call it!' He drew back, still laughing softly to himself, walked to the little pond and then returned to her. 'Would you like to try?'

'What?'

'To kiss—*properly*, as you call it.'

Jeanne tensed. 'That's very forward.'

'A man has to be.'

'I see,' said Jeanne, fixing, with great effort, her regard on the horizon.

'Well?' came Ludo's voice, almost challenging.

'I—I don't know. The poems, the messages,' she began, but Ludo had come to her, his hand taking her shoulder and gently tugging.

'A man has to be…*very* forward.'

'But perhaps I *am* in love,' said Jeanne, confused. She heard herself, weak and pitiful. 'For there are some stories that are born to live. And live they do—like stars.'

'Sorry?'

'I don't know,' struggled Jeanne. She felt Ludo's warmth on her neck, his breath, his smell, Paris. His lips pressed softly onto hers, so much unlike Edouard's and that was the most surprising, most enchanting thing. The difference—she had never thought it possible. A whimper escaped her and Ludo seemed to press harder, more forcefully. And suddenly the heat and her mouth aflame, sending shivers and waves through her body. Her tongue responded—it was like sherbet exploding in her mouth.

It was too—too devilishly good. 'No!' she whispered, her voice hoarse and she pulled herself away. 'I'm sorry—I'm sorry, but I have a love.'

'He isn't here,' returned Ludo, pulling her back to him. 'Love *me*.'

'Oh, God.'

But Jeanne did not have to give way. For suddenly a sharp drawn out yelp pierced the silence, echoing off the walls.

Ludo wheeled round. '*What the!*'

Jeanne shook herself and stood beside him. Together, they peered into the darkness.

'What was it?' she said, afraid.

'Don't be silly!' said Ludo, almost angrily. 'It's—'

'Oh, *thank you*!' came a girl's voice.

'Good God—*that's Cécile's voice*!' whispered Jeanne. 'Whatever is the matter?' And then she remembered—the bedroom, the three friends, the discovery. 'Oh, *dear*!' Another voice, this time from below, announcing the beginning of the fancy dress competition.

'I have to change,' said Jeanne, quickly.

'And I think we'd better leave our friends to it,' added Ludo, his voice irate.

Jeanne could hear the excitement grow from the party room as she changed. There were cheers, followed by laughter. She heard Cécile's voice—back again—and then a loud *hear hear*—Edouard's. She slipped off her cotton dress, hastily folded it—Soumia's voice filling her head with reproach as she did so—and slid on the black, linen dress and red blouse decorated with cascading rows of tiny, gold-coloured medallions. Then the waistband, wide and black and embroidered with strange little symbols—fish, rings, hands. Finally, the tiny silk slippers, petite and supple on her feet. In the reception room, they were chanting her name. She checked herself in the mirror. The headscarf—she put it on. And—again she heard Soumia's voice, the countless times she'd talked of her youth—the eye make-up, a local concoction made of she-didn't-know-what. One last look. The perfect Berber princess. She wrinkled her nose at her self in the mirror, opened the door to the bedroom and stepped out.

The reception room had turned into a viewing room. A small podium had been placed in the centre whereupon each guest took turn in stepping up for appraisal. When she arrived, everyone's eyes were focused on Edwige Janvier, the class swot and Sarah's slave, now posing in her Arabian dancer's costume and blushing furiously between the claps and whoops. Monsieur Bassouin, acting as master of ceremonies, invited the onlookers to allocate their points for Edwige.

'Thank you, young lady. Applause, please, everyone!' cried Monsieur Bassouin. 'And now, I do believe—*heavens!*' He stopped mid-sentence as his eyes fixed on Jeanne. 'I believe,' he began again, his voice a little shaken, 'Jeanne is at last…*ready.*'

As Jeanne stepped forward and made her way through the onlookers, heads turned and the initial applause petered out into a silence. Jeanne stepped up onto the podium and gave a shy smile. She frowned a little, searched for Sarah's face, which she found, then Cécile's and Edouard's, all three dumb with astonishment.

'What's the matter?' said Jeanne, slowly, softly. 'Is—is anything wrong? Have I forgotten to—'

'You look…' stuttered Edouard.

'Yes?' said Jeanne, beginning to blush uncomfortably. They were going to say she was *different* again to be sure.

'*So much like a native!*' he finally blurted out. 'I would never have thought…'

'What?'

'Even your face!' said Edwige. 'Your skin, your features—most striking.'

'The make-up,' said Jeanne, feeling a surge of panic. Someone giggled. Then a man's laugh. Ludo's?

'I say that Jeanne has no possible contender!' declared Henri, in a loud voice, very much like an announcer at a boxing match. It was the sign for laughter to break out. It felt as though the whole world had erupted, ridiculing her. *Speak to us in local lingo then!* added another voice, mimicking an Arabic accent. *Oh, Aisha!* chimed another. *Oh, Sherazade!*

Jeanne stood on the podium, rigid, unable to move. Her legs felt weak. She began to tremble, her mouth twitched and then, unable to hold it in any longer, she burst into tears, desperately trying to hide herself behind her hands.

'Move away—*let me pass!*' It was *Monsieur* Bassouin, witnessing the poor girl dying of shame, feeling anger well up inside him at their incapacity to comprehend what he himself had understood right from the beginning. He stepped up on the podium next to Jeanne and silence suddenly fell. Glaring, he took Jeanne by the arm and helped her step down. 'Sarah,' he said, turning to his daughter, his voice calm now. 'Put the music back on and ask nanny to serve cake.'

Accompanied by his wife, Bassouin led Jeanne to his study. He sat Jeanne down in his leather chair.

'Pass me some water, my dear,' he said to his wife. 'And a handkerchief, if you please. You'll find one in the top drawer. Poor young thing,' he continued, turning back to Jeanne. 'The fools. I do apologise.'

'I don't understand,' said Jeanne, her voice a whisper. Madame

Bassouin leant over, smiling gently and handed her a glass of water. 'I suppose I felt so silly.'

Bassouin sighed and glanced at his wife. 'You looked absolutely beautiful, Jeanne. Believe me.'

'But they laughed. I wouldn't have minded, but they kept on and on.'

'Listen to me, Jeanne. I am Jewish. I was born in Algeria and grew up there. When I left to take up studies in France, they laughed at me too. My dear wife, too—she had to bear the brunt of other people's—*fear*.'

'Fear?' The word seemed odd and Jeanne looked up, not understanding. 'Did I look so horrible?' she said, sipping on the water. She laughed.

'Not horrible, Jeanne—*different* that's all.'

It was the fifth time that evening someone had said that word. What did they all mean? She stared blankly at Sarah's parents. They were smiling, a mixture of sorrow tinged with regret. She saw Bassouin glance once more at his wife. There was something in their exchange she couldn't quite discern.

'Poor girl,' cooed Mrs Bassouin. 'Come now—dry your eyes.'

15

S ummerfield studied during his convalescence, helped daily by Abdlakabir's children. Once able to walk properly, he ventured out to the city *bibliothèque* and read the accounts of local history. On the sight of French uniforms he felt a wary unease and the fact made him conscious that the native Moroccans probably held the same feeling.

Marrakesh had been born of a mixture of Berber pride and ingeniousness, religious fervour and the will to unite. From the Roman *barbarian*, the Berber peoples had lived in northern Africa since the beginnings of time, a patchwork of tribes and territories. But towards 800, three small Berber dynasties pitted their forces and conquered Egypt, laying claim, as descendants of Fatima, the daughter of the prophet Mohammed, to be the rulers of all Believers throughout Spain, North Africa and the Middle East.

In 1070, one of the warrior chiefs from the western part of the empire journeyed across the Sahara to Mecca and received from his spiritual master the mission to spread the message of Islam. He returned to his native lands, stopped his troops on a plain within distance from the Atlas Mountains and here they made camp. They built a palace, mosques and the first of the 20-foot high red clay and earthen walls that would little by little form the fortifications of the city of Marrakesh, which translated as *Land of God*. He named his state the *Almoravide* confederation, one of his greatest achievements not lying in conquest, but in the construction of a system of underground irrigation bringing water to the city from the Atlas Mountains, a hundred kilometres away.

In the second half of the twelfth century, another Berber dynasty, the Almohades, seized power, advancing northwards as far as Grenada in Spain in response to the Castillon *reconquista* of the

Muslim-settled peninsula. It was at that time that the Koutubia, the seventy-metre high minaret juxtaposing the grand mosque in Marrakesh, was built on the ruins of an Almoravide palace and the dynasty reigned for another century, masters of North Africa. They were finally toppled, under attack from both Christian and Arab crusaders, and definitively overthrown. The Arab invaders settled on the coast and on the plains, but would never succeed in conquering the Berber mountain tribes and the Berber Tuaregs of the western Sahara.

Later, in the fourteenth and fifteenth centuries, the Spanish crossed the Straight of Gibraltar and founded colonies in Oran, Melilla, Ceuta and Tangiers. Summerfield learnt that throughout the centuries of Turkish-controlled Islamic rule in Africa and the Middle-East, the kingdom of Morocco was the only nation to retain autonomy and it kept close links with the British, one of its oldest allies. This against the threat of French expansion in Africa, until the late nineteenth century when both Germany and France laid claim to Moroccan territory. In 1911, French troops entered Fez and provoked a political crisis between the two powers, resulting in an agreement that gave France the right to dominate Morocco while German influence was allowed to spread in central and eastern Africa. Thus began French rule under the General Lyautey, in the beginning co-existing with the traditional authorities and then inexorably more direct in rule, until French functionaries occupied the totality of the key decision-making bodies—law, commerce, communications, government and the military.

It was while in the library that Summerfield also informed himself on the French presence in the city. Two garrisons, three courts, a chamber of commerce, two sporting clubs, four banks, an expatriate hospital, the station, an electrical generating plant, a water works, a main post and telegraph office and several sub-offices, a town hall with annex administrative buildings and five schools. There were two institutions for higher studies catering for the French expatriate community. And it was upon reading this that Summerfield decided to visit them and search for the young woman.

Before he could, however, Badr contacted him with a message from Abrach. Receiving him in his lodgings, Summerfield thanked the young man for watching over him after the incident asking him if he would buy him some new clothes, his former shirt and headscarf having been soiled in the struggle with the gendarmes.

He liked Badr and was filled with a mixture of gratitude and curiosity for the young man. For the more he knew of Badr, the more enigmatic he became. Summerfield recognised some shared traits of character, though he was also aware that Badr possessed a certain hardness in his soul that Summerfield, however tough life had been by British standards, could never rival. It was something approaching revenge. And Summerfield also recognised that this singular demon spelled danger. The particular blend of education, religious belief and ideology in Badr made him feel uneasy. It was a provocation. He couldn't help feeling—and suspected that Badr too—that this would one day lead him to an early encounter with death.

Abrach's fresh instructions were that Summerfield now write a letter in return to the young woman. There was a list of points to be covered. There was to be no poetry—just simple, clear exchange. Abrach seemed to want to retain that certain distance, Summerfield reckoning that the big guns were being set up in readiness for the next round of messages. The merchant was once again using Summerfield to play with the fish—reeling in, letting out slack, reeling in, slacking off. The strike was only a question of time.

Summerfield asked Badr to wait while he penned a letter in reply. Such correspondence required no great thought and in thirty minutes the job was done.

I thank you for your letter and my deepest regret for not having had the possibility to answer sooner, though the words that I now write have been in my mind and on my lips every day.

Even if I do feel at times so very close to you, you are correct in assuming that I do not belong to your entourage. For the present, I must remain what you described as a mystery and my apologies if this causes any discomfort. It is, however, a momentary necessity.

Be assured that the time will come for us to meet—I greatly desire this. However, in reply to your questions, I can tell you that I am a reasonably wealthy man, having succeeded in my professional vocation and possessing a good education. I will also add that I am older than yourself and a man of honour.

You seem surprised at having been chosen, and this invokes a certain surprise on my part, too: for know that your beauty is absolute and that my choice knows no doubt. Finally, with respect for your request for a photograph, I ask you to keep the image of me that you yourself have made—it is what your heart has defined, in all clarity, and is the clearest of pictures.

I wish you well and encourage you in your studies. I shall write again soon.

Warmly and sincerely yours.

When finally Summerfield sealed the letter in an envelope and handed it across, Badr looked at him strangely. There was the trace of a frown on his face.

'Yes? Is there something wrong, Badr?' said Summerfield, his voice betraying a sense of irritation.

'You have just shown what is wrong,' replied Badr. 'I detect reticence in your voice, anger in your body.'

'Rubbish,' said Summerfield, curtly, feeling anger now at himself.

'You are troubled, Mr Summerfield.'

'I still feel the pain from the gendarme's stick,' answered Summerfield. 'And how many times must I tell you, Badr—my name is *Harry*! Go now—give this text to our patron.' Badr hid the letter carefully away inside his shirt and gave a wry smile. He was about to leave, when he turned at the door.

'*Académie des Jeunes Demoiselles de Sainte Suzanne de Marrakesh*,' he said, as though replying to a question.

Summerfield raised his eyebrows. 'I didn't ask anything, Badr.'

'Ah,' said the young man, distantly, glancing to the floor and then straight into Summerfield's eyes. 'Then it was written that I should say it. Please—*Harry Summerfield*—be discreet.'

Summerfield stared back into the young man's steady gaze and nodded.

The square before the *Académie* was deserted when Summerfield arrived. A large clock on the ornate central façade chimed seven a.m. The sky was milky white and it would surely rain.

Summerfield, dressed in some clothes that Badr had given him, sat down on the kerb some fifty yards from the main gates and waited. His arm was still strapped and hidden inside his loose-fitting shirt, making him look as though he were an amputee. Through the fragrance of the thick grass of the lawn in the middle of the square and the nearby orange groves, an occasional waft of sweat rose up from the clothes. Sitting with hunched knees, he drew his headscarf around him, covering his lower face and nose and waited.

In his pocket, he had a message. *His* message, written almost three weeks ago upon reading her first simple line. The night before he had dreamt of the moment he would see her. He would take her aside, unveil his face and hand over the message. It was a wild, illogical scene he had invented and he knew it would never happen like that. But still, upon leaving his lodgings, he had slipped the message into a hopeful pocket. One never knew.

Towards seven-thirty, an old man appeared, teetering on his twisted limbs and sat down with some difficulty in front of the large wrought-iron gates that Summerfield noticed were padlocked together. On the other side of the warped gates a nun appeared, a rope in her hands. But far from telling the beggar to leave, she unlocked the gates and promptly wound the rope around the useless lock and handed the ends to the old man. She made a quick prayer with clasped hands, the old man nodded and gave the Muslim gesture of salutation in return. Once gone, the old man settled himself comfortably on his haunches, glanced around him and spotted Summerfield. For a few seconds, the old man remained immobile. Could he be blind, too, thought Summerfield and felt a little uneasy. Perhaps he had taken him for a rival. At last the old man gave him a nod and Summerfield returned it with a vague gesture of his free arm.

Ten or so minutes later a woman appeared, dressed in a dark brown coat and ankle-length dress, probably an external teacher and Summerfield witnessed the first in a series of strange ceremonies the old man was to undertake until the bell rang for lessons an hour later: the woman stopped, bent slightly and handed the man a morsel of bread which he deftly stored away in a pocket of his clothes. The words *Dieu vous bénisse*—God bless you—reached Summerfield from across the silent square, probably the only words of French the old man knew. Upon this, the old man slackened the loose knot on the length of rope, the gates drew open, the woman went inside and the old man immediately tied the knot again and pulled the gates shut. From his viewpoint, Summerfield frowned. Why on earth didn't they just leave the gates open, he wondered. It was at that point, that the first drop of rain splattered onto his hand.

It was raining steadily when the students of the *Académie* began to arrive, first in ones and twos and then in clusters until the flow was constant. Summerfield was wet through. He smelt worse than ever, the dampness mixing with the heat of his body and permeating the space around him with a pungent staleness. He hardly saw any faces. The young ladies of the *Académie* wore their hoods and blue capes or else were escorted by helpers holding large umbrellas. Cars stopped and pony traps arrived, jostling for a space close to the gates. Through the downpour, the old man kept slackening off the rope, pulling it tight and pocketing the objects offered him by the charitable young ladies—food in his right-hand pockets, coins in his left. Damn it, swore Summerfield silently, wiping the wet from his face, the old codger must be making a fortune! The bell rang. Summerfield realised his escapade had been fruitless. And—*rather stupid*. It would have been much more profitable to arrive in the afternoon and watch the students *coming out* of the building, face on. Foul-smelling, sloshing about in the muddy street, he made his way back to the main avenue and hailed a calash.

Freshly washed and in his own local clothes—clean apart from a brownish stain on the left shoulder, vestige of his wounds— he returned in the afternoon and took up position. Again the old man was there at the gates. Had he remained, wondered Summerfield? They exchanged looks again and the old man gave him a gummy smile which carried, thought Summerfield, much smugness. At least there would be no more rain.

At five o'clock the square filled with awaiting transport. There was even a bus. The bell rang and the students flooded out. This time, instinct made Summerfield move closer and he studied the faces from a reasonable distance.

His mind had formed an idea of who he was searching for. Neither tall, nor petite, Abrach had said. Extremely pretty. Dark hair and brown eyes. Graceful—like a gazelle. Different maybe. He was searching for someone who stood out from the rest. Summerfield could feel his mind calculating as he passed from face to face—no, no, no not that one, *ye*...no, neither!

And then he saw her—the young woman. Dark hair, slightly wavy, too far to clearly see her eyes but probably dark, too. Smiling, laughing with a group of friends. She had a special way of moving, conscious of her limbs and free flowing. Confident and beautiful, said Summerfield to himself—could it be her? Summerfield's heart juddered and he felt himself stepping forward. He *wanted* it to be her. The little group chatted loudly. The young woman said something and the others laughed and someone said 'Oh, Sarah!' *Her name*, thought Summerfield triumphantly. And then again, the nagging uncertainty—*could it be her?* He began to walk parallel to them at a distance of some twenty yards, luckily none of them yet sparing him a glance. And then a car drew up and a young man stepped out. The little group halted. The young man approached, black hair gummed back, wearing beige slacks and a blazer—rather debonair. He stooped forward and kissed three of them on the cheeks and then, in a gesture that made Summerfield wince with surprise, he kissed the young woman—Sarah—on the lips. Her friends whooped and the man took her forearm and pulled her away towards the car. Summerfield felt as though he wanted to shout out and checked himself. What a fool! What a *stupid fool*! Just then he caught another regard—the glaring, questioning eyes of a gendarme standing directly opposite him. Summerfield faltered and stopped. The officer flicked his head and Summerfield, now feeling worse than he had that stinking morning, walked away.

It was very late before Summerfield managed to rid himself of his sourness. It was a mark of just how unreasonable his heart had become, his mind jumping to wild conclusions. First, that it was indeed her—*the one*. How could he possibly be sure? And secondly, if it was indeed her, that the young woman should not already have a man in her life—for indeed, none of her correspondence had ever mentioned the word *love*. Lastly, if it were her, why indeed should he have expected her to notice *him?* Summerfield returned suddenly and sharply back to the reality of things. He sighed and fished for a cigarette, tossing the match in disgust out of the window. He was a foreigner, rather a strange bird at that, and employed by a patron to write text and nothing else—he should expect nothing, especially from this dangerous game. Hoping he had found her was only making his spirits worse. The sooner he got it over and done with, the sooner he could be free to move on.

16

Jim Wilding arrived in the last week of March, 1939. Summerfield met him on the very platform he'd seen him off on, almost eight months before. They shook hands vigorously. He had changed, toughened somehow. Wilding's face and arms were burnt a dark brown, his skin leathery and he looked older. He had also lost weight.

'You'll fatten up in Marrakesh,' joked Summerfield and Wilding quipped back.

'You too, Harry—you look as though you haven't eaten meat in days.'

Summerfield laughed. Come to think of it, he hadn't.

They hailed a taxi, an old Ford pick up with a cabin salvaged from a calash bolted to the back, and headed towards the hotel. Wilding couldn't prevent himself from craning his neck and staring at the city.

'It's civilisation, Harry—I'm not used to it. This is luxury compared to where I've been.'

'I'll show you my place sometime,' answered Summerfield. 'It's an eye-opener, Jim.'

'Sure it is,' said Wilding, leaning out of the window to view a flowerbed and its luxuriant foliage. 'But at least there's colours—*and* people. God dammed, I nearly went nuts out there. The only things I had to talk to most of the time were a camel and a Bedouin.'

'*Tuareg*, Jim—they call 'em Tuaregs, here. Bedouins are from Arabia.'

'And the most communicative was the camel!' continued Wilding. 'I even ended up asking him for his opinion.' He sat back in his chair and beamed. Summerfield saw that Wilding was a happy man and it made him feel good too—and to speak in English after so long: that was a relief. 'You haven't changed,

Harry—at least not in character,' said Wilding, studying him. 'Harry—I'm really glad to see you again.'

Summerfield smiled. 'We've got lots to talk about, Jim. I think we'll both see how much we've really changed.'

The hotel made Summerfield hesitate. He stopped in the entrance lobby, feeling somehow foreign, almost unwanted. Wilding continued walking, then realising, turned back. Summerfield was standing, gazing up at the ornate ceiling with its electric fan and brass trappings, overcome by the luxury of it all.

'Yep—me too,' grinned Wilding. 'You know—most of all, I haven't slept in a real bed for almost seven months. I'm afraid I'll never wake up once I'm in it.'

'I feel a bit strange,' said Summerfield, distantly.

'Well you won't after a drink or two. C'mon—that's something else I missed out on.'

They sat in the hotel bar, in leather seats that neither of them could get used to. The taste of cold beer was acrid, dry. Quaintly, Summerfield's first reaction was that he didn't like it. Wilding must have noticed his grimace, for he raised his glass and grinned.

'Remember that beer in Gibraltar, Harry?' Summerfield grunted. 'Seems like a lifetime ago.'

'And Spain,' added Summerfield. 'I'm glad I wasn't enrolled. Things have completely turned round.'

'I read a rag about a week ago,' said Wilding. 'They said Catalonia was on the point of being attacked.'

'Attacked? Good God, it's been overrun—a month ago. That and the Basque territory. It looks pretty desperate, Jim.'

'Well—at least it'll bring an end to the killing, Harry. As for the wider effects, coming back I overheard people talking about Germany. Couldn't understand the French but for a few words, but I think I got the gist of things.'

Summerfield nodded. 'Everyone's gearing up for war in Europe, Jim. The French are talking about mobilising their reserves. Hitler's making noises about reclaiming lost land in Poland.'

'They'd be idiots if they thought war was the answer.'

'Right enough. Problem is—maybe they are idiots.'

Wilding sipped on his beer, rolling it over his tongue and swallowed. 'And what if they do decide to go to war, Harry? What about you?'

Summerfield raised his eyebrows. 'D'you know, Jim—that's a good one. I hadn't even thought about it.'

'Don't blame you,' added Wilding. 'It somehow seems so unbelievable. Only twenty years ago they were butchering each other—you'd have thought they'd learned.'

'I suppose I'd go back,' said Summerfield, continuing his train of thought. He surprised himself. 'D'you know—I *really* think I would.'

'And fight for all those things you found so unjust,' quipped Wilding, raising his glass.

Summerfield shook his head and grinned. 'It's home, Jim. I'd almost forgotten my roots being out here. Meeting up with you again has woken me up.'

'And now it's my fault! Harry—you sure are one ungrateful guy. It was me who saved your skin from Spain, remember?'

'Now, now Jim—you only pointed me in a direction and, as they say out here, *it was written.*' He raised his glass.

'Hogwash!' returned Wilding, grinning and they drank.

It was good to be in Wilding's company. While Jim went downstairs to send a couple of wires, Summerfield took the first bath he'd had in six months. It was so soothing, he nearly fell asleep and it was the water filtering through his lips that brought him back from total submersion. Spluttering, he pulled himself up, climbed out of the bath and dressed. His clothes, the same clothes he'd first worn when arriving in the city, smelt foreign and stiff against his fresh skin. Surprising himself, he realised that he felt much more at ease in his Moroccan attire—the *jellaba* and loose fitting trousers. He looked in the bedroom mirror and shook his head.

Wilding came back and himself took a bath while Summerfield read the two neatly ironed newspapers lying folded on the lounge table. When Wilding finally re-appeared, dressed in a light grey suit and freshly shaven with his hair gummed, Summerfield let out a laugh.

'Good Lord, Jim—the theatres on Broadway don't open until ten!'

'You better get smart, too, Harry—I got us an invite—news spreads fast around here. I've been invited to a society dinner and I'm taking you along too.'

'I couldn't do that, Jim—I'd end up making a scene.'

'Just say you're American, Harry,' returned Wilding with a wry smile.

'Well when is it? I haven't even got a suit.'

'No need to panic, Harry. It's in three days' time. And I can lend you a suit.'

Summerfield suddenly gave a mischievous grin. 'No, Jim—I think I've got just the right clothes I can wear. I'll show you—see what you think of it.' Wilding cocked his head and Summerfield continued. 'But I'll have to take you on a visit of my district first.'

'Pleasure, Harry—but please, I'd like to eat good food tonight and get some good sleep. Buzz me sometime tomorrow.'

The following day, Summerfield neither saw nor heard anything of Wilding. He supposed the American was seeing to business, sending back reports to the States and his employers. Summerfield spent his time seeing to all the routine chores he'd left accumulate for the past weeks and when they were seen to, journeyed to the European quarter with its shops catering for the expatriate community to enquire for a suit. His wild thought for adopting local dress to the invitation had met with some resistance from his wiser self, but it only took a brief discussion with two tailors to discover that buying anything was beyond his means. Perhaps he would take up Jim's offer to fix him up with a spare suit, after all.

Summerfield phoned the hotel mid-evening and after waiting a full five minutes was finally connected with Wilding's room. Wilding, his voice slow and heavy with sleep, yawned into the phone.

'Harry? Jesus, I'm sorry—must've slept for a solid twenty hours. What time is it?'

'Eight,' replied Summerfield. 'I thought you might be attending to business.'

'I was, Harry—serious business. My shut eye.'

'Sorry to wake you.'

'Naa,' protested Wilding. 'Good job you phoned. How about meeting up?'

'Tomorrow, Jim. Take a cab to the entrance to the *Medina* and I'll meet you there. No suit, Jim.'

'Okay. Is ten-ish fine?'

'Ten's fine.'

The *Djemaa El Fna* square had a splendidly lazy atmosphere about it in the morning. Its wide open space seemed deserted compared to the thronging mass of the night. Here and there people crossed it in ones and twos, an occasional patrol cutting an orderly, rectilinear path across its space.

The March sun began to warm the stone and earth, which turned from orange to fuchsia to pale pink. Stray dogs wandered in circles, sniffing the detritus of the night before. Men picked at wood and paper and left-overs from the night.

Summerfield saw Wilding arrive in a calash and watched as the American paid and stepped down onto the compacted earth of the square. He noted that Wilding had heeded his advice and was wearing the casual clothing he probably wore in the field—beige slacks, ankle boots, a bush hat and a blue, canvas jacket. The trap pulled away and Wilding stood for some seconds, nonetheless obtrusive in his western clothes, searching for Summerfield. The American looked at his watch, took a few steps and turned round to search once more. Summerfield sensed a little nervousness in Wilding's movements and smiled to himself, wondering whether his friend would notice him. As expected, Wilding's presence soon acted as a magnet. A couple of men approached him, stopped to say a few words and continued when Wilding shook his head. Then the children, appearing as if from nowhere, tugging at Wilding's clothes. However intensely Summerfield had been looking at his friend, Wilding had still failed to notice him. It was time to appear, thought Summerfield, observing Wilding's growing irritation.

Summerfield rose from his sitting position hardly ten yards away and walked over, shooing away the children. Wilding span round and gesticulated.

'*Go away, you.*'

'I just saved you from being pick-pocketed!' said Summerfield in return. Wilding's jaw dropped and Summerfield laughed. He moved closer. 'Jim—it's me—*Harry.*'

'*What in Christ's name*—' began Wilding. 'Have you *seen* yourself, Harry?'

'I can't, Jim—I'm invisible. I was sitting ten yards away.'

'So you saw me being attacked, then, you crazy bastard.'

'*Attacked* is a little strong, Jim. And I did eventually step in to help.'

'You're nuts,' said Wilding, shaking his head.

Summerfield guffawed. Maybe Jim was right. 'Come on—let's get going before a whole crowd turns up. Follow me—and remember: you've just hired me as your guide.'

'*Nuts,*' repeated Wilding, stepping behind Summerfield and lowering his voice. 'You've gone native.'

'It's a defence mechanism, Jim. Camouflage. I do it so well now, that it takes a very shrewd local to find me out.'

'It'll get you into trouble, Harry.'

'Already has—but funnily enough, not with these people.' Wilding cocked his head, but Summerfield beckoned him on through a gateway and into the intricate alleyways of the souk. 'This way, Jim. It's a bit of a hike to my place and I still get lost in this maze. By the way, why not call me Hassan while we're at it.'

'Because your name's *Harry*, Harry,' replied Wilding, flatly.

'Might save us some trouble, that's all,' returned Summerfield and then, sotto-voiced, 'I wonder what *would* happen to me if they found out. Hadn't thought of that.'

'Christ, you *are* nuts. You're a danger to be with, Harry—sorry, *Mustapha.*'

'Hassan,' corrected Summerfield.

'Jesus Christ, *Hassan*, then!'

'Just Hassan will do, Jim.'

Summerfield wound through the tightly packed streets and

alleys, Wilding following closely behind. From time to time, Summerfield stopped to offer a few explanations. 'And on our left, some say the oldest vestige in the city—thirteenth century—the equivalent of a chapel. And that,' stopping before a chaotic, dazzling display of powders and roots, 'is liquid soap. Incredible, is it not?'

'You mean they put that muck on their skins?'

'I agree the colour puts you off a bit—but it's made from olives and very good for a healthy complexion. Just think if someone decided to commercialise that back home, Jim. *Liquid soap!*'

'Wouldn't work, Hassan,' replied Wilding, playing the game. 'It's more slippery than slippery soap. How could you hold it when getting into the tub?'

'You've got a point,' said Summerfield, shrugging his shoulders. 'Pity, though. And that,' he continued excitedly, pointing at a pile of small, white, roughly stacked rectangles, 'is jasmine. Bars of the stuff. And over there—powdered gazelle horn.'

'What's that for?'

'They say it's an aphrodisiac, but people also put it on wounds.'

'And what about that black stuff?' enquired Wilding, as if his eyes had just come alive. He prodded a woven basket with its pasty metal-grey content.

'They pronounce it *korl* though I don't know how it's spelt.'

'My guide in the desert had some around his eyes. First time in my life I saw a guy putting make-up on.'

'Not make-up, Jim. It's their way of protecting their eyes from the desert glare. They haven't tinted glasses here. If they didn't put that on they'd go blind.'

'Hey—now *that's* strange!' Wilding had caught Summerfield's mix of excitement and curiosity and couldn't stop now. He delved into another basket and held aloft what appeared to be a small, prickly catapult tied in string.

'No idea,' shrugged Summerfield and glanced across at the merchant who picked one up, opened his mouth for Wilding to reveal a set of dark brown teeth and began to scrub. 'A toothbrush!' said Summerfield.

'Obviously effective,' laughed Wilding. 'I'll take one.'

At last, after Summerfield had made a detour just to witness Wilding's retching at the foul smelling chicken market, they resurfaced into the glare of the open streets.

'This is the biggest garbage yard I've ever seen,' said Wilding, squinting. He searched in his pocket for his sunglasses.

'This is home, Jim. We're nearly there.'

'Charming,' commented Wilding as they walked on. 'No offence, Harry—*Hassan*—working in this mess is fine, but when it comes to living…'

'You'll be surprised, Jim. And *Harry* is fine, now. I should think everyone is used to seeing me around here by now.'

'Well, at least that's something. Tell me—how did they take to an Englishman wearing fancy dress?'

Summerfield chuckled. 'It's really very practical clothing, Jim. You should try it.'

Wilding smiled and shook his head. 'No thank you, Harry. We've all got identities—I'm happy with the one I've got.'

'And I'm happy with having several, Jim. D'you know—the kids have got into the habit of calling me *Laurens*! T.E. Lawrence—dunno how they learnt of him, but they liken me to Lawrence of Arabia!'

'Another crazy Englishman, Harry.'

Side by side now, the two men slowed their pace and sauntered along the outskirts of the medina and into the outlying residential spill, Summerfield pointing out the oddities—the little shops and houses with their cluttered shelves and makeshift windows and doors made from salvaged wood and glass. Occasionally, groups of boys passed noisily, saluting Summerfield. And Summerfield, using the Arabic he'd picked up, returned a few words which made them laugh.

Wilding threw him a respectful glance. 'I'm impressed, Harry.'

Summerfield shrugged. 'Maybe they're just laughing at my accent. Imagine it, Jim—an Englishman, already an exotic item in these parts, speaking with the strangest accent they've ever heard, in a language which isn't even their own.'

'They're Arabs, aren't they?' enquired Wilding.

'That's what I thought in the beginning too. In fact, we should remember that the Arabs invaded this country centuries ago, Jim. Most of these people speak two languages, even three if you count those who speak French. They call it the *Tamazight* language, the language of the Berber tribes.'

'So you're speaking to these kids in their dialect?'

'Well—the language is dying in the big towns, but they're still pretty proud of their origins. I speak some Arabic which is the lingua franca of North Africa. It's like calling a Scot or a Welshman, a Saxon,' continued Summerfield, returning to the former subject. 'The Saxons and the Angles—the English—were invaders—'

'*Whoa!*' exhaled Wilding, slapping Summerfield on the shoulder. 'Hold on, Harry. Now I understand why you get on so well here—you're just as complex as them. Why you guys just can't call yourselves British and be happy with that, I don't know. In the States, we see the big picture—everyone's an American, *period*.'

'Maybe,' answered Summerfield, 'but scratch a little under the surface and you'll come up with Irish, Italian, Mandarin, German, Swedish and I don't know how many other affinities. Isn't that right?'

'Where d'you get that information from, Harry?'

'Books, Jim. Only books and words—but I imagine it's true.'

'Well maybe it is,' conceded Wilding. 'And you're something of a bookworm, if I remember—a writer, right?'

'A bad one, Jim. Phoney verses for phoney dreams. And then I let politics get in the way.'

'Not anymore, Harry. You haven't once mentioned all those ideals you held in Gibraltar. You've changed.'

The two of them turned into Summerfield's quarter and Summerfield pointed at the tree which marked the street in which he lived.

'If you need a pee, go ahead,' said Summerfield, ruefully. 'The locals use it as a urinal.' He glanced across at Wilding who raised his eyebrows, but remained silent. Perhaps the American was getting used to things. Before they arrived at the tree, Summerfield tugged on Wilding's arm and they halted. 'And we'll get Mrs Oudjine No. 1 to cook us a meal.'

'Number 1?'

'Mr Oudjine has two wives, Jim. He's quite well off for these parts. Come on—the butcher's is just over there.'

Farther on and squeezed between a hardware stand stuffed full of boxes of rusting bolts and nails and a weaver's workshop dripping with spools of multicoloured thread, was the butcher's. Summerfield felt Wilding falter and he turned. The expression on Wilding's face was one of horrified incomprehension.

'Harry—you can't be serious. We'll die of the plague if we eat that stuff.' Summerfield frowned and followed Wilding's regard. True—he was now looking through Jim's eyes and noticed, as he had done that first time he'd set eyes upon the place, the grim display of heads and entrails on the rickety little stand in front of the shop. A swarm of fattened flies buzzed merrily from head to head, occasionally shooed away by the owner's son brandishing a cluster of palm leaves.

'Yes, I see what you mean,' murmured Summerfield, his voice sounding philosophical—'Though I still haven't figured out if the heads are actually for sale. I presume so.'

'It's—it's *unclean*,' spluttered Wilding.

'Apparently not—the animal has been killed according to Islamic law,' returned Summerfield. 'In we go.'

They walked passed the display of heads—two goats, two sheep and a cow sporting an extremely large pair of protuberant eyes which seemed to enquire questionably at them as they entered the little shop.

'*Salaam*,' said Summerfield, smiling at the owner who returned salutations. 'Meat, please, Abdul—for Mrs Oudjine to cook,' he finished in French.

The butcher disappeared momentarily, leaving Summerfield and Wilding alone in the tiled room. It looked freshly washed but for the fact that Abdul seemed to have forgotten the skirting board and corners where a thick, black strip of grime had colonised the joints in the tiles. Wilding gave a worried frown and then froze. Summerfield glanced at him and the American nodded in the direction of a small window in the wall that gave out to a back yard. Summerfield grimaced. In the middle of the small, dim yard, was a five-foot pile of heads and carcasses, the gleaming white bones streaked with pinkish blood.

'Sheer butchery,' quipped Summerfield, lamely.

'I think I'm gonna be sick, Harry.'

'Not in here,' returned Summerfield, 'It's unhygienic.'

'For me or for the meat?' gagged Wilding, mirroring Summerfield's grimace.

Abdul came back, holding a large flank of meat wrapped in a linen cloth and laid it out on his workbench. Wilding peered over—thankfully it looked spotless. 'And will the family Oudjine be sharing the meal with you?' asked the butcher, his curved knife skitting away a couple of stray flies.

'No, but add a little on for the family, if you please.' Abdul's knife cut into the meat with a soft hiss and he smiled. 'Mutton, *Sidi* Summerfield—a beautiful beast I slaughtered only this morning. May God provide Mrs Oudjine with the necessary respect and dexterity in her cooking.'

'God is almighty,' replied Summerfield, respectfully lowering his head.

The day drew on and the sun blazed for two hours before commencing its descent into mid-afternoon. The odour rising up from his neighbour's kitchen rose deliciously into the still air, filled Summerfield's rooms and wafted up to the roof where they sat under a makeshift canopy Summerfield had rigged up.

'Regal,' commented Wilding, accepting a mug of freshly pressed orange juice. 'I must say I prefer to be up here than down there, Harry. Thanks.'

The two men sipped on their drinks and smoked under the shade. Summerfield briefly outlined the horizon with its minarets and rooftops and the conversation turned to work.

It turned out that Wilding's prospecting in Mauritania had proven fruitless. He had covered an area of desert almost the size of France, carrying out countless studies and boring countless holes. No oil, although he had discovered phosphate and magnesium deposits in some quantity. His job now was to return one last time to oversee the last bore holes and write a full report. Wilding said he intended to send it back to the States beginning of June. And then? He was hoping they'd send him home, but they could also order him farther south into sub-Saharan Africa and the west coast, maybe Portuguese Angola.

'But before they do that,' finished Wilding, his voice sounding determined, 'I'll put in for some vacation and come back to see you. How about taking a trip together towards Libya? They say it's a great place for treasures and ruins.'

Summerfield nodded. 'Why not—good idea. It all depends on how things turn out in Europe, though. Libya could turn into a dangerous place—I don't see Mussolini keeping quiet if Germany goes to war.'

Wilding groaned. 'Well—Algeria, then. At least the French will treat us well.' Summerfield let out a laugh and Wilding glanced enquiringly. 'Anything I said?' Summerfield grinned and shook his head. 'Well—tell me about your work then. How are you paying for this palace, Harry?'

'I write, Jim,' replied Summerfield.

'Well, that's damned good, Harry. It's what you wanted to do, right? What's the paper?'

'The *newspaper*?'

'I figure you do get paid for writing.'

Summerfield nodded and added, evasively, 'Oh, something local that's all.'

'Interesting. What sort of articles?'

'Oh, this and that.'

'This and that,' echoed Wilding and remained silent a few seconds. 'Hey, Harry—I can't believe a guy isn't hiding something when he says *this and that*! Either it's top-level stuff and you're showing that famous British modesty or it's so lousy you're ashamed to tell.'

'It's writing,' answered Summerfield.

Wilding leant forwards. 'So tell me. I'm genuinely interested, Harry. Can't pals ask questions anymore?'

Summerfield felt himself reddening. 'Love letters, Jim. I write love letters.'

Wilding looked at him, silent, and then guffawed. 'Jesus! And they pay you for that? No, c'mon—I can't take it any longer. Come up with the goods, Harry. What's the real story?'

'I'm being serious,' said Summerfield, growing irritated. 'Honest.'

Another silence. Wilding looked apologetic.

'So who for?'

'A man.'

'*What*?'

'No, no…' Summerfield shook his head. 'Not that, Jim. A gentleman who happened to fall in love with a lady. By chance he overheard me speaking French and then, somehow or another, I ended up being offered a job writing.'

'This is like a novel,' chuckled Wilding.

'Well,' hummed Summerfield, 'More than you probably think…'

'God—you're not—'

Summerfield held up his hands as if to ward Wilding off. 'Well, no—*yes*. You see, I don't know her—haven't even seen her, but—'

'But you've *fallen* for her! Hell, this *is* a novel, Harry.' Wilding sat back, rubbed his hands and lit another cigarette. 'So tell me—why doesn't this man do all the smooching himself?'

'She's French. And he's a local. And locals aren't allowed to mix with French women.'

Wilding's expression suddenly changed and he bowed his head. 'Harry—this could land you in a hell of a lot of trouble. All these disguises, all this bizarre, illicit business.'

'I'm just beginning to realise,' answered Summerfield, acknowledging his friend was right. 'In the beginning it was just a little money to keep me going.'

'And if the authorities find out—'

Summerfield sniffed. 'And how could they? Everything's done very carefully, Jim.'

'Nothing ever remains secret for any amount of time—unless it's locked up in the Tower of London and even then.'

They were silent for a few moments. 'He's a merchant—a rich one,' said Summerfield finally. 'He must be influential and I think it's probably thanks to him that the people around here accept me.'

'You're going to find yourself caught between a pair of pincers, Harry,' said Wilding, warning in his voice. 'Any move you make and the jaws will snap tight.'

'Well—I'm on *his* side for the moment. He's my patron.'

'A merchant you say? What's his name?'

Summerfield shook his head. ''Fraid I can't tell, Jim. Confidentiality and all that.'

'You mean you're loyal to an Arab when you should be mixing with the French?' Wilding exhaled. 'I don't understand you, Harry.'

'His name's *Abrach*—that's all I know,' surrendered Summerfield. 'And keep it under your hat.'

'*Abrach*? Strange name. And what d'you know about the lady?'

Summerfield shrugged. 'Not much.' Wilding pulled a face. 'No—honestly. It's all done through several go-betweens. But I do know she's young and I do know where to find her. In fact, I think I have seen her—but she was with another man, young like herself.'

'God—that poor bastard, Abrach. Poor you!'

Summerfield waved his hand. 'No, don't worry about me, Jim. In any case, I can't totally be sure it was her, even if she did fit the description. But when I saw the girl with her boyfriend I understood they were in love—you can tell. And a voice said to me: okay, just in case, time to retire from the fight, time to step back and just concentrate on the job.'

'Well that's something.'

'And I'm almost on the point of stopping the contract. If it was her, now I know she's taken. I'd be leading poor Abrach into a dead end.'

'So what are your plans?'

'Move on?' Summerfield paused, weighing up the rhetorical question. 'Maybe I'd like to travel up into the Atlas and explore a bit. After that—' Summerfield shrugged—'Who knows?'

They remained silent for some time, scanning the view from the roof, each lost in his thoughts. Finally, Wilding sighed noisily.

'Those damn fools—can't they see they're pulling the world towards another world conflict. Harry—I'm not interested in fighting.' Summerfield looked at his friend, nodded and remained silent. Another sigh, this time impatient. 'Harry— I'm *worried*. You're going too far with all this.' Wilding made a sweeping gesture at the city and then his voice softened. 'Come back to your own people. It's not too late. Remember that job in Southern Star?'

'Jim—you worry *too* much. I'm only interested, that's all. When you look at things from their perspective you see things you can't normally understand. Have you ever stopped to think what they feel? What it's like to be under foreign rule in your own land?'

'Nope,' said Wilding, directly. 'I haven't. And I don't want to. I'm here for a job, only another few months maybe, and then I'm going back home. Of course it makes me feel kind of uneasy—and I suppose, if I were to think hard enough like you, I'd understand. But I really don't think dressing up in rags and looking like something out of Ali Baba's cave would make me any wiser.'

'It must be nice to have a time limit,' said Summerfield, without anger. 'A contract.'

'I suppose it makes things easier,' nodded Wilding. 'But you can give yourself one, too.'

Summerfield looked at Wilding and after a few seconds, smiled a little ironically. 'You're right, Jim. I listened to you before and it took me away from Spain. Maybe I should take heed again—wait out the summer and then go. Maybe it's time to return to being a westerner and accept my role.'

17

The following evening, Summerfield made his way to Wilding's hotel and the suit that awaited him. He'd thought about Wilding's opinions and although a natural part of him wanted to rebel, he had to agree that the American's logic was a simpler solution. Discussing with Jim Wilding, it was almost as if he had looked at himself from a distance and seen, as Jim had done, how far removed from reality he had become. It was all quite embarrassing.

Wilding was putting on a tie when Summerfield knocked. Jim looked very suave, very much the American movie star.

'They'll probably ask you for an autograph,' grinned Summerfield, entering the room.

'Suit's in the bathroom, Harry. Try it on—shouldn't be too much difference in size—it shrank a little during a rainstorm in Mississippi.' Sure enough, the suit, a light beige cotton affair fitted him rather well. Only his shoes—his cracked and dusty brown, leather ankle boots—looked a little conspicuous. 'Well, they'll have to do, Harry. I can't help you there.'

'I'll put it down to English eccentricity—or bad dress sense. The French love poking fun out of that one.'

They took a motor cab to the expatriate district. It was the first time Summerfield had been there and was surprised by the sudden orderliness of mown grass and tree-lined avenues. After a stretch of parkland, a buffer zone keeping out the squalor of the city, the cab turned into a residential sector of large, whitewashed houses and stopped. Getting out, Summerfield craned his head and sniffed at the air.

'Everything okay, Harry?' said Jim, seeing off the taxi.

'It's that smell,' commented Summerfield, humming to himself. 'Funny.'

Wilding inhaled. 'Herbs,' he commented. 'Rather a change

from downtown manure.'

'Nice,' said Summerfield. 'Like a mixture of pepper and lemon. Smells like…' but he couldn't put his finger on it. 'Can't remember what, though.'

'Come on—mustn't be late,' said Wilding, pushing him forwards.

The house was not, as they had expected, a grandiose mansion, but a rather functional, rather prim and practical piece of architecture built to a standard design like the twenty or so others in the avenue and with a wide, shady veranda at its base. The garden was large, hesitating between landscaped and tended, to wild and sand swept. Several wheelbarrows and an array of gardening tools lying near a shed were evidence that the gardener had a daily struggle on his hands. It was useless to store the tools away.

At the gate, Wilding tugged on the bell, which despite its large size, let out a high-pitched tingle. Summerfield looked at Wilding and stifled a grin.

'For God's sake, Harry,' hissed Wilding. 'This is top-level. High society.'

'Sorry, Jim –it's the nerves,' grimaced Summerfield. 'I can feel the rebel bubbling inside. Events like this make me want to throw custard pies and break furniture.'

'Jesus—get a grip, Harry.'

A servant appeared at the house and walked stiffly down the pathway to the gate. His master had obviously told him to put on a good show.

'Good evening, gentlemen. May I have your names?'

'*Salaam alikoum. Chnou smitek?*' said Summerfield.

The servant's face froze in panic. His master hadn't told him about this. Summerfield smiled back and Wilding scowled. 'My name is Mohammed, sir,' returned the servant, confused.

'*Ana min Sidi Summerfield, Mohammed,*' continued the Englishman and nodded to Wilding. '*Sidi* James Wilding.'

'I pray, please enter,' bowed the servant and opened the gate.

There were magnolias in the garden and the setting sun cast a red glow over the gorging flowers. Summerfield made a compliment which made the servant's eyes shine with pride.

Wilding prodded Summerfield in the ribs.

'I'll try to make an effort,' said Summerfield. 'Don't worry.'

'Whenever someone says that, it's exactly what I do—*worry!*'

They were led through the front door and into the hallway and asked to wait. Standing there, they heard voices from a room to the right, a low babble of French. Wilding inspected the black and white tiled floor, arranged in a criss-cross style, while Summerfield contemplated the stairway with its potted plants and green carpet. A painting, probably a family ancestor, though maybe a French official of some sort, hung on the wall with a sprig of thyme inserted into the top right corner of the frame. He was just about to draw Wilding's attention to it when a neatly dressed little Moroccan lady hurriedly appeared.

'*Madame,*' greeted Summerfield, bowing.

'Oh no—I'm just the help,' replied the woman, declining to return Summerfield's smile. 'This way, gentlemen. *Monsieur* is with the other guests in the drawing room.'

The host, a sharp featured, intelligent-looking man in his mid-fifties came to greet them.

'*Philippe-Charles Lefèvre,*' he intoned, taking extreme care to speak slowly. 'Head of Regional Administration.'

Wilding shook hands and Summerfield noticed Lefèvre's hunched shoulders, a characteristic of long hours spent at the desk.

'And this is your French-speaking colleague?' said Lefèvre, turning from Wilding to Summerfield and giving the quickest of glances at his shoes. 'British, are we not?'

'I'm afraid so,' returned Summerfield in French.

Lefèvre's mouth gave a curious smile. 'I believe we are allies, Mr Summerfield. Waterloo was a long time ago, was it not? In any case,' continued the sharp-minded host, turning to his two guests, 'do come in. I'm so glad you could come. And—rest assured, Monsieur Wilding, many of my guests speak English and would no doubt be interested to make your acquaintance. Drink?'

The next quarter of an hour saw Wilding and Summerfield introduced to the small circle of guests. Fresquin, the head of the post and telegraph services, had a loud, enthusiastic voice but was diplomatic enough to murmur that he was relieved to see someone different.

'One of the disadvantages of living abroad,' he intoned. 'Always the same faces—and my goodness, I've had enough of Bridge talk. What brings you to Morocco....'

Jean Bassouin, the president of the Chamber of Commerce, greeted them in English. Summerfield took an instant liking to him. Small, witty and full of energy. Lefèvre's wife, dressed in a pale lemon yellow dress and looking rather pale herself, smiled delicately and proffered her hand—to kiss or to shake, it was unclear. Summerfield shook it and Wilding, gleamingly handsome, gave a *baise main*.

'So quixotic,' commented Summerfield.

Wilding grinned back, his eyes sparkling at Madame Lefèvre. 'We Americans have a bad reputation for manners. I just wanted to show that we can rival the Europeans when need be.' Madame Lefèvre's skin suddenly became a blotchy red and out of the corner of his eyes Summerfield saw a look of concern pass over the face of the maid who happened to be passing by loaded with a tray of empty glasses.

Several other guests, including officials from the banks, the church and the education authorities were presented. Majorelle, the painter-gardener, had also been invited but was unfortunately held on other business. Finally, Lefèvre turned to Wilding and Summerfield.

'Right—I'll leave you to mingle. I'll introduce you to Colonel Le Guédec later—he hasn't yet arrived. Should be here for dinner. Oh—and then there's my daughter and her friend, Jean Bassouin's girl. If they ever decide to come down from the bedroom, that is,' he added sourly.

Lefèvre left and they were just about to head for the drinks when Madame Lefèvre intercepted them.

'Mister Wilding—do you play bridge?'

'Well—I—' started Wilding and before he knew it, Madame Lefèvre had embarked on a lengthy description of the local club, obviously excluding Summerfield from any show of interest. Summerfield frowned, caught Jim's glance of alarm and grinned.

'I'll 'er—leave you to it, Wilding. Just getting a drink.'

Summerfield made his way to the maid who still viewed him with the frosty mistrust of a goose watching over her flock of goslings.

'*MaRHabi!*' said Summerfield, cheekily—'*Welcome!*' The maid wasn't impressed. Maybe irony didn't have the same intonation in Arabic. 'A whisky, please,' he added, rather petulantly. 'May I ask your name?'

The maid handed him across a glass. 'You have muddied my carpet, sir,' she replied, tersely.

'Oh dear!' Summerfield stepped back and looked at where he had been standing. 'I'm so sorry—would you have a mop or something—I'll clean it up.' The maid looked at him in horror, but Summerfield was already stooping to pick up a few crumbs of earth.

'Soumia! *What's going on?*' It was Monsieur Lefèvre.

'No—no—it's nothing,' said Summerfield, picking himself up. 'It's my fault. I'm afraid I've given *Soumia* more work to do.'

'Good God, man—it's why we employ her,' said Lefèvre, raising his eyebrows. 'Please—dinner is being served.'

The dining room was spacious, extremely well arranged with nineteenth century rustic furniture—obviously family heirlooms—and painted a pale yellow, much like Madame Lefèvre's dress. Two tables had been arranged to form a large square covered with a dark blue silk cloth. There were candles, sprigs of magnolias and several eating instruments that Summerfield had never seen before. There was some dithering as the guests, like jockeys jostling before the starting line, moved to and fro before the seats, only to be placed and replaced by the umpire, Madame Lefèvre.

'*Garçon, fille, garçon, fille…*' she thought aloud, trying to find a pattern in gender. 'Oh, dear—Mister Summerfield—more boys than girls, I'm afraid. You'll have to sit between the Colonel and Mr. Fresquin.'

'They don't bite?' said Summerfield, but nobody seemed to understand the joke.

'Yes, of course,' said the hostess, quickly. 'Please sit everybody,' she announced, herself sitting down next to Wilding. It seemed as though the American had made a friend and Summerfield thought: God, how dreary an existence she must have. It was true that for once, Summerfield's novelty was outgunned by Jim Wilding's. Not only was Jim a handsome bugger who seemed to shine out like an exotic animal among the middle-aged French civil servants, he was American—a being from a far-removed continent where film stars got out of limousines on every street corner and beggars could become millionaires within a week. If he were honest with himself, Summerfield felt rather cheesed at this. And as a result, he felt even more rebellious—a great bubbling turmoil in the pit of his belly that threatened to boil over. He felt himself fidgeting and with the greatest effort, tried to restrain himself from saying something *déplacé*.

'Are you comfortable enough, Mr Summerfield?' inquired Madame Lefèvre, momentarily bringing a halt to her stream of words to Wilding.

'Thank you, yes. It's the suit,' added Summerfield, sitting upright. 'It's hard to get used to one again.'

'Harry got used to wearing native clothes,' commented Wilding, a little smirk on his lips. 'Very much the *Sheikh of Arabie!*'

To Summerfield's surprise, everyone seemed to find this extremely funny. Everybody that is, except Jean Bassouin, the president of the chamber of commerce, who nodded agreement.

'I wore such clothes when in the field in Algeria. Extremely useful.'

'Exactly,' added Summerfield, thankfully.

'Yes, but *native!*' boomed Fresquin, holding his large stomach from quivering. At that moment the dining room door opened.

'Ah—the youngsters!' said Bassouin.

Summerfield froze in his seat.

'I thought you'd taken root up there,' commented Monsieur Lefèvre, not bothering to look around.

It was *her*—the young woman he'd seen outside the gates of the academy—with the young man she'd kissed. Such was Summerfield's surprise that he failed to notice another young woman behind them, taller, much slimmer and almost eastern in her features.

'Welcome, welcome,' said Madame Lefèvre in a silky voice. 'Please, let me introduce you to our special guests this evening. Mr Wilding from America and Mr Summerfield from England. They're here for petrol, I believe.'

Wilding stood up and shook hands. Summerfield, still overwhelmed, remained sitting and only stood up when he caught Lefèvre's frown.

'Sorry—awfully sorry. You're—'

'Sarah Bassouin.' Summerfield glanced at her father, his ally and felt himself reddening. 'And this is my fiancé, Henri.'

Summerfield turned to the young man, hesitated for a second, taking in his fine features and freshness. For a moment, Summerfield's shadow got the better of him. It *was* her—the secret addressee. And it was hopeless. Accept, said a voice in his head. Summerfield nodded. 'Pleased to meet you both. I'm Harry Summerfield.'

'And this,' said Lefèvre, 'Is our daughter, Jeanne. Shake hands, Jeanne.'

Summerfield turned his attention away from the handsome couple and for the first time noticed the slightly olive skinned, slightly shy-looking young lady as she approached. Curiously, she faintly resembled the young Sarah Bassouin. A humming noise came into Summerfield's head which would, in normal circumstances, be translated as *interesting* followed by *pretty*.

'Jeanne Lefèvre. Pleased to meet you, Mr Summerfield,' she said in English.

Summerfield smiled and bowed his head slightly. 'The pleasure is mine. Your accent is faultless.'

'No thanks to our teacher, Sister Marthe!' said Sarah Bassouin.

'Sarah—a little respect if you please,' said her father, hiding a smile.

'I've done some teaching myself,' added Summerfield, feigning severity. 'And I totally agree with your daughter!' Summerfield glanced round the table. Only Jean Bassouin, Jim and the three young guests laughed in return. *Monsieur* Lefèvre cleared his throat.

'British humour, I believe. *Agnes*—' he pronounced his wife's name with the precision of a surgical instrument—'Please show the children their seats.'

Summerfield found himself facing Jeanne Lefèvre. On her right was Sarah Bassouin's fiancé, Henri and on her left was Jim Wilding, playing, with the utmost politeness, the perfect guest, listening to Mme Lefèvre's incessant monologue and frequently nodding his head. Summerfield glanced again at the Lefèvre daughter, so different, so naturally relaxed and a thought went through his mind that she and Jim Wilding made quite a handsome couple. He in his light grey suit and chiselled, though fine features and she in her pale blue spring dress and dark, flowing hair—tied at the back to reveal rather an elegant neck. Her eyes were large, dark hazel and shone with youth, a blend of openness and wonder but also wariness and shyness at having to mix in adult company. Her nose was rather long and slightly aquiline and it was this feature that struck such a difference with those around her. She looked almost Italian.

A loud *'Ah ha!'* on Summerfield's left—his neighbour, the over-present Mr. Fresquin of the Post and Telegraph authorities —made him start and he immediately turned to observe the reason behind the snort—the tardy arrival of Colonel Le Guédec, dressed in the uniform of the *Gendarmerie.* A shiver of apprehension went through Summerfield followed by what he could only describe to himself as a *slump in his guts*—the empty seat to his right was indeed destined for the Colonel. *Ridiculous*, he thought, cursing the irony of it all: here he was, attending a dinner he shouldn't have been invited to, in the presence of a young woman he'd almost fallen in love with and accompanied by her fiancé, the man who had stolen her from him, and now the arrival of a colonel of the *Gendarmerie* whose men, only several weeks before, had almost beaten him to death.

The colonel sat down, his boots creaking audibly. Summerfield first smelt him—a whiff of *brilliantine* and sharp eau de cologne, and turned his head.

'Pleased to meet you,' said the Colonel, smiling genially. 'British are we? We shall soon, if things get out of control in Europe, be fighting side by side once again.'

'Unfortunately, yes,' said Summerfield, disarmed by the warmth of the colonel's handshake.

Le Guédec inclined his neck in a gesture of reflection. 'Unfortunate. But necessary. The *Boches* are an unsettled lot. Every thirty years or so they deem it fit to invade our country. This time we'll sort them out once and for all.'

'You seem certain there'll be war,' came Lefèvre's voice, leaning forwards to look down the table at his interlocutor.

'Spain is almost finished,' said the Colonel. 'I can only see this as a beginning of wider unrest.'

'But at least the Russians won't have a foothold in Western Europe,' said Fresquin, joining in the conversation with his loud voice.

'*That's something!*' said Henri, the young fiancé immediately reddening at his spontaneous contribution to the conversation.

The colonel hummed, neither for nor against, and it made the youngster's comment stand out even more for its eagerness. 'And what about the Anglo-American view of things?' he added, looking directly across at Wilding.

Wilding withdrew his attention from Mme Lefèvre and looked at the colonel, leaving her conversation to continue for a second or two alone, hanging in mid-air.

'Well, Colonel—as you know, the United States is more concerned with its own area of interest in the Pacific,' answered Wilding, refraining to take position. 'I don't think we'll be seeing any U.S. intervention in your affairs. But perhaps Harry can provide a better answer—he was in Spain, after all.'

'Spain? Really?' Suddenly, it seemed to Summerfield that the entire room had zoomed in on him. He looked accusingly at Wilding.

'No, I—' began Summerfield, but it was too late. It was a strange thing that when people wanted to hear something, they would have none of it until they had got what they wanted. Summerfield was now projected onto centre stage and there was a moment's silence filled with expectation. Summerfield coughed politely.

'I assure you, my part was minor—really of no significance. Jim, I think you'd—'

'What side?' said Henri, rather directly.

'Did you go to the front?'

'And what about the Moorish troops—massacres, I heard.'

'And the bombing—there were terrible reports in the papers.'

'A new and terrifying way of war—*terror*!'

It was the sign for a general outbreak of discussion, coinciding with the arrival of the orange *sorbet* starter. Summerfield was overtaken by events. He was suddenly the centre of a whirlpool around which everybody offered opinion, countered opinion with argument and raised the stakes until it seemed that every fresh comment was met with a louder voice. Summerfield looked at Wilding and met his eyes. Wilding looked a little bewildered.

'I didn't know it'd have that effect,' he said, low-voiced and in English.

'I believe we're witnessing two of the favourite pastimes of the French—eating and arguing. And *all at the same time*—the best thing that could happen.'

'I thought we Americans were loud,' frowned Wilding. 'But this—this is *chaos*!' Mme Lefèvre tugged at Wilding's forearm. 'Excuse me, Harry,' said Jim, raising his eyes heavenwards.

Summerfield found himself quite alone, observing the heated conversation, wincing whenever Fresquin's voice, sounding like a cannon, boomed over everyone else's. And then, suddenly, a softer voice, quite detached from the rest, reaching him from somewhere. It was Lefèvre's daughter, Jeanne.

'Mr Summerfield—is it true?'

'What's true?' said Summerfield, trying to concentrate.

'That you fought for the Socialists?'

'No,' said Summerfield.

'Then, Franco?' She looked a little distraught. Summerfield shook his head. 'That's not what they said.'

'It's not what I said, either,' answered Summerfield. 'I tried to tell everyone, but nobody would listen.'

'To what?'

'I said nobody would listen,' repeated Summerfield, unable to resist the pun.

The young woman looked startled, like some gazelle caught in the middle of a hunt. And for a split second she looked quite astonishingly beautiful. 'No—I—I meant *what did you want to tell us*? Oh! Oh, *I see!*' She reddened and forced a smile.

'I wanted to fight. I even went to Gibraltar to cross the frontier—but my contact never turned up.'

'Father said you'd spoken with Orwell.'

Summerfield snorted. 'I doubt Orwell would ever speak to me. No—I heard him speak once.'

'Oh, dear.' Jeanne Lefèvre shook her head.

'Disappointed?' said Summerfield. 'Sorry. I wish I could be more interesting for everyone.'

The young woman remained silent for some moments and Summerfield returned to listening to the heated exchange. They were now onto the subject of analysing German military strength. *We have the best arms in the world*, Colonel Le Guédec was saying, in an attempt to soothe Mme. Bassouin's worries. *Don't worry— Jean won't be called up. Too old! No—it'll rather be our young Henri here—oh, dear, did I say something wrong?*

'So what were you doing with Mr Wilding in Mauritania?' It was Jeanne Lefèvre's voice, returning to him. Summerfield frowned and refocused.

'I wasn't with Jim in Mauritania. And that's another thing—' He saw her open her mouth, only for her words to be blotted out by a sudden exchange between Fresquin and Mr. Lefèvre. Her look turned from concern to an apologetic smile as Summerfield grimaced in an effort to hear her and then acceptance.

'So what do you do, Mr Summerfield?'

'I write—and yourself?'

'I study.'

Summerfield smiled. 'It seems easier when it's monosyllabic! We understand each other.' She smiled back, a trace of dimples and Summerfield felt a mischievous tingle inside. She was rather surprising, this one. A little snobbish, of course, but then how

could she be otherwise with such parents. But, came a voice at
the back of his head, she *has* something. And then the voice of
irony—she has *potential*.

The main course was served, Mohammed assisting the maid,
Soumia, with serving the wine. Several drops were spilled; little
crimson splashes, rather like blood, thought Summerfield, but
nobody took any notice. Lefèvre would no doubt say later it was
hard to find properly trained house staff in the region.

Business was discussed. Jim Wilding was obviously more astute
than Summerfield had thought, for his American friend, with
much skill and diplomacy, oriented the discussion towards petrol.

'The prospecting in Mauritania doesn't seem to have brought
good results,' he replied in answer to the colonel's questioning. It
seemed to have good effect. At least the Spanish, now in control
of most of the region, wouldn't get their hands on any royalties.
Wilding shook his head and sighed, seeking out Jean Bassouin.

'The British are lucky to have influence in Arabia—the British
Petroleum and Shell companies have struck what seems to be a
limitless source of oil out there.'

'The British have always been accompanied by a sort of sixth
sense,' said Bassouin. 'Or a lucky star. They have a certain feel for
business—rather like you Americans. I'm afraid our Latin cultures
do not have the same edge when it comes to making money.'

'*Business opportunities*,' replied Wilding, softening the impact of
Bassouin's opinion. 'And that surprises me,' he added, showing
interest, 'for the Mediterranean peoples throughout early history
practically invented modern trade and economics. It's in your
blood. The world would never have evolved without the Greek,
Roman or Phoenician merchants—and not counting the latter
explorers like Vasco de Gama and Columbus.'

'History is a series of revolutions,' offered Lefèvre. 'Empires
are built, they grow and then they fade. A greater time for us will
come again.'

'And maybe sooner than you think,' said Wilding, nodding
his head.

'Oh? In what way?' Bassouin leant forward, followed by
Lefèvre, Le Guédec and Fresquin.

'You have the answer right under your noses—well, about five hundred kilometres to the east to be exact: Algeria!'

'The princess without a crown,' quoted Bassouin. 'Four times as big as France and potentially the richest country in Africa.'

'I know certain French oil companies are drilling out there, in the middle of the desert,' added Wilding.

'They have even begun to exploit the oil,' added Bassouin.

Wilding nodded. 'There's probably more than enough. Trouble is, there's a lack of means and technology. You need help.'

'And the United States might propose it!' said Fresquin, blurting out what everybody had been thinking.

Wilding smiled. 'You have insight, Mr Fresquin.' And then, serious, but his voice light and suggesting. 'And why not indeed?'

'Because it is French territory—and French wealth,' said the Colonel.

'I agree. But that doesn't stop an American company exploiting the oil with the French and taking a percentage of the deal.' Several frowns appeared on his listeners' faces. 'It's not important to have all the cake,' explained Wilding, more aggressive now. 'Everybody can have a slice. It's something we call *joint venture*—a new concept. Working together, with one company the main leader, taking the lion's share, and the other accepting a smaller part in exchange for their help.' Silence while the listeners mulled it over. 'Or sub-contracting—that's another field in which there are limitless possibilities. You see—the French authorities give a US company—'

'US or other,' reminded Bassouin, attentively.

'Or other,' echoed Wilding, with a little smile—'Gives *a company* the right to explore and exploit a business activity in return for a levy or a share of the profit.'

'But why would the French government want foreign businesses in Algeria?'

'Ah ha! Good question!' said Wilding. 'That's where the beauty of it all lies—you see, the French government would come out winners.'

'How?'

'Simple! They wouldn't need to pay a cent. It's the contractor who puts the money up front, buys the equipment, pays the workers, refines the oil—all very costly, all very risky. What if oil isn't found? Think of the hole in your pockets. France would have total control over the contract and over any decisions while the US company—or *other*—would do the work. Not only would France earn profit from the oil exploitation, if you think about the savings it would make, it would constitute an even bigger profit. Everyone wins. Especially France.'

Jean Bassouin seemed to retract slightly, as though sinking into a carapace. He was obviously intrigued by the idea and Summerfield understood that inside the genial little man's non-committal exterior, a thousand thoughts were buzzing through his mind. Slowly, carefully and with the same lightness that Wilding's voice had carried, Bassouin spoke up.

'I can perhaps put you in contact with an ex-colleague of mine in Algeria, Mr Wilding. Would you be willing to talk to him as you have talked to us this evening?'

'Sure,' said Wilding. 'I'd be only to pleased to exchange ideas. After all, we can all help each other.'

'When an American says that, it's time to start thinking 80/20,' said Fresquin, smiling. '80 percent for America and 20 percent for the rest!'

'Perhaps not in this case,' said Bassouin, thinking slowly aloud. 'What do you think, Mr Summerfield? What's the British viewpoint? After all, you're in this with your colleague, are you not?'

Wilding darted a glance at Summerfield. Summerfield hesitated, sat back in his chair and gave a secretive grin. 'I'm just an observer,' he said, looking at Bassouin, and then, in turn, the rest, lingering a little longer to look Lefèvre's daughter in the eyes. 'I believe the meat was excellent, the wine marvellous and the conversation interesting—but I think I need to stretch my legs a little.'

'So British!' said Le Guédec, '*Filer à l'anglaise*! But in fact, you're quite right. I'm feeling a little stiff-legged myself.' He turned to face Mme Lefèvre and inclined his head. 'May we have ten minutes before dessert, Mme Lefèvre?'

It was the sign for a general scraping of chairs, something that produced a gasp of alarm from the maid, Soumia, no doubt concerned with the more practical matter of waxing the tiled floor once the evening was over.

The guests broke up into twos or threes, but Summerfield wanted to be alone. They had been sitting for nearly two hours—the odd thought came to him that he wasn't used to chairs anymore—and the conversation, or moreover the role playing, had bored him. What an effort to behave correctly— he was all in. He rose, took his glass and sauntered out in the direction of the others who had headed for the veranda and cigars. But he didn't stop. Instead, he thanked Mohammed who was standing at the door holding a box of tobacco and took a ready-rolled cigarette. He lit up, exhaled and stepped down from the veranda into the garden.

'What's that nice smell, Mohammed?' he said in Arabic, turning back to the servant.

'Savory, *Sidi*.'

Summerfield hummed thoughtfully. 'Very pleasant. Oranges?' he inquired further, nodding in the direction of the far end of the large garden. The servant smiled back and nodded. 'A good job,' complimented Summerfield again. 'May I?'

'Of course, *Sidi*,' replied Mohammed and Summerfield sauntered on, a few steps down the gravel pathway and then stepped onto the thick, dark green expanse of grass. It had been freshly cut, but was so thick and wild, that bending down, Summerfield quickly retracted his hand. The blades were like miniature shards. He brought his palm to his face and in the dark observed a small blob of blood, almost black, on the surface of his skin.

'Did you hurt yourself?' came a voice. It was Lefèvre's daughter.

Summerfield sighed.

'Just a small incision,' he said with effort, turning.

'When I was little, I once ran barefoot on the lawn—I still have a little scar on my foot.'

Summerfield smiled and relaxed a little. She was less than bothersome. Just then the maid passed by with an oil lamp and matches.

'Are they getting worried?' commented Summerfield, raising his eyebrows.

'No,' Jeanne shook her head, shyly. 'Probably mother wanting things to be perfect.'

They stood in silence for a moment, watching as Soumia disappeared into the darkness, a series of halos lighting in her wake, left and right, as she lit the garden lamps. Summerfield exhaled with contentment.

'Very pretty,' he murmured. 'And have you always lived here, *Mademoiselle* Lefèvre?'

'Yes,' she replied. 'Father has quite an important function now. He rose through the *Administration*.'

'He seems a very intelligent man.'

Jeanne nodded. 'He is very good at his job. And he certainly works a lot.'

'Does that bother you?' asked Summerfield, noting a little regret in her voice. 'If you don't mind—' he added, prudently.

'No, of course.' The young woman took a step forward. 'Let me show you the garden.'

'Shouldn't we go by three? Perhaps someone else would be interested—Jim perhaps.'

'Soumia, my nanny, will be watching over us. We can come to no harm here, Mr Summerfield.'

'I meant—' began Summerfield and then checked himself. Her innocence was absolute. It made him feel a little sad. 'A pleasure,' he added. 'Let's go.'

They strolled past a huge old magnolia and into an area dedicated to orange and lemon trees. The smell, in the warm air, was treacly and strong.

'They were here before the houses were built,' informed the young woman. And then, changing subject. 'And if I understand, correctly, you *do not* work with Mr Wilding.'

'That's right. It was a little difficult to hear in there.'

'So you're not prospecting for petrol?' she continued rhetorically. 'You write.'

'That's it—and you, if *I* understand correctly,' said Summerfield, cheekily echoing her words, 'study.'

'Yes.'

'At the *Académie*.'

'That's right—how do you know that?' The young woman looked surprised.

'Well, didn't your friend, Sarah, say something about it?'

Jeanne Lefèvre inclined her head and raised her eyebrows. 'Perhaps—she at least mentioned Sister Marthe, our teacher, if I remember correctly.' A little laugh. 'And what do you write, Mr Summerfield?'

'Oh!' said Summerfield, his conversation with Jim Wilding coming back to him. 'It's not important.' He glanced across and saw that the young woman was a little taken aback. 'What *is* important,' he added, repairing the damage, 'is that my dream is to publish poetry.'

'How interesting.'

'Yes,' said Summerfield, not without irony. 'I don't know if I'll ever succeed, but at least I'm trying. And in any case, it's a direction.'

'A direction,' voiced the young woman.

'A path. And even if it's not the right one, it will inevitably lead to another—perhaps even a crossroads.'

'You speak like an Arab, Mr Summerfield. They are full of such contemplation.'

Summerfield laughed. 'I've grown to like them. I—' he checked to see if he hadn't shocked her—'I enjoy their company. They are far removed from what we Europeans think.'

'I agree,' said Jeanne Lefèvre. 'I suppose it's because I've lived here all my life, but I feel very close to them. I almost consider us one and the same.'

'I don't suppose some would be happy with that,' grinned Summerfield. 'The colonel, perhaps.'

She laughed. 'Oh, the colonel is a fine fellow. Very nice—like an uncle at times.'

'But he has to do his job,' commented Summerfield, ruefully. 'And very thoroughly, no doubt.' He stopped himself. His young companion was looking at him curiously. 'I apologise if I sound cynical,' said Summerfield, lighting another cigarette. He offered it across but the young lady shook her head. 'It's just that I saw some of his men in action in the city. *Thorough* is a light word to use.' She looked baffled. Summerfield shook his head. 'Doesn't matter. Adult things.' At this, the young woman reacted.

'I *am* an adult, Mr Summerfield. I'm twenty-one—nearly twenty-two. Soon, I shall be leaving for France and university. You can talk to me of such things—I *do* understand.'

Summerfield was about to apologise once more, when they entered a small, lattice-work enclosure. It was the smell, the sudden razor sharp nip of scent that filed his nostrils. Somewhat startled, he looked around as if searching for something. It was a small, luxuriant herb garden. Thyme, chives, mint, cumin, pepper and cutting clear through the rest, that delicious smell—what had the servant called it—*savory*.

'This is—' he began, his look of bewilderment turning to a smile—'this is heaven!'

Jeanne Lefèvre giggled and held a hand to her mouth. 'You look like a little boy! Who is the child *now!*' she added, somewhat impertinently. 'Oh, I'm so sorry.'

'No—no, don't be sorry,' smiled Summerfield. 'I deserve it. It's just so wonderful—it was like entering Eden or something!'

'How do you know Eden was like that?'

Summerfield held up his hand. 'Now that *is* going too far,' he reproached, jokingly. He halted, turning full circle to breathe in the fragrances. 'And you? You mentioned you studied.'

A moment's hesitation. The young woman wrapped her shawl closer to her and she gave a little shrugging motion of her shoulders. 'Well, to use your own words, what *really* is important— although of course my studies *are* important—is...'

'Yes?' Summerfield frowned.

'A wonderful story I am living.'

Summerfield stopped and turned to her, curious. His felt his heart warm and for a second her words, so clear, so truthful and devoid of bad intent, melted a hole in him. 'That's very good,' he found himself saying and he gave a slight nod of encouragement. 'Go on.'

'I don't know why I should be saying this—I shouldn't really,' added the young woman, avoiding his eyes. 'I suppose it's because I've had to keep it a secret for so long. And,' she added, raising her head and with her voice full of curiosity, 'it seems so much easier to speak of it to you—someone different.'

'A stranger,' added Summerfield, nodding, 'Yes, it *is* easier to talk to someone you don't know, or someone from afar about secret things. We feel protected somehow.'

'I think I've fallen in love,' continued the young woman, a little surprised by her own audacity. 'In fact, I've never been in love so I'm supposing I am in love. And it's wonderful.'

'He is a lucky man,' said Summerfield, suddenly feeling a tinge of fatherliness towards his young companion. She was so sweet. She reminded him of a kitten, curling up to sleep.

She laughed softly. 'I've never seen him.'

'Sorry?' Summerfield glanced keenly at her.

'No!' She looked up. '*Never.* It's all so gentle—by correspondence. A most incredible thing happened, Mr Summerfield, though you promise never to tell.'

Summerfield felt his heart seize up.

'*Promise?*'

'*Promise*, of course. But I—'

'Several months ago I suddenly received a letter from a man— in the street, of all places.'

It was like a strong current forming. A current that gathered speed and swirled around a centre point, sucking Summerfield in. Suddenly, thoughts ran at him, shapeless. He smelt the clear peppery lemon scent of the herbs. The very smell on the letters he had received. Not Abrach's scent, but—

'And we kept up our correspondence,' continued the young woman, oblivious to the turmoil in Summerfield's mind. She shook her head. 'Although he hasn't written of late—and I'm afraid. Perhaps he has forgotten. Perhaps something has happened. I'm confused.'

Silence. In a single moment, it seemed as if the whole world had for years meant to bring Summerfield to this point, to this garden and the young woman. A whole stretch of time that made up his life, condensed into a single point no bigger than the tip of a needle, though more powerful than the highest mountain or the deepest ocean. He saw the young woman looking at him. He must have appeared frightening, for he saw her expression inexorably change from one of melancholy to wariness.

'Forgive me,' said Summerfield, his voice sounding shaky. 'It reminded me of something similar, that's all.'

'Oh dear,' fretted the young woman. 'I'm sorry, too. I hope I didn't bring back any sad memories.'

'Not at all,' blurted Summerfield, finally regaining composure. 'On the contrary—you managed to bring me the best memories a man could have. Listen—there is no need to worry. Your story will not end. Not yet. He will be in touch, I'm sure.'

'I do hope so.'

'He will.' Summerfield turned to the garden once more. 'May I take some?' he asked, bending down to seek out the savory. 'This is delicious.'

'I use it to scent my letters,' said the young woman.

Summerfield couldn't prevent a laugh from escaping him. 'The fragrance is so much like you, I imagine. Clear and true.'

'I beg your pardon?'

'Nothing.' Summerfield shook his head. 'Remind me your name.'

'It's Jeanne.'

'Listen Jeanne—' Summerfield put his hand to his jacket and searched an inside pocket—'I talked to you about my writing. I would like to offer you something I wrote—I'd appreciate it greatly if you read it and tell me what you think.' The young woman gave him a strange glance, frowning at his hurriedness. 'A writer needs some objective feedback. I'll never succeed if not.' His hand reappeared holding a folded letter and he offered it across. The young woman hesitated, then took it from his outstretched hand and began to unfold it. 'Not now, though. It's not the right moment,' said Summerfield gently, laying a hand on her forearm. He withdrew it, conscious that she might be offended at the gesture. 'I'll get all embarrassed.' Jeanne folded it back in place and held it in the palm of her hand. 'Look,' said Summerfield, beckoning at the sky. 'The old stars—they live like us. Sometimes hard to see and hidden. Other times shining bright.'

'Silvery points in night's pincushion,' said Jeanne. 'I shall never be bored of them.'

Summerfield looked at her from the corner of his eyes, felt himself shudder with the sudden rush of feeling to his heart. 'That's perfectly true,' he said. '*Perfectly* true.'

18

When all was said and done, and all the guests had left and the lights went out, and the noise of tidying from below—chinks and bumps and chimes—reached her; when Mohammed's voice went soft with Soumia and there was a laugh and unsuspecting smells of the earth and leaves nipped the air of her room in bud, Jeanne reached for the letter, unfolded it with care, her thoughts straying vaguely back to the odd Englishman with his odd shoes and odd behaviour. She read, life coming upon her and she shone like the moon over fields of rippled grass and trees.

If you were a river, then I would be your banks, streamlined and crumbling and flowing with your life. And if you were a river, then I would be your willow, sagging with the weight of love, keeling with desire. And if you were a river, then I would seek your source and trickle on down until from joy I smile. And if you were a river, you would flood me with everything that is woman and I would pledge to carry you from the darkness that is land to sea. And if you were a river, then I would be your swan and grace your course with all the pride and beauty your vitality would have won. And if you were my river, running strong and cutting deep, then I would be your river bed where the souls of all lovers sleep. And if you were my golden river, I would be your reeds and lisp in the wind a whispered song on the ripples in your heart; and if you were a river, then I would be your seasons and thaw you evermore when froze and mellow your flow in every burning day that rose.

19

Abrach sat on the upholstered rear seat of his new acquisition, a 1932 Ford T, and smiled, glancing backwards through the rear window at the billowing wake of dust the car sent up. Summerfield turned, bouncing as the automobile hit a rut on the dirt road. Black shapes, people and carts and animals trudging either side, appeared then disappeared like ghosts in the shroud of sand and dust that reminded him of London fog. He smiled wanly back at the merchant and nodded.

'I thought I would offer you a sightseeing tour,' beamed Abrach. 'Get you out of the city. I'd always wished to own a car,' he added, almost as an afterthought. 'Like the French.'

Summerfield nodded again. Despite the interest he showed in the occasion to visit the countryside, he felt uneasy in Abrach's presence. The man's generosity was great and every time he gave Summerfield something, it was a tug-of-war between a friendship and respect that was still pulling them together and Summerfield's desire to end the contract between them.

Summerfield thought incessantly of Jeanne Lefèvre. Their walk in the garden had been like a dream and the impact of his discovery had taken a day to hit him. The following afternoon, sitting at his desk, the events suddenly slotted themselves into a logical order and the realisation was total and crushing. Had she read his message? Had it been the right thing to do? Once more, he had found himself cursing his impulsiveness. He wasn't even clear-headed about his feelings for her. How could they get in contact? What, how, where, who, when? A hundred questions and for the moment, no clear answer.

And Abrach. An invitation to spend two days touring. Summerfield looked out of the car window at the plain and the distant hills, but his mind soon strayed, almost instantly, to his conversation with Jim Wilding.

The American had warned him. Jim had thought the situation dangerous, destined to fail and Summerfield's intention was to terminate his contract with Abrach before it all got out of hand. But here he was, in the very presence of the man who had chosen Jeanne Lefèvre as the target for his love and he couldn't utter a single word about it. In all appearances, it *had* got out of hand. It was too late. And the more he inwardly cursed himself, the more Abrach seemed to offer him his gratitude and friendship. Fate, it seemed, had in all appearances decided to play a vicious game with his conscience, testing and teasing him so that the more he approached the moment to tell Abrach, the further it wriggled from him.

They passed through a collection of crumbling stores and ragged houses on the road. Abrach tapped on his servant's shoulder and told him to slow down for Summerfield to look.

'Do we need petrol?' he added, once more tapping the driver on the shoulder. And then, turning back to Summerfield: 'I shouldn't want us to end up taking a mule back to the city!'

Summerfield gazed out of the window at the poor little halt on the road, a shanty town of a village in all appearances. Here and there, miserable looking men clustered in groups, squatting by the side of the road with their ware displayed on shreds of blanket and cardboard—one or two bars of soap, a rusting jerry can filled with petrol, a couple of packets of rice or grain. Midway through the cluster of shacks, a checkpoint set up by a squad of gendarmes who, although not stopping them, stared suspiciously at the car and its Arabic and white skinned passengers. Hardly daring to glance back, Summerfield saw one of the military policemen lower his head to speak into a radio but whether it was intended for them he couldn't tell.

Once out of the village, Abrach let out a sigh, then grinned. 'They always make me feel a little uneasy,' he said, smoothing out his gown.

'You're not the only one.'

'Ah, yes—your surprise encounter in the old city,' intoned Abrach, with a note of philosophy in his voice. 'Today, Harry, I should like you to visit my region, my village.'

'Is it far?' said Summerfield. Conversation was expected.

'Not too far, I believe,' answered the merchant. He spoke rapidly to the driver and turned back. 'He says we shall be there in two hours. In fact,' he added, pointing ahead through the windscreen, 'it's over there—in the foothills, a little to the south.'

Summerfield followed Abrach's outstretched finger to a distant, low-lying stretch of land behind which, in layers and shades of grey, the hills grew into the mountains of the Atlas. He nodded and smiled. 'Why does the driver keep putting his fist on the windscreen?' he said, asking a question that had been plaguing him ever since leaving the city.

Abrach raised his eyebrows. It was so natural a gesture to him that he had failed to notice. 'You mean this?' he checked, mimicking the driver and stretching out his arm with fist clenched. Summerfield nodded. 'For stones,' replied Abrach, grinning. 'Other cars, lorries—they make the same clouds as us. It's to stop the windscreen from shattering if a stone hits it.'

'I see,' nodded Summerfield and, as if to back up Abrach's explanation, a passing lorry automatically sent the driver's fist as a wedge against the glass. 'Interesting. Does it work?'

Abrach raised his eyebrows again and looked heavenwards. '*Inchalla*. I've never been hit by a stone.'

They drove on, the leaf-spring suspension bending and bouncing over a particularly rutted section of the road. One such pothole lifted the driver off his seat and his head smacked with a loud, dull thump on the sparsely padded roof. As if to make up for the embarrassing event, he began hooting aggressively at the walkers on the roadside, followed by a string of abuse when a goat strayed suddenly across their path. Once again, on relative flat, Abrach's face became serious.

'And now business, Harry. It is time,' he said, his eyes glazing over wistfully for a fleeting moment. 'We must now recommence our correspondence with the young woman. And I ask you, Mr Summerfield, not to spare any passion.' Summerfield glanced away and nodded. 'But first, I received this,' continued Abrach, reaching inside his gown and bringing an envelope from his pocket. 'A rather strange message from the young woman in question. It seems she mistook someone for myself. Hence the necessity—the rather *urgent* necessity—to speed up the proceedings before she escapes.'

'Escapes?' said Summerfield, surprised by the merchant's use of words.

Abrach laughed. 'Of course not—just a figurative remark. I imagine you can interpret this as a mark of my concern. The young lady has been in my heart far too long for me to want to give her up for someone else.'

Summerfield took the envelope from Abrach's hand. 'We may have to concede that it is possible,' he said, waiting for Abrach to give him a sign to open it. The merchant nodded, both for Summerfield to read the message and in answer to his words.

'A younger man—a Frenchman, no doubt... She is bound to meet plenty of young suitors in her milieu.' Abrach seemed lost in his thoughts for some seconds, then exhaled. 'Yes, very likely Harry. But I am philosophical. I see this as a test and as a challenge, both for her and for me. If she is true, and what she writes is what she means, then I shall one day win her.'

'If you have not already won,' said Summerfield, unfolding the message and breathing in the faint scent of savory. It made him smile. He looked up to see Abrach staring at him. 'The exchange of words has been very encouraging,' he explained, with tact, looking the merchant in the eyes. 'Perhaps it was an error to have made a break in the process.'

Abrach's face hardened and his eyes drew almost shut. 'No,' he said, pinching his fleshy chin. 'No, I believe it was the right thing to do. Read and perhaps you will see my point.'

Steadying himself against the jolting car, Summerfield donned his spectacles and held the paper with both hands. He had to read through the message twice.

I recognised it was you. Such words do not come from any man, nor even any particular man. They are words brought in from the desert and the mountains as if by magic, blown in on the winds to take their place on paper. And the wind shapes your writing, with its loops and attack and lines and dots. Why had you never told me your name? Why the secrecy? Once again, I ask you to meet me. I am burning; a candle whose flame now dances and falters in the wind, then ignites and burns bright. Write soon. Tell me where we can meet.

Summerfield did not wish to raise his head. His heart drummed wildly. Letting out a sigh of irritation, trying to control his emotions, he feigned reading a third time. Thank God she hadn't written his name—perhaps she had forgotten it. His heart winced. Between his shoulder blades, the sweat turned cold and made him shiver. And at the same time, he burned, for she had answered him, recognised him. It was all so damn close to Abrach finding out that a stab of panic darted through him. It was time, said a voice. Tell him—*now*.

'Well?' It was Abrach's voice, bringing him back.

Summerfield looked up, searching the merchant's eyes for any sign.

'You look shocked, Harry. Are you all right? Not nauseous or anything?' Summerfield shook his head, which didn't stop Abrach from giving the driver a sign to slow down.

'Surprising, that's all,' offered Summerfield, inwardly cursing himself for his cowardice.

'Exactly!' returned Abrach. 'Do you see? What a terrible twist of fate—the very moment the young beauty falls in love—for that is surely what her words tell us—she meets someone, some unknown man, and wrongly believes she is the presence of her correspondent! Terrible!'

'Awful,' said Summerfield, half-heartedly.

'Terrible!' repeated Abrach, shaking his head. A small grin appeared on his lips. 'And all very intriguing. Irony has always been a faithful companion. It adds a little spice to it all—a test, as I said, of my intention to have her.' Abrach fixed his eyes on the horizon and the coming hills and was lost in his thoughts for some seconds. 'That is why you must write as you have never written before, Harry. I will give you gold for your words.' Summerfield shook his head, but Abrach insisted. 'Write a poem, Harry—and enter the girl's heart like a key to a lock. Turn that key, Harry Summerfield, a perfect fit, well-oiled and making metal melt to tender substance. I must have her heart completely, Harry. And *then* I shall meet her—as she requests.'

They journeyed the last hour in silence, only the driver, occasionally swerving to miss a pothole or traveller, uttering oaths. The road began to climb, at first a soft slope and then a serious of abrupt bends as it wound its way into the hills. The pale gritty dust of the plain gave way to the pale, powdery pink of the hills. Here and there, sparse and almost desperate clumps of grass shot up and clung to the scree between the rocks, becoming lush and thicker as they got higher. The driver put the little Ford into low gear and they moaned and whined down into a valley and up the other side. A plateau, dotted with trees and then another descent into another valley. Abrach turned to Summerfield and grinned.

'Nearly there.'

At the bottom of the valley, the road turned into a track by a small river. The trees grew thick and the grass tall and the deepest green. Little fields appeared, like dominoes, stacked above one another on the slopes of the valley.

'There,' said Abrach, clutching Summerfield's forearm and pointing. 'The village.'

'Where?' Summerfield squinted out at the slopes of the valley.

'Look carefully, Harry—*there*—to the right. Do you see?' Sure enough, Summerfield began to make out the shadow of the rooftops and walls of an otherwise perfectly camouflaged group of edifices, built using exactly the same matter as their natural pink surroundings. 'Spring has come early to the Atlas,' murmured Abrach, his voice unable to disguise a note of joy. 'This time of the year, further up into the mountains, it offers one's eyes so much beauty of colour that it almost makes one weep.'

The track narrowed before they came to the village, too narrow for the car to follow. Abrach signalled for the driver to pull up and, once at a halt, left the car and accompanied Summerfield for the remaining three hundred yards or so.

It was a well worn path, steep and straight, up through a slight gully that trickled with a rivulet of water.

'From the hills,' explained Abrach, delighted that Summerfield was interested. 'In winter, with the storms, the path resembles a small waterfall. There is a shallow well in the village, too. It becomes so full it spills over.'

'Don't they stock the water? For summer?'

'Alas, no, Harry. It is not in our tradition. The people here do not, like you Europeans, think continuously of the future and plan ahead. When there is plenty in the present, they take what there is and when there is none in the future, they do not take any.'

Summerfield nodded understanding and motioned to the trees. There were children sitting in them, observing silently as they climbed. 'I see we are being watched.'

Abrach laughed. 'You can be sure they have been watching ever since we appeared on the crest of the first valley, Harry Summerfield. It is also in our nature—an instinct.'

Nearing the village, they were met by a couple of stray dogs who scampered down from the first houses and sniffed at their feet. Abrach spoke something in *Tamazight* and gave them each a rough pat on the rump which sent them zigzagging crazily back towards the houses.

At last the little path, wide enough for two mules to climb, levelled off and Summerfield found himself standing at the entrance to the village. From here, he could see the track wind its way past several other houses, all identical, rectangular edifices made of blocks of wattle and stone. The roofs were flat and made of wood, also covered by a layer of wattle which in some places flowed over the walls like petrified leaves. From his viewpoint, several houses looked as though they were in ruins.

'A fire?' he said, remarking the blackened walls.

'One could say fire,' said Abrach, his voice carrying a certain sourness. 'One could also say that the families left for the towns and cities in search of work and left their houses in abandon. That would be true for some other villages, Harry. Not this one. Not here.'

A woman appeared, young and with a shiny khaki coloured skin. She was barefoot, dressed in a bright red and blue dress and her face and head were uncovered except for a thin blue headscarf. Several trinkets hung from a sash around her waist and chinked when she moved. Summerfield thought she looked much like a European gypsy.

'Do not forget, Harry,' remarked Abrach, between greetings, 'that the Berber people are not Arabs. While we follow Islam, our women keep the traditional ways. They are venerated for their beauty and their difference and are allowed a certain freedom of expression that the women of the city cannot have.'

The woman, introducing herself as Fatima, beckoned for them to follow her and she led them into the small, shady entrance yard to her house, only to reappear seconds later and invite them inside for tea. Abrach took off his shoes and Summerfield, nearly tripping over a stray chicken that suddenly ran under his feet in panic, stooped to do likewise. They entered through a small, lopsided door and were soon submerged into the almost total darkness of a large room.

A noise from the corner—a sort of moan—made Summerfield peer into the shadows. Abrach spoke in return, still in the Berber dialect that Summerfield, despite the odd word, couldn't understand. A candle was lit. The aurora spread out to reveal a table, a teapot and glasses and, last of all, the origin of the moan—a toothless old grandmother, smiling the broadest smile he'd ever seen and either side of her, cradled in her arms, two small toddlers looking at him with incredibly round eyes. Abrach stooped, went through a rather ornate gesture of greeting and kissed the old lady who cackled. Summerfield stepped forward, bowed his head out of respect and shook her hand.

'Please,' said Abrach, gesturing to the floor and a cushion. 'Sit down. The mistress of the house, Fatima, will serve us tea.'

They drank in silence, Abrach occasionally uttering encouraging noises to the old lady's comments. Summerfield did not know what the subject was, but it seemed mundane in nature. Then, rising suddenly and with a gesture of thanks, Abrach beckoned for Summerfield to follow. Emerging once more into the light and squinting furiously, Summerfield found himself suddenly confronted with the entire village, including a gaggle of children complete with running noses, wild tufts of hair and bruises. He grinned and still silent they grinned back, almost mimicking him. A man holding a stick, whom Summerfield judged to be in his mid-sixties, suddenly appeared and the group of silent onlookers parted, leaving a space for him to approach. It was the village chief, a shrewd-eyed little man, tough and wiry despite his age, his chin adorned with a neatly cut, brilliant white goatee.

'Come,' said Abrach, turning to Summerfield. 'Let me show you where my parents lived.'

They took the main path through the village, past tiny enclosures where goats and chickens milled, bleating and clucking fearfully at their arrival. There were very few men to be seen and Abrach explained, as they inspected the village, that most of them had either been drafted or were working afar, in the towns and cities. They stopped momentarily in front of several houses and the grain store which looked almost new.

'Good,' beamed Abrach, swapping a few words of dialect with the chief. He turned back to Summerfield. 'I have not forgotten my roots, Harry. I provide money for them to rebuild and maintain the village. It will not disappear.'

'You say *rebuild?*' asked Summerfield.

'That was my word,' replied Abrach and declined to explain further.

'And this,' said Abrach, coming to a halt before a large, open space, 'was where my parents lived.'

Summerfield hesitated, glanced at Abrach and followed the merchant's eyes to the spot. The earth was smooth and rounded and undulating—obviously the mark of walls or foundations. He wanted to ask what had happened, but the silence that had suddenly come over the small group made Summerfield close his mouth. It was almost like a mark of respect. Something unsaid that meant that it was not time to talk. After some moments, and with a little shrug of his shoulders, Abrach turned away and continued his visit.

When the tour of inspection had finished, Abrach led Summerfield apart, back down the slope to the small terraced fields. The place burgeoned with life, bright green shoots sprouting up in abundance from the red earth—wheat, maize, carrots, potatoes. Taking care to keep to the irrigation walls, they made their way down to the river, greeting and returning the greetings of the gaily dressed women working the crops. At last,

Abrach stopped on a rock above the shallow river and sat down. He looked about him, exhaled heavily and smiled.

'We shall wait here, Harry—they will call us when the food is ready. We are invited.' Abrach gazed out from his perch for a long time, his eyes, noticed Summerfield, shining bright as they took in his surroundings. At last, turning to him, the merchant gave a melancholic sigh. 'Here I spent a lot of my time with my friends, boys from the village. How we played! And then, later on and as an adolescent, I sat here for hours and read until sunset. A travelling teacher passed by thrice a week to instruct me. He pushed me hard, Harry. Made me read until my head ached and my eyes wept from fatigue—but I thank him. It was how I succeeded in entering higher studies.'

'Your land is very beautiful,' said Summerfield in return, complimenting the valley with a nod of his head. 'I was also born and lived in a valley—but one completely different from this.'

'No doubt filled with your famous green grass and rain and fog!' laughed Abrach.

'And quite a bit of sun, too—as I remember,' added Summerfield, surprised at how defensive he sounded. 'At least from June to August.' He remained silent for some seconds, recalling the Kent Downs as if from a storybook. It all seemed so unreal—the prim fences and green meadows, hedges brimming with life, the lanes and the shire horses, the village post office and the country pub by the duck pond—like a model village one saw in the southern seaside resorts, Brighton or Margate. He turned back to Abrach. 'It's good of you not to forget your roots. I imagine they appreciate your help.'

Abrach smiled at him, a little sadly Summerfield thought, and looked up across the valley to the outline of another village. 'It is quite normal for a man to wish to send money back home to his village. Even more so to his family.'

'The old lady?'

'My aunt,' replied Abrach. 'She has trouble remembering me these days,' he added, his voice trailing off.

'And your parents? Brothers?' said Summerfield, lighting a cigarette. He saw Abrach offer a glimpse of a smile and then he turned his head.

'I know of a boy from this village, Harry. Would you like to hear his story?' Summerfield nodded assent. 'Well,' continued Abrach, giving a sign for them to sit, 'the boy's name was *Abslem*, Abslem El Rifni to be exact. I knew him from when I was child. We climbed the same trees, swam in the same river and fought each other behind the same houses. He once hit me on the back of the head with a sheep's bone destined for the dogs. I bled profusely and a large, painful knot of a bruise was on my scalp for many many weeks. Needless to say, Abslem was duly punished by his father and believe me, he could not lie down on his backside for many weeks either.

And then we drifted apart for some years. I went off to stay with an uncle in Fez to study medicine. Abslem, who also wanted to study medicine, left the village to study in Rabat, in the north.

Abslem's family was very well seen by the villages in the valley. Indeed, he had noble blood, his father descending from a tribe which in former times ruled most of the area. Abslem was proud of his origins and not for one instant did he spend a day in the city without offering a prayer for his family and the village he had left. One day, he would return. You see, he had plans to set up a medical centre for the people in the foothills. They had always relied on the religious teachers, sorcerers and elders to administer remedies, though sometimes injuries—those that cause broken bones, for example—could not be properly cured. It is why we see villagers, sometimes children, with curiously deformed arms and legs where they were inadequately set. It is also,' added Abrach, 'perhaps one of the reasons why the people in the hills and mountains take their time about things. In the city they would say they are slow or half-witted, but it is really their way of reducing the risk of accidents.'

'And Abslem?' said Summerfield, interested. He leant forwards.

'Abslem, yes…. Well he graduated at the age of twenty-six, a doctor, and initially gained experience working as an assistant at the medical school in Rabat—at that time a Franco-Spanish institute. It did not matter that he was not allowed to practice fully as a doctor—the colour of his skin decreed this. What was important was that he had successfully finished his studies and was able to learn from his environment. This he did for four years, never ceasing his letters to his village, never forgetting to send back every week a sum of money from his savings.

But cities are strange places, Harry. Great cities are home to that which is most refined, but they also act as a magnet for everything that is sordid or malevolent or rebellious. It is often in the cities that the idea for revolution is born and in the countryside that it grows. You see Abslem became interested in politics and notably the Arabic cause. And for some strange reason, at that precise moment in history, certain individuals suddenly became aware that they all had an identity. That they were just as capable as their European masters—remember, the French practised direct rule—that is, every position of power was held by a white skinned official from metropolitan France—and that they had a right in the running of their country. Let me remind you, Harry, our previous discussions. We are in 1921, when Abslem was working as a medical assistant in Fez, when the Berber tribes of the northern Rif—and this region too—chose to rebel.

So Abslem, upon hearing of the revolt, decided to make his way as quickly as possible to his village, firstly in order to look over his family and secondly, driven by a sense of destiny, to see what his role would be. His expertise in medicine proved extremely valuable. Once back in his homeland, he found himself solicited by both the Berber tribesmen and the French army. It was his code of professional ethics that made the decision for him and he spent long weeks travelling the mountains and valleys, sometimes following the armed tribesmen, sometimes the columns of French troops, and always respected because his help and skills knew no boundaries of race or nationality.

One day, he decided to make his way back to the village to visit his family. He wanted to see if they were in good health, planned to spend a month with them and wait out the winter weather before rejoining the armies. He travelled for four days, skirting the base of the Toubkal and on the last day, descended the valleys to his village through the night.

He arrived at his village just before dawn. There were no lights in the houses of those who would be rising to tend the sheep and goats. There was no smoke rising from the chimneys. No barks from the dogs, warning the villagers of his approach. All was silent. Still, Abslem continued on his way, descending the opposite slope of the valley on his mule, every step of his animal a closer step to home and his family. On the horizon, the sky turned from black, to purple, to lilac and the first rays of sun pushed up over the mountain summits.

In Abslem's valley, the day did not come—at least not immediately. His eyes could make out the shadows where the village lay and still no lights. Perhaps, he thought, it was through security—the villagers not wanting to draw any undue attention to themselves. The air became lighter, carrying with it the strong smell of wood and the hearths. And then dawn came. Hardly four hundred metres from his village, the grey light of dawn filtered across the valley to show him what remained.

For a while he sat on his mule, at a halt, and wondered if the light was not playing tricks on him. He even wondered if it were the fatigue of his weeks in the field and the strenuous journey back. But no. It was his village—a collection of charred walls and collapsed roofs. Spilled belongings littered the slopes around the houses, as if the insides of each house had been vomited outwards into nature. Here and there, clothes caught in the trees fluttered in the morning wind. They reminded him of bodies and Abslem's feeling of shock was suddenly replaced by one of fear. He descended from his mule and led the exhausted animal, falling and then rising, up the slope to the village. Seven weeks before, he had seen old uncle Youssef sitting on his porch and cutting sticks for the fire. Several months before, his father had mother had welcomed him with open arms and embraced him till his cheeks hurt with their kisses. He called out, but there was no reply, Harry. The village was deserted, pillaged and his father's house a gutted ruin. Of the main living quarters, three walls remained standing and what had once been the pride of the village, the coloured glass windows, were now empty, yawning holes. Treading carefully over the debris—it had rained and his lower legs soon became black from the charred wood and mud—

Abslem thought he recognised some of his parents clothing.

He found them, along with ten or so other bodies, in a dip in the ground behind the village. There were also the carcasses of animals—goats and several dogs. A thin layer of earth had been hastily shovelled over them, but the rain had washed most of it away. Despite his training, despite the fact that he had seen to many wounds over the past weeks of fighting, some of them terrible, he felt sick at what he saw, Harry. The word you would use is *macabre*, is it not? Arms implored the sky, faces twisted in pain, days of being exposed to the open air having bloated and blackened them into horrible masks. He hardly recognised his father, his mother, his two brothers, his sister. But it was them. My poor friend Abslem stayed there three days and three nights, the time it took to cover the bodies, the time it took for a few of the mistrustful, terrorised survivors to return. Abslem, my friend, had nothing left. And that, Harry, is the story…'

Summerfield did not speak straight away. He returned Abrach's gaze, his feelings deadened. Had Abrach been recounting his *own* story? It seemed very likely.

'And Abslem—did you know him well?' he probed.

'Very well,' said Abrach, emotionless. 'He was a dear friend.'

'And after? What did he do?'

Abrach changed position and stretched his legs before him before returning to his squatting position. 'And after, my dear friend Abslem decided to find out who had been responsible.'

'And?'

'The order had been given by a young and rather ambitious captain in charge of a company of legionnaires. In return for the ambush of a French logistics column and in order to put an immediate halt to the rebellion, all villages sympathetic to the cause of Moha Ou Hammou Zayani were to be 'pacified'. Rather a sinister euphemism, don't you think, Harry? Burnt to the ground or murdered are hardly expressions to be used in the newspapers back home in France. Naturally, those whose houses were to be burnt objected. I remember Abslem's father having an old musket—a century-old thing bought off a wandering Moor. I believe Abslem's father tried to defend his house with the very

same musket. Not much worth when faced with mortars and
Hotchkiss machine guns.'

'I think I would have tried to seek out those who committed
the killing,' said Summerfield. 'And I would have given them the
same treatment.'

Abrach smiled, sadly. 'Can one kill a hundred-and-fifty men,
Harry? Should one seek revenge on the Corporal who pulled
the trigger, the Sergeant who put the torch to the house or the
politician who ordered the *pacification?* That is the entire problem,
Harry. And I believe Abslem chose the man in charge of the
troops on the ground. His logic was that an educated man such
as an officer should have had the moral and intellectual duty to
refrain from uneducated acts of barbarism.'

'And did he find him?'

'The responsible is still alive, Harry.' Abrach turned and looked
at him with painful irony. 'And now working as the government
administrator for French Southern Morocco. He lives, no doubt,
barely three miles from where you and I live, in his comfortable
house in the expatriate quarter in Marrakesh, with his family
and with his servants. Every day, he is driven to his office where
he doubtless spends long hours making difficult administrative
decisions for the well-being of his territory. And as for Abslem El
Rifni—I believe he died years ago.'

20

I t was unbearable. Summerfield spent the rest of the day closed deep within himself, as though he had pulled a blanket around himself and curled up in a corner for refuge. His mind had tripped like a switch and, in electrifying clarity, had at once understood: the man ultimately responsible for the burning and killing in Abrach's village was none other than Philippe-Charles Lefèvre, the neat, round-shouldered, snobbish and intelligent little man in charge of regional administration—Jeanne's father.

Early the following morning, Abrach led him on foot, up through the valley, on a short trek before the sun became too hot. Again, Abrach mentioned the necessity of acting fast and suggested that once back in the city Summerfield set immediately to the task of writing. Troubled, slow to react, and in answer to Abrach's questioning, Summerfield offered a lame excuse of not having slept well on the straw mattress provided him for the night.

'Ha!' laughed Abrach, clapping him on the shoulder. 'The English adventurer!' Summerfield smiled wanly and continued, head bowed, as they climbed the track towards the next village. 'If you take the opportunity to travel through the mountains to the desert—and one day I would like to offer you this as a gift— you will have to get used to the conditions!' Again Summerfield looked up and smiled briefly in return, the perfect hypocrite.

He was surprised by Abrach, for despite his large frame he proved very nimble and very sure-footed on the steep rocky paths. In the beginning, Summerfield had stepped out in long, rapid paces, putting energy into each step and subsequently becoming almost breathless on the crest of the first rise. With Abrach leading, Summerfield's eyes naturally fell on the merchant's feet and he began to study him. Strangely, Abrach seemed to put no effort at all into his step. It was rather the lack of force that provided the perpetual motion—like a pendulum in a clock. The merchant's steps were short and regular and light, declining the temptation to stretch and heave across the gaps where the rock had broken, but instead strictly following the contour of the terrain, hugging to it and almost making it his own as though he and the hillside were one single force. The same rhythm, foot after foot, step after step.

Summerfield copied and soon found, despite initial reticence from his legs—and he realised a behaviour that was somehow particular, somehow profoundly linked to his European values in his resistance—that he was able in this way to spare his breath so that his lungs also moved in harmony with his effort. It was almost hypnotic and he was glad, concentrating on the ascent, that his mind was busy from other preoccupations.

In the approach to the next village, the same phenomenon of the little heads popping up above the rocks and crests, shapes hidden in the trees—the children were watching them. Abrach waved, only once, and his free hand rattled in the large pockets of his *gandora* striking something metallic.

'Sweets, Harry. I bought two tins in Marrakesh. French sweets from Vichy. It says so on the lid.'

'D'you think they'll appreciate them?' said Summerfield, now stepping in line beside the merchant.

'I do not know of any child who does not appreciate a sweet,' replied Abrach, confidently.

But this time, he was wrong. When the first gaggle of wild-haired toddlers met them at the entrance to the village, Abrach presented a tin of sweets, unfastened the lid and handed the drops to the expectant little hands. One by one, the hands popped the sweets into mouths. And one by one, the expression on the children's faces turned from delight to one of horror, several of them fighting for breath and opening their mouths to promptly spit out the foul tasting drops. Summerfield looked across at Abrach and his dismay and broke out laughing. Taking the tin from the merchant's hand he read the words on the pale blue lid: *goût extra fort menthe verte—double-strength spearmint taste*. No wonder they spat the stuff out—it was as if the children had popped fire into their mouths.

They were welcomed at the chief's house and served *msemen*—traditional pancakes dripping in honey—together with the inevitable welcoming glass of sweet mint tea, the water for which Abrach supplied from his own gourd.

'For the English guest,' he explained. 'Water from the city. I would not like your unaccustomed insides to experience a week in bed, Harry.'

It was ten o'clock when they began to make their way back. To see them off, a group of girls formed an aisle and began to sing. They listened politely for a few minutes, Summerfield enchanted by the girls' attempts to appear coquettish despite the difficult conditions of hygiene in the villages.

Again, Summerfield was reminded of the Romany image. Some of the girls, the younger ones, were bareheaded, the older, adolescent girls wearing only a light headscarf knotted at the back in pirate fashion. Their dresses were bright green, blue or red smocks with many beads and tassels, faded through countless hand-me-downs and sometimes either too baggy or too tight. They wore woollen tights or leggings, mostly black and holed and cut off at the ankle. Several of them sported hands and faces made up with the intricate swirls and patterns of orange or henna ink which Abrach informed were to make them even more attractive to possible suitors. They sang, or chanted a curiously melodic series of songs, at the same time counting the rhythm with little shuffling movements of their feet and clapping their hands. Even this was so unlike the European way of clapping, for their little hands came together without clasping, palms flat and with a slight, outwards circular motion to produce a curious dampened clicking.

'What are they singing about?' said Summerfield, leaning his head towards Abrach.

'Oh,' smiled Abrach, wistfully, 'They are women's songs of the fields—asking when their love will come, when the rain will fall and when the crops will flourish.'

On the point of leaving, a sudden loud clucking came from

the girls' mouths—a high-pitched shriek that Summerfield had sometimes heard in the poor districts of the city. A hand, followed by others, reached out to point at him. Summerfield glanced at the merchant whose expression turned from one of attentiveness to glee.

'They would like you to sing before you go, Harry.'

'Sing?'

'Most of them have never seen a white man—let alone an Englishman. They know you are different and they are curious. Me too, I may add. What indeed do the English sing about?'

'Oh, dear.' Summerfield hesitated. 'I suppose we sing mostly about the sea—after all, we live on an island.'

'So sing them a sea song,' urged Abrach.

'The only one I know,' said Summerfield, 'Is...' And with that, he commenced, before the suddenly embarrassed and wide-eyed group of girls, to give a rather enthusiastic rendition of *Bobby Shaftoe* together with sailor's jig. Abrach howled with laughter and when Summerfield had finished and a sudden silence descended on the valley, applauded loudly which set the girls off giggling and shuffling coyly on their feet.

'I think several of them have fallen in love with you, Harry,' said Abrach, clapping him on the shoulder. 'Let us leave.' And with a series of waves that lasted the most of three hundred yards, the two of them set out on the path back to Abrach's village.

It was in the early afternoon, during the car journey back, that Summerfield's mood soured as he returned to thinking of the complications of his relationship with Abrach. It was indeed an extremely delicate situation.

As the car, this time Abrach giving free licence to the driver to decide upon the required speed, bounced, slewed and jolted over the dirt tracks back to Marrakesh, Summerfield fell deeper and deeper into introspection. At first he closed his eyes and made out he was sleeping and then, unable and unwilling to cover it up any longer, he turned to Abrach and looked at him with hardened eyes.

'You are troubled, Harry,' said Abrach, almost a remark.

Summerfield remained silent, holding his gaze. 'I noticed it often during these past two days.' Abrach's face saddened slightly, almost as if he knew. 'You have something to tell me.'

'Yes,' said Summerfield, the muscles on his jaw tightening. He nodded. 'You have treated me well, Abrach. You have become like a friend as well as a patron.'

'I believe we touched on this subject before, Harry. I wondered, at *that* moment, if there was something else you wished to say.'

'You were perhaps too trusting in me.'

'Trust should never be doubted before it has chance to grow. It lasts right up until the moment it does not.'

Summerfield nodded silently once more, dropping his gaze and then looking back up. 'I have some trouble with the mission you have given me, Abrach.'

'You have written well, Harry. I believe it is thanks to you that I am so close to my heart's goal.'

Summerfield shook his head, somewhat summarily. 'I know—I know. You already told me.'

Abrach stared and then his face suddenly broke into a smile that Summerfield could only describe as fatherly. 'I shall not prevent you from saying what you have to say, Harry. I shall not judge.'

'I—thank you for your tolerance,' said Summerfield, uneasily.

Abrach waved his hand. 'It is a virtue we have. Sometimes too much of a virtue for our people,' he added. 'Please, continue, Harry.' The little car went over a hollow in the road, slumped on its suspension and bucked as it came out.

'It's a question of values,' Summerfield went on, steadying himself against the arm rest—'*my* values.'

'Ah—values!' Abrach gave a little laugh. 'As we live and gain experience, some are lost and others gained.'

'And some remain until the end,' said Summerfield. Abrach tilted his head and nodded agreement. 'It has come to the point where—where through having to read the young woman's messages, I have almost come to understand her.'

'It's as though you know her,' added Abrach.

'Yes.'

'I have the same feeling,' said Abrach. 'And I suppose we both do. She is very true, is she not? Very naive—in a good sense of the word. We should all be naive, Harry. Like those children back in the villages. We should not become cynical and bitter as adults. But we do. Unfortunately. Life is like that.'

'Precisely. And I wish to remain naive in some respects,' said Summerfield, seizing the opportunity. 'Like those children. While I appreciate your goal—'

'My goal?' interrupted Abrach, his voice suddenly becoming cynical.

'Love is a very altruistic thing.'

'But sometimes we may use *love* to permit us to do many things, Harry. Many crimes are committed in the name of love. It is a grand excuse.'

'I'm not saying your search is a crime, Abrach,' said Summerfield, a little confused. 'And my trouble is not just with the fact of writing. You know the situation in Europe.'

'So you, too, think war is the only way left.'

'No. I don't think that. I wish there were some other way. But everything points in the direction of war, Abrach. I will have to go back.'

Abrach laughed. 'Oh, how you have changed, Harry. Is it the influence of your American friend you mentioned?'

'It is my decision, Abrach,' replied Summerfield. 'Maybe I have changed. One of the things I have discovered—or *rediscovered*—is who I really am.'

'You wear Arabic clothing!' said Abrach.

'Beneath which lies an English skin. Abrach—thanks to you I have grown to love this country. I also love your people. But,' he shook his head, 'I am fundamentally British, born on an island with, as you said, its fog and rain and green hills. I've thought deeply, Abrach. I cannot let anyone attempt to harm my birthplace. If I were five thousand miles from home, I would return to defend it.'

'You will be fighting for politicians you do not believe in, Harry,' intoned Abrach. He paused. 'Though I understand. In the past—and perhaps even in the present—I am doing *exactly* the same.' Summerfield frowned and Abrach held up a hand. 'Oh, it does not matter now, Harry. I will perhaps explain at another moment.' The merchant remained silent for a while and then looked back at Summerfield. 'Firstly, you plan to leave if the situation worsens in Europe. And secondly, your values tell you that any further work to ensnare the young lady is wrong. Is that it?' He looked enquiringly at Summerfield and Summerfield nodded in return. Abrach sighed, passed a hand over his brow and mopped away a bead of sweat. 'I cannot force you, Harry, for I can understand these arguments—both of them. Please understand that I, too, have had to ask myself many questions concerning the young Frenchwoman. My mind is constantly aware of the *moral* argument to the issue. Later, I hope, we shall have the opportunity for me to explain, in further detail—*other* details—my desire for this person.'

'Thank you,' said Summerfield, firmly, though Abrach once more held up a hand, this time almost as a sign of warning.

'But! And there *is* a *but*, Harry. My condition of acceptance is that you write that one, last message on my behalf.'

Summerfield shook his head. 'I can't.'

'A poem,' said Abrach, unflinchingly. 'A poem, Harry Summerfield. And after that—a long-lasting respect and friend-ship between us born of my gratitude and my respect. I shall ask no more and shall expect nothing else. You will be free.' Abrach leant forwards, close to Summerfield's face and stared at him, his eyes sparkling. Summerfield returned the regard, bit his top lip and gave a brief, closing nod of his head.

'All right.'

21

They sat in a hollow by an orange grove, barely a mile from the school, by a stream that fed the fields. It was part of the ancient underground irrigation system and this particular section lay uncovered, the flagstones having been unearthed years ago to tile a landowner's floor or build the walls to a house.

They were hidden from view. Craning one's neck, just above the lip of the depression, a patchwork of wheat and maize could be seen, dotted with date trees and wells, stretching across the plain beyond the city until, in sharp contrast, the sand took over. Here and there, donkeys sauntered slowly in the fields driven by little dots of children. The women bent towards the earth, dug, stood up to stretch, then stooped again to work.

They had walked in awkward silence, meeting up along a path behind the *Académie*. And now they sat in awkward silence, shy, full of what to say but unsure of how to say it. It was like having the answer to all your dreams, all those moments of desire and conviction and determination, suddenly answered, suddenly made real—and accompanied by a thought, half-dread, half-lack of assurance, that it was all too soon.

Summerfield smiled. Jeanne Lefèvre, in her uniform and conscious of it, smiled in return and they simultaneously looked away.

'Lunch lasts for an hour and a half. I have to be back for two,' she said, glancing at her watch.

'We'll get back on time,' said Summerfield softly. 'Tell me—when did you understand it was me?' Their eyes met. She noticed the little glint of irony in Summerfield's expression, the sad and merry lines around his grey eyes and she laughed and it was as if the stiffness had suddenly gone from her.

'Straight away,' she said, nodding her head. 'The reference to water, the river—stones.'

'I was hoping you would. I had kept it in my pocket for some weeks—a mad thought that one day I'd hand it to the woman I was writing to.' Summerfield leant forwards. 'I almost gave it to your friend—Jean Bassouin's daughter.'

'Sarah?' Jeanne's voice rose, a little indignant.

'I thought she was you.'

Jeanne frowned. 'But you *knew* who I was.'

Silence. Summerfield leant back again, fished in his pocket for a cigarette he had rolled before coming. 'Jeanne—I want to tell you something.'

'I asked at the hotel for you, but you weren't there. I met your friend, Jim Wilding.'

'I must tell you something,' continued Summerfield, trying to lead her back from her tangent.

'I made up a story about handing you a book—I think he thought it strange that I wanted to see you in person.'

'Jeanne—'

'It's how I found out where you were—it's only if he asks you any questions—'

'*It wasn't me.*' Summerfield exhaled. His voice was calm, flat. Jeanne looked at him questioningly, her deep brown eyes widening slightly. 'That's what I had to tell you. Before we go any further.'

'I don't understand.'

'Okay—' Summerfield shook his head—'No, I'm not being very clear. It *was* me—I *did* write those words.'

'You just said you didn't.'

'Let me explain.'

'I wish you would.'

'You see—the letters—in fact I *didn't* know who you were.' A fleeting look of panic followed by a barely controlled uneasiness came over her face—it was like an ebbing wave. 'Don't worry,' added Summerfield. 'It doesn't mean that I wasn't true. It's just—just that in the beginning I was writing on another person's behalf, but the words *were* and *are* mine.'

Silence. Summerfield could see her mind working fast to comprehend. She fought for some seconds, unsure of whether to speak, whether her words were the right words. And then she found them, almost flinched.

'You were making it all up.'

'No—*yes*, in the beginning. He gave me a description, told me of his feelings towards you. I imagined you. It's why I confused you with Sarah—in some ways you look quite alike.'

'My God.'

'And then, little by little I understood who you were. I learnt to appreciate *what* you were—your thoughts and your words. I'm sorry.'

Again some hesitation, searching for clarity. She looked at him very directly.

'And this man? What if it's *this man* I've fallen—' she hesitated, checking herself—'*and not you?*'

'Of course it's me,' said Summerfield, his own voice now carrying a pitch of indignation.

'This is awful—'

'It's confusing—'

'No, it's awful!'

'I apologise,' said Summerfield, lowering his eyes. 'I'm sorry—but I thought it was right to say this.'

'Of course you were right.'

'I don't want to trick you, Jeanne.'

'You did, though.'

'God, yes I did—in the beginning. But then something happened—it was that one single line you sent back. Barely ten words—so simple. They snapped something in me. You were—you are—the most beautiful woman I've ever come across, both in mind and in body.'

Jeanne blushed. She seemed quite totally lost.

'Really,' she finally said, neither question nor affirmation.

'What?'

'Thank you,' she blurted. 'I…' She looked down, then focused on the thick dusty leaves of an orange tree. 'I suppose I meant to say…um—*thank you*,' she said again.

'Ah.' Summerfield pulled a face. 'I think I understand.'

'Yes,' said Jeanne, looking at him.

Summerfield returned her stare and nodded.

'*Good*.'

He wanted to reach across—was this the moment? But then again, it was almost as if it was expected of him. The rebelliousness bubbled inside him. Damn—*I'm twenty-eight! Stop dithering, man.* 'Look—Jeanne. It's…*it's time we went back*,' he finally offered.

She seemed as surprised as he. 'Yes,' she answered hurriedly, looking around for belongings she didn't have. 'I suppose it is.'

Summerfield rose and helped her up. He noticed the shape of her legs beneath the cotton dress of her uniform, the white socks rolled at the ankle and felt his heart wince with longing and with pity. The poor girl—he'd really made a mess of things.

They stood now, heads above the hollow and with a view of the fields. Jeanne flattened out the creases in her dress.

'Harry—I want us to continue writing. We'll leave the messages here, under a stone or something. Or look—in the wall over there,' she said, pointing to what looked like the remains of the old irrigation channel. We'll use secret names like secret lovers.'

Summerfield nodded. 'I think I understand. Yes, I'd like that, too. It's all a bit of a shock—again, I'm sorry.'

Jeanne gave a slight shake of her head and smiled.

'It can't be easy for you. And I appreciate your honesty.'

'But not only write,' added Summerfield, doubling back on the conversation. He became suddenly serious. 'But *see* each other again.' And with that, he leant forwards, rather stiffly, and kissed her on the cheek.

A moment's silence. 'Thank you,' said Jeanne, softly and as she lowered her head she smiled.

They began to walk, climbing out of the hollow and taking the path back through the orange grove.

'I should like to tell you about this man I mentioned,' said Summerfield. 'Just to make things fair. I have to write one last message on his behalf—when you receive it, know that it was I who wrote it. After that, if you do wish for us to end, then I will understand and respect your decision.'

Jeanne grinned, almost cheekily.

'Send the message first. *And then I'll see*.'

Summerfield stopped in mid-pace for a second, head to the side, observing her. She really was unique, this one. She really was quite wonderful.

The day passed, and another. The recollection of their first meeting was shed in the turning of the days—like a tendril of cotton clinging to a branch in a breeze, fluttering then gone. There were moments he remembered with absolute clarity suddenly lost, erased from his memory no matter how hard he tried to bring them back. The gaps became wider, information non-retrieved. A hollow. But there were other instances when her smile came back to him, a gesture, a puzzle piece of eye or arm. A warmth. He found himself thinking that two days were too long. And another thought, creeping into his sleep, that he was hardly good enough for her.

Later that week, Summerfield accompanied Jim Wilding to the station in what the American hoped was his last trip to Mauritania.

'If all goes well,' said Wilding, as they took a last beer together at the hotel, 'I'll be back in six to eight months. I've wired back home for some vacation and I can't see them refusing it. Remember, Harry—Libya, Algeria. Hey,' he added, as an afterthought, 'I could even show you back home—why not the States?'

Summerfield agreed, carried along by Wilding's enthusiasm. He felt light, optimistic—anything seemed possible at that particular moment, and the question of where he would find the required money, or even if he would still be in Africa, didn't dent his sense of contentment. He looked back at Jim Wilding and grinned, conscious of the fact that every two minutes or so Jeanne Lefèvre came into his thoughts and that she made him feel like smiling.

'Good,' said Wilding, giving him a curious look. 'I'll keep you posted.' The American sat back into the deep, leather seat in the hotel lobby and sipped on his glass. 'By the way, Harry—how's the reading going?'

'Reading?'

'Yeah—that book, uh—what was it? *Fleurs something* by Baudelaire. The book Lefèvre's daughter gave me for you.'

'Oh, that.' Summerfield sat up. '*Les Fleurs du Mal.* Yes, curious thing.'

'Most curious,' smiled Wilding, trying to eke out a clue. 'When they told me Mrs Lefèvre was calling for me, I thought it might have been the mother. Thank God it wasn't.' Summerfield hummed in reply. Wilding sipped. 'So?'

Summerfield looked up. 'So what?'

'So what was it all about?'

'The book?'

Wilding pulled a reproachful face. 'She was cute.'

'Different,' said Summerfield, non-committing.

'Not as pretty as Bassouin's daughter.'

'Different,' repeated Summerfield and saw Wilding sigh, giving up on the chase. 'And what about Jean Bassouin?'

'Ah,' said Wilding, happy to change subject. 'Well, he's an interesting guy. I'll meet up with him again to talk business. I think I convinced him, if not the others. He's very forward-thinking.'

'And quite of a free spirit, too. I appreciated his views on this country.'

Wilding tilted his head in agreement and was lost in what Summerfield recognised as a momentary lapse into nostalgia. The hands on the lobby clock were turning. He would soon have to leave.

'We had fun over the past two weeks, Harry. It was good to see you.'

Summerfield nodded and smiled. 'Likewise.'

'And you've changed yet again, Harry.'

'Changed? Goodness, you're keen-eyed.'

'Have to be, Harry—searching the ground for clues is my job. Yes, changed—ever since you left for a couple of days with your boss.'

Summerfield placed his empty glass back on the table. 'Abrach. Yes, I suppose it's relief,' he said, reaching for his tobacco. 'I finally managed to tell him about my wish to finish the contract. And it's thanks, in part, to you, Jim.'

Wilding held up his hands. 'Any decision is always ultimately the choice of its taker—or should be.'

'A pity, though,' continued Summerfield, still thinking of the merchant. 'He's been good to me. A good man, all told—*honest*. He seems to have lived quite a lot, although he doesn't directly say it. Hopefully, one day, I'll introduce you to him.'

Wilding nodded. 'Fine by me. When I'm back next time. I also mentioned him to Bassouin—if he's such a rich guy, then Bassouin should know of him. Maybe we can all meet up.'

'You told—*Bassouin?*' Wilding sat back, shocked. 'But you *knew* it was bloody delicate,' returned Summerfield.

Wilding hesitated, for once lost for words. 'Hell, don't worry, Harry—I just mentioned his name.'

At the station, they shook hands as Wilding boarded the train. The whistle blew and the steam from the ageing locomotive belched in protest at having to set to work.

'Sorry about that, Jim—back at the hotel, I mean,' said Summerfield apologetically, from the platform.

Wilding cocked his head. The train creaked slowly away. 'That's ok, Harry. I should've kept my big trap shut. Things'll be fine, though. Next time I'm back, we'll all meet up.'

'Fine,' said Summerfield. 'Take care. Let's hope you don't find petrol!'

'Here's hoping,' Wilding called back, grinning as he held aloft crossed fingers. 'By the way—I'll be sending you an envelope!'

'*What?*' The train whistled once more, gathering speed and Summerfield creased up his face in an attempt to hear.

'An envelope!' shouted back Wilding, grinning again. Summerfield mimed incomprehension. 'You'll know what to do with it!' added Wilding, laughing and then he was gone.

On his way back now, Summerfield walked the length of the colonial station and instead of turning right towards the medina, suddenly changed his mind and headed for the district where the *Académie* was located.

It was one-thirty in the afternoon and the streets were almost deserted. The air was warm-to-hot, but a dry breeze from the plains occasionally buffeted his skin, making the walk tolerable. He was filled with a sudden urge to be near her—in a place which had known her presence.

Nearing the *Académie*, he took to an adjacent road dotted with a row of bungalows destined for the families of the military and what looked like a depot of some sort, deserted but for a couple of lorries and a wandering dog. The road soon dwindled to a track and rose through a thicket of thorny, thirsty-looking bushes before giving a view from its crest of the large plain filled with its fields.

Summerfield hoped he would somehow find her there, in the grove they had chosen as a meeting place, even if—and giving his watch a glance just to check again—the time allocated for her lunch break had come to an end fifteen minutes before.

Picking his way through the increasingly dense orange groves, he arrived in the little hollow and stood for a moment, still and silent. The grass looked flattened and there were traces of footprints in the dust by the old irrigation wall. Perhaps they were from their meeting, three days before. But then again... He smiled, a warm feeling running through him that perhaps she had been there, just minutes before. Instinctively, he looked for a sign and his chest heaved a little in disappointment when he couldn't find any. The word *failure* darted quickly through him—what if she didn't care? What if she wasn't thinking about him with the same intensity as he thought of her? He exhaled, swore silently at himself and exiled the nagging thoughts from his mind. Lowering himself into the sunken irrigation channel, he ran his hand over the ancient bricks, tugging gently. At last, in roughly the spot to which she had pointed, one came loose, filling the palm of his hand with pale pink grit. Strangely, he took the utmost care with placing it on the floor of the ditch, afraid that it might lose its shape and be unable to return to its niche. He crouched down and peered into the small cavity—there was a paper inside, folded into a small, thick, uneven square. On it was written *For Magpie from Jay*—the pseudonyms they'd given themselves. A rush of joy swept through him and he smiled.

I meant to say so many things, to meet you on the same level. This time, Magpie, the stone that you are proved lighter and clearer than the water. I forgot my ways, the strong current that I believed I was and became a fish, darting under rocks, shy in the shade of the water plants, evasive. I shall do better. But I am happy—for even hiding, along my silver sides flashed the reflection of you, the stone.

Summerfield sat in the hollow and read the message three times. From his pocket, he brought out a pencil and a notepad that Abrach had offered him some weeks before. A kind of drunkenness filled him; a happiness for everything simple on earth, the simplest and most truthful being the fact that Jeanne Lefèvre had entered his life, a presence in half the moments of his days.

I recognised you, dear Jay, and we met, briefly by the river that was you, our tongues timid with numb words. We talked for so few minutes and when you were gone that day, and evening drew on, I remembered your face in the shade of the orange trees and the crescent moon of your smile. For hours I remembered and lit candles in the night. And, stargazing, as solitary travellers do, the wind blew in from the south and I opened my mouth, sucking in the air, sucking in you.

When can we meet again? Give me the day and I shall be there.

When he had finished writing his reply, he slid back into the trench, carefully folded his paper and wedged it firmly into the back of the cavity. Then he replaced the brick, filling the edges around it with a little earth and climbed back out. He stood there for long moments, smoking a cigarette and looking out, his eyes unfocused, over the shapes in the fields on the plain. And then, turning and full of warmth, he picked up several small, flat stones from the floor of the hollow where the grass didn't grow and arranged them in a little stack at the foot of the nearest tree as a sign.

That evening, when he sat at his desk in his room, long and empty moments ticking by over the empty sheet, he realised it was more difficult than he had thought. One last poem, Abrach had said. It was as if his mind had split the question in two, a clear division between the words he wrote on the merchant's behalf and those born of his own true feelings. He could no longer invent for something he saw as unreal, of no use.

Several times, he rose and paced the room, pottering about with useless tasks or else spending long minutes at the window, smoking. He concentrated on the professional which rose reticently inside him, only to be turned back by some inner refusal, like a door closing in its face. He grew angry with himself, consequently crushed and ripped the sheets of empty paper and threw them into the bin. He slammed his writing desk shut and gave an almighty kick at his shoes. One took off, shot across the room and hit a saucepan, dislodging it from its hook with a loud clatter.

'I don't want to do it! Jesus, I *can't!*' he shouted, only for a voice to rise up from below—his neighbour Abdlakabir.

'Is everything all right, *Sidi* Summerfield?'

'*Yes!*'

'I heard you calling to Jesus.'

'I've lost something, that's all.' And then, calming down, suddenly grinning:'thank you, Abdlakabir—I'll find it.'

'I hope soon,' came his neighbour's voice.'My wife wishes to sleep and we can hear your footsteps.'

'Oh, God—is it that late? *Sorry.*'

Silence came over the house. Summerfield made an extreme effort to tread softly. After a while, the muffled, almost baritone snores of Abdlakabir's first wife rose up from below.

He recuperated what he could from the bin and sat back down at his desk. It was approaching midnight. The words came quickly, mechanically and without emotion—a ten-line poem, remarkably resembling a set of Noel Coward lyrics etched deep in his memory together with tootling piano. Something about *my love and the birds.* He didn't re-read. Instead, he copied out the text in neat handwriting and slipped it without further ado into an envelope. Tomorrow, he would hand it to Badr.

The following morning, rising rather fuzzy headed, he took a hasty breakfast of leavened bread, honey and olives which he washed down with tea, and then took the envelope to a group of boys squatting on the corner of the street.

Even now, after so many months, Summerfield still wondered what on earth went through their minds all day long as they sat and waited—they seemed a permanent feature of the street, as innate as the lamp posts or the pissing-tree. Still, Summerfield at least provided them with weekly errands—sometimes a request for tea or water, other times running messages destined for Badr when Summerfield was too lazy or busy to seek him out. Today was such a day. He descended the narrow stairs, crossed the courtyard and wife No. 2's collection of cooking pots and stepped into the shadow of the side street. Summerfield approached the boys, their blank faces turning to a scowl, almost mistrustful, then recognising him, becoming broad grins.

'*Laurens!*'

'*Summerfield,*' he returned, as he always did, but they insisted on calling him otherwise. Aware that they hadn't received any schooling, it was rather intriguing to wonder where they had heard of T.E. Lawrence. Perhaps the legend had travelled orally across the expanse of North Africa to reach these hopeful ears. Summerfield stood before them. 'A note—for Badr. Important.'

'How much?'

'A kick up the backside!' returned Summerfield, shaking his head. 'All right—a glass of orange juice for each.'

'*Crayon!*' said a gloomy-looking youth, the leader, in French.

'Imad, you can't write—what use is a pencil?!'

But Imad would have none of it. '*Crayon!*' repeated the youth again, frowning.

'All right, all right—I'll give you a pencil. Now, hurry up—it's a very important note. Be back before Midday prayer and I'll give you two.'

Returning to his lodgings, Summerfield changed out of his *jellaba* and donned his trousers, shirt and boots. He had decided to walk to the orange grove in time perhaps, and with a little luck, to see Jeanne and he didn't want to unsettle her with his local attire.

His journey on foot was hardly a journey at all. It was almost a dead moment, like any trip between home and an important event. He failed to notice the squad of soldiers practising drill in the square, missed the spectacle of two little boys cheekily mimicking them and the subsequent attempts of the drill instructor to send them off with a series of theatrical gestures. Summerfield's mind flitted like a swallow in a summer's eve— her, him, doubt, certainty, hope, impatience. He didn't see Jean Bassouin drive pass and wave. He missed a snake charmer feeding a mouse to his cobra.

Once more in the orange grove, this time for midday. If she were to come then he would see her. He ducked down, slid under the low-lying branches onto the cool, thick grass and noticed that his little pile of stones had gone. For a moment, startled, he wondered if someone else—wandering children perhaps—had found their secret place and dislodged the stones, the brick. And then his eyes rested on something—a little pyramid-like structure made from twigs and tied together with blades of grass. A sign. The warmth gushed into him. Her warmth. He stooped, picked up the tiny pyramid and studied it for some moments in the palm of his hand. Delicately, he placed it aside and went immediately to the tumbledown wall, his hand drawing, as if from memory, a gentle arc until it came to the loose brick. It came away more easily than before. And there was a note inside.

Your words fill me with happiness, though they also scare me—for how can I rival them and the feelings they carry with them? When I try to rhyme, I write discord and when I try to think I fall into dream. These are strange days, my Magpie. I am supposed to answer questions, write essays, concentrate on mathematical problems and be the dear daughter. I cannot think. It seems our meeting has since cast a spell on me and I drift, and let myself drift, like a leaf in autumn. I fall into whatever breeze or gust will take me, careless and uncaring where I am carried. Sometimes the leaf comes to rest under a gaze—my teachers, friends, parents. And they speak, but like a leaf, somehow dead and on its way to another place, I do not answer. They enquire if I am ill. They tell me to wake. But like an autumn leaf, I cannot wake. I am scared, Magpie. Scared of the strange, turbulent current in which the leaf finds itself—and the scariest of all: that this world, this beyond world, is more real than the life surrounding it.

A second, more hurried note—on a separate scrap of paper, the writing more slanted, with several crossings out. She must have been late for studies.

I wish to meet you again. And once again, I cannot think, my mind a total blank! What is this feeling that I am feeling? What is this sliding, this falling? It's as though the moon has turned upside down and the sun appears at night! When, you ask? I don't know. All I know is that I want to see you—to talk, to see if all this is real. This week, I cannot—obligations, as you said. It makes me angry—with myself and with those others who have regulated my life, my time. Next week, yes. Tuesday. I am supposed to have a late piano class which I am determined to skip. Write, my Magpie. For although I cannot come to our secret place for several days, I will imagine your words hidden behind the stone, waiting for me.

Summerfield stayed for a long time. Midday stretched into afternoon and he fell into a gloominess that surprised him, sending his hopes of ever seeing her plummeting, not like a leaf from a tree, but like the tree itself, cut at the base. It was ridiculous of course. He even recognised that it was a wilful fall, the bizarre, wistful melancholy that pulsated through his head and body so deliciously pleasurable.

At four-thirty, he rose out of his lethargy, carefully placing the little wooden structure she had made him inside the pocket of his jacket and took the path through the orange grove towards *the Académie*. He would catch a glimpse of her as she left at five. It was all so simple. But when he approached the building, he saw, from the shade of the trees, a profile he recognised, standing with his back to him, barely fifteen yards away. It was Abrach.

Summerfield's immediate reaction was to sink further back into the shade of the orange trees and from there he watched. The merchant was dressed in a beige, linen suit, the first time Summerfield had seen him wearing Western clothes. It looked very odd, but Abrach's build and posture were such that it was unmistakably him. He had taken up position in much the same place as Summerfield had several weeks previous—opposite the main gates, too far for anyone to notice him in detail against the sun, close enough to make out the students as they left the *Académie*. To Summerfield's dismay, Abrach's position also meant that he could have no way of getting closer without being seen. And from the orange grove, Summerfield was too far to be able to see Jeanne clearly. He hesitated for some seconds, his breath short and rapid, silently cursing the merchant and weighing up the risk. And then, realising that it was useless, he withdrew deeper into the grove and slipped away.

When at last he arrived back at his lodgings, his spirits as black and thundery as a winter's day in Northumberland, he found the boy, Imad, waiting for him.

'Oh, God—the *pencils*—I forgot!' Summerfield gestured an apology and cursed his forgetfulness, suddenly realising that he'd spent an entire day in his search for her. The sour-faced youth dipped a hand into his *jellaba* and brought out an envelope. 'What's this? A reply? Good God, that was quick. Come,' said Summerfield, beckoning for Imad to follow. Upstairs, Summerfield opened his writing desk and pulled out the first two pencils that came under his fingers—fine, forest green affairs, made in Germany. Imad handed over the letter and snatched the pencils from Summerfield's hand.

'*Orange juice!*' scowled the boy.

'*Bugger off!*' was Summerfield's curt reply.

Intrigued—for how could Jeanne have written him a reply so quickly—Summerfield sat down without taking off his boots and opened the envelope. It was from Abrach. His heart sank.

> *Dear Harry,*
> *I thank you for your effort. But this is not a poem of love, it is a dancehall song. And such a song is not what is needed at this precise moment. Re-write, Harry. Re-write—and quickly!*

In his current state of mind, Summerfield's first reaction was to think: *write it yourself!* And then, as various scenarios went through his mind, some involving physical violence and others involving sudden disappearance, Summerfield's mind inexorably turned mischievous. The old rebel fluttered its flag within him and rose to its feet with a malicious grin on its face.

Write a poem, Harry—and enter the girl's heart like a key to a lock. Turn that key, Harry Summerfield, a perfect fit, well-oiled and making metal melt to tender substance. That was what Abrach had told him. Well then, you shall have your key—and she shall know that it is me.

On the desk, before his eyes, was the tiny, delicate pyramid. The blades of grass, wound around the twigs to lock the joints, had already blanched in the dry heat to a pale green. He did not eat that evening. Every now and then, his eyes rising from the scribbled lines, the discarded ideas, he glanced at it until he grew familiar with every notch and every grain. He imagined her fingers, the movement of her hands and wrists as she had joined the little sticks together. He wrote one poem and two texts, fell asleep for an hour and then woke up, an alarm in his unconscious compelling him to re-read and proof. One of the texts he discarded without further ado, leaving a remaining page of prose and the poem.

He compared the two, employing the critic in his mind, viewing them both from various stylistic angles and finally made a decision. The trouble with poetry was that it was alive. It changed shape and grew. Left for a day to repose, it would ask for something different, complain that one of the words was not telling the truth, that another was an intruder. Left for a week, it might demand amputation and even metamorphosis. Left for a month, it would appear clumsy. Returned to after six months, it might appear, at last, as the perfection it had promised it would be all those months before. He chose the prose.

Exhausted, pushing himself beyond the limit of his groaning tiredness, Summerfield forced his hand back to a fresh sheet of paper and copied, with the utmost care, the last draft of the text which he then placed inside a new envelope. And with that, Summerfield blew out the candle, dragged himself over to his bed and, not bothering to undress, fell asleep.

Upon rising moon you came to me, a chill that I might lose you, and the day empty. I dream thus, in the late hours, in the deepest corner of sleep, that most ancient and secret part of ourselves. I know it is a sign of love. For it is an extreme, the other being a certitude like an oncoming wave. We turn to the sea and travel with the swell as it turns to a surge and, just as the wave forms and the crest unfurls, we turn our backs to the breaking sea, take one last gulp of air and dive in its flow, rushing towards the shore, tumbling with the sound of laughter through the roar. And then, tangled on the sand, still smiling, with the ebb dragging and lifting the sea sediment from under us back towards the forming waves so that it feels as though the ground is slipping backwards with us. We open our eyes, those in love, and see the world from the point where the wave crashed and foamed: the film of water, the sparkle of sun on a grain of sand, a tiny mosaic of shells that form sizzling pearls and beads, a joyful bubbling from the air holes. And rolling, the sky is a royal blue and somewhere the sun blinding. We bask for a few moments, stretch, sigh. We were caught in love's wave and another will follow.

22

Another midday lost. Another occasion without Harry Summerfield that sent her heart and spirits crashing.

She clenched her teeth and, with the utmost effort, turned to follow *Sœur* Marthe into her quarters. Sarah Bassouin sent her one, last look of sympathy to which Jeanne pointed hurriedly in the general direction of the orange grove. In return, Sarah gave her an imperceptible nod of the head and disappeared. Blast her parents, blast Sister Marthe, blast her preparation for university which, as everyone had decided on apart from herself, had taken up her lunchtimes and evenings.

Love. It was the strangest of feelings. Not even Sarah's description fitted exactly. Perhaps, Jeanne had concluded, everyone experienced it differently. And the worst was the uncertainty. If she were truthful, she didn't know for sure that this was it—that *love* that everyone, from school friends to parents to film idols, spoke about. It was very painful.

Jeanne seemed to float in an almost permanent state of *beyond*. In all appearances, she was absent. Her body seemed a hollow, ghostly vehicle for what seemed to her just a cloud of feelings, hardly thoughts, but waves of euphoria—as high and tremendous as they were violent and crashing. For when the wave receded she was dragged into a horrible emptiness for long, terrifying minutes. It was a state of sheer panic—as though she would certainly die and never see him again.

Her mother and Soumia were now totally convinced she was suffering from some mystery illness contracted in the *Académie* biology labs. And of course, Soumia's wagging tongue (and naive belief in anything deemed *scientific*) had meant that Jeanne's mother came to know of the *Bubonic plates*—a further warping of Soumia's initial *tictonic plague*. Goodness knew how Soumia's mind worked, Jeanne had thought when having to explain to her mother. Perhaps, she had added silently, her mind wandering for a few moments, Soumia was in love too. Permanently.

Sister Marthe's individual maths lesson dragged on and dragged on, an hour stretched beyond shape so that every minute seemed like ten. The old nun explained algebraic formulas with such intense verve, and was so taken away with her pedagogy, that she hardly paid attention to Jeanne whose mind repeatedly defied any attempt at being influenced by logic. *But what about love?* it argued. *What about poetry?* Nothing else mattered. Everything from geological rock formations to the theory of the atom appeared so minimal in comparison, so ridiculous and unreal, that it hardly deserved a footnote in her present list of priorities.

Gazing into the distant plain from the window of Sister Marthe's living quarters, Jeanne saw the spread of the orange groves and imagined that Sarah had already accomplished the mission conferred upon her of checking for messages. She noticed a cloud edging across the blue sky and thought she saw in its hollow the shape of a man. A bird flew across her view. They were signs, she thought. Her days were full of them. It was as though, for the first time in her life, she had suddenly become aware of nature around her.

'*Exercise three*,' said Sister Marthe, in a tone which implied she was repeating herself.

'I beg your pardon, Sister Marthe?'

'The exercise, Jeanne,' puffed the nun, reaching for her water spray.

'What about *love*, Sister?' Jeanne started as though her body had suddenly received an electric shock. She was amazed at such a remark coming from her own mouth and her hand went to her lips in a tardy attempt to stuff the word back. Sister Marthe, too, looked shocked, her eyebrows raised in such a questioning frown that it sent her forehead wrinkling into a score of folds beneath her coif. She looked like a bulldog. At last the pump wheezed and spluttered, sending a sprinkle of water onto the sister's face.

'Did you say something about—*love*, young lady?'

Jeanne remained silent, giving only the slightest nod of embarrassment and looked away. For the first time, she saw the limits of the nun's room—the dark green paint on the walls, a couple of framed diplomas from the University of Nantes, the little polished oak chest of drawers with its lace mats, the fading collection of photographs and several crucifixes including one with a hand-painted porcelain effigy of Jesus. It wore a smile that captured Jeanne's attention. It was a mysterious smile—the sort of smile that came of nostalgia and mellow memories, a sort of inner serenity. As though, in his last moments on the cross, Jesus had assessed his life and had come to the conclusion that it had all been worth it. Jeanne frowned, uncertain if her eyes were playing tricks on her, uncertain if her feelings were sending her once more towards the crest of a wave.

'You're looking at that smile, girl,' came Sister Marthe's voice, strangely confiding. Jeanne looked round and was surprised to see the old nun smiling with something approaching glee. 'So you can see it, too!'

'Yes,' said Jeanne, unsure of how to react.

'I bought that in Lourdes on my first pilgrimage before taking up orders,' said Sister Marthe, placing the maths book, in a gesture that brought Jeanne much relief, cover down, in her lap. 'There were dozens of them in the shop—all porcelain figures of Christ on the cross. But this one—this *particular* one—had such a different expression on his face from all the rest.'

'Perhaps the craftsman had made a mistake.'

'You're using *logic*!' reproached the nun, suddenly laughing to herself. 'What I've been trying so hard in the last hour to make you use!' Jeanne laughed too. She suddenly felt very close to the old lady, as though they were sharing, just for a few moments, something unique. 'But what if we look beyond logic for two minutes? We could say the craftsman made the mistake on purpose. Perhaps like Da Vinci and *La Joconde*. Perhaps he, too, was having his moment of fun. But perhaps he was simply painting what he knew everyone would overlook—that representation, that simple, almost idiotic look on her face that is so clearly the look of someone who is head over heels in love that all the art critics, with their rolls of degrees and years of portentous books failed to notice! A little,' added Sister Marthe, almost murmuring, 'like the look you have on your face now, Jeanne.'

Jeanne sat back. 'Oh dear, do I look that stupid?'

'I'm afraid so. But don't worry—those who are not in love cannot see it. They just think you're ill or half-witted.'

'My parents, for instance.'

'Perhaps. But we could also,' added Sister Marthe, continuing excitedly, 'look even further.' Jeanne pursed her lips. 'Yes. We *could* say that this particular face was meant for us. A unique sign, a message intended for two people happening to be together at the same place and at the same time among millions of others and in the context of time and history. It is love in Jesus' face that we see.'

'Sister Marthe—this is far removed from logical thought. Are you all right? The heat, perhaps?'

'Don't be silly! I'm just allowing my mind to stray, that's all—and no impertinence, young lady. We are all, even teachers, allowed to imagine and sometimes what is imagined is nearer to the truth than any logical calculation can be.'

'But you've never spoken like this.'

'Of course not,' replied Sister Marthe, sharply. 'Could you imagine a class full of young post-pubescent girls, their minds filled with Clark Gable, fads, horses, Balzac and jazz music understanding all this? I certainly can't.'

'Sarah Bassouin, though.'

'Oh, Sarah Bassouin! Heavens above—*yes* she is a good girl. And *yes*, she is in love. But Jeanne, there are many kinds of love— many burning shadows that the heart pursues. Sarah's is one that approaches friendship more than anything else, a love that grew steadily and peacefully and without hindrance. I suppose we could say that Sarah's love is healthy and written. It is a love that brings only happiness. Whereas others…'

'Yes,' said Jeanne, leaning forwards and resisting the temptation to openly admit to suffering from the other case.

'Others experience true love. Though—' Sister Marthe suddenly stopped herself and pondered for intellectual thought— 'though perhaps on reflection, the first case is the *real* true love after all. Oh dear, all so confusing.'

'Yes!' said Jeanne, indeed looking rather confused.

'I beg your pardon,' said Sister Marthe, suddenly realising Jeanne's plight. 'Where was I?'

'True love.'

'Oh, yes—*or not*. But in any case, a love that is born from the highest summit and the deepest ravine. One that, because it is almost impossible to obtain, causes both the greatest joy and the most profound sadness. It is a love born of being apart. A love that inspires great words. That offers one a closeness to spirituality and to God that no one else can hope to achieve.'

'But does it succeed?' By now, Jeanne was feeling quite distressed. Sister Marthe's words seemed so laden with doom.

'What? Oh, of course! But it depends.'

'On what?'

'It doesn't depend on *what*, my girl. It *depends*—that's all. Heavens, you look at such a loss, dear girl.' It was true. For some reason, Jeanne was suddenly filled with the overwhelming desire to burst into tears. 'What is meant,' continued Sister Marthe, her voice suddenly returning to a calm sense of logic, 'is that such love always succeeds, whether it be for only three days or thirty years. Nothing is certain. But what *is* certain is that it is worth living such a unique experience—not for anything on earth would I say the contrary.' Silence. The *Académie* bell clanged dully, a sign that lunch break was over. 'Oh dear—we haven't eaten,' said Sister Marthe, matter-of-factly.

'But you—how do you know these things?' The question had been on Jeanne's lips since the beginning and she wasn't afraid to ask anymore.

Sister Marthe looked directly at her and then at the crucifix. 'My dear girl—I had a youth as well, you know.'

'But you…but you can *still* recognise these things.'

'Because I am still in love, my dear.' The old lady looked away and clasped her hands. 'It has never left me. For some years I kept the chagrin of my love and then, then I decided to keep only the joy of it. And now I love in a different way,' she added, glancing once more at the crucifix and smiling, much in the same manner, Jeanne thought, as the odd expression of serenity. 'Every day I am filled with happiness. And now,' said the old lady, clearing her throat. 'Let us return to class, shall we not?'

Jeanne rose, gathered her books and followed Sister Marthe to the door. At the threshold she turned and, biting her lip, looked enquiringly at the old teacher.

'Don't worry, young lady. I understand—and I shall accordingly be tolerant with you. I have great faith in your ability to pass the entrance examination. Go now.'

It had been a tiring day and once Jeanne had finished dinner she disappeared upstairs to her bedroom with a series of yawns that sent her parents exchanging glances. Closing the door behind her, she was caught between busying herself with homework, reading the message Sarah has retrieved for her or falling onto the bed to rest. She chose the latter, her body drained of strength and lay there on her back gazing up at the ceiling.

Her mind wandered—Sister Marthe, the conversation and the delightful discovery. She suddenly felt a very deep liking for the old lady and found it hard to imagine how she had managed to wear such a mask of authority and narrow-mindedness for so long. And then Sarah, the surreptitious handing over of the message under the desk and later, their hurried few minutes of conversation in the toilets. For Sarah had had quite a fright, crossing paths with a tall, heavy-set native who had given her the oddest of looks as she emerged from the orange grove. It was as though he had been expecting someone. His eyes had seemed enquiring, returning constantly, in the few short seconds that Sarah hesitated on the path, to her hand and the folded message before gesturing an excuse. Jeanne had thought the mystery man the messenger she had become accustomed to, but the physical description didn't fit. A loose-fitting suit, Sarah had said. A large face, placid if it hadn't been for the circumstances, and the trace of a moustache. Next time, they would go to the hollow together, for safety. And permeating her thoughts, a flitting presence every few moments, Harry Summerfield. She wondered what he was doing, imagined his face and for some reason saw him sitting in a café, sipping a tea and smoking, his gaze looking out into the crowd, directly at her.

At last, with great effort, she crawled to the side of her bed and withdrew the envelope from her satchel. She felt her heart immediately beat faster. Unlike the other messages, Harry's did not smell of orange essence but paper and a slight hint of sweat. Sometimes the paper showed a crinkle where his palm had rested in the heat and humidity of his lodgings in the old city. There was something dark, savage and forbidden about all this—so remote from her genteel surroundings. One day, she hoped he would take her there, secretly and there they would lay, his arms around her, with the smells and noises of the old city reaching them from outside.

She unfolded the note, glancing across at her bedroom door to check it was locked, and read.

Dearest Jay,

I write with news that you will soon be receiving a message through the usual channels. It is the last message written on behalf of my benefactor, though I hasten to add that the words are true and directly from my own thoughts and feelings for you. I have made it clear to the concerned that it will be the last message. Try not to have any negative feelings for him, for he is a good man. Hopefully, I shall soon be able to speak to you about all this.

The days pass with an emptiness I had not thought imaginable. Each time I return to the grove, my hope surges with the thought that perhaps I will find you. That we may share precious moments in each other's company. I ache just to hear you, just to see you and it seems as if my evenings, these all so long evenings, are taken with reading and re-reading your words. Your little pyramid—greatly appreciated—takes place of honour on my desk and it has become a symbol of my hope in seeing you soon.

In fact, I believe we have a secret helper in the guise of our W. I received an envelope from him today, intended for your father, with an accompanying note apologising for the loss of his address. Do you see? W has entrusted me with bringing it to your house—sacré W! I intend to inform your father of my visit, planned for Thursday of the coming week. I hope, with all my heart that he will invite me to stay to dinner so that we may at least be in each other's presence for a few stolen moments.

Lastly, I would like to thank you, Jay, simply for being alive and for filling my thoughts and days. May Thursday come with great haste.
Dearest, warmest regards,
Magpie

Jeanne lay back, the letter held close to her, a feeling of warmth spreading throughout her body to culminate in an overwhelming smile. She laughed aloud, her mind suddenly filling with Sister Marthe's remark about the Mona Lisa and felt herself shake with joy. She must look so very silly, but she didn't care.

Surely enough, the following day upon arriving at the *Académie*, the smartly dressed young Arab—*Mercury*, as Jeanne had fallen into the habit of calling him—brushed past her in front of the gates and slipped her an envelope into her hand before disappearing.

She carried it with her through the morning, as she had done with the others, slipped out of view inside the waistband of her dress. Instead of hurrying to lunch before Sister Marthe's planned blank exam, she went to the toilets to read. Again the smell of orange essence as she pulled the letter from its envelope, but this time she associated it with Harry. It was a beautifully written message and the reference to waves fell with such coincidence and such signification with the very thoughts and emotions she was experiencing that she thought it a sure sign. The uncertainty she had felt over the last few weeks evaporated. A certainty filled her. Almost destiny. He was the one—Harry Summerfield. And it frightened her.

Another coincidence—Sister Marthe's blank geography exam, the subject of which was wave formation! As Jeanne's mind grappled with the scientific aspect of the question, it also worked in parallel with great wonder at the turning of events. It was strange how everything seemed to lead back to her heart—as though the whole world was helping her to achieve her dream.

23

'How *is* Mr Wilding?' enquired Mme Lefèvre, nodding for the servant, Mohammed, to leave them.

Summerfield shook her hand, conscious of the eagerness in her voice for the American and also the total lack of concern for himself. 'He's fine, Mme Lefèvre. He sends his regards. And also apologises for not popping in before leaving.'

'Such a gentleman,' said Mme Lefèvre, her voice almost a whisper. 'Come. I believe you have an envelope for my husband.'

Summerfield followed her across the chequered floor of the entrance hall and remembered the last time he'd been there, the evening of the dinner, and his deliciously serendipitous meeting with Jeanne. Passing the dining room, he caught a glimpse of Soumia, the house maid and her customary frown of distrust. He gave a nod of his head and smiled, but she didn't seem to recognise him. *A madhouse*, he thought silently and felt a sudden pang of pity for Jeanne and her stuffy surroundings. No wonder she wanted to go to Europe.

Mr Lefèvre was in his study, pouring over some documents on his desk which he hastily arranged as Summerfield walked in. How could this anodyne, frail-looking little man be the cause of murder and of burning, thought Summerfield, almost shaking his head. Lefèvre rose, straightened his shoulders with a grimace and walked over. His first reflex, noted Summerfield, was to give his shoes a glance.

'Ah yes, the Englishman—Mr *Bonnyfield*.'

'*Summerfield*,' corrected Summerfield, following Lefèvre's regard. His boots were crinkled but shiny—he'd made an effort to buff them with some of Abdlakabir's sheep's fat.

'Please, do sit down—my apologies. I believe you have a document for me.'

Summerfield nodded, a little taken aback by the man's

abruptness. He sat down in one of the linen armchairs just as the telephone rang. Lefèvre remained standing, a clumsy silence filling the room and finally he picked up the receiver. Summerfield's mind flashed momentarily with the village in the foothills and the sound of Abrach's voice.

'What? A guard on the house? Two?' said Lefèvre, turning his back on Summerfield and dropping his voice. 'Most appropriate. Who, you say? Yes. No, no I can't say as I have. Hmm. Good— well keep me informed. Goodbye.' Lefèvre placed the ear-piece back on the telephone set and once again an embarrassing silence filled the space between them.

'Yes—' another clearing of the throat—'a tea, perhaps, Mr Summerfield?'

'That would be nice. Milk, please. I haven't had a proper tea in ages.'

'It must be difficult for you,' answered Lefèvre, at last sitting down and Summerfield wondered if there was any irony in the man's voice. 'Tea, Soumia—with *milk* for our English visitor.'

Again the silence. Summerfield noticed that Lefèvre was staring at him with unfocused eyes. Was it is his jacket? A stain, perhaps? he wondered and then realised that Lefèvre's gaze was for the large brown envelope he was still holding in his hand. His first reaction was to hand it across, but then, on second thoughts, he refrained—keep the old trout on the hook, he said to himself and smiled at the Frenchman.

'How is Jeanne?'

'My daughter?' Lefèvre frowned, seeming to have difficulty in understanding why he should ask.

'And her friend,' added Summerfield. 'They were at the dinner you invited Mr Wilding and I to.'

'Ah, yes—exact. *In good health*, I should imagine.'

'Good,' said Summerfield. 'And what about the situation?'

'Nothing to report,' said Lefèvre, as though speaking to an official and then hesitated. 'You do mean Europe.'

'That's right.'

'Umm.' Lefèvre pondered and Summerfield understood he was weighing up the risk of starting a conversation. 'Worsening,' was all Jeanne's father said, choosing to stifle it. 'Is that tea coming, Soumia?' he added, calling out. As if by a trick of a hat, the housemaid suddenly arrived with a tray and served tea in rather a Moroccan style, from great height and with a noisy bubbling as the liquid hit the porcelain cup. Lefèvre, he noted, declined the offer.

'The letter,' said Lefèvre, as Summerfield picked up his cup and sipped. Goat's milk—the tea had rather a sour taste.

'Yes,' said Summerfield, placing back the cup and picking up the brown envelope. Lefèvre leant forward. 'Jim sent it through several days ago,' added Summerfield. 'I'm afraid he mislaid your address.'

'Yes, quite,' said Lefèvre, 'You informed me of the fact. May I—'

'It's probably something about his findings and possible business.'

'Well, Jean Bassouin's really the man for that. Still—'

'Shall I take it to Mr Bassouin in that case?'

'No, no!' Lefèvre's voice could hardly contain its irritation. 'Please—Mr Summerfield—I *do* thank you for bringing it, but I have much work to do.'

'Of course,' nodded Summerfield.

'Especially given the gravity of the events in Europe—you do understand.'

'Of course,' repeated Summerfield and at last, wondering whether Lefèvre would implode, handed across the envelope which the Frenchman immediately opened. The documents were extracted and then there was a silence as Lefèvre read. After a few moments, Lefèvre looked up.

'It's *all* in English!'

'Oh, dear.'

'No—hold on. There's a note in French.' Lefèvre's eyes peered closely at the small, hand-written note, not of Jim's writing. 'Apologies…' read Lefèvre, skipping the formalities, 'I know that Harry Summerfield has had translating experience—perhaps he can help. *Perhaps he can help!*' repeated Lefèvre, sitting back with a fatalistic sigh. The Frenchman lifted his spectacles and rubbed his eyes. 'Well, Mr Summerfield—when can this be translated by? And I imagine you will also be charging a fee.'

A deadline and a sum were arranged and Summerfield was just saying to himself what a crafty blighter Jim Wilding was, when Mme Lefèvre walked in with—*Jeanne*.

'Jeanne!' spluttered Summerfield, standing up.

'My *daughter*,' said Mme Lefèvre, looking momentarily lost. 'Jeanne, that's it. You remember her.'

''Er—of course,' said Summerfield, regaining his composure. 'We had a very interesting talk.'

'About the garden,' added Jeanne, walking across to him. She wore the most wonderful smile. 'Harry—I may call you Harry— Harry simply loved the magnolias.'

'Yes—magnificent,' returned Summerfield, conscious of the fact that from somewhere outside, from quite afar, Jeanne's mother was saying something about the English and their gardens. 'So— how are you, Jeanne?'

'*I'm well*,' said the young woman, her eyes large and soft and, from Summerfield's point of view, most moist.

'Yes,' he replied, his voice trailing off.

'*Yes*, what?' It was Lefèvre, bringing him back from flight. 'Mr *Summerfield*?'

'What? Oh, excuse me. I suddenly felt a little tired. I do apologise.'

'My daughter is complaining of tiredness too, at the moment,' said Mme Lefèvre, her voice sounding a little anxious. 'You young people. It's probably all that free time you have.'

'Work never makes one feel tired,' added her husband, gruffly. 'At least not me.'

'Papa—wouldn't it be nice if Mr Summerfield were to stay to dinner!'

Lefèvre looked as though a glass of water had been thrown in his face. 'Can't this evening, I'm afraid,' he said quickly. 'Too busy.'

'Oh, *Philippe-Charles*—it's so nice to have company!'

'No, sorry. Can't,' replied Lefèvre, shooting a glance at his wife. 'I really am too busy and Jeanne has to study. Remember—the exam is only three weeks off.'

'Please, papa. I can practise my English with Mr Summerfield.'

'Mr Summerfield also has work to do,' said Lefèvre, avoiding his daughter's plea. He stooped down and picked up the envelope. 'Mr Wilding's translation.' He stepped forward and, without looking Summerfield in the face, handed it back. An uneasy silence filled the room. Lefèvre began to pace and then he came to a halt, his voice irritated then softening as he looked at his wife and daughter. 'Well, what about Sunday, then? How's that? You can bring the translation.'

Again a silence, saved by Mme Lefèvre. 'Sunday is a good idea. We can prepare something special to eat. Much better than what we were to eat this evening.'

'Good!' growled Lefèvre. 'That's settled. Now, you will excuse me—I have to work.'

Summerfield leant forwards, shook Lefèvre's hand and let himself be ushered out. It all seemed so completely unfair. He'd only said ten or so words to Jeanne. He tried desperately to find some way of lingering a little longer and hit upon the magnolias.

'What about the flower garden, then? How are they?'

'How are *what*?' said Jeanne and her mother in unison.

'The magnolias, of course.'

'Oh!' Jeanne suddenly realised and was about to continue when her mother butted in.

'*Dead*!'

'Oh, God.'

'*Dormant*, in fact,' added Mme Lefèvre. 'Now, say goodbye to Mr Summerfield, Jeanne. She must do her homework,' she added as an aside. 'You'll see him on Sunday. Let's say seven-thirty.'

'Seven-thirty,' repeated Summerfield, hesitantly. 'Thank you, Mme…' He turned as Jeanne approached him and held out her hand. Her face wore the deepest look of sadness he'd ever seen— sadness mixed with anger.

'A pleasure, Jeanne…' he managed to utter and then Mohammed appeared to show him out. 'Goodbye.'

'Goodbye, Harry…Summerfield.'

Once outside, the evening swallowed him. He found himself feeling the loneliest of poor mortals in the world and despite the warm June air, he shivered. He gave the Lefèvre house one last glance and began to walk. It was anger more than anything else. Anger and frustration. *Those silly old fools.* He felt like a sinking ship, its keel ripped off—plunging down, down into the cold black waters. But then, for some reason, he felt his pace slowing and he came to a halt at the second lamp post in the leafy avenue. He gave it a soft punch with his fist. It was strange, for it wasn't the idea that first came to him, but his body that acted before his mind had time to form a thought. He swung slowly round, his hand pivoting on the lamp post, a full circle and a half and found himself facing back down the avenue. Slowly, surely, he began to walk back towards the Lefèvre house.

Thank God there wasn't a dog, he found himself thinking, as he stole around the edge of the garden, past the tool shed and its litter of awaiting forks and spades to the back of the house. He had waited until the last particles of clarity in the evening sky had gone before climbing over the fence. It was almost pitch black now.

Standing behind the magnolias—not as 'dead' as Mme Lefèvre had said them to be—he spied the upper floor. There were several soft lights on in the bedrooms and one of them was Jeanne's. But which one? *Jesus, you must be barmy*, he heard a voice say to himself. *What if Mohammed found him out*—he'd be after him with a pitchfork or worse—a scimitar or something! *Don't be ridiculous* said another, more composed voice—he hadn't set eyes upon a single scimitar since arriving in Morocco. Perhaps they didn't use them here. He ended the conversation with himself abruptly, choosing instead to study how to get up to the first floor windows without breaking his neck.

There seemed plenty of holds, the house was not overly high— he had a natural fear of heights—and there was, of all things, Mohammed's ladder lying in the grass beside the conservatory. It wasn't very romantic, he thought, climbing up a ladder. Hardly Shakespeare. Still, it was safer. After a few moments of self-encouragement, he moved forwards, crossed a short patch of open lawn and came to a crouch beside the ladder. Carefully, silently, he put it into place beneath the first window and began to climb. Halfway up, he froze—the scree of a night hawk, terribly close, almost made him lose his footing. Heart pounding, he stepped softly up the last eight rungs, craned his body and peered over into the dimly lit room. *Jesus fucking Christ!* It was Mme Lefèvre, in a lemon yellow bed robe, putting some sort of ghastly night cream onto her face. Immediately, Summerfield ducked down and scampered silently back to the foot of the ladder. Once more on the ground, regaining his breath, the next question was what other window? He desperately hoped Jeanne's parents were still sharing a bedroom—imagine if he were to fall face to face with old Napoleon, Jeanne's father! It would put a fatal end to any translation of Wilding's document. Be logical, he told himself. What sort of wallpaper, what sort of curtains would a young woman and a miserable old pen pusher have? His doubt got the better of his confidence. No ladder climbing, he concluded, weighing the risks—he'd have no chance of escape if he got it wrong. Instead, keeping to the shadows, he picked up a handful of earth and sifted out the pellets. Returning once again to the wallpaper theorem, he chose the third window and threw. The pellet clicked against the window pane. He threw another, missed, and another, tensing, ready to merge into the bushes.

As if a prayer had been answered, Jeanne's face appeared momentarily at the window. One last throw. A pause. Jeanne reappeared, her fine features looking anxious, searching beyond the window into the night. And then she looked down, saw him, frowned, brought a hand to her mouth and then smiled. The window slid up with a little sigh and Summerfield, stepping rashly out onto the lawn, beckoned for her to come. She nodded, held up two fingers and then disappeared again. Two minutes stretched into what Summerfield imagined were five—among the longest five of his life. And then, sliding carefully through the rear door onto the veranda, Jeanne appeared and came silently to him.

'Well,' said Summerfield, softly.

'Well,' whispered Jeanne, putting a finger to her lips. 'You're *mad!*' They stood for some seconds, exposed in the light from the moon, their eyes discovering themselves—he in his crumpled suit and shirt, the collar of which had come loose from the initial climb and she, in a light summer dress, bluish in the night light but probably a shade of green. They moved consciously towards the shadows, their eyes drawn to each other—she, the shape of his jaw and the shadow under his lips, he her left ear, the way a strand of hair curled behind it to a point on her neck—focusing, unfocusing—skin, nose, lips, eyebrows— coming together, she on his eyes and he on hers. It was like some tremendous swell in the sea, a deliciously warm coaster that made them simultaneously rise to a smile. A moment was lost forever, inexplicable how it passed, and suddenly they were in each other's arms, their lips pressing gently, nudging like two cats meeting in the night.

Slowly, still clasped, they edged towards the farthest corner of the garden by the great magnolia and stood there, breathing in each other's scent, nudging each other, rubbing skin against skin. They did not move. They were the quietest words either of them had ever said, sometimes silent, sometimes just a murmur of a murmur, a millimetre away from each other's skin.

'I have dreamt of this moment.'

'I have written books about it in my head.'

'Your skin smells of lemon and pepper all mixed into one.'

'Your lips are soft and giving.'

'Generous to one who is herself generous.'

'Night stay longer than you did yesterday.'

'Keep the stars aloft and the moon burning bright.'

'Like a tiger's eyes in the night.'

Soft laughter.

'Did you receive the message, my love?'

'I did.'

'He was a good man and now it is finished.'

'Does he know of us?'

'No-one knows. One day I shall tell him.'

'When it is time. Will he suffer?'

'Greatly, my love.'

'And will you suffer?'

'Not as much as he, I fear.'

'And so suffer. Such is the price of truth.'

'This is the truth.'

'It is.'

24

His heart was at the centre of the world. It babbled to him, trickled, radiated and danced in a language so illogical from that which came out of his head, but which seemed a thousand times truer and more meaningful. It connected to portentous things, so important and obvious like the stars, the night air, Jeanne and just simply being alive.

As he left the Lefèvre house behind him, he passed under the soft yellow glow of the single electric street lamp that lit the avenue and turned back, one last time, to send a smile in Jeanne's direction. Lights shone from behind the shutters of the upstairs windows and he wondered, hoped, that she had returned uncaught to her room. Turning again to his path home, the darkness turning silvery blue from the demi-lune, he wondered what she was doing then. Was she feeling so whole that her heart spilled over into a private chuckle of joy? Was she re-reading his message or simply remembering the perfection of that moment when their lips touched? Was she, like him, just astonished by the weightlessness that seemed to lift him by the collar and carry him over the ground? He laughed, felt a wave of warmth ebb through him and whispered 'I love you' into the night air.

The warm glow stayed with him as he walked past the rich, well-kept houses of the expatriate French. It stayed with him as the air grew colder and the distant ranges of the Atlas turned black and merged with the sky. It stayed with him as, nearly four hundred yards away and crossing a small plot of unbuilt land, where a track led off left onto the plain that stretched until the mountains, he noticed a squat-looking shape among the weeds and thorn bushes: a car. There were people in it. Lightless, the car looked too small for the shapes inside. Unconsciously he looked away and his feet changed direction, his body turning slightly right, back towards the road and the avenue. No sooner had he begun when the tinny opening squeak of a door reached him. He glanced back. A shape had appeared. Summerfield halted. The shape beckoned for him to come over.

'Harry,' came a soft, low voice. 'It is I, Abrach. Come.'

Summerfield frowned, his heart now emptied of love and taken by what he could only identify as a clear sense of uneasiness.

'Abrach?' he called back, hesitantly, his voice, almost forced by the night hour into a murmur. 'Is it you?'

'Come, Harry,' said the shape and moved closer into the moonlight. 'I would like to talk to you.'

Summerfield gave a shrug, glanced behind him, and walked towards Abrach. They shook hands and Summerfield saw the merchant's face and the smile. As they trod carefully towards the car, two other shapes left it to wander off among the bushes—Abrach's men, Badr perhaps, though Summerfield could not be sure.

'Please,' said Abrach, inviting Summerfield to get in. They sat down on the back seat and Abrach closed the door. It smelt slightly of mildew, the scent of men cramped for a long time in a small space and Abrach, noticing it too, leant his large frame forwards and rolled down the window a couple of inches.

'So?' said Summerfield. 'Please tell me, Abrach—were you following me?'

The merchant sighed and rubbed his face in his hands in a gesture of weariness before looking up.

'Not exactly, Harry.'

'I suppose—' began Summerfield, becoming increasingly aware that he was trapped, 'that you…'

Abrach let out a soft laugh and looked empathetic.

'Poor Harry. Let me save you the ordeal. Yes—yes, I know for certain that you were in the Lefèvre house this evening. I cannot for sure guess the reason why you returned there, but I have a very sharp feeling that it was not for the company of our Administrator, *Monsieur* Lefèvre.'

Summerfield nodded and a fleeting grin came to his lips. Abrach continued, his generous face earnest and somehow odd.

'I will not keep you long, Harry. And forgive me if I scared you a few minutes ago. You must have been surprised to see me.'

Summerfield gave a groan for confirmation.

'I must tell you something important. I beg you to listen carefully,' continued Abrach.

Summerfield weighed up the situation. An urge to just leave the car gave way to resignation. He'd have to face his sentence sometime.

'Go ahead,' he said, wondering if the merchant would refuse to pay for the work he'd recently completed.

Abrach nodded, business-like and clasped his hands, the earnestness removed from his eyes and replaced by a steady calm.

'The story of Abslem El Rifni was a true story, Harry. And I think you concluded that Abslem was I. You see,' he added apologetically, 'I'm not one to make a good story-teller, which is why I needed your services to win the young lady's heart.'

'You said it was a question of race,' said Summerfield.

'Among other factors, yes,' replied Abrach. 'Nonetheless, love was the arm I chose. Do you understand?'

'I suppose you mean that it was better than choosing guns and bombs,' nodded Summerfield.

'But the effect could have been devastating,' resumed Abrach. 'If things hadn't…become complicated.'

'The real goal was her father, then? Right from the start,' said Summerfield, avoiding the insinuation.

Abrach's mile was fleeting, wiped away by something distant, something cold.

'Yes. That man—that young captain, so bloated by ambition and belief that it poisoned his sense of humanity—was Lefèvre. Lefèvre who ordered the burning which gave rise to the killing. Lefèvre who even these days—no doubt almost every day—signs his name at the bottom of orders of arrest, of imprisonment and even execution.'

Summerfield gave a shake of his head.

'He is—what's the word—rather emotionless. At least, he gives the impression he couldn't give a damn for anything other than his duties to the Republic. But actually putting hatred into his work—I find that hard to believe.'

'Not hatred, Harry. He doesn't need any hatred. Lefèvre is a committed servitor of the French State. He is one of the élite. From birth, he has moved through circles that call for a certain obedience, a certain blindness—schools that manufacture the engineers, soldiers, functionaries and politicians of France. Nothing must stand in the way of the *République*—neither the Boches, neither the English and certainly not the poor, indigenous and uncivilised peoples of its colonies. Their revolution was founded on blood and massacre, on the elimination of whole classes and the destruction of opposing ideas. Do not forget, Harry—that it is still a young republic. Barely a hundred and fifty years separate France from its bloody change.'

Summerfield remained silent and eventually sighed.

'You know about Jeanne and I.'

Abrach nodded.

'Yes.'

'Did you have your men follow us?'

'No. At least, not so closely as to interfere with your privacy. No, I understood, Harry. Your eyes and your voice gave me the clues. The way the light danced in them whenever you thought of her while we talked. The way your voice grew soft, the way the words you wrote became full of so many other hidden hopes.'

Summerfield dropped his gaze.

'I'm sorry.'

Abrach shook his head.

'I think you understood from our previous conversations that I would not blame you. It is so, that's all.'

'And your plan? Why not place a bomb under Lefèvre's car? Why not lay in wait with your men and ambush him? Why not a bullet?'

Abrach sat back and looked genuinely shocked.

'Me? Do you think I am such a man to want to kill in cold blood, Harry? I gather that you have not understood me—not at all. The question did enter my mind—a long time ago—and I even tried to get near to him to pull out a gun. But I couldn't. It is not what I, as a good man, can do. And in any case, he is very diligent, very prudent. Mistrustful. He would have smelt that something was coming.'

'But Jeanne? You wanted to get at him through her? Kidnap her.'

'I wanted—*want*—to meet her. To explain. How else could I get so close? Every letter that arrives is checked by Lefèvre—personally. She has to know the truth, Harry.'

'No—no, I don't believe you. There were other ways.'

'Have her before me, that young, lively, lovely young woman and just tell her of the crimes her father has committed—that she is the daughter of such a man. For me, there is little more agonising than knowing that you have failed in the eyes of your children. That the love in their eyes has been replaced by reproach and by disgust.'

'You're right—I *don't* understand you, Abrach,' frowned Summerfield.

'I try,' said Abrach, softly. 'But what does it matter. You—the complication that has suddenly arisen—means that I have to act now before your heart forces your tongue to talk about things you shouldn't; before she talks. Before Lefèvre hears of it. And before he surrounds himself with guards and sends out the dogs to find me.'

'Is this why you're here? Not so much for me, but for her?' Abrach remained silent. 'You're planning on doing something this night?' pressed Summerfield, his voice becoming urgent. 'I beg you, Abrach—don't.'

'I must. I will talk with her. And when this is over, you will be there in the morning to explain and soothe her.'

'You can't,' urged Summerfield. 'She'll be hurt.'

'Trust me—it is unwise to use such a word, I know—but it is all I have. Trust me. My intention is not to harm her.'

'Harm her? You'll frighten her to death!'

'You are emotional, Harry. I suggest you return to your home and drink some of your whisky to calm your anger. I must do this—I thought you would understand. I ask you to remember what Lefèvre did to my family.'

'I know, I know,' mumbled Summerfield, feeling torn. 'But, Jeanne.'

'I promise I will not cause her any harm. Now go. And tell no one. I'm sorry, Harry—but remember that I will be able to find you easily if need be.'

Summerfield looked back at the merchant, opened his mouth to reply and then closed it. The threat was subtle, but understandable. If he understood clearly, he had no choice.

'It's a pity I have to terminate our contract like this, Abrach,' he murmured, conscious of his weak, if not defiant attempt at striking back.

Abrach sent him a faint and rather sad smile.

'As you say—a pity, Harry. I greatly appreciated meeting you. You were different. I will see to it that you are paid. Now, please go.'

25

Harry had been gone for almost an hour now. They had held each other until midnight and then, with the sound of Soumia's voice reproachful, calling for her to go to bed, the painful leaving. Every time they had pulled apart, a strange, irresistible force brought them back together again into physical contact. He could not leave. Their bodies did not want it.

Her arms needed his skin, his lips needed hers. And as they both realised that each embrace lead them closer to the last, their kisses became more desperate, their hold on each other more painful until, like claws, their fingers had dug deep into each other's arms, shoulders, back and buttocks, sending such burning shards of desire through them that she had felt like fainting. She had whimpered like a puppy, his hand covering her mouth to hush her and then he was gone, one last look with such an odd expression of desire, fear and pain all mixed into one, that it had frightened her.

Alone, it seemed as though he had drugged her, for Jeanne stood rooted in the exact spot where they had held each other, her mind and body limp, heavy and unresponsing. She could not think. No words came. Just that pulsating heat, pushing through her, somehow holding her upright.

And then, after uncertain minutes had passed, the terrible loss, the sucking out of her of life. How she plunged. How empty her existence suddenly felt. She grew afraid, flashes of catastrophe filling her mind—an accident on his way back. A misunderstanding, a quarrel and then the moonlight on the raised blade as it struck down into the flesh between his shoulder and collarbone. He would be there, helpless and lonely, his body lying in the shadows of some back street, dying without her.

In her room, it was Soumia's voice, a forceful whisper, that interrupted her.

'*Bed, Mademoiselle!*' the housemaid's voice hissed from behind the door. 'Turn the light off!'

'Yes,' she replied, fearful of how her voice sounded. 'Sorry, Nanny—just reading my notes one last time.'

'*Studies!*' she heard Soumia's voice, murmur irritably, her voice trailing off with an inaudible story as she disappeared into her room.

Jeanne walked to the open window and breathed deeply. Harry was somewhere out there, walking back home, perhaps already in his rooms. She smiled out into the night, eyes closed, calm now, and then switched off the lamp before going to her bathroom.

She stood for long moments before the mirror, studying herself, occasionally giving an involuntary shake of her head. Was this the person in love? she heard herself saying. Was this really herself? Her skin was red where they had kissed and her lips hurt. Her pale green dress clung to her from the heat, both that of the June night and that of their bodies. It formed a patch of criss-crosses across her stomach, creases marking the place where they had pressed against one another. Slowly, she undid the buttons and peeled the dress away until she stood in her underwear. She felt moist between her legs and in a moment's private embarrassment, she understood that it was not perspiration, but wetness from herself, her sex. And as if to strengthen the sudden discovery, she suddenly felt aware of the physical, the fact that she had swollen, like a flower in bloom, and that she was so full and burgeoning that she ached. It was more from curiosity than anything else that made her fingers automatically seek out the flower, explore and then withdraw, wet and lubricated. She brought her finger tips close to her face, shyly breathing in their scent, studied them as she rubbed the liquid between thumb and forefinger, thinking how strange and wonderful and foreign it seemed. Again she shook her head, looked back into her reflection for her eyes to catch another detail—the marks on her waist and upper arms, purplish stains where Harry's hands had clutched her. When she remembered this, her head swam and her breathing became rapid, little spirals of desire darting through her heart and belly to her sex and sparkling out through her thighs to her lower legs in ever-increasing density. Again she felt weak, her hand automatically reaching out to steady herself. She was different—her eyes looked eastern as they narrowed with desire, her skin that tint her parents did not have, the blackness and thickness of her hair that was theirs neither, but Mediterranean. She was different—wild and burning like a gypsy. She was different—and proud of that difference. She was full of love, brimming so much with desire, a woman, not a girl and for a time, a few seconds perhaps, a few minutes, long minutes, so free. The feeling took her by surprise—a long, ever-rising and at the same time deepest surge, something more powerful than she had ever felt. An uncontrollable trembling came to her thighs and then the huge surge of convulsive energy, a bursting star. She held her free hand to her mouth and bit into her flesh. Her body throbbed, she leant forwards, hands on the washbasin and breathed as well as she could. And then, looking up, emptied, her eyes welled with tears, tears of happiness and exhaustion.

It was two o'clock before she finally padded across her bedroom and slipped beneath the cotton sheet. The night was cool and still. An insect bumbled lazily in the darkness and then left, back out through the half-open window of which she was too tired to rise and close.

Her last thoughts were of Sarah and a strange conversation, real enough for Jeanne to think that it had occurred, so dreamy that it also seemed part of her mind's fall into sleep. In it, Sarah was telling her that her father had mentioned how she looked so unlike the other Europeans. A little too beautiful, a little too finely featured. *Pied-noir.* Jewish extraction, almost—like Sarah. In her dream, she and Sarah became sisters. They lived in the same house, not far from Harry's rooms and strangely there was no mother. They all spoke in a bizarre mix of languages, sometimes French, sometimes English and at other times—totally comprehensible despite the fact—in an odd babble that sounded Spanish, but wasn't. In her dream, Jeanne separated her letters, those written before Harry had told her, and those he had written after and hid them in different locations, her unconscious bringing back reality, for she had done exactly that the evening before—and making it all the more surreal. At last, her tiredness tinged with an exquisite sense of well-being, Jeanne's mind drifted into sleep.

It was strange, but Jeanne felt his presence long before she opened her eyes and saw. A voice from somewhere inside her told her it must have been four o'clock and if she had opened her eyes straight away, she would have been surprised to see that it was exactly that. She whispered softly from her sleep: *'Is it you?'* A noise, the movement of the curtains and a warmth treading lightly across her room. *'Have you come back?'* She felt herself smiling. There was no reply. She forced open her eyes, let out a sigh and raised herself on her elbows, half-expecting to feel Harry's lips brush against hers. Standing at the foot of her bed, hardly six feet away, was a stranger.

The seconds were without end. She did not move. Neither did he. She saw his eyes, made all the larger and striking in the dim light, wide and white and initially just as shocked as hers. He was dark-skinned, tall and heavily-built and she wasn't sure, given the darkness, that he had a moustache. The fear crept upon her slowly, as did the realisation of the situation. He must have noticed, for his face began to change, turning from one of curious interest to one of fear itself—fear that she would panic. It was this face, and its desperate plea for calm, that forced Jeanne's fear to rise even further, even faster. He held out first one hand, then another—palms outward—and when this failed to calm her, moved forwards. It was like a twig snapping. In a split-second, she had crawled back, still facing him, frantic until her lower back wedged painfully into the iron bedstead.

'I know you are the daughter of Philippe-Charles Lefèvre, my child, and I want to talk to you,' said the stranger in a soft, strained voice. 'After all, I have a letter in which you said you wanted to see me. Remember?'

Jeanne stared back, unable to open her mouth.

'I want to talk to you about the truth. About what your father did and the awful things that he does everyday to my people.'

Her fear had taken over and only a silent scream for help filled her mind that emerged as a growing whine from her lips. The stranger's eyes glared wide and he brought a finger to his lips.

It was then that first Soumia's voice, then Mohammed's, gave a muffled shout from behind her bedroom door. The man grimaced, almost in pain and then his face hardened.

26

Two days had passed and the strange, intricate whine of dawn prayer reached Summerfield like the wind creeping through a crack in the door. He opened first one eye, then the other, felt a surge of well-being seep through him and stretched gloriously in his bed. The word *Jeanne* came to him before anything else, her name more than just a person, but a state, a philosophy, a reason, an absolute. He grinned, stretched again, followed it up with a loud groan of pleasure, and rose.

He had slept all of four hours, woken in the night by the sound of an explosion in the east and the crackle and patter of gunfire. At first, he had automatically linked the incident to Jeanne and had spent a fraught ten minutes, worried nauseous, cursing the fact that there was no way to contact her, before Abdlakabir called up from below gleefully informing him that the independence fighters had struck a military depot near the old palace.

He felt curiously energetic. Perhaps it was like that—four hours or eight, with anything in between either too little or too much. He put some water to boil, gave yesterday's bread a squeeze to check its edibility and dipped his finger into a jar of honey and olive oil that Mrs Abdlakabir No. 2 had given him the previous week. The taste was soft and smooth and indecisive, still strangely foreign to Summerfield's tongue, though wholesome. He dipped in his finger another time and sucked it as he walked over to the window and drew back the linen cloth that served as a curtain.

Night still reigned—just. Gun metal in colour, it subsided slowly and turned an ever-clearer shade of purple before his gaze. The prayer seemed to last longer than usual. Once, from the rooftop, he had seen the district Imam beginning the ascent to the top of the minaret before prayer. Small, bent-backed and with a smooth clarity of skin that gave him a most benevolent aurora, the Imam had been lugging a large, copper megaphone over his shoulders. Summerfield had watched as the old man, obviously used to the ritual, turned about-face and wriggled through the small, ancient entrance to the minaret backwards and then disappeared with a scraping sound.

Summerfield let himself be carried on the wave of his good spirits, his mind busy with memories of Jeanne and their long and heady embrace barely forty-eight hours before. She was so close in his thoughts that he smelled her scent, felt the warm press of her belly against his groin. His sex began to stiffen and he stepped back with a grin, not wishing Mrs Abdlakabir No. 1 or anyone else for that matter to witness his noble erection.

It was precisely at this moment, which also coincided with the water coming to boil, that he heard muted footsteps in the street below. They hurried closer and then two dark shapes, huddled together as one, scurried into view. It was all too quick for Summerfield to register. Preoccupied with the boiling water, he stepped back, walked over to the stove and took the pan off the hob, only to hear a dim knock on his neighbour's door below, followed by a silence then more footsteps.

Summerfield cursed under his breath, annoyed at the fact that the disturbance had caused a dramatic wilting of his member. He stood still, listening, the pan still in his hand. Then came the sound of someone coming up the steps to his door. A moment of alarm shot through him, his mind flashing back to the *gendarmes* and their flailing sticks. Quickly, he replaced the saucepan and looked around, desperately seeking a weapon. A soft knock. Summerfield seized the saucepan again, slopping the steaming water onto the floor at his feet.

A voice, hardly a murmur, said: 'Harry Summerfield—it is I, *Badr.*'

'Badr?' Summerfield relaxed. 'Good God—just in time for tea.'

'Let us in—*quickly.*' Badr talked louder, his voice carrying a sense of urgency and Summerfield immediately moved to the door, drawing away the bolt.

'What? Abrach, too?' Summerfield's eyes fell on the merchant's ashen face, his eyes bloodshot and swollen with pain. 'My God! Whatever happened? Jesus Christ—*your head*. Come in—quick.'

'Abdlakabir is bringing medicine,' hastened Badr as he helped Abrach through the door to Summerfield's bed.

Summerfield closed the door behind them and hurried over. He darted a glance at the merchant. Several, small rivulets of some pink, viscous matter ran from Abrach's hairline down across his forehead. He had obviously been hit with an object. There was no other trace of injury, but why so much pain? 'Where is he hurt? Show me. I have some medicine left.'

'His hands,' said Badr, grimly, looking towards the door. 'I only hope we were not followed.'

'Followed?'

'The police, Mr Summerfield.'

'Shit.' Summerfield opened his mouth and there came another knock. Badr moved forward, one hand quickly lifting a flap in his gown to produce a pistol, and carefully opened the door. It was Abdlakabir, trembling with the effort of having carried a steaming basin up the steep stairway. Badr quietly thanked him, mumbled something quickly so that Summerfield couldn't hear and closed the door, bringing the basin and a bag over to the bed.

'Master,' whispered Badr, gently tugging on the cape that covered Abrach.

Abrach looked up, distant, tears falling silently from his eyes.

'I thank you, Badr. I am afraid it is dirtied,' he hissed through clenched teeth.

Badr shook his head, glanced at Summerfield.

'I am sorry, Mr Summerfield. We had to act fast and your rooms were closest. I will see quickly to the wounds and then we shall be gone.'

Summerfield hesitated. He felt quite useless.

'Please—is there anything I can do?'

Badr gave a little grin and said calmly: 'As you said—a little tea would be a good idea.'

Summerfield nodded and turned, glancing back as Badr carefully pulled away the cape that covered the merchant. Abrach was in what remained of a yellowish suit, stained with sweat, singed as if by flames and rather too small for his frame, the strength of his arms having the effect of shrinking the sleeves. The sleeves—Summerfield shuddered—were almost black, stained up to elbows in blood. And then the merchant's hands. Summerfield swore, too fascinated by the sight to move. From the upper knuckle to the tips, Abrach's fingers were an unrecognisable bunch of tangled keys. They were so unlike fingers that Summerfield stared on, discerning what he thought were fingernails, discovering a flattened and embedded gold ring, until Badr's voice, both firm and surprisingly gentle, brought him back.

'Master—please look away,' he said to Abrach, bending towards the merchant's hands and exploring how he could disentangle the mess. 'Abdlakabir has bought ointments and gauze, but nothing else.'

'Wait—' Summerfield breathed deeply and stared at Badr. 'I have some morphine—Abrach left it when he took care of me.'

'God is great,' breathed Badr with relief and nodded for Summerfield to fetch it. 'It was fate that made him leave it.'

'It was help and concern for a friend,' said Abrach, suddenly looking round, his eyes avoiding his hands, and giving Summerfield a painful smile. He turned his head to the side once more. 'Though Allah might also have had a part in it,' he added, respectfully and not without a hint of humour.

Summerfield returned, gave Abrach an encouraging nod and prepared the syringe, screwing the little needle to the glass cylinder with trembling fingers.

'Sorry—I've got the shakes a little. Here we are.' He pushed the needle carefully into the aperture of the small phial of liquid morphine and drew back the pump. 'You do it, Badr.' Badr looked at him and shrugged. Summerfield turned to the groaning merchant, fighting a sudden urge to be sick. 'Abrach, how do we do this?'

'Lower hands—two doses. Look for the vein—no, not that one.' Summerfield drew the needle across Abrach's hand, glancing up with amazement at the man's calmness—how Abrach could actually look at his own destroyed fingers and at the same time direct operations was beyond him. 'That's the one. Please, Harry—quickly now. I believe I'm going to faint.'

Summerfield pushed and felt the needle pop through Abrach's skin. Abrach didn't move—it must have been minimal compared to the pain of his fingers. Immediately, Summerfield applied pressure to the syringe and the liquid emptied, almost stubbornly, into Abrach's swollen vein. He quickly handed a piece of cotton to Badr, took the young man's thumb and pressed it onto Abrach's skin where the blood had begun to form a bubble. Then the other hand. A strange, almost female laugh escaped Abrach's lips.

'You're as good a doctor as I, Harry. I thank you.'

Summerfield looked up into Abrach's exhausted eyes and smiled. And then Abrach fainted.

Badr tried as best as he could to bathe the shattered fingers, disentangling them one by one and setting them straight. The little finger on the left hand was almost completely severed and hanging on by a shred of skin. Badr deftly cut it off, carefully placing the bloody digit on a rag on Summerfield's bed. Abrach's gold ring, twisted and flat, was removed using a pair of pliers, the snapping sound as they cut the metal sending a shudder through Summerfield. Once finished, Badr wrapped the merchant's hands in bandage and stood up. He gave Summerfield a wild glance, suddenly gagged and walked to the adjoining room where Summerfield could hear him taking a series of deep breaths. Presently, he returned, looking calm and determined.

'A friend will soon arrive with transport. We had to abandon the car—too obvious.'

'What's going to happen? It's something to do with Lefèvre, isn't it?' said Summerfield, walking across to the drawer and taking out his flask of whisky. He offered it to Badr who frowned and shook his head. Summerfield took a nip and screwed back the cap. 'I *knew* nothing good would come of the idea!'

'Friends will take Abslem to a doctor. I hope they manage to get through the checkpoints. The police—'

'What a mess,' said Summerfield. He sat down. 'This was no accident.'

'They spotted him—he was caught.'

'Who is *they*?'

'People, the police—it is of no matter. We were on a mission,' added Badr, curtly.

'A mission? The explosion—was it you? What are you—revolutionaries or something?'

'A mission of observation,' redirected Abrach, who had gained consciousness and was listening. 'A simple act of tourism.'

'And the police nearly amputated your hands?' Summerfield shook his head and snorted. 'Please—Abrach—*Abslem, if it's your real name*—tell me the truth.'

Badr glanced anxiously at Summerfield then at the merchant and Abrach tilted his head squinting with pain, as though conceding.

'The last time we talked, Harry…I should have known it would cause her alarm.'

'I knew it,' said Summerfield again, drawing breath and fighting back the urge to curse the man. 'Jeanne—is she all right?' he asked. Then: '*She* did that to you?' Summerfield was nonplussed.

Abrach shook his head. A whimper escaped his lips and he gave a shake of the head as though reproaching himself.

'I should have listened to you, Harry. It all went terribly wrong.' The merchant slowly shook his head again, a gesture of sadness mixed with bitter irony. 'After all this time, Harry. After all this waiting. I brought disaster upon myself in a moment's impatience. I thought your hearts would spell the end of my plans.' Abrach's voice hardened and grew bitter. 'What a stupid fool…'

'And Jeanne—are you sure she's all right?' repeated Summerfield.

'I believe so. I can hardly comprehend it was me,' continued Abrach, suddenly thrown into gloom.

'A fucking mess,' repeated Summerfield, angrily and turned away. He imagined Jeanne and the state she must be in and silently cursed Abrach.

Abrach, the morphine deadening his senses, looked up with glazed and distant eyes.

'It was not in my nature, Harry. I was not meant to do this. But I did. I am sure to lose everything now. As if my family wasn't enough.'

Summerfield stared back, lost for words. He shook his head in a dismissive gesture and smartly stood up as the sound of more footsteps came from outside.

Badr walked silently to the window and peered carefully out.

'It is Radoin,' he said, and hissed to the figure below. Returning to the bedside, he gave Summerfield a glance and knelt next to Abrach. 'Master, Radoin has come with help. He will take you to a doctor—one of our friends. Go with him now. I will see to Mr Summerfield's discomfort for I fear you have lost much blood on his sheets.'

'Doesn't matter,' said Summerfield, mechanically. 'Take care of Abrach—that's the priority, I suppose.'

'This Radoin will do,' repeated Badr, giving him another meaningful glance. 'Do not fear for Abrach. I will join him later and ensure he is looked after. Quickly now—the police must not find you,' added the young man, lifting the merchant to his feet.

'I thank you, Harry. Forgive me. I did her no harm,' grimaced Abrach.

Summerfield gave a wave of his hand.

'Don't be foolish, Abrach. It's me. I—I *apologise*.'

'Apologise?' said Abrach with effort and halted in the doorway. Summerfield thought he saw laughter come fleetingly to the merchant's eyes—that and a faint glimmer of bitterness. '*Whatever for*?'

Summerfield watched from the window as Badr and the third man, Radoin, led Abrach away and disappeared around the corner of the street. Hardly a minute passed and then Badr came back into sight. He gave a quick glance up at the window and nodded to Summerfield before taking to the stairs.

They worked in silence, folding the soiled bed sheets and gathering the detritus of their hasty work including the severed finger that Badr deftly wrapped in the strip of cloth and placed in a pocket. Despite Summerfield gesturing to the contrary, Badr began to wash the bloodstains on the floor and carpet. Once finished, the young man cleaned his hands and joined Summerfield.

'I will ask your neighbour to burn all this when I go.'

'Thank you, Badr,' nodded Summerfield, pushing across a plate. 'Eat—I'm afraid it's yesterday's bread, but the honey makes it edible.'

They chewed in the morning stillness and Summerfield noted, despite Badr's education, the young man's eating habits that betrayed humble origins. When the bread was finished, Summerfield poured more tea.

'Tell me what happened, Badr.'

'I saw you talk to Abrach—I was one of the men in the car. He insisted on meeting the young woman that night. And like you, I tried to dissuade him.'

'I didn't know he could be so blind.'

'When one has suffered one often is,' said Badr, almost introspectively. 'Our presence coincided with the arrival of a police guard.'

'Oh, God,' said Summerfield. 'I heard Lefèvre on the phone—so that was it.'

'Abrach tried to get away.'

'And was caught.'

'Yes,' murmured Badr. 'He spent all of yesterday in the special detention centre. By the time we knew of his whereabouts and got organised, it was too late.'

'The explosion, the gunfire—it was you.'

Badr nodded. 'We had to get him out. Abrach—*Abslem*—is very influential. He regularly has contact with Zayni's successors who still resist the French in the mountains.'

'What—what happened to him?' asked Summerfield, timidly. 'His *hands*…'

'Have you never heard of the methods they use to extract information?' said Badr, grimly. 'I was told Lefèvre paid a visit. We cannot be sure, but it was probably he who finally gave consent to go ahead…'

'With torture?'

Badr nodded. 'We cannot prove what happens behind those walls,' he added, bitterly. 'They say that accidents happen. Abrach's happened to involve a winch. From what I understand, they forced his hands into the teeth,' he added, his voice turning almost to a whisper. 'They slowly, purposefully crushed his fingers.'

Summerfield shuddered. 'That's—*sickening.*'

'It is usually effective, I am told.'

'You got him out, thank God—the poor bastard.'

'We lost two men in the process, Summerfield. Altogether, this has been quite a disaster.'

The two men remained silent for some moments and in the stillness they heard the sounds of the city begin to stir, the distant clang of a police car.

'I'm afraid most of this is my fault,' said Summerfield, unable to hold it in any longer. 'Badr—*I'm the one* responsible for Abrach's actions.'

Badr straightened up, returning to the shrewd and alert, his habitual traits. 'I think we are no longer obliged to call the master *Abrach,*' said Badr, without emotion.

Summerfield lifted his head and looked at the young Berber.

'He told me about the village and a family—obviously *his family.*'

'Do you know what Abrach actually means?' added Badr. 'He has lived many years under that name. It means a cover, a blanket under which the people of the mountains hide from the cold. And he is also very good at the trade he chose to hide behind. Abslem is a very rich man by our standards.'

'And a benefactor to the cause.'

'Do not blame yourself for what happened, Harry Summerfield.'

Summerfield let out a bitter laugh and shook his head.

'How can't I? You both know how I feel about Jeanne Lefèvre.' Summerfield dropped then raised his gaze. 'I betrayed him, Badr.'

'You did what was asked of you.'

'No—I betrayed him.' Summerfield lit a cigarette and exhaled noisily. 'The poor bugger. It's not only his fingers that are mashed. And what,' added Summerfield, his mind suddenly falling upon the obvious, 'will he do to me when he's in good enough shape? I deserve to be shot.'

'You are a man very sensitive to guilt, Harry,' said Badr, almost bemused.

Summerfield looked up and glared at him.

'I do not think it all so necessary,' added the young man. 'I repeat: you did what was asked of you.'

Summerfield frowned. 'I don't understand.'

'Perhaps Abrach's heart was indeed captured by the young woman. What is certain is that it was sick with the loss of his family. What happened between you and Jeanne Lefèvre just added the pressing element of time into things, that's all. At some moment he would have confronted her. It was written.' Badr seemed to hesitate, pulled softly on his immature beard and sighed. 'Abslem El Rifni was of noble family—a warrior family. But he was also a cultured man. He studied at university—almost an unknown thing for a Moroccan to do. He is also, as I'm sure you are aware, a very warm-hearted man. Unfortunately for him.' Badr rose, wiped his hands on his gown and gestured to Summerfield. 'I would have had no hesitation in putting a bullet in Lefèvre's neck. And now, after this, I do not doubt that Abslem El Rifni will either.'

27

Jeanne sat on the veranda, staring emptily at the khaki form of the policeman quivering in the heat by the gate. He had been there since lunch, replacing another, and had hardly moved. Her mother tapped her on the forearm and offered her tea.

'Poor girl. All this has so upset your capacity for study.'

Jeanne sighed and turned her head. It all seemed so unreal.

'What do you think?' added her mother. Jeanne frowned, unsure of what she was referring to. 'Will you be *ready*?'

It took a second or two for Jeanne to realise. She felt like shouting—how her mother could speak of her studies when she'd nearly been killed!

'Yes, mother. I'll be ready.'

'Good. It will please your father to hear it.'

The silence came again and Jeanne, bothered by her mother's presence and the overbearing attention to her as though she were some sort of a diseased victim, made it difficult to return to her books. Her mind wandered to Harry. How she wished he were here to hold her in his arms. He would know how to comfort her. She would heal in his words and in his embrace.

Time chimed from behind her in the hallway. *Housebound for a week*. It was so ghastly. For the first time in her life she saw just how awfully boring her parents and their lives really were. They lived in a routine of silences and staid formalities, from breakfast until night, a never-changing agenda of words and acts that must have been repeated tens of thousands of times over their twenty-two years of marriage. *Nice weather today. Le fond de l'air est frais. Bisous. How is Mrs Lefèvre this morning? Take care, chérie. I'll call from the office. See you at 5. Allez—au travail. Allez—time to check the housework*. And the worst, the *very* worst, was that they didn't even seem to notice. Father was driven to work and *Mater*, with the new preoccupation that seemed to interfere annoyingly with her schedule, tried to mother her until, come afternoon, and evidently satisfied that she had done her bit, she returned to her routine, pottering about the garden rectifying Mohammed's work.

Jeanne had never known so much tedium. After two days, it was so strong that it smothered the effects of Thursday night and the stranger's intrusion. Only Harry's presence, only his memory was strong enough to carry her through. She bore him like baby, though the warm, glowing weight filled her heart not her belly. She felt like shouting his name into the air and writing it on every page of every book. And tomorrow, Sunday, he would come to dine.

The thought of seeing him again made her feel light and giddy. How she hoped they could find a few moments alone to hold each other. She would tell him what had happened, the whole horrible story and he would kiss her softly and cradle her head upon his shoulder. She imagined the touch of his fingers in her hair, soft protecting strokes as he soothed her, the hardness of his muscles as she held onto his arms.

Lefèvre came back punctually at 6.15 and, saluting the police guard, approached the house with an habitual *I'm a little late— Sorry—work at the office* to which her mother replied *only a 'little' fifteen minutes, chéri—welcome back*. Jeanne shuddered. How her mother could keep up the hypocrisy of it made her feel angry. It was as though her father were returning from a crusade instead of an office.

Lefèvre sat down, took off his hat which he placed neatly on top of his briefcase and leant over to kiss his wife on the cheek. He seemed to forget Jeanne in this ritual. True, she was usually upstairs in her books when he came home.

After a few moments of enquiry into his day at the office, Jeanne's mother called for Soumia and drinks. It was yet another habit—the *apéritif* upon returning from work.

'Everything in order? Nothing to report?' said Lefèvre, looking at the two women and giving a wane smile. 'Office talk, I'm afraid. Takes some time to switch off. So?'

'*Bien*,' said Jeanne's mother. 'Jeanne has been trying to work and assures me she's on form for her exams. Nothing to worry about.'

'Good. And yourself, *chérie*. Hard day?'

'Oh, the usual. Mohammed's such a clumsy hand at pruning. You'd think he'd have a clean cut.'

'The Arabs have a reputation for using the blade,' commented Lefèvre. 'Though not our Mohammed, *chérie*!' It seemed to make them both laugh and Jeanne squirmed uncomfortably.

'He's not an Arab, father.'

'What?'

'He's of Berber origin.'

'Quite,' muttered Lefèvre, giving his wife a grimace. 'Ah, drinks. Thank you, Soumia.'

The chink of the ice in their glasses was like the chiming of the clock in the hallway—somehow institutional. As was the sigh of contentment her father let out after the first sip. She shivered. She felt even more disgust for her father than the man who had tried to abduct her.

'Mother—what are we going to eat tomorrow? Perhaps Soumia could try to make something English for Mr Summerfield—'

'*Good God!*'

'I'm sure that would please him.'

'Good God!' repeated Lefèvre. 'I'd completely forgotten him.'

'Tomorrow is Sunday, father.'

Lefèvre snorted. 'Well we can't invite him under these circumstances. We'll have to call it off.'

'*Daddy!*' Jeanne nearly jumped out of her seat in alarm.

'No—I'm afraid we can't. Impossible. After everything that has happened.'

'I'm not a cripple, father.'

'As I can see. However—this is really not the time for gayness and chit chat. What happened was a very serious affair. You require calm and silence, my dear.'

'You brute!' shouted Jeanne, unable to contain herself and slapped her books shut.

'Jeanne—*whatever?*' gasped her mother.

'Doesn't matter, *chérie*. She's fraught. Shock and all.' Lefèvre placed a hand on his wife's arm to soothe her. 'Afraid we have to be firm here.' He turned to Jeanne and looked steadily at her. 'I understand your condition, my girl. Mr Summerfield will just have to come another time.'

'When?'

'Difficult to say.'

'When?' demanded Jeanne and she saw her father's eyes harden.

'*When* you have managed to completely calm down,' he replied slowly.

Jeanne looked away from those eyes and then suddenly remembered.

'And what about the document? Isn't it important?'

'I'll send Mohammed to pick it up,' answered Lefèvre with a wave of his hand. 'Where does the Englishman live, anyway?'

'Mr Wilding mentioned he had lodgings in the old town,' said Mme Lefèvre, taking care with her voice.

'The old quarter? Good God—what's he doing there?' Lefèvre's face creased into something approaching disgust. 'He'll catch something.'

'Sarah's father lives there too,' added Jeanne, secretly outraged at the direction the conversation was going. Her father made a humming sound that suggested he wasn't quite in accord with all of what the Bassouin family stood for.

'Mr Wilding also mentioned that Mr Summerfield was something of an artist,' added Mme Lefèvre, this time her voice carrying a hint of excitement.

'And a *Socialist*!' added Lefèvre. 'Look what they did to France in '36! He started telling us about his intentions of going to Spain. Well—that's a lost cause in any case.'

'He can't be very well off,' said Mme Lefèvre, sneaking a glance at her daughter.

'Mummy!'

Her mother gave a little laugh and grinned.

'I *knew* it!'

'What?' Lefèvre suddenly seemed quite lost.

'Jeanne,' continued her mother, wagging a finger. 'I *knew* you had a little inclination for our Englishman!'

'Good God!' exclaimed Lefèvre, once again.

'How dare you!' shouted Jeanne and felt herself turning a blend of red and white—embarrassment and fear.

Her father sniggered and then became serious.

'My dear girl—how sweet. I suppose it's the age—I'd forgotten.'

'Or didn't notice.'

'Don't you *understand*, Jeanne?' said her mother, looking sickly sweet. 'It's only normal to have feelings at your age. It's as though one were trying to *feel* how it is to be in love.'

'Well I'm *not* in love,' protested Jeanne.

'I should jolly well hope not,' scoffed Lefèvre. 'Especially with him. The man's a pauper—one just has to look at his shoes. And he's Anglican. *And* he's much older than you.'

'Seven years,' said Jeanne, feeling wretched. It was as though she were betraying him. Why couldn't she declare what her heart so wanted to shout aloud?

'Seven years, is it?' said Lefèvre, shaking his head. 'That's like a man of eighteen falling in love with an eleven year old. Rather unpleasant, if you think about it.'

'But I'm *not* eleven.'

'So you *are* in love with him?' smiled her mother, knowingly.

'No—*no*.' Jeanne sat in silence, wrenched between telling the truth and bowing to her parents' ridicule. It was useless. Even if she did say yes, it would only make them more intolerant towards Harry. '*No*,' she said, finally.

The evening drew on and Jeanne, her body heavy with gloom, retired to the spare bedroom to rest before dinner. The world was against her—her parents the minions of all the bad luck and unhappiness piling upon her. She felt as though she were alone in the middle of a sandstorm that clogged her movements and her heart, slowly burying her. She wanted *Baudelaire*, her teddy. But she couldn't even fetch him, her bedroom off-bounds while the police had carried out their investigation. Soumia was clearing up the mess and Jeanne imagined her trying to sponge away the stains of those ghastly hands on her bed. She shuddered at the thought. Maybe her parents *were* right. Maybe she *was* ill with the shock of it all.

Her eyelids grew heavy. She felt the heat upon her skin. Fever, perhaps? She thought again of Harry, wished she could reach him, tell him. She felt so lonely. In the hallway, so distant, it seemed, she heard Soumia's voice, low and hurried. She was talking to her mother. With supreme effort, Jeanne strained her ears to listen: *in the room,* said Soumia's voice—*awful.* And her mother's voice, in reply, an appeal for calm. And then Jeanne's eyelids closed. The next moment, unable to determine exactly how long she'd been asleep, her mother knocked at the door.

'Come down to dinner, Jeanne. Quickly now—your father is hungry.'

Her father ate hurriedly. Mother had not been exaggerating. Hardly had Jeanne begun her second mouthful than her father was wiping clean his plate, completely engrossed with the operation and oblivious to Jeanne's stares. Her mother caught her eye and a fleeting glimpse of apology came to her face. It was one thing Jeanne and she had in common—the value they placed on table etiquette. Lefèvre, head bowed, swabbed his lips and mechanically took a swig of wine from his glass before returning—the transition was striking—to a position of utmost poise and dignity.

'I sent Mohammed off to find the Englishman. Shouldn't be so difficult—can't be that many whites living in the poor district.'

There was a silence, Jeanne restraining herself to be led into any show of emotion. She must remain calm, she told herself. Only then would they let her get back to the *Académie* and her friends and, hopefully, Harry.

'We'll invite the chap next time Wilding is back from his field studies. Not that long, I believe.'

'That *would* be nice,' chimed Mme. Lefèvre and turned to Jeanne. 'Wouldn't it, dear?'

'Yes,' said Jeanne, sullenly, without looking up.

Her father cleared his throat.

'Soumia and Mohammed have tidied the mess in your bedroom, Jeanne. And mother has checked. It seems you may return to sleep there—if you wish.' Jeanne looked up. 'That is, if you think you won't be too bothered. I think it may be a good idea to lock the window for the time being.'

'Thank you, father.'

'And…there's *something else*, Jeanne.' Her father's voice sounded odd. Jeanne placed her fork down. 'Soumia found some letters while she was cleaning your room.'

Jeanne's heart missed a beat.

'Letters?'

'Yes. A dozen or so. *These* letters.'

Lefèvre's hand moved to his lap and produced a bundle tied together with string. He placed them on his wiped plate and looked keenly at her. Jeanne felt the blood drain from her. She began to shake.

'In normal circumstances,' came her mother's voice, 'We would simply have left them where they had been found.'

'You—you've *read* them?'

'The last bears a signature—*Abrach*,' said Lefèvre, his voice emotionless. 'Tell me Jeanne—is there a connection with the person who broke into your room?'

'I—' Jeanne's voice faltered. She felt like dying. Thank God they hadn't found the ones bearing Harry's name.

'During questioning he said his name was *El Rifni*,' continued Lefèvre. 'But, it is essential that you tell us the truth.'

Silence.

'Perhaps,' whispered Jeanne. 'I'm—I'm not really sure.'

'Did you have a liaison with this Arab, Abrach?' Her father's voice was cold and direct and Jeanne felt herself flinch.

'No, father.'

'It *is* the truth?'

Jeanne raised her head, the shame bringing tears to her eyes.

'Yes, father. I'd never seen the man. The messages arrived at the *Académie*—I don't know how.'

Lefèvre studied her for a few seconds, glanced across at his wife and then let out a sigh.

'Well, that's some good news, at least. However,' he continued, his voice changing back to a stern calm. 'The fact remains that this Abrach has been sending you—sending you the most *perverse* correspondence. Why in earth's name didn't you tell us? '

'Love letters,' said Jeanne, the words escaping her lips as though it were the most natural occurrence in the world.

'Tacky. And smutty,' said her father, mechanically. 'Hardly the sort of letters your mother and I exchanged. Naturally, I would have been surprised to learn that they had been written by the Arab who introduced himself into your room. But *Abrach* is an indigenous name. It is quite improbable that a native knows how to write so well and yet—there are mistakes that no Francophile of good education would make.' Lefèvre placed his hands slowly on the table, letting his words sink in. 'I will remain calm, Jeanne. But I now demand that you tell us all about this. Before anything else happens.'

Saturday passed and with it, a visit from Sarah Bassouin and her father. While Jean Bassouin joined Lefèvre and Colonel Le Guédec, Sarah joined Jeanne in her room, officially to revise for exams.

The door closed and with Soumia's footsteps returning downstairs, Jeanne's first reaction was to fling herself into Sarah's arms and cry. She had never felt so miserable in her life. Everything had soured and gone wrong. The world was against her.

They sat on the side of the bed for some minutes, holding hands. Sarah's words of comfort turned inexorably to the *Académie* and all the gossip. Sister Marthe had suddenly become lyrical, giving them, of all things, love poems to study; several policemen had questioned old *Quasimodo* at the gate; Aude's brother had joined the army and entered officer school at Saint Cyr. Henri had arranged for a honeymoon in Biarritz in August and the best of all, the very best and most important—was that *Cécile had lost her virginity*. At this, Jeanne let out a shriek.

'Who with? How?'

'With Edouard.'

'*Edouard*!'

'In his parents' attic.'

'Edouard?' repeated Jeanne, incredulous. 'The shy, dithering stamp collector! But he kissed *me*!'

'Cécile says he's a lion in bed—though perhaps that's

Cécile's imagination.'

Jeanne remained silent, her mouth agape, only for a surge of self-pity to then rush through her. '*But what about me?*' She felt her eyes begin to sting and the imminent bubbling of tears. 'Everybody's living and *me*—I'm just confined to this prison—*rotting*! Sarah—what an awful existence. I feel like dying!'

'Nonsense!' said Sarah, raising her eyes heavenwards and once more taking hold of Jeanne's hands. 'You're living an adventure! All the girls are dead jealous. Oh, don't worry,' she added hastily, 'I haven't gone into any details. But everyone knows about the incident. Everyone knows you're in love. Even Sister Marthe!'

'Oh, God!' Jeanne shuddered and let out a wail of despair.

'Jeanne? Are you all right?' came her mother's muffled voice from below.

'Yes!' called back Sarah. 'Just tackling algebra, Mme. Lefèvre!' Sarah led Jeanne back to the bed and sat her down. 'Look—I've something for you. You see—a letter. It's not over, Jeanne. Your love still comes to the orange grove and soon you'll be able to see him.' From under her dress, Sarah pulled out an envelope and handed it across. 'A bit sticky, I'm afraid,' apologised Sarah. 'Had to peg it to my suspender.'

'Have you read it? Everyone seems to be reading my things.'

'Of course not,' frowned Sarah. 'I wouldn't want you to read mine.'

'But you *showed* me yours,' said Jeanne, sniffing. 'Even the intimate bits. When Henri put—'

'That's different,' interrupted Sarah. 'We're betrothed. Nothing can stop us. Now, open the letter.'

Jeanne began to un-peel the seal, stood up—a reflex—and extracted the letter alone by the window. Sarah began to busy herself with the maths books though Jeanne knew she was observing her.

There were Harry's words and Jeanne's heart brimmed so suddenly with joy that she had to steady herself. It was like lifting into the air inside an aeroplane.

Dearest Jay,

I am fraught with concern and so desperate because I cannot hold you, comfort you. I am aware of what happened and I feel so terribly angry. Not least because part of this is my fault. You see—I know the person who gave you such a terrible fright. I am sorry, so sorry, my dear. Even if I am indirectly responsible, it is as though I had caused the pain. I imagine the horrible scene. Forgive me.

The hours pass in emptiness and I learn. I learn that time is a poison, that when you are not there to soften the days, it sours my thoughts and spirit to the darkest of moods. You seem to be the only true thing in this life. A truth kept from me by these awful events. And my world is a lie without you.

But listen to the breeze in the morning. See how the sun makes the flower burst. Feel the sigh of the stars on your skin from their lonely distance. And you will understand that I am standing by your side. That, if you turn your head slightly, you will see me smiling. That, if you close your eyes and reach carefully into the shadow, you will touch my lips with your finger tips and feel their tender caress upon your skin.

I will go to the orange grove every day, my love. And I will wait. And one day you will come.

The softest of kisses,
Magpie

'You're not going to cry again, are you?' said Sarah, distrustfully, bringing Jeanne back to reality. She shook her head in a daze. 'Thank God,' added Sarah. 'Look on the bright side, Jeanne. All this waiting will surely turn you both into fiery beasts when you finally get round to making love.'

'Sarah—*you dirty so-and-so!*' cried Jeanne, picking up a cushion and clubbing Sarah on the head.

The cushion fight lasted a full five minutes and sent them collapsing onto the bed, breathless and soaked in sweat. They lay side by side, letting out whimpers and giggles.

'My parents found some letters,' said Jeanne at last.

'Oh, dear.'

'Yes, but thankfully not those signed by Harry. I really can't fathom why I chose to separate them. But I'm grateful.'

'Rather. The other man—' Sarah's voice was soft, curious. 'D'you think he loved you? What a strange way of going about things.' Jeanne hummed an acknowledgement. 'What was he like?'

Jeanne raised herself onto an elbow and looked at her friend. 'Who?'

'Come on—the man who entered your room,' insisted Sarah.

Jeanne lay back and grimaced. 'Quite tall, portly, dark-skinned, a native—hands that would…would crack a neck in two with no problem,' she added, her mind flashing with the image of her father. 'I think he was the man who followed you in the orange grove.'

'*Urgh*.' Sarah shuddered and reached across to take Jeanne's hand. 'Must've been hideous. And rather scary—almost in a pleasant sort of a way,' she added, in afterthought.

'What d'you mean?' Jeanne frowned, perplexed.

'A dark shape in the night, entering your room. A man. A native. He comes to your bed and observes you in your sleep.'

'Sarah…'

'His hand, perhaps. Perhaps he reached out and touched you in your sleep.'

'Sarah! You're really strange!'

'It's like in a book,' defended Sarah. 'Just imagining, that's all.'

'Well, imagine the worst fright you've ever had and multiply it by a hundred. That's what it felt like.'

Sarah sighed and was silent for a moment. 'Yes. I'm sorry, Jeanne. Listen—I'm terribly hot. Let's go down to the kitchen for a glass of lemonade.'

'Good idea,' said Jeanne and rose, her mind still perplexed. Perhaps Sarah wasn't altogether wrong. There had been something exquisitely exciting about it—like falling out of a tree and gripping on to the last branch. Her heart pounding in her chest. Fear and exhilaration.

Mother was not to be seen. She and Soumia had probably left for the market to shop for fruit and vegetables. Jeanne and Sarah made their way to the kitchen and served themselves lemonade from the larder.

'Ludovic—Henri's friend, you remember—'

'Yes, I do,' said Jeanne, gulping down the bubbles.

'Returned from the United States. He said they've got

machines that create ice.'

'Heavens—we could do with that here.'

'Rather. Apparently, only the very rich families and only the very few have them. They're called *refrigerators*. They put food and drink in them and it keeps it fresh for weeks and weeks.'

'It must be fun to live in America,' said Jeanne, distantly. 'They seem to be dancing all the time. At least, that's what the films show us.'

The kitchen was a welcome break from the heat outside. The girls sat and took off their shoes, their toes touching the cool floor tiles until they warmed and only then placing their soles fully upon the surface. Both drew their dresses up above their knees and sat there, insouciant, sipping on their lemonade.

In the silence, they could hear the low rumble of the men in the adjoining study. Unconsciously, Sarah stood up, opened the window and craned her neck.

'Probably talking about the war,' whispered Sarah and pulled a face which was meant to imitate a stuffy Le Guédec. Jeanne rose and joined her. She could hear the men's conversation, distinct words despite the muffled tones. Her father was speaking:

'*Abslem El Rifni, Colonel.* Then Le Guédec, with his slight stutter: *yes, I've s-set up road blocks. Informers—locals working for us. They report to Lieutenant Feldsman. An Alsatian—good man, v-very thorough.* Her father again: *It's astonishing how the past catches you up. I had no idea—.* Jean Bassouin: *the revolt turned quite brutal, I believe.* Lefèvre: *had to set an example—if not, the whole country up in arms. Quite,* affirmed the Colonel: *and my men will s-see to it that El Rifni is hunted down and arrested, rest a-assured. In the meantime, I propose keeping up the safety measures. Someone to accompany my daughter and the house staff,* came Lefèvre's voice. *And a permanent guard on the house and at the office, Philippe-Charles, don't you think?* A murmur of affirmation. *You'd think they'd have learnt their lesson. Oh, the occasional gesture of discontent. D'you call murdering police officers an occasional gesture of discontent? I want that man removed, his possessions confiscated. Unacceptable—Should have raised the village to the ground years ago—all of it. Get the army to see to it now, will you? Sorry?* said Le Guédec, hesitant. *Destroy it—completely. It might even flush the madman out into the open...'*

Jeanne drew back from the window and served herself another glass. Her father had been pitiless, though she supposed he was right. When she rejoined Sarah at the window, the men had changed subject. As Sarah had so rightly guessed—the war in Europe. Her father's voice, though, sounded more determined than on previous times the subject had been approached. *'It's almost a question of weeks, gentlemen. The only official thing remaining is the rubber stamp on it all.* Bassouin: *blast Hitler and his mad designs. All of Europe will be set on fire.* Le Guédec: *a little alarmist, Jean. If we and the British can get enough modern equipment to the right places in time, then we'll knock them out within a month.* Lefèvre: *they say the nature of war has changed.* Le Guédec again: *tanks and engines and planes—unstoppable. Berlin is a two-hour flight from Paris and two day's driving. We have the best-equipped army in the world, gentlemen. The most men under arms, the biggest tanks, the fastest motorised units.* Bassouin: *and young Charrier has joined up—officer material. Might just finish his training in time. I fear it may generalise,* said Lefèvre. And Le Guédec: *mobilisation is only a signature away from reality.'*

The sound of a knock on the study door. It must be mother coming back. Jeanne peered into the hallway. It was Mohammed, a large brown envelope in his hand. The study door opened and Jeanne heard her father's voice, preoccupied:

'Ah, yes—thank you, Mohammed. Put it in the tray, would you. I'll see to it later.' Mohammed briefly disappeared, conversation at a halt and then reappeared, closing the door behind him. Immediately, from behind the wall, the sound of the three men speaking in low, grave voices started up again. From the kitchen the girls listened on for a few moments more. Lefèvre's voice became predominant. Jeanne heard her father distinctly: *'we must begin to put our native troops on a footing. More training. Paris demands a Moroccan brigade.'* She drew away and closed the kitchen window, giving Sarah a furtive glance.

'I know what you're thinking, Jeanne,' said Sarah, nodding. 'I only hope they don't begin their silly war before my honeymoon.

Come on—I suppose we'd better return and start revising,' she added, glumly.

'You revise first. I have to write a letter,' said Jeanne, her face glowing. 'For Harry.'

28

S ummerfield sat in the dusty café—more of a drinks stand than anything else—and unfolded his copy of *The Times*, oblivious to the distrustful glances and low growls of the local men. Hardly a year ago, he would have been afraid, taking the behaviour as threats and it sent a slither of mild surprise through him that he should now not care. He cleared his throat and, as if to underline his complete insouciance, sent a neat, compact ball of spit out into the dusty road. His coffee was served and he thanked the owner in Arabic.

The Times was a week old, though looked a lot more. Somehow ending up in a stand at the railway station, the heat had baked crisp the sheets. It made an awful noise and looked outrageously large in the cramped place. Irritated by this, a vague promise to write a letter to the editor on the subject came and went fleetingly from his head.

The title on the front page read *Roosevelt appeals to good sense, Churchill attacks Chamberlain*. So, thought Summerfield, after years in the wilderness, the old war dog is making a come back. Further down, two other articles: *B.E.F. geared up to go* and, in the oddly officious style of *The Times*, *Mr Hitler receives enthusiastic ovation during Danzig speech*. Finally, a footer nestled next to an advert for Burberry Mackintoshes, indicating banishment to page two: *Spain: capitulation talks under way*.

So it was all over. Or almost. Summerfield searched in the pocket of his *jellaba* for a ready-rolled cigarette and lit up. *Over*, he repeated to himself and felt neither anger nor regret. Rather surprising, he realised, given that barely two years before he'd given up a life in England to fight in Spain. He raised his eyes for a brief few seconds and gazed out, unfocused, on the past he'd almost forgotten. *I wonder what Wilding is up to?*

Summerfield allowed himself a further half-hour of reading

before finally rising. He left *The Times*, neatly folded, on the rickety table in the street café, wondering who would pick it up. As an afterthought, it could have come in useful for the loo.

It was an important day. And Summerfield realised that perhaps it was why he'd deliberately tried to appear so carefree—to stop the excitement from getting a grip. Today was when Jeanne would at last be free to meet him at the orange grove.

Arriving at his lodgings, the threat of world war, Abrach, lack of any income and his future in Morocco were relegated to unimportance. Of the utmost importance, however, was the worry of the hole in his left boot, finding a pair of dry socks and having a shave.

He washed thoroughly, rubbing a bar of jasmine upon his skin to smother the smell of summer sweat. Shaving took longer than he'd planned—he didn't want any cuts what with his blunt razor. And none of the socks he'd washed upon waking were yet dry, the sun having chosen to dawdle behind the cloud. He padded downstairs barefoot, knocked on his neighbour's door and asked if he could use their hob, which was permanently lit, for a while.

Abdlakabir, his eyes alight, was only too helpful, insisting also that his first wife give his hair a quick tidying with a pair of clippers which, judging from both the design and the rust, Summerfield imagined to have come straight out of ancient Egypt.

'Is she young?' enquired Abdlakabir, watching on as his dour first wife appropriately manoeuvred Summerfield's head in a series of jerks.

'I've told you—I'm after a job, Abdlakabir,' replied Summerfield, shaking his head, a gesture that provoked a rather sharper jerk than usual and a warble of discontent from Abdlakabir's wife.

'Is she one of us? If so, I may take you aside and tell you a few worthy and useful things,' persisted his neighbour.

'It's a post on a local newspaper—*translating*,' continued Summerfield, secretly thinking of Jeanne and her heavenly face. Come to think of it, she did indeed possess some of the unique elegance of the Berber women.

'And will you offer her a present?' came Abdlakabir's voice.

'A present? *God*—I forgot!'

'Ha-ha!' triumphed Abdlakabir and clapped his hands. Even his frosty-faced wife allowed a trace of a smile to come to her lips. '*A job indeed*, Mr Summerfield! No present, you say—then you must find her one.'

'What could one give the most beautiful woman in the world?' said Summerfield. 'Her beauty renders all the gold and jewels of the earth as rusty and un-shining as the clippers your good wife is using on my hair.'

'A poem,' said Abdlakabir. 'Write her a poem.'

'That I have done many a time,' answered Summerfield. 'She has bracelets and necklaces made of my words.'

'Then flowers.'

'Mere baubles, my friend, for she is the Flower of All Flowers.'

'A ring—no, not a jewel, you have said that already,' said Abdlakabir, seeming to run dry of ideas.

'And a ring would spoil her lovely fingers, my friend, the only ring possible being the Sacred one—and that time has not come.'

'That time has not come,' echoed his neighbour, now scratching his head. 'I am lost, Mr Summerfield. I can think of no present fit for such a princess. But how do you gain a woman's heart in your country? Try that.'

'*Chocolates*? In this heat?'

A final jerk, a final snip and Abdlakabir's first wife released her grip on Summerfield's head.

'I am empty of ideas,' groaned Abdlakabir, taking Summerfield's plight most to heart. 'And I cannot remember what I did when I was young.'

At this, his wife gave a grunt and to both their surprise, began to speak. 'My husband, who has momentarily lost his memory. Who no longer remembers how to woo the beauty of woman, other than offering her a goat, a roof and a stove to work over. If our Lord permits, I would suggest that such beauty as Mr Summerfield describes can only be honoured with simplicity. For beauty is often so simple and unexplainable that it deserves to be offered that what it is.'

'Explain, oh wife!' demanded Abdlakabir. 'You have not spoken thus since our beginnings.'

'You did not ask me to,' replied his wife, tersely. Once again, her face drew cold and blank and she pulled her gown around her as she stepped across to a crate in the corner. The two men looked on in silence as she bent down, rummaged inside and brought out a small, darkly polished mahogany box, its edges beaded in intricate patterns of mother-of-pearl. She wiped it free of dust with her sleeve, smiled the smallest trace of a smile and opened it. With the tip of her index finger, she pressed downwards on something inside and, with the box in one hand and holding aloft the outstretched index finger of her other, she motioned across to Summerfield.

'Look,' she said, placing her finger before Summerfield's eyes. 'It is so small, so delicate, so simple, yes?'

'Yes,' nodded Summerfield, looking up into her eyes and smiling.

'But also so intricate. And its meaning goes much beyond any gold or jewel or flower. For it is those and much more.'

'The hand of Fatima,' smiled Abdlakabir, leaning across. 'Yes— why didn't I think of it?'

Stuck by the simple moisture of the skin to her fingertip, Summerfield marvelled at the tiny little hand, hardly bigger than an orange pip, delicately worked in silver thread into a pattern that seemed without end, spiralling back on itself and continuing once again.

'It is beautiful,' murmured Summerfield.

'Like the woman you will see.'

'Tell me—where can I find one. I don't have much with what to pay.'

'It is for you to offer her,' said Abdlakabir's wife and her eyes softened momentarily before turning back to stone. 'And in return, I will keep your hair that the old clippers have cut. I shall stitch them onto my cushions for decoration and for a while at least, they shall keep their yellow.'

It was nearing midday and Summerfield returned his gaze once again from the distant plain to scan the path through the orange trees. *Nearly time*, he told himself and hoped she wouldn't meet with any problem.

The leaves had changed from a spring green to thick and dark, almost black. Everywhere, clusters of little oranges, looking more like limes for the moment, sprouted from the branches, hard and strong and impudent.

There had been no note in the little cranny in the ditch, but Summerfield knew that Sarah, her friend, had been there for he had discovered another little structure made of twigs that Jeanne had probably made when confined to her rooms. The tiny bits of wood had been tied into the shape of a heart. It was all so sweet, it had almost brought tears of happiness to his eyes.

Jeanne did not come gracefully into the hollow. He heard her approaching, a hurried rustle of leaves and snapping twigs and then she lurched into the grove, nearly losing her balance. She was out of breath, a radiant smile coming and going between gulps of air. Summerfield reached out and took her hand. They clasped each other, pressing their bodies forwards, tight and inseparable. Her waist felt so small and childish and Summerfield felt a surge of something approaching paternalism flood through him. He would protect her, carry her through time while she grew into life. They pulled apart, eager to look at each other, as though they'd forgotten, as though they were checking that all was real.

'So you came!' said Summerfield.

'And you, my love!' replied Jeanne. They stood, full of too many words, mute, shy.

'I—I want to hold you.'

'Yes—hold me.'

Once more they held close. Summerfield could feel his breathing against hers, the way his chest moved, the rise and fall of her ribs and the inexorable synchronicity of their movements. He imagined them making love in much the same way. He kissed her softly on her cheek, then her lips and again. She seemed to hesitate, falter, and then she turned to him and their tongues met. A little whine, as though sipping champagne for the first time, came from her mouth.

'It's beautiful!' she whispered.

Summerfield pressed harder and her body went limp. This time she whimpered. Summerfield's sex hardened and he pulled back slightly, not wishing to alarm her, but she pulled him towards her. They kissed for a long, long time.

'I love you.'

'*Je t'aime.*'

Eventually they withdrew, slowly, as if prising apart two magnets. Summerfield couldn't help but stare at her and she reddened.

'What's wrong?' Summerfield laughed with enchantment, but Jeanne flushed darker, misunderstanding. 'I'm not pretty? I know I'm not the most beautiful—'

'No, no!' Summerfield shook his head and pressed her hands in his. 'You silly girl. You're—you're just *so beautiful*. I wanted to look at you, that's all. Make sure you were real.'

'*Well, I am*. And I was thinking the same thing, Harry. It's like—like being in a dream.'

'Then dream on, my love.'

'Yes—' Jeanne looked away, suddenly shy and a smiled burst upon her lips. 'I want this to last forever.'

'Come,' said Summerfield, tugging softly on her hands. 'Lie next to me. Close your eyes and rest.' Again she hesitated and Summerfield smiled. 'Just a few minutes—come.'

'I—I've never lain next to *anybody*.'

He pulled her gently, leading her to the side of the grove where the ground formed a gentle slope. He sat down and Jeanne, still standing, gave a little shrug of her shoulders.

'Come, my love. Sit. Please,' he said, putting pressure on her arm. It was like coaxing a foal. Finally, she gave in, bent down and turned to sit down beside him.

'I've brought you something. Here—' He probed carefully into his pocket and brought out a folded piece of wax paper. Jeanne looked at him, shy and inquiring. 'It's for you,' he said. 'It's nothing grand. Open it, Jeanne—be careful, though.'

Jeanne's fingers—so slender, he thought, observing how they moved—took the small packet and gingerly prodded the little flaps.

'It's like a little letter,' she grinned. 'One of your poems.' She had opened it fully, parting the folds with her fingertips like the petals of a flower. She peered and a little gasp escaped her lips. 'It's wonderful! So intricate—*I can't explain*.'

'The women here use it as a talisman.'

Jeanne nodded. 'Yes, Soumia has one. She says it protects her. But this—this is *miles* more beautiful than hers. It's lovely. Where did you get it, Harry?'

Summerfield looked at her and smiled. 'From somewhere I didn't expect at all.'

Summerfield lay back and she followed. Above them, they could see the clear blue sky beyond the canopy of leaves, the pattern of the sun on the shade. In the distance, a donkey brayed insolently for a few moments and then was calm. A bird fluttered noisily into the grove and chirped in surprise.

Summerfield let out a sigh of contentment and reached for Jeanne's hand. They clasped together softly and tightened. He watched the rise and fall of her body as her breath came and went, the little shiver every now and then and the pressure of her fingers around his. Unable to resist any longer, he leaned over and kissed her softly on the forehead, her eyebrows, the tip of her nose, her lips, her chin, her neck. Her breathing became rapid and she changed position, craning her neck for more. Her skin was salty to his tongue. Moving down, into the little hollow at the base of her neck, his tongue licked up the moisture in the V of her blouse—one button, one little ivory button separating him from the discovery of her breasts, one small, but tenacious barrier. Jeanne straightened then relaxed and Summerfield hesitated, wondering if this was resistance. Then down, a deft flick of his thumb and forefinger and the button gave, snapping open the thick, white cotton to reveal the hidden skin of her cleavage and the cream-coloured silk of her bra. She was pale in these parts. So striking the difference that Summerfield gazed in awe. She was breathing so deeply now that at every second breath her bra came away from her skin, a fraction of an inch, to reveal the dark aureole surrounding her nipple. Summerfield pushed inside, eager but tender, nudging away her hand that had suddenly come to rest on her chest, his free hand snapping open another button before she could resist and parting the material. It was as though he were watching his fingers through another's eyes, detached and fascinated as they worked their way across the plump little rise of her left breast, prising beneath her bra strap and edging across cooler and cooler skin towards the bud of her nipple. He touched. It was hard and erect, almost bursting. Jeanne whined and a moan escaped her lips. More space—he forced away the bra cup and slipped in his hand to encompass her breast. As he squeezed Jeanne shuddered, perhaps in pain, he didn't know, but it excited him.

'Kiss me,' she whispered. 'Kiss me.' Summerfield moved his head towards her lips and parted them with his tongue. 'Kiss my breasts,' she added, rectifying the request and Summerfield obliged, removing the encumbrance of her bra and flicking the tip of her nipples with his tongue, each in turn, then sucking, biting softly until Jeanne's body arched and rose from the ground and she let out a soft, girlish yelp. It was the first time any man, anybody, had brought her to that unique and heady summit.

For a long time they lay in silence, immobile. Summerfield's sex was stiff with desire for long, almost painful minutes before it subsided to a delicious state of semi-erection. He still held her hand, sticky with sweat, in his. Words of love came softly from their lips and it seemed, in that moment, that they would not be separated by anything. And then the time. A sudden panic with Jeanne rising to peer at her watch. A sigh of relief. Not yet. Still fifteen minutes before she had to get back.

'I don't want to leave you, Harry,' she said.

'Stay with me, then. You are—' Summerfield shook his head in amazement. 'You are a jewel, Jeanne. And I feel so damn humble before you.'

A wide, bashful smile shone on her lips and she shook her

head. 'No—you're the beautiful one, Harry. Really.'

'I thought we couldn't say that for a man,' teased Summerfield.

'I was thinking of the whole of you,' she replied, earnestly and then realised. A sound of reproach. And then her eyes grew distant, her face blank. She shook her head, sadly. 'I cannot stay. Must go back. Oh, *damn* school, *bother* exams.'

'What about the next time? When can we next meet?'

'And *damn* my father!' she added, desperately. 'It's like being a prisoner. And the war—it's all he ever talks about. They're preparing, Harry. It's a foregone conclusion. Official.'

Summerfield frowned, grew cold and focused. 'If it is, I shall have to return to England.'

'No,' she whispered.

'I've thought about it, Jeanne.' Summerfield shook his head and sighed. 'I have to go back. I can't stay here and watch.'

'It's not our war, Harry. It's the war of stuffy old politicians and madmen. Not ours.'

'The fact remains that I'm British and my country—*I don't want to fail her.*'

'And is dying for her the answer?'

Summerfield remained silent, perplexed—how could a woman understand that? he thought. It was somehow ridiculous, yes—but somehow…somehow *necessary.* 'Come with me, Jeanne. Back to England.'

'Not to England—*my studies.* Father intends to send me to France.'

'France? Don't you realise that *that's* where the war will be? No, come with me and we'll be free and alone to do what we want. You can study in England.'

'And see you march off. And wait endlessly until you come back—if you *do* come back. Oh, Harry!'

Summerfield exhaled noisily. 'I can't *not* go,' he added, finally. '*Don't you understand?*'

'No, I don't.' A silence overcame them, the twittering of a bird seeming entirely out of context, mocking.

'I have to go, Jeanne,' sighed Summerfield, at last. 'It's like a—*like a voice* from somewhere inside me. *Unexplainable.*'

'Harry—perhaps it'll all be called off. Perhaps they'll find a way.' There was a note of conciliation in Jeanne's voice, desperation even, and she leant closer, her hand gripping on his.

'You'll wait for me. Here. And I'll come back once it's finished and then we'll be together. It's simple!'

She looked at him, fear and love and longing mixed into one, and they drew together.

29

She was wearing a silver chain around her neck with the sweetest silver crucifix and next to it, hanging on a silver thread, the hand of Fatima. Summerfield watched her, almost in reverence, captivated at how such a beautiful being could exist at all, as she reached behind her neck and unclasped the chain. The movement accentuated the shape of her breasts through her blouse—her waist and flat little tummy. Summerfield looked on, smiling broadly. His head shook in wonderment. A sad little smile appeared on his lips as she stepped forward with cupped hands and offered him the necklace.

'I can't,' said Summerfield. 'It was for *you*.'

'Please,' whispered Jeanne. 'I love you so much, I would give you everything I have.'

'And I too.'

'I want you to wear it, Harry. I want you to be protected and with God's help you'll return safely from this stupid war that is coming.'

'And you, my love? Don't you think I am worried sick with the thought of you leaving for France? I feel powerless, ridiculous. With money I could take us both far away.'

'Money,' murmured Jeanne. 'My parents have money and they live in a pretence of happiness, a prisoner of it. Do you know why my father doesn't ask for a posting back to France? Because he wouldn't have his servants and his soldiers and his power. That's why.'

Summerfield pulled a face. 'Well, a little of it wouldn't do any harm. I'm looking for steady work, Jeanne—maybe teaching. I want to be ready for us. I want to offer you a good life.'

'You are my good life, my love. I feel so strong that all the annoying and bothersome problems that can happen have no effect. You lead me through my days, Harry. I am yours, for you save me.'

'Come,' said Summerfield, feeling as though his feet were
going to lift from the ground and send him floating among
the branches of the orange grove. He took her cupped hands
which she poured into his, sending the silver chain slipping
into his fingers. He kissed her softly on the lips and then her
hands. When he raised his head their eyes met and locked
with such intensity that he felt a fire rising from somewhere
deep inside his stomach, the flames of which licked his eyes
and made them shine with tears of happiness. He raised his
hand, letting the necklace trace the shape of her shoulders
beneath her blouse and she shivered. Then, brushing across
the open neck, slipping down into the smooth curve of her
chest and beyond, the silver wriggling into her breasts. Jeanne
giggled, squirmed a little and closed her eyes. She whispered
something he could not hear and he murmured something
back, equally as incoherent, the language of love, a noise with
more meaning than any word.

He wanted her, here, now. Wanted to violate this sweet and
innocent beauty with his manliness. Pulling her down suddenly
into the grass and dried leaves of the hollow, their lips met with
ferocity. He clawed at her blouse, her bra, forcing apart the
hindrance of clothing to seek her breasts, her belly, her armpits,
her mouth and once again her belly. Her hands gripped tightly
onto his shoulders, holding on as though afraid to fall into
some precipice without him. And then her skirt, a movement of
protestation, but his hand prised open her knees and slid upwards
into the overwhelming, intoxicating softness of her inner thighs.
Her sex was hot, her knickers drenched and his fingers slipped
beyond into her open cunt, her flower, the Sacred. Jeanne let out
a cooing sound, like a bird and the instinctive thrust of her pelvis
pushed against him. She came with a cry like a note of music
and called out his name. The silver necklace fell onto her belly.
Fumbling clumsily with his trousers, his sex lumbered forwards
into space and Jeanne stared momentarily at it with a mixture
of fear, surprise and expectation. And then he mounted her,
suddenly gentle, nudging her legs farther apart. Again their eyes

met, a fraction of a second, and he kissed her eyelids, each one, tenderly and he entered her. A gasp escaped her lips, a little cry and she winced. Softly, very softly Summerfield pushed into her and withdrew, pushed back and withdrew. The pain disappeared from her face, but she was still tense, still afraid of what would happen. He spoke in whispers to her, loving words that soothed and encouraged. She was tight around him and his sex quickly ached with a need to release its load. The surge of orgasm seeped inexorably up from his balls, buzzed along the shaft of his sex and gathered in force and energy at the base, ever swelling from the gathering charge. He gasped once, twice and withdrew from her to discharge over her thighs, his back arched, as if the wild animal were gripping onto the neck of its prey. Jeanne let out a little cry as she watched, a cry of awe more than anything else. Summerfield stared back, aware that his face would probably scare her and lowered himself onto her body with a kiss. There was blood on his hand—her blood.

'I have spoiled you, my love,' he whispered.

She shook her head. She was crying. 'You have made me alive. I'm *so* happy.'

'I totally, incredibly love you, Jeanne,' murmured Summerfield and in a spontaneous, unconscious gesture, took a linen handkerchief from his pocket and gently rubbed it across Jeanne's sex. 'Look,' he said, softly. She smiled at him, unsure and peered with him at the pinkish red stain on the cotton. 'This is your beauty—your passage into womanhood. I am honoured, my love.'

Conscious of their nudity, they quickly dressed, Summerfield giving her the handkerchief and turning his back as she tucked it into her knickers. Once finished, he took her hand and they sat together, knees drawn, leaning against each other.

'What if I'm pregnant?' she said, at last, her voice as surprised as it was fearful.

'No.' Summerfield shook his head, though wasn't entirely convinced he hadn't left a trace of him inside her. 'And in any case—I would love a child from you.'

She grinned, shyly and she rubbed against him, her hand

clutching his. 'If we had a baby, I wonder if it would be *métissé?*'

'A mix of colours?' Summerfield frowned.

'Some tell me I look like a Moroccan girl. And they all think it, I'm sure.' Summerfield looked at her for several moments, inquisitive. 'Come on, Harry,' she said, nudging him, her voice sounding weary. 'You've noticed how different I am from my parents. Even my school friends—apart from Sarah, and she has Jewish-Algerian blood. It's evident.' She shook her head, sadly. 'How stupid of me not to have noticed before—and those ridiculous comments from my father of how I had the Lefèvre chin, the Lefèvre nose—it was all so cruel.'

'Nothing is proven, Jeanne,' said Summerfield, momentarily lost for any pertinent words of comfort. 'Sometimes it's a natural reoccurrence—you know, like an ancestral reminder of where we all came from.'

'Will you still love me if it's true?' whimpered Jeanne, suddenly filled with self-pity.

'Oh, Jeanne. I will love you even more! Don't you understand? You're beautiful—*different*. That's part of why I'm head over heels for you.' He shook his head. 'I could *never* have married an Englishwoman. Not even a Frenchwoman. This skin you have, like a milky, tender olive—I could travel its surface for a lifetime and still wonder at it.'

Jeanne laughed. She kissed him, went silent and then squirmed. 'Did you say *marry?*'

Summerfield was caught by surprise. He turned his eyes to her and saw all the softness and beauty and hope in the world. He could see a future and she was in it. 'Yes—I did. I want you, Jeanne. *Marry me, then.*'

'When?'

'Now.'

Jeanne looked at him, her eyes startled then softening. He voice was hoarse, a barely audible whisper. '*Yes.*'

'Good. Then we are married.'

'What about rings?'

'*Damn!*' Jeanne laughed and Summerfield looked around him. 'We need a ring!' he said, rising to search the floor of the orange grove. 'None here.' Jeanne rose and joined in the search. 'Oh, bother. We'll have to do without, but—hold on.' He leapt across to the irrigation ditch and disappeared. A few seconds later he had reappeared, grinning broadly, and clambered out. Approaching Jeanne he held out his two, tightly clenched fists. 'Some species of animal offer gifts to their mates—a sign of love and of eternal togetherness. This is such a gift, Jeanne. Choose.'

'Which one?' said Jeanne, in incomprehension.

Summerfield shrugged his shoulders. '*Either*—they both mean the same, but are different. *Choose.*' Jeanne tapped his left hand and his fist turned in on itself and opened palm up. 'A pebble, Jeanne. This is my gift with which I now marry you.' Jeanne laughed in delight and took the small, round stone and held it to her lips. 'And this pebble is mine,' said Summerfield, opening his other hand. 'Kiss it, too, Jeanne. Give it luck and love evermore.'

Jeanne stepped forward, lowered her head and kissed the object in his palm. 'And now kiss me, silly!' she said, giving his shoulders a shake.

30

Lefèvre was sitting at his desk, working on two things simultaneously: the draft of the call for mobilisation in French Morocco—in fact, a modification of the one from Saint Louis, the French West Africa HQ in Senegal—and a letter to the *doyen* of the Sorbonne, an old school friend, requesting Jeanne's entrance to 1st year studies in October.

He stopped to lean back and stretch his aching shoulders. The fan on the ceiling had ceased revolving—hadn't noticed. *Damn*—no wonder he was sweating.

'Corporal—what's happened to the ventilation?' he called out and a muffled voice, an oddly out-of-place Corsican accent, called immediately back from behind the closed door.

'Electricity, Sir. It's the genny—ran out of juice.'

'Logistics is Dubrot's job!' snapped back Lefèvre, to no one in particular. 'A breakdown in the middle of the afternoon!' he added. '*Quel âne!* Corporal,' he called again.

'*Sir.*'

'Bring me some coffee. And while you're at it, bring me a native with a fan or something. *Monsieur* Bassouin will arrive at 4 p.m.—it's like an oven in here.'

'Yes, sir.'

The sound of the corporal's hobnailed boots resounded off down the flagstone corridor and Lefèvre carefully mopped the bridge of his nose behind his glasses. The envelope, with the translation inside, caught his eye and he suddenly remembered he had to hand it to Bassouin, something he'd forgotten to do at the house what with their conversation. He reached over, placing it on a corner of his desk, then, on second thoughts, replaced it directly on the edge in front of his two papers, making sure it was correctly aligned at a right angle to the wall. He sighed, exhaled a stream of recognisably overheated breath, and pondered over his two papers. Which one? he caught himself saying aloud, and chose the letter to the Sorbonne. He didn't want Bassouin to know he treated private affairs at the office.

A few minutes later, there came a knock at the door. It was the corporal. He entered, saluted, turned and tugged on the tunic of a native carrying somewhat maladroitly a tray with coffee in one hand, and a large, cumbersome date palm branch in the other. He advanced slowly, at a shuffle, so as not to upset the tray.

'Corporal—can't you just help the man out a little?' said Lefèvre with a scowl. The corporal returned the scowl, though directed at the native, took the branch from the man's hand and dropped it disrespectfully to the floor bedside the window.

'Thank you, corporal.'

'Yes, sir.'

The Moroccan placed the tray down and served tea, after which, to both Lefèvre's and the corporal's bewilderment, he picked up the palm branch and began to sweep the floor.

'You arse!' exclaimed the corporal, darting an apologetic glance at Lefèvre. 'I told you to fan, not sweep.'

'Perhaps, corporal, the man doesn't speak French. Where did you find him, anyway? He's not one of the usual boys.'

'The others are taking their nap, sir.'

'Nap!' exploded Lefèvre. 'When in God's name will they understand our way of doing things!'

'It's pretty damn hot, sir.'

'Well *we're* working, aren't we?'

'Just goes to show, sir,' muttered he corporal, meaningfully. '*Indigènes!*'

The native, standing quite still with the large branch in his hand, wore a look of total passivity.

Lefèvre seemed lost for a moment. '*Well show him what to do, corporal!*'

'*Sir,*' cracked the soldier, once more swiping the branch from the man's hand and immediately fanning the air. He finished off by stabbing a finger at him and placing the makeshift fan back in his hands. 'Now you. *Yallah!*' For a second or two the man's face was still a mask and then it broke into a broad grin to reveal a row of stained and uneven gums. 'Yallah!' said the corporal, once again and the man set to work, Lefèvre hastily placing paper weights on his documents before they scattered. The corporal left, closing the door behind him and Lefèvre went back to his letter, a little unsettled by having to share his office with an Arab—what did the British call them—*punkahwalla*: El Rifni's men could be anywhere.

Lefèvre finished the letter after hesitating somewhat over the closing formalities—didn't want to appear too familiar. After all, he hadn't seen de Frazenard for almost ten years. He sealed the envelope with the official stamp of the *République*, something that brought a sigh of satisfaction and flicked it into the out tray ready for posting. Turning now to the declaration of mobilisation, Lefèvre caught the native staring fixedly at him, something that sent an uneasy shiver across his shoulders. The scene with El Rifni still filled his thoughts almost permanently. He hadn't slept soundly since that night, his wife complaining that he repeatedly uttered the most alarming grunts at around 3 o'clock in the morning. In his office, Lefèvre rose, telling himself that his wife could jolly well sleep in the spare room, and opened the door to find the corporal asleep standing up.

'Corporal.'

'Sir,' said the corporal with a start.

'I'm opening the door. For the air.'

'Yes, sir. Pretty damn hot, sir.'

'Quite.'

Bassouin arrived at three minutes to four and walked straight in without knocking.

'They're massing troops on the Polish border!'

'What? Who?'

'The Germans!' replied Bassouin. 'I've just received a communiqué from Saint Louis.'

'I say!' Lefèvre sat quite rigid, uncertain what it meant. Even he had thought a solution possible.

'They say they're on manoeuvres, of course.'

'Well, that's a relief,' said Lefèvre, relaxing. 'We're not ready.'

'That's what they say—wouldn't trust Herr Hitler an inch of a thumb. Anyway—how are things?'

'Hot,' said Lefèvre, darting a glance at the native, who had stopped waving his branch. 'Dubrot got his lists in a twist.'

'That or the military pinched the reserve.'

'Hell—nobody informs me of anything!' squeaked Lefèvre. 'Good God, I'm in charge here! Who gave the order?'

'HQ in Saint Louis.'

'Well how do you know?'

'The advantage of working next to the communications centre, I'm afraid. I get all the latest sporting results before anyone else, too. Damn good of you to have lent me an office down there, Philippe-Charles. Most obliged.'

Lefèvre let out a grunt and reached for the envelope. 'Here, Bassouin—before anything else. I'm afraid I forgot to give it to you the other day. It's Wilding's translated report.'

'Thanks,' replied Bassouin, accepting the envelope. 'Let's hope we can find a way of working with our American friends. Might upset the British, though.'

'They'd deserve it,' said Lefèvre as Bassouin withdrew the document. 'They've already snapped up the Middle East.'

'Umm—untyped,' murmured Bassouin, pulling out the sheath of pages.

'It was in English.'

'Hand-written—quite neatly done.' Bassouin paused. 'Oh, dear. The odd mistake—masculine/feminine. Did Wilding do this? Didn't know he wrote French.'

'I had that British chap, Summerfield, translate it for us. Had the cheek to ask payment for it.'

'Well, for him it's work, I imagine. No—not at all bad. He was a copywriter, wasn't he?' Bassouin placed the papers back down on the desk, but Lefèvre didn't answer. 'What is it, Philippe-Charles—anything wrong?'

'Just looking,' muttered Lefèvre, leaning across. 'Hadn't bothered to take a peep at it before—thought it might be confidential. That—that writing…'

'As I said—quite neatly done, all told,' said Bassouin, frowning. 'It's a bit hot in here, that's true. Would you—'

'*Odd*,' said Lefèvre, abruptly, and shook his head. 'It reminds me…reminds me of something. Of—' Lefèvre suddenly sat down, ashen faced.

'Are you all right?' said Bassouin, himself leaning forward. 'Shall I get the corporal in here?'

'That writing. This is not Abrach's. Or even *El Rifni's*—it's *his*!'

'Summerfield?'

'The letters—this document: *the same hand-writing!*' wheezed Lefèvre.

31

They came for Summerfield just after dawn and the heavenly morning reminiscence of making love to Jeanne. He had just enough time to peer at the face of his watch—5.15 a.m.—before the front door imploded.

'What the!'

'*Debout*! Get up!' Rough hands gripped him and pulled him from under his sheet. 'Filthy bugger's stark naked, sergeant!'

'Give 'im his trousers.' Completely bewildered, Summerfield felt a bundle hit him and fall to the floor—his clothes. It was then that he fully realised the predicament and suddenly became bright red. 'Put 'em on, you dirty git. And quick.' Summerfield bent down slowly, with as much decorum as he could gather, and began pulling on his trousers as the gendarmes looked on. 'Bloody English and their weird manners—quick, I said!' repeated the sergeant. 'And you.' He turned to a corporal. 'Search the place. Get all the papers you can find.'

Once dressed, Summerfield looked on, helpless as the corporal and another gendarme systematically rifled his belongings—the chest of drawers, his desk, the kitchen hob, upturning the mattress and chairs, breaking his shaving mirror.

'I'm a British citizen,' he said at last. 'I want an explanation. I demand to be taken to the British authorities.'

'We know who you are. And the nearest British presence is in Casablanca, five hours' train journey to the north.' Summerfield dropped his gaze. 'No luck, Mr. Summerfield.'

The two soldiers came back from the writing room, their arms filled with stacks of paper. 'Found all this.'

'Good,' said the sergeant. 'Take it downstairs. And handcuff our *Anglish* friend here. You never know.'

'We're allies, sergeant. There's going to be a war and we're on the same side.'

'Oh, yes?' replied the soldier, flippantly. 'Passport and papers?'

'Over there,' nodded Summerfield, in the direction of his jacket.

'I'm arresting you, Mr Summerfield. We'll need to ask you some questions. Don't cause us any trouble.'

'*Monsieur* Lefèvre—the Administrator—he's a personal acquaintance,' offered Summerfield, lamely.

'And my old auntie's Edith Piaf,' said the sergeant, shaking his head. 'Come on—move.'

The street was eerily quiet, all windows shut. Summerfield supposed they must be watching through the cracks, fearful of the gendarmes. The sergeant got into the rear seat first and the corporal bundled in Summerfield next to him. The car, a small, khaki painted Hotchkiss, pulled away with a whine and disappeared around the corner.

Summerfield had already seen the police compound from the street—an art deco affair, much like an airport bungalow complex, whitewashed and with porthole windows. What he hadn't seen before was behind the building. The little Hotchkiss passed through the checkpoint and barrier and drew up in a wide arc in front of a series of roughly built, thick-walled blocks surrounded by rolls of barbed wire. They could have been houses from any of the local villages were it not for the bars at the tiny, square windows, hardly large enough for a child, let alone a man, to wriggle through. There was a well nearby and above it, housed in a derrick, a well-oiled winch that sent his stomach momentarily churning.

'Prison,' said the sergeant, the trace of a smirk across his lips as he saw Summerfield's look of fear. 'But first, we'll fill out some forms.'

In a cramped office adjoining the first block, a lieutenant was busy swatting flies. His khaki tunic was a single patch of sweat and his fair skin was blotchy red—obviously a recent arrival to the country. He turned upon the sergeant's barked arrival, the fly swat in one hand and his other, in a recognisable tic, reaching for his fledgling moustache and rubbing it for reassurance.

'Summerfield, sir.'

'What?'

'Arrest number 234E.'

'Quite—quite,' muttered the young lieutenant, in a daze. 'Apologies, sergeant. The heat—can't seem to get it together...'

'All the same in the beginning, sir. Takes a while.'

'And then you become as crazy as everyone else in this place,' said Summerfield, turning to the lieutenant, sure that he had found an educated equal.

'*Silence!*' shouted the sergeant.

'Lieutenant, I only want to—'

'Silence, I said!' Summerfield suddenly felt as though his stomach had been blown out. He fell to his knees and groaned like a wounded animal.

'Neupont!' it was the lieutenant's voice. 'Did you really have to kick him?'

'Sorry, sir—the heat. And that bastard had it coming.'

'*Enough*—help him up. He's a British citizen.'

They carried him to an armchair and sat him down. Bent double, Summerfield wheezed like an old man, desperately fighting for breath.

Still obtrusively holding the fly swat—Summerfield flinched, imagining through tearful eyes that it was a stick or something—the lieutenant came forward with a glass of water. 'This might help,' he offered, feebly. 'Sergeant—fetch the forms. I'm afraid you'll have to share with the natives, Mr Summerfield. Lack of space...'

Barely ten minutes later, Summerfield found himself on a foul-smelling earthen floor, worn as hard as concrete by successive years of occupation. He was conscious of two other people in the cell, though couldn't bring himself to raise his head and look. A long time passed, cut now and then by the low, growling voices and the sound of spitting. A couple of times, the balls of spit hit him on his shoulder and back, involuntarily or not, but Summerfield could only lay still, recuperating his strength.

Finally, he took a breath and with gritted teeth heaved himself up onto his elbows. The pain ebbing, his senses returned—notably his sense of smell and he grimaced at the acrid stench filling the cell. His eyes searched and found the dented and rusty bucket in a corner. Opposite it, their faces empty and their eyes full of resentment, were the two other occupants. Summerfield stared back at them, gave a slight nod of his head and pulled himself first into a crouching position and then upright, immediately thumping the ceiling with his head. This seemed to amuse his onlookers and they broke into a long, high-pitched cackle of laughter, only stopping when the guard cracked on the cell door with his stick. Summerfield stood, hunched in the centre of the silent space. The cell was bare but for the bucket, a bowl full of greyish water for washing, a pile of straw and the two other inmates. He sighed, turned in a full circle—something which brought a hint of curiosity to the two other faces—and gave a cheesy smile.

'What does one do in such a place?' he said in English. 'Eh?' He looked directly at them. 'What does one do?' The two men glanced at each other and Summerfield sensed them relaxing. He wasn't French—or Spanish. And had no quarrel with them. 'Salaam allikoum,' he said finally, placing a hand on his heart and bowing slightly.

'Allikoum salaam,' they said in unison, tied, by their tradition, to do no other than reply to the greeting.

Summerfield gave them a wry smile, once again looked around the cramped space and chose a spot as far away from the bucket and its rank content as possible. He tapped the ground with his boot, tested the wall and sat down. It was like this, in total silence, that the next two hours passed.

Prayer was said towards midday. It broke the monotony. Summerfield looked on, a spectator to the ritual, which still seemed so complex with its flurry of robes, bows, kneeling, standing up, kneeling again and chanting. There was almost something artistic in it, artistic and military in its well-defined execution. He nodded respectfully as one of the inmates caught his eye, though was thinking how wonderfully simple and pragmatic the Christian way of prayer was. And perhaps, how also devoid of commitment.

Prayer finished, the sound of keys clanged against the iron locks on the doors. Lunchtime. Presently, the door to the cell opened and an old Arab, flanked by an enormously gangly gendarme brandishing a truncheon, shuffled in and placed a bowl of rice on the floor followed by a large, tin mug of fresh water. The door closed again.

Much to Summerfield's surprise, and with a shocking disregard for the decorum of just a few minutes before, the two native inmates lunged forwards and began scooping out fistfuls of rice as though their lives depended on it. Any second thoughts on hygiene rapidly disappeared and Summerfield too stuck in, plying out wads of the gluey substance and cramming them into his mouth. Before the bowl was completely wiped clear, Summerfield deftly snatched away the tin mug and, looking steadily at the dumbfounded looks of his fellow inmates, was the first to gulp down the cool, fresh water to the halfway mark. Summerfield sat back on his haunches, feeling like a victor in the 100 yard dash, and in a majestic gesture, held out the mug to the others.

Sleep. He hadn't eaten in any great quantity, but the consistency of the rice (held together, it had seemed, by some sort of fatty paste), together with the heat, made his eyelids drop like a stone in water. Just a matter of time, he heard himself saying. *Patience.* In the evening, he'd be free of this terrible mix up. A loud fart started him, mid-afternoon—his own, involuntary and the result of having gulped the rice earlier on. The two others in the cell didn't stir, sleeping deeply. Summerfield's eyes closed once again.

At five o'clock, another clanging of keys, squeaking of doors and the faint waft of exterior air reaching them for a few, relieving seconds. Bread—luckily cut into three slices. At least they wouldn't have to grapple for it. More water. Which seemed to give the sign for the inmates to relieve themselves into the bucket. This they did in a most discreet fashion, squatting on their haunches, backs to Summerfield, pulling up their *jellabas* and deftly slipping their members from under their pants. When it came to Summerfield (he'd been holding it in for almost an hour now), the fact that he was wearing trousers made urinating seem the most obscene and flagrantly voyeuristic act. He had to stand up, of course, head bent, unbutton and then unleash his loud, sloppy jet into the nearly full bucket. The looks on the others' faces seemed to confirm the generally held local belief that the Westerners were a crude and rather barbaric race. Summerfield did not feel very proud and tried to make up for this by rapping on the door in order to empty the bucket. To no avail.

'The window,' said one of the inmates at last—the first words exchanged since the beginning of the day. Summerfield frowned and again the word was repeated, followed by a gesture of throwing.

Summerfield picked up the bucket with outstretched arms, making it all the heavier and more cumbersome to carry to the window. It must have contained a full five pints of urine and luckily for now, nothing else.

The window was set high, just below the ceiling and just above his shoulder level. He would have to give the container a mighty swing to get the contents out—and well-aimed too. He practised the gesture, taking great care not to spill any of the contents. The two other inmates prudently stepped back into the opposite corner. *One-two-three*—Summerfield launched the bucket—which immediately slipped out of his grip, thudding against the bars with a *WooOingg* as the contents slapped crazily around the circular surface, shot towards the bars and the open air and then decided to make a u-turn and flood both the cell floor and himself. *'Fuck, bollocks and fucking bollocks!'* thundered Summerfield, stepping back. Too late. A wave of the foul-smelling brew slapped full force into his chest. The inmates once again howled with laughter, but immediately fell silent upon observing the rage in Summerfield's eyes. He gave the cell door an almighty kick. *'Let me out of this fucking hole!'* There was no answer. Again he shouted, and again he gave the door a kick followed by a diatribe against the French, which finally resulted in the sound of footsteps in the corridor. The slit in the door snapped open. Summerfield found himself staring into the mad eyes of the sergeant, something that immediately silenced him. Neupont's upper face cracked into a hideous grin. A moment's silence and then a foul, gelatinous spray of phlegm hit him full in the face. Summerfield remained silent, in utter stupefaction, while the sergeant glared back at him with eyes filled with the utmost hatred.

'Sergeant?' It was the lieutenant's voice, in the corridor.

'Sir!'

'Is it our British fellow?'

'Yes, sir. One of the wogs attacked him.'

'Oh, dear.' The lieutenant's face appeared nervously behind the slit, sweating. '*Urghh*—the animals. They've covered him in—and what's that *awful* smell?'

'They chucked the piss pot at him too, sir.'

'You're a liar, sergeant,' said Summerfield, in a hoarse whisper, too dumbfounded by the man's dislike of him. 'Lieutenant—I need to change. Wash. And I demand access to a telephone— contact a man called Jim Wilding.'

'Quite,' said the lieutenant, glancing to his side and the sergeant. 'Um—sergeant thinks it's too dangerous to open the door. Might make matters worse. Wait for a bit and let things calm down.'

'I want to get out,' said Summerfield, controlling his anger and forcing out his words. '*Now*, lieutenant. You're not going to torture me—not like the others. I'm a British citizen. I need to contact Wilding. You see—I *saw* the winch.'

'Winch?' The lieutenant looked away, probably towards Neupont and pulled a face. 'A touch of heatstroke,' he murmured. 'Listen Summerfield, if there's anymore trouble meantime, call and I'll send a squad. I'm sorry—'

'I want you to let me out!'

'*Monsieur* Summerfield—'

'*Now*, you fluffy-chinned, useless idiot. *Don't you realise?*' shouted Summerfield. The lieutenant seemed frozen by sheer panic of indecision before the sudden outburst. It was the sergeant's voice, barking a reprimand, that made the young officer start. He gave a little shake of his head and shut the slit. '*Now!*' repeated Summerfield, but there was no reply.

He had never felt so enraged, so humiliated in his life. For an hour, he paced to and fro the length of one wall, demented with anger, a continuous stream of obscenities growling from his throat and occasionally erupting into fits of shouting. He failed to notice the token gesture of sympathy from his two cellmates who, extremely nervous, huddled together in the opposite corner, but who at one point tentatively rose to push the water basin towards Summerfield.

Food was not served. One by one, the other cell doors opened and closed but not theirs. The two Arab inmates wailed in protest.

'And what about us?' shouted Summerfield.

'Too dangerous,' came the reply. 'When you've calmed down.'

'I *have calmed down.*'

'Not enough! That'll teach you.'

And then night came. The smell in the room was unbearable. Occasionally, a ripple of hot wind blew in from the south, a nauseous wave swelling the stench into the very depths of Summerfield's guts so that he gagged. His fellow inmates stared at him in disgust and resentment—it was his fault they hadn't eaten—until they finally turned their backs on him and huddled down to sleep on the straw. Summerfield lay awake in the dark for a long time. His last thoughts were a question that kept nagging at him over and over—would Badr rescue him from the nightmare as he had done for Abrach? There came no answer.

5 a.m. prayer woke him up, an awful collective droning from the cells, far removed from the hypnotic, snaking chant from the city minarets. And then the door opening. A corporal was there, holding a bucket of water. Which he instantly threw over the supine Summerfield.

'You *pong*,' said the corporal, masking his nose.

'And you fuck off,' said Summerfield, weakly.

The corporal tutted melodramatically—he must have seen it

done in a film—and shook his head. 'No breakfast for you, I'm afraid. *Manners* is important.'

Another half-day of stench, monotony, near-vomiting from the smell and the now constant murmurs of protest from the two other inmates. But towards mid-afternoon a sudden scurrying, a sudden sound of boots on the earthen floor. The cell door opened and the corporal re-appeared, this time holding two buckets full of clear water. Next to him, a native, who bent down and laid two neat piles on the floor—one made up of a towel, a *jellaba* and a bar of soap; the other, two army billycans filled with food, bread and a mug of water.

'Get washed quick. There's a visitor. And you two—' he stared fiercely at Summerfield's fellow inmates. '*If you touch that grub—*'

The door slammed shut and immediately Summerfield grabbed for the soap and plunged his arm into the water. But then he stopped dead. No, he wouldn't wash. Let whoever it was breathe in the filth as much as he'd done. He wouldn't cover it up. So he ate, looking steadily at his two downtrodden inmates.

Ten minutes later the cell door opened, the corporal frozen to the spot, his eyes threatening to bulge out of their orbits. To Summerfield's surprise, in stepped Jean Bassouin who immediately let out a cry. '*Bon sang! C'est quoi cette puanteur!*'

'*C'est moi,*' replied Summerfield, standing up and grinning cynically. '*I'm* at the origin of this stink. Or maybe it's them,' he added, glaring at the corporal. Bassouin automatically offered his hand. 'No—don't shake it. You might catch something. I even revolt myself,' said Summerfield. 'And these poor bastards,' he said, turning to the two native inmates. 'They've had to put up with this for almost two days.'

Bassouin frowned, lost for a moment and then seemed to wake up. '*This is shameful*! An insult to France and the Republic—who the hell is responsible for this?' The corporal's upper lip began to shake, but he remained silent. 'Clean this filth—*immediately*!' added Bassouin, roaring despite his slight size. 'And inspection of all the other cells, while you're at it. Get the officer in charge.'

'He was on night duty, sir. He's sleeping.'

'Then wake the idiot up!'

The corporal ran off, leaving the cell door open and without guard. Bassouin seemed quite unperturbed, only stepping back into the corridor to gulp in a breath of clean air. 'Out you come, Summerfield,' he motioned. 'I most sincerely apologise.' And then, in Arabic, his words directed at the remaining inmates. 'You will have to stay here, I'm afraid. The cell will be washed clean presently.'

They walked along the corridor as the corporal and the young lieutenant, bleary eyed and with his shirt hanging out, arrived. The lieutenant was pulling furiously on his baby moustache.

'Unpardonable!' was all Bassouin said, the lieutenant's face turning very pale. 'Clean up that filth. I'll inspect the others after I've spoken to Mr Summerfield.'

Bassouin took Summerfield out of the cell building towards the administrative quarters and an office. There he gave orders for fresh clothes to be brought, for Summerfield to be lead to the shower rooms and for a guard to be placed at the door. On no account were they to be disturbed.

Summerfield showered blissfully, groaning with the simple but miraculous pleasure of water and soap. When he came out, he was given a towel and a uniform minus the insignia and his soiled clothes were taken to be washed.

Bassouin was waiting for him in the office with mint tea and biscuits. Summerfield noticed that he wasn't sitting behind the desk, but on one of the two chairs in front of it. Taking the other chair, he felt a surge of respect and friendship towards the man, mixed with great relief at finally being free from the cell.

'I am deeply grateful, Monsieur Bassouin—*Jean*. Thank you,' said Summerfield, finally. 'They wouldn't even let me contact Wilding.'

'And I apologise, once again, Harry. This was not at all desired and I deeply regret the treatment.' Summerfield nodded back and Bassouin recognised the look in his eyes. He gave a little flick of his head. 'Yes—and I shall see to it that those responsible are sanctioned.'

'Who gave the order to arrest me?' inquired Summerfield,

sipping on the tea. 'Lefèvre?'

Bassouin nodded. 'I was with him when—when he recognised your handwriting. The translation, you see—he put two and two together.'

'You don't seriously think I was responsible for the events.'

Bassouin raised an eyebrow. 'Directly, no—of course not. However, you *were* involved. A smart-minded lawyer could turn the indirect into the direct.' Summerfield opened his mouth to protest, but Bassouin continued. 'The ultimate outcome was an infraction into a leading official's home with intent to kidnap and assassinate. All the evidence leads to the conclusion that it was all part of some plot.'

'Maybe. But I swear I wasn't aware of Abrach's—El Rifni's— intentions. I assumed he just wished to talk to the Lefèvre family. I'm as much a victim in this as anyone else.'

'To what measure do you associate with El Rifni—or Abrach, as you call him?' Bassouin's voice had changed in tone to one of calm officialdom and it unsettled Summerfield. He felt himself withdraw warily.

'In the beginning I knew him as a patron. I was there to work for him. True—I grew to appreciate some of his traits. He seemed quite a philosopher—sort of bitter-sweet.'

'Like a man who had suffered and who had stepped back to take stock of life.'

'That's it. It appealed to me. And then, as my feelings for—for…'

'Jeanne.'

'Yes—grew… I came to see him as a competitor, a threat.'

'Didn't you realise the complexity of it all? The chances of success—for both of you—very slim indeed.'

Summerfield grunted ironically. 'A rich Arab and a poor Englishman—I suppose both of us were off to a bad start for Lefèvre's daughter's heart.'

'That's not exactly what I meant,' said Bassouin, sending Summerfield a reproachful glance.

'Yes, I know. I apologise, Jean. However, I can vouch for the sincerity of my own feelings towards Jeanne. I love the girl. And I believe she loves me.'

'It's rather delicate,' said Bassouin, lowering his gaze. 'You see—I *know* you're innocent. And Lefèvre, too, acknowledges the remoteness of you colluding with El Rifni in this affair. He is willing, Harry. Willing to let you free.'

'You mean I'm *not* free?' Summerfield frowned and put aside the tea.

'He is willing,' repeated Bassouin with a sigh. 'If you agree to put an end to your relationship with his daughter and return to England.'

Summerfield let out a cry. 'I don't believe it! We're halfway into the twentieth century and—and the idiot tries to bribe me. *With that!*'

'Rather old school, I must admit,' murmured Bassouin.

'No—eighteenth century!' added Summerfield. 'It's ridiculous, absurd.'

'But those are his conditions.'

'And a refusal on my part?'

'Then you'll have to stay here and let the incredibly dull and methodical administrative process take its course. An investigation. Questioning. Unfortunately, I believe some of their techniques are quite persuasive—could get a man to own up to anything.' Bassouin leant forwards and drew breath. 'Look, Harry. In all objectivity, if I were you, I'd accept.'

'I didn't expect you, of all people, to say that.'

'Accept and you'll be free. Don't you see?' Summerfield shook his head. '*Free*,' repeated Bassouin, as though the word were self-evident. 'If your love is so great, then nothing will stop it, will it?' A mischievous smile at once came to Bassouin's lips. 'Do you see?'

'You mean? But the deal is—'

'I propose you read Voltaire's *Candide*, Harry!' said Bassouin, with a gentle smirk. 'Please—try to be a little less naive. There are some things that no law can even attempt to control.'

'But—*principles*, Jean!'

'I'm not saying *do*. I'm saying *if*. *There* is all the difference.'

Summerfield sat back and gazed out of the window. A squad of native troops marched by in the near distance. 'I would like to take Jeanne to England with me. Away from the war,' said Summerfield, distantly.

Bassouin hummed. 'I'm afraid there will be no place to hide from *this* war, Harry.'

'Give me five minutes to think,' said Summerfield, after some moments. 'And then I'll agree.'

32

The gate opened with a rusty squeal and Summerfield stepped out, pausing slightly to turn and stare frostily at the guard as it closed back again.

It was mid-evening, Bassouin having immediately arranged for Summerfield's release some two hours before. He had even offered to drive him to his lodgings but Summerfield, soaking up his new freedom and desperate to enjoy the air, preferred to walk back.

The sun was low on the horizon, ready to submerge below the skyline and a cool breeze had blown in from the east and the mountains. Summerfield opened his mouth, almost lapping in the wonderful freshness and his gait took on a cheery swagger as he walked steadily past the police compound, through the barracks and housing district for the French administrative personnel of lower rank, and into the outskirts of the city.

In the distance, he caught a glimpse of the old city walls, their pale pink now ochre in shadow. He wondered what had happened to his flat, his belongings and hoped his neighbour, Abdlakabir, had had the wisdom to repair the lock and close everything up. He must repay the man, he told himself, and suddenly grew nostalgic—he would miss him when in England.

Turning past the outer limits of the expatriate quarter, with its schools and sports clubs, he began to concentrate on Jeanne and how he would approach the issue. Would she finally accept and agree to go with him to England? It seemed their only chance of being together in the long run. It would mean great sacrifice on her part: leaving her parents, her studies, her links with Morocco and her friends. All that for an out-of-work Englishman about to join the army and fight someone else's war.

The fact of thinking of her so intensely led him to alter his way home. He found himself heading for the *Académie* and the orange grove. Although only a matter of two days, it seemed a lifetime since the last time he was there. He wondered if there would be a note, wondered too if the traces of their love-making would still be there. His mind filled with her and his heart began to beat erratically and swell. He was in love—and it hurt not to be with her.

He crossed the square, hesitating for a moment to look at the dormant *Académie* building with its overly ornate gates, now firmly padlocked. His eye caught the regard of a beggar—strange to be here at this time of the day—and, further on along one of the avenues, a road sweeper, his head covered in a *cheiche* so that only his eyes and nose were apparent. Summerfield continued, up onto the grass verge surrounding the square and along the sandy path that forked three ways, one of them through the trees of the orange grove. In the distance, the sound of an engine choking into life. A lorry. He took no notice, and stepped into the grove. And then the sound of footsteps. He stopped, irritated. If it were the damn police again, he'd really go mad.

'*Look here—I've just been—*' he said aloud, turning on the footsteps. The beggar hesitated for a moment, his face caught between a snarl and a smile and then he stretched out a hand. Automatically, Summerfield searched the pocket of his army fatigues, forgetting he had been taken from his lodgings without time or thought to take any money with him. Just then the lorry appeared in view.

'I'm terribly sorry—' he began. The beggar's face turned ugly. 'I'm telling the truth,' said Summerfield, with determination.

The lorry drew up beside them. He frowned, glanced at the driver, back at the beggar and then froze.

'*Good God!*'

Suddenly, there were three of them on him, dragging him towards the back. He let out a shout and his mouth was immediately covered by a grimy hand. He resisted, his feet clawing at the ground, before the third man gripped his legs and he was carried, powerless, to the tailgate and bundled in. The lorry immediately bucked in a cloud of smoke and dust and pulled away. For a split second he pulled free, tugging on the tailgate and managing to pass his head and left shoulder free. His vision, in that second, was of the *Académie* and a slender shape standing before the gates, looking at him, her face white with shock. Was it Jeanne? *Jeanne!* He tried to shout but was wrenched back, his voice turning to a cry of pain. And then all was darkness.

33

It was the old knot tier, *Monsieur Quasimodo*, emerging from his rickety shelter in the orange grove, who stumbled across the young woman. He hesitated, momentarily lifting his cape from his head as though it would help his old eyes focus better. The shape he saw on the side of the road whimpered. An arm suddenly twitched. It was a European, he could see from the clothes. Frowning, he shuffled over.

Jeanne lay in a heap on her side. She was silently crying. The old man peered closer. The young face, pale, though not so foreign, streaked in tears and grime, was the saddest face he had ever seen. She was trembling. Again, he hesitated. He looked about him as though sensing trouble and made a clucking sound. His old arthritic knuckles reached down and stroked her hair. The girl flinched and for the first time, her eyes looked up and met his.

'I know who you are,' he said, mumbling in French. 'Do not be afraid, my child. Come. Get up now.'

Jeanne lay there for a long time, looking into the old man's milky eyes but seeing nothing. Her thoughts were an emptiness of desolation. She shook. They had taken him away.

'Come,' repeated the old man. '*Viens. Lève-toi.*'

She tried to rise, the effort triggering another spasm of tears. She felt so stupid. 'They—they took him,' she said, sure that the old man wouldn't even understand her. 'A lorry. Men.'

'I heard a row,' said the old man in his curious voice.

'Did you see them? Did you see them?'

The old man shook his head.

'We must phone the police,' whimpered Jeanne. 'He's in danger.'

'Was it your love?' asked the old man. '*The foreigner?*'

Jeanne's eyes widened. 'Yes. How did you know?'

'He is kind. He leaves me food, a little money, something to read when he comes to see you.' The old man grinned gently, showing his black gums. 'And he calls me *Sidi—Monsieur—*but not *Quasimodo* like the girls do.' He saw her sudden shame and cackled. 'And there is another man, a big man, one of us. He came to ask about you and your foreigner. His hands,' whispered the old man, suddenly holding up his own petrified claws, 'Were misshapen. Bent like the branches of a sickly tree. He tried to hide them under his sleeves but I saw them.'

'*Oh, God.*' Jeanne suddenly felt nauseous.

'You know him,' said the old man. 'He is dangerous, *n'est-ce pas*? Come. Let me help you, *M'moiselle.* You are suffering.'

When Jeanne arrived at her parents' house, her mother was waiting at the gate. Jeanne threw herself into her arms.

'They've taken him. It's so awful,' wept Jeanne as her mother helped her towards the house. Suddenly remembering, she turned to the police car. Her father was talking to the officials on the curb. Inside the car was the old knot tier. He was looking out at the rich houses, the well-kept gardens. He seemed confused. '*Merci,*' cried Jeanne. '*Merci, infiniment, Monsieur.*' Both her father and the policemen fleetingly turned their heads to look at her. Her father raised an eyebrow and scowled.

'Come, Jeanne. Come inside and tell me everything,' said her mother, squeezing her arm.

'You must order the police to take action,' said Jeanne's mother, once Lefèvre had joined them.

Lefèvre sat down opposite them and clasped his hands. 'The man is a scoundrel. Do you *realise*? Summerfield tricked our daughter into falling in love with both him and a criminal—a *known terrorist*. Summerfield's idiocy nearly got our daughter killed—not to mention me.'

'He is a citizen—a white citizen—a European and one of us. It is our duty, *Philippe-Charles.*' Her mother's voice was almost plaintive. Lefèvre's sharp features seemed to grow even more angular. He rubbed his head, re-arranging the few strands of brill-creamed hair across his scalp.

'Oh, bother,' he finally ceded. '*Of course* I'll give the order. It's my duty—*even for Summerfield.* But, don't be under any illusion—it was probably El Rifni. And if it was, then our young and romantic fool is probably now lying in a ditch outside town with his throat cut.' Upon this, Jeanne let out a loud wail and relapsed into a spasm of sobbing. Lefèvre looked uncomfortable, embarrassed. 'For God's sake, Jeanne, pull yourself together!'

'I don't think you realise,' said Mme Lefèvre, tersely, 'Just how deeply Jeanne felt for the young Englishman.'

'Well I hope it didn't go *too* deep,' replied Lefèvre, cutting short his wife. 'Do you really understand?' He raised his eyebrows, looking icily at his wife. '*Do you understand*?' he repeated.

His wife's jaw froze open. 'Oh, God. Please—*not that*!'

I'd never thought of it before, said Jeanne to herself, gazing up at the ceiling of her bedroom. The sedative the doctor had administered had made her drowsy and heavy limbed. I'd never thought of it. How, in the old times, a woman could actually die of a broken heart. And some actually did. Will I die? How great must sadness be to actually kill you? Does despair get so much, so choking, that it constricts the lungs, the throat? Or does the heart just refuse to go on living anymore? *I wonder…*

The bedroom door was locked—Daddy's idea. The window, since that awful night, barred. It was to protect her, but also themselves. She realised they thought she might do something stupid. And…the thought had in fact crossed her mind. Suicide or running away.

She should try to find him. She should. But truth was, she was scared. She had no idea how to survive outside. In fact, the country she had lived in for twenty years she hardly knew. Through all her books and studies, she could rattle off the *départements* in France, the postal codes of all the main cities, historical facts from Pépin le Bref to Napoleon III, the streets of Paris and where the chic shops and stores were located. But she had only ever been to Paris twice in her life. In truth, she was a foreigner in France and a foreigner in French North Africa. She felt so alone, so weak and lost and useless. She felt the nausea overcoming her again, the same sickening rush of bile as when that feeling of fear seized her stomach and made her gasp for air. It came suddenly and she leant over the side of the bed to retch into the bucket Soumia had placed there. She called out then stopped herself, feeling totally miserable. *I want to die*, she whimpered and began crying herself to sleep.

34

For a long time, blindfolded, Summerfield lay on the floor of the lorry, bucked and thrown, the roaring and whining of the transmission hammering his ears and head. He had no idea where they were heading and after an initial attempt at tracing the path of the lorry in his mind, he gave up. All he could think of was Jeanne and the look of total incomprehension on her face as she saw him and he was filled with the sickening sense of panic that he would never see her again.

In the darkness, time took on another dimension. It dragged tortuously on, as though he were wading against strong current. Was all this Lefèvre's doing—some Machiavellian plot? Or was it Abrach out for revenge for what he'd done? He could not move, his hands bound, his body wedged tightly between what he took to be a wooden crate and the weight of someone's legs pressing down on him. He wanted to shout, to run, but couldn't. He thought of Bassouin, of Jeanne and of Wilding. For some strange reason, his mind played the nasty trick of jealousy and he imagined the latter two, meeting up, Jeanne in a state of panic, Wilding only too willing to offer a consoling shoulder and then…The thought of losing her was agonising and Summerfield fought, without much success, to wipe the images from his mind. In the end, he gave up, sliding into the inevitable, his mind flailing futilely one last time before he sank into a profound sleep.

When he woke, there was silence. Only the sound of the wind, fresh, as it buffeted the tarpaulin of the lorry and whistled through the cracks in the wooden floor. He stirred, tried to stretch as best as he could and shivered in the cold air. There came a murmur of voices from outside his blackened and closed little world.

Suddenly, he felt himself being rolled on his side and hands reached down to grab him. He was dragged roughly to his knees and the thought came to his mind that he was to be executed, left there miles from anywhere, bound and rotting beneath the sun. His heart thumped audibly in his ears and raced so fast that he became breathless. A whimper escaped his lips and behind the blindfold, thick tears began to soak into the metallic smell of the material covering his eyes. He felt hands untying the knot, the darkness clearing and then the breathtaking pincushion of a moonless, star-studded night sky. So they wanted him to see it all, the thought came to him, the end: *the bastards.* Then suddenly:

'Harry—how are you?'

'Badr—is that *you*?' Summerfield squinted into the darkness and a tall, thin shape appeared.

'It is me, Harry. Perhaps I can offer you some tea. We have travelled far.'

A few minutes later, Summerfield found himself sitting cross-legged opposite the young man who was serving him a glass of thick black tea, a vague and slightly ironical smile on his lips. Badr finished pouring and brought the glass to Summerfield's lips. 'Drink, Harry. It will do you good.'

'I could drink better if my hands were free,' said Summerfield, controlling his voice. The silence of the huge sky somehow commanded him to speak softly. He also wasn't sure about Badr and the situation. He thought it wiser to play neutral.

'It is unfortunate, Harry, but I must keep your hands bound until we reach our destination.'

'May I ask why?'

'So that your mind does not force your body to do something it would regret. You will be untied when we are safe—I promise you.' Badr leant forwards once more and let Summerfield sip from the glass. 'Perhaps you would also like a cigarette. You smoke, I believe.'

Summerfield nodded and remained sulky while Badr produced a packet, lit up and placed the cigarette in Summerfield's mouth. It was a local brand—black tobacco—and tasted like earth. He inhaled and, clumsily, he removed it between clasped thumbs. 'You know that you have committed a crime, Badr—you and your fellows here. The Americans would call it a kidnapping. At first, I thought it was Lefèvre's men.'

'Seen from another perspective, Harry Summerfield, you have been both abducted and saved all at once.'

'I had been freed. Bassouin intervened.'

'Bassouin is one of the better of the worse evils running our country,' said Badr. 'Though I imagine there were terms attached to your freedom.'

'Terms he recommended me to violate,' added Summerfield. 'You are worse than a band of thieves, Badr. Have you any idea of what my intentions were, what I had to do? You took me from her.'

'The Administrator's daughter,' grunted Badr, non-committal.

'Jeanne,' rectified Summerfield. He shook his head. 'You have absolutely no idea, have you?'

'I have an idea that Abrach was courting her when you took her from him.'

There was disbelief in Summerfield's voice. 'You know that's not true. You were the one who told me, Badr!'

'Perhaps I was speculating. It happens to a man, Harry.'

'Badr—what's happening? Why this? You've become bloody strange. And for God's sake free my hands—we're friends, aren't we?'

'Friends not yet, Harry Summerfield. And maybe never. We worked together and we have a certain mutual respect. But the word *friend* is invalid.' Summerfield pursed his lips and looked away, swearing under his breath. Badr offered him some more tea which he at first refused and then begrudgingly accepted.

They sat in silence for a while, watching as the other men— three in total—sat in the shadows of the lorry and smoked, talking in low, mono-syllabic voices around a tiny flame that occasionally peeped from its hole in the ground. Then Badr spoke, his voice changed, softer now and, thought Summerfield, less aloof. That was one thing that really annoyed him about the young Arab—an intellectual snob and from a poor background—the worst sort. And maybe, he added, as an afterthought, quite like himself.

'Harry—the world has suddenly changed and Abrach—El Rifni—has realised. I wonder if you have?'

'You mean the war?'

'The impact of it, Harry.'

'Britain and France will be at war with Germany.'

'The impact for *this* country, Harry. *Our* country. Have you thought of that?' Summerfield frowned and an imperceptible smile showed fleetingly on the young man's lips. 'I don't blame you, Harry. And for the moment, most of the French government in Morocco is also thinking the same. Nobody has actually thought of what it means for this land. Or for all the colonies, for that matter. This will be a war that will change the world.'

Summerfield nodded. It was true. Both he and all the rest of the Europeans were locked onto Europe, the centre of the world. For Badr and El Rifni, the centre of *their* world was Morocco. Summerfield frowned. 'You don't think we'll lose?'

Badr shrugged. 'Only Allah knows the outcome. And in any case, either way things will change. Both for the French and the British empires. You see—everyone suddenly needs us. The French have begun mobilising their North African troops, the Americans are promising future financial aid, Germans in white cotton suits have appeared asking for meetings with those connected with the nationalist cause.'

'You're a Socialist, Badr—and so are most of those in the independence movement. You can't seriously endorse a Fascist influence in Morocco.'

'Of course not,' said Badr. 'But we could accept their money and arms for the good of the cause.'

Summerfield grimaced and turned away. 'Even you have turned cynical!' he spat. 'And in any case, what in the hell has it all to do with abducting me? I demand my freedom. I demand that you take me back—*now*.'

Badr raised an eyebrow and poured some more tea in such a deliberate fashion that it appeared to Summerfield the greatest gesture of irony.

'I'm afraid that is out of the question, Harry. We have to keep you away from Marrakesh for a while.'

'How long is *a while*?'

'Only Allah knows,' said Badr, once again.

'Look—in all due respect,' replied Summerfield, irritated, 'leave Allah out of it and tell me. How long?'

'Two days or two years,' answered Badr, offering Summerfield his glass.

'What do you mean?'

'If Lefèvre is eliminated in two days' time, you will go home. And if it takes two years, then you will return in two years.'

'But I've nothing to do with that!' shouted Summerfield, unconsciously trying to stand and falling backwards. 'And what about the war? I've got to get back to England!'

'Some of your politicians are saying exactly the same as last time—that it will all be over for Christmas. Maybe you'll miss it, Harry.'

'This isn't at all funny, Badr.' Summerfield was pale with rage. 'You have no right to keep me here!'

'You know too many things about us, Harry. You cannot go back.'

'I *must* get back, Badr. Can't you understand? For Jesus' sake—I have to see Jeanne. I have to convince her to come with me to England.'

'I suggest you pray to Jesus to make things happen quickly, Harry. That is all I can offer. I will do the same to Allah—and hopefully, you will return to your love and your war the way you want it.' The young man rose then and began to walk back to the lorry. Summerfield let out a roar of frustration and anger. Badr shook his head, murmured something to his men and Summerfield's mouth was promptly gagged.

Towards late afternoon, the sun cooling to a copper globe two-thirds into its fall, the lorry came to another halt. Badr helped Summerfield onto his legs and he wobbled slightly before dropping down onto the gritty ground.

'We will not stay long, Harry,' said Badr, gently pushing him by the elbow. 'Pee behind the lorry and then come this way.'

Summerfield craned his neck to where Badr had gestured. Some fifty yards away was a small cluster of pathetic looking hovels—three lopsided shepherd's huts in a state of semi-ruin. He nodded begrudgingly, stepped behind the lorry and relieved his painful bladder.

Walking towards the huts, Summerfield wondered why Badr had chosen to stop in such a place. Perhaps it was to eat again, he thought. The first hut was empty, a large gaping hole yawning in one wall where the mud bricks had crumbled. He caught a glimpse of a flapping strip of material and the frame of an old cupboard before he felt Badr squeezing his arm and leading him on. The second hut, one wall painted a fading pea green, looked in sturdier state. Badr stopped before the weathered door and gave Summerfield a slight push.

'Please go in,' he said, loosening the gag on the Englishman's mouth and urging him on with a flick of his head. 'And close the door behind you. We will leave in five minutes.'

Summerfield looked mistrustfully back at the young Berber. Again Badr motioned with his head. Summerfield stepped forwards, lifted his tied hands and pushed. He slid inside the cool dark interior and with difficulty turned and closed the door, a last slit of light and Badr's face promptly shut out.

'Harry,' came a voice.

'Abrach?' His heart missed a beat. 'Is that you?' Summerfield looked into the darkness and became aware that several small candles were emitting a feeble light.

'I am here. Sit.'

At last, his eyes growing accustomed, Summerfield discerned Abrach's large shape sitting in a corner on—of all things—a red leather armchair one would normally find in a hotel lobby. One of its armrests was disembowelled and its stuffing flowed out. Immediately, Summerfield noticed the merchant's hands, their odd shape wrapped in two great wads of cloth like a pair of boxing gloves. He looked into his eyes—sad, weary eyes—and sat down on a wooden box.

'Abrach—*Abslem*—you must get me out of this.'

'No salutations, Harry? I believe we were once almost near to friendship. Is this how you greet your benefactor after so many weeks?'

'And I believe our working relationship finished some time ago too,' said Summerfield, stonily. 'Are you going to kill me?'

'What for?'

'Because I know too many things.'

'Not as many as you could imagine,' replied Abrach, a spark of his former self punctuating his weariness. 'No,' he added, looking down. 'No, I will not have you killed—how could I do that to a man who helped me. No, just remove you for a while, that's all. Somewhere safe.'

'Safe for you,' said Summerfield. 'Don't you remember? I was going to leave this bloody country in any case. There's a war to be fought.'

'*Your* war. If you still hadn't realised, Harry, *our* war has been going on for nearly forty years.'

Summerfield remained silent, suddenly tired of letting himself be drawn into argument. 'I suppose I should enquire how you are, Abrach.'

'Abrach or Abslem, whichever, Harry. Rather than me commence, tell me yourself. How am I?'

'You're being cynical, Abrach,' said Summerfield, surprised by the merchant's tone of voice. 'You never were.'

'We change.'

'Yes.' A silence. 'We change.'

'So tell me, then, Harry Summerfield. What do you see before you? Do you see a man proud of the business he managed to build? A man more or less tolerant and content?'

'How am I meant to interpret this irony, Abrach?' shrugged Summerfield. 'It speaks for itself. I see your clothes, dirty and worn and the way they tell me you have lost weight. I see your face that has lost its shine—a beard where a neatly clipped moustache once made you look like a Hollywood film star. Is that what you want to hear?'

'Is it not the truth?' replied Abrach. 'Do we not judge by what we see?'

'You were a fine and intelligent man. A merchant and a benevolent and most generous man.'

Abrach laughed softly and his eyes glittered with reminiscence. 'I remember the times we walked and talked, Harry. They were good times. I was like a teacher and it was amusing to see how you got along.'

'A good student, then?'

'A good student, yes,' said Abrach, tilting his head slightly. 'But it is over. And I am no longer a merchant. They ransacked my shops, burnt and stole my stock. They even confiscated what I had in the bank—they can do anything they want if you are an Arab or a Berber.'

Summerfield grunted. 'I can believe that. They made me wallow in my own shit in prison for three days—a *European*—so I can believe, all right.'

'So you see, if you were to ask how I am, Harry...I would reply that I have lost many things: my family, my wealth, my identity, my house, my shops, even the use of my hands. And I fear, Harry, that I am also losing my faith in humanity. My look upon this world is no longer one of wonder and enchantment. It is not with generosity that I look upon people. And while I lose these things, I feel that I am gaining something else—call it cynicism, call it disgust. Harry—however hard I try to fight these new possessions, I know that I cannot win back the old Abrach, the old Abslem. It is terrible, Harry—but I can feel that vengeance will win my soul. I cannot stop it.'

'It will lead to killing,' said Summerfield, tiredly.

'And probably to my own death,' added Abrach. He sat back and raised his head a little, as though contemplating the moment it would come. 'So before the last of any good of me goes, I want to thank you for the past and all the good moments and your work—and of course your help. The fact that we are both foreigners here bound us together, I think. And now I ask you to accept your imprisonment. Badr will see to it that it will be as free a sentence as is possible.'

'Weeks? Years?' said Summerfield. 'And this?' he added, holding up his tied wrists.

'Only you can know,' replied Abrach, irony in his eyes. 'When you no longer wish to escape you will realise that you are free.'

'Riddles,' said Summerfield, shaking his head and grimacing.

'Life is often made up of them,' answered Abrach. 'Have you not discovered that yet? Go now. You will hear my name, no doubt, but you will not see me.'

35

Once again, Summerfield found himself on the floor of the lorry as it jolted along an endless series of dirt tracks in the now total darkness. Again the anger came back to him with the realisation that Abrach had had no intention of setting him free. His rage lasted a long time and he bit so hard into the material binding his mouth that it was soaked in his spit while his tongue was now as dry as the sand and dirt on the road.

The hours passed and at last his anger faded to a feeling of bitter acceptance. His mind turned to calculating. He judged they had been driving for five hours in all since the halt with Abrach. They hadn't slowed. There hadn't been any police checkpoints. Obviously, Badr knew the terrain and had taken to the remote paths worn through the rocky, sandy gravel plain over the centuries by caravans and nomads. And while the noise inside the lorry was almost infernal, he knew that the vastness of the space outside would swallow it up. No one would hear. Where could they be taking him? The hills? Maybe Abrach's village? No—they'd gone too far for that. And not in the same direction. The position of the North Star had told him that. They were heading inexorably south east, despite the twists and turns due, no doubt, to obstructions on the tracks. They would have to stop, sooner or later, for petrol, thought Summerfield. And then maybe a chance of getting away. It was a hope. For the next hour, his mind set about planning the best course of action, all the time his eyes fixed steadily on Badr, perched on a tarpaulin above him, observing the darkness. It was not to be. The dreadful monotony of the trip even overcame the noise and little by little, no matter how hard he fought, Summerfield's eyes closed shut and he fell asleep, long before the lorry began the steep climb into the mountains.

He awoke, shivering, well before dawn. Carefully, he edged his head to a position where he could see a little over the tailgate. The immediate view was one of a blackened mountainside dotted with the shadows of trees and, beyond that and further into the distance, a series of crests and tops, black and jagged against the petrol blue sky. The silence was both powerful and at the same time frail in the dimness. There was a slight haze in the air, the morning mist of the Atlas Mountains. He turned to look at Badr and immediately one of the young man's eyes popped open. He nodded with a vague smile, though Summerfield did not respond. He was angry again—angry at having slept through the possibility of escape.

Badr approached, which seemed to give the sign to the others to wake and begin preparations for breakfast. The young man stooped down, drew back and seemed to look at him with an air of regret. Summerfield frowned.

'Come, Harry. Please join us for breakfast. I'm afraid you'll have to wear our clothes—though I believe you are used to them. Indeed, you like them.'

'Why?' attempted Summerfield from behind his gagged mouth. Again he frowned.

'Your clothes are dirtied. You've pissed yourself, Harry. It is not your fault. Come.'

Summerfield felt wretched, but at least he was in clean clothes.

'You'll need a *cheiche*, too,' mentioned Badr, squatting near the driver who, frying pancakes, was observing Summerfield curiously from above the tiny flames of his fire. Badr climbed into the lorry for a few moments and reappeared. 'Here,' he said, offering his two hands to Summerfield. 'Blue or black?' Summerfield didn't look up and reached out to take one. 'A true *homme bleu*,' said Badr and laughed.

They ate *msemen*—pancakes soaked in honey—washed down with bitter-sweet coffee and Summerfield felt better. After a while, his shame overcome, he raised his eyes and met those of his captors. They showed neither mockery nor interest, their only preoccupation being that of eating and they returned Summerfield's regard with encouraging nods directed at the rapidly diminishing pile of pancakes.

Once replete, Badr snapped a command and the little band of men began at once to gather their belongings and cover up the traces of their halt. The lorry was loaded and Badr helped Summerfield, his hands once again tied, up onto the tailgate and into the back. A last check to see that nothing had been forgotten and Badr gave the order to continue. The lorry was started using a crank and spluttered into life with some difficulty due, no doubt, to the thinning mountain air. The frail, yellow headlights seemed to struggle with the mist, swallowed after ten metres. Within three minutes—the time it took for the engine to turn regularly—they had ground into gear and were bouncing perilously upon a track that lead straight up the slope of a mountain valley.

Once again Summerfield found himself in the position of captive, the brief moment of camaraderie born of a common hunger now forgotten. He was forced back down onto the floor of the lorry, jolted painfully for some minutes then struggled up, despite Badr's command to the contrary, to search a place among the baggage. Badr's eyes were full of anger at Summerfield's show of rebellion and Summerfield returned his stare, his own eyes filled with resentment. It was Badr who finally dropped his eyes, his mouth twisting cynically.

The track rose steeply into the flank of the mountain and continued straight onwards, defying the sheer slope and rocky outcrops. Top heavy, it leant outwards towards the empty precipice on its chassis at a worrying angle, intending at any moment, it seemed, to topple over and crash down into the valley floor.

Summerfield closed his eyes and offered a silent prayer and when he opened them again, Badr was grinning at him.

'Each to our own religion,' shouted Badr above the noise of the engine.

'There is only one God,' returned Summerfield. 'Even for an atheist like me.'

'He comes even to the most disbelieving—when they *need* and when they *want* Him.'

Approaching the crest of the valley, the little lorry pained and struggled on a last outcrop and then stalled. A stream of abuse, followed by a stream of excuses for such foul blasphemy came from the driver's cabin. The sudden silence was strange, immense and all-embracing, as though some silent hand had suddenly taken them in its huge palm.

'Start the engine,' ordered Badr, irritated, conscious of the effect of the silence on his men who seemed to baulk.

Once again the lorry spluttered into life, sliding back as the driver missed gear. Summerfield shouted in alarm. An awful grinding and the driver finally punched into first, pressing down with force on the accelerator. The lorry bucked forwards, slewed, slammed into a deep rut and stalled again. Another stream of abuse, this time Badr's voice rising above the rest to threaten the driver. He jumped down, removing a revolver from under a sack and with a nod towards Summerfield handed it across to his companion. He disappeared round the front and an argument flared up. Summerfield heard the dull thump of the young man's fist on the driver's head and then there was silence.

'*Yallah!*' ordered Badr and the engine automatically chugged into life. The driver waited, gunning the engine and then— Summerfield supposed Badr had walked ahead and was directing operations—hit the accelerator. The lorry lurched forwards, sending Summerfield crashing painfully into the tailgate. The lorry bounced once, twice against the rock and lurched third time over with a great *thhtongg* as the leaf-spring suspension hit the chassis and then sprang back into shape. A cheer rose up from the cabin followed by a wild burst of laughter—a sign of released tension. The driver's voice rose above the rest and gave thanks to the Almighty for having helped them on their way. Badr reappeared, having rapped the driver's door with his fist, a sign to move on. He hoisted himself up into the back of the lorry, gave Summerfield a brief glance and lit a cigarette. After a while, he glanced again and, catching Summerfield looking at him reached across and let the Englishman take a pull. They grinned.

Dawn came without them noticing and cast a purplish veil over the mountain side, enough to make out the trees and vegetation. Somewhere down in the valley a dog barked and a distant sound of prayer whined eerily up from an unseen village. From the back of the lorry, Summerfield peered out and saw a distant light flicker and fade—the first fires were being lit.

Not long after, the sun began to rise and the black silhouettes of the mountains were suddenly projected upon them, seemingly within hands' reach. Summerfield's jaw dropped and he moved instinctively forwards towards the tailgate. His captor moved with him, but a glance from Badr, understanding what was happening, sent him back to his seat. Instead, Badr knelt down beside the Englishman, steadying him with his arm.

'It is grandiose, is it not?' said Badr, gravely, but Summerfield didn't reply.

He had never seen anything like it. And when, suddenly, the sun peered over the crests, hovered hesitantly for a few seconds then burst into the valley, Summerfield felt a strange, exhilarating surge of emotion rush suddenly from feet to head and his eyes filled with tears.

'Don't worry,' said Badr, his voice unusually gentle. 'You've been through a lot in the last forty-eight hours.'

Summerfield shook his head, wiping his eyes. 'It's—it's so bloody beautiful. Almost as beautiful as England's hills,' he added, hard again. Badr looked at him, paused then nodded a wry smile.

As they drove on along the rough track, level against the hillside now and then down into a higher valley, Summerfield's eyes were filled with a glorious pastiche of colour—rich pink, emerald green and the clearest sapphire blue he'd ever seen. There was something there he couldn't quite put his finger on— something in the air and light and he felt confused. Before he could realise, the trauma of the last few days seemed to evaporate from his mind. Jeanne appeared, her face as clear and present as the mountains, and he felt sure, quite absolutely sure she was thinking of him at that precise moment. They loved one another and it was going to be all right.

The sun was midway in the morning sky—Summerfield judged it to be around 9.30 a.m.—when the lorry stopped on a small plateau and Badr unbolted the tailgate. He beckoned for Summerfield to follow him. Standing next to the young man, he followed Badr's outstretched hand towards where the track petered out and disappeared to a steep, rocky path.

'This is where we're going, Harry Summerfield. We have two days' walking ahead of us before we arrive.'

They began to unload the lorry and before it was completed a team of mules appeared on one of the paths high up where a deep gully formed a gash in the mountain side. Badr went out to greet them, scaling the steep little path with small, rapid steps until he reached them. There were four mules in total and two tribesmen, dressed in pale blue robes and armed with rifles. Badr spoke with the muleteers for a few moments and Summerfield thought he saw him nod in his direction. He watched them, strangely thin shapes—the effect of the sharp perspective—descend the path with precaution until, barely a hundred yards from him, they took on their normal form. When Badr wasn't looking, one of the muleteers gave Summerfield a hostile grin and, levelling the barrel of his rifle at him, mimed a shot.

A long, strenuous ascent for the first two hours left Summerfield breathless and sweating and somewhat angry. His captors, taking the opportunity to brew some tea and smoke while he recovered, didn't seem in the slightest bothered by the rugged terrain. He felt useless and weak—a westerner among these men built of pure muscle and sinew.

The journey began again, through a pass in the jagged crest and then down, following a vertiginous goat track of loose stone. Several times he slipped and, unable to stabilise himself with his arms, fell painfully on his back—something that produced howls of laughter from the muleteers. The track led to a large rounded belly of smoothened rock, which they crossed, this time Badr holding Summerfield by the arm, until they reached the valley floor.

This they followed for another two hours or so then, once more, they took a track up into the next mountainside. The same pattern of events repeated itself throughout the day—a steep climb followed by a perilous descent followed by a valley and then another steep climb. Once they crossed a small wood and cement bridge over a torrent that in winter would have swollen and raged a full four metres deep. One of the mules stopped half way, refusing to go any farther, frightened by the height and rushing water. It took four men, two pulling and two pushing, and a full fifteen minutes, to finally get the beast moving.

Towards the end of the afternoon, after a long break to rest during the hottest hours, they entered a gorge and followed the winding path of the torrent for a mile or so before it opened out into a wide, undulating valley. It was then that Summerfield noticed the little shapes, spying them from a distance—children. Heads popped up from behind rocks or looked out from tree tops, but they never came close and when Summerfield caught their gaze they immediately drew back like crabs scampering back under rocks, coy and frightened. Perhaps, wondered Summerfield, they had never seen a white man before—quite probable given the remoteness of the valley.

It was a sign that they were approaching a village—perhaps their village—and a feeling of relief and even gaiety filled the men. They picked up their step, drew back their shoulders and took on the nonchalant air of warriors returning from patrol— something that made the little children, dotted about the hillside, giggle with pleasure. Summerfield muttered under his breath at their joy. He had lost weight over the past four days, looked grey from tiredness and worry. Approaching the village now, suddenly appearing from out of its mountain camouflage, he felt almost ashamed of himself. He looked like a criminal, his hands tied and his look haggard.

The village was a large collection of mud and wattle houses, stacked one upon each other on an earthen outcrop to one side of the valley. Crowning the village was a Kasbah and a large, imposing granary. The village was the colour of the mountains, pinkish beige, and seeped into them unnoticed if it were not for the windows with their white surrounds.

It was a rich valley. Summerfield imagined that many thousands of years ago, a glacier had pushed its way between the mountains and deposited a deep layer of sediment and rock which, through time, had created the patchwork of flat pastureland and large protuberant mounds—boulders covered with luscious grass and trees. A system of irrigation channels branched off from the now shallow torrent and formed the irregular rectangular dykes marking parcels of laboured land containing almond trees, maize, carrots, turnips, olive trees and wheat. Here and there, wells had been bored and women and young girls, sometimes with the help of mules, carried water or bundles to and fro between the fields and the village. When the group of men passed, they either refused to look at him or else their regard displayed an immense distrust, almost fear. Curiously, there were no men or boys. Summerfield called to Badr who was walking at the head of the band of men.

'Talking,' replied Badr, looking over his shoulder. 'Or doing business. The boys? They are the heads you see from behind the rocks—they are shepherds.'

'But why do the women do all the carrying?'

Badr stopped and turned to Summerfield, a little perplexed and obviously wondering if it was criticism. 'Because it is their role,' frowned the young man. 'And because the men leave for the towns to earn money. This is how it has been for a long time. This is how it is.'

'And schools?'

'There are no schools, Mr Summerfield. Not here. There is a Mullah. But the Berbers have an oral tradition and can remember all that is passed down in history. But there are some boys who are taught to read the Koran.'

'Like you.'

A trace of a smile came upon the young man's lips. 'Like me,' he echoed. 'The Mullah took me as his student—he is rather disappointed that I didn't return to take his place.'

'He's still in the village?'

'He's very old. And even less tolerant than he was before,'

grinned Badr. 'You will see. He tests me as if I were still eight years old. And he will test you, no doubt.'

'I can't wait,' said Summerfield, with irony. 'And what about these?' he added, nodding to his bound hands. 'I feel like a criminal.'

Badr dropped his gaze and resumed walking for some moments without looking back and then stopped again. He approached Summerfield, produced a knife from under his gown and deftly cut the rope, finishing it with a glance that carried a warning. 'If you try to leave us, I'm afraid you will be killed, Harry. It is like that.'

Several dogs began to bark as they entered the foot of the village and a mule brayed indignantly. Badr swapped blessings with several men they came across, speaking a dialect in which Summerfield could hardly pick out several words. They were pointed towards the summit of the village and the Kasbah.

'Good,' said Badr, turning to Summerfield. 'The *Kaïd*—the war chief—is here and expecting us.'

The winding track led up past forty or so squat houses to a small clearing, evidently the place for ceremonies of different sorts and a bartering space for passing caravans. Several olive trees gave shade and it was under one of these that Summerfield sat for what seemed like an eternity before a messenger arrived with an invitation to enter the Kasbah. Summerfield rose and was escorted by the two armed muleteers, Badr having stayed ahead to speak with the Kaïd.

The Kasbah was almost a village in itself. They entered through an archway and an enormous, sculpted door. Summerfield glanced up at the imposing walls of the fortified house, immediately conscious that the Kaïd and his family were not only people of high political importance, but also extremely wealthy. It was the only group of buildings in the village to have glass windows, for the most part a thick, opaque green, while the central tower contained more intricate patterns of various blues, greens, reds and yellows. The walls were made of the same pinkish beige wattle as the houses in the lower village, but crowned with a series of symmetric patterns made of squares and diamonds.

Summerfield was escorted through a series of extremely narrow corridors, some open to the sky, some enclosed by a section of planks and woven date palm leaves to form a roof. A final corridor gave out to a small courtyard, which they crossed, disappearing into a pokey, rather lopsided aperture in the farthest wall. This led immediately to a steep set of stairs and a first level— empty—then a second, containing several old women who didn't bother to cover themselves. A third, then a fourth set of winding steps led to a large, furnished room lit by green, red, blue and yellow beams flooding inwards from the windows and lighting up the swirling cloud of dust particles in the air. Summerfield's immediate reaction was to wrap the lower part of his headscarf around his mouth and nose, as though confronting a sand storm and he stood there, his two guards behind him, in the middle of the room and waited.

A few moments later Badr appeared and beckoned for him to follow through another doorway. Summerfield discovered the floor of the adjoining room to be covered with carpets, in some places forming several layers and mostly blue or yellow and decorated with the strange, almost runic designs of the Berber culture. There were cushions, too, a chimney, a series of large chests where Summerfield imagined the bedding and valuables to be stored and an intricately carved mahogany table inset with mother-of-pearl; around it, four squat chairs, of French design, looking oddly out of place. But even more striking, even more ostentatious, was the central piece in the room—a very large and ornate oak wood wireless set. It looked like a cross between a gothic church steeple and a Bentley Speed 6 radiator grill. And it was not plugged in—for the simple reason that there was no electricity. Summerfield stifled a grin, turned to the Kaïd sprawled in his chair and followed the man's restless eyes back to the wireless set. He had the distinct feeling that if he laughed now, it would be his very last.

'This is the Kaïd, Ahmed Youadi, the chief of the entire valley as far as the eye can see,' announced Badr, in a low, respectful voice. He turned to Summerfield. 'He is a very powerful man, Mr Summerfield, naturally very wise and also very lacking in patience. Believe me—it is best to keep to the law of the valley.' Summerfield's eyes returned once more to the chief and he nodded slightly. Ahmed Youadi—a small, bearded, muscular man in his mid-fifties—made a gesture of welcome and followed it up with a tersely spoken declaration in local dialect. 'He says he hopes you will learn to understand us,' translated Badr. 'And abide by the rules of our religion and of our tribe. Until then you have only two simple things to do—eat the food he offers you and obey the words he speaks to you.' Badr kept his gaze levelled at Summerfield. 'You may now thank him.'

The trace of a frown appeared on Summerfield's face and then he turned to the chief. 'Thank you. And may God guide me in His wisdom.'

Chief Ahmed Youadi answered, rapid and unsmiling. Summerfield looked enquiringly at Badr. '*And may Allah provide Ahmed Youadi with tolerance,*' informed Badr, a hint of a smile appearing on his lips.

36

Jeanne lived in an unreal and relentless dream. Her health alternated between the deepest depression and an emotionless resignation that her life was worthless. She had never felt such emptiness could exist. A physical emptiness for Harry that rose up from the depths of her body and expressed itself in fits of tears in which she whined like a wounded animal.

She was often sick, able to go two days without touching her food and subsequently lost weight. One evening her father made her sit at table for three hours in a face-to-face duel until she finished the food on her plate. She retched. And this had sent Lefèvre into a rage she could never have thought possible. Sure that she was doing it on purpose, he had confined her to her bedroom for three days. At night Jeanne heard her parents arguing vehemently.

All this time, Jeanne thought of Harry. A thousand times, she went over and over their letters, the times they had been together, their touches. Each time, she went searching for the smallest of detail and her mind lingered for an eternity so that it almost became real, only then to realise that it was the deepest, most hollow presence.

She began to receive visits. Sarah popped by, announcing her forthcoming trip to France for the wedding. Cécile, still as mad as ever, came with Edouard to tell her they were now engaged. And then Sister Marthe called by with Jeanne's exam results—*obtenu avec mérite*. Jeanne caught her parents exchanging knowing glances and wondered how long it would be before they announced she would go to France to study.

Every day, Jeanne asked for news of Harry. Several reports of a man resembling Summerfield had come in: a face in a car in a village to southeast, a man at the central station in Marrakesh.

Someone who, when questioned, turned out to be a German archaeologist, Lefèvre adding that it was a lucky coincidence for, given the worsening situation in Europe, he could now place the man under surveillance. But no real concrete sighting of Harry. The good point was that nobody had been found which ruled out the possibility of murder. They must have hidden Summerfield away, concluded her father, difficult to find. The country was half uncharted. There were even places, her mother had tried to reassure her, where the Berber tribes were living in complete autarchy, in much the same conditions as they had hundreds of years ago. There was no way the authorities could search all these remote places. All they had to do was wait and hope that a rumour would lead to the right ears. This did not reassure Jeanne.

The summer holidays proved an ordeal of heat and boredom. Everyone seemed to have left. Jeanne's father, given the crisis, was unable to take time off and her mother never travelled anywhere without him, so the prospect of them spending a week by the sea in August, as they habitually did, was ruled out.

Jeanne's health failed on two occasions, mostly through lack of regular nutrition. On these occasions, she was administered food and vitamins by a nurse her parents paid to stay in the house the time it took for Jeanne to regain her strength. They were days spent gazing over the top of a book she could never finish, her eyes inevitably drawing to the distant mountains and the feeling that somehow, somewhere, Harry must be there. In the garden, in the shade, Mohammed kept watch on her armed with a long stick. Outside the gate, a policeman watched permanently over the house from the shade of a date tree.

The night was the worst. Lefèvre thought it likely that Abrach—*El Rifni*—would attempt to kidnap her again. After all, he had done likewise to Summerfield—most probably to prevent him giving information to the authorities. Jeanne, despite all her father's clinical calmness, sensed her father was scared. Both for her and most of all for himself. What vile things had he done to make a man hate him so much, she wondered. Life was awful—a continuous string of betrayals and truths that constantly tried to defeat her belief in the goodness of things. How long would it be before she gave in? How long before she became like her parents?

One day, mid–August, her mother summoned her to the living room. A fresh cup of lemon tea was waiting for her together with a *corne de gazelle*, her favourite cake that positively oozed sugar and honey and so sweet that it made her teeth ache. Her mother must have asked Soumia to make them especially for the occasion.

'Sit down, my dear,' said her mother. Jeanne did as she was told and accepted the tea. 'Good.' Her mother brushed away a stray hair from her brow, flicked away an imaginary something from the top of her pale green summer dress and took a deep breath. 'Now, your father and I have arranged things, Jeanne. You will not have to worry about that.'

'About what, mother?' inquired Jeanne, a distant flame of hope flickering in her. Was there news of Harry?

'Your studies, of course,' frowned her mother. 'Your future.'

'My future. Oh.'

'You sound as if there won't be one,' said her mother, tersely. 'For goodness' sake, please change your attitude, Jeanne. It is quite unbecoming of a young lady of your standing. Life is full of unpleasant events. We just have to turn the page and start reading anew.'

'That's not very comforting, mother,' said Jeanne. 'Have you ever experienced something as horrible as—'

Her mother pursed her lips—that almost incriminating expression of hers—and raised a hand. Jeanne remained silent, feeling like a little girl, scared as always by the authority her parents wielded over her.

'Your father has decided you will undertake law studies.'

'I'm not interested in law.'

'He wishes you to enter the Administration.'

'Like him.'

'For the status and the security and the safety.'

'Security I can understand,' said Jeanne. 'But *safety*?' Jeanne grimaced. 'What safety?'

'That if ever you cannot find a husband—' Jeanne's eyes widened. Was she hearing correctly? '—you will still have an opportunity to make a career.'

'Haven't you both realised?' Jeanne could contain her anger no longer. 'Harry Summerfield is—*will be*—my husband.'

'Mister Summerfield has disappeared, Jeanne,' answered her mother, remaining calm. 'And one day, quite soon—you'll be surprised—he will disappear from your thoughts too. It's sad, but that's how it is.'

'He will never, ever disappear from me,' said Jeanne, solemnly.

'When you are faced, in the weeks or months or years to come, with a man—for example, *Ludovic*—and he begins to court you. How will you explain that you…that you are—how should we say…?'

'That I'm what, mother?' said Jeanne, defiantly.

Her mother's voice was icy cold. 'That you are no longer a virgin—that you lost your pureness with a foreigner who then disappeared. How will you explain that, Jeanne? *How?*'

Jeanne was stunned. She had never expected her mother could say anything ever like it. She felt like screaming, like crying.

'What if I'm still pure?' whined Jeanne, fighting desperately.

Her mother shook her head and again pursed her lips.

'We're not that stupid, girl. Your body has changed. Your hips are woman's hips now—that's how it happens. Your attitude too changed not long after that awful Arab tried to kill us. You have— *haven't you?*'

Her mother's gaze was too intense to face.

'I wouldn't tell anyone about it,' said Jeanne, miserably.

'Rubbish! You don't have to tell anyone—especially a man! They know about these things. They can *smell it*, like a beast smells meat.'

'That's *horrible*, mother.'

'It's how things are. Life is—life can be so…' her mother hesitated, as if she was fighting back the urge to cry herself— '*So disappointing*,' she said, breathing in at the same instant. She remained silent for a few moments, regaining composure, and when her calm, grey stare had returned, she said. 'So there you are—law studies. Everything has been arranged.'

'I suppose the teachers will be old women spinsters,' said Jeanne, gruffly. 'And I'll be housebound forever.'

'My dear,' said Jeanne's mother, shaking her head. 'Don't you understand? Don't you remember? You will not be staying here. Morocco is a country that has done you more harm than any good. We shall proceed with the initial idea to send you home.'

'But *here* is my home.'

'No, Jeanne. *France* is your home. It is your country, your real roots, your duty.'

'Mother—I do not look like you or like father. Why is that?' attacked Jeanne.

'Oh, not that old rubbish again! You will make me extremely angry, Jeanne, I'm warning you.'

'My skin is different, my eyes, my features. I could almost be— be one of the natives if I stayed in the sun for longer. That's why Soumia has been so insistent all these years! And was it you that told her to do that? Are you ashamed of me, mother?'

'I don't know what you're talking about. You're hysterical, Jeanne, an idiotic child. Now be quiet!'

'No! No I won't. I've had enough of being quiet, of shutting up.' Jeanne could contain herself no longer. She felt a surge of anger and hatred for everything around her rise up inside. 'What did *you do*, mother—all those years ago?'

'What do you mean, Jeanne? You're—you're quite mad all of a sudden.'

'Did you do something stupid, too, mother? Worse than me perhaps? Something that is forbidden? With a native, maybe?'

Jeanne's mother let out a cry of anger and indignation and promptly lunged forwards. Jeanne felt the sharp, dry slap on her cheek and drew back. Her mother had never done that, never in twenty years.

'You—you *hit* me, mother.'

'I slapped you,' replied her mother, mechanically. 'And justly so. I have never been so insulted in my life. To insinuate that I, of all people, could have slept with a native. Disgusting!'

'They are people—just like us. We're not better, mother, just different.'

'You young fool,' said Mme Lefèvre and shook her head. 'You know nothing of the world, do you? Absolutely nothing…' She paused, her mouth moving slightly, undecided as to talk further. 'Your father and I… We—' Her mother stopped herself and drew breath. 'You will attend the university at Bordeaux. You will study law. You will stay at your father's sister's—aunt Géraldine. There your supposedly different colour of skin—and different features, for that matter—will not be so out of place. After all, *historically* they have a lot of Spanish and Moorish blood in them.'

Jeanne looked at her mother with hatred. She was just as bad as the Blackshirts in Europe.

'And one more thing, Jeanne. Remember that we have also decided this for your own good. Your health will only get worse if you stay here. Memories—bad memories—are best left behind in life.'

'And when do you intend to send me?' said Jeanne, sullenly, defeated.

'The first week of September—term starts at the beginning of October. That will give you time to acclimatise and get used to European life. I've also arranged for you to meet up with Sarah and her husband who have planned to honeymoon in Biarritz. It'll do you no end of good. Go now—our conversation is finished.'

The remaining weeks went so quickly and Jeanne was filled with a strange, conflicting mixture of emotions. Sadness, always sadness when she thought of Harry and their love for each other. Anger at her parents for this ultimate bullying of her life. Fear and excitement at the thought of discovering France and Europe and all the new people at university. She felt like both running away towards the mountains and running away from her ordeal in Morocco. Mother had been right on that point. A bad memory was like a heavy anchor, dragging her backwards towards what could have been, what should have been and all the mistakes. She could no longer bear the pain and something inside her urged her on towards a light, a new beginning. Maybe going 'home' as mother had called it—France—would provide her with just that new light, that new beginning. But it would never happen.

It was the 2nd of September. In the night, Jeanne had heard her father on the phone: German tanks had entered Poland. Jeanne's affairs—two large travelling chests, a hat bag and two suitcases lay at the foot of the stairs ready to be loaded onto the calash that would take her to the station. Mother and Mohammed were to travel with her to Tangiers where they would say their goodbyes. A day's voyage would take Jeanne to Marseilles and then a train would take her across France to Bordeaux and her aunt's. Accordingly, Jeanne's father had freed himself from the office for a couple of hours and was to meet them at the station for her departure.

Next morning, the calash arrived and the driver, assisted by Mohammed, duly loaded the vehicle. Jeanne went back upstairs to give her bedroom one last glance. Her teddy bear, *Baudelaire*, was propped up under the sheets and, tears suddenly escaping from her eyes, she rushed over and gave him hug. Even him, the soft and comforting presence through the past ten years or more, she was leaving behind. Downstairs, the crying took a turn for the worse. It was Soumia, nanny and housemaid, who first began sobbing, then crying and then, in true Berber tradition, wailing. They held each other tightly for several minutes, Soumia whispering dialect into her ears, probably a prayer for safe keeping and protection. When they drew apart, the maid's eyes flickered momentarily over Jeanne's body. A fleeting look of complicity came across Soumia's eyes and she nodded.

The journey to the station took Jeanne through the expatriate quarter, so quiet and genteel, into the outskirts by the city walls, pale pink in the glaring sun. People went about their daily work and routines in the streets and squares, oblivious to the change in her life that was about to take place. She took in the colours, etching them in her memory, certain that Europe would be eternally overcast and grey. Finally, arriving at the station, a throng of porters and beggars came to them and Mohammed had to push them away. Father, together with a policeman for a guard, met them at the ticket office. They went through to the platform with the swathe of porters, joined now by a gaggle of hopeful shoe shiners, paper boys and a snake charmer believing them to be tourists. Lefèvre was stiff lipped, uncomfortable and parsimonious with his words. 'Good weather. Not too hot. Have you got a coat within reach for the ship?' were his remarks. Jeanne's mother, however, was more talkative, emphasising the thrill of returning to France with all its monuments, culture, cinemas, theatres and such. At last, the train pulled in belching smoke and hissing steam. The porters became agitated, as did the fifty or so others attending their passengers and a kind of a mad and frantic jostling briefly followed for first access to the compartments.

'Goodbye, my darling,' said Jeanne's mother. 'Write or cable as much as possible. I shall phone for aunt Géraldine at the post office in two days. Goodbye, my dear. Take care.' She kissed Jeanne, held her close for a brief, lonely second or two and then it was her father's turn.

He stepped stiffly to her and sighed. It probably meant a hundred things—love, forgiveness, apology, regret maybe. He held out his arms. And then came a voice.

'*Monsieur* Lefèvre. *Monsieur Lefèvre!*'

Lefèvre turned round. 'Oui. C'est moi. *Qu'est-ce*—?'

An army officer—a lieutenant—strode up to him and with a gallant gesture excused himself before Jeanne and her mother. His suavely gummed hair had come loose in the apparent rush and a lock fell down over his eyes. He flicked it away.

'Sir. Excuse me, sir, but important news. I thought it might be urgent, seeing that…' he nodded towards Lefèvre's wife and daughter.

'Yes, yes. What is it? Is there trouble with the line? Have the tracks been sabotaged or something?'

'No, sir. More important than that.'

'Well, what is it then, for God's sake?'

'Sir, the war—in Europe. France has just declared war on Germany. England is to follow. It's started, sir. We're at war!'

Lefèvre hesitated, his eyes growing wide and then promptly narrowing shut. He looked at his wife, at Jeanne and cleared his throat.

'Porters!' he shouted above the cacophony. 'Take those bags back off the train immediately. The ladies have decided not to leave.'

37

The light grew mellow, September came and life and the valley re-adapted to the change in season. Summerfield had been lodged in a small room in the Kasbah for the first week, his actions limited by a thirty-foot length of rope tied in such an intricate knot around his wrist, it was impossible to undo. Thus he was at least able to exercise his legs, pacing to and fro between a small, sunlit courtyard, the roof of an edifice below and his living quarters.

He shared his room with Badr and Rashid, brother to the man who had driven the lorry on the perilous journey up into the mountains. Badr stayed much of the time with him that first week, talking or reading or spending long moments of silence, almost meditation. They spoke sparingly, as if they had consumed their words on the journey and nothing was left to say. Instead, it was an occasion for the silence to speak to them and between them. A silence that Summerfield's senses grew to understand and befriend, for it was hardly silence at all: prayer, from before dawn, filling the valley with its nasal, mesmerising meanderings, trickled like a stream running to him from afar. Then the barking of dogs, waking up the other animals, the chickens, the mules and the goats—an undecipherable cacophony of bleats, brays and counter bleats. There were voices too: the dampened murmuring of male voices from within the Kasbah walls and the occasional chirping of female voices as they walked up from the fields below the fortified house with their heavy loads. The crackle of fires being lit and the chink of kettles and tea pots brewing tea. And even the air itself seemed to resonate, every particle carrying with it the particular ringing of the mountain air, a pure, still presence that had the effect of calming Summerfield's irritation, his worry.

Badr came and went and came again, sometimes bringing Summerfield some tobacco to be smoked in a rudimentary pipe made of a hollowed out chicken bone; other, rarer times, coming back with a real cigarette. After a while, Summerfield began to break the cigarette in two and offer the other half to Badr. And although the young man didn't smoke, he never refused. And then the young man returned a final time with news that he would be leaving for the city for several weeks. Upon hearing the information, Summerfield felt a strange tinge of regret—could it be real friendship that was beginning to find root in him? Summerfield's mind switched almost immediately to the grim understanding that yet another person was being taken from him, that he would soon be alone again.

When he awoke the next morning, Badr had gone. *What was he, this young man*—captor, saviour, traitor, philosopher, friend? Difficult to say. When Summerfield's mind returned to Jeanne— something he had painfully though deliberately exiled from his thoughts over the last ten days or so—he was filled with an anger that infiltrated his lungs with an acid air of longing. It was Badr who had commanded the kidnapping; Badr who had tied his hands and pinned him to the floor of the lorry. And yet, despite this, despite the violence of the act, Summerfield couldn't help feeling that deep down, Badr was good, that the young man had acted against his true nature.

Rising from his bed of straw and linen, he noticed that his hands were free, the rope cut in the night. He imagined the wry smile on Badr's face—on the one hand showing trust, on the other, knowing that Summerfield was bound to want to escape.

It felt odd to be free—his limited movements had set the boundaries of his universe and created a comfortably known world that included three rooms and as many people. For an hour or so Summerfield remained in his quarters, listening, wondering if anyone would come to check. And what about breakfast? Would Abdul, the driver's brother, arrive as usual and serve him tea with bread and honey? The sky grew clear and no one came and Summerfield realised that it was he who would have to move.

Treading softly, he made his way down the confines of the corridor that led from his sleeping quarters. He followed his nose more than anything else, the faint waft of mint and saffron brewing in tea pots. He got lost. The Kasbah was such a labyrinth of corridors and chaotic floors. He stepped out into open air—or a least a ledge—some fifteen feet above the ground in the Kasbah walls and let out a gasp. He felt himself toppling forwards and clutched at the earthen walls to stop his fall. A fattened goat—maybe a pregnant female—was looking up at him from the rocky slope directly below. It bleated, defecating in the instant that followed as if to accentuate the insult. Standing in the opening, having found his equilibrium now, Summerfield surveyed the hillside below, empty on this western flank but for several low-walled and scattered shepherds' shelters. A brief, exhilarating sensation of freedom suddenly overcame him. If he wanted, he could run—*now*. Run and join Jeanne in Marrakesh. And then it disappeared—the feeling—snuffed like a candle with only the acrid bitterness of the smouldering wick remaining. He suddenly felt a desperate emptiness—an emptiness that overcomes a man who suddenly realises he is completely alone. He found himself about to cry and angrily swore at himself, pushing back abruptly to walk back the way he'd come.

Finally, Summerfield came upon a group of tribesmen in a wide, low-beamed room and sat down near them, his back turned. They seemed to have been expecting him and a low exchange of jokes at his expense followed before one of them threw a spoon to grab his attention. They beckoned him to take what he desired to eat and drink and then rose to wander off.

Summerfield's days passed in such a way. He was no longer a prisoner tied to his cell, but although free to wander and observe, was met with such mistrust and hostility that he didn't dare go further than fifteen yards from the Kasbah walls. A couple of times, he was spat upon. On several occasions he was insulted— or at least they looked and sounded like insults. They were the lowliest of peasants he'd met so far—grossly impolite, dirty and showing an extreme lack of intelligence in their incapacity to overcome their perception of him. It was he who had spent time in a French colonial prison, not they. It was he who'd been beaten by the gendarmes. It was he who'd been forcibly abducted. He felt angry—anger against the whole bloody lot of them, the French and these people alike.

Nostalgia of England and the company of Englishman overcame him and he suddenly saw them as the most trustful, straightforward and honest people; maybe sometimes hypocritical with their dislike of anything vaguely intellectual, snobbish in their inherent understanding that they were quite naturally superior to the rest of the world, obsequiously over-polite, sneeringly class-bound and annoyingly always bloody right. But what clarity, what sincerity and what empathy—an Englishman would not hesitate, not for the slightest second, to help anyone in need. An Englishman would not hesitate, not even for the time it took to say *Jack Robinson*, to see the difference between what was right and what was wrong and gauge his actions accordingly. God, how he missed them. Them and the greenness of the hills and fields, the drizzle and changing skies; them and the morning paper over breakfast and the genteel civility of daily existence. Two thousand miles away, a completely different planet away. Summerfield looked wretchedly up from his sitting position, his mind slowly focusing, channelling his thoughts into grim determination, one single aim: to escape, to be free. While winter swept icily up the valley and froze the earth and the tribes hibernated, Summerfield waited and planned his escape.

38

He had been gone for almost a whole day and understood he was running in circles. The bastards knew it. He was trapped. And they didn't even bother to come after him.

On one side an impossible climb up a sheer face of scree. On the other, a system of fortified shelters—shepherds' huts with guards—spread out at intervals just below the crest of the first valley. Going south, keeping to the riverbed, there were always villagers about. Whenever someone spotted him—women or children—they pointed, letting out a whoop and breaking into laughter as if playing a game of hide and seek. And if Summerfield knew that they would not dare come closer, he also knew that not far behind them, on the valley slopes, there would be men training their rifles at him, playing with his silhouette in their sights. And to the north, the coomb where the valley found its source—a huge horseshoe of a cliff face scarred with ravines, where hundreds and thousands of years ago the glaciers had formed a wedge to gouge out the valley. Only the night would help him. And this night he would try.

In preparation, he hadn't eaten for two days. He had tucked his food away under his clothes in anticipation of the flight through the mountains. He stole a gourd left on a stone wall and a knife from an empty kitchen. He gathered together his clothes, made a bag from his cover that he could easily sling over his shoulder and found string, a shred of matchbox and a dozen matches. And then he waited, a whole day in his room, his mind an inner rehearsal of how he would slip through the line of sentinels and head towards the west.

He planned to keep on going until he dropped, as far ahead of the valley tribesmen as possible so that he could rest a couple of hours and gather his strength. With luck he would retrace the rough track the lorry had climbed and use it as a guide towards the plains, the first village and a telephone. From there, a call to the British embassy in Casablanca. They would surely alert the authorities and hopefully send someone out to fetch him.

He was so determined and the itinerary etched so deeply in his mind, that the thought he could fail was as frail and distant as the thought of ever seeing Jeanne again. She was making preparations for France and her studies, no doubt. Perhaps engaged to some rich civil servant's son? And what about the war? It seemed he had been in the valley for years and nobody here had even mentioned Europe, the news. A faint hope that perhaps it had all been called off came to him and he looked out from the small window of his room to the dying sun over the mountain crests and smiled: *wouldn't that be perfect!*

Night came. He went to the inner courtyard at around nine-ish, complaining of tiredness and took his food back to his room. This time he ate it—a hot meal of cooked wheat, olives, potatoes and a few shreds of tough chicken meat. After that, an apple, which he slipped into his pocket.

The silence of the mountains fell and the voices grew low and calm. The odd dog barked in the distance, a final territorial gesture, and then grew silent. A baby howled from somewhere in the village—hunger or fright—and then nothing. The voices disappeared. A faint snoring from somewhere along the corridor. Summerfield, tensed like a bow for the last few hours, rose silently and gathered his things.

He found his way to the yawning hole in the Kasbah walls—a path he had memorised over the last week, even following it with his eyes shut to test himself. The cold night air surprised him, sharp and defiant. He swore under his breath and carefully slipped down into the darkness, trembling from a slight attack of vertigo. Once on the ground, he crouched among the rocks for several minutes, letting his eyes grow accustomed to the darkness. High above him, to his right, the moon was a thin blade in the sky, a million stars for company. And then he set off.

For several hundred yards he followed a shallow ravine towards the valley floor and then struck off left, up a gentle slope littered with low bushes and boulders of quite considerable size. To his right he spotted a shelter, a glimmer of a flame sending shadows dancing around the walls inside. He sank lower, on all fours and the odd thought that perhaps he might be mistaken for a marauding animal—did they have bears here?—crossed his mind. Summerfield—the trophy adorning the Kaïd's chimney breast, the Englishman they managed to bag one night in September! He began to laugh, his nerves brittle and checked himself. He continued from boulder to boulder, the slope growing steeper. He was sweating now despite the cold and he smelt himself in the clear nip of the air, something like the odour of tea in a tin. And then he stopped dead. Directly in front him, barely thirty feet from the shadow of the boulder was another shelter, a squat stone edifice. From the window protruded a rifle—the guard had obviously laid it there on the ledge. Summerfield could hear the low murmur of voices—two of them. One rising high and almost woman-like while the other, deep and mocking, repeated the same word—incomprehensible to Summerfield—as the other spoke. The way ahead was blocked, his efforts reduced to nothing. He sank back into the cover of the rock and retraced his steps. Several moments passed until he got his chest to stop heaving. Keep calm. Once again, he took a breath and slipped out onto the mountain slope, away from the guards and horizontally across the flank of the mountain. He judged that he would need a good four hundred yards to be safe before he could begin to climb upwards again.

This time he felt the certainty that he would find a way through the line of watch posts. His eyes had scrutinised the flanks of the valley for long, concentrated moments and had seen nothing. The way up looked clear and the flicker of hope that perhaps he had found the breach in their defences sparked into a flame and brought strength to his arms and legs.

The climb was difficult, across open terrain littered with small rocks, scree and the odd ghostly bush. Perhaps that was why they hadn't bothered to post anyone there—they'd thought it too difficult, too open. He almost crawled up. Every heave towards the top was a slow, deliberate and careful gesture, the danger that of setting a flurry of stone and rock clattering down the slope. His breath was regular and deep and he could see the crest approaching, a black serrated ramp that led to freedom. And after? He wasn't thinking of after. All that mattered was reaching it. It spelt victory. It spelt rejoining his people and his language and maybe, with it, the chance to find his way to Jeanne. It was almost as if England were just on the other side—a matter of a single step from one side of the valley into another: this one hostile and burned by the fierceness of Morocco, the other green and fertile and mild.

Up onto the flank, stopping once to roll over and drink and calm his burning throat. Then onwards again, like a cat stalking a prey. He could feel himself grinning—*the crest nearly there*. Barely ten yards from his goal, he halted, judging it wise to gather his strength for a few moments before the ultimate effort. He felt happy, elated and fought to keep it from sending his heart drumming even faster. More water. Several minutes went by and the concentrated effort that had taken him up the flank of the valley ebbed from his mind and body. It was then that the pain came, like a new priority claiming top of the list. It was his hands and legs and feet. They stung as if he'd been caught in a swarm of wasps. Peering closer, Summerfield could see that they were smeared with a dark, metal smelling liquid—blood. And he hadn't even noticed. He was immediately reminded of the crest and told himself he would look to his cuts and bruises later, in the daylight of the next morning. One last glance around him, tensed against the mountainside, and then in a semi-crawl, struggling to keep his impatience from breaking into a run, he moved forwards. Ten yards, seven yards, five yards—he began to smile, feel the trickle of relief and victory begin to form a soft and intimate laugh in his throat. Then suddenly, a faceless silhouette stood up in front of him: a sentinel. Summerfield stopped dead, squinted. The guard let out a grunt, no trace of surprise in his deep voice. *The crest*, said Summerfield to himself, filled with panic. He struck off abruptly to the right, trying to detour the black shape as though he were facing an adversary on a rugby field. The sentinel moved to block him. A laugh. Summerfield twisted again in the opposite direction, breathless, his body inevitably headed for a crash course but the disadvantage of climbing upwards slowing him down to walking pace. It was no more a collision than a bumping into. Another laugh, deep and mocking. Summerfield whined in frustration and heaved with all his strength. The sentinel did not move. He pushed again, weaker and weaker until he was practically leaning on the shape, motionless. Summerfield could see no face, just the black indentation in the man's headwear where his eyes should have been, just his smell, earthy. An arm moved lifting up an object—a blade—and Summerfield stopped breathing, expecting the arm to slash down upon him, cleaving his head in two. Instead, another laugh and suddenly Summerfield was pushed back. He slipped on the stones, fell some five yards and picked himself up. He advanced and was pushed back again and suddenly realised that they would not kill him. *They couldn't*—their orders were to keep him alive. One last time, Summerfield heaved himself forwards, ripping his sack from his shoulders to gain in agility. This time, the silhouette, grunting loudly, gave him an almighty shunt which sent him tumbling chaotically down the slope a full hundred yards. Summerfield knew he was beaten. He got up unsteadily, sobbing in frustration. Glaring into the darkness at the silent sentinel, he turned and began to walk back down to the valley floor swearing every filthy English insult he could think of until the night swallowed him.

His face was buried in his mountain coat of roughly woven wool. The air was sharp and icy and he was shivering. He'd spent a miserable three hours picking his way across the valley, stumbling and increasingly aware that he was trapped. It was hopeless. The ridges of the mountain valley were laced with guards and sentinels and they had known, from the day they had freed his hands, that he would have no chance of slipping through the defences. For that was what they were—not so much a system implemented to stop him getting out, but a way of warning the valley tribes of anyone wanting to get in.

He couldn't remember if he slept. He just remembered a last glance towards the stars above him, millions of silvery pricks in the black of the sky. He saw a shooting star and, as he had done as a child, made a forlorn wish. And when dawn came and his shivering intensified, he knew for certain that such hopeful wishes did not come true. He was still there, a prisoner, far from the woman he had fallen in love with, far from his home, far from a war he was bound to miss. A despair he had never known fell upon him and made him feel hollow—like a single husk of wheat left over after the harvest. He felt so miserably alone and useless. He began to sob, hating himself. Once again he buried his head beneath his woollen coat to black out the reality of the day.

If time passed, he didn't notice, but the silence was long and solitary. And then a voice, a girl's voice, far off and almost unreal. And then something touching his head—a hand, tentative then prodding. He didn't want to come out—he was so ashamed.

'*Sidi*?' came the childish voice, softly. '*Sidi*?'

Slowly, shyly, Summerfield uncovered his face, squinting into the light. He was met with a smile, fresh, young and impertinent. It was a girl, maybe fifteen—of age to be married. He saw her eyes, large and brown and smeared black with kohl.

'Wake up, *Sidi*,' said the girl, noticing his tears. He must have looked awful and for the first time her impish smile wavered with embarrassment.

'I wasn't sleeping,' replied Summerfield, helplessly. 'Who are you? Why have you bothered me? You know who I am.'

'*Raja*,' said the young woman. 'My name is Raja.'

'Raja,' echoed Summerfield and rolled his eyes heavenwards. '*Hope*, for God's sake—her name is *Hope*!'

'You are the white man.'

'The Englishman,' replied Summerfield, 'the *prisoner*.'

She didn't seem to understand the emphasis upon the word. Instead she held out her hand, small and dirty and the colour of a brown olive. She wanted him to stand. 'Come she said,' not letting go. 'Come, *Sidi*.'

'I feel like staying here and dying,' answered Summerfield in English, and the tone of his voice must have touched her, for after a moment's hesitation she tugged on his unmoving weight. Another tug and Summerfield rose unsteadily, his muscles painfully bearing the strain. 'All right, Raja—I'm up now. *Saved by a girl*—I suppose they sent you, but who bloody cares. I'm starving.' He brought his hand to his mouth and made a gesture for food and she smiled.

'Come, *Sidi*. Food.'

She led Summerfield in a zigzag through the rocks and scrub, holding his hand, stopping every now and then for him to get his breath back. He realised something was wrong. His chest was pounding and he had begun to sweat. Breathing was like sucking in flames. He would have liked to ask her how she had come to him—was it the guards or was it indeed God that had sent her? But he didn't. For by a small brook, twisting down towards the valley river—he remembered the dazzling clarity of the water before he fell—the world went completely black.

For some time, some days, maybe even a week or more, he passed from the unconscious to moments of consciousness, woken by what he failed to understand as his own smell and the burning inside his body. For these brief seconds and minutes, it was as though every muscle of his body had been tied into ragged knots that on the slightest movement, sent shards of pain through his body. He had never felt anything like it and he shook so violently it made him cry out in fear—he thought he was dying. And then he would lapse once again into a coma, the smell hard on his tracks, into the throes of what he would later learn was dysentery. He would also learn in the weeks to come that he was as close to death as could be and that if it hadn't been for Raja, her unshakeable and devoted care and the fact that she contacted Badr to come urgently to him, he probably would have been buried in the valley.

Once, when he opened his eyes to see Badr peering worriedly at him, he heard the young man's voice say in English. 'The war, Harry. France is on fire.' He remembered muttering something stupid along the lines of 'so I'm not the only one, that's a relief' and then falling back into darkness, a single sentence, permanently looping in his mind: *on fire, on fire, on fire…*

Then one day, miraculously, Summerfield opened his eyes and the world seemed different. His head was clear, free from thought and torment. The first thing he heard was the twitter of a bird and he saw, from his bed of straw and linen, a small white-crested finch looking inquiringly at him from the ledge of an open window. It darted off in a single wing beat leaving a smell of incense in the air, a mix of sandalwood and cinnamon. Summerfield felt better, felt strangely real and strangely alive. And he smiled. When he turned his head, he could almost feel the presence, the warmth of another human being. It was the young woman, Raja and the grin on her face was as wide and ripe as the morning sun. She stretched her hand to him and touched his shoulder and he took it in his.

'I remember you,' said Summerfield, as though returning into a past so distant it seemed unreal. '*Hope*. Thank you.'

'And you have a friend here,' said Raja, smiling.

'Badr—yes!'

'So that makes *two* friends, *Summerfield*,' added the girl, unable to pronounce his name properly. 'Badr and Raja.'

The girl's words were simple, but the meaning seemed so important to him. He wasn't alone in this godforsaken valley. He wasn't hated. And two people, two *foreigners*, had stayed with him through his illness, helped him through the darkness. It was an unexpected gift.

The days passed and Summerfield's strength began to return. Raja informed him that he had lost a lot of weight, though couldn't say exactly how much—something approaching four jars of olives. Summerfield accepted this—after all, a jar of olives was as good a measure as any other. Badr popped in several times a day, stopping with him the time it took to share tea and give any news that happened to have entered the valley.

The news was indeed bleak. Denmark and Norway had capitulated. France was being overrun. British, French and Belgium troops were being forced into an enclave near the Belgian coast. There were heavy losses and on last accounts, the

French were launching a desperate counter-attack near Arras. As the news came in dribs and drabs and Summerfield began to build up a fuller picture of the disaster, his mind went wild with worry for Jeanne. She suddenly came back to him in all the stark clarity of their last days together—her face, the voice, the way she smelt and the loving touches they had given each other. She became more real than real and he even called out her name, helpless, more than a thousand miles from her and the hell in Europe.

For several days he struggled with this. Once again, his nights were torn into shreds and his health took an abrupt turn for the worse. Raja bathed him and lifted his head to water as she had done before. And then, as suddenly as his fever had returned, it disappeared. And with it the constant thoughts of Jeanne. Summerfield had let go. He had let her drift from him. Her face and her presence which had been so startlingly near simply vanished and only a vague and distant shape that was her, like a ship on the horizon, lingered as a permanent feature. In retrospect, Summerfield thought this sudden disposal incredibly cold blooded but Badr, wise despite his youth, told him it was pure survival instinct. He was powerless and his mind had decided to save his body by cutting her out of him.

39

It was unthinkable. The expatriate community listened in helplessness as day after day the news came in of the situation in France. It was worse and worse. With stunned realisation, it became clear that defeat was highly probable.

Jeanne's father was rarely home these days. An emergency committee had been set up to deal with the crisis, but there was nothing much they could do but wait for further news. Wait and pray that some miracle would happen.

Jeanne was amazed at the pace of events. She could remember standing on the platform of the station ready to leave for Europe as if it were Monday. In the days that had followed the outbreak of war, Marrakesh had seemed full of soldiers. Where they had all suddenly come from she didn't know, but she did know that her father had something to do with it. Full mobilisation had come soon after. French Morocco was to raise two divisions of troops and it looked likely that one would be sent to Europe. Talk of border skirmishes in Alsace reached them through the wireless and newspapers. British planes had dropped leaflets over Berlin. Italian troops were massing in Libya causing alarm in colonial Algeria. It was like a huge bubble that was about to burst. And meanwhile, Poland had been invaded and overrun in seventeen days, left to its own as the Allies hesitated, prepared, still hoped.

Edouard had left for Europe, making Cécile a permanent feature of Jeanne's daily life and her days were no longer empty, boring stretches. The expatriate women were busy. They raised funds for the war effort, kept a look out for German and Italian spies, knitted various items of clothing to be sent to French soldiers in Europe and organised rare-metals collection points. As April turned, Denmark capitulated without resistance and Norway was the target of British and French raids to counter the Nazi invasion. And during this time, Jeanne and Cécile shared tears, though both for different reasons. Jeanne's love had already died, whereas it was the likelihood that Cécile's would be killed in the ensuring weeks that sent her into despair. And others left too. Suddenly, the only men not in uniform were either civil servants or boys. And someone else. Someone tall, foreign, modern. Someone who looked so naturally self-assured. Someone who possessed a deep, meaningful and very listenable voice. It was Jim Wilding.

As May came with the awful news they had all been waiting for—the invasion of France—Wilding had appeared in Marrakesh. He was taking a break, but he also was there on business before continuing on to Casablanca and Rabat. His government had contacted him to go north and feel out the French colonial authorities. And it was in this role that Wilding arrived in the city, meeting up with Lefèvre and Bassouin and the other leading officials of the protectorate. And it was also how he came to be invited for dinner at the Lefèvre house and how he once again met Jeanne.

'The whole world is about to go to war again.' Jeanne heard the American's words resound solemnly in her father's study as her mother, scrupulously dressed and made up, knocked and entered carrying the tray of drinks that Soumia would otherwise have brought into the room. Conversation immediately stopped. From the hallway, Jeanne peered in and saw her father's look of irritation and surprise as her mother placed the tray on the table. There were the usual group of father's colleagues—Jean Bassouin, Fresquin in charge of the post office and communications, Colonel Le Guédec and several new faces—French army officers. She saw Wilding, sitting relaxed and cross-legged in his chair. He turned his head, perhaps conscious that someone was looking in, caught her eye and nodded with a little smile.

'Are you enjoying yourself, Mr Wilding?' came her mother's voice, full of concern for the American visitor.

'Yes, thank you very much,' interrupted Lefèvre's brusque voice. 'Now, if you would kindly—'

'And you must stay a little to chat after you've finished with the serious talk,' added Mme Lefèvre, unperturbed, darting the handsome American a reassuring glance.

Wilding nodded. 'With pleasure. And Jeanne—' he turned slightly and smiled again towards the hallway. 'Is she—?'

'Yes, yes,' rasped Lefèvre. 'Perhaps later, *Monsieur* Wilding. *D'abord, nous devons*—please translate, Jean.' He waved his wife away. 'Thank you, *chérie*—for the drinks.'

Mme Lefèvre walked calmly out, closing the door softly behind her and caught sight of Jeanne at the bottom of the stairs. 'You startled me, Jeanne! Did you hear? Mr Wilding would like to chat with me—us—after drinks. So charming, so *American!*'

'There's a war on, mother,' replied Jeanne.

'Is there? Oh yes, I was forgetting—for a *moment*. So nice to have a breath of fresh air in the place, don't you think?' And with that, her mother floated away, all lemon-yellow pleats and furls and with a hint of rose petal perfume in her wake. Jeanne watched her depart, an undisguised grimace on her face.

It was two more hours before the men adjourned their meeting and another thirty minutes before Soumia led Wilding to the patio giving out on the rear garden. Under the shade of the mighty magnolia—Mohammed's pride—Jeanne sat with her mother who had fallen asleep. Her mother stirred slightly when Wilding arrived and her magazine, *Vogue*, slipped slowly from her lap to the ground. A little moan escaped her gaping mouth, her eyes remained closed and Jeanne put a finger to her lips.

'A pity mother had to attend to war business,' said Jeanne.

'Indeed,' said Wilding, sotto-voiced and Jeanne thought she saw the hint of a smile in his eyes. 'Perhaps we should talk elsewhere. She looks so—'

'Silly?' whispered Jeanne.

'Peaceful,' replied Wilding, shocked at Jeanne's cheekiness.

Jeanne rose slowly, taking pains not to make any noise and the two moved off along the garden path. From the upstairs window, Jeanne caught a glimpse of her father looking out at them.

'He's probably getting changed for the office.'

'Yes. He mentioned he was almost living there these days,' said Wilding. 'By the way—good to see you again,' he smiled and offered his hand.

Jeanne took it. It felt very big and reassuring, a little rough. She supposed he indulged in manual work. She wondered what engineers actually did when they looked for oil and wondered whether to ask.

'How is Harry?' said Wilding and the question caught her off guard. She halted and felt a cold shiver pass through her.

'You mean you haven't heard?' she said, turning to Wilding and almost whispering.

'Your father mentioned he was unreachable. But I imagine you are in touch with each other.'

A spasm of grief swept through her and she suddenly felt like crying. She wanted comfort in this American's strong arms, but instead stepped back.

'For once, father is rather right. *Unreachable*. Harry was abducted.'

'*What?*'

'It's been a horrible year, Jim. Complicated to explain. I was nearly killed—my father too. A local terrorist apparently. Then my parents—they found out about Harry and I. It's—it's been one disaster after another. Awful. I feel so ashamed.'

Wilding's hands moved helplessly. 'Hell. I feel ashamed, too. I should have kept contact. I sent him a cable—must've been all of five months ago or maybe more. Jesus, how stupid and thoughtless of me.'

'No,' said Jeanne, shaking her head. 'It's not your fault. I should have tried to inform you, I just didn't think. You were Harry's friend and you might have been able to help. God, how stupid of me!'

'That makes us both stupid!' said Wilding, shaking his head fretfully. 'But who took him? And *why?*'

Jeanne felt suddenly quite frail, sapped of all energy. Her mind had managed to block out Harry and now, with Wilding, the awful memory of the events was back and tormenting her.

'I'm sorry—I—feel a little ill,' said Jeanne. 'Got to sit down a bit,' she said before turning off at a tangent to seek out a garden bench. She only just made it, reaching out to steady herself at the last moment. Wilding, following closely, took her elbow and eased her down. Glancing up at her father's window, she saw that he had gone. Thank God—she didn't want any more recriminations.

Wilding remained standing, for once a little lost. 'Can I do anything? Should I wake your mother?'

'Oh, dear *not that!*' said Jeanne, surprising herself. She looked up at Wilding and burst out laughing. 'Excuse me, Jim. *Please excuse me*—I think I'm just a little nervous that's all.'

'Well I thought it was funny too,' smiled Wilding. 'I think she kind of likes me—*a lot.*'

'It's because you're different. Something to brighten up the boredom of her life, I suppose.' Jeanne looked timidly away. 'And mine, too.'

'It's a nice compliment,' said Wilding, cocking his head. There was almost a frown on his face, as though he were trying to figure her out without success. 'You must be damn sad about Harry. An awful hard trial to go through,' he added. 'Listen. How about a fresh drink in town? I have a car. It would do you good to get away from your parents a while.'

'I can't. They keep me cooped up here—for my safety, they say.'

'It wouldn't be for long. An hour or so and you'll be with me. What better protection?' he added, mockingly. 'Come, we'll inform Soumia and I'll leave a message at your father's office just to let him know.'

'No, I'm sorry, but I can't.' Jeanne was adamant. She shook her head sadly and remained silent for a few moments. Pensive, she asked: 'D'you think you could find Harry? Send out someone to search for him?'

Wilding sat down and clicked his tongue. 'I could try. Does anyone have an idea of where he might be? Look, I don't want to appear glum, Jeanne, but there is a fair chance that he might have been killed. God, I hope not. But there are still places hidden away where they haven't even seen a white person.'

'No one knows,' murmured Jeanne. 'He could be up there in the mountains. He could be dying of thirst in the desert.' She suddenly caught her breath and stifled a sob. 'God, I'm so weak, so stupid. I'm sorry.'

Wilding shook his head. 'I'll try to get a couple of local people to ask around. Don't worry. I'll also contact the British embassy when I get to Casablanca. Maybe they can help.' He paused. 'Jeanne?' Wilding's voice had suddenly become grave. She looked up, wiping a stray tear from her eye. 'It seems to me you're doing yourself a hell of a lot of harm. Almost as if you couldn't break free from the thing. You've got to turn the page, Jeanne. No disrespect for you and Harry, but—things will start happening for the better.'

'Yes,' sighed Jeanne. Her mother had told her the same thing, but it seemed somehow different coming from Wilding. She believed him. 'Yes, you're right.' Again she looked at him and her eyes stayed. For the first time she noticed the lines on his face, his blue eyes, darker than Harry's but good, strong and honest eyes. She felt like a little child before him, this big, knowledgeable American. She felt herself beginning to go red. Slowly, almost like an animal that had finally given up and acquiesced, she lowered her head and brought it to rest on Wilding's chest. There was a moment's silence. He was stiff, unmoving. And then she felt it. His hand moved. It came to rest on her hair. He was stroking her, soothing her and it felt so reassuringly beautiful.

40

Strangely enough, letting go of the wild and hopeless dream of seeing Jeanne again also killed any further thought of escape from the valley. For a while resigned, a sort of gloomy lethargy took hold of Summerfield. And then, one day, the heat of the oncoming summer waking him from his afternoon sleep, he realised he had accepted.

He felt lighter, not entirely joyous, but definitely unburdened of his persistent and painful self-reproach. He was in a valley in the Atlas Mountains, God knows where exactly, and unable to leave. He had tried but failed, but at least he had tried. And in any case he was powerless to change the events that were happening a thousand miles away in Europe. He wasn't free, but he was sure he had a friend in Badr. And he was sure someone had saved him, taken care of him and brought him back to getting to grips with life—it was Raja, *Hope*. And her heart was as big, almost as overbearing, as the great burning sun that hovered over the valleys. That was a sign.

Time passed and Summerfield grew stronger, both physically and mentally. He began to laugh again. He took to sitting outside on a pile of cushions and skins, soaking in the sun while sipping tea, and soon became something of an attraction.

At first the children came. It took them two days to get within talking distance. Little heads began popping up from behind the rocks and tall grass, curious and hesitant before darting away as soon as Summerfield spotted them. It became a game. Little by little they came closer, letting out shrieks of fear and glee as he waved his hands with a shout. They were so close now that he could see their faces, and this was when the shrieks were replaced with almost hostile looks from the boys and the shyest, coyest of looks from the little girls. Unlike the Arabs in the city, their faces

were uncovered and they wore bright colours of red, yellows and
greens, resembling gypsies who roamed Europe in their caravans.
The children stood together in groups of three to four and not
knowing how to approach him further, began to sing, each group
competing with the other and advancing closer a few yards after
every verse. It was enchanting. When they had left to return to
their families and homes, the strange, sad, bittersweet melodies
stayed for a long time afterwards in his mind.

At the end of the second day he was lost in a gaggle of them,
mostly boys this time, having been put to shame by their sisters
the day before. They surrounded him, smiling hesitantly and
gaining confidence as Summerfield made them draw their names
out in the earth.

It was thanks to them that an idea began to form in Summerfield's
mind. By the river, there was a rutted clearing neither used for
crops nor grazing. It was worn and dusty and dotted with several
clumps of thorn bushes and the decaying stump of a large and
solitary olive tree. The left side of the clearing sloped downwards
for twenty yards or so before plummeting into a little ravine that
gave onto the river. On closer inspection the patch of ground
was like a cheese full of holes—snakes, mice, rabbits, foxes. The
occasional whitened rib cage and discarded animal skull also
pointed to the fact that it was used as an occasional tip. And it
was here that one day Summerfield took it upon himself to lead
a group of twenty or so giggling, babbling and laughing children
to initiate them in the game of all games—*football*.

The ball he had made from a bundle of newspapers Badr had
supplied him with, wrapped in consecutive sheets around an
inner core of wood and bound together with a web of string.
The notion of goal posts was quickly understood. The fact that it
was forbidden to touch the ball with the hands was completely
ignored. In this way, the first attempt at a match resembled
some sort of mediaeval variant of rugby with children running
everywhere punching, pulling, kicking and screaming. A large
cloud of dust swallowed up the small, thrashing players which
at least allowed Summerfield to have an approximate idea of
where the ball actually was. And it was when the dust for some

reason settled and the children became quiet, that he was able to understand that the ball had been reduced to a few shreds of paper, a stream of knotted string and the wooden core looking like a discarded coconut.

The following morning, Raja took Summerfield to see her grandfather who happened to make some of the finest gourds in the valley. Summerfield described what he was looking for. Raja's aunt lent a hand with her sewing kit. By the time the sun had retracted its midday claws and the light became soft and golden, Raja returned to Summerfield with a new football—not exactly round and not exactly inflated, but something that could be kicked and something that rebounded off the ground, albeit at a sometimes crazy angle. Summerfield was overjoyed. He took Raja in his arms and embraced her and she went a dark purple with embarrassment.

Over the next week Summerfield organised a series of matches between groups of children that he separated into teams wearing different coloured neckerchiefs. Parents began to watch, as did the village dignitaries from afar. The Kaïd, Ahmed Youadi, watched the battles for the ball with barely disguised pleasure from his parapets in the Kasbah. The village Mullah frowned at the scene with barely disguised fierceness. Very soon, a long forgotten law was invented that forbade any organised ball games for prolonged periods and Summerfield's enterprise promptly outlawed.

The emptiness lasted four days and the silence in the valley seemed incredibly deafening and downright sad. On the fifth day, sitting on his seat outside, Summerfield cocked his head and listened. From the distance he heard the sound of childish whoops. He rose from his chores and craned his neck, straining to pinpoint where the sounds were coming from. In the distance, across the other side of the valley, a group of tiny dots were running wildly about a patch of abandoned field kicking a ball. The children had rebelled. Summerfield grinned. And his grin turned into a laugh. It was the beginning for Summerfield; the beginning of his acceptance of the valley and of his love for the people of the mountains.

41

News of Henri's death came to them on the 14th of June, the day German troops occupied Paris. Jean Bassouin called by to announce it to the Lefèvre family at lunchtime. Apparently, Sarah's husband had been engaged in the Abbeville sector when his armoured column had been attacked from the air. They didn't know where the body had been buried. Sarah had sent the wire from Rouen where she was attempting to get a ship across to Southampton.

Jeanne was fraught. Despite the sad news, her thoughts were immediately for Sarah. Was she safe? Were there bombs? Jean Bassouin, Sarah's father, was deeply moved too. It was the first time Jeanne had ever seen her father show any emotional sympathy, all the more so because he put a protective arm around his friend and colleague. Bassouin, desperately guilty, called himself a fool—he should have repatriated his daughter at the start of it all. No one ever thought it would turn out like this and so soon. Lefèvre, making excuses about it being better to concentrate their minds at the office, led Bassouin away to his car and the awaiting police escort.

Alone now with her mother, Jeanne waited until Soumia had cleared the table and brought them tea on the veranda. When she spoke, she was afraid her voice might betray some of her happiness despite the terrible news.

'Mother. Mr Wilding has asked me to accompany him to visit the banks.'

'What? Oh…' her mother seemed to have been dreaming, weighed down by the news. 'Terrible, terrible times,' she muttered. 'What will happen to our dear country?'

'Mother? Mr Wilding,' repeated Jeanne. 'He wishes me to interpret at the banks. He has some financial business to look into.'

'*Monsieur* Wilding, you say?' her mother had suddenly regained her senses. 'He asked *you*?'

'You can't speak English, mother.'

'I didn't mean anything by it,' lied her mother. 'I was just thinking it would be wiser, in these times, to have a chaperone with you. Poor Sarah. Soumia, perhaps. Or even,' she added, matter-of-factly, '*Me*.'

Jeanne smiled fleetingly. 'Mother, it's quite obvious that you like Mr Wilding.'

'I—' Jeanne's mother stopped herself, as though any words would only confirm her daughter's insinuations.

'But think of daddy,' continued Jeanne. 'How hard he's working and how preoccupied he is. He needs you, you know.' Her mother looked at her, shrewdly. 'And think of what he would say if—'

'Jeanne—you have turned out to be quite Machiavellian in your way of dealing with people.'

'No, mother. Just stating the obvious, that's all. In fact, Mr Wilding said he'd be round at 1. Which means…'

'That you have barely five minutes to get ready,' said her mother, pursing her lips. 'And no make-up, Jeanne. Men get strange ideas in their heads when they see blush on a woman's cheeks.'

'No, mother,' called Jeanne after her, as she went inside the house.

Wilding arrived at 1 p.m. sharp in the black Citroën the French authorities had lent him. Why were they treating him so officially? wondered Jeanne as she descended the steps under her mother's watchful gaze. Wilding got out and sent Jeanne a welcoming smile. She felt suddenly quite self-conscious. True, she had put on a new summer dress—a cream cotton affair, sleeveless and slightly *décolleté*. Perhaps it was a little too much. Too late now. Wilding had opened the car door for her and she stepped inside, her hem riding above her knee so that Wilding had to look away.

As they drove towards the bank district, Wilding informed her that whatever she was to hear had to remain confidential. She was to swear by it. *Solemnly*, he laughed and made her draw an imaginary cross across her heart.

'You see,' he added, glancing across at Jeanne. 'Things are turning out pretty difficult and pretty complex too.'

'You mean in France.'

Wilding nodded. 'I'm sorry, Jeanne, but it looks sure that France will lose this one. And when they do, things will become extremely complicated—in France, but also here and in the other French colonies. Have you heard of someone called De Gaulle?' Jeanne shook her head. 'Not many people have. But they will do. Pretty soon. He's in the military—a high-ranking officer.'

'And why will we soon hear of him?'

'Because he's setting himself up as the future saviour of France.' Jeanne frowned, feeling quite lost in it all. Wilding nodded. 'That's right. Some say there'll be a civil war—the old lion of Verdun, Pétain, who wants to control what he can salvage from the German invasion and De Gaulle, who wants to continue the fight until the Nazis are kicked out.'

'So we should all be on *his* side, then.'

Wilding smiled. 'Not so clear and not so easy. What if Britain loses against the Germans? It's a bit like backing a horse in a race with no clear favourite.'

'But who's gambling?' said Jeanne.

'Who?' The answer seemed so evident. 'Why, the United States of course. The world is changing right under our feet, Jeanne. We have to be very vigilant. Imagine a world under Hitler—a return to the dark ages. We don't want that to happen if we can help it.'

The banks were closed during the afternoon heat, but Wilding had arranged a series of meetings with the managers at three of them. He introduced Jeanne as his assistant though she knew two of the people and had to politely remind Wilding of the fact. Oh well, she was still his assistant, if just for a day, joked Wilding, unsettled.

In fact, he needed her just for opening formalities. Once these were done with, he told her to wait in the managers' offices while he consulted various documents and accounts. Alone, Jeanne found all this very intriguing but thought it better not to ask any questions. Two hours later, Wilding had finished his tour and they got back into the boiling car.

'Wow!' Wilding let out a yelp. 'The steering wheel's as hot as hell!'

'The seats too,' said Jeanne, squirming uncomfortably.

'Should have left it in the shade this time. My apologies, Jeanne. Let's go before we frazzle like eggs!'

As he pulled away, air mercifully filling the interior, Jeanne said: 'Jim—could I be your assistant sometime again?'

He looked across and grinned at her. 'Sure—with great pleasure. You were perfect.'

'What about that cold drink you offered?' said Jeanne.

'That was yesterday,' replied Wilding, playfully.

'I think we've deserved it today.'

He looked at her. Jeanne held his gaze for a second then turned away.

'Sure. I think you're right,' said Wilding.

They bought cold drinks—orange and beer—from one of the remaining petrol halts still open. Seeking shade, Wilding drove to the city outskirts and drew the Citroën up beneath a cluster of date palms giving blessed shade. Opposite them, in the distance, the Atlas rose majestically into the simmering air.

'We must be mad,' said Jeanne, letting out a giggle. 'The only ones outside at this time of the day. I hope I don't get heat stroke.'

'Then drink,' said Wilding. 'Here. Would you pass me a beer, please?'

Jeanne leant down to the floor of the car and the paper bag containing the bottles. She was conscious of a large damp patch of sweat across her back and wriggled the material of her dress free.

'Here, Jim. I'm afraid I'm a little sticky. Excuse me.'

'No need. Me too. I feel as though I'm melting like an ice cream.' His eyes rested on her shoulders and darted to her open neck where the sweat had gathered in beads. He took the bottle with a nod, still looking at her. There was an uneasy silence. 'Aren't you going to drink too?' he said, softly.

'Mm. Yes,' said Jeanne, feeling a little lost.

'You know, Harry was a great guy. A friend. He was—*is*—very much in love with you, Jeanne. I hope—I hope you'll find each other again.'

Jeanne glanced down, shyly. She felt odd, as though it was not what she had wanted to hear. Somehow, it seemed as though Wilding had betrayed them both, broken the rules of their playful afternoon. A pity. It had taken her away from it all. 'Yes. I do too,' she murmured.

And then, suddenly a finger—an index—touched her softly on her neck. It was Wilding's. She looked up, startled and slowly sat back. She expected Wilding to remove it but he didn't. And she didn't move either. Instead, the finger traced a slow, soft zigzag across her open neck, joining up the beads of her perspiration one by one until, lower now, he reached the material of her dress. His finger inched down, nudging under the cream-coloured cotton and gingerly explored the beginnings of her cleavage before once more travelling back up to leave her skin. Jeanne held her breath.

'Mmm. Yes, you are pretty hot, Jeanne,' said Wilding, calmly. 'And beautiful with it. Lucky Harry. How old are you now?'

'Twenty-two,' replied Jeanne, breathing freely now.

She couldn't fathom the American out. Why had he withdrawn his finger? She felt no guilt. In fact, if it weren't for Jim's constant references to Harry, she wouldn't have thought of Harry at all. It was awfully cold of her, but she just wanted touch—human touch, a man's touch—and everything would be all right.

'You can do that again if you want,' she said, avoiding his eyes. 'I liked it.'

There was a moment of hesitation, Jeanne still looking down and then the finger returned, more playfully now, re-tracing a ticklish path through the cool gleam on her skin. She looked up into Jim's smiling, understanding eyes and then leant over, again placing her head on his chest, the movement making his hand slide down softly onto the rise of her breasts.

'I'm so damn sad, Jim. I want to live. Just to live and have some protection, some happiness. Love me—please love me.'

It was the second time she'd made love to a man and she still didn't know the comfort and bliss of a bed. She remembered Wilding's hand on her wet bra—her sweat—and Jim's breathing that became heavy and strong. The next moment they were kissing and it seemed as though all the weeks of despair and pain had transformed themselves into a wildness she had never thought herself capable of. Her hands had clasped Wilding's body, pulling free his shirt to grasp at the matted hair of his chest. Their tongues were frantic—she realised it must have been the first time in a long time for Wilding too. Their mouths still locked, they had struggled in the confines of the car, his left hand entering the funnel of her open legs, her right hand fighting with the buttons on his flies until she pulled his penis free. His fingers had been thick and skilful and eager, slipping into her heat, her wetness and moving in small, rapid circular motions across her lips and clitoris. A whine had escaped her, gathering in length and intensity. She hardly knew herself. How her hand grasped the weight of Wilding's sex. It felt large, powerful, and manly. She had never done it before, but the movement came instinctively, as though she had been programmed to carry it out from some unspoken part of her femininity. A rhythmic gesture, pressure on the shaft of muscle. She watched it under her hand as she experienced first her orgasm—a piercing rush of heat, an unbearable pleasure that made her laugh uncontrollably—then his. She cried out when he came, more of shock than anything else. Three spouting jets of liquid which—she swore—jumped a full foot into the air and slapped heavily down onto his trousers, her dress. And then the bubbling afterflow, oozing over her hand, hot and sticky, smelling like the forest after rainfall, ammonia and dark earth. She had felt a little disgusted at first. Then curious and finally almost spellbound as Wilding held her for ages in his arms.

They had cleaned themselves in the water of one of the irrigation channels trickling through the date palms. And then he had driven her away, into an abandoned oasis across the plain. It was here they made love in the heat and shelter made by the car. She lying on his jacket, he cradling her head above the ground so she could see the movements of their bodies. He didn't have any contraceptives and at first, through sheer fright, she clamped her legs together and resisted his efforts. For several moments, kissing wildly, it seemed they were wrestling.

'Jim. Harry—I'm not,' she whimpered, afraid that Wilding would reject her.

'Doesn't matter,' said Wilding, looking at her strangely. 'No worry,' he had said, his voice hoarse and cracking above his whisper. 'Trust me. I want you.' She hadn't understood what he'd meant, but his eyes looked into hers, hard and truthful, and she felt herself opening wide for him, a cradle for his hips. Jeanne was all feeling, the pleasure of presence and contact rather than sexual peaks. She felt Wilding's sex inside her and how her own muscles gripped onto him, the movement of his body and the clash of hip upon thigh. She felt his heat and smell against her shoulders and neck, the sweat on his back, slippery under her hands. And she felt him coming, his whole body stiffening and quivering as though electric, and she cried out in fear before a voice said to her *it doesn't matter, it doesn't matter*. She abandoned herself to his orgasm, the only moment of any importance in the world being this one. Soon after, while they had lain for long, silent moments in each other's arms, he had asked: 'Did you want me to stay inside of you? Jeanne—did you want that?'

Jeanne hadn't replied immediately. She was confused by the question and her own behaviour. At last, she said: 'Yes. I suppose I did. My life, Jim. It's meaningless. Only you now make it important.'

Wilding smiled and laughed softly. He looked away, his blue eyes searching the mountains and then turned back to her. He kissed her lightly on the lips. 'Jeanne. I've just thought of something. It's all so—so goddamn obvious. Why don't you become my wife?'

Jeanne was feeling faint again. Her head was an eddy of excitement and torment: excitement because Jim was in the salon with his parents and Jean Bassouin. Torment because Jim was to leave that afternoon for Casablanca. Once again, her life seemed to be a succession of rising and falling waves. Hope and happiness that crashed into loss and despair.

She waited outside the closed door, hearing Jim's voice low and measured, so low that she couldn't discern individual words. A shriek from her mother told her that it was Jim asking for her hand in marriage. And then her father's voice, clear and nasal after initial surprise.

'Well, I—our daughter certainly seems to have a penchant for Anglo-Saxons. Whoever would have thought?'

'Oh, Philippe-Charles!' Her mother's chiding voice. 'But isn't it simply lovely?'

'Of course, *chérie*. Mr Wilding—James. It would be an honour for us.'

'Take Jeanne to America, Mr Wilding,' came her mother's voice again, this time breaking into a sob. 'Take her away from the war.'

'It's a probability, Mrs Lefèvre.'

'What do you think of all this, Jean?' came Lefèvre's voice.

'I think we should invite Jeanne in to see what she has to say. But I think it's a happy moment. If only my poor daughter could be here with us.'

The door opened and her mother appeared, her mouth crooked and trembling between a smile and a grimace of tears. 'Darling *chérie*, please come in. Mr Wilding has just announced us your wonderful news.'

Jeanne leant forwards and gave her mother a kiss. She wondered if her mother's tears were from relief rather than happiness. Relief that her daughter would be spared a life of unmarried shame, relief that the family would keep its reputation intact. Jeanne breathed deeply and stepped into the salon. Vaguely, she saw her father making a nodding motion, Jean Bassouin smiling through his sadness. But they were on the periphery of her vision, almost unreal, onlookers to the focus of her attention, all that seemed true and glowing and lovely—Jim. A smile took hold of her body and seemed to fill her with the sun. She approached him and he held out his hand for hers. They kissed.

Wilding was to leave that afternoon in the Citroën Lefèvre had lent him. Thankfully, Jeanne's parents had let them alone for their last hour together. Unable to go up to her rooms, they sauntered around the house and garden and back again, their arms locked, their conversation light and sparse. Occasionally, they came to a hesitant halt and kissed. Twice, Wilding pulled her into a hidden corner and they kissed more savagely, their hands running desperately over each other's bodies, seeking the slightest breach in their clothing, the smallest of access to bare skin. Their last moments were frantic attempts to hold back time.

'It's been growing in me steadily,' said Wilding, on one occasion. 'A feeling that I was attracted to you, wanted you. But Harry—I couldn't have done that to him. I'm kind of guilty about that, Jeanne.'

'Yes. I know,' she had replied, frowning. 'Me too. In a way, I've betrayed him, but I have no regrets—I must live, I must love. And to survive I have to escape this dreadful boredom, this prison my parents have built. Know that I love you, Jim. And that probably, for me too, I have been wishing for this. You are an exceptional man.'

'We'll go to America one day. When my job is done.'

'How long must I wait, Jim?'

Wilding shook his head. 'Not long—I *hope*. My job has been put aside for the moment and I'm a government man—working for the Yankee dollar, as we say. There are things…things to do with the war they want me to see to.'

'Oh God,' Jeanne inhaled. 'Let there be no danger.'

Wilding laughed. 'Hell, why should there be? No, the US is keeping out of things in Europe. We just want to make sure our interests are seen to, that's all. No one has any reason—or *right*—to harm me. In ten days I'll be back. We'll marry as quickly as possible and you'll be an American citizen. Believe me, Jeanne. In the times that are soon coming, it'll be the best protection anyone could hope for. Now kiss me and say goodbye, my lovely Jeanne.'

That evening, while Jeanne and her parents sat in the salon after dinner, she said a silent prayer to keep Jim Wilding safe from harm. He had promised to phone as soon as he reached

Casablanca. Jim was full of reassuring gestures like this. He was doted with a sort of feeling for others and planned ahead so that fears were dispelled and doubts transformed into trust. So different from Harry, she found herself thinking, her mind going off at tangents. Harry, poor Harry, was—had been—someone so spontaneous, like a leaf that placed trust in the wind to lead him to the next decision and the next event. She did feel remorse. Her love for him had been so immense, but maybe all first loves were like that—intense, desperate, and unachievable, doomed to magnificent disaster.

She sipped on her sweet wine. Father had lately initiated her into this evening ritual—cognac or whisky for the men, *Muscadet* or *Rivesaltes* for the ladies—an unsaid message that he had accepted her into adulthood. She was one of them.

Her mind meandered, back and forth to Jim journeying north and Harry—ironic this—probably a prisoner in the south or already bones bleaching in the sun. Perhaps there were people, she thought, that were necessary encounters before the real and total happening occurred. Even if she had thought her love for Harry everlasting and strong, even if they had given each other their whole souls; even if they had written those beautiful words—it was only part of a process, a step towards Jim Wilding, a trial in which she had learnt the bittersweet taste of love and the incredible folly of passion and desire. It had awakened her, made her realise who she was and prepared the path towards her destiny, the encounter with Jim at a moment she was at her lowest.

Sitting in her armchair, she distantly watched her father switch on the wireless set. A faint noise of music and fritter and the strange other-worldly noises as he fine-tuned the frequency reached her ears. She saw it now: her destiny with Jim as the future Mrs Jeanne Wilding, a life in America, studies perhaps or a devoted mother, a large house, sunshine but not the fierce dry heat of Morocco. No dust, no sand whipping in on the desert winds. America. Newness and comfort and safety. When would her parents pay visit? she began to wonder, when her father held up a hand and called for silence. The news was about to begin.

The tremulous, tinny voice—that of the institutional radio speaker, Pierre-Maxime Deschamps—crackled from the radio cabinet. Lefèvre turned up the volume.

'It is with great chagrin, but also relief for millions of French people in this time of suffering, that on this day of the 22nd of June, 1940, the Armistice has been signed. France is in defeat before the German forces. But it is also in honour. For our *patrie* has in part been saved. From the Spanish border to Franche-Comté to the border with Switzerland, a Free Zone has been declared. Members of the new government together with Marshal Pétain state that the Empire will remain intact and under complete French rule, as well as the Fleet which is required to protect it…'

The announcement was brief, concise and with no mention of the torn remnants of the French army, the hundreds of thousands of prisoners or the rest of France occupied by the Nazis. It ended abruptly with news that the German government had offered a peace treaty to the British. And then the strident, martial anthem of the *Marseillaise* began to play. Jeanne and her parents remained silent, motionless for a few seconds. And then Lefèvre stood up, followed by his wife and Jeanne, as the anthem ran its course. There were tears in her mother's eyes and she broke into a sob as the hymn reached its final, tragic and glorious chorus.

'I wasn't informed,' said Lefèvre, shaking his head dumbly. 'They gave me no idea of the scale of what was happening. Why?' His voice rose, filled with incomprehension and almost pity, for his own plight or that of his country or both. '*Why*, in God's name?'

'And what about De Gaulle?' said Jeanne, promptly clasping a hand over her mouth. Her father turned abruptly to her.

'De Gaulle? Who told you about him?'

'Jim,' she replied, somehow feeling not in the least intimidated by her father anymore. She felt grown up. 'He talked a lot about the situation. I know quite a few things, actually.'

Lefèvre let out an irritated gasp: 'Good God, my own daughter knows more than I do—the Administrator officially in charge of this damn area! I don't believe it!' Again he shook his head, a gesture that reminded Jeanne of a dog emerging from a river and shaking off the water. 'And yes—*what about De Gaulle*, indeed? I wonder if Bassouin knows—Le Guédec, too.'

'Can I suggest the BBC,' offered Jeanne.

'Don't be impertinent, Jeanne,' said her mother sharply.

'No. No, she's right,' said Lefèvre.

'What?' Her mother looked as though she'd received a slap in the face.

'Of course she's right,' added Lefèvre, frowning at his wife as though confronted with a village simpleton. 'But it's in English, damn it!'

'I can understand,' said Jeanne, daring to interrupt. 'I can translate.'

Her father stood with his mouth open for a few seconds. 'Good God. Quick—the tuner. What's the frequency? *Chérie*—' He shouted over his shoulder to his wife—'Get a glass of whisky for me—double. And a glass of wine for our daughter!'

An hour of listening later, including much re-tuning as the radio crackled and spat and struggled to keep hold of the BBC, and they had a much different picture of what was happening. There were many other people in the salon now. Lefèvre had summoned the other expatriate officials and notables and events strangely took on an atmosphere of a festive working group. Those who had trouble understanding English strained to pick up the odd word and waited impatiently for Jeanne to give her translation. She felt elated in her new and important role and knew from the nods and smiles of encouragement from her father that he was proud of her—at last.

Every twenty minutes, the BBC was re-broadcasting De Gaulle's speech of 18th June—the call for continuing struggle against Nazi Germany. Given little attention earlier on in the month, the speech had now gained in importance. Jeanne felt shivers run through her when De Gaulle's voice, solemn and charged with emotion, urged them to fight on as Free French Forces, the forces of Good against evil, fighting for the free world. He told them to make their way, by whatever means, to England.

It was all so confusing, thought Jeanne, looking at the faces around her for signs of fellow incomprehension. Everybody seemed to be calling themselves Free French, though for completely different reasons. It was her father who eventually dropped the volume on the radio and called for attention.

'The question now is what to make of all this,' he declared. 'What are we to do?'

'With all due respect, the last question shouldn't have to be asked at all,' said one of the gathering. It was the otherwise jovial bachelor, Fresquin, head of the *Poste et Télégraphe* services. He wasn't so jovial now and the change made Jeanne feel quite uneasy. 'The order is clear. Our government, with the Marshal probably at its head, has ordered us to carry on as we were.'

'But who *is* our government?' said Bassouin. 'And to what degree are the Marshal and Free France under German influence?'

'Didn't you hear? The *official* French sources clearly said that our loyalty is to France and our empire. An upstart in London, a Colonel who suddenly promotes himself to general and proclaims himself the saviour of France, isn't going to tell *me* what to do.'

'A traitor,' came a comment from the rear. 'He didn't stay in France for the rest of the campaign. Many troops were killed because they believed that defeat could be avoided. De Gaulle evidently thought that all was lost as early as mid-month.'

'Some would call that intelligence, courage and insight,' returned Bassouin.

'Look, Jean. We are all aware of your Jewish origins,' said Fresquin. 'If you're afraid that we'll suddenly change into Nazis and hand you over just because we choose the Vichy government, you're mistaken.'

'My religion has nothing to do with it!' It was the first time Jeanne had seen Bassouin angry. 'Just remember that my son-in-law has died for France. I'm sure he wouldn't like to see half of our country suddenly swallowed up by Germany.'

'Try to look logically at the situation,' added a young army captain. 'I urge you to stop taking a personal stance in all this.'

'I am not—' began Bassouin.

'Gentlemen, please. Calm and order. Calm and ORDER!'

rose Lefèvre's voice, struggling against the sudden outbreak of shouting. He gave his wife an urgent glance. 'Get the food in, *chérie*, get the food in, for heaven's sake!'

But cakes and sweet wine did not calm the storm. There were several arguments, rather heated, going on between groups of officials. Someone—Le Guédec, perhaps—gave someone else a push and received a push in return. A glass was broken. Suddenly, a loud electronic wail, rather like a police siren, filled the room followed by a deafening screech of feedback. It was Lefèvre at the radio, volume knob turned on full. When he switched it off, a high-pitched ringing remained in the air. Faces slowly unfolded from creases of pain. Lefèvre breathed deeply and exhaled.

'I propose we continue this at the office. Gentlemen—please. We cannot allow ourselves to get emotional in such a crisis. Some of you were ready to kill each other, it seemed!' Several listeners laughed and Lefèvre held up a hand. 'Colonel, Captain. Inform your men to wait until morning for clear orders. For the moment, everyone must keep calm. *Monsieur* Fresquin—I'm placing a platoon of legionnaires around the telegraph system for protection. Let's proceed to headquarters now and leave my ladies to peace. Is everybody in agreement?'

There was a general nodding of heads, followed by a raised hand. It was the young captain. 'But what do you think, sir? As Administrator—'

'To be discussed later,' said Lefèvre.

'No,' came another voice, surprisingly Bassouin's. 'As head of this region, your opinion would serve as general guidance for us all.'

Lefèvre hesitated, shifting uneasily for an instant. 'You put me in a difficult position, *Messieurs*.'

'We insist,' said the captain, followed by murmurs of agreement from the others.

'Well, I.' Lefèvre cleared his throat. 'I repeat that it is essential we discuss the subject at headquarters, but if you want a quick personal opinion, my instinct tells me that De Gaulle is right. My head says wait and see. The question is: how long before Germany takes over what Pétain has managed to salvage? How long before the Italians invade Algeria from Libya? How long before officials arrive from Vichy, under pressure from the Boches, and begin implementing those heinous policies that we have so far managed to stop?' Lefèvre stopped and in the silence audibly drew breath. 'I am a hard man, gentlemen. You are all aware that I will tolerate no opposition to French interests here or anywhere else. But I am no fatalist. I cannot accept that France is defeated for good. I cannot accept that even the smallest square metre of our fair country is occupied and controlled by foreigners.'

'So you are with *De Gaulle*.' It was Fresquin again.

'I didn't say that.'

'You are ready to revolt against the Vichy government, *our* government—the government of France.'

'No! No, I didn't say that! Gentlemen, *please* keep calm,' said Lefèvre in an attempt to stop the speculation. But it was too late. Once more, there was an outburst of shouting from the gathered men. Lefèvre gestured for his wife and Jeanne to go and as they closed the door behind them Lefèvre began to plead for the men to take leave. In the hallway, Soumia appeared, looking worried.

'A telephone call, Madame. From Mr Wilding. I hope we are safe.'

'Don't be silly, Soumia,' said her mother, as composed as ice. 'Jeanne—you may take the call upstairs away from the broo-hah. Now, let's get the gentlemen's coats ready, Soumia. And make some sandwiches for Monsieur Lefèvre. The night will be long, I fear.'

Jeanne ran upstairs, suddenly uplifted with the thought of talking to Jim. Good, true Jim—he had promised he would call. She went into her parents' bedroom with its sad, over-orderly decoration and picked up the receiver.

'Jim. Hello, my darling. It's me, Jeanne.'

Wilding's voice came back to her, weak in volume from the distance, but nonetheless deep and reassuring. 'Hello, Jeanne, my love. I've just arrived—no problems on the road. The checkpoints took one look at my papers and passport and let me through without any hassle.'

'Hassle?' said Jeanne. It seemed a nasty-sounding word.

'Trouble,' corrected Wilding. '*Problems*. I'm to meet several officials here starting this night. I need to rest a little before. And I've just heard the news in the hotel lobby. France is defeated.'

'We listened in earlier. And to the BBC. Father convoked his colleagues.'

'Is everything ok? You sound a little nervous, Jeanne.'

Jeanne sighed. 'It turned into a very big argument. The BBC is re-transmitting De Gaulle's call for resistance. He wants us to side with him.' Jeanne heard Wilding make a humming sound, as though he were thinking aloud.

'What's your father's standpoint, Jeanne? Forgive me, but it's important.'

Jeanne hesitated, struggling for a few moments to clear her mind. 'He's quite objective—as usual,' she said. 'But he really seems to think that De Gaulle is right. It caused quite a row.'

'Jeanne, my dear, listen to me. I don't want to alarm you, but you have to listen. Are you listening?'

'Yes, Jim. I am,' replied Jeanne, a pinprick of fear entering her. 'Go on.'

'You can expect trouble. When such a situation arises and beliefs are involved—political ones, national ones—then there's bound to be a little upheaval.'

'Do you mean demonstrations? Shooting?'

'Maybe not. But I wouldn't say no, either. I've also spoken to the American embassy here in Casablanca. They're telling any American citizens in the country to stay at home and keep off the streets just in case.'

'Oh, don't worry, Jim. I'll be doing that too.'

'But your father's position makes you and your mother potential targets, Jeanne. I think it's more than just staying inside the house. If your father has declared his standpoint, then sooner or later his hierarchy will send someone down to make him change his mind. If he doesn't…'

'Oh, God.'

'But that's not for now. No panic. See how things go. But please prepare your bags and be ready to leave at the slightest sign

of danger. Your father may be setting himself up as a potential
enemy of the Vichy government. Jeanne?'

'Yes, my love.' Her voice almost a whisper.

'Tell me that you're all right.'

'Yes, yes, I'm fine, Jim. I—I miss you. I wish you were here
with me.'

'I do too. I want to take you away from this mess, Jeanne. I'll
try to be as fast as I can. Maybe leave a couple of days before I
planned. I have to go now, Jeanne. I love you.'

'I love you, Jim.'

'I'll phone tomorrow.'

42

June ruled over the mountains and the valley. At 4.30 a.m., the inhabitants rose with the rising of the sun, Morning Prayer floating like the smoke of the first morning fires, slow and bewitching. It was the time Summerfield loved the best—the first hesitant opening of the eyes, the freshness of the air in his nostrils, the smell of earth and that soft grey-blue light of the dawn—night time like an outstretched arm, clutching the day as they inexorably parted in opposite directions.

For the first time in his life, Summerfield felt the strength of time—its great, massive presence gathered in a palpable tranquillity he had never thought possible. There were no chiming bells, no ticking clocks or racing second hands. No train whistles, idling motors or background babble of the crowd. The people of the valley awoke, washed, talked softly, ate. They followed the sun as it rose and obeyed time by following it obediently at its own pace. In Europe, Summerfield had the feeling that men tried to outpace time itself—a constant race to beat it at its own game. They rushed to shave and to eat. They pulled on their clothes and tugged on their shoes, sometimes forgetting keys, wives, children and kisses. After that, they ran to the bus, tram or train arriving at the office without a glance for the trees and sky. One did not think of nature—except for brief excursions into worry over the rain soiling one's suit or a longing for sun and a holiday break. Europe was ruled by the clock, against the nature of nature itself. Somehow, it was madness. Somewhere along the line, Summerfield thought, it spelled doom for the industrial man. The machine was setting the rules for its owners and not the other way round.

With obedience to the rise of the sun came lightness. There was work to do of course. But what did it matter if Summerfield

arrived ten minutes late to the task or thirty? The work would
be done or not done—for there was always tomorrow to finish
off what couldn't be done today. What absurd and utter madness,
he concluded, thinking then of the old maxim. *Don't put off*
for tomorrow what can be done today. It was like cramming life
into a sardine tin. Here, in the valleys, nobody put a number to
their lives—an hour was an hour, one part of a day—nothing so
sacred—and one died when one died and everything in between
was life and nothing else. We are wrong, he told himself, to
look too deeply into things. Scientific measurements—average
lifespan, production rates, timescales—put the daily pressure of
deadline on our minds and made us do inhuman things; like
thinking of three things at once, dealing with four problems
at the same time, staying after hours at the office to finish
the job and dashing after pay rises—causes of stress, stomach
ulcers, wrong to others, heart attacks and aggressiveness. For a
man with time on his hands, free to stay in bed or work until
he wished and when he wished, was generally not an angry,
frustrated man.

These days, Summerfield helped Raja in the fields although it
was against the custom. Here, the usual was for the boys and
young men to look after the goat herds, taking on the role of
shepherds. The older men tended to men's affairs—counting
the harvest, trading and negotiating, praying, talking politics and
occasionally taking up their arms. The women did everything
else: weaning their children, shepherding them and setting them
to work on helping with the daily tasks. They laboured the fields,
carried bundles of firewood on their backs to the home, cooked
meals, ensured the water supply and the washing and countless
other tasks. The men looked upon Summerfield with surprise
and mockery. Then the looks became reproachful and almost
dangerous. Raja, hearing rumours that some of the men, their
hostility fuelled by the religious leaders of the valley, were thinking
of confronting Summerfield, advised him to stop helping.

Where to invest his energy? Although not pressed by the
urgency of time, Summerfield felt pressure from his own self-

pride. He did not take long to find himself new employment. The idea came to him when exploring the winding paths that cut through the maze of village streets and houses. There was one particular place where the stench became so fierce that he retched, turned around and quickly backtracked to the village square.

He saw Raja walking up the slope with a bundle on her back and she must have noticed his grimace, for she asked if he was all right.

'No,' said Summerfield, pulling another face. 'I think I just found the village latrines!'

'Oh, the gully,' said Raja and smiled. Her beige eyes sparkled with mockery. 'Don't worry, *Sidi* Harry—you'll get used to it.'

'But people just squat there and—'

'Pee and poo,' said Raja, cackling with laughter.

'Not only men. I saw a woman just hitch up her skirts—in broad daylight!'

'And people do not do this in England?'

'Well, sometimes…*only if necessary*. They did about three hundred years ago, I suppose.' Raja laughed even more, shaking her head, quite too theatrically Summerfield thought. She was a cheeky one. And then it came to him. 'Hold on! I've just had an idea!'

'Like the football game!' chirped Raja.

'Orderliness and cleanliness,' replied Summerfield. '*Public toilets.*'

'What's *public toilet?*' inquired Raja.

'*Public toilets,*' said Summerfield again in English. 'No—don't worry. The word doesn't exist in your dialect—or at least I don't know how to say it. I mean a place where everyone can—*do their business.*'

'But we already have a place.'

'The place is a stink hole—unhygienic. Things like that brought on the bubonic plague in England. No, I mean a place where people are hidden from view and where they can sit.'

'Sit? *What for?*'

'For *comfort*, of course—are you stupid?'

'Are *you* stupid?!' retorted Raja. 'You want to change us. But you don't understand that this is how it is done—and it doesn't bother anybody. It's natural and as long as you take care to hide your—'

'*Thank you*, Raja,' interrupted Summerfield, bringing the conversation to a halt. A frown appeared on his brow and he refrained from launching into the offer of an argument. The young girl would surely beat him—she had a character like a lioness. 'We'll see,' was all he said and walked away. 'We'll see...'

He began by choosing the place—a square patch of almost level land at the bottom of the village bordered by a screen of twisted and ragged old olive trees. It was both visually sheltered and also subject to a constant breeze coming up the valley from the south, enough to drive away the swarms of flies. He then, once again under the gaze of a growing number of curious children, began to dig a series of ten holes, three feet deep, in a straight line south to north. He stopped at five—a sudden stratum of rock lying barely four inches below the earth rendering the task impossible—and dug the other holes where he began so that the whole formed an L-shape. It took him three days. Channels linked the holes together. He lined these with a thick local mortar people used to make bricks for their houses. Badr, back from his affairs, showed him how to mix it. From the channels, he traced a line to the future cesspit some twenty yards away. Here, he made the children place pebbles and stones in a square that measured some twelve-by-fifteen feet—the outline for the pit. It was at this point that the village Mullah appeared, leaning on his stick to view events. The children dispersed slowly, wary of the tutoring stick and Summerfield had to finish off placing the pebbles himself. The Mullah cleared his throat.

'And pray tell me, Englishman, what you have in mind? A fortress, perhaps? A *Houses of Parliament* for the village?'

'Your humour is of great strength today,' replied Summerfield, taking pains to adhere to the strange protocol of formality one had to follow when addressing the Mullah. 'Not such a grand edifice, I'm afraid. No—nothing lowlier than a toilet.'

'A toilet? Is it not too large a toilet for your individual use, or perhaps our food is so at odds with your foreign stomach that your needs are so great?'

Summerfield, still smiling, dropped the last pebble into place. 'No, Respected Mullah. I am building a large toilet for everybody's use. It will make the village cleaner, help with keeping modesty and provide comfort.'

'It helps, perhaps, with making us more civilised,' intoned the religious teacher, ironically. 'And may I ask who gave you permission for this venture? You steal our soil for western edifices which none of us know how to use. Perhaps, when finished, you will be so kind as to demonstrate to the entire village?'

'I regret that I have not asked, having believed that the ground was destined for no use. That I apologise for.' Summerfield looked sharply into the little man's shrewd eyes. 'Respected Mullah, are you against the idea?'

'I am against heresy, Englishman. Be careful that your construction does not overstep the ancient laws of the valley that is all.' The old man stood as straight-backed as possible and turned away. 'Oh, and by the way.' He glanced stiffly back. 'By what means do you intend to evacuate the waste? I see that you have built channels and are planning a pit. But it seems you have overlooked the water supply. Goodbye, Mister Summerfield. And yes—*good luck!*' And with that, the old man hobbled away with what seemed a cackle of doom lifted straight out of a pirate pantomime.

Summerfield sighed and sat down before his plans. He rolled himself a cigarette—thick, black local tobacco and a thin slip of rice paper. Damn, the old goat was right. He'd completely overlooked the water supply needed to evacuate the water. The nearest well was a hundred and fifty yards or more away in the village. The nearest stream of equal distance and the river beyond any practical distance at all. A small, grubby boy with inflated cheeks sat down beside him to sniff in the stray smoke and share in Summerfield's despair. Summerfield gave him a glance and shook his head.

'What's you name?'

'Mohammed.'

'Yes, I suppose it had to be,' said Summerfield: 'The first son, aren't you. Well, Mohammed, I have a lot of work to do. Would you like to help me?' The little boy nodded, unsmiling. 'Good. I see you're enthusiastic. In fact, I have a great amount of work to do—and I don't know if it will all turn out worthless doing it.'

'Why do something if you know it might fail?' said the boy, the first sentence since sitting with him. It was rather a brutal one at that.

'Ah, I see you speak. And wisely, too,' added Summerfield with a wink. 'Why?' he pondered. 'Because I'm *British*, that's why.'

'Hum.' The boy grunted and squinted at Summerfield. His cheeks looked larger than ever—like a gerbil filled with sunflower seeds. 'All right.'

'You mean you *believe* it?'

'You said the same when you invented the game with the ball,' scowled Mohammed. 'And you were right. This lucky *British* you speak of. It is bigger than our luck. I wish to be British too.'

Summerfield laughed. 'Then from now on, Mohammed, I say that you are an honorary *British lucky*. If I ever get out of this place, I'll write a letter to the embassy about you!'

'What's an embassy?' enquired Mohammed, losing the thread of things. Sometimes what the Englishman said was so silly that he couldn't understand. 'And why a letter?'

'No worry. Just consider yourself lucky, that's all. First, we need stones—big ones and flat. Like this,' said Summerfield, using his hands to outline the shape.

'Why?'

'I see you are logical-minded too,' said Summerfield. 'Too logical. For the thrones, of course!'

'Kings have thrones,' frowned Mohammed.

'You'll certainly feel like one after sitting on them. Crapping in comfort, Mohammed, it's the only way. In fact, we'll all be kings after this. The rest—the water and this big hole—well I haven't the answer as yet. But it'll come. I'm *British*.'

'Me too!' grinned Mohammed, unsure of the Englishman's riddles but certain of his newly acquired power.

Little Mohammed showed him a quarry behind the village that until then Summerfield had been oblivious to. It wasn't exactly slate, but another stone that resembled it in colour if not texture. There was a tool, rather like a garden hoe but much stronger lying near the stones and apparently for communal use. The little boy lifted it with strong arms and brought it down sharply on a block. A puff of smoke, as if a bullet had struck it, exploded in the air above the impact and a small, clean, vertical crack appeared.

'Excellent!' shouted Summerfield. 'Here, now you've shown me how, let me finish it off, Mohammed.' He lifted the tool and brought it down in the cleft left by the boy's initial strike. Immediately, a sheer slice of rock broke off and fell on its side among the debris. 'Well, it works. Now all that's left is toil and sweat.'

The next day saw Summerfield and his helper back at the quarry, slicing rock. Mohammed brought along his younger brother who helped at the olive press. More importantly, their father was a muleteer—and the brothers had borrowed the communal animal for the early afternoon.

With the borrowed mule, several trips back and forth from the quarry to the construction site were enough. The temperature was fierce and the valley was deserted. The two brothers watched, sometimes scowling, sometimes grinning, as Summerfield showed them how he wanted to place the cut stones—one vertical larger stone either side of the hole and two thinner, flat stones horizontally across the top, half a foot apart and straddling the three-foot hole beneath. By the end of the second morning, the latrines had been formed, the seats ridden of any sharp protrusions and the ten structures tested for strength and reliability. Several adjustments had to be made for the end five destined for children and the aged. But judging from the frowns on the boys' foreheads, they still hadn't realised what they were for. When Summerfield took them through a simulation of their use, grimaces and rasps and all, they broke into an unstoppable fit of giggling and laughter. The next morning, Mohammed and his brother arrived at Summerfield's door at 6.30 sharp—at the head of ten other children eager to set to work on the *British throne toilet* as they had now baptised it.

Summerfield and the small army of children began digging the large cesspit. Raja appeared, providing them with drinking water and looking at Summerfield, he noticed worriedly, with nothing short of glowering adulation. Badr, too, once his work was done, lent a hand, joking that even the tribal Kaïd, leader of the whole valley, didn't possess such a magnificent set of thrones as this. And then, once again the village Mullah paid a visit. Hobbling into sight and nearly toppling into the deepening hole, he steadied himself on his stick, his mouth setting into a thinly disguised smile of disapproval.

'I see that you have not yet thought about water, Englishman,' he said, tutting fretfully. 'And even if you do find an answer, who do you think will administrate the construction? Clean out the system, ensure the hygiene of the thrones, dig out the mess when it blocks and deepen the throne holes when they have been too often used? And what about the possible abuse of Holy Laws? There is much more to this than you have thought, Mister Summerfield.'

The crowd of workers stood silent and motionless. Summerfield looked steadily at them before turning to the Mullah.

'Respected Mullah, many hundreds of years ago, the kings and savants of your great religion were among the first to provide the civilised world with proper hygiene and waste evacuation. Their marvellous work eradicated disease and brought purity to the world when London was a stink hole of plague and filth. If I can help this valley, being inspired by your farsighted forefathers, then it will not be heresy.' The Mullah remained silent, chewing on a wisp of his beard, thinking. 'And indeed I must thank you, Respected Mullah,' added Summerfield.

'Thank me?' The old man raised his eyebrows. All eyes turned to him and his face fought between relentless animosity and a concession of pride.

'Yes, *thank you*, sir. For I, Summerfield, am a dreamer. Since the beginning, I have been dreaming at every moment during the planning of this construction. And your sharp insights and criticisms have made me stop and think—because every dreamer requires a realist to ensure the success of a project. Children—

everybody—I propose to applaud our Respected Mullah for his indirect help!' The army of workers broke into—not as Summerfield had expected a round of spontaneous clapping—but a jubilant song interspersed with yelps and victory whoops. The old Mullah, at first distrustful, then embarrassed, finally seemed to decide it was best to extract the most from the lost situation and broke into a series of toothless smiles and elegant gestures of acknowledgement.

Summerfield ate with Badr that evening. The young man was obviously impatient to tell him something and when he gave the news of the French defeat and subsequent armistice, Summerfield felt a strange sense of disinterest overcome him.

'That's terrible,' he said, forcing emotion into his voice. 'This tajine is really good, by the way. Who made it?'

'Raja and her mother,' replied Badr, scratching his goatee.

'Mmm. Delicious. You know—Raja's a lovely girl. An awful character, though. How old is she now? Fifteen? Sixteen? I caught her looking at me in a strange way this morning. I hope she isn't…'

'Harry, I don't understand you. Not so long ago you were filled with anger at not being able to join your war,' interrupted Badr, shaking his head. 'And now, you talk about food and young women. And by the way,' added the young man, parenthetically, 'Raja is destined to be my wife. We were chosen for each other when she was nine and I fifteen.'

Summerfield froze. 'Hell—sorry, Badr.'

'That's how it is. We could already have married, but I wish to wait until she is seventeen.'

'No, not that. I wouldn't have thought. You'll make a fiery couple.'

'She has temperament. But, Harry, you are avoiding the subject.'

'The war?' offered Summerfield. Badr nodded. Summerfield put down his plate and cleaned his fingers. 'Yes, you're right. I feel very bizarre, my friend. It's as though I'm not concerned anymore, as though it all belongs to another time, another world. Not my world.'

'The destiny of France, perhaps. But England, Great Britain—your country?' The young man ladled another portion of vegetables onto Summerfield's plate and handed it back to him. '*And* Jeanne Lefèvre.'

'Good God…' Summerfield raised his eyebrows. He had surprised himself. 'Yes, I'd… I'd almost forgotten,' he said distantly.

'Perhaps you have deliberately pushed all that into forgetfulness, Harry. Perhaps it is too painful to think about.'

'You may be right, Badr. Do you have any news?'

'She did not leave for France.'

'That's something.' Summerfield withdrew into silence. 'And Abrach—*Abslem*?'

'I cannot say much, I'm afraid. But I believe he is continuing the struggle against the French. Things may change now. No contact with Lefèvre—ever since the event. The Administrator is protected twenty-four hours a day.'

'He should have killed him when he had the chance,' said Summerfield, shaking his head.

'It wasn't how he wanted things to happen, you know that,' replied Badr, washing his hands in a bowl that smelt faintly of oranges. It reminded Summerfield of the letters. So long ago it seemed. 'Abrach wasn't a man intent upon murder—he was too good for that. He just wanted Lefèvre to admit, to repent.'

'You said *was* a good man,' repeated Summerfield.

'Yes. I said *was*. What he has experienced has…has turned my master into a bitter, vengeful man. I am afraid he will become like the people he wishes to defeat—merciless.'

'And you still fight with him?'

'I fight for a wider purpose, Harry. And I hope, in the deepest part of me, that he will see the truth and change back to the generous man he was before.'

Summerfield put his plate back down with a grunt. 'Badr, you are an intelligent, courageous and honest young man. But you are flying so high with lofty convictions that you fail to see the reality of life. Your naivety is as dangerous as Abrach's cynicism. Take care—please. As a friend I ask this of you.'

The young man smiled sheepishly and sat up straight. 'Enough of me and my failings, Harry. And may I remind you that you are one to speak of naivety! But your war? You didn't answer me.'

Summerfield thought for a few moments, inwardly trying to summon up his true feelings. They wouldn't come. He shook his head. 'I don't know,' he exhaled. 'As you said, maybe I don't dare thinking about it all—it will hurt too much. But then again, I feel unburdened of it all. I'm—I'm almost *at home* here in the valley. If I were free to leave tomorrow, then I would probably return to defend my country. But I am not. And as every day passes, my skin changes a little in colour, my mind begins to think as you do and my tongue manages to speak your strange language better and better.' Summerfield paused, stunned by a sudden revelation. 'Good God, Badr! *I'm almost happy here.*'

'Almost?' said Badr, cocking his head and smiling faintly.

'*Almost,*' repeated Summerfield.

The cesspit to the *British throne toilet* took a further day of digging to finish. They had to pull out Summerfield and his two small helpers using knotted ropes. The children, Raja, Badr and now a growing gathering of curious adults cheered when his head appeared, gleaned in sweat, from the hole. Climbing out, Summerfield noticed the old Mullah on the edge of the crowd. He was staring at him with unsmiling eyes.

The next two days saw screens made of brushwood and discarded wicker go up between the thrones, so that only the head and shoulders of the adult user could be seen. The children liked this idea, inventing a game involving peeking around the screen and frightening the hapless occupant.

The problem of water supply remained, however. It nagged Summerfield at night, crept into his sleep. He thought of setting up a sanitary unit whose task would be to carry water in buckets and clean away the waste for a fee. But this was no good. It would make him a boss and anything as absurdly outrageous as being an employee would never be accepted by the tribes' people. He thought of prospecting for water nearer the pit, but the work would be gigantesque. He also thought of the mule and having it bring water regularly to the throne room, but he'd probably have to hire it or buy it from its owner and he had no money. When Summerfield's dreams became so full of toilets, flushing water and the threat of rotting faeces that it began to wake him long before dawn, he decided to take a break from the project for a while. Perhaps, like writing, the idea would gestate in his mind and pop up as a perfect solution when it wanted to.

Badr came to him next morning—with a manly lurch to his walk. Under his arm was a long, rolled rug that looked surprisingly stiff. Sitting on his cushions outside his hut, Summerfield looked up sure that something was on the young man's mind. A solution for the cesspit, perhaps?

'Good morning to you, Harry.'

'Hello, Badr. Is something the matter? Can I offer you a tea?'

Badr sat down. 'No, thank you,' replied the young man, brusquely. 'Harry. Today I have decided to teach you something.'

'Oh—I thought it was the cesspit,' said Summerfield, mildly. 'And what, pray tell me, Badr, do you intend to teach me?'

'I remember that at one time you were ready to fight in Spain.'

'My convictions at that time, Badr. Yes—yes, I was.'

'And how exactly were you going to fight?'

Summerfield frowned and sat up. 'What d'you mean *how*?'

'With your hands, perhaps? With your fists? Or maybe with a pen!' Badr let out a brief guffaw.

'Now look here,' began Summerfield, aware that the young man was mocking him. But he didn't have time to finish.

'Today I will teach you how to use a rifle,' said Badr.

'A rifle? You mean a gun?'

Badr stood up, giving his head a little shake of regret. 'Harry, the world has suddenly changed. It is at war. How would you be able to defend yourself if you don't know how to use a rifle?'

'Can you trust me?' frowned Summerfield. 'After all, I'm supposed to be your prisoner. I don't understand.'

'Prisoner you say!' Once again, Badr guffawed, but this time followed it by a slow scratching of his beard. It was a sign that Summerfield had hit on something. Badr smiled tersely. 'You are no longer our prisoner, Harry.'

'What?' It was Summerfield's turn to stand up. 'You mean I'm free to go?'

Badr nodded. 'The chief and the elders have decided. They think it dishonourable that they should keep you from your country's war. If you wish, you are free to leave, Harry. But one other thing—the chief and the elders also consider you as one of their people. They—perhaps the right word is—*appreciate* you.'

'Well.' Summerfield took a few steps, turning on himself, feeling a little lost. 'That's—that's very pleasing to hear, but…but now I have to make a decision.'

'Take your time. Their decision is not an invitation to leave the valley today.' Badr sighed and looked across the valley to the mountain peaks. 'If you decide to remain, then you may have to one day defend this valley along with your brothers.' Summerfield looked at him. 'The French, Harry. Though they have been defeated in Europe, they still have their empire. And this long war between them and us, they still want to win. They are becoming very active in the foothills. Patrols have been sighted in the higher valleys. Opinion is that they are preparing a campaign.'

'I've never fired a gun in my life,' said Summerfield, distantly. 'Though I'd like you to teach me. It would be an honour.'

Badr beamed. 'It is also an honour for me. And as a sign of our trust and friendship, I have brought you along a very special gift.' At this, the young man placed the rug on the dusty ground and delicately unrolled it. 'For you, Harry—a Lee Enfield Mark II 303. A British rifle, almost a legend. Still one of the best in the world.'

'How on earth?' said Summerfield, gaping. 'How did it get here?'

'It's always been in the village. Some say it was brought up by a caravan in the early part of the century. Others say it was smuggled in from British spies in the 1927 uprising, happy to see us fight the French.'

'In any case, it's a superb gesture, Badr.' Summerfield felt overcome with feeling. 'I thank you,' was all he could manage.

'Take it. Pick it up—it is not loaded and I took care to remove the bolt.'

Summerfield bent down and lifted it. 'That's heavy. Much more than I thought,' he said, surprised by the weight.

'Come,' said Badr, cheerily. 'You will see how it kicks!'

That evening, eating some salted semolina and vegetables he had prepared, Summerfield's ears still rang with the sharp crack of the Lee Enfield and the strange aftermath of echo, almost like a tear of lightning, that had whorled through the valley. Badr had been right—the old rifle had a beastly character. His shoulder hurt like hell from the fierce recoil. After Badr had taken him through much theory, making him adopt various firing positions, bracing himself, assembling and reassembling the mechanism, loading the stubby magazine and going through various cleaning techniques, Summerfield's first shot almost sent him falling backwards and the bullet upwards. God knows where it had landed. Because ammunition for the British rifle was scarce, he could only fire off five rounds. By the fifth, Summerfield felt proud—for he was able to hit a boulder some three hundred yards away that Badr had designated. True, it was quite a large boulder. But Badr had assured him it was encouraging.

As Summerfield ate his simple meal, he kept glancing at the Lee Enfield lying on his cot with the bolt removed. A faint smell of cordite still emanated from it mixed with bees' wax that Badr had administered before handing it over to Summerfield. And then his thoughts turned to his conversation that morning and his newly obtained freedom. He could simply go. However, before his mind went down this labyrinth of thought, there was a soft knock at the door. Summerfield rose and opened it.

It was the old Mullah. Summerfield started in surprise.

'Are you not going to welcome a guest inside?' said the old man and Summerfield relaxed a little. There was no trace of animosity in the old man's voice.

'Of course, Respected Teacher. Do come in. Please, sit. Can I offer you some mint tea?'

'With pleasure, Mr Summerfield. But make it China tea. And may I suggest you add a little of that English habit into it.'

'You mean milk?' Summerfield frowned and felt a distant sense of mistrust flicker in him.

'I would like to try,' nodded the old man, delicately. 'And I see,' he added, sending a glance at the Lee Enfield on Summerfield's cot, 'that our young Badr has initiated you in the art of shooting.'

'My apologies,' said Summerfield, hastily covering it up.

'No need, no need. It is a custom in these valleys for a man to have an arm. Though a crime, I must add, for a man to use it unless he is attacked or unless he hunts.'

'Of course,' nodded Summerfield, putting the kettle on the fire. 'Both our religions forbid murder.' A few moments of silence overcame the two men, a sort of uncertainty about what to speak of. 'The weather...' offered Summerfield then changed his mind. 'Have you come to dissuade me about completing the thrones?'

'Very direct,' nodded the Mullah and sighed. 'No. Rather I have come because I am still not totally convinced.'

'Then you have indeed come to voice your disagreement.'

The old man sat back and folded his arms, his stick slipping out of his arthritic knuckles and sliding gently to the floor. 'Please, Mr Summerfield. I have come because I want you to persuade me.'

'Can't you be persuaded by yourself?' said Summerfield and softened his tone. 'I think you have seen the progress in construction, oh Respected One. You know the reason why I wished to build them.'

'Really?' The old man gave a knowing grin and showed several missing teeth. 'You say you wanted to build this edifice for the health and hygiene of the villagers. Is that all?'

'It's enough, don't you think?' said Summerfield, beginning to feel irritated. 'That and what the French would call *pudeur*. We can't have womenfolk baring their backsides in broad daylight.'

'To my knowledge, this is not currently the case,' returned the Mullah, frowning sternly. 'If there have been cases of indecency, then I'd like to know who.'

'There has been no indecency,' replied Summerfield, increasingly interested in the verbal skirmish. 'It was just a turn of phrase of mine.'

'I feel relieved,' said the old man. 'It *is* true that the occasional wild young boy will tend to flaunt his nascent snake from time to time, but our people are generally good and proper. So tell me—what else made you want to build the edifice?'

Summerfield paused, the time it took to pour the water into another kettle containing tea. 'I needed something to do, oh Mullah. That is the truth. I could not work the fields—I now know why and I accept the rule. But my body and mind were restless. A man must have a goal.'

'Ah, good!' beamed the Mullah, his wrinkles making his skin look like an old prune. 'We agree on something at last.'

'I wanted something to do. And it was when I came across the public gully that the idea came to me.'

'Humm,' pondered the Mullah. 'Yes, I suppose I can quite understand you. I try to avoid the area, but it is sometimes necessary to…use the gully myself. At my age! I can hardly squat anymore and when the cold east wind blows straight down the gully between your buttocks and you have to get some cheeky young boy to hold you while you do it, I can tell you it is most embarrassing!'

'Especially for a man of your status, oh Respected Mullah,' nodded Summerfield.

'Especially,' echoed the old man.

'Am I right,' probed Summerfield, carefully, 'that you think the construction might be of use after all?'

The old man shifted in his seat. 'First, some of your English tea, if you please.' Summerfield poured, added milk, stirred and handed the bowl across. 'I thank you,' said the Mullah and took an alarmingly loud slurp of the scolding liquid. There was no reaction of pain or surprise and Summerfield raised his eyebrows with a tinge of respect—the old badger must have a throat made of iron. 'Let's say that I am beginning to be persuaded,' continued the teacher. 'Though, how should I say it…' The Mullah's voice suddenly took on a delicateness much like honey, insinuatingly rich. It seemed to be pointing Summerfield in the direction of a request. 'I am still not entirely, one hundred per cent convinced—even if so many *others* are. However, if…'

Summerfield looked at the old man and found himself mimicking his nod of encouragement.

'I see,' said Summerfield, with the feeling that something was about to dawn on him. 'Perhaps…'

'Yes?' nodded the old man, energetically.

'Perhaps, if you would honour me with a *favour*?' said Summerfield.

'If I can,' replied the old man, once again aloof.

'By accepting the honour of being the first to try and test the construction,' said Summerfield.

The old man let out a sigh of agreement. 'I would indeed be inclined to accept this honour, Mr Summerfield. When?' he added, rather quickly. 'We wouldn't want anyone to cheat and get there first! It would spoil things.'

'Absolutely. What about in two days' time. I must first find a solution for the water supply.'

'Ah, the water!' The Mullah looked suddenly defeated and a look of what could only be described as sadness overcame his face. It lasted a full three seconds before being replaced by a fleeting grin. He made to stand up and Summerfield had to help him. 'A solution will be found, *Inchalla*,' said the old Mullah, accepting his stick that Summerfield held out to him. 'Where there is a will. I bid you good night now, Mr Summerfield. You are indeed a very persuasive man.'

'As indeed you are too, oh Mullah,' returned Summerfield with a respectful bow. 'And also a man of action,' he called out as the old man hobbled off into the darkness.

A hot breeze filled the valley, blew nonchalantly for a morning then disappeared. A balmy heavy weight of heat settled in, making beads of sweat appear on his brow at every movement.

Summerfield made plans. He would meet the Mullah in the evening, at his convenience, in a day's time. Together, they would inspect the works and Summerfield would demonstrate how to use the new fangled thrones before leaving the wise old man to satisfy his business. A bucket of water would suffice for the test phase. The following day, sure that the Mullah would have spread the good word, Summerfield would announce the identity of the man that had been the first to successfully test and use the thrones. Hopefully, he could then announce their opening for general use with the Mullah's blessing. Perhaps some other dignitary would endorse the project too before what was sure to be a rush of children and their parents. And the water? The best bet would be to ensure that everyone brought along their own supply and be responsible for cleaning away the waste. It was the simplest, easiest solution. If the project proved a success, then perhaps he could persuade the elders to build an overhead irrigation channel—a sort of pipeline—from the well up in the village to the site, though it would mean much work and require many resources.

The morning drew on and the heat became stifling. The women in the fields took frequently to the shade, wrapped from head to toe in robes as protection. Summerfield still couldn't fathom out how they managed to do this. For Europeans, the slightest hint of sun and heat provoked a systematic discarding of clothes. Here, it meant the opposite: the tribes' people covered themselves up.

As Midday approached, the weather became unbearable and under general consent, it was decided to abandon the fields and slopes and stay inside until the heat subsided. From his shaded doorway, Summerfield watched, undecided as to go and check the installations once again. The valley filled with a sort of thin, simmering smoke that was hot mist for an hour. It then melted before his eyes, replaced by seething strata of heat that sizzled and blurred over the ground until it hypnotised him. When he shook his head to gather his wits, beads of sweat were projected into the air. He drank water, fanned himself and looked on. He thought he saw Badr in the kaleidoscope of heat, bent double and scurrying quickly among the village houses. The figure gave a brief wave in his direction and then disappeared. Summerfield drank tea, resigned to sweating profusely and hoping the perspiration on his body would cool him down.

Raja appeared, swathed in robes of royal blue cloth. Once inside, she uncovered herself in silence while Summerfield blew noisily and groaned, a sign of growing irritation with the situation. A faint smell of cloves and cinnamon and a deeper, musky smell came to him. It was Raja's body smell.

'You are angry, *Sidi* Summerfield. So moaning and angry against this weather.'

'I should bloody-well think so,' grumbled Summerfield in English. 'This is unbearable, Raja! I've never known it to be so hot—not even in the plains or in Marrakesh.' He returned to dialect. '*Can't you*—can't you *do* something!'

She let out a laugh and looked mockingly at him. 'The French have a reputation for weakness and complaining in such weather—I didn't know the English were worse!'

'But look at you!' retorted Summerfield. 'You're wet!' The young woman stepped back and tried to look at herself. True, there were large patches of damp covering her dress. 'Doesn't it bother you?'

Raja touched one of the patches under her arms. 'No. In fact, I didn't even know it was there. We have to live with it.'

Summerfield poured out two cups of water, exhaled noisily and tut-tutted. 'I can't understand you all. You're beyond comprehension. All of you.'

'The villagers?'

'Everybody! Everybody living south of Plymouth.'

'Where's *Plymmut*?'

Summerfield didn't take any notice of her. 'Why you stand this awful environment is beyond me. Why don't you move north? Why don't the hundreds of tribes get it into their heads that there is better, more clement weather somewhere else? Why don't you just move, for heaven's sake?'

Raja poked out her tongue and looked sullen. 'How do I know? I'm a woman and my work is to make the fields provide us our food to eat. I know about the fields, but I have no answer to your stupid, unnecessary questions.'

'They're not stupid. *You* are! If you thought about these questions and actually *did* something, then you wouldn't have to ask them again.'

'Now you are impossible to understand!' retorted Raja, her voice rising to a shout. 'Go and ask the Mullah, go and ask the Kaïd, but not me.'

'You said *I* was angry,' said Summerfield, aware that he sounded quite childish. However, it felt quite good to have someone to whom he could let off steam and rid himself of his irritation. He suddenly felt quite malicious. 'Now *you are*, Raja—*angry!*'

'I'm not!'

'You are!'

'I'm not, not, not!'

'You are, are, and are!'

They looked at each other, surprised by the outburst, and suddenly fell into laughter.

'This is silly!' said Raja, giggling.

'*We* are silly!' added Summerfield, triumphantly. 'And thank God we are. Imagine if we had to be serious all the time.'

'Imagine if we had to answer questions like yours all the time,' continued Raja.

'Now don't be cheeky, Raja!' said Summerfield, lapsing back into irritation. And so continued another round of arguing until Raja, at this point her words becoming an uncontrollable high-pitched babble of Arabic and Berber dialect, rose in disgust, wrapped herself in her robes, slammed the door shut and walked away.

'Open that door!' shouted Summerfield after her, but in vain. 'Come back and open that *bloody door!*'

He decided to go out and brave the heatwave. Pacing irritably about his small hut was worse than sitting and sweating it out. Stepping out of his dwelling it felt like he almost walked into a wall of heat and took an involuntary step back. 'Holy God Almighty!' he blasphemed, lowering his shoulders and walking into the cauldron.

Down by the construction, the vegetation had turned beige, petrified in the windless heat like fossils. A solitary cat, a mangy grey and white tom, sat panting under a thorn bush. Its mouth was so far pulled back in the effort that it looked as though it were grinning. Summerfield winked at it and stooped down to touch one of the toilet emplacements. *'Ow!'* The cat suddenly started and shot past Summerfield. '*Bloody hot!*' spat Summerfield, himself scared by the cat's sudden movement. He exhaled noisily, gave the site a look and turned to go: 'And this damn heat will dry up all the water in any case,' he mumbled, as he walked back to his hut.

The sun changed. White and powerfully aggressive in the afternoon, it seemed to cook in its own heat and turn a strange, watery yellow verging on pink. As evening came, it seemed to swell as it fell slowly in the sky. It became orange, a great shimmering, hovering globe—Summerfield had never seen it so big. He sent up a silent prayer for wind and urged the night to be fresh. Captivated, occasionally wondering why nobody had paid him a visit since Raja, he watched the hours go by as the sun sank, vermillion, in the violet sky. The air did not change. It was as stifling as it had been all day. With the sun, and fatigue of his struggle against the heat, his eyelids sank and eventually closed shut. While he slept, nature prepared itself.

He awoke with a shout, blinded by the electric white of the flash of lightning. A terrifyingly close clap of thunder roared overhead. Summerfield swore and rushed out of bed to close the door of his dwelling. He paused, cocking his head. What was that strange noise—like distant hooves thudding on the ground? It got louder and louder. It seemed to be approaching the village. There was a single, unexpected gust of fresh wind that disappeared as quickly and surprisingly as it had come. And as the storm exploded overhead, looking out, he saw the sheer wall of water moving inexorably towards the village. He had just enough time to dash outside and retrieve his seat and cushions before the first fat drops stung his skin. He slammed the door behind him and watched. Through the slit of his window the rain hit the ground like bullets, spattering dust and debris. It was as close to apocalypse as he'd ever been. The noise was deafening, the sky black, enraged. He cursed with every rip of thunder and as the water began to drip increasingly through the cracks in the roof, he seriously wondered if he would survive the storm. He began to sing *Jerusalem*—very loudly—interrupting it with alternate bouts of swearing and praying. He was in the middle of a prayer when the door shot open. A large, masked shape pushed through the doorway. Summerfield let out an instinctive roar and braced himself for struggle.

'It's me! *Badr!*' came a muffled shout. 'I've been knocking for ages! Get your rifle, get your belongings—you must shelter at my house. It's safer!'

In the morning, the valley awoke later than usual. An unreal calm filled the air, like the aftermath of a great gathering. When Summerfield and Badr looked outside, they saw a valley strewn with the flotsam and jetsam of the storm—clothes, stones, rocks, shreds of material, young trees, utensils, roofing tiles, wooden beams, uprooted bushes, the charred shape of a mangy dog lying on its back with its paws outstretched. It looked like a battlefield. Only the river, down in the trough of the valley, bubbled and rushed, bloated happy with the water from the summer storm.

'What a mess,' commented Summerfield. 'I seriously thought I was going to die. Thank you, Badr. I wonder what shape my hut is in.'

'I'm afraid you should think more of your *public toilets*, Harry,' said Badr. 'I wonder what shape *they're in* after all this.'

Surely enough, as the two men picked their way through the debris down towards the clearing, they saw that the screens had completely disappeared, no doubt blown or washed away to the other side of the valley. The gullies leading from the compartments had crumbled and the thrones themselves were mostly down. The cesspit was a pool of brackish water. But there was something else, something different—a large array of heavy urns, some two hundred of them placed in files, four deep behind each emplacement.

'Are these yours?' said Badr, perplexed.

Summerfield shook his head. 'I've never seen them before.' The two men approached. 'They're full of water,' said Summerfield, mechanically. He looked at Badr, puzzled and their faces lit up as it simultaneously dawned on them. 'Do you know what this means?'

'Water supply!' shouted Badr and spontaneously embraced

the Englishman. 'You have your water supply—for two weeks at least!'

'But *who*?' said Summerfield, stooping to rap one of the great urns. 'Hold on—looks as though some of them have some sort of a sign on them.'

Badr crouched akimbo and looked up. 'It's the Mullah's mark—they belong to him.'

'The old devil!' spat Summerfield.

'*Please*, Harry!' said Badr. 'Such irreverence.'

'Oh, I'm sorry—a purely Christian reflection, Badr. The *old saint*, then. Yes…the old saint,' he repeated, glancing up the hill towards the Mullah's quarters.

43

Nearly a day passed before Jeanne heard the sound of her father's voice again in the hallway downstairs. She hurried to the landing and peered over the banister, shocked by the greyness of her father's face. For the first time, she noticed how old he looked.

'It's scandalous,' she heard him mutter and he looked up, seeing her for the first time and gave her the trace of a smile. He cleared his throat. 'I'd like to have a word with you all—mother, Jeanne, Soumia and Mohammed. Please assemble in the sitting room. I need to freshen up a little first. Oh, and pour me a large drink, *chérie*,' he added, nodding briefly at Jeanne's mother. 'Anything as long as it's strong.'

They gathered, as Lefèvre had ordered, in the sitting room, Jeanne and her mother sitting, Soumia coyly accepting a seat herself and Mohammed, uneasy with breaking the rule, declining the offer.

'*Madame*,' said Soumia, unable to maintain the silence that had settled over them. 'I was just thinking that a nice tomato salad would be—'

'Soumia,' said Mme Lefèvre, pursing her lips and giving the maid one of her silencing looks. 'The moment is grave and tomatoes won't help.'

'Sorry, *Madame*.' She looked down and clasped her hands. 'It's just that ever since a while, if I may dare, things have been—'

'*Thank you*, Soumia,' sighed Mme Lefèvre, pausing to consider whether to reprimand the woman. She decided against it. 'Perhaps we could send you off to De Gaulle in England as a secret weapon—you'd talk the Germans to death!'

For a moment, Soumia's eyes grew wide sure that Mme Lefèvre was serious.

'Mummy was only joking, Soumia,' said Jeanne.

'But she never jokes,' replied Soumia, involuntarily and clasped a hand over her mouth. 'I'm so sorry, *Madame*. It just came out.'

Mme Lefèvre looked sternly back and was about to reply when her husband entered.

He had freshly washed and shaved and there was a livid nick on his blue-ish chin from which a bubble of blood had coagulated. Jeanne wished he wouldn't gum his thinning hair like that. It made him look messy and somehow clownish. Maybe she should ask mother to tell him about it. Her father cleared his throat and remained standing, his glass in his hand.

'I'm afraid the situation is all rather confusing,' he said and added, with a smile of irony, 'or perhaps it's all too clear. The protectorate high-commissioner and the administrative authorities have pledged allegiance to the government in Vichy. It is the official, legally recognised government of France and our empire.'

'Yes, that *is* clear,' said Mme Lefèvre, immediately conscious of her shallow remark.

'However,' continued Lefèvre, sending her a telling glance, 'even though all French citizens have been asked to comply to this act of allegiance, a minority is still in favour of De Gaulle. Morocco is in limbo—if only for a day or two.'

'The silence is very odd,' said Jeanne. 'There are even no cars.'

'Didn't your mother tell you?' said Lefèvre, shaking his head. 'We've advised people to stay off the streets until things are clearer.'

'Because of possible demonstrations,' said Jeanne, answering her father. 'I talked to Jim and he told me—'

'Yes,' said Lefèvre, holding up a hand. 'Jim Wilding was good enough to speak to me too. He seemed worried for you—not surprising given the state you're in over each other. Either people will comply, or there'll be unrest—hopefully minor in nature.'

'And he thought you might be in danger, too, father.'

Lefèvre looked at his wife and gave her a fleeting grin of reassurance. 'For the moment, no one has said anything. I will comply with orders from above, carry on as usual. I can't see how voicing a fleeting opinion would land me in any great trouble, after all.'

In the afternoon, sitting on the veranda and finishing off a pair of mittens for the prisoners of war in Europe, Jeanne heard a sharp crack in the distance. She put down her needles. It had sounded like a small banger, dry and harmless.

'Mother?' she called and Soumia arrived. 'Ah, hello Soumia. Did you hear that? Get mother for me, will you. Don't wake father, though.'

Soumia nodded, looking worried and as she turned to scurry away, there was another solitary crack, followed straight after by a *poc-poc.*

'Gunfire!' said Jeanne, rising. She strained her eyes towards the distance and the centre of the old city. When her mother appeared moments later, they saw a thin blue trail of smoke rising to the left of the tall tower of the Koutubia mosque. It was somehow unreal: long, heavy seconds of silence broken by isolated cracks and followed by some other sort of guns with their flat *poc-pocking* sound.

Then Lefèvre appeared in his dark green dressing gown, looking tired and anxious. 'I've just had Le Guédec on the phone. It seems someone shot at a police vehicle and hit the radiator.'

'That must be the smoke,' said Jeanne.

'A lot of smoke for just a radiator,' said her father. 'Wrong colour, too.' He shook his head. 'I don't understand.'

'The shots have intensified,' said Jeanne's mother. 'And now they're coming from over there too,' she added, pointing towards the western part of the city. 'It's very worrying, Philippe-Charles.'

Lefèvre rubbed his chin, wincing as he touched the spot where he'd cut himself shaving that morning. 'Mother, get Mohammed to assemble the bags in the hallway.' Jeanne looked at her father. 'One never knows,' he said back. 'Oh, and make sure you've got your belongings—any jewellery, money, that sort of thing. I'll take a look at the car.'

'Father?' It was Jeanne, her voice trembling.

'Yes?' Lefèvre turned round, inquisitive and annoyed at having been interrupted.

'Jim said he'd be back earlier than planned. He wants to help us.'

'When?'

'Tomorrow. Late morning with a bit of luck.'

'Then pray that things won't get too out of hand before he gets here.'

Jeanne stayed on the veranda. She had already prepared her things after the phone call to Jim two nights before. Suddenly, the shots in the distance ceased and however much she thought the silence would be broken once again by the crack and *poc* of the guns, it wasn't. Silence reigned once again, strange and fragile.

She watched her father, dressed now, walk down to the front gate and approach the gendarme standing watch by the black Panhard. She couldn't hear what they were saying, but the gendarme shook his head several times. Her father's gestures were at first appealing, then sharper, authoritative, but the gendarme remained adamant, beckoning over a second gendarme from the light truck parked under the trees of the grassy central alley to the avenue. He had a sub-machine gun slung under his arm and Jeanne noticed his slow, lilting gait, a little like the marching style of the legionnaires. Perhaps he had once been one. Her father's voice was higher now and she heard the words *ordre* and *impensable—unthinkable*. The two paramilitaries, towering over the small, balding figure of her father, remained unperturbed. It was almost as if they were mocking him. Then a car appeared, driving fast up the avenue towards them and tearing up a thin cloud of dust in its wake. It came to a sharp halt with a high-pitched squeal and Colonel Le Guédec stepped out. The two guards immediately saluted. There was a brief, low-voiced exchange of words and Le Guédec led Lefèvre aside by the arm. The two gendarmes turned their backs and walked nonchalantly over to their truck. Jeanne watched on. Le Guédec produced a sheaf of papers, seemed to be explaining something. Her father looked quite pale, shook his head. Le Guédec persisted, pressing the papers into her father's hand and producing a pen. Whatever was going on? At last, with a gesture of futility, Lefèvre read the papers, glancing up occasionally into the Colonel's, his friend's, eyes. He signed, handing the papers back in disgust. However, their handshake was long. Lefèvre kept the Colonel's grip and spoke something before giving the hand a final, firm shake. The Colonel turned, looked back towards the house and caught Jeanne's gaze. He smiled, nodded and gave her a brief salute.

'The Colonel very nicely brought me some papers I'd forgotten at the office,' explained her father, as she and her mother met him downstairs. 'Those dolts who were supposed to be looking after our safety wouldn't even let me touch my car. A good thing Le Guédec arrived.'

'The papers,' insisted Jeanne.

'Yes.' Lefèvre exhaled heavily. 'Well—good news. My superiors have offered me a long period of leave. I didn't want to sign, given that there is much work to do here at the moment, but the Colonel persuaded me. It's for the best.'

'Long period of leave? What does this mean, Philippe-Charles?' said Jeanne's mother. 'Is anything wrong, *chéri*?'

Lefèvre remained silent, his mouth set in resignation and then gave a sigh of exasperation. 'I was rash enough to be objective about the situation,' he said. 'This so-called long period of leave means I have been replaced by a Vichy official. I'm too much of an embarrassment—that's what Le Guédec said.'

'And what side is *he* on?' said Jeanne, feeling angry.

Her father gave her an ironic smile. 'Things aren't so easy for him, my child. He was very proper, very gentlemanly—and he's probably saved us quite a lot of bother. He will let me keep the car and he's sending us to his mountain lodge to stay. He will keep our whereabouts to himself—he gave me his word.'

'Mountain lodge? What about our house in Mogador?'

'The sea ports are tightly controlled,' said Lefèvre, a hint of fatalism in his voice. 'I'm afraid I would be arrested there.'

'And where is this lodge—and how comfortable is it?' said Mme Lefèvre, almost indignantly.

Lefèvre gave her a little glance and refused to answer the second question. 'It's in the Atlas. Quite a way up, apparently. Le Guédec had it built at the time the last lion was killed in 1922—he participated in the hunt.'

'How beastly,' said Jeanne, angrily. 'The last of a noble race—

tens of thousands of years just finished off with a hunting rifle. God, I hope Jim will know what to do.'

Waiting was the worst of all things, Jeanne came to conclude. She had been sitting for hours, her head becoming increasingly jammed with worries and thoughts that she couldn't shake off. A single, irritating question kept returning to her mind every three minutes or so: *when would Jim arrive?* She double-checked her packed belongings, which Mohammed then carried down to the car in readiness for their departure. Perhaps Jim would come with them? Perhaps he would ask her to stay and accompany him south. And what if he could marry her there and then and take her with him to America? There were so many confusing and difficult arguments going on in her head. So many uncertainties.

Soumia was coming with them. Not Mohammed. That at least was certain. There was no space in the car and in any case, the loyal gardener was entrusted with staying behind at the house to look over it while they were gone. A long period of leave, wondered Jeanne. How long actually was this long period of leave? Two weeks, three? A month? Little by little it dawned on her that her father's career was ended and that very likely it was the last they would see of Marrakesh for some time.

Her father and mother were downstairs, behind the closed doors of the sitting room, discussing options and decisions. Where would he eventually take them? Not back to France, that was sure. England? Too perilous a journey. Perhaps French East Africa which seemed to have sided with De Gaulle. Chad seemed another planet away and didn't exactly inspire her— people said it was just one, monotonous stretch of open sand and nothing else. Damn the war and people's stupidity. Suddenly, a wave of nostalgia filled her and she began to cry. She'd always lived here. What about her friends? What about the places she knew so well? It all seemed so definitive and brutal. She'd miss them terribly. One name came back to her: Sister Marthe. The *Académie*, she thought—all those memories. She had to see her, had to say goodbye.

It took her father two phone calls and ten minutes of negotiation with the gendarmes to obtain permission. A police van appeared outside and Jeanne's father escorted her to it.

'Please, gentlemen,' he said, gravely, looking into the officers' eyes, 'Take good care of her. She's my only daughter. She is to be back in one hour.'

As the police car drove away, Jeanne caught a glimpse of her mother in an upstairs window, looking vacantly into the distance.

'What's in the bag, *'moiselle*?' enquired one of the policemen, nodding at her lap.

'Oh, only letters and some objects for Sister Marthe. They're so dear to me and I want her to have them. She helped me so very much.'

The streets were deserted. It was all very eerie and Jeanne felt a shiver pass through her. The city had been dormant for three days now and she was surprised at how much debris could accumulate on the streets after such a short time—twigs, paper, balls of grass and thorny bushes blown in from across the plain, cardboard, the odd faeces, a dead cat. A couple of carts lay abandoned, their owners no doubt having led away their donkeys to pasture while the curfew lasted. By the military quarters, there was a car parked in the middle of the road with a flat tyre. There was something hanging from the nearby lamppost.

'I wouldn't look if I were you, *m'moiselle*,' came the policeman's voice, suddenly, but she did.

Jeanne gasped. '*Awful, horrible!*'

'Please turn your head,' ordered the policeman but she couldn't keep herself from gaping. It was a body hanging slack from a rope. They passed the corner and Jeanne saw the face, a native, swollen like a great purple ball. She shuddered and felt sick.

'Better stop,' said the driver pulling up some twenty yards farther on. This time Jeanne looked straight ahead, not daring to look round while he got out to inspect the corpse, remained for a few moments and then rejoined the car. 'We'll deal with it later,' he said with a grimace and slammed the door shut.

'Why?' said Jeanne, trembling. 'Why would someone do that?'

'Someone taking advantage of the curfew to settle an old vendetta,' answered the policeman, mechanically. 'That happens.'

The academy looked somehow old and worn without the noise and colour of its students. The old knot tier, *Monsieur Quasimodo* was nowhere to be seen. A policeman escorted her to the large warped gates and pulled on the bell. Several dull clangs later and a sister arrived, in all appearances walking sideways towards them as though distrustful and ready to run.

'*M'moiselle* has come to see Sister Marthe,' said the policeman. 'She has an hour—no more. We'll be waiting here.'

'And you might like to offer her something to drink,' added the second officer. 'The young lady has just had quite a shock.'

Jeanne followed the sister, whom she recognised as one of the lower school teachers, to the entrance to the main building. She had aged. Maybe it was the light. In any case, she remembered taking piano lessons with her when she was barely into her teens. What did they used to call her? *Nosteratu*—that was it—on account of her long, claw-like fingers. Glancing down, Jeanne could no longer see why they had called her that. The sister had the most normal set of fingers ever.

'Sister Marthe has just finished prayer. I will tell her you are here, *Mademoiselle*.'

Jeanne waited a few moments and then the door opened again and a silent, beaming Sister Marthe appeared and took her in her arms. Jeanne felt the tears sting her eyes and then plop onto her cheeks. They held each other for a long time before sister Marthe drew back, wheezing and still looking at her with the broad smile on her lips.

'You look superb, Jeanne. Really—a fine young woman.'

'Thank you, Sister Marthe. And you look wonderful, too. Honestly.'

'Oh, no,' said the sister, reddening. 'The events have taken the shine out of me, I'm afraid. It brought back some sad memories of the last war, you see. I had two brothers.'

'Oh, I'm so sorry.'

Sister Marthe held up a hand and shook her head. 'No. It's me—becoming sad and whimsical again. Come. We shall have tea. Tell me what has happened to you.'

For the first time in over a year, Jeanne sat in the sister's dark green room—her office and bedroom all in one. The old nun's water pump—how she remembered that awful wheezing sound in class—sat on the dressing table. Her framed diplomas from Nantes looked tarnished and yellow now. And the crucifix was still there, the peaceful, benevolent smile on Jesus' face despite the pain. Jeanne thought it reminded her of Sister Marthe herself. How she hid her pain to give love and understanding to others. How, despite the assessment of her life with all its trials, it was all worth it.

Jeanne recounted her story, leaving out very many details so as not to shock or offend the old sister. When it was over, Sister Marthe said: 'So what happened to your great love, the Englishman?'

'He—he was taken away.'

'That's a pity. So you found an American?'

'No. Well—yes. Well—' Jeanne faltered, taken aback by the sister's directness. 'I didn't do it on purpose.'

'I didn't say you did,' puffed Sister Marthe, finishing off her tea. 'And in all honesty, the truth wouldn't shock me in the slightest. Remember—I was a young woman too once.'

'Sister Marthe.' Jeanne looked down, then raised her head to look steadily at her. 'I don't wish to speak too much about the details. It has been hard for me—to forgive myself and move on, putting hope in a new life with Jim Wilding.'

'I understand, child,' whispered Sister Marthe. 'And I think you're very brave. Well!' she suddenly exhaled, changing the subject. 'As for me, I must say I find it rather strange not to be teaching. How long all this is going to last only the Lord knows. I'll tell you a little secret though,' she continued, leaning her large weight towards Jeanne. 'I'm reading a lot. Poetry!'

'Really?' frowned Jeanne, finding it difficult to understand why it should be a secret.

Sister Marthe raised her eyebrows and whispered. 'Don't

tell anyone, but I smuggled in a book by someone called Yeats. Heavenly—and so romantic, so passionate!'

'Sister Marthe!' Jeanne sat back in surprise.

'Yes,' said the nun, a look of confession coming across her face. 'Naughty of me. You see—I have to forgive myself, too. And of course, I do tell *Him* about it.'

Jeanne squeezed Sister Marthe's forearm and in the same movement, picked up her bag and handed it across. 'Could you please keep this for me, Sister.'

'Of course—what is it?' frowned Sister Marthe.

'Letters, little presents. Most of my love for the Englishman is there—and his too. I don't really understand why, but I think you're the person I would most like to have them.'

'I shall hide them away,' said Sister Marthe, smiling benevolently.

'Sister Marthe?'

'Yes, child.'

'I don't have much longer. Would you accompany me outside. Just a short walk. Please?'

The two police officers gave their assent and watched as the young woman and the old sister walked slowly across the square in front of the *Académie* to the beginnings of the orange grove. Jeanne held sister Marthe's hand and led her carefully through the trees. At one point, they passed the old knot tier's shelter, sagging and lopsided now, a few belongings scattered in the grass and sand.

'I wasn't aware he lived here,' said Sister Marthe, sadly. 'If I had known, I would have offered him a space within the walls and provided meals.'

'I'm not sure he would have accepted,' replied Jeanne. 'He was a little strange. Though he helped me when I needed it. I'm afraid something bad might have happened to him because of that.'

They moved on, through the thickening trees until they came to the other side of the grove and the great plain before the distant mountains.

'Let's sit for a few moments, sister. I used to come here a lot.'

'It's very inspiring,' said the old woman, wheezing heavily as she placed her weight down on a large flat stone. 'Silly me—I forgot to take my pump with me. Still—beautiful mountains. I can see them from my room.'

They sat for a few, silent minutes. Strangely enough, Jeanne's head was empty of thought. She had imagined, while picking their way through the grove, that it would bring back a flood of memories, but she somehow felt peaceful and empty of worry. It was as though the memories of the place belonged to another person, another life. At one point she rose mechanically and sauntered down to the old irrigation channel.

'Be careful, Jeanne,' called Sister Marthe after her, but Jeanne had already dropped down into the ditch despite her dress and heels.

She took a few paces along the channel, glancing down to see the dust covering the shine on her shoes, feeling the old bricks with her fingertips. One, two, three—she came to the place, the loose brick. With her thumb and forefinger she prised it out, dislodging a small flurry of dust and sand. She looked into the cavity behind. There was no note, no message, just a few larger grains of stone and wood. Otherwise smooth. She inserted her hand and it was cool inside. A sudden urge to leave something there took hold of her. She thought for a moment, perplexed, then unfastened her earrings and placed them hurriedly inside. Then very carefully, conscious that Sister Marthe was looking on, she replaced the brick in its place.

'There,' she whispered and turned to rejoin Sister Marthe. 'Please, sister—help me out.'

Sister Marthe pulled her out of the channel with surprising strength and beamed knowingly. 'One day he'll come back.'

Jeanne smiled fleetingly in return and looked away in embarrassment. 'And I will be long gone.'

There was more shooting as the evening drew on. Lefèvre joined Jeanne and her mother for dinner. He had news.

'I was on the phone with Jean Bassouin. He says there were incidents in the poor districts of the old city—apparently local independence fighters. They're obviously all too happy with the situation and are hoping fratricide will occur. I suppose that fanatic, El Rifni, is among them too. Strange thing while with Bassouin—the phone clicked—someone listening in. And then the line went dead.'

'Mr Bassouin is a nice man,' said Jeanne, remembering her visit to his house in the old city. 'I hope he'll meet up with Sarah again.' She caught her father give her mother a glance. Lefèvre looked uneasily out of the window and cleared his throat.

'Jean Bassouin went further than me with his opinions. He became rather emotional—that idiot Fresquin's incessant goading, of course. Looking for personal vengeance of some sort. Bassouin openly declared support for De Gaulle and mentioned leaving for England through the Spanish enclaves on the coast. I hope nothing will happen to him.'

A heavy silence overcame the room, cut by the sound of chinking cutlery and Lefèvre's unnerving habit of letting out a soft whine whenever he chewed his food. Jeanne's mother gave a grimace and looked apologetically at her.

'Any news from Jim Wilding, my dear?'

Jeanne shook her head slowly, the thought of him so far from her making her want to cry. 'No news, mother. He said he'll be here tomorrow and I trust him.'

'I hope so,' said Jeanne's mother, her voice suddenly heavy with tiredness. 'I do hope he comes to help us.'

Jeanne suddenly awoke in the dark—she had been dreaming that Jim had had an accident. Her bedside lamp clicked and the glare made her draw away. It was her mother.

'Time to go, my *chérie*. Wake up now.'

'Where? What time—' began Jeanne, averting her eyes from the light. 'But Jim is coming. An accident?'

'You're still asleep, my dear. I don't understand. Please. It's time to leave—clothes on now.'

Dressed, Jeanne stood in surly silence in the hallway as her parents moved quickly to and fro with last minute preparations. Soumia shoved past, laden with cooking utensils and foodstuffs.

'I'm not going,' said Jeanne aloud. 'Mother, father—I'm not going.'

'Don't be silly now,' came her mother's voice from the sitting room. 'You'll make father angry.'

'I refuse to go. Jim said he would come and I'm going to wait for him.'

'You're coming with us,' came Lefèvre's voice, sounding urgent. 'We don't have much time. Le Guédec came by an hour ago. He said it was imperative we leave—immediately.'

'No. You don't understand. I'm staying. Leave me with Sister Marthe. I'll wait.'

'They'll catch up with you, Jeanne. They'll know where you are.'

'They? Who's *they*?' Jeanne couldn't believe this was happening.

'The *milice*, the gendarmes, the police—*them*,' shouted Lefèvre, suddenly appearing in front of her. His hair was dishevelled, his shirt hanging out where he had hastily dressed. Jeanne thought he looked ugly. 'Bassouin has been arrested. And not only because he's for De Gaulle. Some fanatic among the staff is a damn anti-Semite.' Jeanne stood quite still, shocked. 'Don't you understand, girl?' Her father's face was close to hers. He shook her. 'They're full of hatred. They'll lock us away or do something stupid. You said you'd seen a man hanged from a lamp post. Do you want that to happen to you?' Jeanne felt as though she was in the midst of some horrible dream. She shook her head slowly. 'Then you will come with us. *Now*. There is no refusing.'

Ten minutes later and Jeanne was out into the fresh night air, her mother ushering her towards the awaiting Panhard. Mohammed started the engine and immediately jumped out to make way for Lefèvre.

'God—the map! Have you got the map?'

'What map,' said Mme Lefèvre, her voice filled with panic.

'*Have-you-got-the-map?*' repeated Lefèvre, hardly containing his anger. 'The one Le Guédec gave us. How the hell do you expect us to find the way if—'

'It is here, *monsieur*, it is here!' shrieked Soumia, drawing it out of a bag. 'Are they coming?'

'Give it,' ordered Lefèvre. 'And do be quiet.' He looked about the car, checking everybody was in. 'Mohammed?' The gardener stood on the roadside, shivering. 'Close the house as quick as you can and stay inside. Keep the doors locked. I advise you not to make a move until a few days.'

'Oui, *Monsieur* Lefèvre,' nodded Mohammed.

'Mohammed—thank you. Do be careful. I'll try to send you word. And please make contact with Mr Wilding. Tell him where we are going. It's very important.' Lefèvre wound up the window, grunted into gear and drew away. Through the rear window, Jeanne smiled bravely back at Mohammed, a lonely shape becoming smaller and smaller.

44

A squad of soldiers in loose formation stood idly before the house. Their rifles were slung over their shoulders and they were wearing those quaint steel helmets with the slight rounded crest that reminded him of film footage of the First War. Whatever had happened was over, thought Wilding as he drew up.

He got out stiffly, a night's non-stop driving and a dozen or more checkpoints behind him. Coming into Marrakesh, his eyes had literally closed and he was sure he had driven sightless for any number of seconds before opening them with a realisation of the danger.

Immediately, a gendarme stepped up, an officer. 'What do you want? How did you get here?' Two questions that Wilding's sluggish brain had trouble deciphering, let alone reply to. He made a faint gesture of incomprehension and his hand went to his pocket.

'Passport,' he said. 'And official papers.'

'*Anglais*? Sergeant!'

'*Américain*,' said Wilding quickly. He handed his papers across and watched the two men study them.

'You are working for the American government,' the lieutenant said in hesitant English. Wilding nodded. 'Why do you come here?'

'The Lefèvre family are friends. I am their daughter's—Jeanne Lefèvre's—fiancé. Have you arrested them?'

The lieutenant gave a brief shake of his head. 'They ought to be. They left Marrakesh early this morning before we arrived.'

'I want to see,' said Wilding, holding out his hand for his papers. The lieutenant, stony-faced, handed them back and gestured in the direction of a group of police officers in the garden. 'You must check first with them. You need the man in civilian clothes. He is in charge.'

Wilding walked through the gate, his senses now awakened as his mind raced. He had told Jeanne to stay and wait for him. Something serious must have happened to make them leave so quickly. He hadn't banked on things getting out of hand. He swore inwardly, angry with himself and Lefèvre. Just *five more hours*. Why hadn't they kept still? The garden was littered with papers and clothes. The front door was ajar, the frosted glass that was a feature of its upper structure shattered.

The gaggle of police officers went inside before he could accost them and he followed in their wake.

'Jesus!' he let out a cry. In the hallway was Mohammed's almost naked body, lacerated and bleeding from a dozen or more wounds.

'You are?' The inspector was a middle-aged man with sandy-coloured hair. Wilding had a feeling they had already met. He handed across his passport and papers with the official US seal and introduced himself.

'James Wilding. American envoy to southern Morocco. I'm here to find out about the Lefèvre family.'

'Yes. Thank you, Mr Wilding. I think I know you. We met once at the Lefèvre house on a dinner occasion.'

'Pleased to meet you again,' said Wilding, thankful he had been recognised. 'A pity about the circumstances, though.' The inspector followed Wilding's gaze to the oddly positioned body on the floor and pulled a face. 'When I saw the mess in the garden and the state of the door, I thought it might have been an attempt to arrest Lefèvre.'

'You know of his convictions?' said the inspector.

Cautious, Wilding gave a shrug. 'The region has been in some uncertainty over the past week or so.'

'Not so uncertain. The orders from the *Métropole* were clear.'

'That is correct,' said Wilding, playing safe. 'So this wasn't any of your men's work?' he continued, turning the conversation back to the ghastly scene.

'I don't think torture of this nature is our way of doing things,' said the police officer, distastefully. *Not yet*, Wilding heard himself say, but kept quiet. 'No, this is the natives' work. Probably El Rifni.

I wouldn't be surprised.'

'The man who called himself Abrach?'

The inspector grunted ironically. 'I see you know the file.' His eyes returned to the corpse. 'I suppose you knew the odd job man—something of a gardener, I believe.'

'Mohammed,' said Wilding, morbidly drawn to the face. Half the man's nose was missing, sliced off by a blade of some sort.

'Poor devil. They obviously didn't kill him quickly. They wanted information of some sort. Most probably Lefèvre's intended destination.' The inspector stopped and looked sharply at Wilding. 'You wouldn't know yourself, I suppose.'

Wilding shook his head. 'No. And that's bad. Very bad. I was due to meet up with Lefèvre's daughter.' He held up his left hand. 'We're engaged.'

'I'm sorry,' said the inspector, with a slight bow of respect. 'She would have been safer with you.' He gave Mohammed's bloody corpse a last, rather blasé glance and motioned with his chin. 'I wonder if *he* told them anything before he died.'

Wilding shook his head sadly. 'Dear God only knows.'

45

L ate afternoons, Summerfield would sit with the old Mullah and watch over the valley. From their viewpoint they could see, spreading east to west, the string of five villages that made up the tribal territory. Two of them, their own—that of Aït Itmolas—and Tichkit, stood out as richer, fortified villages and centres of discussion, decision and commerce. The best saffron harvest came from Medwala. The best warriors from Zemghort. Imi-n-Fala claimed that their women were the most beautiful in the valley and Tichkit was ready to fight for its reputation for the most succulent olives in the Atlas. The Mullah had taught him how to pronounce the names in the local accent, though continued, in the odd lessons he gave Summerfield, to deepen the Englishman's knowledge of Arabic. In any case, Summerfield concluded that the villages were as much an allegory of the Berber penchant for difference and bickering as they were of the federating pride and warriorship against all foreigners, including the Arabising influences of the cities and plains. Devout Muslims, but staunch upholders of their proper identity, the Berber tribes of middle and southern Morocco had never been totally tamed by anybody—from the Romans to the Vandals, Arabs, Turks, Portuguese, Spanish and still the French.

Summerfield had grown to like and respect the old man, his generosity after the storm proving the catalyst for a relationship that went beyond that of man-to-man and deepened into something approaching father-son. It was not without its complications. Regularly meeting for discussion, and sometimes joined by Badr, they also regularly disagreed. On more than one occasion, what started out as a Berber love of verbal sparring ignited into a full-blown argument over habits, customs, the usefulness of football and circumcision, British world domination ('a little *dépassé*' Summerfield had remarked), excision of women in the plains and to the Mauritanian south, freedom and independence, even the value and virtues of salt.

On such occasions, it would suffice for the fiery passions and tongues to pay heed to their eyes. For looking out over the grandiose serpentine stretch of the great valley, they could not fail to be influenced by any feeling other than awe and serenity. Abrach had once told him, a long time ago, that he would find God in Morocco. Perhaps he had been right. For it was difficult to think that God was nothing other than real when faced with such beauty.

One day, the old Mullah dropped his mask and his sharp, accusing features became softer as they sat looking out over the fertile valleys. He paused for several seconds, turning to look at Summerfield. He seemed to be weighing the Englishman up.

'My days are filled with moments in which I wonder about all this,' he finally said. He raised one of his hands, so covered in liver spots it was hard to discern his real skin, to gesture at the landscape and beyond. 'Over the years, I've come to sharpen my conclusions to two points, *Sidi* Summerfield. Two things that I've come to realise are my truths which no other thinking can alter. The first is that as I advance in life, I have become increasingly aware that although we learn, acknowledge and take into account that much in the world is grey and unclassifiable, it is increasingly important to keep on separating the greyness into either black or white. For in the end run there is only Good—loving humanity, respect for people and nature, tolerance and forgiveness—and there is only Bad—exploitation of people, nature and resources, merciless ambition and heinous acts be it in the family, the tribe, at work or in a wider struggle. Admitting to the greyness means joining the ranks of the Bad—all those here and outside the valley—the millions—who are too scared or too comfortable to take up position. It means joining the ranks of the cynical adult. It means betraying the childish quality in us that is idealism and hope, Mr Summerfield.'

Summerfield nodded and smiled. Was it a message the old man had saved only for him? In any case, it appealed to the moment.

The expanse of nature before them demanded a binary choice—Good or Bad; and anything else than what lay before their gaze was nothing other than bad.

'And the second conclusion?' continued the Mullah, scratching his beard. 'Would you like to hear an old man's ramblings?'

'Not ramblings, Respectful One. An old man—well, *yes*.' Summerfield laughed and nodded at the Mullah. 'What will you tell me now?'

The old Mullah smiled at the Englishman's impertinence and his voice became soft. 'I will say a timelessly repeated thing—that when will Man understand that God is something over and above all frontiers, politics and religion? He is all around us, at the centre of everything innate and living, the sky, clouds, mountains, deserts, rivers, cities, the living creatures and Man himself. God sees no difference in Man, but watches on as Man continues to divide and differentiate, creating shadows in his heart in order to assuage his hatred and frustration of himself, as a human, onto the excuse of others.'

'A lot of us are weak in this way,' said Summerfield.

The old man frowned and touched his arm. 'He is saddened by this, Harry Summerfield. And more—He is angry. The world will see horrible things and there will be such terrible justice at the end of it.'

When Badr came back to the valley in July with news of Mers-el-Kébir—British ships and planes had bombarded the Vichy French fleet moored in port, sinking a score of ships—Summerfield had climbed to the rocky outcrop to ponder the consequences. When the torment came once again to haunt his sleep, sending his nights into sleepless reproaches for losing Jeanne, Summerfield sat in the sunrise on the valley slopes and found peace of mind in the rising gold and much wise soothing from nature. He had said, remembering his conversations with his friend, Badr, that he almost thought the valley his home. And now the *almost* was doubt-free. The valley *was* his home. And the time would soon come when he would have occasion to prove it.

He was now generally accepted as *The British One*. This differentiated him from being French and therefore an enemy. It also meant that he was, as from Mers-el-Kébir onwards, an enemy of the French as well as the Germans. No one in these parts knew much about the Germans, except that word-of-mouth spoke of them wanting to invade much of North Africa and wanting to spread much havoc. Apparently, the Germans had nothing against the native peoples and even encouraged them to rise up against their old colonial masters in the sphere, namely the British and the French. This led to a tricky balance between how to speak of things to Summerfield. They were complicated times with complicated consequences.

Summerfield was also known as *The Builder* or *The Ingenie,* a perversion of the word *engineer*, difficult to pronounce by the Berber tongue. For his ambition had not limited itself to municipal toilets. Summerfield had also attacked the problem of infrastructure, suggesting after the violence of the summer storm that the tracks criss-crossing the valley from village to village should be paved in some way to avoid the otherwise muddy quagmire. The idea was voted a good one, though unreasonable in terms of workload. Labour was short, being required for the multitude of other day-to-day tasks in the valley and it was judged, not without reason, that the tracks were not bottomless and would sooner or later wear or wash away to the underlying rock. People were willing to sink up to their knees in mud for a few years rather than spend precious time, effort and resources not to. It amused Summerfield rather than angered him. For he saw in such odd logic, the weighing up of what was bearable and what was priority, a deadly sort of logic set in the value the Berber tribes gave to time. The mud would last two to three months. Their empire and culture had lasted two thousand years. The road building would last six to eight months. Many things could happen in between. It was better not to venture too far ahead into this unknown quantity of risk. Therefore, concentrate on other, more practical and controllable things in the meantime.

Summerfield's mind and body had then turned to building a school. With the Mullah's help and blessing, he refurbished and extended a crumbling shed on the edge of the village that in the past had sheltered goats. He made a series of basic wooden benches and glazed a wall so that things could be written on it in paint and rubbed off as necessary. The biggest problem was convincing both children and parents that it was useful to attend. Summerfield decided to get around this by doing a tour of the fortified village and the immediate valley and speaking to them about it. *But when will our children have time to work in the fields?* said the parents. *Why do they have to know about Europe and America? It will surely make them even more insolent than now!* But Summerfield talked. And he explained. He drew pictures. He argued. He threatened to close the public toilets. And he almost gave up in the face of such stubborn resistance. It was when waking one morning to see the old Mullah struggling up the slope towards the Kasbah and slipping in the mud that the ultimate idea came to him: it would save the old Mullah from certain accident and, at his advanced age, certain death.

This time, instead of knocking on doors, Summerfield nonchalantly began to mention the old man's frail legs and risk of broken bones to the children. It was the children, once again, that proved the best way to move the mountain. The word spread. And the word took on a multitude of different shapes and meanings: *the Mullah would die if he continued to climb up the slopes to visit the villagers; the old man already had a broken ankle and was telling no one so that he could continue his teachings; the Mullah was kept awake at night by the pain of his old aching muscles; the poor old dignitary had already written his will in preparation; the glistening stones and soil were not, in fact, the mark of autumn rain, but the old Mullah's sweat that poured out as he climbed the various steep slopes and gullies.*

The project finally met with acceptance. It meant that Summerfield had to share the building with the Mullah, but the end result was worth it. The children received religious teaching and they also received lessons in English, geography, theatre and history. Trouble was, none of the children could write, but they had magnificent memories born from an aural aptitude that had been handed down in poems, chants and songs for thousands of years. Thus, content with his half-won victory, Summerfield spent three afternoons a week in the role of teacher.

One evening, having helped Raja's father with tanning leather, Summerfield climbed the slopes to his favourite lookout, a rocky outcrop that gave him an expansive view to both the eastern and western reaches of the valley. He sat down, pulled out his tobacco pouch and stuffed a wad into a small, etched, hollowed out bone that the men used as pipes in the region. Thankful that the cool mountain breeze momentarily blew away the awful smell of the tanning from his skin, he lit up using his box of matches. He studied it for a few seconds, the picture of the lion and the French words, conscious that it was a long-removed link from Marrakesh and the civilisation of cars and telephones, trains and boutiques. He didn't know which day it was. It made him laugh.

After some minutes looking out across the wide, majestic space and breathing in the air, he noticed Badr, winding his way up the slope below. The young man was wearing a pale blue shirt and *cheiche*. He had slung his rifle over his shoulder, a German Mauser and in his hand he carried another rifle—Summerfield's Lee Enfield. He watched the speck getting closer, the young man's features becoming palpable and then stood up to greet him the last fifty yards or so.

They embraced and Summerfield noted with respect that Badr showed no trace of breathlessness. Badr was an athlete—like all the others in these mountains. Lithe, sinewy bodies that knew no greed, as hard and lean as the lives they led. They sat down. Mirroring Summerfield, Badr produced his own pipe and began to plug it with thick, black local tobacco.

'Beautiful,' commented Summerfield, making a waving gesture at the valley. 'I don't know what day it is, but I certainly know the month!' He chuckled. 'September is magical in this place. I've never seen such light, such life.'

'It is *Turday*,' informed Badr with his deplorable English accent and grinned at the wince it produced on Summerfield's face.

Some things never changed—despite the schooling. 'The harvest time is coming,' he added. 'We shall all be working extremely hard in the coming two months. You will see the true meaning of the word *exhaustion*.'

'As a young lad,' said Summerfield, nodding at his friend, 'I worked in the fields picking hops.'

'Hops?'

'*Houblons*,' said Summerfield in French, but Badr didn't know the word. 'What we make beer with.'

'Ah!'

'It was damn hard work too.'

'It will be good to compare,' said the young man. 'Here—take your Enfield,' he added, passing the heavy rifle across as though it were the lightest of sticks. 'It is not only the harvest that will exhaust you.'

'Oh?' Summerfield looked keenly at Badr, a little pinch in his stomach.

'Last week I was in the foothills to the west. The war in Europe hasn't stopped the French objectives here in Morocco. I saw columns of lorries in the plains. Many soldiers. There were aeroplanes too. They are setting up a base, Harry.'

'An offensive?'

Badr sighed, letting out a stream of smoke and shook his head.

'This has been going on for almost forty years, Harry. They are like rabid dogs—they won't give up. They started in the north, then the south. The mountains—the High Atlas—are all that remain. We have no minerals here. We have no precious metals. What do they want if it is not just domination and subjugation?'

'Electricity, maybe,' said Summerfield. 'They will build reservoirs and dams to produce electricity for their industry and infrastructure. It is progress.'

'*Their* progress. The old Resident-General, Lyautey, an old man who loved this country like his own, found other ways. He was an old warrior, true, and fought many battles with us—but he believed in leaving us our traditions and our lands. Now things have changed.'

Summerfield remained silent, feeling helpless. He shrugged his shoulders. What could he tell the young man? That it was in their interests too? That the two worlds could learn to live side by side? That maybe, in a hundred or two hundred years, Morocco would be free again? He felt suddenly guilty of his Europeaness, his whiteness. They had dominated the world for more than two thousand years, restless and driven by the obsession with wealth and a damned curiosity. Somehow it all seemed natural and at least indisputable, unstoppable.

'So you bring me my rifle,' said Summerfield, finally. He too let out a sigh. 'Will there be a battle?'

'No. Not like you think. No big battles like in the books and films. We cannot fight their numbers. We cannot even, for long, stop their offensive. But it is time to take you on a patrol. Maybe you will find the occasion to practice your shooting some more. We are adept in the art of skirmish.'

46

Two days later, Summerfield found himself part of a small column of fifty men. They left before dawn and the heat that would settle fiercely on the slopes. As they picked their way along the tracks westwards and into the next range of valleys, Summerfield saw a woman's shape at the window of a house. It was Raja and she had risen to bid her farewell to Badr—a few low-voiced words, a nod, a gesture. It was a poignant little separation and made Summerfield's throat seize for an instant. He wished, like his young friend, he had a woman to say goodbye to; a love to look forward to returning to.

The light was a violet-blue and made everything seem almost unreal—like a Hollywood western backdrop. The smell of thyme nipped the air, mixed with the occasional fetid waft of animals cooped up in their stables. The inevitable dry bark of a dog coughed at them as they passed a shepherd's dwelling and continued monotonously long after they had mounted the western flank of the valley and followed the crest. At one point, looking out over the landscape, Summerfield picked out a similar column setting out below them, a dark centipede of men zigzagging slowly as it picked its way along the serpentine tracks. As day broke and the two columns advanced, one above the other on the flank of the valley, Toubfil, their lanky, unsmiling leader gave the order for a song. For a mile or so before they parted direction, the two columns marched on, one on the high track, one on the low track, echoing each other with verse and chorus.

Summerfield felt the excitement in him, buried deep out of reserve but also pulsing regularly in his head and veins as, part of the band of tribesmen, he had murmured his contribution to the song. He had never shot at anyone before—*and shooting at a Frenchman, a European, one of his own?*—and wondered

if even he could. A nagging voice inside him suggested that
he had no reason to do so. At one point, aware that he was
growing annoyed with the internal battle, he resolved himself
to concentrate on the precise moment, the journey *to* and *if* and
leave the decision for later.

They ate from their provisions for the first two days—pancakes
and salted semolina. They must have covered ten to fifteen miles or
so and Summerfield's legs ached with stiffness from the incessant
climbs and descents which had caused his knees to swell. On the
third evening, Toubfil bought a goat from an isolated shepherd,
carefully choosing the animal from the herd, superstitious of the
markings and avoiding anything that might present a sign of ill-
omen. They ate it, roasted on a spit behind a crop of boulders,
and it was delicious.

That night a young messenger from the *Gral-eb-naa* tribe who
inhabited the area slipped into their camp with news of French
troop movements. Hardly had Toubfil begun to question him
when a light—a warning fire—flickered in the distance, indicating
French presence. Toubfil, rising from his subdued conversation
with the young messenger, seemed to scan the blackened horizon
for a moment as though checking for a decision. Finally, he turned
and gestured in the direction of the fire. *Yallah*, he said tersely and
was off before the majority of the column was on its feet.

The young *Gral-eb-naa* tribesman—Summerfield guessed he
was all of thirteen years old—led them at a fast pace through the
darkness despite his bare feet. Before long, Summerfield found
himself panting and had to halt. His rest lasted a full four seconds
before Badr's shape doubled back along the thin track and tugged
on his arm. His friend spoke no words, but the glare from his
eyes indicated that it was forbidden to stop. Summerfield nodded,
gritted his teeth and pushed on.

The column climbed upwards, taking to a steep, zigzagging
and sometimes crumbling path. Only once did Summerfield
look down at the sheer slope and the dark abyss below and it
was enough to make him tremble. Pulling himself together, he
focused on the man in front, copying his exact pace and footing.

An odour of sweat and fear and leather hung about the column as they climbed on. Someone further on farted involuntarily in the effort and Toubfil hissed a reproach. At last, the column reached the crest of the mountain and, not stopping, continued on down the other side at an even faster pace. Summerfield calculated that they had been on their feet for almost twenty hours and wondered if someone had to collapse before Toubfil ordered a halt. He wondered if it would be him. Everything ached—from his lungs and the painful rubbing of his rifle on his collar bone to the stab of effort in his thighs and calves at each step down the steep path. A blister on his right heel burnt like hell.

After two more hours of forced march, coming to a small hollow between two valleys, Toubfil finally brought the column to a halt. The men eased themselves down with a series of sighs and drank. Badr picked his way to where Summerfield lay sprawled against a tree stump and flicked his head as if to ask how he was. Summerfield pointed to his legs and winced. The young man nodded in the darkness and gave him a grin with his shocking white teeth. He sat on his heels in front of Summerfield and seizing a leg, much like a sports doctor, began to massage the knotted muscles. Summerfield fought to contain his groans— half-pleasure, half-pain.

Almost immediately, Toubfil sent off a messenger, a man named Rahul, to make contact with the other column and the order was passed on in silent gestures to sleep. Summerfield closed his eyes and even before Badr had finished his massage, he fell into deep unconsciousness.

An hour or two later the movement of his chattering teeth awoke him. A cold, cutting breeze was blowing in from the high ranges to their east, permeating his layers of clothes and even the animal skin that Badr must have covered him with in his sleep. Normally, the tribesmen would have lit huge bonfires of bracken and wood to heat up the air. This time there was only a small mound of pebbles under which a dim glow of embers suggested fire. It was kept alight for tea, the tribesmen's sugar-high fuel. Toubfil was kneeling there, looking out into the distance and the darkness. After some deliberation, Summerfield picked himself up and moved over. Toubfil turned his head and gave a surly nod as Summerfield sat cumbersomely down. Summerfield shivered violently and cursed himself. The warrior would surely think him weak. But Toubfil said nothing. Instead, he reached for a headscarf, picked out a large pebble from the mound and rolled the hot stone in the material. He handed the bundle across, gesturing urgently to Summerfield with his head. *Choukran*, said Summerfield, taking it and holding it with his two hands to his chest. *Choukran*.

The men did not wait until dawn. As if the early Morning Prayer had programmed them over the years, they rose fifteen minutes before the first streaks of light appeared in the eastern sky and had already drunk their tea and chewed their bread in the space of ten minutes when Toubfil gave the order to march. The dim clattering of rifles and a few gruff murmurs were all the sound they made. Searching for Badr, Summerfield tucked the wrapped pebble inside his clothes and followed his back as the column of men plodded once more upwards and south. At one moment looking up, Summerfield saw more flames on a distant mountain slope.

'Another warning fire?' he murmured, pulling himself up to walk by Badr.

Badr shook his head. 'It is a burning village, Harry. There are no warning beacons on that slope. At least we know where the French soldiers are.'

An hour later, Toubfil held up his hand to halt. The fifty men froze without noise. Toubfil's large, bony hand, silhouetted against the grey-blue sky, made a flattening motion and all of sudden, Summerfield found himself the only man standing. He looked around him, bewildered. Then Badr pulled him down and put a finger over his mouth. Seconds passed and then came the grunt of Toubfil's voice as he rose. *Salaam allikoum* came the greeting from behind a hedge of thorn bushes and the first shapes of the men of the second column pushed through into the clearing.

For thirty or so minutes, Badr disappeared to join Toubfil and the leader of the second column, a shrewd-featured though handsome-looking warrior, Saïd. Dispersed throughout the rocks and bushes, the ninety or so men snatched at the occasion to close their eyes while their leaders discussed the next course of action. Summerfield, shivering again whenever they stopped, lit up a pipe and smoked miserably in the numbing wind as he lay prostrate between two old and fallen sections of tree trunk. Oddly enough, he remembered a breakfast scene from years ago when he'd been at grammar school in Tonbridge. It was a ritual to take tea, muffins and scrambled egg before beginning lessons with, as the fluffy-chinned, braying-voiced pupils were called, the *wild ones*. So strange, he thought, hearing laughter in his mind's eye, so *English*. *So bloody strange and English and lovely…* Had he really messed up his life? he wondered. Have I really wasted what I thought was meaningless and dull? I could murder a bloody muffin right now.

Toubfil, Saïd and Badr—the three leaders—came back among them, bent double and picking out men for their respective assault groups. Saïd tapped Summerfield on the shoulder, but hardly had he done so when Badr appeared and spoke something rapid and in dialect to Saïd. *Waha*, nodded Saïd and gave Summerfield a brief smile followed by a sign to join Badr.

Grouped into three clusters, each group received a murmured lecture from their respective leader. Badr, the youngest of the three and almost the youngest of his hand-picked group, seemed to have the older men's immediate respect and attention. It dawned on Summerfield that the young man's absences from the valley must have won him much experience in whatever mysterious actions he got up to; much more than any of the older tribesmen among them.

Badr used a small piece of stick to draw out the lines of the valleys before them, stabbing at the earth to indicate the village that had been set aflame. He proposed that the French troops were logically heading for the next village, some five kilometres east—'over this mountain,' he said, nodding upwards and behind them. 'This is where we want to engage them.' The men nodded silently. Badr's voice grew grave, his eyes turning into hard, black stones. 'Saïd's group will act as bait. They will run like a herd of scared goats—up here,' he said, tracing a line with his stick. 'We and Toubfil's men will act as snakes, hidden in the rocks on both sides and ready to strike. We will not confront them at close distance. They will try to advance—they are determined. Every time I give the order, you will fire and then move back to where I tell you to go. There may be artillery—know that now. Very important: nobody is to remain behind. If anyone is injured then we either take him with us or, if he is unable to be moved, we shall be merciful by finishing his life. It is a dishonour and an ignoble threat to our families to be taken prisoner. Does everyone understand this? Yes? Then let us go forward—some of you with God's blessing and others, like I, with the blessing of free man. Come!' Summerfield rose with the others and stood behind Badr. '*Sidi* Summerfield,' muttered Badr over his shoulder. 'I remember once in Marrakesh how reckless you were. It resulted in you nearly getting beaten to death. Please, Harry—this time, no silliness. Stay with me and obey me. It would be no glorious ending you are searching for to die on these foreign slopes! Remember that you are destined for a greener, more English heaven than this.'

An hour's climb and twenty minutes descent lead them to their positions, some two kilometres downstream from the village of Itdirzt. A mule sauntered by as they crept behind their respective rocks and Summerfield recognised the rider as Rahul, the messenger Toubfil had sent out two days before. Despite Summerfield's smile, Rahul remained cold and un-answering as he continued on down the valley track, rocking gently towards where Badr supposed the French scouts would encounter Saïd's men.

Badr drew Summerfield towards him and a small hollow crested by natural parapet of debris and stones.

'This is good to rest your rifle on,' said Badr. 'How are you, Harry?'

'I'm fine,' said Summerfield. 'A little thirsty, though. And damn hungry too.'

Badr grinned fleetingly and reached into his pocket. 'Here—a pancake I bartered for a bullet. Eat.' Summerfield nodded in gratitude and began chewing. 'You will probably tremble, Harry.

We all do. It's a mixture of fear and excitement. Indeed, most of the time, mostly fear. Do not worry. If you cannot aim, then do not shoot. It is a waste of a good bullet.'

'So what do I do? Throw stones?'

'No, Harry,' grinned Badr. 'Just pray and swear—hopefully, doing this will help you aim.'

A long hour passed and then the sound of shots echoed up the valley path. Ten or so followed by a spaced two or three. Badr raised his hand—the sign for them to get ready. Further shots rang out in varying intervals, cutting into the silence that had overtaken the valley.

'You see that point there,' said Badr, softly. 'Where the rock pushes out by the old tree.' Summerfield nodded. 'Point your Lee Enfield just there—this is where they will poke their heads round I am sure. Ours are the only rifles capable of precision shots.'

'And you trust me to be precise,' said Summerfield, ironically.

More shots and shouts reached them—Saïd's men retreating. From his position, Summerfield saw two shapes suddenly appear and he tensed, squinting through the sights. Badr grasped his forearm and Summerfield looked up, startled. The young man shook his head. The shapes were two of Saïd's men, retreating, as planned, up the track that led to them. A minute later, another appeared, limping heavily. The cries were coming from him—a mixture of pain and frustration, as he pulled himself up the steep track. A light automatic clattered from the rocks behind him. He looked round at something, flung the rifle from his shoulder and began scrabbling crazily up the track.

'It's Ali,' hissed Badr. 'They will kill him.'

It was then that the two khaki clad soldiers appeared bent double and advancing. They did not shoot and Badr understood immediately.

'They want him alive. Open fire, Harry—too bad for the plan!' Badr raised his hand—the signal to fire. The sound of Badr's shot made Summerfield's ears explode. His eyes seemed to see everything without seeing—his trembling hands, Badr's hand pulling back the bolt, the sliding click, another explosion.

The cracks of other rifles as Badr's men also opened fire. 'Shoot!' urged Badr, shaking Summerfield violently. 'They're catching up Ali.' Summerfield brought the Lee Enfield up to his shoulder, saw a shape and fired blindly. The rifle bucked painfully into his chest and he swore. Badr again loaded and fired—one of the French soldiers went down out of sight. 'Got him!' spat Badr. 'Harry—concentrate on the second.'

The next Summerfield knew was a strange humming over his head—like an insect flying past. He cocked his head, curious. 'Harry—what are you doing?' Badr's face was red and angry. 'Get down—they're shooting at us, don't you realise?!'

'Christ!' gasped Summerfield. He sank down and inched his eyes towards a hole in the parapet. He could see a dozen or so other huddled shapes moving up the valley path, stopping, ducking, disappearing only to rise and move forward again. There must be a whole platoon of them—the advance guards of the French attack. He looked to his left—Badr was sliding down, loading, sliding back up and firing at a regular rhythm.

'Do as I do,' he said, without glancing at Summerfield.

'Shouldn't we be moving back?'

'Not before Ali is safe.'

Summerfield felt dazed. His mind wandered blankly for several seconds and then unconsciously, he pulled himself up, aimed and fired. And again.

'He's over there,' said Badr. 'Thirty yards in front, behind the rock. He can't walk.'

Summerfield peered over the parapet, searching for the unfortunate Ali and then span round, letting out a shriek. 'Fuck! My back—they've shot me!' Badr grabbed him, turning him roughly onto his stomach.

'Not a bullet, Harry. A splinter of rock.'

'It hurts like hell!' ranted Summerfield. He felt himself explode with rage '*Those fucking Frog bastards!*'

'*Harry!*' Badr, his eyes wide, motioned for him to remain calm.

'How fucking *dare* they!' roared Summerfield, beyond reasoning, lifting himself off the ground. 'How *fucking dare* they!' From the fear of a few seconds ago, he stood up, his hand working furiously on the bolt as he fired off three rounds oblivious to the whizzing, buzzing bullets flying past him from below. And then his legs crumbled from under him and Badr was pinning him down.

'You're mad, Englishman! You'll be killed!' He raised his hand again, gesturing for his men to pull back.

'And Ali? We can't leave him,' wrestled Summerfield.

'Ali will not speak.'

'You said—'

'Ali is dead,' said Badr, coldly.

'*Dead*?' Summerfield stared into Badr's eyes. 'What…?'

'I had to, Harry. It is the rule. Poor Ali. Come now!'

And before Summerfield could speak, Badr had hauled him backwards, out of their position and was tugging him back to a second line of fire.

The combat seemed to last an eternity. It was a game of hide and seek. The French troops advanced, Badr and his men shot at them and they disappeared only to reappear closer than before. Again they moved back, without losses. There was silence for a while and Summerfield imagined the French troops must be recuperating from the hard climb. But the real reason for the lull soon became apparent: the drone of an approaching aeroplane filled the valley getting closer. They saw it roughly two kilometres away, a silver-winged bi-plane like something out of World War I.

'Don't be duped, Harry,' said Badr, sensing Summerfield's smile of irony. 'That thing has machine guns on it—and probably bombs too.'

'It's a disaster, Badr—a fucking disaster.'

'It usually is,' said Badr. This time it was himself who smiled ironically. 'I wonder where Saïd and his men are. They were to join up with Toubfil on the eastern slope.' No sooner had he said this, when a muted shout was heard. One of Badr's men had signalled the approach of a messenger. A shape crawled into the depression where Badr and Summerfield lay. Once again it was Rahul, his face creased with severity under a mask of dust. He had a blue, blood-soaked bandage wrapped around his left hand. Summerfield thought he observed a lack of thumb and his stomach squirmed.

'Orders from Toubfil,' rasped Rahul, his voice in tatters. 'Pull back silently and disperse. All groups to return home.'

'And Saïd?'

Rahul jerked his bandaged stump towards the opposite hill, almost a kilometre away. The French bi-plane glittered for a second and then disappeared into the cleft of the valley. Moments later, the faint metallic *tat-tat-tat* of its machine-guns reached them. Rahul hawked and spat grimly. 'Saïd will play with the aeroplane for a while before darkness comes.'

Over the next hour, Badr's men moved back in twos and threes, back over the crest of their slope and melted into the valley beyond. The firing was sporadic, the main interest having moved to the events happening in the next valley where French light artillery had now joined the roving aeroplane in rooting out Saïd and his men.

Once out of range of French marksmen, Badr tended to Summerfield's back. It was a small, horizontal wound, roughly half an inch wide—nothing serious, though painful enough when Badr extracted the shard of stone and rubbed a herbal mixture on the oozing blood. It took all of five minutes and then Badr hauled Summerfield to his feet, took his rifle and headed him westwards.

They walked in silence, their spirits muted. It took time for Summerfield to be able to look his friend in the eyes for what had happened to Ali. Terrible as it was, he finished by convincing himself that Ali had met with a quicker and safer death than if he had been captured.

Summerfield followed Badr into the night, the stinging sensation in his back a sorry reminder of events. Altogether, it was an empty, rather shameful end to his first taste of combat. He had shown though, if not through courage but anger, that he could face hostile fire and moreover, shoot at men—French soldiers—he had previously had no reason or desire to harm. It perplexed

Summerfield: he had been willing to fight in Spain for a greater, wider cause and all that he had experienced over the last few days was a very personal affair indeed.

It was a long, desolate return to the valley. On the second evening, they met up with Toubfil and a group of ten of his men. They ate together, relieved to have different company and swapped stories of the fighting. Toubfil had strayed from his position opposite Badr under pressure from the French advance and when mortar shells began coughing and exploding around them, had ordered a retreat. His men had scattered, melting into the maquis and the gorges that were a feature of those parts. Toubfil, together with his *ten faithfuls,* had pushed through an encircling French patrol, killing a sergeant in the process and had then followed a dried out riverbed to an isolated farm. They had kept their distance, for another group of men were billeted there along with a French officer and three Legionnaire scouts. Toubfil hadn't tarried in making a wide circle around the hamlet, but not before he and his men had seen the disturbing sight of a tall, heavily built Arab with oddly crooked hands, pawing over a map with the French officer. A cripple, said Toubfil and one of his men said the Berber word for *scarecrow* and added *devil* for good measure.

On hearing this, Summerfield looked directly at Badr, but the young man refused to return his stare. Instead, Badr breathed deeply and spoke to Toubfil.

'So the devil is working for the Vichy French? Did you see his face?'

Toubfil spat and shook his head.

'The monster had a hood covering his head—though I will remember his hands when I see him. My dagger will remove them for him.'

'Unless they remove you first,' said Badr, grimly.

At last, four days after the failed ambush, Summerfield followed Badr, Toubfil and the men over the last crest, past the look-out posts and into their valley. It seemed sweet and sunlit and welcoming and an audible heave of relief came from the men as they set down a zigzagging path towards the distant Kasbah. Little by little a crowd gathered as they approached and Summerfield spotted Raja looking keenly at Badr among the returning men with deep and satisfied eyes.

47

Le Guédec had been right. The hunting lodge was far from anything: a man-made oddity drawn with the lines of a city-dweller, nestled in a large, wooded hollow on a valley side with no other sign of life as far as the eye could see. A man had been waiting for them at a point where it was obvious a vehicle could go no further—Le Guédec must have arranged things in advance with typical precision. Lefèvre had abandoned the car, hiding it in a copse of trees and covering it with brushwood with the help of Le Guédec's guide. A gruelling five-hour climb up a steep and eroded goat track had finally led them to the lodge. It was larger than Jeanne had imagined.

There was a main building—a two-story affair with a spacious patio that was covered by a sagging wooden awning to keep out the sun in the hot months. It had obviously been unfrequented for quite some time—two maybe three years—for the paint was a pale, whitish pink, speckled and flaking like a sunburnt skin. There were two bedrooms, thick with dust. The curtains looked as though they'd been gnawed at by animals and hung in jaundiced tatters. When Soumia opened the shutters, they saw that the floors were littered with the husks of long-dead insects of every sort—flies, beetles, spiders, dragonflies and some strange, unknown creatures that must have been indigenous to the mountains. Downstairs, the small dining room and living room that looked out into the terrace were even filthier. Huge strands of dust, like lank cobwebs, sagged and swung from ceiling to floor, over the wooden chairs and the leather sofa—God knows how Le Guédec had managed to bring it here—traps for hundreds of dead flies. There were droppings everywhere—mice and rats—the disembowelled cushion on the sofa evidence of their presence and lastly, by the fireplace, the skeleton of a bird with a mummified head, feathers sticking oddly at angles from the carcass.

Outside, some twenty yards or so to the right, two, long, low-lying huts served as servants quarters, tool sheds, kitchens and stables for the mules that Le Guédec must have used to ferry provisions to the lodge and return his hunting trophies to the foothills. The cluster of buildings had been built among a score or so of pine and nut trees, and at the bottom of the wooded hollow was a small, bubbling spring that formed a pool before trickling through a niche in the rock and disappearing downwards towards the valley floor. A two-metre-wide pathway of smoothened rock and pebbles leading down the mountainside indicated that in the winter months the spring probably gushed with force and formed a waterfall.

Exhaustion from the journey—a harrowing experience of fear, worry and ravines that had made her stomach turn to jelly—turned to determination as Jeanne witnessed her mother breaking down at the sight of their new and rudimentary lodgings. It was the final drop, of course, the detail that made the strain of the past few days manifest itself in a fit of uncontrollable sobbing. But it had been her mother first and it gave Jeanne something to turn her mind away from her own desperation.

Their initial discovery over, she helped Soumia make tea and sat her mother on the terrace in one of the wooden chairs while they set energetically about the cleaning with a couple of old brooms found in the servants' quarters. Here, Jeanne's father was engaged in conversation with Le Guédec's man, probably organising supplies, she imagined. Money was exchanged. Glancing up from her work, Jeanne saw a long faded red bundle being handed over and, as part of the material flapped away in the breeze, the nut brown, polished stock of a hunting rifle flashed momentarily in the sunlight. For some reason it sent Jeanne's thoughts momentarily spinning towards Jim and she felt a stab of panic in her chest—Jim who must be going mad with worry, looking for them, uncertain. Thankfully, she was wrenched away from the painful thoughts by a sudden shriek from Soumia. Another dead animal had been uncovered—the dusty, petrified carcass of a snake.

'Oh, *M'moiselle!*' fretted Soumia, as Jeanne disposed of the husk with wary though angry strokes of her broom. 'I want to go back to Marrakesh. I don't want to sleep alone in the stables with all the creepy crawlies!'

'Don't be silly, Soumia!' scolded Jeanne. 'Of course we're not going to let you sleep out in the outhouses. How could you possibly think you wouldn't stay with us here?'

'*Really*?' Soumia's face wore an exaggerated grimace of surprise mixed with gratitude. 'Really, *M'moiselle*? I don't believe you—*Monsieur* Lefèvre—'

Jeanne shook her head in exasperation. 'You remember those *tictonic plagues*, Soumia? *Plates*, in fact, and it wasn't *tictonic*, either, but—'

'The one's you studied at the *Académie*, oh Lord!'

'Well, these mountains are made up of them. They might pull apart any minute, Soumia. If you slept in the outhouses, then there's a risk the earth might split open and you'd disappear!'

'Oh!' shrieked Soumia, bringing her hands to her head. 'Ohhh!'

'*That's* why you're going to sleep here—with us! After all, *who* would do the serving?'

'Oh, thank you, *M'moiselle*. Thank you!' replied Soumia, oblivious to the irony.

'Now let's finish off our job, Soumia,' said Jeanne, conscious that her voice had grown huskier, more authoritative.

'And I shall help,' came a voice from the doors to the patio. It was Mme Lefèvre, her mother, her face ruddy and streaked with dried up tears.

'Mother—'

'No—I'm fine now, Jeanne. Thank you. I feel so silly—just a little over-tiredness.' And then, as if recognising her daughter's command of the situation: 'Tell me what to do now.'

Two hours later, after several trips to the spring and back with buckets of water and much dusting, sweeping and scrubbing, the main room and its adjoining study were as clean as could be. Jeanne called for a downing of tools and arched her aching back, pausing for a second to peer into the large wall mirror Soumia had just finished washing. She giggled. Was it the light or the dust or fatigue that made her hair look streak with silvery hair?

'Mother, Soumia—look, I'm as old as you are now!'

Soumia laughed. Her mother said: 'Cheeky girl!' and they went outside to tea that Le Guédec's man had prepared.

Lefèvre joined them. There was a loaf of bread and a half-opened tin of concentrated milk to accompany the thick, black mountain brew. Jeanne ate without much concern for manners and heard her mother tutting in the background. Her father sighed, as if to silence his spouse and Jeanne could almost hear the words *there are more serious problems to worry about, chérie*, escape his lips.

Lefèvre tried to sound reassuring and made a pun about the three-star comfort of the place. Then, on a more serious note, 'We'll be fine, here. Le Guédec's man—Hattim is his name—' the guide momentarily looked up and flicked a glance at them—'is here to bring us supplies. His family lives over in the next valley and can provide us food. I'm paying for it of course,' added Lefèvre, as though the fact added to the strength of the agreement. 'And we have a gun, if necessary. For hunting,' he continued, quickly meeting the three women's eyes.

'*Monsieur*? Will we be here long?' asked Soumia. 'Those tictonic plates, insects and snakes, sleeping…' she began, only to fall silent at the frown appearing on Lefèvre's face.

'Whatever is she babbling about?' said Lefèvre, shaking his head. 'We'll be here for as long as it takes,' he continued, answering what he thought was her concern. 'You'll have to put up with the insects and snakes. And as for *tictonic plates*?' he shook his head again and looked to Jeanne for assistance.

'Soumia is worried about being obliged to sleep in the outhouses, Daddy.'

'Of course not,' waved Lefèvre. 'You'll sleep in the main house with Jeanne. The important thing is to remain together.' Soumia let out her breath, a kind of exhaled thank you and Jeanne thought she saw the trace of a smile on her father's lips. She had never seen him like this before and it suddenly occurred to her in a strange awakening truth that quite apart from being a senior official, a man and an administrator, he was a person, her father, someone who might have feelings after all. Lefèvre seemed to notice her regard, for he looked at her, a little puzzled, a little embarrassed. 'And James—Jim—will surely find us,' he said.

'Do you really think so, Daddy?' Jeanne sat up and the eagerness in her voice betrayed her desperation.

'He's a very capable sort,' said Lefèvre, keeping a professional edge to his voice. 'He has connections and the advantage of being American. What's more—I'm sure he'd want to get back to his darling fiancée as quickly as possible! Who wouldn't?'

'That would be—*be the answer to my dreams*,' said Jeanne, unable to contain her thoughts.

'But when that will be, we can't be sure,' warned her father. 'The thing is to remain calm and concentrate on our time here. I'm quite sure we'll see winter come and we have to prepare ourselves for that. It can be very hostile here.'

'There's certainly a lot of cleaning and repairing to do,' joined in Mme Lefèvre, breezily. 'A month at least!'

'This is my main expectation,' said Lefèvre, brushing aside his wife's light remark. 'The fact that Jim Wilding, with his influence and above all his passport, can accompany us safely out of here.'

'But where?' added Mme Lefèvre.

Lefèvre shrugged. 'I supposed I'd have to try to get to England; or more practically, Chad. Bassouin mentioned that De Gaulle had ordered the gathering of Free French forces there. As for yourselves—my deepest hope is that James will put you on an American ship and sail you to the United States, far away from this unpleasant mess.'

'Poor *Monsieur* Bassouin,' said Jeanne, distantly. 'He didn't get away, I fear.'

'*Poor* France,' echoed Lefèvre, continuing with his train of thought. 'Our Lady torn in two…There will be unmentionable crimes before she is able, once again, to be one. Unmentionable crimes…'

48

September turned to October and the myriad of little fields and orchards in the great valley failed to ripen. From his dwelling, Summerfield noticed the tribe's people rising with the Morning Prayer only to stand and gaze at the expanse of cultivation, a silent hope in their hearts, their eyes straining to see if the crops had fattened in the night.

Calling by one day, Raja shook her head in exaggeration and fretted. Copying the older womenfolk, her voice went into a high-pitch warble. 'The olives are like lifeless marbles, the carrots like toys for a girl's doll, the wheat as stringy as the unkempt grass in old Aïcha's shame of a garden, the apples only fit to rust metal!'

Summerfield, raising his eyebrows at the young woman's theatrical show, though at the same time conscious that worry was nagging at everyone's mind, nodded in sympathy.

'This will be a dried meat winter if it continues for any longer,' he said. 'People have to eat and the flocks will be decimated.'

'What do *you* know?' said Raja, suddenly turning against him. Her face scowled with anger and she raised her chin—another exaggerated gesture, playing adult. 'Ha! An Englishman with his rain and parks and overfed stomach!'

'What?' Summerfield couldn't believe his ears. 'Why do you scold me so, Raja? Have I not expressed concern? I am one of you now—a member of the tribe that must eat the fruit of this valley!'

Raja seemed to be struggling for words. Summerfield frowned. He had the canniest feeling she would burst into tears—which she promptly did. 'Oh, terrible life, terrible life—I hate it!' she wheezed, caught between letting her tears flow and hiding her face. The tears finished by getting the better of her and the young woman wailed alarmingly.

Summerfield stood up, feeling helpless and Raja tottered towards him. Her final step sent her into his arms. 'Oh dear,' said Summerfield, confused. Women—the strangest, most complicated creatures. 'Poor Raja, poor girl,' he soothed. 'Whatever's the matter? *Tell me*,' he said, holding her tightly. He felt the weight of her head on his shoulder and the moisture of her face seeping through his shirt to his skin. That smell of hers—the faint musk of her sweat, cumin, cinnamon and a flowery whiff of rose that came from the herbal perfume the women in the valley used—reached his nostrils and he inhaled. '*Tell me*, Raja,' he urged softly, but she remained silent, her tears turning to a sniff and they stood there, the man and the girl, for several long and silent seconds. The awareness of her body slowly and inevitably dawned on him— the press of her firm and plump little breasts on his stomach, the hard, bony curve of her hips against his legs—and for an instant his body involuntarily awakened. His hand moved to her ribs and edged to the soft, pulpy base of her left breast. He felt a faint stir in his groin and a twinge of heat spasm through his penis. 'Oh!' Summerfield breathed heavily and pulled himself away. 'Raja'—a little cough, his voice irritated now— 'For God's sake, tell me what the matter is? I can't *guess*!'

'*Badr*!' she finally hissed in a whisper.

'Badr? Is he *ill*?'

'It is like an illness. I'm so in love. *We* are so in love—but I cannot have him. I want to be his wife and the pain in me is so great. Summerfield—'

'Another year, I believe,' said Summerfield, realising that it was the last thing she wanted to hear.

'A year!' she wailed. 'Twelve months more of this agonising longing. And what if we die between times? The French will come after the snows have gone. Their general knows where we are. Oh, hateful! Why *does* he do this to me?'

'Who?' said Summerfield, suddenly lost. 'The general?'

'*Badr*, that's who!' seethed Raja. 'Does he deliberately play games? Does he use his lofty values to make a crazed and beaten woman of me? He is like a rock to me—cold as a stone that cannot be broken. Oh, these men! Oh, you are so cunning, so wicked! May God discover the truth and burn you all!'

Summerfield stood back. After all, it was certainly within Raja's inflammable capability to send a left hook flying towards him. 'And me?' he found himself retorting. 'What about *me*? The loneliness of *my* nights!'

Raja stopped and looked at him, her face creased into a mixture of incomprehension and curiosity. Everything with Raja was exaggeration. 'What loneliness? You mean—?'

'Me too, Raja—I suffer. I have the memories of a great love that night after night become drier and drier. They leave me with an emptiness like a starving belly. Raja—I haven't kissed a woman in—' he felt himself move towards her and held himself back. She seemed to realise this and her eyes opened wide in surprise.

'So *this* explains your irritable, mean nature, oh Summerfield!'

'*Mean*? Me?' Raja could indeed have punched him.

'The way you scowl at me and the other women as you pass. Receiving a hello is like extracting gold from donkey's dung!'

'Raja!' squeaked Summerfield.

A grin appeared on her face, slow and spreading and making Summerfield feel excruciatingly embarrassed.

'So that's it!' she said, triumphantly, her grin baring all her teeth and even the hole in the side of the lower left row. 'Summerfield—you are doing things with your hands! And it is so unsatisfying, so empty!'

'Don't be ridiculous! I'm English!' said Summerfield, aware that his defence sounded just as hollow as his vacuous masturbation.

'Harry Summerfield—you are *sad*! You need a wife, maybe,' said Raja, completely cured of her own chagrin now and her voice carrying the certainty of one of the village gossips. 'Or maybe, there are the goats that would help you out?'

'Raja!' Summerfield moved forwards and she squealed, backing out of his hut. Laughing, she gave a little skip and then turned one last time. 'Thank you, Harry. Talking to you has made me feel much better now!'

'And we could talk more, Raja—you have exactly the same problem as me! Hands *indeed*!'

'Don't be stupid!' Her face blackened once again. 'I'm a child of God!'

'Exactly,' sent Summerfield. 'With all our oddities and imperfections! Ha! And *take that!*'

Raja did not reply. Instead, she gave a terse, semi-obscene gesture with her tongue and hurried off towards the village.

Days in the valley became dreaded days of waiting. At first, after the months of labour and care and watering, the people of the valley waited with excited expectation for a return on their effort. But as the days passed and nature was seen to be reluctant, a sense of irritation entered their expectations. The crops and orchards replied with a recalcitrant silence—a stony disobedience in the face of the villagers' hopes and a refusal to answer their prayers. A noticeable trace of worry entered their faces as they gazed out over the expanse of the valley. The fruit was examined, the soil tested. People gathered by the village wells and took to tasting the water to discuss whether that had anything to do with it. A rumour flickered and smoked that it was God's answer to the works that the Englishman, Summerfield, had undertaken and it was quickly smothered by the old Mullah and his cane of wrath.

Every day brought with it its denial—*why us? Why does the valley merit this punishment?* And its anxiety—*what will we eat during the blizzards? Will the others have more than I?* The Kaïd called for a meeting with the leading figures of the valley to discuss the problem and the measures that could be taken, but the nagging truth that was on everyone's lips remained unspoken: in the end run, they were powerless before nature. They could invent techniques and explore the wisdom of their elders and gather hay for readiness to feed the animals they would have to slaughter in the winter, but they seemed so small in comparison with the greatness and finality of nature's swing.

Summerfield, relegated to being an onlooker—he had none of the agricultural skills required to deal with the problem—saw the people of the valley sink slowly and inexorably into the great fatalism that characterised their culture and which constituted one of the most noticeable differences with his own. *It will rain—if God wills it*. Or *we will starve, if it is to be so*, were expressions he began to hear a hundred times a day.

A western culture, he concluded, cogitating on his observations while walking through the unyielding terraced crops, would act differently. In Europe and in America, they had long since tried to wrestle destiny from God and from Nature, His daughter. For hundreds of years man had been making experiments and building inventions of wood and iron and now plastic and rubber and synthetics—Man's alchemy to reverse control. Faced with a problem, the European mind and body flung themselves desperately at the solution, unsure of where they would end up, but certain that it would at least be somewhere. And moreover, somewhere that might give them even a little more edge on the impalpable ingredients of life they could not seize and that could never be completely mastered. For how to explain miracles? How to explain the complete and unexpected twist of fate that sent Man and Nature into one and then sent them exploding outwards from each other in disruption: freak weather, strange events, signs and omens and happiness when everything pointed so strongly towards failure and pain. Summerfield could not discern what approach was best or even if there was one which was stronger than the other. It was different and that was all. And maybe, in the end run, he concluded, the best was a meeting of both worlds—a willingness and trust that would leave God and Nature to open up the path to good outcome; while at the same time searching and exploring to take up the challenge of responsibility over one's own destiny. At some point along the way, the two would undoubtedly meet and great things would perhaps result.

At last, two weeks into October, the order was given to begin to harvest what was possible before it rotted on its branches and in the fields. It was an occasion for everybody, from the youngest child to the oldest grandmother to put their backs into the earth and reap the resources they had planted.

But the atmosphere was morose. Singing, half-hearted. People toiled and then went to bed instead of talking by an open fire. Songs were silenced. Laughter was as spare as the crops that lacked. The autumn would be hard and the winter harder still.

As the last carts and baskets were unloaded into the fortified granaries that topped every village along the valley, Badr was asked by the Kaïd, Ahmed Youadi, to set up a series of patrols to observe the outlying mountains. Men in groups of ten were regularly chosen to climb the tracks and paths for any sign of the French and also to forage for any food that might be more abundant in the neighbouring valleys. Summerfield's time duly came and he shouldered his Lee Enfield and trudged off with the rest of the men and a three-day absence from his home.

They did not encounter the French, only a reconnaissance plane that they once watched from the safety of the *maquis* humming lazily through the valleys. They would probably not see it again before the spring for October and early November brought much fog and heavy downpour that made flying too hazardous and too unproductive.

As Summerfield patrolled with his small band of adopted brothers, he mulled over the fact that he was single. Approaching thirty-one now, he had only really known two women in his life, not counting the occasional visit to the tarts in Stoke during his first writing assignment as a young man. It was all pretty depressing. Two love affairs and not much fun in them either, all told. Elizabeth, the upper middle-class *femme fatale*, whose ravenous sexual appetite was a necessary cure for her fits of depression; Jeanne, the young beauty, innocence stepping out onto the path of passion, the necessary discovery of the truth about herself and her deepest desires. Poor Jeanne, he heard himself saying as he followed the mesmerising rhythm of his companions' footsteps. How he had lifted her hopes and broken her innocence. He shook his head, as though shaking free his sense of guilt: no, it had been pure love, the best and on the contrary it had been sublime. He had had nothing to offer her—nothing material in any case—and she had taken his love and desire with equal passion.

He refrained from dwelling too long on her—it would only

increase his emptiness—and instead thought about what Raja, *the little imp*, had said. It seemed he had a reputation for grumpiness. Strange, he had never thought that the womenfolk actually wanted him to look at them. In fact, he'd made a determined effort, in order not to cause anyone any offence, not to. They were, after all, supposed to do nothing before they were married. Or perhaps the Berber tribes were different. Perhaps, like many other peoples, they accepted religion as a useful set of laws and spiritual guidelines, but tolerated a little swaying from the path as part of the natural process of things.

The women, he mused, finding conversation with himself becoming very interesting indeed, were in reality very coquettish. Most days, they took pains to adorn their skin with intricate henna tattoos. Wearing red, orange or royal blue was an everyday occurrence too, mostly in scarves and belts worn over their black working robes—nothing like the glum strictness of the city women. The kohl they applied on the lids of their eyes, although serving to ward off the sun, also gave them a sensual look, highlighting the clearness of their green and hazel eyes. From a wary, almost aggressive initial exchange of regards, Summerfield had glanced up at times to see the most impish of sensual shines in their eyes—Raja herself being the epitome of feminine sensuality in the valley. Beneath their clothes, he had sensed firm, ripe bodies made supple and strong through their work in the fields and soft and smooth from the unguents and oils they took care to cover their skin with at night. And it was their smell that at times made his head turn and that, strangely enough, fuelled much of his solitary pleasure at night.

But what did the menfolk do? Summerfield found himself asking. And how did they view all this? Like most things, he concluded, what you are immersed in on a daily basis throughout the years becomes unnoticed or accepted as usual behaviour. Men and women courted and married like anywhere else. Like a game of fly-fishing, they sent out alternate lines that skipped and brushed the water's surface in varying degrees of colour and light until, at one particular moment, the allure of the magical and dancing fly triggered the ancient instinct to thrust up to the surface and gob the hook. Fish, considered Summerfield—from the strong-bodied trout to the muscled, deadly pike—actually *knew* they were being duped, but the attraction of being caught and consumed was all-hypnotic and senseless to resist. As for the young and single, true—there had been cases of what Raja had referred to as *pleasure with the goats* and probably a bit of harmless groping among the rocks with either sex. Indeed, it was one of the old Mullah's functions to oversee that these particular activities were discouraged and suppressed. But mostly, the young warriors-cum-farmers seemed content to stay within their own gender and seemed to find what pleasure they required in talking and smoking and sharpening their shooting skills. Music, too, proved a harmonious substitute for any lack of sexual activity and often poetry handed down from ancient times stretched many a night into the light of dawn.

Coming to rest on a rocky outcrop, Summerfield sat with the rest of the patrol as they promptly lit up their pipes made from hollowed out bones. He passed a wad of black tobacco to a companion who lacked and nodded silently. Yes, thought Summerfield, gazing out over the endless sea of misty crests before him, Raja was right. I'm quite a sad case, all told. And maybe her advice was good: I do indeed need a woman.

The night came suddenly and unexpectedly and brought with it a rolling series of clouds that dropped low across the crests to hug the slopes. Their leader, a small, wiry man whom the others called by the French-sounding nickname *Hatif*—the hasty one—ordered a fire to be lit among the rocks. As the cold turned from sharp dry to piercing damp, he showed Summerfield how to lean against the heated stone and warm his clothes. It was very welcome, for Summerfield found himself yearning for the heat of his hut and covers and cursing the very fact that they were out there in the freezing wild.

He could not sleep. Perhaps an hour passed before the warmth inside his coat faded and he rose to warm himself again only to find that the fire had died out. He returned to his spot, lying down once more and trying in vain to plug the holes in his sleeping arrangement from the icy damp. Restless, he wondered if the others were having the same problem, though a quick peek from beneath his layers of cloth told him otherwise. Hard buggers, he told himself, glancing at the scattered bundles that were bodies and feeling a tinge of envy at the snores that were coming from several of them. It'd take him years to get used to these conditions.

His discomfort turned inexorably towards irritation and his irritation towards anger. It was impossible—he just couldn't sleep. Finally, shivering now, he rose and began to get his limbs moving to generate heat. To the left, some five yards away, he came across one of the sentinels who glanced nonchalantly up from his position and nodded.

'I have to piss,' muttered Summerfield as he stepped past. 'Freezing!'

'Where is your weapon?' murmured the figure, a note of reproach in his voice.

'Oh—back there,' replied Summerfield, softly. 'Safe. Can't pee with a rifle in my hands.'

'Better that than die pissing,' mentioned the shape, giving a visible shrug.

'Bollocks,' replied Summerfield, sourly in English. 'And don't fall asleep,' he added before slipping past the sentry into the mist.

After ten or so yards, Summerfield thought he had gone far enough. He was a little warmer now, thank God, and standing still was at last bearable. He stopped thinking, listening to the eerie silence—in fact noise—of the mist. If he concentrated hard enough, he could hear it—a faint, hypnotising patter like something crackling softly on a window pane. Little by little, the grey darkness drew shapes in the rocks and, feeling a tinge of nervousness creep up on him, his eyes strained to discern the path back. He took two, three careful steps and then juddered to a halt barely three feet from a yawning precipice. '*Jesus Christ,*' he exhaled, almost immediately subject to the reeling, uncontrollable signs of vertigo. Feeling his arms begin to flail in panic, he promptly sat down, a painful jab of rock into his coccyx, and edged backwards, safely away from the abyss. Now he did feel like peeing, he muttered, and turning onto his hands and feet to a crouching position, edged back towards the camp. Five more yards, obviously in the wrong direction, and a hand clamped on his shoulder.

'Very funny,' he murmured, expecting the sentry to be grinning into his face. Turning, something suddenly smothered his mouth—a cloth—and he felt himself being dragged back. His eyes went wild, straining to get a glimpse of his unseen attacker and a searing pain shot up his back and face. If he struggled, his neck would be snapped.

For a dozen yards, unable to call for help, he was half pushed, half dragged across the slope, sure that at any moment he would be shoved over the edge into the void. And then, roughly forced to the ground so that his face lay pressed into the cold, wet grit of the rocky mountain slope, a series of whispers.

'Kill him.'

'No—make him talk.'

'Kill him, I say.'

'I know this man.'

I know this man—the words came as a miracle to Summerfield's ears. It spelt a thin slither of hope, a chance of survival.

'I recognise his eyes. This is no Arab, no Berber.'

'So we can kill him. The French do not have to know.'

'The legionnaire is apt in smelling death wherever it occurs,' whispered the voice. 'Leave him, I say—or else you will be the one who takes the place in which you want him to be.'

Lying there, shaking uncontrollably, Summerfield then felt the thin, sharp tip of a knife touch his Adam's apple. It sent a tremor down his chest and deep into his stomach. The grip on his mouth slacked and the cloth disappeared.

'You have angels that follow you even in the dark,' said the voice and Summerfield, certain now who it was, raised his head slightly to look at the blackness that was Abrach.

'*God*,' shivered Summerfield. 'I thought it was all over.'

'So did I,' said Abrach, glancing at the man holding the blade to Summerfield's neck. 'As with most of the butchers one can hire, their sense of reflection is sometimes limited to sudden, primary gestures. It can be useful.'

'What—what are you—?' began Summerfield and tried to raise himself up on his elbow only to meet with ungiving resistance. He saw Abrach's oddly shaped fingers rise to his lips—like knotted twigs—and gesture silence. Summerfield, powerless, closed his eyes in acknowledgement and returned to his prone position. 'You were sighted,' he whispered. 'working for the Vichy French.'

'The most despicable of men—just below these murderers I hired to help me.'

'To kill your own people? I cannot understand, Abrach.'

'To kill them if necessary if they get in my way. You know my target, Harry.'

'Lefèvre?' Summerfield frowned. 'But he's in Marrakesh.'

'Was,' said Abrach from behind the *cheiche* wound about his face. 'Until he foolishly decided to choose the Free French. It was probably the biggest mistake he ever made—that, and destroying everything I ever had.'

'You've lost your senses, Abrach—I just can't understand,' whispered Summerfield.

'A man does something wrong,' grunted Abrach, moving his face closer so that Summerfield could smell his breath. 'And he expects some form of punishment. That is justice. But when the punishment goes on and on, disproportionate with what he committed, intended not only to punish but to humiliate, to ruin and to destroy him…it breeds vengeance like a disease that has no vaccine.'

'Is there no goodness left in you, Abrach—the man whose heart ruled with intelligence and wisdom?'

'You speak like a mountain Mullah,' said Abrach, grinning slightly. 'I see my decision to imprison you here has had an effect.'

'So the cynical finally won over the hope?' said Summerfield, breathing again as Abrach finally drew away.

'I once told you it would get the better of me—and in all truth, Harry Summerfield, I cannot remember much of who I was before. It is of no matter. Like you said, too—death will get me. But not before I get Lefèvre and—may I add—his *family*.'

Summerfield felt as though he'd been touched with a live wire. '*Jeanne?*'

'Perhaps. I do not know for sure, but would a father leave his daughter in a hostile city?'

'She's here? In the mountains?'

'Perhaps,' repeated Abrach. 'I believe they talked to a certain Le Guédec and made arrangements. That's what his manservant said at least.'

'Mohammed? Where?'

'That is what I am here to find. Obviously, you don't know either.'

'Leave her alone, Abrach—please.' Summerfield stared into the man's eyes. 'It was not her fault.'

'You're the one to blame, of course, Harry. You always wanted to save the world, sacrifice yourself. Thus be it.'

'No,' hissed Summerfield, suddenly afraid and conscious of a renewed pressure on his throat. 'That's not what I meant. Don't you see—you *cannot* kill. You said it yourself.'

A strange, soft, almost woman-like bubble of laughter came from Abrach. 'My dear Harry Summerfield. You try, you try and that is good. Though too late, my old friend,' continued Abrach, his face turning to stone. 'Presently, I have discovered that my entire life was meant to lead to what I am about to do. I see no other reason for existing.'

'In reality,' said Summerfield, suddenly clear and calm. 'You are out to kill *yourself*.'

Abrach looked back at him, unflinching and sighed. 'It is time to return to your brothers,' he said. 'You have been away for too long. It would be a pity for them to fire into the mist and kill you by mistake. Leave, Harry. And say nothing. My men can pick you out at six hundred yards and are itching for blood.'

'And Jeanne? Promise me, Abrach. For old times' sake.'

'I never was who I was,' returned Abrach, gesturing for his man to lift the blade from Summerfield throat. 'All that counts is now. I can only promise you that my punishment will be without mercy.' And with that, rough hands pulled Summerfield to his feet and gave him a push. 'It is that way. And thank God that you have been spared.'

Abrach and his man disappeared silently into the mist and Summerfield, the tension released, suddenly broke down into a fit of uncontrollable sobs. A voice came to him.

'*Sidi* Summerfield? *Sidi Summerfield?*' It was the sentry, calling out from the left.

'It's me,' Summerfield called back, stifling his tears. He took a few heavy, lurching steps, maybe five, six yards, and saw the vague barrel of a rifle nudging through the grey.

'Is it you, *Sidi* Summerfield? I heard voices—are you all right?'

'The sad past,' said Summerfield, sniffing heavily. 'I was only talking to myself.'

'Talking to yourself, oh strange Englishman.'

'Yes. About the saddest past you could ever imagine.'

49

Towards mid–November the first snows came—like the harvest rather late and sparingly. The wind, however, with a force and iciness that Summerfield hadn't thought possible, was plentiful. It drove in from the summits, sweeping low through the valleys with an eerie moaning and cut through walls and clothing alike. Over the coming weeks, the pink earth that had risen in powdery clouds during the dry months alternately became a quagmire, liquid and thick when it rained or snowed, and a painful, almost impracticable rutted crust when it froze. Wrapped in their clothes and skins, people were hard to recognise now and Summerfield found himself looking out for their gait and how they held themselves rather than their faces. There was the old Mullah, hobbling along with his concave back, Raja with her lilting cheekiness, Badr with his long, slow and careful steps.

The first heavy snow finally arrived in the last week of November, turning the valley into a sumptuous and dazzling white. The wind died down and for a while children whooped and shouted as they played in the fresh and compact powder.

And it was once again Summerfield's turn to join the other men on patrol. This time, the column of twenty men and three heavily-laden mules was headed by Badr. Before they left, his friend gave him an intricately tailored fleece to wear. Judging from the quality, it must have cost the young man a considerable sum, but all Badr did when faced with Summerfield's objections was to comment on the Englishman's inexperience of proper cold and a gory explanation of what frostbite could do to a man's protuberances if unprotected.

The ritual leaving of the village at dawn took place, with the men's coughing muffled by their headwear and long scarves. As they stamped about bringing warmth to their bodies, waiting for the order to leave, Summerfield saw Raja standing at the doorway to her mother's house. He waved to her and she grinned, looking sad. She said something that was lifted away by the breeze, and then Badr appeared, walking over to her. The young couple stood close without touching and a silent message was passed between them. After a few moments, Badr turned to join the group of men and Summerfield saw Raja's head drop with tears and turn away. He felt desperately sorry for her, somewhat irritated at Badr, his values and unwavering self-discipline and told himself he would have a good man-to-man talk with him about it all. Who knows, thought Summerfield, perhaps a Christmas marriage might be in the offing.

Headed by Badr, the men and animals formed a loose column and with last waves and goodbyes, trudged off in the snow up the valley slopes. Once away from the village and a good hours' walking behind them, the young leader called for a halt. Badr sat his men in a semi-circle around him and, squatting, told them the news.

'We shall be gone for longer this time, my brothers,' said Badr, pulling characteristically on his now fully grown beard. 'Five, maybe six days.' There was a ripple of a collective groan, then silence. 'There has been talk of sightings,' he continued and the atmosphere suddenly became measurably different, the men leaning forwards. 'As usual, the rumours are conflicting. The messenger from the A-Auri says a hundred or so men with mortars. Someone else, from the tribe of the Toubkal say thirty at the most. And yet another says only a handful. Whatever their number, we can rightly say that they are there for three reports cannot lie, at least about their presence.'

'And us?' said a man—Taffu—an eager shine in his now uncovered eyes.

'I will lead you to a place where they were said to be heading. We are to meet up with the Toubkal men and join up to force the French away.'

'So we shall see fighting?' said Summerfield.

'It is very likely,' replied Badr, avoiding his eyes. 'The winter is our ally. It has been our companion for thousands of years in these mountains. Now is a good time to teach the invaders a lesson.'

'Before they teach *us* a lesson in the spring!' spat a tribesman.

'Before they *try* to teach us a lesson in spring,' corrected Badr, with unaccustomed bravado. He looked steadily at the man behind the comment. 'We will see how your spirit changes once we see them running for their lives in the snow.'

They sweated as they walked despite the cold. The strain on the muscles of Summerfield's legs was ten times worse than usual and during the first day he suffered enormously from cramp. At one point, he slipped and his knee came out of its joint only to slip back with a horrendous clumping sound. One of his comrades produced a balm from a small, glass jar that burnt like fury on his skin but which helped calm the stabbing soreness of what was likely to be a trapped nerve.

During camp that evening, Badr came to him and suggested he return to the valley with one of the men. Summerfield refused, playing down the pain and hopeful that the morning would see things better. As evening set in and a cold blue light sent them into shadow, each man burrowed a deep hole in the snow and lit some dry sticks, alternatively changing position every now and then to warm their bodies. Somewhere around ten o'clock, they ate some salted meat and bread that they heated over the flame before rolling themselves up in multiple layers of clothes, prayer mats, covers and sacking off-loaded from the mules. To Summerfield it was a night of uncomfortable shifting as he fought to find both evasive warmth and comfort. He would lose consciousness for twenty minutes only to wake suddenly, as though hardly a second had passed, shivering. He was grateful to be shaken by one of the two sentinels at around three if only to move. It was his turn—two hours of watch until five.

The next day followed in much the same way. Muscle-burning hikes up tracks made perilous by the snow and ice, descents into neighbouring valleys, stumbles and falls, the relief of the rest periods and boiling tea. Once they thought they heard a plane, but it was only the wind making a strange droning noise as it drove through the crags around them. They were so high now that there were no longer any trees. In the summer, Badr told him, as they trekked, the place was a mountain desert, arid and the colour of golden sand with only lizards for company.

On the third morning, they once again gathered around Badr before they set out. There was a sense of hard lucidity about the young man as he talked to the men, over a half of them double his age.

'The next three hours will see us in the area where the French were heading,' he informed them. 'I want your guns ready at all moments and your courage firm. There is a small group of buildings—up there and this is where I believe they will be.'

'I knew the buildings,' said a man, his mouth almost toothless. 'They spent March and September there years ago and hunted cats, and many times laughter could be heard ringing in the valleys around.'

'That is the place,' nodded Badr, gravely. 'With God's will, the chance will be ours to show them how the tribes are truly warriors, that this land is ours.' There was a general murmur of agreement and several muttered prayers. 'Remember, winter is our ally. We must use the snow and the clouds; make the cold our sword as we drive them out.'

Clenching his teeth against the stubborn pain in his knee— every time he bent it to step upwards, a knife blade seemed to enter his cartilage—Summerfield followed Badr as he gestured back along the line of men for them to distance themselves and keep low. He gratefully accepted a sturdy stick from Badr and found himself wondering when he should speak to him of Raja. Finally, two hours of hard slog took them to a small plateau that looked down onto a series of natural terraces carved into the rock of the adjacent slope. The terraces cascaded down into a valley they could not see the floor of until, at last, the tree line appeared just above the clouds.

'We are here,' said Badr. The men squinted, searching the uniform whiteness. 'Down there by the trees,' indicated Badr, pointing. He brought out a pair of captured binoculars from his sack and began checking the terrain. 'The French planted the pines here years ago when they built the houses.' He grunted a laugh. 'They are the only trees for miles.'

'Do you see anything?' said a man, gruffly.

Badr shook his head. 'The buildings are hidden behind the copse—too far away to see anything else. We will go down. Unload the provisions and put the mules to rest. Harry—you will stay to guard them.'

'I cannot guard mules,' said Summerfield at this. 'I know even less of these beasts than I do of winter warfare.'

'Harry—your leg.'

'I insist on coming, Badr. And Youssef,' he continued, looking round to find the youngest member of the patrol, 'is barely past adolescence. His family would be devastated if ever anything happened.'

Badr held his gaze for some moments, thinking, and then nodded assent. 'Let it be.'

They ate, out of sight behind the crest and out of the cold wind. Curiously, after they had finished, the wind suddenly died down only to be replaced by a gentle snow fall that sent Summerfield into warm recollections of Christmas walks in England. This he soon forgot as Badr gave the order to split into two groups and descend the mountain slope by separate approaches. Thankfully, Summerfield found himself just behind his young friend. The thought that it was only his second time in any sort of action crossed his mind and still in some doubt over his potential reaction preferred Badr to be close by to guide him.

Every fifty yards down the slope, Badr gave the sign to halt while he swept the wooded terrace below with his binoculars. They crouched as they moved, sometimes almost on their backsides as they slid over and between rocks, sometimes up to their thighs in snow when it became deep. Barely half-way between the crest and the cluster of pine trees they received a series of signs from the other group descending on their right.

'The men of the Toubkal,' muttered Badr and gave a brief smile, almost of relief. 'They have joined us, moving up from below, slightly east.' He brought the binoculars to his eyes and after several moments handed them to Summerfield. 'Here, Harry. Look.' Badr nudged Summerfield to the right direction. 'Mmm—they look like insects down there. They should take more care. If we can see them—'

'They know what they're doing,' answered Badr. 'I trust.' He took back the binoculars and once more gave the sign to advance.

The stonework of the buildings suddenly came into view through the pines, grey pinkish patterns. Two, maybe three buildings, one set apart and obviously serving as stables and store houses. Another four hundred yards and they would be there.

'See the smoke?' whispered Badr, asking Summerfield to confirm.

Squinting through the eyepieces, Summerfield saw a thin, almost transparent wisp rising from behind the trees from what would have been the roof. He nodded, feeling his heart suddenly beating heavily. 'A fire—there's someone there.'

Badr relayed the information to the groups and a soft, muffled series of clicks told Summerfield that the men had released the safety catches on their rifles. The raiding party split into sub-groups and Badr sent two of them skirting to the left and right. Once in position he gave the sign to close in. His eyes, thought Summerfield, looked glazed and wild— maybe the effect of fear or apprehension—and wondered what his own looked like.

At last they were among the trees, thirty or so yards from the first set of buildings. They waited a while, caught their breath and listened as the snow began to fall more heavily, great feathery flakes that made it difficult to see anything with any precision. There was no noise coming from the buildings, at least from this distance. Summerfield watched Badr tugging nervously on his beard. 'Forwards,' murmured the young man and Summerfield followed, his Lee Enfield ready, his senses too occupied by the forthcoming attack to notice the sharp pain in his knee. They crept silently up to the walls of the outhouses and paused for final preparation. Was it the cold stone or the situation that made Summerfield's fingers tremble numbly? The other groups should now be in position, he thought and wondered why Badr was waiting. Then, sticking close to the walls, he found himself moving forwards behind Badr as they advanced on the main building. Suddenly there was a noise, a movement and a loud shout. A shot rang out and Summerfield fired too, lashing back the bolt to reload. Then chaos—a volley of detonations from all sides as something moved in front of them in a blur whining like a demented banshee. Summerfield saw it, a bucking bundle of movement and fired again. There was a hideous yelp. More shots. 'Stop!' shouted Badr. 'Cease fire, damn you! *Stop!*' The mountain rang and echoed with the diminishing waves of gunfire until silence came upon them. Badr craned his head carefully and peeked around the corner of the wall. 'A goat,' he exhaled. 'Curse it—a goat!' Summerfield relaxed and involuntarily stepped forward only for Badr to pull him back. 'Careful, Harry. We don't know what else there is.'

From the left, a group of three advanced through the trees and came to a halt taking up firing positions. Those to the right called from behind the outhouses and there was a sudden, human moan. Badr moved carefully forwards, around the wall and into the clearing, his Mauser kept levelled. The goat, which must have taken a dozen or so bullets, laid twisted and torn, one of its hind legs missing. And then their gaze went towards the house and froze. Summerfield let out a gasp. The windows were blown in, the doors hanging off their hinges. And in front of this, barely three yards from the entrance, were three wooden staves topped by three severed heads.

'It can't be,' said Summerfield, breathless. '*It can't*—' and his eyes rested in disbelief on the ghoulish sight. The heads were a greyish purple, eye sockets sagging in something resembling a medieval scene of sorrowful repentance, the whole a criss-cross of blood and matted hair. However disfigured, they were unmistakably the heads of Lefèvre, his wife and Soumia, the Lefèvre housemaid. Several yards to the left were their headless bodies, shot through with holes and lying on top of one another in a heap.

'Dear God,' said Badr, 'this is not the work of the French,' and as he glanced at him, Summerfield felt his stomach churn uncontrollably and he was immediately sick.

'It is custom,' said Badr, once he had led Summerfield into the building. 'In the northern Rif in 1921 they trapped the Spanish army on the plains and laid out two thousand heads on branches cut from the trees.'

'Barbarians,' spat Summerfield.

'A custom—and perhaps unfortunate,' said Badr, looking uncomfortable. 'But to change the subject, I am thinking of something else—*someone* else, to be exact.'

'*Jeanne*!' Summerfield suddenly looked up. Suddenly, he could hardly breathe. 'Do you think –?'

Badr nodded and shouted an order to search the house. They listened in deadly silence, eyes turned upwards as the sound of footsteps trod heavily through the upstairs rooms.

'Nothing,' shouted a voice. 'But four beds. Objects. Different clothes—women's clothes.'

'She was here,' said Summerfield, dazed. He shook his head. 'Jesus Christ, she was here. How could I—'

'You should not feel guilty, Harry,' said Badr, sternly and reaching across gripped his arm. They looked at each other. Badr shook his head. 'You didn't know. *No one* knew.'

'I knew Abrach was in the area—I should have told you,' said Summerfield, irritably. 'They were massacred. It's—it's *disgusting*. No pity or chance of escape. What *insane* vengeance.'

He heard Badr rise and walk away. Outside the Toubkal men had arrived and he could hear Badr engaged in conversation. A few moments later, the young man returned. 'It wasn't them. They didn't know there were Europeans here. I think—' Summerfield raised his head from his hands and looked at Badr—'I think it might be Abslem El Rifni after all,' finished Badr, guiltily.

'*Abrach*,' whispered Summerfield, 'Why didn't I believe him? God, I didn't actually believe he could do such a thing. Remember that time he was seen, Badr? *Toubfil* came across them. Why?' he asked, stunned by their—by *his*—ineptitude. '*Why* didn't he kill him then? None of this would have happened.'

'Jeanne Lefèvre must be with them,' said Badr, 'Unless…'

'Unless she escaped,' finished Summerfield. He snorted. 'Escaped! And in this!' he added, with an angry gesture at the mountains. 'Four hours in this and she'd die of cold.'

'Four hours have long since passed, Harry, I'm afraid. The killing probably happened sometime yesterday evening. The heads—they are frozen.'

Nonetheless, Badr ordered search parties off to explore the mountain slopes from east to west. He refrained from mentioning finding a body, but Summerfield knew that it was the principal reason behind the action. Finding a tool, Summerfield began to dig the hard earth behind the outhouses and was joined—he was grateful—by three other men in his group. When it came to hauling the bodies to their graves, he couldn't bear to look. One of the men, Taffu who had shown so much cynicism at the outset of the mission, brought along the heads and reverently matched them with their respective bodies. When it came to piling the earth and stones on the bodies, Summerfield noticed that the Lefèvres' ring fingers had been severed, though whether it had been the murderer's or Taffu or one of the Toubkal men, Summerfield was beyond caring. His mind was singly focused on Jeanne. To think that she had been here, he repeated to himself under his breath, that she had been sitting in exactly the same armchair as I had been only a few minutes ago. When all was finished, Summerfield said a prayer and then the three men who had help him dig stood back and spoke in Arabic for Soumia's grave with its upright little stone turned towards Mecca. She would never have hurt a fly, Summerfield heard himself saying, it was all so horribly unjust.

When the search party came back two hours later, Badr came to him with news. Nothing had been found. Just the trace of movement in the snow heading south, and discarded shoes, women's, two of them at an interval of twenty or so yards. Badr produced one and asked Summerfield if he recognised it. Summerfield shrugged despondently.

'Could be. Who knows. I wasn't aware of her wardrobe, you know.'

Badr shook his head sadly and gave a little sigh that betrayed his powerlessness. 'There are some letters, Harry—and her belongings. Perhaps you would like to take some of them with you.'

'What?' Summerfield looked up, still dazed. 'Oh, yes. Thank you, Badr. That's...that's very thoughtful.'

'We must go, Harry. It is time.'

'The French?' said Summerfield. 'You're right. In any case, I don't want to stay here.' He shouldered his Lee Enfield and then turned to look at his friend. 'So what do we do, Badr? Give me five men and we'll track them.'

'Have you seen how the snow has fallen, Harry? It would be difficult.'

'But not impossible. There must be enough tracks left to lead us to them.'

Badr remained silent, scratching his beard. At last, with another little sigh, his eyes met Summerfield's. 'Our mission is not over. We were to engage with the enemy. Abrach is with the Vichy French and therefore he is one of them—an enemy. I say two more days. We can follow what we find. After two days, Harry, we shall turn back and return home.'

'And if we don't find her?' said Summerfield, looking directly at him.

'The valley is your home, Harry. You must return there.'

50

Her nose was fractured. Every time the monster pressed against her she cried out in pain. It seemed to excite him. As a result, he usually ejaculated quickly, grunting, lifting his heavy weight off of her on his grotesquely twisted hands and wiping himself on her clothes. He was wordless, left her, lumbered away.

They had raped her four times since they murdered her parents: once by a second man, shortly after they had killed her father, three times by the man they called El Rifni that she recognised as Abrach, the same mad beast who had once tried to abduct her. In the beginning, she had resisted him. Her fractured nose, the bruises and scratches and the gash on her neck were proof of that. And then, the fourth time, she had stopped struggling out of some inner instinct. Survival. She had succeeded in distancing herself, as though she was not there and her body not hers, just a mechanism, an orifice for her attacker to use. Her mind was empty and removed and thus her senses deadened, only the sharp stab of pain in her upper face and the nagging burning sensation in her sex reminding her she was part of some macabre experience in the realness of things.

They sat her on a mule and covered her with shrouds of materials and skins—the same on which Abrach wiped clean his penis after taking her. She was conscious of a smell, could not discern whether it was him or sweat or the tanned skins, but the very thought of it made her gag so that she could not hold down the food they gave her.

They travelled slowly, in a column of twelve men, headed somewhere west—towards the Vichy French or towards his camp, she was unsure. Once, she looked at him as he moved roughly inside her, caught his eyes for a fraction of a second and thought she saw the glimmer of a genteel character that he might have once been: remorse, a wordless apology—and then, shocking in its suddenness: coldness, hatred, as though her aggressor himself had removed his mind and senses from the ultimately mechanical act.

She thought of killing herself. The rope that tied her wrists would not prevent her falling from the mule and pushing herself off into the precipice. But something kept her going—something that, at moments, she hated even more than her captors for keeping her alive.

Alive was something that sent shocking images to her mind. They came suddenly and she shook them away just as brutally. Images of first Soumia, hysterical, yelling and whooping in that strange way native women did though this time through utter, uncontrollable fear. They had lifted her skirts—the sight of her nanny's fattened thighs shocking her—and laughed. Her mother sobbing uncontrollably, clinging to her father, then wrenched free as she and Soumia were dragged to the left of the patio and promptly shot. Her father's high-pitched, almost feminine scream of anger and the sudden force with which he momentarily tore free and lunged at Abrach. She would never forget. Never forget either the look in her father's eyes when Abrach began shouting at him, his grotesque hands raised barely centimetres from his eyes. That regard, sideways at her and unflinching, as though what Abrach was ranting about didn't matter in the slightest—utter resignation mixed with apology and a desperate message of fatherly love. And then the pistol shots, three at point-blank range in the chest which sent her father's body spinning towards the others and the other shots—maybe seven or so—from the men's rifles. Pieces of body flew apart and speckled her clothes. Hysterical, she had been dragged inside by Abrach and his adjutant and raped. When they pulled her out into the clearing, the blood streaming from her nose and neck, she had a blurred view of three headless bodies and remembered asking herself, dreamlike, where the heads had gone.

As they plodded through the deep snow, she fell into a trance, her gaze distant and unflinching on the whiteness below her feet. The notion of time slipped away, punctuated by those ghastly memories. What was it that had forced her to stay alive? What could be worse than what she was suffering, what she had seen? Was it hope? Or was it fear—fear of dying that kept her going, a fear that would enable her to endure the worst of human suffering in a futile attempt to put off the nothingness of death a few moments longer? It was all very odd.

Her mind took a meandering turn into her past. It was not her, the smiling girl in a cotton school dress. The laughter, the friends as they walked coming together, jostling boisterously and then parting again, were from a thousand miles away, another life. *Another person*. Faces came to her and voices too. Not words, just the rhythm and tone of happy voices: Sister Marthe, her dear friend Sarah Bassouin, Cécile so loopy, so carefree and Edouard who had had a crush on her and her mother's mockery. Harry. Harry Summerfield, her first true love. So foolish and impossible. Gone now. She shook her head involuntarily. Those days did not belong to her. It hadn't been her. No—life began after Jim came into her life, after she had become an adult. How, she thought, would she ever be able to tell him? The sudden shame made her shudder and guilt pushed the air from her lungs. How would Jim ever forgive her for what had happened? Perhaps, she should never go back to him. Perhaps she should live a life of loneliness and keep the secret locked inside her old age. But what *was* this— she surprised herself—was she *hoping*? Hadn't she just projected herself into the future and the afterworld of the nightmare she was living? Again, Jeanne shook her head, but this time conscious that she had just stumbled upon the reason why she could not kill herself. It was Jim: the thought, the certainty almost, that they would meet again.

On the second day, rising before dawn as the snow began once again to fall, she felt something was different. It was minute, almost imperceptible, but it was there: the feeling that something was to happen. It was like a forthcoming presence. She winced in pain—she was smiling. Was it Jim? Was Jim Wilding coming? Jeanne's breathing became rapid. Perhaps she was going mad, she thought, but her eyes darted around her at the mountains.

He was here, in the air and in the snow. His strength and good humour, his self-confidence that could blow away the darkest of thoughts and problems was…was *seeping into her* from everything around. And then she felt herself flying, but as she turned her head, she saw that she wasn't—she was falling. Abrach had shoved her and now he stood, his huge silhouette towering before her against the mountain as her smile went blank and she turned again to stone and steel.

The fires were doused, little comfort against the shivering cold, and once again she was heaved up onto the mule as Abrach and his men set out. She was trembling uncontrollably. Abrach roughly covered her with yet another cloak and spat into the snow as if ashamed of such a gesture before his men.

They were going downwards now and the snow had stopped falling. A quietness settled in, so great among the mountains that it almost constituted a noise. After an hour or so, they halted and words were exchanged between Abrach and his men. To Jeanne, half listening, half present, they seemed gabbled, heated words. Perhaps they had decided to kill her after all, she thought, absently. They were pointing at things in the distance—directions. And then, as suddenly as they had come to a halt, they were off again, plodding towards the right and continuing the sunken track downwards. That strange, impalpable presence returned to her then. Jim was trying to reach her. He was far, but he was trying to speak to her and she heard in her mind his rich, deep voice and a warmth suddenly touch her shoulder.

There was a man slightly in front of her whose job it was to keep a hold on the loose reins around the mule's neck. Once, scared, the mule had refused to move forwards and first he, and then with the help of several other men, had whipped and pushed the creature until it decided to move. The mule's indignant braying still filled her ears. The man wore a maroon coloured turban, wrapped in many layers around his head so that it took on an almost conical appearance. Only his eyes, greyish brown and churlish, showed from behind the shroud as he repeatedly looked round to check—the idiot—that she was still there. She supposed that he did this more through fear than anything else, Abrach having entrusted him with guarding her. Or perhaps, she thought, Abrach knew that she had thought of ending her life. She wondered what the muleteer would do if she suddenly jumped down and ran. As she thought about this, the ragged column passed through a terraced olive grove, the trees stark and leafless and grey. It was a sign that they had shed their altitude and were entering the fertile heights.

Once through the deserted grove, they halted. Ahead of them, the indentation of the track disappeared between two rocky outcrops some thirty or so feet high. The sound of Abrach's voice, a low, muffled murmur, reached her as he discussed with his adjutant and another man. The large shape, almost clumsy, seemed to hesitate, pondering the oncoming terrain and then turned back to look at her. She met his eyes for an instant and held his gaze and then he turned back towards the track. There was a gruff assent and his left hand came upwards, mittenless and livid in all its hideous disfigurement to wave the column on.

Jeanne thought suddenly of Jim, the situation and shuddered as she fought back the tears. In answer to her noise, her muleteer glanced back through the slit in his shrouded head, his eyes condemning. And then he stumbled. She wondered, in that split second, what punishment Abrach would dole out on him. But he fell heavily, something red spouting from his stomach. And then a loud crack. The mule bucked crazily and Jeanne saw herself falling through the air, over the mule's head. The snow seemed to race towards her and when she hit it there was a crumpled sound to the blackness before her eyes. It was then that she realised— they were under attack.

The shooting became deafening and wild. Around her, Abrach's men ran for cover. Several of them yelped or grunted, toppling to the ground. One man held aloft his arm, his wrist pouring blood and seemed to be wailing an incomprehensible prayer. She screamed and her voice turned into a continuous moan as terrified, she witnessed the massacre around her. Wherever her captors ducked, they could not escape. To the left of the outcrop, zigzagging shapes. I'm going to die, she repeated, holding her head between her hands, *I'm going to die.*

It was impossible to calculate how long the combat lasted. There was much shouting, the thin, pitiful wails of the wounded, the bizarre fluttering, zinging sound as bullets whirled through the air around her. The shots became sporadic. Two men crawled frantically away and bolted, flinging their weapons behind them. And then silence, the smell of cordite, an odd shot. Jeanne raised her head, saw something move into her line of sight and gave a horrified gasp. It was Abrach, lumbering towards her, his large, mangled hands flapping madly in the effort to wade through the snow. And then another shape, to her left, looking at her— distinctly blue eyes—only to step forwards and bar Abrach's way. The great shape swayed to a halt and turned to face his captor. Huge clouds of condensed breath billowed from the monster's open mouth. He lifted his exhausted head to confront the blue-eyed warrior and Jeanne saw the most grotesque look of surprise come across his face.

'Is it *you* to be the one to release me from my burden?' implored Abrach, breathlessly.

Slowly, the warrior lifted his heavy rifle towards the man's face and Jeanne had the most horrifying certainty. A detonation. Suddenly, half of Abrach's head tore away, the disintegration sending a spray of pink liquid hissing into the snow, the great body jerking and falling. It landed heavily and flailed, once, twice and then was still. Jeanne held her breath, numbed, certain she would be next to die.

51

Slowly, deliberately, on her hands and knees, she began to crawl away. Summerfield dropped the Lee Enfield.

'Jeanne!'

She looked back at him, over her shoulder, like an animal, almost a nonchalant curiosity in the gesture and Summerfield hesitated.

'Jeanne?'

He heard his own voice, perplexed, as he caught sight of her bruised and empty face, the layers of clothes and skins—a stray animal responding vaguely to a half-forgotten name. Was it her? Slowly, so as not to scare her, he unwound his headscarf and attempted a smile.

'*Jeanne…*' His voice was soft, foreign sounding and he was suddenly conscious of the reality of his clothes, the weathered colour of his skin. She raised herself and sat on her knees, unsure. 'I suppose I've changed,' he said, weakly.

'Harry.' The answer came as a whisper. She began to sob gently. 'Harry.'

They held each other tightly, silent as Badr's men went through the dead bodies for loot.

'Where is Badr?' said Summerfield at last and had to repeat himself, almost a shout.

'Wounded,' came a reply.

'God! Where is he?'

A raised hand, an impatient gesture. 'Over there.'

Summerfield got up, wincing from the sharp pain in his knee, and in turn helped Jeanne to her feet. She looked stunned and wavered groggily. Summerfield half led her, half pushed her to a group of three men, one of whom he recognised as Taffu, squatting by a body. Summerfield fell to his knees.

'Oh God, oh God—*Badr!*' The young man opened his eyes and winced. There was a thick, black bubbling of blood just under the young man's right lung. Summerfield glanced away only to see that Taffu had a pistol in his hand. '*No!*' shouted Summerfield.

'It is the rule,' murmured Badr, looking resigned. 'The tradition…'

'To hell with your stupid bloody tradition.' Summerfield snatched the pistol from Taffu's hand.

'Harry,' fought Badr, attempting to move.

'Shut up,' hissed Summerfield. 'You're my friend. You lead us. We have to take you back.' Summerfield looked around him. 'Tie him to a mule.'

Taffu's mouth, until then agape, snapped shut. 'We need them for the girl and our trophies.'

'The guns, gold and trinkets can just fuck off,' threatened Summerfield. 'If you don't do as I say you'll get some English anger on your fucking plate.' The men frowned in incomprehension, glancing at Badr for any sign of command. 'Do it!' yelled Summerfield, waving the pistol. At last, with begrudging silence, two of them left to fetch a mule.

Light, the snow swirled in lazy circles as the small column trudged eastwards. The men were happy, having tasted battle, victory and taken loot and there was much chattering that made Summerfield frown condemningly. How they could swap such disproportionate stories of bravery and with such insouciance— while Badr agonised—was beyond him. He suddenly felt sickened, weary of this fickle people and their childish joy.

Muttering oaths in English at the tribesmen's jabbering, Summerfield led the two mules that carried Jeanne and Badr as the column picked its way through the snow-bound tracks. Badr's moans of pain had set Summerfield's nerves on edge and he felt relieved though guilty when his young friend sank into unconsciousness.

For the most part Jeanne was sullen and brooding. At one point, she looked up and said, mechanically: 'It was you who executed El Rifni.'

'He's dead,' returned Summerfield, avoiding her eyes. 'I was afraid, angry…'

'You killed him in cold blood, Harry.'

'I thought he'd harm you,' muttered Summerfield. And then, after a long silence: 'Yes, yes I shot him—in cold blood if you like. I have no qualms. Just—just *shocked*, that's all.' He glanced at Jeanne and her expression showed neither acceptance nor condemnation. She had withdrawn into her silence.

It was late when Jeanne spoke again. They had climbed through a pass and were descending a valley. The winter white made the pink rock milky, almost translucent like a shade of jade, and a weak setting sun gave watery shine to the land. Summerfield thought he recognised a familiar outcrop and was about to check this with a tribesman, when he heard Jeanne's voice, timid and shaking.

'Harry, they—'

She held her breath and Summerfield, seeing that something was wrong, took to her side. He felt like touching her, though feared that if he did her emotions would ignite, she was that tense. Suddenly, she continued, a spurt of words delivered in a weary monotone.

'They did horrible, terrible things to me, Harry. And my father, mother… Soumia's screaming…'

'They were criminals,' said Summerfield, 'fanatics. I'm glad they died.'

'Terrible things,' she repeated. 'The horror of it all.'

'The brutes—you're badly beaten, Jeanne. Don't worry—the women of the valley—they have ointments and lotions that can heal you.'

'Harry—they…they *abused* me.'

The word came out as a squeak, somehow quaint and old-fashioned and it sent a shiver through Summerfield.

'In the beginning, two of them. Then only Abrach.'

Summerfield felt the air sucked from his lungs. He was sinking for her.

'No, my poor darling. Oh, no…'

'After the first two times, I just—just switched off. Yes, like a light—switched off.' The unsettling chuckle in her voice, her

snapping nerves, scared him, angered him. She turned slightly
then looked away. 'What if—what if I'm *pregnant*, Harry?'

'I'll cut them into pieces—fingers, hands, ears, bollocks and
bloody tongue—' spat Summerfield.

'He's dead, Harry. Remember—you shot him in the face. That
sound!' She laughed, a deranged little squeak. 'When the muck
hit the snow. Like fat sizzling in the pan.'

'*Jeanne*. Please—*stop*!'

Her face froze suddenly as though Summerfield had just
slapped her.

'Stop you say? After everything they did?' Her voice trailed
to a whisper, fell silent and then she burst into tears. 'I'm sorry,
Harry. So stupid. I'm not brave, not brave!'

Confused, Summerfield stumbled a few paces then turned
back. 'But you *are* courageous. So very brave, my darling. Very.'

'Please, Harry. Please—*avoid* that word.'

'I didn't—'

'Just don't say it. *Please*,' she said, coldly.

When they settled down to camp that night, Badr awoke in great
pain. Summerfield hollowed out a hole in the snow, making a wall
to protect them from the wind, and while Jeanne sat huddled and
morose in a corner, tended to his friend.

Summerfield grimly peeled away the layers of clothes to reveal
the wound, difficult to locate due to a great amount of clotted
blood. He fetched some boiled water, conscious of the smallness
of his act, and set about cleaning the ragged hole in his friend's
strangely white abdomen. The only chance, he concluded, would
be to return to the valley. How he hoped they knew how to deal
with such wounds. Lastly, he gave Badr some opium mixture and
wiped his friend's brow, so burning hot despite the cold. Drifting
in and out of consciousness, the young leader babbled words
in a dialect Summerfield couldn't understand. Once, their eyes
met and Summerfield saw the strange, milky glaze in his friend's
regard, a beaten, weary look that he now knew to recognise as
the resignation before death. Suddenly, Summerfield felt so tired,
so powerless, that he was unable to control the tears that began

to roll down his cheeks. He sobbed silently, kneeling beside his friend and started when he felt the lightest of touches on his cheek. It was Badr, his hand raised, a look of tenderness in his eyes momentarily warming through the pain.

'Dear Harry... *After*—care for Raja, will you?'

'One more day, Badr,' whispered Summerfield, taking hold of the young man's hand. 'Hold on for one more day and you will be fine.' Badr gave an almost imperceptible smile of irony. Summerfield fought to hold back his tears. 'We're nearly home, Badr. I promise.'

'My beard...' whispered Badr.

'What?' Summerfield leant forwards, his ear nearly touching the young man's lips. 'What did you say?'

'My beard,' repeated Badr.

'*Beard*?' Summerfield frowned.

'Oh, Lord, how it itches! And I can't damn well scratch it.' Badr attempted a laugh which turned to a painful moan. A long minute passed before he was able to breathe correctly again.

Summerfield shook his head sadly. 'You young fool, Badr. It never really did suit you, you know...' But the young man was silent, having once again drifted into unconsciousness.

They set out at 4 a.m., too cold to sleep for more than twenty minutes at a time and pressed to return to the valley. From the hesitant, unsure outsider, uninitiated in the ways of the mountains and command of men, Summerfield had become a leader. It was he who, deciding it was time to march, gave the order to raise camp. And it was he who, leading the two mules at the head of the column, picked the path back to the valley with now instinctive confidence. The men followed. There was no resistance to his role and they seemed to go faster. Maybe it was the fact that the terrain now became recognisable as their own, the confidence that came to men who knew that they were nearly home.

After three hours of journey, the day began to rise and the sky turned from black to indigo to cobalt blue. Summerfield called the column to a halt and ordered tea to be brewed and the remaining rations distributed. While fires were lit and water boiled, he scanned the landscape behind them with Badr's binoculars, one of the lenses of which had been shattered by a bullet during the combat. Nothing. They had not been followed.

Once assured, he then turned to Jeanne. With hot water he moistened his *cheiche* and began to softly bathe her face, gently patting the cuts and bruises and stroking them whenever she winced. She did not look at him and Summerfield was glad for this. Her description of what had happened during her captivity had left him incapable of any form of verbal help. As a man, a member of the male race, he felt ultimately ashamed, as guilty as her former aggressors and somehow dirty. No wonder, he reflected, she was so distant, so detached. How could she not be? He was surprised then, upon finishing to wash her wounds, that she glanced up, offering a brief though—as he judged— sincere smile.

With no unnecessary tarry, they were once again on the path back. One more crest to overcome and the next mountainside would be theirs.

'I'm sorry, Harry,' blurted Jeanne at one point. 'For having been so sharp.'

Summerfield, turning to her, pulled a face as much in embarrassment as anything else. 'I was an idiot to have used that word.'

'It's not—not *fitting* anymore, is it, Harry?'

'Is that a rhetorical question?' quipped Summerfield, but she did not seem to notice the irony and he shook his head. The poor girl was completely vacant, as though her senses had been killed along with her ideals. 'You know, Jeanne, that word I used—it came completely spontaneously. There was no other word I could find for a person so—so dear to me. It had nothing to do with—with what we lived before. I know that life sent you off in a different direction after they took me.'

Jeanne raised her head and looked at him, briefly inquisitive.

'I have a bundle of letters, Jeanne. I'm afraid I read them.'

'Letters?' Jeanne seemed to be coming back from afar.

'Jim and all that,' said Summerfield, humbly. 'I'm aware of what you both mean to each other.'

'How?' Jeanne looked confused.

Summerfield made a silent gesture as if to say *don't worry*. 'I accept that, Jeanne—you and Jim. Part of me has grown so old over the past two years. Sometimes I feel as though life is a continuous peeling away of idealism—just to reach the inner truth of disillusionment that is the reality of it all.'

'But how did you get them? And where are they?'

Summerfield pursed his lips. 'Here.' He dug into his knapsack and brought out the bundle, tied together with a slither of material. 'Please—take them back. They're yours.'

She took them, hesitantly as though unbelieving, then clutched them to her. She began to sob.

'You see, we reached the hunting lodge and I saw—' he paused, failed a breath—'*everything*. When we discovered that one of the occupants was missing—probably you—I wanted absolute proof. I found the letters on a shelf beside your bed.' Summerfield fell silent and watched as Jeanne's body heaved with little spasms of grief. 'We both have something to shed tears over,' he added, resigned.

Four hours later and the column had climbed the slopes to a ridge that led down to the valley and home. The tribesmen let out a series of whoops and embraced each other and Summerfield caught sight of the village through the haze. His heart surged with joy and a lump came to his throat, a mix of relief, hope and a strange, desperate sadness. Instinctively, he turned to search for Badr and approached the young man's body lying limp across the mule.

'Badr. Wake up my friend. Wake. Can you hear me? We're home. You're going to get better. You're saved.' The young man did not move. 'Badr?' Summerfield peered closer, noticed the deadened eyes, the ashen skin and drew back. Badr was cold.

Jim Wilding stood on the quayside at St. Louis, French Senegal and watched as the Portuguese crew, shepherded by a moustachioed young bursar, finally opened up the gangway for the passengers to board. He drew a deep breath, felt a certain puzzled sadness come over him, and then nodded to the porter waiting by his luggage to follow him on ship.

Paying off the porter and locking his cabin to stand on deck, Wilding felt the whole past four months slowly lift from him. Giddiness took hold of him and he had to brace himself against the ship's rail. He'd tried everything: embassy contacts, friends, informers, the military, even appealing for witnesses for anything they had seen on the day of Jeanne's disappearance. He could have stayed on, he thought, his mind dwelling momentarily on his return to the States. But if he hadn't found her, it meant that she was either dead—he winced at the word—or had been spirited away to some remote area beyond his reach and influence. He knew it was almost hopeless and, in that calm and thoroughly logical way of his, had mastered his emotions, knowing full well that it would only lead to unnecessary pain and ill health. He'd left contact details in Marrakesh, just in case and had even paid for the off-duty services of a police investigator to routinely follow things up. Now was a moment to look towards the next step in things—his enlistment, training and hopefully active service. It was only a question of time before the United States entered the conflict. After that... He cocked his head, closed his eyes as he breathed in the sea air. After that, the next step—and strangely enough, despite the improbability, despite the cards stacked against him, Jeanne seemed a sure part of it.

Raja did not appear for ten days. Passing her parents' house, one could hear the constant chants and wails of distress that accompanied Badr's death. If it wasn't Raja herself, it was her mother. And when their tears ran dry, a relative or neighbour was invited to stay and produce the sounds of mourning. Little gifts of coins, trinkets or, more precious in these desperate times, food were given for the service. Such was the tradition.

Watching her house from the small, squat window of his dwelling, the January wind moaning up the valley, Summerfield remembered that Raja hadn't wanted to believe him—the usual reaction of denial in such circumstances. For finally, he reflected, we are all invulnerable, a permanent and lasting presence until the sudden *gone*. And like a kind of unreasonable logic, we somehow think our loved ones are immortal, as we do ourselves; and death doesn't come tomorrow, after all—it is remote and seems rather nearer the impossible than the probable. One day, when death does come, our childish logic is ripped up and thrown away. And we are left with an empty space—the chair where he sat, her voice that filled the room—and a nagging, deepest questioning of the possibility that something else—another place, another life—in all superior, human calculation must exist after all. Raja had refused, despite the innate sense of fatality etched into her culture, the inevitable. In the end, Summerfield had had to call in one of the tribesmen who had fought with him to persuade the girl. And finally, ceding to the truth, Raja had pummelled out her pain on Summerfield, writhing like a viper when both he and her parents tried to wrestle her away.

And then the burial, the old Mullah's voice whipped away in the wind. Badr's body, wrapped in a white linen shroud was laid on its side in a shallow grave, head turned towards Mecca. Supported by helpers at both arms, leaning against the wind, the old Mullah chanted prayers while the womenfolk wailed and the men lay stones and earth over the body, slotting them into place like tiles on a roof so that they formed a slight though elaborate mound. The body finally covered, a flat stone was laid upright where the head rested and turned profile towards the Holy City. Summerfield, standing apart, stayed on, as did Raja at the graveside, and watched the mourners drift away, heard the lamentations fade until they were alone in the whistles and moans of nature.

Summerfield had approached his friend's grave: Badr who had acted as his messenger, who had taught him so much, protected and befriended him with so much simplicity and sincerity. He spoke in English, intimate words, and Raja glanced at him red and dirty cheeked, her eyes hostile as though she were ashamed that Summerfield should see her so weakened. For some reason he found himself reciting the Lord's Prayer. Though the words were out of place he carried on, for the lilt and intonation of the prayer were beautiful sound to any event. And then he had gone, touching Raja on the shoulder as he walked away and she, shuddering as her tears once more began to fall.

So the days passed and Summerfield watched from his window, worried for little Raja and guilty too as she disappeared from the life of the valley. If only he had paid more attention, perhaps spotted the killing aim before the shot, pushed Badr to safety. The haunting thoughts and hypotheses came frequently to his sleep.

They called him a hero now, the English warrior who, with such temerity and calmness, had stepped up to the monster Abrach and coldly blown his head away; the hero who had dared to defy tradition through his love for his friend; Summerfield who had defied—though no names were ever given—his fellow tribesmen and their duty to finish off Badr on the field of battle. Summerfield who had saved the white woman; Summerfield, the uninitiated foreigner who took command of the men in combat and who led them safely home. Summerfield who, in all his humble magnificence, refused to accept the spoils of war and who preferred his men instead to inherit the trophies.

It troubled him—the salutations, the stories and the visits. The children playing in the snow chanted his name, the men smiled fiercely as he crossed paths, the yarns became ever bigger of feats he had never committed. And most of all, the bragging among the tribesmen, the belief that they were now invincible. Winners of the moment, thought Summerfield, unable to face the inevitable and devastating defeats of tomorrow. For the French soldiers would come. It was as inevitable as the spring.

Abrach—El Rifni—also troubled his mind. The monster of the mountains, they called him, though only Badr had ever known how he had been before. Summerfield had closed his eyes when he pulled the trigger. The sound—how did Jeanne describe it? Like fat sizzling in the pan. An awful, nagging sound he would never forget. And the oddest thing of all—Abrach himself. Sometimes, the confusion was such that to Summerfield's mind the man he had killed wasn't Abrach at all. The genial, generous man who had sponsored him in his penniless, early days in Marrakesh was a different being altogether from the hideous, misshapen bulk who had led the murderers to the hunting lodge and Jeanne. Summerfield had confronted a stranger, the *devil geist* of a man that had once been Abrach. And now both he and Badr were gone—the two men who had once shown him their friendship and allowed him to survive. It was a strange, haunting feeling. And a lonely one.

Meanwhile, Jeanne had taken possession of his bed while he slept on a pile of hay on the floor of his dwelling. She convalesced quickly, the ointments and potions the village women administered miraculously making her bruises vanish almost overnight, smoothing away the cut on her cheek, healing the pain in her lower abdomen. Cured physically, realised Summerfield, but still and probably for much longer desperately ill inside.

Indeed, Jeanne had withdrawn completely into herself. There were days when she said nothing at all. She lay on Summerfield's bed or else huddled, knees drawn, by the fire, avoiding him. Summerfield was patient. He ensured she was kept warm, received daily visits from the women and gave portions of his meagre food to supplement her own. She was moody, regularly goading him, scared at the thought of carrying child, then unsettlingly silent for long periods of time. The only real attention she offered was towards the small bundle of correspondence she had retrieved. It began to annoy Summerfield. It wasn't so much the thought that she had fallen in love with Jim Wilding—that he had accepted—but rather the way in which she almost worshipped the letters, making a rather histrionic demonstration of protecting them whenever anyone got too close to her. She read them at least three times a day in what Summerfield soon realised was a sort of ritual. Read, smile, put them aside, hide them, cry, grow angry, feel reproach, sleep—only to wake again and repeat the process. Summerfield felt powerless. He felt angry. What had she done with his own letters he had so tenderly sent her all that time ago?

Outside, the weather reached a peak of severity towards the end of the first week of January and then calmed. The old Mullah informed him the snows had stopped and would not come again until the following November. Sunshine peeped occasionally through the clouds and in some places the thick white crust of snow began to melt. Towards mid-month it drizzled then rained for two days and the village paths were turned into a quagmire.

Then, one day, Raja showed her face again, slipping head bowed out of her house on the pretext of a chore, only to return an hour later, noted Summerfield, with her head held high and the permanent frown of sadness replaced by a look of quiet determination.

It got warmer. The people got hungrier. Up above the village behind the fortified walls of the Kasbah, the granaries were now nearly empty. The Kaïd placed armed guards in front of them and his men distributed increasingly smaller rations to the people of the valley. The same words could be heard twenty times a day—never had there been such a hard and empty winter. A child died, then another. The curious hollowness around the eyes that accompanied malnutrition was present on many faces. Dogs and cats began to mysteriously disappear. In December, most of the valley's fowl had been slaughtered and now it was the turn of the goats and mules. Towards the end of January only the fittest, finest beasts were kept to regenerate the herds in spring while the others were killed, cut up and distributed equally among the families. Desperate prayers were said, imploring God to see the seeds safely through the frozen days until the thaw. Great hope was placed on the early spring crops of millet to bring the valley back from starvation. Along with the other men and boys, Summerfield went hunting for any game—rabbits and wild goats, but also birds and mice that could be boiled and stewed. Excepting the guts which were fed to the few dogs remaining, nothing was thrown away and everything from head to tail consumed. A man from a neighbouring village was stabbed while attempting to kill a cat and both owner and thief spent a week in the Kasbah locked in separate cell rooms.

Summerfield, unable to stand the heavy silence of Jeanne's presence, paid a visit of respect to Raja and her family, glad to breathe freely. Sinking mid-calf in the mud as he crossed the stretch of track between his abode and Raja's house, he caught sight of her mother waving to him from the window. Finally, extracting his foot from a particularly tenacious muddy hold, he stepped up to the threshold and edged his way to the window where he found himself almost nose to nose with Raja's mother.

'Salaam, *Lâlla* Tizni. My deepest respects,' said Summerfield, clinging onto the sill so as not to fall back into the mud. 'And to Raja, too. Pray tell me, where is she? I would like to speak to her.'

'She is by the fields, clearing snow,' replied the woman, with that curious warbling voice that Raja seemed to have inherited. 'And your help might be most welcome, perhaps.'

Summerfield frowned. 'Ah. Well, I will go.'

'Yes, go.'

'Yes,' said Summerfield, hesitating. Mrs Tizni seemed rather odd today, he thought. Perhaps the prolonged crying. '*Salaam*.' He bade goodbye and edged carefully back along the wall.

He picked his way along the edge of the track where the

rocks and stones made walking easier and descended towards the
first set of terraces on the valley side where Raja's family had
sown their crops the previous November. The olive trees stood
twisted and grey and he surprised himself with the thought that
in another month or so they would bud into colour. He had
almost forgotten the striking beauty of the greens and pinks that
lit up the mountains.

He spotted Raja before she saw him, a small, vigorous bundle
of black, squatting as she pushed away the snow with a plank of
wood. The squelching of his steps informed her of his presence
and she looked up as he came within talking distance. She stood
up. Her legs were brown with mud up to her knees and she
was sweating from her work. Summerfield could smell her sweet,
spicy odour.

'Raja,' he said. 'Hello.'

'The hero,' she replied, terse-lipped. The theatrical frown she
used to express discontent cut deep into her forehead. 'May God
care of you.'

'And you yourself, dear bereaved Raja.' Her frown relaxed
and she seemed a little embarrassed. Summerfield stood silent,
watching her, aware despite the layers of clothes she was wearing
that she had lost quite a bit of weight. 'Your mother proposed I
might help.'

'She would propose that to a mule and I might accept.'

Summerfield sighed deeply, glancing away and then back at
her. 'You look thinner.'

'Surprising,' commented Raja, picking up her plank of
wood again.

'The pain was great for me too, Raja. I have also come to pay
my respects.'

Raja hummed and looked down. 'I thank you, then. Now,' she
continued, squatting down, 'I must continue with my work.'

'And I will stay and help.'

'I do not need help.'

'You do,' insisted Summerfield.

'I don't,' answered Raja, beginning to heave the plank into
action.

'It looks heavy.'

'I am a Berber woman. I know how to do a man's work.'

Again Summerfield sighed deeply and exhaled just as noisily.

'Your mother said I could help Raja and not the donkey I have sitting in front of me.'

'Oh!' The young woman let out a little gasp of shock. 'You haven't changed, you English. Even your old self comes back through the hero.'

'I am not a hero,' said Summerfield, shaking his head. 'It's what people want in order to turn their minds from their empty bellies.' He glanced aside and caught sight of a rake propped up against an olive tree. He stepped tentatively across and took it.

'Harry—I did not accept your help.'

'Your mother said I was to.'

'Maybe you are lying. I will ask her later and then apologise if necessary.' Summerfield edged closer to her, upturned the rake and began pushing away the snow. 'No, I said.' Summerfield continued, grunting as he pushed with all his strength. 'I said *no!*' repeated Raja.

'And I say *yes!*' he finally shouted. 'Raja—you stubborn, naughty child—'

'I am not a child!' she shouted back, her voice rising to a high-pitched wail. 'I'm a widow—a *woman!*'

'You are!' returned Summerfield.

Raja rose, holding the plank between her two hands and approached him.

'Raja—what d'you count on doing? Don't—'

Too late. She was against him now, pushing at him with the plank with all her force. Summerfield felt ridiculous and wondered if anyone up at the village was looking at them. And then, with one almighty heave, Raja sent Summerfield slipping. He let out a shout, desperately flung out his arm to grab Raja, missed her and plunged back first into the quagmire with a loud slap.

'You cow! You sheep's arse of a woman!' he shouted, his anger worsened by the fact that it was impossible to extract himself from the mud. 'Help me, for Christ's sake!'

'Do not blaspheme the Prophet!' said Raja, her initial gape of surprise turning into laughter. 'Oh, no! Summerfield, you make me—make me laugh!' Her voice cracked into a joyous screech and she shuddered with the effort, her eyes streaming with tears. 'Oh, how stupid you look. Oh, poor proud Englishman!'

'Just help me,' said Summerfield, his anger subsiding as her screeches became contagious.

'It's the first time I've laughed for two months!' said Raja, bending down and trying to reach across with her hand. 'I can't.' She leant forwards, picking up the rake and offering the handle to Summerfield who had at last managed to wriggle his back free to reach a sitting position. 'Pull.' Summerfield pulled and Raja let herself fall. She landed with a splat beside him and rolled onto her side.

'You did that on purpose!' whined Summerfield, himself now laughing.

'Of course,' giggled Raja, her face covered in smears of rich brown mud.

'And how, oh stubborn woman, are we to get out of this now!'

Minutes later, having crawled, slipped and wriggled like snakes, they were sitting breathless in the snow beside the little field. Their laughter had subsided, only Raja, obviously still thinking of the picture he must have given, letting out a low unrelenting chuckle.

'Look at us,' said Summerfield, making a grimace as he glanced first at her then himself. 'We're filthy.'

'I don't care. It was so funny,' said Raja, suddenly timid. 'Thank you, Harry.'

Summerfield caught her regard for an instance, those jet black eyes that sparkled a little, just like before. A warm, baffling feeling shivered through him and he leant towards her, ever so carefully, so that his shoulder momentarily touched hers.

'We have both lost something, Raja—and the pain was so great.'

'Badr was a splendid man, Harry.' Summerfield nodded. 'When I think we were to marry in the spring—after all this time and waiting…'

'It is sorrowful.'

'It was written. It had to be.'

'Raja, *please.*' Summerfield shook his head. 'Do not echo what the elders say. Express what you really feel and do not cover up life's injustice with easy words about fate.'

Raja looked up and he thought she was about to retort, when her eyes softened again.

'I feel,' she said, tentatively, 'like the sky has collapsed. Like the stars were killed. That the world about me is without light.' She gave a strange little sound, like a hiccup. 'At least, it was like that for many weeks. And then, one day I decided to go out.'

Summerfield nodded. 'I watched you from my window.'

'And I noticed that there was colour,' continued Raja. 'That the smallest of things—birds, the children, rabbit prints in the snow—were real. I knew then that Badr was part of it and that he had left to become the details around us. I knew that it was impossible to bring him back to the village.'

Summerfield studied her, surprised more than anything else. 'Raja—I didn't know you could speak like that. Why? Why do you pretend to be a strong, unthinking woman all the time?'

'Because I am!' said Raja, suddenly switching back. 'I'm both. But women cannot show thoughts or deep ideas about things.'

'With *me* you can,' said Summerfield. 'In fact, it's what you've just done. I'd much prefer a wife who could be both brave and funny and with whom I could talk with about serious things too.'

'A wife? You?'

'Well, yes!' frowned Summerfield. 'Am I that undesirable?'

'You have the white woman.' Raja's face took on a trace of cheekiness.

He let out a guffaw. 'No—no, not that.'

'Some say you knew her from before?'

'You know perfectly well I did, so there's no need to ask a question,' said Summerfield.

'Well, if a man lives with a woman under the same roof,' answered Raja with hardness in her voice, 'in our traditions it means only one thing.'

Summerfield waved her away.

'What's more, it is *sin* if you are not married.'

'I tell you I—we—are *not*...' Silence. Summerfield battled for his words. 'Not *you know—doing things*.'

Raja hummed and clucked her tongue. She scratched her cheek with grimy fingers. Summerfield suddenly had the feeling she was bothered by something, but couldn't quite pin it down.

'I think you were once in love with her, am I wrong?' she probed, feigning disinterest.

Summerfield shrugged his shoulders. 'We both were. Terribly in love. I could have died for her—and very nearly did.'

'Then why don't you love each other again?'

'Raja,' sighed Summerfield, leaning back to look keenly at her. 'You're very curious.'

'A woman who isn't might be a man in disguise!'

'Who made up that silly saying?'

'Me,' replied Raja, smiling cheekily. 'Shame on you for calling me silly.'

'Well,' resumed Summerfield, shaking his head again—really, this young cat was beyond his understanding—'Time passed, things happened, we changed, fate—'

'*You* said fate was—'

'I *know*, I *know*,' rectified Summerfield, irritably. 'What I meant was that she found another love. A *better* love.'

'A *better* love than yours?' chirped Raja, half-amused, half-flattering.

'No need to mock me, Raja. I can tell you it damn well hurt—as much as Badr. I say a better love because I know the man and he is good. And if ever she manages to return to him, he is intelligent and wealthy enough to offer her a good life.'

'I do not need wealth,' said Raja and checked herself. 'So—perhaps yes, you were right. We have both suffered.'

'Our hearts died,' added Summerfield. 'But somehow hearts manage to come back to life—like the seeds of a wilted flower.'

Raja gave a little grunt and clucked her tongue again. 'So, here we are.'

'What d'you mean?'

'Oh, nothing,' said Raja, falling into silence. Then: 'So if I understand, the white woman—Jeanne—she has no desire for you?'

'Raja—I've just *told* you!' Summerfield felt exasperated. What *was* she after?

'And you have no desire for *her*, in that case—am I wrong?'

'Stop asking me if you're wrong,' said Summerfield, irritably. 'Because you want to convince yourself that you are right!'

'Well?' Raja's voice too had grown irritable. '*Do* you?'

'Why in heaven's name—?' began Summerfield and then stopped. Could it be—*could it be* that Raja was *jealous*? Good God! At that moment, he looked at her looking at him and realised she hadn't so much lost weight through grief as through change. A change in her body. The past four months had seen her shed her adolescence. Gone were the full, rounded forms of her body and face and now—she was right—she *was a woman*.

'Wait,' he said, feeling confused. 'Let me think.'

She was silent, the fact that she didn't ask why, only confirming Summerfield's realisation that she wanted a clear and truthful answer in order to make a—*God*—he and *Raja*! The idea suddenly hit him like a lump of mud in his face.

'And so?' inquired Raja, her voice trailing to a murmur as she looked away. 'What is your answer to that question?'

Summerfield looked across the melting whiteness of the valley to the sea of mountain crests beyond and then back to Raja. Was she anxious? In any case, she showed no signs. He felt as though a heavy chain had just been lifted from his neck.

'In all honesty,' he replied, talking to her half-turned face. 'Neither my mind nor body show any desire for her. Jeanne left me many months ago. And she has a bright and happy future waiting for her.'

'I would want one, too,' said Raja, turning back to him. There was a look of almost apology on her lips and in her eyes. 'My parents called me Raja, the Arabic word for *Hope*—and I do.'

'Some might say that you want happiness too soon,' said Summerfield, giving nothing away.

'Badr loved you as a man would a brother,' replied Raja, softly. 'Sometimes I think he *knew* what would happen—that he could not marry me sooner because he knew his life would be short.

He would give his blessing, I know.'

Her eyes became soft, then sad, finally turning to slits of laughter.

'Especially to a very muddy, very dirty man like you, Harry Summerfield!'

She laughed and so did Summerfield and spontaneously they placed their hands on each other's shoulders and pushed each other away.

54

The first days of February arrived and only the caps and crests of the mountain heights kept their snow. But if the air grew warmer in the day, it still froze the landscape at night. Summerfield would wake in the morning to find the ground before his home a rutted and dangerous scarring of frozen mud and sheets of ice. Food was very scarce. He hadn't eaten meat in almost two weeks and things were so bad in the valley that the order was given to bake the mule dung into flat cakes, mix in a few grains of cereals recuperated here and there and use it as a substitute for bread. Having at first grimaced and baulked, Summerfield had finished by eating it if only to fill the vacuous emptiness in his stomach—in fact, it wasn't that bad. Jeanne had flatly refused.

They spent most of each day together, Jeanne gradually regaining the habit of using words and although they were mostly bitter or sad, Summerfield was relieved that she spoke at all. Some of the change in her Summerfield understood as desperate relief—her periods had come and pregnancy, by some miracle, avoided. To get her active and away from her dark thoughts, he took her with him when he visited or worked the fields. The women found her curious, both beautiful and frightening and some even showed animosity for the things she had gone through, believing she was a bringer of shame and bad luck. In these cases, Raja or one or two of the braver womenfolk would harangue the others with a long and guilt-laden tirade until they apologised.

The worst was the evenings. Time seemed elastic with Summerfield sitting by the fire and Jeanne on his bed. He had long ceased to try to offer words of comfort which she only spat back at him. He could understand her pain. But it was more difficult to understand that she needed to unburden herself of her hatred in some way and that he happened to be the nearest, most available person on which to do this.

One evening they had a row which pressed faces up against the windows of the neighbouring houses. After resisting her anger for almost an hour, Summerfield had become enraged, searching in his belongings for a pebble—one of the two they had pledged themselves to each other with nearly a year and a half before—and thrown it through the open window into the night. She ended up screaming and Summerfield had had to step outside and huddle against the porch until she calmed down, embarrassingly conscious of the looks he was receiving from the dark. She repeated the word *prisoner* hundreds of times before she fell silent and Summerfield, shivering in the cold, imagined she must be feeling what he had felt during his first months of capture in the valley.

Only, technically, she wasn't a prisoner. No one, not even the Kaïd, had ever said she must stay. If anything, she was a burden— an extra mouth to feed that only bit the hand that fed it.

With growing certainty, Summerfield realised that he would some day have to take her back to her people, to what she called civilisation. That she could not survive, mentally, or physically in the valley for much longer. The problem was where he could take her. The winter snows had cut the valley off from the outside world. His understanding of events had stopped at the German and Italian offensives in Libya and the summer invasion of Russia. No other real news had arrived since Badr's tragic end.

As the days passed, Summerfield tried to piece together what he knew of French activity and possessions in North Africa. Going west towards the Moroccan plains or north towards the border with Algeria was out of the question: Vichy troops would be on the lookout for insurgents or any sign of Free French opposition. Going south, via Ouarzazate and following the coastline was equally as hazardous. Perhaps there were Spanish enclaves, though it was probable the Spanish authorities would hand them over to the French. More than that, even if they did cross the border and manage to travel freely through

Mauritania, they would only arrive in Senegal which as far as Summerfield remembered had pledged allegiance to Pétain. The only possibility then seemed first southwards, to the tail of the Atlas Mountains, then strike eastwards across the desert near Zagora or perhaps the northernmost corner of Mauritania and Mali. After that, directly east, across the Sahara into the southernmost part of Algeria and into Chad where eight months ago, Colonel Leclerc had established his base for the Free French forces operating in Africa. It was a bloody long journey, thought Summerfield. He'd never been in a desert environment and thought that Jeanne hadn't either. He also wasn't sure that he would be able to communicate if they needed help. Did they speak his strange mix of Arabic and Atlas dialect? French, perhaps? And what about supplies and means of travel? And a final point was Raja. How ironic, he thought, that at a moment when happiness seemed to have blossomed between them, he should understand that it was time to go away. It amounted to her suffering another 'death', another absence and he was sure the effect on her would be devastating. Several days of pondering and lonely walks, at times giving way to fear, other times to logic, and Summerfield decided to see first the old Mullah and then the Kaïd for their advice.

The old Mullah, suffering from a cold and swathed in shawls and scarves so that he looked like a pile in a jumble sale, thought it risky but advised him to seek the answer in his heart and in God. Only He could offer Summerfield the best advice and a true course that he should follow in spite of the consequences that could arise. 'It is only when one *wants*,' reminded the old man through a fit of wheezing, 'that things become probable.'

The Kaïd, Ahmed Youadi, on the other hand, was more pragmatic. At one point, the warlord took him aside in a private room so that they could speak alone.

'I can see three reasons why you should go, Summerfield,' the Kaïd confided. 'One—by leading the white woman away from us, the French will have one less reason to attack us. Two—when the French do attack us, which they will, and soon, they will win.' He shook his head. 'We cannot stop aeroplanes and artillery.'

'The villages will be burnt to the ground,' said Summerfield, suddenly alarmed for Raja and her family.

'I believe not.' The Kaïd offered a sour grin. 'I will inform them that the warriors who wish to fight will leave the valley and confront them at a place of their choice. I am perhaps a proud man and willing to die gloriously, but I have enough mercy and intelligence to spare my people and our history. It will last long after the vain few hours of a battle we cannot hope to win. And what is the use of you being captured here?' Summerfield remained silent while the Kaïd stoked up two pipes and passed one across. A deep, noisy suck: 'And third—' he continued, gravely—'You have proved yourself, Englishman. You have helped us in your work and in your words, risked your life for us, shown your love for your poor brother Badr and also shown a certain tenderness for one of our women—Raja. It would break her heart even more to see you die or made prisoner here than attempt to escape and hopefully survive.' At this, Summerfield made to talk but the Kaïd held up his hand. 'The white woman does not belong here, Summerfield. Her misery is written on her face like a black banner flying in the wind. I do not want her here. She will bring us worse luck than bad luck.' The warlord looked Summerfield directly in the eyes, making him flinch. 'And there you have my final, true word on the affair.' Summerfield nodded, not without a nagging feeling that the Kaïd was hiding something from his feelings, and returned the man's fierce stare with his own clear regard. 'What's more, I will give you a guide—Moulay—a man who grew up here, led caravans through the desert, fought in the 1925 uprising and decided to return. He knows the ways of the sea of sand. And two mules—one for Moulay and one for you and the white woman.' He paused, blowing out a thick cloud of smoke. 'Summerfield—*Harry* Summerfield—I am glad we met. Now go and tell Raja Tizni of your decision. That is all.' And with a wave of his hand, the Kaïd gestured for Summerfield to rise and leave.

It was early evening when Summerfield trudged back from the high walls of the Kasbah. The tobacco had made his stomach feel even emptier and he could hear it rumbling and grumbling like the distant approach of thunder through his shirts. He felt increasingly helpless. As though any attempt at explaining to Raja would inevitably end in tears and conflict. He wondered whether to attack the subject immediately or leave it until the evening, but was unable to decide. As usual in such circumstances—a typical failing that he recognised—unable to plan correctly, he resigned himself to acting on the moment and adapting if need be to a changing situation.

Down by the stream, which had ran clear and fast since the beginning of the previous week, was Raja. As everyday, they had given themselves a meeting time and place. It was one of their favourite spots. For three months hidden by a slab of snow and only the sound of trickling betraying the river's presence, the warming had caused the thick white cover to cave in along its course. Arches had formed from which stalactites dripped and disappeared smacking sunlight off the water. Like children, they usually sat and threw stones in an attempt to knock off the shards of ice. They laughed at the slightest grimace, the silliest of words. Sometimes they held hands. They made plans.

This time Summerfield felt unusually heavy, as though his heart had taken on ballast. It even affected his walk and his smile. As he approached her, the burden soured to a growing sadness.

To her usual black—still three months of mourning to go— she had added several blue and red ribbons, strips of material that fluttered in the breeze. Her skin had become bronze in the sun and snow and as he came to her Summerfield noticed—not without a pang of remorse—that she had made an effort to accentuate her eyes with kohl and blue shadow. She looked young and healthy and ripe with happiness. She rose and they stood for a few silent seconds at arm's length, looking at each other. He held out his hand and touched hers briefly and it made him laugh inside how she looked guiltily about her upon this gesture, as though some elder might see the forbidden act.

'Come, Raja' he said, motioning with his head. 'Let's walk a little. I have something to say that is difficult for me.'

'That there is no hope of ever eating meat again?'

Summerfield shook his head. 'Don't be silly, Raja.'

'That there is a certain word in your head that trickles down to your mouth that forbids your tongue to say it?'

'Raja!' Summerfield laughed, unable to resist the playfulness. 'And what would that forbidden word be?'

'Oh, come now,' taunted Raja, turning profile to let the wind mould her gown about her body. 'Wouldn't it be something beginning with *L*?'

'You mean *Lights*?'

'Oh! You ass!'

'*Letters*?' Summerfield goaded her. 'Or *Ladies*?'

'You snake!' Raja's voice was theatrical, that of a hurt little girl.

Laughing, Summerfield apologised and tugged on her arm which made her slip a little. She shrieked and this produced a further bout of laughter. When it died down, and their steps had taken them to water's edge, and when Summerfield had cursed at himself in silence, he said:

'Raja. Dear Raja—I am to leave the valley.'

She stared blankly at him, but when he didn't answer, she said: 'But this is not funny.'

Summerfield shook his head slightly and lowered his eyes.

'I have to go away, Raja. I have to take Jeanne back to her people.' He glanced up again, lips pursed, apologetic. She shook her head slowly, several times, unable to speak and he noticed a tear forming in her left eye that began to smudge her makeup. 'I'm sorry, my dear Raja.' Summerfield felt awful. 'It is all I can say.'

For a moment, the young woman clenched her teeth, fighting back her anger. 'If I were a man, I'd hit you, Harry Summerfield.' Then her arms waved in a gesture of futility and she clasped her hands. 'But I'm a woman and all I can do is cry or suffer silently or want to feel you against me. Harry, for the love of God—hold me.'

Summerfield stepped forwards, and against the tradition, clasped her against him. They were both shaking and he could feel her breath against his chest, rapid and fighting the urge to cry.

'I love you, Harry—do you understand?' she said, a whimper turning to a hiss.

'Yes, my lion cub. Yes. Raja, I—'

She drew apart, her fingertips pressed against his lips and he remained silent, looking at her as she held on, her eyes shut tightly as though in desperate prayer.

'I want to go somewhere warm, Harry. Somewhere we can sit and hold hands without being afraid.'

Summerfield shook his head. 'We cannot go to my home, neither yours. People will see.'

'Please, Harry. I cannot bear to let you go like this.'

'*The shelter*—not far from here. And there's a fire—we'll be warm.'

Together, they picked their way up along a winding path made slippery by the thaw, past the sacred tree whose worship was a vestige of the old Berber religions and into an area that served as pastureland in the spring. Another ten minutes and they were at the door of the small shepherd's hut. It gave in grudgingly and with a loud creak. Inside, it was dark until Summerfield, fumbling with his matches, found a candle, then another and lit them. Raja dug among the loose kindling lying by the small fireplace and with a series of cracks and snaps stacked it in under the chimney. Almost as quickly, Summerfield leant forwards with a another match. It fluttered then went dead. He struck another. This time, a dry leaf caught and then a small flame leapt from a stick and caught another. He drew back and stood by Raja, watching the flames grow strong.

They seemed hypnotised, but it was more through fear than the butterfly movement of the flames. At last, cursing himself for his childishness, Summerfield held out his hand to touch Raja's arm. He turned and she turned to him. Slowly, surely, they edged together until the pupils of their eyes were big and black in the orange glow. Summerfield could smell her again, both her body and her breath. It came on his skin in little gasps, hot and smelling almost of gun powder. His hands moved down her arms, resting an instant on hers and then back again, this time pressing against her belly through her blouses. Her eyes were big and wide and wild, black stones whose strength and youth scared him a little and then his gaze fell on her mouth. Her lips were compellingly ruby, a full ripeness he had never seen the likes of and he was suddenly aware that Raja was beautiful and that she was somehow alive in order to be kissed by him. Their heads drew together, a twinge of electric as their noses touched and then they drew away, two snakes in a charm. Her belly, round and warm pressed against his hands, nudging him towards the slow, heady expanse of her unheld breasts. Through the cotton layers he felt their sweet soft rounded base, touch then not touch, touch then not touch. Again, he felt himself falling, his forehead touching hers, their noses, and their lips barely an inch apart, hot and almost painful with desire. They came together softly, hesitantly, pressing against each other, touching tongues that sent a shiver through his body. Summerfield felt that strange, powerful feeling of manliness enter him, the calm strength and assurance that preceded the moment before taking a woman. She was seventeen, six months away from eighteen and her girlish body turned woman teased him with excitement. Raja whimpered and he felt her hands firmly clasp his.

'We cannot, Harry,' she whispered.

'Are you afraid?' he answered softly. 'My love, I will be soft with you.'

She gave a little flicking motion of her head. 'No, not afraid. It is what I want. But I am virtuous and this means for me the greatest of gestures, the most beautiful of gifts between a man and a woman. Do you understand that, Harry?'

'I understand,' said Summerfield, kissing her softly. 'Though the toughest thing to satisfy. You are beautiful, Raja and you cannot estimate how little you are away from being loved. I want you.'

Still gripping his hands, Raja buried her face into his chest and remained there, unmoving for several seconds. Finally, she drew back and smiled.

'Come—let us sit before the fire,' she said, leading him across the small open space of the refuge. 'Take off your jacket, Harry and your shirt. Sit.'

As he obeyed, she herself stood before him, her fingers

reaching for the buttons on her blouse. With a smile in her eyes, shy for a moment, she gripped onto her shirts—three layers of them—and slowly, not without difficulty, pulled them up, over her breasts that shook with the effort then came to rest and then over her head. For the first time, Summerfield saw the hard, round cheekiness of them, young and curving slightly outwards, the whiteness of them against her brown skin and the way they tapered to a point at her nipples, a deepest ruby brown, discs the size of dark copper pennies.

'I can give you this gift, but we cannot touch for it is forbidden. For love—that most beautiful gift—we must wait. Because if you love me, you *can* wait.'

She sat down opposite him and drew close so that they both sat, their legs entwined. Summerfield took her face in his hands and with his eyes travelled the clear curves of her shoulders to the full hang of her youthful breasts. He was won by her sweetness and her honesty and he loved her.

'Promise you will accept the rule,' she whispered.

Summerfield smiled. 'Usually rules are the only things I have an insatiable urge to break.' Raja laughed softly. 'Though this time, my dear Raja,' soothed Summerfield, 'so young and so virtuous as you are, I accept.' He leant forwards, breathed in her scent of cumin, musk and cinnamon and her lips came to him, subservient and hungry and they kissed for a long time and with much tenderness.

That night, Summerfield told Jeanne of his plans. For the first time since the ambush, he saw her come alive, the hope rushing back to her and a look of gratitude came to her face.

'Thank you, Harry. I'd die if I were to stay here. Once again you've saved me and I am grateful.'

'It is the right thing to do,' was all that Summerfield replied, his mind preoccupied with the nagging thought of losing Raja.

It all went very quickly. The Kaïd's man, Moulay, came to Summerfield's house and briefed them on what they had to expect. Certain rules were laid down and agreed to: that they should not question his decisions; that they should remain as calm and as quiet as possible at all times; that they were to strictly follow his rules on the drinking of water; that in extreme heat they should cover their skin entirely with clothing and bathe once daily using the sand and that if they got separated they were not to attempt to look for him—he would find them. Summerfield was given twenty rounds of ammunition for the Lee Enfield and four old gold coins that they should use for their various needs including buying their way out of danger if required. Miraculously, several slabs of salted meat were produced from the Kasbah storerooms and hidden away in their saddlebags wrapped in cloth. They carried two large goatskin gourds for water and Ahmed Youadi was reassuring: the desert was rich with water if you just knew where to find it.

The snow disappeared and the first buds of February peeped through the soil and on the branches. On the day of leaving, a great crowd gathered to see them off. This was partly the Kaïd's idea, for he wanted as many people to see the event as possible— it gave all the more chance of the news reaching the French and persuading them not to attack the valley under the pretext of Jeanne's presence. Some people turned up to see the white woman leave and with her, they hoped, the bad spell that lay over the valley. But the majority of people turned up to say goodbye to Summerfield, the outsider, the Englishman, who had learnt their ways and fought by their side. The man who had brought strange games and edifices, not to mention ideas, to the valley and who had provided so much content for fireside gossip over the last two years that it would serve for decades to come.

The old Mullah with his helpers was there, as was the Kaïd and his personal bodyguard of warriors. Tears were shed and shouts of encouragement shouted over the clamour. For two hours that morning, the hunger that haunted five hundred bellies was forgotten as the two mules and three people set off south.

Summerfield was stricken with a feeling of fear that gave rise to nausea. He had looked everywhere, calling in at her parents' house, neighbours, the river and even climbing up to the refuge. Raja was nowhere to be seen.

The wild thought went through his head that perhaps she had done something reckless, decided to kill herself or follow them or simply run away from the pain of it all. Yesterday, one last time sitting next to each other, semi-naked in the warm refuge, their caresses becoming increasingly tender and poignant. They had talked about the future and their hopes and she had finally let the tears run from her. Coming back down from the mountain slope and having to part ways had been agony. And now, added to that was the awful thought that she might be dead.

The Kaïd was impatient. There were many other things to do in preparation for the desperate and telling spring that was fast arriving. He sent men looking out for her and wanted things to begin on time. His heart pounding, Summerfield gave the Kaïd an imploring glance and received an irritated nod of assent: ten more minutes. Hurriedly, Summerfield left Jeanne and her look of surprise to scour the village one last time for Raja.

It was by the great rock that he found her. The same rock beneath which she had first come across him, a captive shivering with sickness and empty of hope, all those many months ago. He recalled how she had introduced herself with such innocence and yet with such cheekiness: Raja—*Hope*. The girl. The grin. The sign.

She was sitting on her haunches, huddled against the cold and Summerfield thought he could hear her muttering. His noisy approach startled her and she let out a shriek of surprise. For a few seconds they could not move. In her eyes was the deepest sadness he had ever seen and for a rare instant he felt the vulnerability she so brashly hid, the femininity behind the daily mask of humour and hardness. Then, in a split second, she rose and he was moving towards her, taking her into his arms. A cry of pain and of loss came from her, and Summerfield felt his own eyes smarting with tears. Their mouths sought each other, desperate and wild and their bodies pushed against each other almost fighting. He squeezed her breasts, took her buttocks in his hands and pulled her against him in a parody of love and desire. They kissed long and hard. And then they grew silent, as though their love-acting had spent their bodies like the real, the godly. They held onto each other, stumbling then stabilizing, tottering then firm. He placed his hand softly in the folds of her dress between her legs and felt the heat of her sex. He heard her sigh. With his other hand he stroked her face, traced the contours of her forehead, eyebrows, nose, lips and chin which she mirrored.

'Do you remember, Harry? That time I found you?'

Summerfield smiled sadly and whispered a yes. 'You were an answer to an unspoken prayer,' he said, softly and kissed her lips.

'I was a girl. I knew nothing about life. I had not the slightest notion of what men meant or did or what love was. But my secret is—do you want to know my secret, Harry?'

'Tell me,' said Summerfield, rubbing gently against her.

'My secret is that I knew, from that very moment I saw you there, beaten and ill and strange in your foreignness, that I loved you. I kept it a secret, Harry. Or else I did not know what the voice in my head was saying. But I fell in love with you the instant you looked up at me.'

Summerfield withdrew slowly from their embrace and looked deeply into her eyes and felt he had touched something beautiful in her. He smiled. 'You reassure me. And make me feel strong. Wait for me, Raja and one day I will return.'

'I will wait, my dear Englishman. May God protect you...'

55

Moulay was a small, hard, sinewy man who considered speaking an unnecessary waste of breath. On the index finger of his right hand was the largest ring Summerfield had ever seen—a smooth, round chunk of ivory stained yellow. The rare times he did speak, it was for two reasons: giving orders and proffering opinion in the form of either fathomless wisdom or the shallowest of nonsense—Summerfield could never guess which. Moulay swore that the more people spoke, the more breath they used up and the shorter their life became. And that was it. The longest flow of words from his mouth in nearly three days.

'So if you spoke only twenty words in your lifetime, you'd live until five hundred and three, is that it?' Summerfield had teased, having become increasingly irritated by Moulay's taciturn monosyllables.

'What the camel imagines, the camel drivers guess,' replied Moulay, mysteriously. Summerfield rolled his eyes heavenwards and turning his head, vainly sought Jeanne's support. But she was looking away, back towards where the valley might lay and Summerfield exhaled gloomily. What might take three months of travelling had got off to an agonisingly tedious start. He could only guess at his companions' thoughts, rendered more difficult by the fact that Moulay seemed to live with his face permanently covered by his *cheiche* so that only his eyes showed—Summerfield hadn't even seen him unwind it for eating and cringed at the thought of what crusty debris might lay behind the headscarf. And Jeanne's continuing and obstinate self-imposed isolation. He'd hoped her spirits might lift upon leaving the valley but despite the odd flicker of emotion, she remained generally morose and unwilling, lost in her thoughts of Jim and her trials. All in all, Summerfield began to think that he had greatly sacrificed something for her in leaving the valley and that she was unquestionably the most ungrateful person he'd ever met.

So they travelled, both during the first hours of light or the dusky hours of evening so as not to be seen, picking their way down ravines and mountain flanks and through the great labyrinth of the gorges of Tedrha which made them seem so puny and unimportant. Teasing Moulay was the solution Summerfield now favoured in an attempt to make the man communicate. But Moulay was a veteran of the desert caravans and silence seemed to be his second nature. He was sand, a vast stretch of silent sand and his eyes would dart expressionless away from Summerfield's when under attack and lose themselves in a distance Summerfield could not perceive.

The day after leaving the valley, they had heard a bi-plane buzzing lazily in the vicinity and, watching from the cover of an overhanging rock, had seen it dip its nose into the myriad of valleys, disappear in silence and then resurface with a low-pitched drone as it struggled for altitude in the thin mountain air. They had not been seen and Moulay ordered that they should cut down even further on the time they spent journeying during the daylight hours and instead wake an hour earlier at three in the morning. Summerfield hoped that the Kaïd had been good to his word and sent news to the Vichy French forces of his intention to face them in the open. He couldn't bare the thought of Raja's family being shelled and his mind was constantly plagued by the fearful image of the young woman running from the explosions only to have her back hit by shrapnel. He could almost hear her screams at these moments. He wished he could have real companions with whom he could speak and distract his mind.

Moulay may have been a dire travelling companion, but Summerfield recognised the man's skills in orienteering. Working without a compass (Summerfield had acquired one some days before in exchange for a slice of salted meat and occasionally checked their guide's calculations), Moulay led them by the stars or the shadows the sun produced from the rocks and trees.

Sometimes he knew the path and made an abrupt and somewhat indecent gesture with his riding stick for the direction to take. Other times, Summerfield watched with growing fascination as Moulay's otherwise expressionless eyes moved and oscillated with calculations and intuition, darting across the terrain and summing up the right track to take. He almost seemed to see *beyond* what lay before them, retro-plotting their course according to a combination of criteria: time, direction, danger, ease, possible escape and weather. And Moulay never failed, even if, at times, Summerfield had to bite his lip to keep himself from questioning the chosen path. What seemed an impassable sea of boulders revealed a sandy-floored track; what seemed to be a stomach-churning precipice turned out to be a gentle series of steps down the flank of a mountain. On several occasions, just before dawn would break, the wily guide led them to secret places that he swore only he and God and the animals knew about. They were often small paradises lodged in the rocks or at the bottom of ravines, bubbling with clear water and emerald coloured reeds. In one such place, Moulay plucked fish from the pools and in another, a tree that Summerfield had never seen, gave perennial fruit—small, yellow buttons that tasted like raspberries to the tongue. Gradually, Summerfield's mood changed, his respect for Moulay's strengths overcoming his dislike of Moulay's weaknesses. However, his teasing didn't stop—it was a way out of the gloom, a distance he made between the hopes for his life and the harsh reality of Jeanne's burden of guilt and pain.

The landscape changed. Treeless and craggy ravines gave way to pine groves and smoothened rock. In some places, the maroon-coloured stone looked like ball upon ball of polished wool flowing downwards into valley streams and Summerfield imagined there must have been much volcanic activity in the area many thousands of years before. Then came fertile earth, rich and dark red and carpeted with the greenest grass he'd ever seen. One morning and one night more and then the earth became pink and fine like sand. Wild olive trees scattered the gentling slopes and the spaces between summits became wide and windy. After the fifth or sixth

day of travel, Summerfield lost count and took his mark instead
on the terrain and the direction they were headed. Then, one day,
after setting out at their customary 3 a.m. and circumnavigating
a plateau of jagged black rock, they mounted a gentle hill to see
before them, in the first indigo of the day, the vast expanse of
the Saharan threshold—a plain criss-crossed by the shadows of
tracks and rivers, scudding clouds of oases, dark green against
light beige, and the scattered rectilinear patchwork of isolated
villages. Summerfield's breath left him and disappeared upwards
into the greatness of the space and the vast horizon. Again, before
the omnipotence of nature, the certainty that God existed came
to his lips and he offered up a prayer that made Jeanne look
curiously at him and Moulay frown in incomprehension.

'English,' commented Summerfield, giving Moulay a cheeky
wink. 'Just my humble thanks to the Almighty for the beauty of
this land.'

'May God be praised for His miracles,' chimed in Moulay and
sank to his knees in Morning Prayer, bowing to the east across
the desert plains.

The next day, barely ten miles out on the plain, Moulay led them
to a small outcrop of rock that contained many caves—perhaps
once troglodyte dwellings, imagined Summerfield—and left
them there with food and water. Taking the two mules, Moulay
rode silently away, gesticulating in that obscene way with his stick
towards the south.

'Ksar-Tazzr,' he said, turning back to them. 'A village. No
more mules,' he grunted and Summerfield saw in his eyes that
he was grinning.

'But when are you coming back?' asked Summerfield, in
mountain dialect.

Moulay shrugged his shoulders. 'When God permits,' he
answered and trotted off across the dusty earth with the mules.

It was the first time Summerfield had been alone with Jeanne
since they had set out from the valley. It felt strange. She lay
sleeping in the shadow of the cave and Summerfield watched
her with something approaching curiosity. Her face had tanned

during the days of travel despite their avoidance of the hottest hours and once more he was conscious of the features that set her apart from a purely European physiognomy. He remembered how she had suffered from this difference and he remembered, during those furtive meetings in the orange grove, how he had reassured her of her beauty. It was the shine of elegance that comes of mixed blood—the finishing touch of something southern, something eastern in her and it still made him perplexed, still made him spellbound. Had she made love to Jim? he wondered and saw himself, seemingly years ago, the first to unfold the petals of this rare flower. He shook his head involuntarily, a gesture of perplexity: they had been so madly in love. And now the love he felt for Raja was growing that way too. Did it mean that it was all so ephemeral? That there were other loves waiting for him in life? That what he had imagined as the *One* to whom all the paths in life were meant to lead him were in fact just a series of illusions, mirages that served as destinations on the sprawling clock of days, weeks and years? His mind wandered emptily. Minutes passed and then he shook himself back into consciousness. No, Raja was different: it wasn't just a physical beauty, the foreignness, the *adventure* that her body represented—it was also the sweet, warm togetherness that he felt; a certain compatibility of spirit, a certain *complémentarité*—the French word came quicker than the English—of characters. A woman (*girl*, he had nearly said) like Raja was fun, a challenge and made everyday seem different and boisterous. Their sparring was like making love and underlay the passion of the real act. In this aspect, Jeanne had been different. Coming back to the flower, it seemed the best image for her. He had picked a beautiful poppy, wild but fragile once uprooted and his love for her had been worship, a look from afar, a desire like a bee has for pollen.

Moulay came back five hours later on foot. Summerfield, ready with his Lee Enfield from under the rocky overhang, had been tempted to shoot. Jeanne, for once alert, had whispered to him that she recognised the solitary figure as Moulay and Summerfield had slowly, carefully replaced the safety catch.

'Where are the camels?' said Summerfield, frowning at Moulay as the wiry little man sat down and drank.

'Camels?' Moulay's eyes carried a hint of laughter. 'Why camels? Why not horses?'

Summerfield shrugged irritably. 'So where are the horses, then?'

Moulay shook his head just once, sharply. 'Not horses. A lorry.'

'A lorry,' echoed Summerfield.

An erratic wave of his riding stick towards the south. 'Coming.'

For the first four days, they cut across the flatness of the pre-Sahara in the back of a battered Berliet stacked high with slabs of salt. A small cavity, just big enough for Summerfield to stretch his legs in a sitting position, had been made among the cargo at the back. Anyone opening the tarpaulin would see the roughly hewn slabs and nothing else.

The leaf spring suspension, almost flattened by the weight, made it impossible for them to rest and worse still, he and Jeanne were showered with flakes and salt dust every time they drove over the slightest dip or stone. It irritated their skin, made their sweat like mustard and the only way to avoid this was by remaining completely covered despite the heat. Before setting out, Moulay had ordered them not to speak and so Summerfield and Jeanne communicated with occasional gestures, mouthed words or the expressions on their faces. The main messages between the two of them were *hunger*—a grimace followed by rubbing the belly; and *uncomfortable*—a grimace followed with wriggling on Jeanne's part and a rather overdramatic rubbing of the arse by Summerfield.

The strangest thing was that despite being separated from the driving cabin, Summerfield could hear Moulay and the driver jabbering almost incessantly, and sometimes it seemed—hysterically—from within. Summerfield felt strangely robbed. From having spent nearly ten days mute and brooding, Moulay now showed a will to yap on a par with the most vociferous of village gossips. The driver, he soon found out, was Moulay's cousin and husband to Moulay's sister, Wafa—which also made him his brother-in-law. As time went by, Summerfield learnt of probably most of Moulay's vibrant and extended family—Walid, Torkia, Nour, Sadi, Redouane, Mabrouk, Djelloul and God knows how many others—and also of most of their lives. A house bought here, a cuckold there, Nour's cakes that sold so well, a botched circumcision and Abdelghani's shingles.

Angry that he had to share his time and space with a brooding Jeanne, angry that Moulay had betrayed him, angry that he was far from Raja, angry that his stomach was crying out for food, angry that he smelt like a mature and very salted cheese, Summerfield passed away the tedium by singing to himself, picturing Raja, holding in an ever-present urge to urinate as they bounced over the tracks and open sand and bearing a constant series of painfully hard erections that lasted, quite naggingly, for hours on end.

On three occasions they were stopped at roadblocks set up where the desert tracks converged. Moulay became as silent as stone. In the back, the fear making his heart accelerate, Summerfield closed his eyes and practiced the scenario he had imagined a hundred times—the tarpaulin pulled back, stacks of salt pushed aside, Jeanne's nerve cracking, her cry that betrayed their presence, shouts in French or German, the looming shape of a uniform as the cargo was prised away, then Summerfield's shot, pushing forwards as he loaded again, searching other targets and then—then a blank, his mental rehearsal having avoided what could happen next. During the forced stops, long, excruciating minutes of fear passed in which every noise became amplified and meaningful. Voices in French, orders, Moulay's grunts and the rustle of money passing hands.

The second time they were stopped, Summerfield had had to pull Jeanne to him and smother her mouth with his hand. He could feel her tiny spasms, the hot breath from her nostrils on his fingers, her voice on the verge of releasing a sound. He feared that he would suffocate her. Once out into the safety of the plain again, he released his hold and although she gasped and spluttered, she lingered in his arms and squeezed him for comfort and Summerfield wondered if there was any hidden meaning in it all. He returned the embrace, nerves and mental exhaustion seeking something physical, more animal, more emotional. They spent several long minutes, just like before, holding onto to each other for safety and reassurance, alone in the hostility of it all.

The third time he heard the lorry grinding down through the gears and whining to a halt, Summerfield twisted his body round and peeped through the salt to a crack in the wooden buffer adjoining the driver's cabin. To his stupefaction, the approaching roadblock was not a barricade of barbed wire or a string of soldiers, but a ragged line of what looked like pygmies adorned with grotesquely painted cardboard hats and armed to the teeth with spears and shields. *What the hell*, he hissed, the initial shock giving way to relief as the lorry drew closer. They were boys, an odd mix of what looked like six to twelve year olds. And it was only when the tallest of them, the leader, held out his hand and rubbed thumb and forefinger together that Summerfield understood their novel way of earning money: a road toll. Moulay gesticulated with his stick and threw them insults, but his cousin, more tolerant, reached for something—food or a pinch of tobacco perhaps—and tossed it to the impudent warriors through the open window. The make-believe warriors drew apart, giving a cheer, and let the lorry through.

On the fifth or sixth night, stopping for food and sleep, Moulay informed them that they were two hundred kilometres into southern Algeria and travelling parallel to the Mauritanian and Malian borders. Here, the frontiers merged, unclear and mostly unmarked. The land was a meeting point not only the Vichy French patrols, but marauders, caravans, Spanish deserters, brigands and the fierce Blue men of the nomadic Tuareg tribes. Clashes were frequent and once in a while tribes confronted each other in dispute, only to turn their guns in common cause against the white invaders patrolling the area.

Here the dusty earth and sand of the plains gradually turned from pinkish grey to beige to a fine peppery orange. Sand drifts appeared, then dunes and before he knew it, Summerfield realised they had entered the true desert and that it stretched before them towards the east, unbroken for three thousand miles.

A three-hour drive the following morning and the lorry came to a final halt. This time, as though anticipating the next stage of the journey, Moulay's voice slowed, becoming taciturn as he entered a final conversation with his driver-cum-cousin. One last time, the stacks of salt were unloaded and a narrow passage cleared through the cargo.

Summerfield, helping Jeanne to her feet, squeezed through the slabs of salt and jumped down from the lorry, tottering when he hit the sand, his legs unfamiliar with firm ground. He stretched, groaning from the pain in his knees and after rubbing them vigorously looked up to see Jeanne already upright, profile to him and her head turned in a stare that panned from the tired looking cluster of date palms to the left of the lorry across the immensity of open space that occupied the whole horizon on the right. Summerfield went and stood by her. He whistled through his teeth which made her momentarily turn her head and then back again to the desert. Summerfield had the strangest impression that he was the edge of an inversed beach, looking out not to the water but to the expanse of an ochre sea of sand, rippled and whipped by a million petrified waves that lapped endlessly into the horizon.

'Are we actually going to try to cross that?' he said, turning to Moulay and his cousin.

The little guide gave a curt shake of his head. 'No—not *try*. Just *cross* it, that's all.' His cousin seemed to find this particularly funny and the fact that Moulay had gotten the better of a white man no doubt added to the hilarity. He rolled his head in a series of laughs that resembled a severe fit of hiccups. Summerfield, turning sour, picked up his Lee Enfield and began deliberately to test the sights. Moulay's cousin abruptly shut up, looking disconcerted, then worried and disappeared round the other side of the lorry checking tyres.

'What now?' said Summerfield, content that he had imposed himself.

'We wait,' returned Moulay, begrudgingly. 'My cousin goes this way—' a wave of his stick—'and we go that way'—another wave towards the dunes.

Summerfield shouldered his rifle. 'And what will we wait for?'

'Camels,' answered Moulay. 'Our ships of the desert.'

In among the cluster of palms was a well and while Moulay bartered a transaction with his cousin and waved the lorry off, Summerfield called for Jeanne to help him draw water. He had expected a bucket and a rope, but the well was equipped with a hand pump that offered stiff resistance and squeaked abominably as it drew, coughing out water into a makeshift trough made of a petrol barrel that had been cut in two. After five minutes, sweating, the two of them had managed to fill the bottom of the trough with four inches of cloudy, beige-coloured water.

'I need a damn good wash,' he said, turning to Jeanne. 'But you go first.' She hesitated, a silent, questioning look on her face. Summerfield grunted and then smiled. 'I'll turn my back—keep an eye on Moulay. There's no need to undress— look, I'll show you how.' Squatting, Summerfield unwound his headdress and loosened his robes, making a series of gestures to show her how to wash.

'You know their ways,' she said. 'You're almost one of them.'

'Two years in the mountains,' he confirmed. 'One of them as a prisoner. I had to learn.'

'I suppose one does,' agreed Jeanne and gave a little flick of her head to make him turn away.

Standing there, back turned, Summerfield heard the sound of loosening clothes. Water splashed and miraculously he caught a sudden nip of lemon.

'My God—I've just smelt heaven,' he called over his shoulder. 'What is it?'

'Soap,' answered Jeanne and he thought she sounded pleased. 'Olive and lime.'

'*Soap*?' Summerfield was astonished.

'The women in the village. They gave it to me before we left.' There was a long silence. It was as though she were making a point of her superior possession. And then, in a small, tentative voice: 'You can borrow it if you like.'

'*Super—thank you*, Jeanne,' returned Summerfield, surprised by her gesture and felt himself grinning.

He heard the sound of her hands, wet upon her skin and the soft plop of the soap being dropped into the drinking trough. Instinctively, he turned his head slightly, glancing at her from the corners of his eyes. She was busy, sluicing her armpits and he had a delicious though furtive glimpse of a tit, shuddering as her hand brushed against it, momentarily bulging in the action and then falling back into place, a heavenly hang of a shape. He closed his eyes, looked away and felt his throat go dry: if there was one Godly creation that could rival the beauty of nature it was the curve and movement of a woman's breasts.

After a further few minutes in which he heard a groan of effort, the clang of metal and her hands scooping water—probably washing her hair—Jeanne announced that it was his turn.

He turned round and momentarily froze, a feeling of clumsy timidity suddenly overcoming him. Her face shone creamy-white and had a waxy glow and with her hair pulled back she wore a boyish expression of grumpiness mixed with almost glee.

'Is something wrong?' she said, looking worriedly at her feet. 'Is it a scorpion? A snake? *Where*?'

Summerfield laughed and his embarrassment evaporated. 'No.' he shook his head. 'Just you—it's the nicest I've seen you in a long time. You look beautiful. You seem—*happier*. And it's good to see.'

For an instant, he thought she would close like a book and return to her isolation, but she checked herself, though not without some effort, and forced a smile.

'I think it's your turn now,' she said, pointing to the soap. 'I'll help you draw more water if you like.'

Summerfield pondered the option and grunted. 'No need— I'll use your water. If it has the same effect on me, I'll be a happy man.'

They were sitting drinking the mint tea Moulay had brewed when three shapes shimmered into view on the near horizon— three sets of outrageously long legs, like ostriches, with a fat belly and a giraffe's neck attached to it: the camels had arrived.

One was ridden by a man dressed in the dark blue robes and headgear of the *Tuaregs*—the Berber nomads of the desert. It was no surprise that they were called the Blue men, for when the rider halted before them and uncovered his face, Summerfield observed that the rider's skin was a darker shade of blue, the sweat having washed off the dye of his headdress to the pores of his skin. Seeing Summerfield's consternation, the rider grinned showing a perfect row of gleaming white teeth and rubbed his cheek. He spoke rapidly, in a dialect Summerfield couldn't understand, and Moulay bade him to join them with a cup of sweet tea.

After a long and ceremonious three glasses, they agreed on a price for the remaining camels. Moulay gave the beasts a second thorough going-over, checking for old wounds, gall and any abscesses and then made Summerfield dip into his knapsack and produce two gold coins. How Moulay had known he'd been given them, Summerfield hadn't a clue—for it had been a tacit arrangement between himself and the Kaïd—but he handed them over to the Tuareg rider who nodded politely. Another glass of tea, exceptionally sugary, was made from pouring the rests together. The Tuareg sucked the syrupy mixture noisily before rising sharply to his feet and proffering a long series of Godly farewells.

56

As dusk settled on the horizon, Moulay lashed their belongings and two ten-litre goatskins filled with water to the camels. Before setting out, he made Summerfield and Jeanne stand before the two beasts and gave them a brief instruction on how to ride. They were to climb atop WaRed—*flower*—hardly a name that pictured speed or prowess—a spindly female with a large, brownish petal-shaped spot around the left eye and hence her name.

'Speak to her,' ordered Moulay, 'For she must trust you.'

'What do we say?' said Summerfield, feeling slightly silly.

'Your names. And how much you want her to take you across the erg.'

Summerfield shrugged, translated to Jeanne, who let out a laugh, and putting all embarrassment to the wind, began to charm WaRed with *I wandered lonely as a daffodil* which he thought very fitting given her name. Several tries at mounting—the initial sharp jerk and lift off making them cry out and laugh—and Moulay tied the reins to the pummel of his own saddle. With a last look back, only his eyes showing from behind his headgear, Moulay gave his customary gesture with his stick, a disrespectful upwards thrust that Summerfield couldn't help thinking meant something unpleasantly directed at him, and they set off at a lazy, looping pace eastwards towards the gun grey sky.

Solitary, but somehow *present* was how Summerfield described the desert. They journeyed relentlessly into the sea of sand, leaving the tracks behind them, at first a desert of rocks and stones and strange, twisted trees with bulbous green fruit shaped like bladders that Moulay informed them were called Sodom Apples. At one point, disappearing into a hollow between two dunes, the guide approached one and struck deftly at a fruit with his stick. Immediately, the great bloated bladder exploded with a puff, making Moulay emit a mirthless laugh.

'Don't touch,' he commanded. 'The sap will not leave your hands again. If it touches your tongue, you will be very ill.' His eyes glaring grotesquely, he briefly mimed stomach cramps.

Beneath the loping hooves of the camel, Summerfield caught the glint of quartz in the moonlight, some of the stone perfectly smooth and large, forming strange and angular phallus shapes. During a stop to relieve themselves, he pocketed one—translucent and pink—and while he turned, his eye caught sight of something else, curved and black. He let out a muffled cry, at first sight believing it to be an animal and then, stooping low, picked it up. Encrusted in the black stone was a finely sculptured trace of white, a score of delicate branches seemingly sketched into its surface.

'Good God, it's a fossil—a damn *worm* or something.' He beckoned for Moulay and Jeanne to come over. 'What is it?' said Summerfield.

Moulay shrugged his shoulders. At their feet, scattered in an area roughly twenty feet wide, they discovered many hundreds of them.

'Fish,' said Jeanne. 'Thousands of years ago, this must have been a sea.'

'A *sea*—do you hear that, Moulay?' said Summerfield.

'No,' Moulay's eyes looked stubborn.

'Yes—a sea,' repeated Summerfield.

Moulay shook his head and Summerfield understood that he didn't want to speak further on the issue. Perhaps, he thought, as they re-mounted the camels, Moulay thought they were questioning his faith and thought it very odd.

As they journeyed slowly through the night, the rocks petered out to stones which seemed as though some great hand had scattered them in flurries across the sand. Eventually, they found themselves treading fine sand. Around them, the dunes closed in, becoming uncountable in number, undulating humps and waves—they had finally entered the true sea of sand. It grew cold, much colder than Summerfield had imagined, a dryer, sharper cold than that of the mountains that made his skin prick and pimple. They wrapped themselves in the thick woollen mats that Summerfield had seen Moulay take from the Blue man—mats that apparently served several practical uses: sleep, tea, prayer, blankets, capes, protection against the sand storms, parasol and makeshift tent—and rode until Moulay at last gave the order to halt.

Much as they had done to hide their presence in the snow, Summerfield dug two small, funnel-shaped holes in the sand and lit their fires. He boiled a cup of rice and—Moulay having decided not to eat and huddled against his camel for warmth—Summerfield shared the bland though filling feculent with Jeanne. Having washed their bowls in the sand, they sat in silence for a while, looking at the shadows of the dunes and the incredible quantity of stars.

'I have never seen so many,' whispered Summerfield, leaning across to Jeanne. 'Not even in the mountains.'

'Like pins in a velvet pin-cushion,' returned Jeanne, her voice sounding breathless in the effort. 'We watched them together once before,' she added after a long silence.

Summerfield smiled inwardly. 'That was another life ago. I thought you'd have forgotten the poem.'

'I very nearly have,' she replied, tiredly. 'I do not want to offend you.'

Summerfield shook his head, though inside, he was indeed put out that she should have said it. He wanted to ask what she had done with them, but instead: 'It doesn't matter. A new life is beginning for you.'

Jeanne glanced at him and fell silent once again. She ran a hand through her hair under her *cheiche*. 'Do you think we'll make it?'

'Of course.' Summerfield nodded. 'I'm not ready to die—I have things to do.'

'We could die out *here*,' she offered, emphasising the word. 'It's so inhospitable. There's nothing.'

'I don't feel that. I feel—*strangely comforted* by it all.'

'You're *bizarre*,' frowned Jeanne.

'Not like Jim Wilding,' answered Summerfield, flatly.

'*Not* like Jim,' echoed Jeanne. She pointed upwards to the night sky. 'A shooting star! Did you see it?' But Summerfield was too late. He had missed it. 'I have written a letter, Harry. It is meant for Jim if you ever meet up with him.' Summerfield frowned and a trace of irony appeared on Jeanne's lips. She gave a brief hum. 'I suppose I do believe that you'll survive, Harry. But I have less faith in my *own* survival. Maybe it has something to do with what I went through... I—I no longer have any confidence, you see.' She reached across to her bag and carefully pulled out a small folded square of paper—two pages already frayed at the edges. 'Give this to him if you find him.'

Summerfield hesitated then took the letter with a nod of his head. 'I will.'

He felt the rough grain beneath his thumb and forefinger and his touch lingered a few seconds, enjoying the feeling. Leaning sideways to his knapsack, he opened it and slid it inside. Surprisingly, there was a soft chink of glass and frowning, Summerfield pulled the sack to him and inserted his fingertips further. They pricked against something sharp. Withdrawing his hand, he saw a tiny chip of glass protruding from his fingertip. He plucked it out and peered into his bag.

'*Damn!* The compass—*broken.*' He prised open the sack and pulled out the damaged casing. The needle was missing. 'What a bloody fool,' he hissed, reproaching himself. 'Probably when I got down from WaRed—I should have folded it in something. *Damn!*'

'Is it that important?' said Jeanne. In a gesture that surprised Summerfield, she began to move closer to him—one, two movements—and then settled. Summerfield could feel the sudden warmth of her arm and thigh against his own.

'Important? Yes,' he whispered. 'If we ever get lost in this place. It's the basic tool for survival. Look,' he added, turning his head with some difficulty to face Jeanne's right ear. 'Shouldn't we bed down against WaRed? Moulay—'

Jeanne let out a sleepy sigh. 'But it *smells*,' she whispered. 'And Moulay *smells*.'

'A small price to pay for warmth,' answered Summerfield, but

Jeanne leaned against him, pushing like a cat to find comfort. She unexpectedly placed an arm around his back and sighed. Confused and unable to move, Summerfield let the silence go by. Jeanne grew heavy. Slowly, he inched a mat towards them, hooking it from toe to fingers and carefully covered their two shapes. Her breath became slow and deep, pulsing warmly against his collar bone. She had fallen asleep.

Another day of travel began. When the sun reached ten o'clock, Summerfield, instructing Jeanne to keep a hold on him while WaRed undulated over the sand, used his freed hands to empty his knapsack, placing the objects one by one in the folds of his shirt. The thought had been in his mind since waking and it nagged him—it was important to retrieve the needle. By placing the needle on the spindle inside the casing, even without the liquid to hold it in place, it should give him a few precious seconds in which to take their bearings. He looked twice, his fingers pushing into every fold and every corner of the leather holder but found nothing. The third time, he lost his temper and, causing both Jeanne and Moulay to raise a cry, jumped down from WaRed and emptied the bag in the sand.

'If there was anything in it, you've lost it now,' commented Jeanne and Summerfield swore.

Moulay trotted back on his mount.

'What is it, *Sidi* Summerfield?' he frowned. 'The sun, perhaps, on your English skin?'

'It's no time for jokes, Moulay,' returned Summerfield, irritably, standing back up. He placed his hands on his hips and swore again towards the expanse of dunes. 'Fuck it! My compass, Moulay—*broken*.'

'Oh,' grunted Moulay. 'And perhaps we can repair it.'

'Not a chance,' replied Summerfield. 'The needle's pissed off in the sand.'

'What?' frowned Moulay, unable to understand the English.

'It is lost,' clarified Summerfield in Arabic.

'It is God's will, perhaps,' answered the guide. 'I am sorry it has happened. But trust me, *Sidi* Summerfield—are not the best directions in the desert given by Moulay's undeniable knowledge?'

'Yes, yes,' replied Summerfield, annoyed with himself. 'But the compass was a safeguard.'

'Do not think I did not see you checking my directions in the mountains, Sidi. I did not say a thing because I hoped you would learn to understand that I know from experience and from the land how to go from here to there.'

Summerfield shook his head. 'Moulay—you've never strung more than five words together to me. And now—'

'You are distressed, *Sidi* Summerfield. I see this.'

'Yes,' said Summerfield again. 'Yes. All right—I *know* you can lead us across the desert, Moulay. I did not mean to insult you.' Moulay cocked his head in acknowledgement. 'And I thank you for getting us until here. Let's hope the rest of the journey continues in the same manner.'

'If God wills it,' replied Moulay and raised his stick. 'It is this way,' he said, sourly.

A mile or so after setting out again, Jeanne asked Summerfield a question.

'Do you know anything about the stars, Harry?'

'Why d'you want to know that?' frowned Summerfield, still annoyed.

'You wrote me a letter once. About Cassiopeia and things.'

Summerfield shook his head. 'Poetic drivel,' he replied. 'I know as much about stars as any other dreamer.'

That day, they rode until midday, Moulay informing them that they were so far from anything that the risk of being seen was less than minimal. When they dismounted, by a scattered scrub of thorn trees, Summerfield felt groggy and was about to ask Jeanne to steady him when she herself leaned against him, swayed heavily then fell. Summerfield knelt and heaved her on her back. Her eyes moved lazily and then rolled back to reveal the white of her orbits. She shuddered, gagged and then vomited.

'No!' It was Moulay's voice and he was now beside them. 'Like this!' he ordered, pushing her back on her side. 'She will drown on her bile if not.'

'What is it?' said Summerfield, scared now. 'What's wrong with her?'

'The heat illness.'

'Hyperthermia,' stated Summerfield. 'The sun—I told her she had to drink more. Is it dangerous?'

Moulay shrugged his shoulders. 'She could die,' he said, matter-of-factly, then noticing Summerfield's look of panic, added, 'but only very rarely does this happen.'

Again, Jeanne retched, bringing up a flurry of liquid and whitish lumps of undigested rice. She began to speak deliriously—something about her skin and stars and darkness.

'What shall we do?'

'The mats—give her shade.' Summerfield rushed to the camels and unloaded the mats and his rifle. Checking the location of the sun, he plunged the butt of his Lee Enfield into the sand and draped a mat over it to form a shelter. 'Keep her on her side,' instructed Moulay. 'Give her water and pour some—like this—on the back of her neck. She must not move. She must not be touched by the sun.' Moulay rose.

'Where are you going?' said Summerfield, standing up to face him.

'For help, of course.'

'Help?' Summerfield shielded his eyes. 'In *this* empty desert?'

'There is an oasis I know of—about an hour from here.'

'Why not put her on a camel?'

'She should not be moved—I told you.' Moulay's eyes were steady and Summerfield found himself craning to spot any emotion in them. 'If there is an oasis, there is a well. And if there is a well, there are nomads and help.'

'You're leaving us here?' said Summerfield, in disbelief. 'You said there was nobody for miles?' Summerfield shook his head, his muscles tensed as though his body instinctively knew that something was wrong. 'Where *are we*, Moulay? And for Christ's sake take that bloody scarf off of your face!'

'You are insulting, *Sidi* Summerfield. You should know that a man of the desert does not reveal his face. And, as I often tell you—

we are going east. Towards the mountains they call the Hoggar.'

'Bloody rogues and bandits,' stammered Summerfield in English and then, giving up, frustration sending his voice into a whine—'All right. But what if she wakes? What should I do?'

'Follow me.'

'How?'

'The trace of the stick,' replied Moulay, cocking his head towards his camel. 'I shall tie my stick to the camel's tail. If needed, the trace will lead you to me.'

Summerfield remained silent, glancing at Jeanne who was now moaning softly. At last, Moulay spoke again.

'It is the only way, Summerfield. I will return—I promise. You must stay and protect her.'

Summerfield watched the guide ride off at a fast trot, mount a dune and then pass out of view, the thin irregular trace of the stick disappearing with him. He shouted an oath at the dune, slapped his hands helplessly against his sides and turned back to Jeanne.

Her strange babbling had begun again, cut by fits of crying. The words and noises reminded Summerfield of a spell. 'To hell with it,' he mumbled to himself and, choosing to go against Moulay's advice, decided to move Jeanne to the shade offered by a thorn bush. He took hold of her lapels, smelling the vomit on his hands, and pulled. She was heavier than he thought and in the effort, there was a tear and the collar of her shirt ripped and flapped. At last, he managed to drag her under the loosely woven canopy of branches and went to fetch the mat and his rifle.

The silence was almost total. A slight breeze butted mutely against the dunes and if it had not been for the slight tremor of the branches, Summerfield would have thought nature had stopped. Then WaRed limped into view, Moulay having strapped its hind leg to stop the beast wandering too far. The beast sniffed at a thorn bush, bit into the branches and with a loud, determined groan began chewing. They had the goatskin a quarter full of water and Summerfield unloaded it while WaRed chewed happily. Regularly, he poured some of it into a cup, bringing it to Jeanne's lips and then wetting her nape. At one point she struggled to raise herself and he chided her, pushing down until she gave way and lay still.

'I'm sorry, Harry. I said strange things. I didn't mean to cry.'

Summerfield stroked her forehead and neck. 'I felt awful myself,' he said. 'Good job you fell first, because it was about to be me.' She chuckled slightly and in a sweet gesture, her hand moved to his and clasped it.

Time passed—about thirty minutes, Summerfield guessed. At last, he considered it appropriate for Jeanne to sit up and take a deeper draught of water. She looked better now, the pale, waxy shine to her skin having disappeared and her cheeks now flushed with red. Summerfield rose, walked a few paces then on better thoughts returned to pick up the Lee Enfield.

'I'm just going to take a peep over that dune,' he said. 'Try not to move.'

'Harry—'

'I'll stay in sight, don't worry.'

Leaving Jeanne propped under the bush, Summerfield pushed up the sheer wall of a dune, his feet rapidly sinking up to his shins, his hands burning on the searing sand. He grunted with the effort, like in a rugby scrum, sending a wake of sand tumbling behind him. At last, heaving himself to the top, he looked down at Jeanne and gave her a wave. She looked very small. The dune, Summerfield calculated, was some thirty feet in height. She waved back, looking worried.

Summerfield turned to survey the terrain. Nothing—no sign of an oasis, he thought aloud. *Blast*—the sun was directly above them, impossible to judge any direction for the moment. To the left, the distant grey crags of the Hoggar rose hazily in the waves of heat. Must be east. After ten minutes of scrutinizing the horizon, Summerfield slid back down and returned to Jeanne's side. He looked at her, offered a sheepish smile and drank from the cup she held out to him.

'Mmm,' he said, grimacing at her, 'nice subtle aftertaste of sick in this. Good stuff!'

'Harry!' cried Jeanne and she blushed, making him laugh. 'This

500 Tom Gamble

is a serious situation.'

He shrugged his shoulders. 'True. I wonder where Moulay is.'

'Do you think he was the one who broke the compass?' said Jeanne, distantly, her voice returning, devoid of emotion, to its former self.

'Lord knows,' said Summerfield. 'Couldn't tell if the man is lying anyway—he keeps his face hidden.' Silence. Summerfield looked lazily about the scrub and sighed. 'We'll just have to do what everyone else in these parts does—put our faith in God and let what happens happen.'

Jeanne made a humming noise and once again they fell silent. A fly buzzed wearily and circled off. Twenty yards or so away, WaRed still munched impassively and then, for some reason, stirred.

'Must be the thorns,' commented Summerfield.

'Harry?'

'Hmm? What's the matter?'

'Do you feel it?'

'What?' Summerfield frowned.

'The movement. Like a slight tremor.'

'What d'you mean?'

'Concentrate,' said Jeanne, her voice growing hoarse. 'You can feel it on your skin.'

Summerfield held his breath. She was right. Through the seat of his trousers, he could feel the ground moving slightly. He changed position, placing his hands palm down on the sand. Distinct, irregular tremors.

'Christ—do they have earthquakes in these parts?' he said with a growing sense of worry.

'It's getting worse,' said Jeanne.

'*What the—*!'

Summerfield rose instinctively, an awful sensation of fear dawning on him, and grabbed the rifle.

'Get behind me,' he said, pushing Jeanne out of the way.

His fingers shaking, he adjusted the sights of the Lee Enfield to one hundred yards and slapped back the bolt. A bullet slipped and clicked into the firing chamber. He raised his rifle. The ground trembled now, groaned. Across the clearing, WaRed bucked on three legs and began squealing.

'*Fuck! Look out!*' shouted Summerfield, tensing for the first shot.

Suddenly, in a spray of sand and mad snorting, a group of horsemen broke over the crest of the thirty-foot dune, careering downwards in a chaos of waving arms and high-pitched screams. One horse zigzagged crazily and fell, catapulting its rider. Summerfield stood petrified, the muzzle of the Lee Enfield swaying uncontrollably in his fear. He fired high, the bullet cracking off into the sky.

'*Fuck you!*' he shouted, full of frustration and rage.

A last, horrifying scream and the horses came to halt, stamping and chaffing barely twenty yards from them. There were fifteen or so of them. One shot, maybe two, he calculated. He felt like pissing himself. The bullet—the moment of death—did not bother him. It was the terror the Tuareg warriors communicated. In blue-black, completely covered. On their faces black masks with only two small holes for their eyes. They looked like some satanic sect, demons of the desert. Seconds passed and Summerfield trembled visibly. From somewhere behind him, Jeanne was whimpering. His eyes settled on the leading horse. The satanic rider, the carbine, the sheathed scimitar, the saddle of blackest leather and—dangling jauntily from a rope attached to the pommel, a pair of hacked off hands. On one of them, the index finger wore a large, ivory ring spattered with blood. They were Moulay's hands.

'Jeanne,' croaked Summerfield, making a slight gesture towards her. 'God has let me down. I'm sorry.'

57

The warrior leader gave no name and did not uncover himself. Vulnerable, puny, miserable, distrustful, Summerfield and Jeanne stood before the horsemen as the leader gestured for two of his men to calm WaRed. In the minute or two it took them to control the beast, it slowly dawned on Summerfield that they would not be killed. It troubled him.

'And Moulay?' said Summerfield, at last, avoiding the severed hands. 'Why?'

'He was a traitor and a thief,' returned the masked leader in a growl that sent a shiver through Summerfield. 'The desert has ears and his cousin is a vain, babbling fool. He was to betray you.'

It took some seconds for the shock to sink in. Then Summerfield raised his eyes. 'And you? Don't you want to kill us?'

The leader grunted, spoke some rapid words to his men. One of them, with mother-of-pearl stitched into his mask in a diamond shape, dismounted and approached with a bag in his hand, obviously aiming for Jeanne. Summerfield tensed and stood in front of her.

'He is a tribal sorcerer and knows how to heal your woman. Leave him,' ordered the leader. Summerfield glanced at Jeanne, gave a slight nod of his head and stepped away.

'I asked a question,' said Summerfield, turning back to the masked chief. 'Why not us?'

This time a low, grumbling chuckle came from behind the mask. 'Because we are taking you to the white soldiers.'

Summerfield's hope slumped and he shook his head in defeat. 'Those Vichy bastards, dogs of the lowest sort.'

'Not,' said the leader. 'We are going east. To where the liberators are. They will give us money, freedom for action and arms in exchange.'

Summerfield's mouth fell open. 'I don't believe it,' he mumbled.

His hands came to rest on his hips and he shuffled slightly like a man who had lost his sense of direction. *A bloody miracle!* 'And what will you do with the hands?' he said, motioning towards the grizzly trophies.

'Nothing—throw them to the animals and insects.' The leader began to unwind the rope from his pommel.

'The ring?' frowned Summerfield.

'I would not take a ring that has adorned such a filthy hand,' growled the leader and then tapped a leather pouch on his belt which gave a muted jingle. Summerfield sensed the man was grinning. 'But three gold teeth, yes.' And with that, in a lazy, disrespectful gesture, the masked warrior threw Moulay's severed hands into the sand where they landed with a muffled thump.

For two weeks they rode the desert with their masked escort and not once did they see their rescuers' faces. They rode, talked, ate, shit and slept in their attire. In that time, Summerfield had chance to take stock of the truly gruesome arsenal of weapons they carried lashed to their saddles—spiked maces, scimitars, double-bladed daggers, silver knuckle dusters, carbines, pistols and a particularly vicious-looking arm that consisted in a series of long silver spikes that were inserted one by one on their fingers like some ghastly set of rings. It struck him as barbaric, mediaeval almost.

At one point crossing a desert road that stretched in a straight, gravel line south to north towards the horizon, they spotted a convoy of three lorries some kilometres away—military lorries—and the leader, whom they now knew as Zoubir, had to threaten his men first with oaths, then with his riding crop to stop them bolting in pursuit. Finally, the exasperated chief managed to dampen their enthusiasm by brandishing his mace and cracking it with a loud clang across a wayside panel. It read *Algers 1,000 km* in one direction and, dented by the mace, *Timbuktu 750 km* in the other.

WaRed didn't make it through the Hoggar mountains. A horse gave signs of fatigue by slowing to a dawdle then stopping, refusing to go on. A camel was different, plodding on in exactly the same rhythm until it dropped from exhaustion, unable to rise again. Added to that, the sheer climb and treacherous rock of the Hoggar made her slip several times. The effort killed her. One evening, coming to a spectacular outcrop of orange rock, ragged like a huge termites' nest, she kneeled to let Summerfield and Jeanne dismount and then quietly rolled over and died.

But what was taken from them, gave back to them. The tribesmen, profiting from this boon, skinned the beast and drew great hunks of meat which they let cook for two hours in a hole they filled in with sand. That night, Summerfield noted that WaRed, despite her fragile name, was a tough old beast, not helped by the grit that had permeated the meat during roasting, but nonetheless delicious. As was custom, they ate everything they could, leaving nothing for the following days. It was a mixture of custom and pride, for the warriors were capable of going almost a week without food, their stomachs living off the faith that God would provide for them whenever the next occasion to eat arose.

The magnificent and foreboding crags of the Hoggar behind them, they descended into the great depression that rose yet again to the summits of the Tibesti Plateau some three hundred kilometres to the east. More significantly, the Tibesti constituted the uppermost western corner of Chad.

In the gorges, they met up with another raiding party—some of them wearing the desert khaki of the *Méhari*—travelling in the direction they had come from and Summerfield had the distinct feeling that at last things were happening, the free world was reacting, the tide was beginning to turn. Tacit greetings were offered, tea brewed and information exchanged between the two leaders and then they were off again, in two blue-black and khaki columns, shrouded and masked and forever mysterious.

Again, two days later, they saw other troops. Grouped on a slight rise, they watched a swarm of vehicles—seven of them— crossing the plain towards the north and Libya, spewing up a billowing wake of dust and grit. Summerfield was alarmed to see them at one point change direction and head towards them at two to three miles' distance. The leader of their group waited, his men strung out in a line and Summerfield once again un-shouldered his aging Lee Enfield.

'Are they theirs or ours?' he said, glancing nervously at the impassive leader. 'They will have machine guns.'

'We will see,' grunted the leader, raising the muzzle of his carbine. When the vehicles turned from spewing black beetles to clearly visible shapes, he pulled out a crimson flag from his saddlebag and held it high so that it fluttered in the desert wind. The vehicles slowed visibly and a same banner, of identical colour, was held aloft in the leading car. '*Ours*,' growled the voice from behind the mask.

The vehicles came to a halt barely five hundred yards from them and the Tuareg leader trotted out to meet them. British? French? wondered Summerfield, feeling odd to lay eyes upon white men—his own. He noted that the vehicles—several Chevrolets, oddly elegant with their curved fenders and a couple of transformed Hotchkiss painted in desert beige—were as heavily armed as the tribesmen, bristling with automatic weapons and laden with jerry cans. At one point, the leading car ground into gear and, with the masked leader riding by its side, approached the Tuareg riding party. An officer wearing a khaki *cheiche* and high laced boots got out and walked slowly up to them in a large, loping gait. He was very tall and his legs seemed badly adapted to the sand. He gave the tribesmen a lazy salute and focused on Summerfield and Jeanne and their foreign dress.

'*Sidi* Zoubir informs me you are one of us?' said the officer—a captain—in a flawless public school accent.

'I'm British,' replied Summerfield, feeling odd, 'and this is Jeanne Lefèvre, a French citizen.' He noticed the soldier's pale blue eyes and burnt skin—much like his own.

'Good to meet you, Summerfield,' grinned the officer. 'Captain Barnes—that's B-a-r-n-*E*-s—of the LRDG.' Noticing Summerfield's incomprehension, he added: 'Long Range Desert Group—a riff-raff bunch of marauding Frogs and Brits. We're attached to Leclerc's forward base.'

'Are we near?' said Summerfield, forgetting to return the protocol.

'Listen, Summerfield,' said the captain, suddenly looking a little embarrassed. 'I can certainly *hear* you're one of us, but I don't suppose you have any papers—passport, that sort of thing? Your *clothes*, you see.'

'Papers?' Summerfield was dumbfounded. In the middle of a desert the size of an ocean? 'No, sorry—they were lost when I was abducted from Marrakesh. That was—forgive me, I've difficulty fixing time—over two years ago, I think.'

'Hmm.' Captain Barnes stood akimbo and seemed to be pondering, producing a pipe to help him wrestle the situation. 'Er—how can we *do* this? I've got to check, you see,' he added, apologetically. He was silent for several moments, his forehead creased, then suddenly—and slightly out of key—he began to sing: '*Bob-by Shaf-toe…*'

Summerfield blinked and exchanged glances with the masked Tuareg.

'*Bob-by Shaf-toe—*' repeated Barnes, motioning Summerfield to go on.

'*Went-to-sea,*' echoed Summerfield and the warrior chief let out a grunt.

'*Silver—*' egged on Barnes.

'*Buckles on his knee,*' continued Summerfield, feeling himself flushing red. '*He'll come back and marry me.*' Pause. '*Bo-nn-y Bob-by Shaf….toe!*' As he finished, Barnes, his face lit up with obvious glee, energetically joined in.

Barnes let out a congratulatory chuckle. 'That's all fine for me, Summerfield. Well, these chappies will take you to HQ, I'm sure,' he said, nodding at the warrior chief. 'You'll have to explain your story to the intelligence boys, I'm afraid. You do understand—one can't be too careful what with Rommel's lot and the wops and their tricks.'

'No, no of course,' replied Summerfield, feeling lost. 'Are we far?'

'You'll be in a hot tub of soapy water in about two days from now, I should think,' said the captain, jauntily and added, sotto-voiced while raising an eyebrow at the silent warriors: 'Magnificent creatures, what? Glad they're on our side—put the wind up the devil himself.' Summerfield nodded. Captain Barnes stepped forwards and Summerfield took his hand, firm and dry despite the heat. 'Good luck, Summerfield—*Madam*,' he added, giving Jeanne a brusque and gentlemanly nod.

'You, too, Barnes,' said Summerfield. 'I hope we'll meet again and—sorry if I seem…*distracted*. We've been alone for some time.'

'Hmm—jolly good,' said Barnes, a little embarrassed. He turned and headed for his command car which had already revved into life. 'By the way,' said Barnes, turning back as he jumped into his seat. 'I've got some spare togs in the back—standard khaki desert kit. Would you like them?'

Summerfield hesitated then shrugged: 'Oh, no thanks, Barnes. I'd—I'd rather keep to *these* for the moment.'

The captain gave a curious smile and glanced at his driver who raised his eyebrows.

'Captain Barnes—one last thing,' said Summerfield, hurriedly. Barnes craned his neck. 'What if I *hadn't known* how to sing *Bobby Shaftoe*?'

Barnes raised his eyebrows and grinned.

'Quite simple, Summerfield—I would have got out my revolver and shot you through the eyes. *Spies* and all that.' Barnes laughed, offered one more lazy wave and nodded to his driver who reversed the Chevy in a wide circle, spraying up dust and stones before crunching into forward gear and accelerating off to rejoin the others. Summerfield turned to Jeanne and touched her wrist.

'We're nearly home, Jeanne. You can start getting better—really.'

The next day saw the horsemen gather speed, eager to reach their destination and most probably their rewards. Summerfield and Jeanne rode separately, each sitting behind a warrior and preoccupied most of the time with maintaining balance as the horses alternated between a rapid trot and a canter. They watered briefly at a last well, hidden among a thick clump of date palms, and then set off again, covering another thirty miles or so before the leader gave the signal to halt for the night.

The group bedded down in a loose circle formation, the horses tethered to rocks amassed in the centre. No fires were lit—they would go without a meal this night—to avoid the possibility of drawing friendly fire. Sentinels were posted further out, some twenty yards or so from the main group and changed every two hours.

Summerfield and Jeanne found themselves after their day's separation, sore and aching from the rough ride. They sat down in the obscurity, Summerfield sneaking a hunk of sugared wheat meal from his knapsack. Too hard to break, they took alternate turns, nibbling away at the cake until moist and biteable. As on the three previous nights, Jeanne once more drew close to him and lowered her head so that it came to rest on his shoulder. Summerfield still found it odd, somehow sweet and understood that despite all her suffering she was still in some ways very much a young girl. He released his arm from the press of her side and put it protectively over her. She produced a soft moan of assent. Up above, in the incredible night sky, Summerfield for once spotted a shooting star and he let out a whispered gasp of awe.

'Despite everything,' he said, softly, 'despite my thirty-two years, a soul full of irony and a cynical mind—I can still find stars so wonderful. *Funny that.*'

'Harry?' he felt Jeanne's body squeeze slightly against his. 'I never did thank you.' Summerfield let out an embarrassed breath. 'I was so—so close to dying, so angry, so ashamed. I needed to hate someone—I'm so *sorry.*'

'I hope—' began Summerfield, when Jeanne raised herself on one elbow, craned towards him from below and gently kissed his lips. '*Oh.*' He was silent. She was staring at him directly through the darkness and he thought he saw her eyes form a smile.

'Thank you, Harry. You—you helped me get so much better. I want to live.'

'That's good,' replied Summerfield, sensing the uselessness of his words. He smiled back, into her face and she slid down once more so that her cheek rested on his chest. He closed his eyes for a few seconds, breathing serenely, a feeling of wellbeing seeping through him. His hand inched under the matting used for blankets and found her hand. He took it and she responded, gripping his.

'There is still some sort of love between us, Harry,' she said softly. 'It cannot be denied. But it is an impossible love—at least impossible to transpire into anything else other than that kiss and these hands that hold.'

'I know,' returned Summerfield, his throat dry. 'I know.'

58

Faya Largéa was a small, untidy desert village turned into a sprawling forward base for the Free French forces operating out of Chad in support of the British forces in Libya. It had an airstrip, a fuel dump, rows and rows of tents and was defended by a line of ditches and fortifications and many intricate miles of barbed wire. There was a busy hum about the place and the presence of so many soldiers and supplies had drawn half the nomadic desert population from a two hundred mile periphery to set up makeshift markets and undertake the menial tasks that the soldiers were willing to pay for. It was into this environment that the Tuareg warrior chief led Summerfield, Jeanne Lefèvre and his small column of masked warriors, trotting proudly and rather nonchalantly through a series of checkpoints and dugouts.

Uniformed men, both white European and black North African—Senegalese with their characteristic scarlet fez—turned their heads as they rode by and they received a salute from an RAF officer who, raising his eyes from studying a wingtip of his Hurricane, looked shocked to see them. At a third checkpoint, a hurried phone call was made over the wireless and a sergeant dispatched on a bicycle to accompany them to HQ.

Headquarters was billeted in what Summerfield took to be a post and telegraph office—an uneven, low-lying building of patchy brown clay with barred windows, a tall, slightly lopsided pylon, webbed with antennae rising behind it some twenty yards away. The sergeant dismounted from his bicycle, leant it against a sandbag emplacement and went inside. Minutes later he re-appeared with a small, muscular officer wearing a white kepi of the *Légion* and his right arm strapped in a bandage. Instead of coming to them, he went immediately to the warrior chief and bowed a greeting. They seemed to know each other. Words, in the desert dialect, were exchanged. Consequently, Summerfield's rider nudged him, a sign for him to dismount and Jeanne followed. Quite uneasily, Summerfield noticed the two guards standing watch over the entrance to the building prepare their weapons.

The officer—a lieutenant—stepped over and in an odd, awkward motion, offered Summerfield his left hand. Summerfield shook it.

'*Un britannique, je crois*,' said the officer, nodding. '*Bienvenue à Faya Largéa*—welcome.' Summerfield's rider then leant down, proffering Summerfield's rifle and knapsack. Spotting the Lee Enfield, the officer seemed to withdraw slightly. '*Ah*—I think I will take these. *Sergeant?*' Once the rifle and bag removed, he then turned in evident curiosity to Jeanne. 'Ah—a *French demoiselle*— if I am not mistaken! A sand rose!' he added, quixotically and ushered Jeanne apart. 'I have had reports of your sighting,' he continued, facing them both. 'You must understand that we have to ask certain questions concerning your identity.' He paused, waiting for Summerfield and Jeanne to acknowledge him. 'And very likely you will have information for us that will be of great use and interest.' Again a pause. '*M'moiselle*,' he said, nodding to Jeanne. 'This time, *gentlemen first*. Please come with me to the mess Mlle Lefèvre. You may take refreshments while your companion is being questioned.' And with that, the officer led Jeanne away by the wrist towards an outlying tent. The time it took for Jeanne to turn her head and exchange farewell glances, the sergeant had grasped Summerfield's arm, motioning him to enter the building. At the threshold he halted while a guard searched him. Obviously, he must have smelt badly, for the guard confirmed his check with a grimace.

'*Désolé*,' said Summerfield apologetically, stepping into the cool of the building. Growing used to the dimness, he found himself facing a wall on which a giant tricolour hung, a strange looking cross adorning its middle bar.

'*La Croix de Lorraine*,' informed the sergeant, recognising Summerfield's curiosity. 'You don't know this?'

Summerfield shook his head and suddenly felt very old—like a capsule time had left by. 'I have been—for some years—very *far* from everything.'

'The sign of the Free French Forces,' the sergeant began to explain, when another lieutenant appeared.

'Thank you, sergeant. You may return to your post. I will take him through.' The sergeant saluted, gave a curt nod of his head to Summerfield and marched off. 'Good man,' commented the lieutenant and Summerfield caught a whiff of pine—the young man's eau de cologne. 'My name is De MontSalvert.'

'Summerfield—Harry Summerfield. British citizen.'

'That we shall see, Mr Summerfield,' smiled the lieutenant. 'You will be questioned by both French and British officers—I hope you understand the necessity.'

'It was explained to me, yes,' said Summerfield. 'May I perhaps wash first?'

'I'm afraid not,' said the lieutenant, cocking his head. 'My superiors are very busy people at present. We cannot keep them waiting—this way, please.'

A slight pressure on Summerfield's shoulder towards a door. The lieutenant knocked.

'Enter,' came a muffled, efficient-sounding voice.

The door opened and Summerfield stepped in. He immediately froze, his eyes unable to connect to his brain. Before him, uniformed, slightly greying, sitting in a foldable chair behind a campaign desk, was Jean Bassouin—with as much a look of complete incredulity on his face as Summerfield.

That evening, Bassouin invited Summerfield and Jeanne to dine with him. Sitting opposite the genial man, it was strange to think of Bassouin as a soldier. His uniform—that of a colonel—was ill-fitting and hung loosely about his middle-aged spread more like a gardening jacket than anything else. Summerfield noticed the receding hair and greying temples of his host and found himself shaking his head in an involuntary gesture of amazement. He still couldn't totally believe that they had been reunited.

'Father said you'd been arrested,' said Jeanne, freshly washed and wearing a white shirt and army slacks. 'When we left—we were so alarmed.'

'It was Fresquin and his cronies,' said Bassouin, his face growing momentarily cold. He grimaced and looked down into his plate. 'How could a colleague—a professional companion and fellow civil servant—have done that? I'm still nonplussed by the act. They kept me under house arrest for a couple of days and then took me north on a train. There was talk of me crossing at Tangiers. I suppose I was to be judged once in France—*awful.*' He looked up, noticing his guests' moroseness and smiled. 'But things took a turn for the better, *n'est ce pas?*'

'You managed to escape,' said Summerfield, bringing a forkful of bullied beef to his mouth.

Bassouin shook his head. 'No—sheer luck, in fact. In Tangiers, for no apparent reason, my two guards just walked away—I don't know why. Walked away in the street and left me there. Naturally, I did the same—in the opposite direction!' He laughed and Summerfield and Jeanne joined in, relieved. 'Looking back, I suppose they knew what it was all about and their hearts weren't in it. Nothing to do with political opinions or concern for one's country. Arresting a man simply because he was a Jew… *scandalous.*' Bassouin repeated the word, almost in a murmur and fell silent, letting out a deep sigh. For a moment, lowering his head, Bassouin looked as though he were silently praying. Summerfield glanced worriedly at Jeanne. 'That's why they took her, you see,' said Bassouin, at last.

'Took?' said Jeanne.

'Sarah—my daughter.' Jeanne sat back and Summerfield noticed that her left hand was shaking. 'Rumour has it that she was sent to a camp of some sort near Paris, then to Alsace. At the time, they thought it was just for a few months—time enough for the threat to peter out and the war to calm down. Later, we learnt what the camps were really for.' Bassouin looked up, a watery sheen on his eyes. 'Sarah who loved life, everyone and everything in it,' he said, aware of the futility of his words. 'I have no hope.'

Jeanne leant forwards, at the same time darting a glance at Summerfield, and placed a hand on Bassouin's. The man's face grew soft and tender and he gave her forearm a little stroke with his free hand, much as though he were soothing his lost daughter.

A few moments of silence passed and then, with a change of face, hardened now, Bassouin drew back and looked at Summerfield.

'We must fight this evil, Harry. Fight it and stamp it out like we do a foul insect. Only then can we rest and pick up our lives.'

Summerfield nodded, Bassouin's words making a shiver run through him. 'Jean—I want to help. Don't know how though.'

'Can you shoot—or was that old Lee Enfield just for show?'

'I can shoot,' returned Summerfield, avoiding Bassouin's eyes.

'And you have used it in combat, I see,' said Bassouin, a look of sympathy appearing fleetingly on his face. 'I know how it feels, too, Harry. But we do these things—through duty, fear or simple instinct to survive. And there are those who use a rifle through hatred or doctrine. These latter types, these criminals—be they German, Italian, Vichy French or any other man driven by some mad ideology—must be fought. The light and softness of this world depend on this.'

'A noble cause,' said Summerfield, not without irony. 'Perhaps I have forgotten about causes—I have seen a few men die, you see.'

'You speak English, French—Spanish, too, I believe—and Arabic. You can ride and shoot. You know how to survive.'

'And take a bearing without a compass!' snorted Summerfield, glancing at Jeanne. 'I couldn't find my way across a public park, Jean. I nearly got us killed out there.'

'So you will learn,' said Bassouin, flatly. 'The LRDG—know what that is?'

'We met with a certain Captain Barnes,' nodded Summerfield.

'Barnes—yes, I know him. Very *British*,' said Bassouin with a trace of a smile.

'*Very.*'

'But don't let appearances fool you. The man is a professional soldier and an engineer *par excellence*—it was he who blew up the rail link at Sebha Oasis. Without him, Rommel would have sent an uppercut into Montgomery's balls. Monty wouldn't have liked that,' added Bassouin, shaking his head. 'The British can use your expertise, Harry. More than that, the Free French *need* your expertise. De Gaulle wants us to play a bigger part in the fight. What we have here, scattered about the Chadian desert, is just the beginning of an army that will liberate not only Africa, but France and Europe too at the sides of our British and American allies.'

Summerfield looked Bassouin in the eyes and pondered the words. He felt Jeanne looking at him too, wondered what she thought of it all. *And Raja and the mountains*? said a voice from within him. His heart winced—how he missed them.

'You know, Jean. I—I have become *different*. I feel as though I don't belong here—among the *white men*.'

Bassouin smiled and gave a nod of understanding. 'What did Barnes tell you about the LRDG?'

'He said they were riff-raff,' answered Summerfield, thinking back to the surreal encounter.

'Individuals, free-thinkers, odd-balls, adventurers, lovers of North Africa and the desert,' continued Bassouin. 'They could never fit in with the European rain, the constraint of thought and behaviour, the stuffiness. A few months back, when we took Koufa, a raiding party was decimated by the Italian *Saharianna*. Out of thirty men, only ten got back—and they got back not because they knew how to use a compass, read equations or draw up artillery quadrants. They got back here, most of them wounded, because they were rebels, because they loved this great, wide desert and its peoples and wanted to pursue the fight to set them free.'

Bassouin fell silent, letting his words sink in. Mechanically, he returned to his food and took a couple of mouthfuls before raising his head again.

'And what else would you do, Harry? Stay here and die of boredom? Try to return to Morocco and risk getting caught by the Boches or Vichy patrols?'

Summerfield clasped his hands together. A clock ticked on the wall behind them. The faint sound of music drifted in from a wireless set.

'You were always a convincing man, Jean,' he said, with a smile of irony.

Bassouin grinned. 'I can ensure that you're given a lieutenant's bar on your shoulder tab.'

'Not a pip? French, then?'

Bassouin shrugged. 'Here, we are all the nations of the world. You'll be with British, French, Gabonese, New Zealanders, Tuaregs, Rhodesians, Senegalese, Indians and heaven knows what else.'

'And if I want to leave?' said Summerfield, raising his gaze.

Bassouin chewed for some moments, thinking it over. He drew in his shoulders and inhaled. 'You will have a loose contract. Let's say you are on a par with the Tuareg tribes—not exactly a mercenary, not exactly enlisted, but fighting with us in a common cause until the time comes to stop. I will try to see to it that you have the proper papers.'

Summerfield calculated a while longer, weighing up Bassouin's offer, thinking of what Raja would say—probably scold him, knowing her—then gave a little nod. 'Until the time comes to stop fighting,' he echoed. Then, turning to Jeanne: 'And you, Jeanne?'

Jeanne looked surprised. 'Me?'

'It *is* a good question,' agreed Bassouin.

'I—I hadn't thought about it.'

'Will you be staying—*here*?' offered Bassouin, turning from Jeanne and glancing across to Summerfield.

Summerfield raised his eyebrows and shook his head. 'I don't think so. Jeanne has a priority to take care of.' He turned to her. 'Jeanne?'

'Would you like me to leave you alone for a few minutes?' offered Bassouin to both of them.

Jeanne gave a slight smile. 'Thank you, Jean. But no need—really. Harry and I have talked about the situation. You remember the day I became a fiancée? Now I have Jim to wait for.'

Bassouin swallowed—a sign that the decision had been registered. 'I can get you to Cairo. Things are safe there,' he nodded. A few seconds of silence passed in which the music from outside grew louder—jazz—and then he clicked his tongue, his arms raising and falling in a gesture that meant *so that's it*. 'Harry. I'll introduce you to your new colleagues—a mad, good-hearted bunch of misfits and damn good soldiers by the way. I think you'll find a home there.'

Bassouin rose and Summerfield followed, a little reticently, as though having second thoughts. He wavered a little above Jeanne and she looked up. They remained looking at each for several instants and then she slid her hand around his and clasped it.

'Goodbye,' said Summerfield and with a brief nod, withdrew his hand and walked out.

Once outside, on the flattened sand of the parade ground, Bassouin gently tugged Summerfield aside and for a moment the older man looked a little lost.

'Is anything wrong, Jean? Have you decided not to enlist me after all?' added Summerfield with irony.

'Harry—you know that I appreciate you. Ever since I met you at that stuffy dinner event at the Lefèvre house, your…your *difference* made me like you straight away.'

'It's reciprocal,' said Summerfield, beginning to frown. 'But I don't see what…'

'*Difference*,' repeated Bassouin, inwardly. 'I suppose that just about sums things up. I'm *pied-noir*, you know—a mixture of French, Jewish and Algerian.'

'I remember you saying,' said Summerfield, more puzzled than ever.

'Now that Sarah—my daughter—has gone,' continued Bassouin. 'And that the Lefèvres were so tragically killed. What do you think if I asked for Jeanne to consider me as her—as her…'

'As her *father*?' obliged Summerfield.

'That's correct,' said Bassouin, feigning nonchalance.

'Well—I—I think that would be a very kind gesture,' replied Summerfield, fighting to retain his surprise. 'Actually, she always did mention how close she felt to you. She considered Sarah as a sister. In fact, I even confused them at one time.'

Bassouin smiled, a trace of nostalgia on his face, and with a little gesture gave the sign for them to continue walking towards the officers' mess.

'She *is* different, too, isn't she?' said Bassouin, oddly, as they sauntered.

Summerfield nodded and glanced across.

'A beauty,' he said. 'She's not completely European—not the northern type, in any case. She once told me she had terrible problems coping with that. Apparently her parents would explode whenever she mentioned it.'

Bassouin hummed in agreement and seemed to be reflecting on the shape of his shadow to the left of his brown ankle boot. 'Such a thing could never have been mentioned, you see,' he said matter-of-factly.

'Sorry?' Summerfield straightened up and his eyes met Bassouin's.

'The fact that I and Jeanne's mother once had a fling.'

'You mean—?' Summerfield halted.

'I suppose it doesn't matter now—after everything that's happened,' added Bassouin, holding onto Summerfield's arm. 'The war, the treachery, the loss—it sort of puts things into perspective.'

'Did *Lefèvre* know?'

'Of course. As did my own wife. We chose to hush things up—wouldn't have done any good to our image as the colonial moral keepers of justice and order, would it?' Summerfield grimaced slightly. 'Anyway—that's what was chosen as an argument,' added Bassouin. 'Poor Jeanne's mother—Agnès. I don't think she and Philippe-Charles ever slept in the same bed together again. I suppose that accounted for their lack of any own children.'

'My God,' muttered Summerfield and then, suddenly remembering. 'So what about Jeanne?'

'You mean now? Well—of course I won't tell her. And neither will you.'

Summerfield raised an eyebrow, meeting with Bassouin's steady gaze. Despite his slight size, Summerfield felt suddenly quite intimidated by the look.

'No, of course not.'

'At least—I won't tell her *for the time being*,' continued Bassouin, distantly. 'Let the water run and all that. But, do you know,

Harry—I would just love to be able to walk her up the aisle one day.' He laughed and Summerfield, feeling slightly dazed by it all, echoed him. 'Well, Harry. Here we are.'

Summerfield followed Bassouin's outstretched arm towards the entrance to the officers' mess. There was a large, insolent slogan slapped on the brickwork in whitewash—*To Rommel with Love.*

'Ready to meet your companions? By the way, I didn't mention the odd custom they have when welcoming newcomers…'

59

November, 1942

Several thin black funnels of smoke rose up above the town of Safi on the western Moroccan coast and Summerfield watched, fascinated, as a flight of F4F Wildcats flew through them and roared overhead, past the fort topping the old city, and heading inland. A last look through his binoculars at the scattered houses and farms that announced the southern suburbs of the town and he nodded to the radio operator to give the order to advance. Slowly, in a V formation, the six remaining vehicles of Z patrol LRDG—a mix of Ford F30s and 30 cwt Chevys—crawled towards the first buildings, twin Vickers and Brownings sweeping the terrain with their muzzles.

At two hundred yards they received a pot shot from behind a low lying wall. While Summerfield waved to his left wing to fan out and accelerate, the two remaining Chevys on his right slewed to a halt, a well-practiced manoeuvre, to provide covering fire. In the lead jeep—a Willys—Summerfield shouted '*Step on it*' and the driver immediately ground through the gears, thrusting the little vehicle over the gravel and sand in a charge towards the hidden marksman. At fifty yards, a small, grey figure wearing what looked like a fireman's helmet bolted from behind the wall throwing his weapon behind him in an attempt to run to the cover of a nearby hut. Barely ten paces into his panic-stricken sprint and the figure was hit full in the back by a fierce flurry of bullets from the Vickers and disintegrated, one leg flying off at the knee and the head and right arm jerking free from the torso and kicking up dust as they hit the ground. Slowing down, Summerfield glanced briefly at the mess over the wall, stopping to study the old Lebel rifle the Vichy marksman had carried, its stock snapped off by a bullet. 'Forwards,' he ordered, giving the sign to resume formation.

Safi was a sprawling fishing and phosphate town of ramshackle factories and canneries that looked oddly out of place with the old city. Summerfield could see both from his advancing jeep—the fractured roofs of the factories, hit by shells from the naval forces off the coast and the huddle of ancient buildings rising chaotically to the mount with its fort that overlooked the sea. At 4.30 that morning, after a thirty-minute bombardment from the battleships and cruisers offshore, the southern hook of Operation Torch—35,000 American troops—landed in and around the port and city. Air support, Avengers and Wildcats, strafed and bombed Safi's airfield and communications complexes, moving on to disable Vichy reinforcements heading in from the north.

At the same time, sixty miles away to the south of the city, Summerfield had seen the flashes light up the dawn sky, the wind carrying the weak rumble of the big guns across the desert plain. When they arrived, the city was almost completely under Allied control, most of the Safi garrison now prisoner and milling about on the beachhead under American guard. A few scattered and desperate groups loyal to Vichy remained, carrying on a useless—and to Summerfield, senseless—struggle in the honeycomb of streets up in the old medina.

There was debris everywhere—tyres, crates, clothes, shoes, weapons, empty shell cases, abandoned cars, dead dogs and bodies, mostly civilian. As they drove warily through the suburbs and its shanty town and into the streets of the city, the odd pop of a rifle followed by the crackle of machine gun fire echoed faintly off the sheer walls. A heavier thump in the vicinity, which made them instinctively duck for cover, informed them of the presence of mines. Judging the danger to be real enough, Summerfield and two corporals got out and walked ahead of the vehicles, arms levelled, on the look out for trip wires and the tell tale sign in the gritty streets of freshly turned earth.

Approaching the central mosque, they came across a wide crossroads under the control of a detachment of GIs. In the middle, sitting cross-legged and with their hands on their heads, were twenty or so Vichy soldiers dressed oddly in the pigeon blue fatigues of the beginning of the war. Among them were three German sappers, at the moment Summerfield's patrol group entered the square, being lifted from the others and taken away. Summerfield held his hand high, a sign for the column to halt, and got out. A quick scan of the open space found him what he was looking for—an officer. He walked over, conscious that the GIs were eyeing his Arabic headdress with a mix of curiosity and disdain. Conscious, too, that a strange fish-like smell pervaded the place.

'Lieutenant Summerfield,' he introduced himself, giving a half salute and offering his hand.

'Jesus—wasn't expecting the Limeys here at all,' said the officer, a small, tough-looking lieutenant with a mop of black hair all gummed back beneath his helmet.

'Not really Limeys,' said Summerfield, cocking his head at his column. 'About eight different nationalities in the odd bunch.'

'Oh,' replied the American, looking a little ill at ease. 'Anyway, glad to have you here. Second lieutenant Clanger, 3rd US Infantry division.'

'*Clanger*?' repeated Summerfield, unable to avoid his look of surprise.

The young American officer smiled sheepishly. 'Yeah—that's it, I know. You can't imagine what I get from these guys,' he added, shaking his head at his men. 'Still—kinda hardens you up going through school 'n' that.'

'Hmm,' agreed Summerfield. 'I'll buy that. By the way, wouldn't swap a few ciggies, would you? This black stuff we have is like lighting up creosote.'

As the two men swapped cigarettes and lit up, the sound of an explosion over near the port shook the air.

'*Sardines*,' said Clanger with a grimace. 'We hit beach and ran into a mountain of them rotting on the sand. Had to wade through the shit—which may explain the smell around here.'

'Extraordinary,' offered Summerfield, a little lost at the brash young lieutenant and his odd report of events.

'We're about thirty per cent down on numbers—poor bastards

spewed their insides up and just couldn't go on. And I wouldn't be surprised if the sardines finished by blowing up. Goddamn stench!'

'Listen, Clanger. I hope things get better for you and your men—' Summerfield smiled reassuringly at the American who was now eyeing him suspiciously—'Really. But you wouldn't happen to know where Headquarters has squatted, would you?'

'HQ?'

'I have to report in with some information we gathered. We've just driven in from the east across the desert.'

The lieutenant seemed to ease down and his stance changed from one of *are you taking the piss, Limey* to one of respect. He tipped back his helmet and glanced at Summerfield's insignia. 'You're one of those Desert Rats—thought you looked a bit local in that fez you're wearing.'

'*Cheiche*, actually. But—doesn't matter.'

As Clanger gave him directions, a few inhabitants began to appear timidly at windows and out of cellars. In the space of a few minutes, there was much talking and the beginnings of barter were underway. Summerfield returned to his jeep leaving Clanger, somewhat overwhelmed by the thickening crowd, to police the situation.

Summerfield led his convoy back along the lines through the streets—tarmac now—towards the port. American engineers were busy laying telephone lines and securing defensive positions while columns of infantry and Stuart tanks, freshly disembarked from the secured port, moved up towards the front in the opposite direction. Native Moroccans, in twos and threes, stood warily on street corners, looking unsure if they should welcome this foreign invasion or hide.

They passed the town hall on which the first American assault troops had hung a giant Stars and Stripes. Its façade was pockmarked with bullet scars and the impacts of tank fire. Several windows were black and burnt and a row of charred bodies—Vichy soldiers—lay to the left of a headless statue, watched over—as if they would resurrect and flee—by a Royal Navy detachment with bayonets fixed.

Two more streets and then the telephone exchange building—
Allied HQ. Here too, Summerfield saw that resistance had been
stiff. The roads and pavements were littered with thousands of
spent cartridges and not a single window remained intact in
the street. Large, brownish pools of blood stained the ground
and a good dozen corpses, covered over in tarpaulins—HQ staff
oblige—still lay where they had fallen. To one side of the road, on
the corner of the exchange, was the wreck of a Vichy tank—an
old R35 from before the war and no match for the American
Shermans. Coming to a stop before it, Summerfield and his
men peaked through the curious hole punctured in its hull and
grimaced at what they knew to be hidden inside.

The hour he spent at HQ was fruitless. Once past the security
check, there were too many people with too much to do. Finally,
deciding to leave, it was then that Summerfield chanced asking
the duty sergeant—a huge bull of a man whose helmet seemed
three sizes too small for him—and received the answer he had
been hoping for.

Leaving his men to make their way to the port and stock up
on supplies, Summerfield shouldered his Sten and proceeded
on foot.

A first bar had been ransacked, its innards tipped out of
the gaping window and spilling across half the road. A second
more modest bar, not so farther along the street, was intact. A
small, frayed and faded parasol had been wedged against a chair
announcing it was open for business and Summerfield smiled
to himself—yet another odd and serendipitous event in a war
characterised by boredom, solitude, horror and fear. He walked
up to the open door, removed his headscarf and stepped in.

The interior was cool and Summerfield was caught momentarily
off guard by the dimness. As his sight grew accustomed, he saw
that the bar was painted a pale green. A hastily made threesome of
paper flags—US, British and Free French—had been pinned to
the wall above the shelves of bottles and glasses. It was surprisingly
empty, surprisingly silent: two navy officers, one British, one
American, sat reading revues and sipping orange juice in the

corner; a US Army captain asleep, with his head resting in folded arms. And finally the man he had come looking for—a broad-shouldered, good-looking, well-build chap in his early thirties, approximately Summerfield's age and wearing the uniform of a major in the US Intelligence Corps. He seemed to be waiting, staring at something on the wall. Judging from the expression on his face, he seemed to have been waiting for something for some time. Summerfield stood and watched the man pick up his glass, study the contents and then finish it off. It was at that moment that he glanced up, his eyes a deep, bright blue—unfocused for an instant, then questioning, then widening in disbelief. Summerfield nodded slightly and felt himself breaking into a grin.

'*Jim Wilding*—what the hell are *you* doing in a hole like this? The whole town smells like a ripe sardine.'

They embraced, Wilding's initial shock turning to loud joy that woke the army captain from his sleep with a cry. Finally, he ushered Summerfield to his table, called noisily for alcohol, and they sat, unable to speak for several minutes. Wilding looked in good shape and the neat cut of US officer fatigues gave him a debonair look, something of a cross between Fred MacMurray and Tyrone Power. But it was when he spoke that Summerfield really recognised him. That rich, deep warmth sent his mind back to recalling memories of Gibraltar and Marrakesh almost five years before and he almost felt tears coming to his eyes.

'I won't say we've changed, Jim,' said Summerfield, with a little irony. 'We meet up so rarely that it's too plainly obvious.'

Wilding shook his head. 'Holy Jesus, what happened to you, Harry? Where to start? And me and—' Wilding stopped and a look of pain entered his face for a few fleeting seconds. 'Harry?' He looked away and then back again, raising his eyes to look steadily into Summerfield's. 'I'm afraid I've got some bad news.'

Summerfield returned his regard, noticed the lines of regret on the American's face, the haggard look.

He shook his head slightly—'I know, Jim'—and Wilding frowned.

'There's something for you.' Summerfield's hand went to his battledress, searched for his inside pocket and pulled out a tattered letter. 'Sorry it's in such a state. It's travelled far,' said Summerfield, his voice mellow. 'It's a letter for you Jim—written some time ago—from Jeanne.' Wilding's eyes widened. 'She's all right. Safe. She's in Cairo.'

'My God...' Wilding seemed to collapse, his face muscles sagging.

'She needs you, Jim. She says she loves you.'

Two days later, Summerfield stood on the airstrip with Jim Wilding watching the Dakota going through the flight check. Its two engines coughed and growled and settled to a steady throb. Wilding picked up his kitbag.

'Say hello to her from me,' said Summerfield, taking the American's outstretched hand.

'I will, Harry. I'll be forever grateful for everything you've done for her—for *us*.' Summerfield looked down, feeling himself reddening. 'You're one hell of a swell guy, Harry. Completely mad, but swell even so!' They laughed. 'Gotta go now,' said Wilding, pursing his lips. 'Cairo, here I come.'

'Take care, Jim. See you anon.'

'Hey—Harry?' said Wilding, turning back mid-way to the Dakota. He dropped his kit bag and cupped his mouth with his hands. 'I didn't ask—what are *you* gonna do now?'

'Oh,' Summerfield hesitated, frowned. 'I've done my job. I'm going home, Jim.' Wilding grimaced and brought a hand to his ear. 'I said I'm *going home*,' repeated Summerfield.

'Where's that?' shouted Wilding, perplexed. He picked up his bag again, took a few steps and began climbing into the plane. 'To England?'

Summerfield shook his head. 'No. To the mountains.'

'*Mountains*? *Here*? You're mad, Harry.'

Summerfield grinned and gave a brief wave. 'There's Hope waiting for me there!'

'What was that? *Hope*, you say?' Wilding made a sign that he wasn't sure and gave a sheepish smile.

Summerfield nodded and grinned. 'That's right, Jim—*Hope*.'

60

Many years later, in the near suburbs of Marrakesh, Achik Radoun, a plasterer by trade, was making the last preparations to a wall before lunch break. Achik considered himself lucky. He had a long term contract with a subsidiary of a French parent company with offices based in Casablanca, and at the end of every month sent home three-quarters of his pay to his parents and family. It was his third job for them, travelling south to join in the refurbishment of an old school building that was to be one of those luxury, five-star hotel complexes for Europeans holidaying in the royal city. Achik had never seen so many gold-plated doorknobs piled up in the storerooms, such an extravagant number of containers loaded with toilets and bathtubs so vulgar in their sophistication. It was all so very far from the traditions that had kept his land still wild and untamed for so long.

Rafik, Achik's foreman, shouted up from the overgrown gardens below. 'Hey—Achik—*time to stop*. Prayer time then lunch, my friend—they cannot wait!'

Achik shouted back and was about to leave, when what he took as a twinge of conscientiousness took hold of him. He turned back and found himself frowning.

The room had once been rather small. Only two days ago, the breakers had knocked down the adjoining wall using sledge hammers and it now formed a shockingly over-sized future bedroom suite with its neighbouring bathroom space. Achik looked at the debris collected around him—the thick, faded green tatters of old wallpaper, the broken chairs, scattered rags of clothing, twisted metal, the broken picture frame that housed a faded black and white photo of an old, rather large, Christian nun. She had the faintest of smiles on her lips and to Achik it looked as though she were telling the camera she knew something that no one else did. It must have been her room. What had it once been—a monastery or something? A school? The place had been abandoned since the early seventies, one of the last vestiges of French presence in the great pink city. And now Morocco was growing strong, thought Achik. Strong with tourist palaces and electronic toilet seats. Things were changing fast. So fast that he could hardly recognise certain districts when he returned back home to his family.

Again he heard Rafik's cry from below, impatient but well-intentioned. And again, Achik turned to leave but hesitated. His eyes instinctively sought the only remaining job to do before he was to lay the plaster that afternoon: the plinth. With a sigh, he picked up his crowbar, leant downwards and with a sharp, upwards tug, tore off the fragile wood in one movement. It snapped loudly from its nails and wobbled free to come to rest in a small cloud of dust. Achik nodded to himself, pleased and then froze. There was something pale wedged in the slats behind where the plinth had been. He peered closer, stooped and pulled it free, his heart beginning to pound with the thought that maybe he had found a wad of hidden money. But no—it was a bundle of old papers. Letters, perhaps. With a grin and a look heavenwards, he stuffed the bundle in his jacket pocket and went to join Rafik.

Later that evening, after work, Achik sat on his bunk bed, texting a message to his family on his mobile phone. He waited until the beep confirmed reception and then put the phone aside. He sighed—he was happy. He had eaten well. A good day's work and now a well-deserved sleep awaited him. Most of the other men were now playing cards in the small rest area they had arranged outside the clutter of prefab huts in which they were billeted. He didn't feel up to it. Not this evening. While making ready his affairs for a pre-sleep shower, he suddenly remembered the bundle in his pocket. He stopped with his preparations and, leaning over, sought out his jacket pocket and removed the papers.

There were more than a dozen, he judged, all tied together with a piece of flaking raffia. He brought out his penknife, flicked open a blade and neatly cut it. The papers slid out and he hastily nudged them onto his bed covers. They smelt old and mouldy and the writing, in French, looked as though it had been written with a fountain pen, layers and layers of neat, precise lines. His fingers touched the letters, coming to rest on one that looked in better shape than the others. Prising it open, it ripped slightly at the fold and he held it aloft for a second before laying the flimsy paper to rest in his lap.

'So, what could the old nun have to say?' he said to himself. He squinted at the loops and lines and began to read:

I would dearly love to kiss you, just once, and say: t'was I who writ these rhyming words upon a hook and bit the catch of love myself…

Achik looked up, amazed and a laugh escaped him. '*Incredible! The old devil of a Sister!*' He shook his head and felt somehow enchanted: *Such a cold sacrifice for a life of loneliness, and such a hot heart that should live on…*

61

He had forgotten that when spring came to the Atlas, it was said that God had forgiven their winter and blessed them once again with the purple buds of wild thyme, slopes full of tumbling blossom and valleys rich with the greenest shoots he'd ever seen.

Climbing the paths upwards, his muscles burning and the sweat gathering in beads that rolled down his neck and back, arms and legs, the colourburst made his heart swell with something approaching a sense of complete attachment to the world. It soothed the blisters on his feet despite the regular scolding rub with the ground through the worn and unheeled soles of his army boots. It wet the dry thirst of his mouth.

He made his way instinctively, not in need of a compass or a guide, certain that the valley was somewhere before him, another crest, another dip perhaps beyond. Picking his way through a copse of thorn bushes, counting another hundred and thirteen steps on a thin path through the stones and he saw the crest of his valley barely thirty yards in front and heaved himself forwards in a joyous, though painful scrabble to the top.

Summerfield closed his eyes. The wind came to his face, cool and boisterous and he remembered. The valley and its smells—sweet-dry dust, the olive presses, musk and cinnamon, cumin and sweat, honey and the metallic nip of well water—came to him. The colours and the people, and those like Badr who had died and most of all Raja.

It was not difficult for a man to get lost in a war. The battalions moved on and the stragglers, the injured, the deserters or the unbelievers were left to wander among the chaos of logistics and ruins left behind. It had taken him five months to find his way to the mountains. Travelling by night and early morning, he had swapped his officer's Sten gun for a soldier's Lee Enfield and kept it with him much out of Berber tradition. A warrior does not return without an arm, a trophy. In some places they had fed him, thinking him a liberator. In others, they had run, seeing in his blue eyes and increasingly fading khaki memories of the Legionnaires and colonial Vichy and the German detachments sent south to reinforce Pétain's French. He had lost much weight and his hair had grown too long for comfort. Somewhere along the way, lice had found a home oblivious to the carbolic soap which as the weeks passed wore to a translucent slither and then evaporated. He often scratched. He let stubble grow. When he discovered the first few grey hairs of his early thirties peep through his nascent beard, he shaved. Thus he kept the rhythm up—four days' stubble then shave—telling him of how time passed and how each ritual brought him farther south, farther east and nearer to his home.

He opened his eyes. For several moments, oddly saddened, he could not smile though his senses were full and bloated ripe with what he saw. It was the valley—that great, wide, sweeping, winding cleft in the deep pink mountains that was home to the tribes that had adopted him, to Raja who had saved him, to his heart which had lead him on. He understood then that when the alchemy of happiness is so full, so complete, it simmers into the sweetest of melancholies.

In the distance, he saw what he thought was the village of Zemghort, only the shadows of its clustered, pink wattle walls a sign that it lay nestled on the slopes. His own, Aït Itmolas, was out of view, somewhere below him and hidden by the rocky outcrop on which he now stood. Little shapes moved mechanically in the distance—not the women in their fields but their donkeys munching grass. It must be somewhere near three in the afternoon, rest time—no wonder there was no one about. A yellow finch flew overhead. Gathering his greatcoat which he had used as a blanket in the winter months on the plains, and slinging his rifle over his shoulder, he set off.

The outcrop proved hazardous and several times Summerfield

slipped, grabbing onto the roots of the thorn bushes and ripping his skin. A third time, slipping for several yards downwards over the smooth rock, his heart beating with panic at the height, he decided on another path. Crawling right, crab-like, he made his way across the domed surface for fifty yards and found another path that led round and downwards to the valley.

The first glimpse of the terraced roofs of Aït Itmolas, some three hundred yards off, fuelled his confidence and burnt away the strange, timid apprehension he had been feeling. Stupid questions, silly doubts, like *What if they have forgotten me? What if they don't recognise me? What if Raja has gone?* Then, picking his way through a cluster of large cacti, some of which reached shoulder height, and stepping into a small clearing, he saw a small boy squatting by a pool of water in the rock. The little boy gasped and immediately stood up, a look of stubbornness and fear on his chubby brown cheeks.

'Salaam,' said Summerfield, cocking his head. '*Labess*—how goes?'

The boy's eyes grew wide and wild. He must have been no older than five. They darted to Summerfield's shoulder and the muzzle of his rifle and then back again to his long tangle of hair bleached fair in the sun and his eyes, his eyebrows too having grown white and almost non-existent. Summerfield took a step forwards. For a second the boy's face fought with indecision, then closed firm, and with this he abruptly turned and ran letting out a series of yelps.

'Super,' said Summerfield out loud, and bringing his hands to his hips. 'I've got to start again all over, I suppose!'

He shook his head, braced himself and began once more to descend the slope to the village. He caught a few seconds' glimpse of the tall, squat tower of the Kasbah—three years ago his prison—turned left on the path that wound round a series of huge, moss-covered boulders and exited onto the valley floor and an onion field. The earth was rich here, the pink turned to deep reddish brown and his boots took on the clod weighing down his stride.

Following the irrigation gullies, he came to an olive grove in bloom. On the branches, washing out to hang—great swathes of cloth in different shades of blue, ruby red and black. His heart beating fast now, feeling himself grinning with exhilaration, he cast away his greatcoat. Approaching the trees, he un-slung his rifle and backpack and tore off his faded army jacket, rifling the pockets for his belongings and stuffing them into his trousers. Then, walking up to the strips of coloured cloth he hesitated, sorted, then chose a shirt of indigo blue. He held it up, smelt the waft of olive soap on its rough hemp fibre, checked the size. Okay, he said, and wriggled it over his head.

Once again, he gathered his things. And then he stepped back into the shade cast by the trees. Looking up, he had seen her: Raja. Suddenly timid, suddenly filled with self-doubt, he watched as Raja moved away from an open doorway with a group of women and crossed the ground towards him. She was petite, still had that lilting walk which suggested a boyish character and carried the basket laden with dates with nonchalant ease. A white smock covered her, faded and grey in several places, and she wore a bright blue and red headscarf, the sequins of which glittered in the sun. She was talking and the warble of her words and the twitter of laughter from the women reached him. Raja, the talker, the clown. Raja the sweet one with her boisterous eyes. Raja the beauty with her olive brown skin and fine face. Raja now the woman waiting to be loved. Summerfield felt himself shudder—the weight of time and absence—the beginnings of tears, and he gulped them back, cursing silently, not wishing to make a show of himself. She was the most beautiful thing Nature had ever created. Taking a deep breath, he stepped forwards.

When she saw him, a random glance away from her friends, the world stopped. Her face struggling with an almost agonised smile, Raja suddenly folded up on herself and sank to her knees.

Summerfield rushed to her and bent down, enveloping her in his limbs. He felt her shoulders, her arms, the brush of her loose left breast upon his wrist. She did not speak, trapped between laughter and tears. He placed his hands on her cheeks and brought her eyes to his. They did not seek each other's lips—it could not be done—and instead Summerfield teased away her headscarf to kiss her hair.

'*Habibi* Summerfield—my darling Summerfield,' she whispered. 'I thought I'd lost you.'

Summerfield held her to his chest, like a father clutching a child, and breathed the cinnamon, the musk, the faint nip of wood fire that was her smell.

'As sure as the stars, I knew I'd find you,' he said.

Then, clutching each other they rose as a gathering of children and the curious came. Someone shouted *The Englishman!* And Raja turned to them as she held his arm and said:

'Summerfield, *the Amazigh*—the free man, *one of us*.' And then, to him: 'Will we have a house, Harry?'

'Yes, my love, we shall.'

'And will we have a proper bed, my Amazir?'

'A bed that will be hard to leave, my wild one.'

'And will we have children, Harry?'

'Many,' grinned Summerfield, squeezing her am. 'And I will sing them *Bobby Shaftoe* to remind them of the English sea.'

'And I will tell them of how silly and stubborn you can be.'

'*Raja!*' Summerfield drew back, saw her surprise at his reproach and then clasped the sweet little woman to him again. 'With Hope comes Charity—will you not spare me some? I'd forgotten your beauty was born of both a fox and a dove.'

'Come, my lion, my *Amazigh*—come talk to the Mullah. He will be very happy for he has had time to think of many great inventions for the village.'

Together they walked, under the dust raised by the running children and the harvest song that the womenfolk had begun to chant, across the pale pink earth and the irrigation gullies trickling clear and fast, the orange glow of the eve of evening and the warm, still air of the valley, their home. To the east, the steep slopes turned mauve and to the west, gold. It was an end of a journey, the closing of a book. Summerfield held Raja tight and his mind strayed back afar, across the years, the lands he had belonged to and fought through. How some good men had turned bad and others better men still. It was strange, he mused, looking at the mountains around him, feeling the heat of Raja's warmth, how the present always seemed so—an odd word, this—so *engaging*.

Acknowledgements

Writing itself has always been an adventure for me and something of an enchanting process, where all the dots of a lifetime join up to create a text and a story. Looking back on this journey, I'd like to give special thanks to the following: my grandfather, Alfred Suckling for his wartime tales and inspiration; Joan and Tom, my mother and father, for everything that they were; Tim, Jane and Emily – my dear and adventurous children; Lydie Keo – my love and encourager; Azziz Radouk, Moroccan guide and friend, who led me to the real people of the mountains; Ben Mohammed Zoubir, Mauritanian guide and friend, a true leader whose adventures in the desert I shared; Lahcen Belahcen, a Good man, for his guidance and knowledge of Arabic/Berber culture; Ashaka, my cat, who provided much companionship during *Amazir*; the people and children of the Atlas – whom I keep in my heart; and finally – and not least - Simon Petherick, and his diamond, Beautiful Books.